THE PALADIN

Book One of The Whiteblade Saga

Adam Nichols

MILLENNIUM

Orion Paperbacks
A Millennium Book
First published in Great Britain in 1998 by Millennium,
a division of Orion Books Ltd,
Orion House, 5 Upper St Martin's Lane,
London WC2H 9EA

A CIP catalogue record for this book
is available from the British Library.

ISBN: 0 75281 562 8

Typeset at The Spartan Press Ltd,
Lymington, Hants

Printed and bound in Great Britian by
Clays Ltd, St Ives plc.

No book is ever finished without help. I'd like to say thanks to:

Rozenn Bégasse and Benoit Bleau who very kindly lent me their excellent printer at extremely short notice.

Ryan O'Connor, who introduced me to the marvellous convenience of e-mail.

Ellen Shizgal, who gave me a second home.

The Crockers – Anne, Clayton, Will, Raymond, and Elizabeth – who generously let me have the use of their upstairs nook in which to work.

Marley Morris, who lent me her technology.

Rae Burbige, who, in her usual generous fashion, lent me her flat when I needed it.

Caroline Oakley, my editor, who, with her calm good judgement, helped me to make everything fit together.

Gaile, Martin, and Jade, who coped with me while I wrote – bless them.

Thanks all!

PART ONE

LONG HARBOUR

I

Elinor admired herself in the long shard of cloudy looking-glass she had attached to the wall of her little attic room. The glass was old and broken and the silvering on the back had worn off in spots, but she could still manage to get a fairly good view of herself.

A long, brightly patterned skirt was wrapped about her hips, knotted so as to leave her left leg bared to the thigh. She wore a little sleeveless top of washed blue fabric, which nicely emphasized the swell of her small breasts and left her navel and a hand's span of naked belly visible above the skirt. The top's pale blue contrasted nicely with the length of her dark hair and brought out the blue of her eyes.

From a little box on a rickety table, Elinor reached out a stub of kohl-stick. Leaning her face close to one of the looking-glass's clear patches, she carefully outlined her eyes, giving to them a satisfyingly dramatic presence. Putting the kohl-stick back, she coiled up her long dark hair into a loose mass at the back of her head and pinned it into place with a slim bodkin of carved wood which she took from the table-top.

Elinor pirouetted slowly in front of the cloudy looking-glass and smiled. 'How can he resist?' she said softly, jubilantly, to her reflection in the glass.

'Tonight,' she said. 'Oh, *aye* . . .' And hugged herself and shivered pleasantly.

Elinor backed away from the looking-glass and reached up to one of the slanting wooden beams that crossed the low ceiling of her attic room. From a hidden niche behind one of them she carefully lifted down a small, damp bundle. She unwrapped this and took out a little effigy fashioned roughly in the shape of a man, limbs made out of bits of twisted cloth, wisps of coppery-red hair tied about the featureless head. It had a

3

musky scent to it and squished slightly, like a damp sponge, in her hand.

'Earth below and sky above,' Elinor began, repeating the rhyme that Dame Sostris, the maker of the charm, had taught her. 'Mother Earth and Father Sky. Image of the one I love, made with hair and earth and blood. Hear my pleading, Powers divine, make him love me, make him mine.' Holding the charm before her, she dribbled saliva on to it, then held the thing to her mouth in a long, wet kiss. 'Make him love me,' she repeated. 'Make him *mine*!'

After a moment she carefully wrapped up the effigy again and returned it once more to its hiding place behind the beam. She took a final twirl in front of the looking-glass, smiled to herself, then skipped out of her room down the two flights to the ground floor. She slipped along the short hallway and out into the back room. The evening breeze sighed through the open window that faced the small garden outside.

The twins sat perched on the back of the tattered armchair, their heads together. Elinor could see no sign of anyone else. She let out a relieved sigh. She did not fancy facing her mother right now. Slowly, she started tiptoeing by, hoping to slip into the front room and out of the door before anybody knew she was gone. She put a finger to her lips, shushing the twins, and tried to wink conspiratorially at them as she passed.

'Mum!' Tiss, the elder of the two, cried. 'Elly's tryin' to sneak out again!'

'An' she's all tarted up!' Tass added.

The twins grinned maliciously at her.

Taking a step towards them, Elinor raised her hand menacingly. They scampered off the armchair, out of the open window and into the garden. Elinor turned, disgusted with them, and there stood her mother, Genna, leaning against the doorjamb.

'Don't start,' Elinor began. 'Just don't start.'

Genna stood taking in Elinor's skirt, the flash of thigh it revealed, the pale blue, sleeveless top. 'Tass was right enough. A right tart ye looks, dressed up like that. What *does* ye think ye's playin' at, girl?'

Elinor shrugged sullenly.

Genna's lips were pressed into thin lines of disapproval. She

4

ran a hand irritably through her grey-streaked, black hair, sweeping it back off her face in a habitual, weary gesture.

Grey eyes, greying hair . . . *grey soul*, Elinor thought disgustedly. 'Ye's old and tired and ye understands *nothing*!' she told her mother. But she said it silently in the privacy of her own mind – a habit she had developed, having learned the cost of outright rebellion.

'I suppose ye's off to The Anchor,' her mother said disgustedly. 'After that fella from Shilligen's mob ye've been mooning over?'

'And what if I am?' Elinor flung herself into the tattered armchair the twins had vacated, scowling.

'A barrel house is no fit place for a girl yer age. And ye *knows* Jago has forbidden ye to go there.'

Elinor said nothing.

'Listen to me, Elly girl . . .'

'My name's Elinor, Mother. And I'm no little *girl* any more!'

Genna shook her head. 'Elinor, then. Just listen, can't ye? They're no good, that mob of Shilligen's. Head bangers, the lot of them. And *secretive*! So bloody secretive ye never knows what they might be doing. Don't be going after him, Elly girl . . . It'll only bring on grief.'

Elinor snorted. 'I'm not yer little "Elly-girl" any more! Ye doesn't understand. Ye doesn't understand *anything*!'

'I understand only too well, girl,' Genna said sadly. 'Only *too* well.'

The women looked at each other in silence for a long moment.

'He's going to be mine, Mother,' Elinor said evenly, her voice tight. 'And neither ye nor anybody else is going to stop that!' She snapped out of the chair and stood there, glaring.

Genna stepped towards her daughter. 'I won't sit idly by and watch ye make the same *stewpid* mistake I did! Yer father . . . Jago and I . . . have *plans* for ye, girl. Ye can do better for yerself than some wastrel from a barrel house!'

'Jago's *not* my father.'

'He's been a far better father to ye than feckless Corki ever was!'

Elinor only glared sullenly.

'Listen to me, girl! Ye doesn't know what ye's settling for, getting involved with somebody from the likes of that mob of Shilligen's. Corki was of that sort. And *he* was no more reliable than a harbour cur.'

'*Don't* say things like that about him. You don't know why he . . .'

'Corki was faithless as a spring wind, girl. And it's well past time ye admitted it. He ran out on me, on *ye*, and left us to starve. If it hadn't been for Jago . . .' Genna shook her head. 'And now ye wants to go and get involved with another of them same, useless, *faithless* wastrels.'

'Ye's *wrong* about him!' Elinor snapped, stamping her foot.

'He's a smuggler, girl,' Genna responded. 'Worthless head bangers, the lot of them. This one of yers'll prove no exception. Ye'll see!'

Elinor did not even bother to reply. Turning on her heel, she stormed out through the doorway and was gone outside into the coolth of the early evening.

'Ye'll catch yer death, dressed like that when the night comes on proper down by the quays,' Genna called. 'Summer's a *long* ways off yet, my girl!'

Elinor did not slow her pace, did not look back, did not acknowledge Genna in any way.

'Like talking to a brick wall, talking to that one,' Genna muttered to herself. 'Strong-willed and stubborn as a pack mule, and with no more sense, sometimes, than . . .'

She lapsed into silence, shaking her head. As she stood there gazing at her daughter's retreating form, her face reflected a complex mixture of anger and dismay and uncertainty. And grudging pride. 'Ah . . .' she sighed. 'The poor devil doesn't stand a chance. But what's to become of ye, girl, now that ye's set on this mad road?'

Elinor strode along through the cobbled, dirty Long Harbour streets, an intricate maze of refuse-strewn alleyways and wider roads filled with people enjoying the spring twilight. The winter snows were gone for good now, and the days had warmth in them. There was a feeling of excitement in the air, in the blood. Elinor felt her heart beat faster with it, felt a pleasant thrilling in her limbs.

Her route took her through the hubbub of Market Square,

where there were barrows filled with dark slabs of meat, spring mutton, marbled with white fat and circled by moving clouds of new flies. Winter walnuts, wrinkled apples and onions, herring, codfish, mussels, white cabbages, clams, blue turnips . . . all being hawked loudly.

The autumn markets were far bigger than this, but the cobblestones were still green with heaped piles of discarded vegetable leaves, the air thick with scents. People bustled everywhere. Vendors shouted their wares, shoppers haggled, beggar children scurried about – all in a crowded, swarming, living, excited mass.

Elinor slipped quickly through it all, knowing her way. More than a few men whistled appreciatively at her. One vendor reached out a hand to her in melodramatic supplication as she passed, crying something she did not care to catch. She ignored them all and kept her quick pace, headed towards the quays where The Anchor was located.

In a little, the evening air began to hold the briny-weedy scent of the docks. The harbour breeze was chill on her exposed skin, giving her goose pimples. Turning a corner, she saw the familiar façade of The Anchor before her and paused. She felt her heart skip with excitement, all else forgotten.

Then, repeating Dame Sostris's charm silently to herself – 'Make him love me. Make him *mine*!' – and crossing her fingers for luck, she plunged forward.

The Anchor was one of the larger and more popular barrel houses in the area and even at this relatively early hour of the evening it was already in full swing. Elinor paused at the threshold, standing under the iron anchor above the doorway that gave the place its name, gazing in. The big fireplace at the far end of the spacious, central room blazed away as it did every night, summer and winter, and candles in tall, cumbersome sconces cast a shimmering radiance over everything. The 'musicianers', as her mother would have called them, wailed out an old dance tune and a crowd of people was already well into one of the intricate step dances that had become suddenly so very popular this season. It was stifling hot, and reeked of woodsmoke, candle wax, home-brewed beer, sweat, and the musky, mixed smell of packed, none-too-clean humanity.

Elinor loved it.

Especially this evening. The place simply seethed with boisterous noise and motion, for the same spring fever she had sensed in the streets was alive here tonight. She felt it in her own blood as she hurried in, her eyes sharp and alight, casting about through the crowd for that one special, bright face.

'Oooeee . . .' a voice said from behind her. A hand snaked its way up through the open side of her skirt and tried to slip in past the curve of her thigh. 'If it isn't little Elly.'

Elinor slapped the hand away.

'Make a grown man cry, she does,' the voice said, and was answered by a chorus of male guffaws.

'I'll thank ye to keep yer scabby hands off me, Jons,' Elinor said acidly.

'Now now, little Elly me girl,' the man called Jons replied. 'Don't ye be gettin' *angry* with me, now.'

'My name,' she said, glaring at him, 'is Elinor.'

Jons laughed. He made her a mocking bow. 'Me 'umblest pardon, Mistress Ell-ee-noor.' He was a tall, hulking man, arms thick as Elinor's thighs. He smelled strongly of beer and the acrid reek of stale sweat. Several of his cronies stood gathered behind him, frothy beer mugs in hand, grinning lewdly.

'Smooth as a dream it was, lads, that thigh o' hers.' Jons winked at those near him. 'Think she'll let me have another feel?'

'Try puttin' yer hand on me again, Jons, and I'll cut it off,' Elinor snapped. Reaching for the bodkin that pinned up her hair, she did a quick, complicated flip with it, and in her grip a slim, nasty-looking, polished iron blade winked suddenly in the dancing candlelight.

Jons skipped backwards quickly despite his apparent bulk.

'Try touching me again, ye smelly old fart,' Elinor said, 'and I'll cut off more than just yer hand!' Her dark tresses had come tumbling down, and she flung back her head, brushing her hair away, glaring.

Jons's mates laughed heartily at his expression.

'Now, Elly,' he began, recovering from his initial shock. 'Ye don't want to go waving that little prickler about like that. Couldn't do nothing but get a man angry with a teeny-weeny little prickler like that.'

Elinor held the slim blade loosely, moving it in small circular

8

motions in front of her in the way Corki, her father – her real father – had once taught her. 'Try me!' she snapped. 'Arsehole!'

Jons's face darkened. Slamming down his beer mug on a nearby table, he took a menacing step forward, reaching for her with one huge, beefy hand. Elinor snicked her blade across it, making a nasty cut across his palm.

'Oww!' he roared, skipping away. 'Little bitch.' He sucked at the cut, glaring at her. 'Little *bitch*!'

Elinor stood shivering, her pulse beating a frantic rhythm. He was faster than she had thought.

Jons took another step towards her.

She held her ground, the little knife out before her.

Jons stopped, suddenly, and began to laugh. 'First time anyone's cut me in more years 'n I can remember, Elly me girl. Ye stood up to me good an' proper. Ye've yer daddy's spirit in ye, all right. And he taught ye good. Corki always did have a deft hand with a blade.'

'Elinor,' she said, ignoring his mention of her father. 'My name's *Elinor*.'

Jons nodded. 'All right . . . Elinor.' He sucked at his hand some more. 'Hurts like buggery,' he commented, still laughing.

Elinor relaxed, though not entirely.

'Go on with ye,' Jons said, waving her off. 'Ye've got spunk, girl. I do admire that.'

Elinor did up her hair again, slowly, folding the slim, polished iron blade of the little knife into its wooden casing and pinning up her hair with it. She kept her eye on Jons, still not certain his apparent good humour was real. He smiled back and waved her off again.

'Make him work for it a little, Elinor me girl,' he called out after her. 'Whoever the lucky sod may be!'

She gave Jons no answer, simply turned away and continued through the crowd, scanning, looking for that one particular face.

She stopped momentarily, closed her eyes, and tried to visualize the little effigy that lay tucked up in the rafters of her room – as Dame Sostris had taught her to do it – focusing all her attention, all her energy, all her desire. Holding the small man-shape before her in her mind's eye, she murmured:

9

'Image of the one I love, made with hair and earth and blood. Hear my pleading, Powers divine, make him love me, make him *mine*!'

She opened her eyes, took three steps, and, at the far end of the room from the fireplace, she saw him, saw the brightness of his red hair, the brighter brightness of his face.

Elinor halted. Seeing him actually here before her now, she felt suddenly nervous and awkward. Her pulse skipped. It was all so contrived, somehow, this intention of hers. It oughtn't to be so contrived . . .

As she stood there hesitantly, Annocky got up from the table at which he had been sitting with several others, tossed back the last of a mug of beer, and headed for the steps which led to the Betting Ring upstairs. With him went two men, strangers Elinor had never seen before.

She swallowed her nervousness and headed after him. As she drew near the stairs, however, she heard a voice call her name.

'Business, Elly girl.' It was Mytch One-eye, one of the men Annocky had been sitting with. There were only two of them left at the table now, Mytch and a skinny grey-beard named Pol. 'Better not go up there,' Mytch said. 'Don't 'spect Shilligen would like it much, ye sniffin' about up there after Annocky while they're tryin' to do business.'

Elinor felt herself blushing. She had not realized her intentions towards Annocky were so obvious to everyone. She bit her lip, hesitated, then started towards the stairs anyway, trying to ignore the seated men.

But grey-bearded Pol called out to her, 'Come sit with us, Elly, an' keep us company for a bit. Much the sensiblest thing for ye to be doin', all things considered.'

Mytch nodded. ''T'wouldn't do ye no good to aggravate Shilligen, girl.' He smiled and winked at her with his one good eye. 'Annocky'll be back down eventual.'

Elinor hesitated, then shrugged and went over to join them at their table. At least, seated with them, she wouldn't have to fend off the advances of anybody else. And there was a middlingly good chance they would stand her a beer during the wait.

She only hoped that wait was not going to be too long . . .

10

II

Ah, but he was a lovely man, Annocky was. Elinor lay next to him and admired the line of his sleeping face by the dancing light of the fire. The oval blue tattoos on his cheeks gleamed dark and exotic. She reached a hand gently down and fondled him. He murmured softly but did not wake. Soft and silky and still damp he felt. She snuggled in closer to him under the pile of blankets they had brought against the night's cold. The strong man-smell of him overwhelmed her and the thought of him, hard and big, sent a shiver running through her at the memory of what they had done.

It had seemed a very long while that she had sat waiting for him in the noisy, smoky, familiar chaos of The Anchor. And then he had returned, his face grumpy as he walked down the stairs, muttering to himself about some business matter or other. But the grumpiness had evaporated when he saw her. Elinor felt a little thrill, remembering the transformation that the sight of her had wrought upon him.

And then talk, and beer, and more beer, and eventually to this out-of-the-way place Annocky knew – his special Night Garden, he named it – stepping through the darkness, her heart trembling in her breast, her blood singing with beer and excitement and love.

Mine, she thought, lying there beside him. Dame Sostris's charm had worked. *Mine now. All mine.* She lay close to him, inhaling the aroma of him, watching the endless changing patterns of the fire he had built for them and the twisting shadows it cast upon the uneven walls and thrusting trails of ivy that hedged this little hidden spot – a verdant niche tucked away between two windowless, brick warehouse buildings.

'Come in, my lovely,' Annocky had said softly, leading her by the hand through the little three-board slat that served as a sort of door into his hidden 'garden'. 'I'll build us a fire. And by its bright and dancing light we two shall know each other.' She had shivered, feeling almost she would faint, feeling it was all too perfect: the dancing flames, the dark, trailing masses of the ivy, the protective walls, the stars high and bright and glittering overhead like vast expensive jewellery, Annocky looking at her as if he could eat her up whole.

It made her shiver again now, remembering that moment. Annocky's Night Garden . . . She would never forget its wild charm.

Given a chance, though, she thought, shifting position to get a bit of stone out from under her hip, she might have chosen a more seemly spot than this for her first time. Something softer under her poor back at any rate. And Annocky had been a bit rough, and it had hurt, a little, when they did it at first . . .

But she felt it to have been beautiful, nonetheless.

And he was *hers*, now.

Elinor sighed like a cat, soft and satisfied. Far, far overhead in the cloudless heavens, she could make out the star-shape named the Fisher, the spring constellation that marked the return of the great herring schools, that marked the end of winter, the return of warmth, the beginning of new life and growth and . . . and, now, of her new life with Annocky, away from Genna and bossy Jago – her own person at last!

She felt like an entirely new person, reborn, with a whole and entirely new life before her, free as one of the great white swans that came skeining through every spring and autumn, migrating to new lives. Yes . . . she felt like one of those white swans, who flew free and strong, with their mates by their side.

Annocky's eyes wafted open and he stretched, drawing her closer to him. 'What is ye grinning about, then? Ye's grinning like a cat with a mouse.'

Elinor grinned all the more. 'Ye're my mouse. My very *own* mouse.' She sank her teeth into the solid, lovely flesh of his arm just below the shoulder.

He roared in pain and surprise and rolled backwards, trying to pry her loose, but she hung on until she felt her mouth run with his blood. She let go then and looked up at his surprised face, still grinning, and licked the blood slowly from her lips. His arm showed the double half-moon scars of her bite. Blood welled up where her sharp teeth had cut into his flesh.

12

For a second, he simply stared at her, eyes wide. Then he laughed, a big, solid, deep-from-the-belly laugh, and grabbed her to him tightly, squeezing her with his long sinewy arms till she felt faint.

'Mad woman,' he murmured, easing his hold on her.

'Lovely man,' she replied, snapping her teeth at him.

He squeezed her again and the two of them rolled and struggled and thrashed about in the blankets until both collapsed into paroxysms of laughter.

'Ye're my man, Annocky,' Elinor said, once she was able to talk again. 'Mine. Now and forever. I put my mark on ye. Together, we'll do great things, ye and me.'

Annocky rubbed his upper arm and grinned.

'We'll get a little house down along the Ferthside,' Elinor went on. ''T'won't be much at first. But it'll be *ours*, with nobody else about telling us what to do and not do. And we'll . . . we'll spend evenings together by the fire, or looking out at the stars, or take long walks along the Ferth strand, just us two, arm in arm.' She frowned slightly. 'And I'll find something to do. 'Cause I'm not going just to sit about at home and have babies. Not *that*. I'm going to amount to something, Annocky! I'm going to be better than either Jago or Genna ever gave me credit for. I'm going to . . .'

Annocky's face had clouded over and his eyes turned away from her.

'What?' Elinor said, feeling her heart suddenly lurch. 'What is it?' She knelt over him, her hands on his arms, and shook him. 'Annocky!'

His eyes turned back to her. All the good humour had evaporated from his face. He pushed her off him, sat up cross-legged in front of her, a blanket draped across his shoulders against the night-chill in the air, and sighed. 'Is ye sure ye knows what ye's doing, girl? Does ye know what sort of man I am? There's things ye doesn't know 'bout me an' Shilligen's mob.'

'My mother thinks ye're all a terrible lot. Head bangers she calls ye. Full of secret nastiness. But Shilligen's mob can't be all that bad. After all . . . *ye're* one of them.'

Elinor lay down with her head on his thigh. She reached a hand over his leg and held him gently. 'It's *ye* I want, Annocky. I don't care about yer mob.'

13

He grinned. 'It's me ye has got.'

'And I intend on keepin' ye, too. Forever.'

Again, Annocky's face clouded over. 'I don't know, Elinor . . .'

She squeezed him where she held him, hard.

'Aiee!' he yelped. 'Easy there.'

Elinor held on to him. 'Ye hasn't been lying to me, has ye, Annocky?' she said. 'Ye hasn't been leading me on just so as to get me here to have yer way with me tonight, has ye?'

'No,' he said quickly. 'Of course not.'

'And ye *does* love me, then?'

'Of course.' He reached over and pulled her into his arms so that she let go her hold on him. 'Silly girl. How could ye doubt it?'

'Then ye *is* mine,' Elinor purred. 'And we *will* have our own little house by the waterside.' She looked at him, smiling, ran her fingers gently over his face. The tattoos gleamed exotically on his cheeks. One long braid of red hair dangled across his chest, dark as ripe cherries in the night, and the paleness of the rest of his intricately shaved scalp shone in the firelight.

Annocky smiled, but it was a stiff little smile, and something in it sent a small flutter of unease through Elinor's belly. She arched her back at him like a cat and spat: 'Ye're my man, Annocky, my first, my *only* man. We'll build a life together, ye and I, a good life, a better life than my mother ever imagined. And *nobody* better try to interfere with that!'

Annocky shook his head and reached for her again. 'Little vixen,' he sighed. 'What'm I goin' to do 'bout that temper o' yers?'

She snuggled into his hold and said nothing. Slowly, languidly, she ran her tongue over his chest. His muscles were firm and sleek, and his skin tasted of the saltiness of dried perspiration. Her tongue glided downwards in a long, slow, wet sweep, and she felt him shiver pleasurably.

He reached for her, and they began again.

III

'No,' Elinor said, shaking her head. 'I won't!'

'Yes ye will, girl,' her mother snapped. 'And right smartly at that. Yer father's waiting.'

'He's *not* my father!'

Genna glared at her daughter. 'Yer *father* was a faithless wastrel. Jago has supported us, supported *ye*, for over a decade now. He's a good man, and a far truer father to ye than Corki ever was!'

'Jago's a tight-fisted old fart who . . .'

Genna slapped her, an unexpected, resounding *thwack* that hurt. Elinor stared, hand to her cheek, shaken. It had been years since her mother had hit her.

'I'm going downstairs,' Genna said. She was panting with suppressed and indignant fury. 'Ye straighten yerself up. In a little while – a *very* little while – ye'll come downstairs. Ye'll *not* keep yer father waiting overlong. And ye'll be proper respectful to him. Is that clear?'

Elinor hung her head sulkily, saying nothing out loud, but cursing her mother hotly in the privacy of her own mind.

'Is that *clear*, girl?' Genna demanded.

'I'm not a little *girl*, Mother!'

'Then stop acting like one, ye silly, spoiled thing! Jago's got something very special to tell ye.'

'He's not . . .'

'Leave it, girl. Just *leave* it!' Genna turned and stalked out of Elinor's attic room.

Elinor wanted to hit something, hard. She *hated* that way her mother and Jago ordered her about – as if she were a child. But she would not have to endure it for too much longer now. Not now she had found her Annocky. A little thrill went through her. *Her* Annocky. Let her mother and old Jago rant as they liked. She would be gone soon enough from all their interference. Gone and free to start a real life with Annocky, just the two of them, in their little house by the water. She ached for it.

'Elly!' she heard her mother shout up from below.

'Coming,' she called back sullenly. She took a quick look at herself in the mirror. Her cheek was splotched an ugly red where her mother had slapped her. It still stung a little. She rubbed at it gingerly, shook her head.

'Elly!'

She did not answer. Craning to see her reflection in the cloudy mirror, she tied up her hair – Jago liked to see it down – then turned and ducked out of the low doorway and down the stairs, as slowly as she dared.

Jago was sitting in the back room that served as his office – a big, craggy-faced man with hard, dry hands and a soul to match. 'Took ye long enough,' he said by way of greeting.

Elinor glared at him in sullen silence.

'Jago,' Genna put in quickly, coming to stand next to his chair. 'Don't start with her.'

He waved her to silence. 'Aye, woman. All right. Now don't crowd me.'

Genna hesitated, then backed away and sat on another chair. Four had been set up, Elinor saw, forming a little rectangle. They were chairs of Jago's making, but mismatched, discards from his workshop, each with some little flaw or other that made them difficult to sell. It was typical of the man, she thought, that he would use such discards at home rather than craft a proper set. Here he was, a master carpenter, yet their home was furnished entirely with mismatched odds and ends.

'Sit,' he said to Elinor, pointing at one of the empty chairs.

Elinor baulked.

'Sit!' Jago barked.

She sat.

He ran one hand over his balding head and regarded Elinor in silence for a long moment. Then: 'Let yer hair down, girl. It makes ye look old when it's up like that.'

'I like it this way,' she replied.

Genna leaned forward. 'Now, Elly . . .'

Jago waved her back again. 'Let it go,' he said. Looking at

Elinor, he sighed. 'Ye always had too strong a will in ye, girl. Always wanted yer own way and nothing else.'

She said nothing.

Jago shook his head, threw up his hands. 'It all comes from having yer ears stuffed with nonsense by that Corki.'

Elinor stiffened, but a cold glare from her mother kept her from saying anything.

'No telling what silly notions he might have put in yer head with those stories of his,' Jago said, 'before he ran off and abandoned ye.'

Elinor lurched up half out of her chair. 'They were *wonderful* stories he told!'

'They were *stories*, girl!' Jago snapped. 'Full of lies and exaggerations. Not fit for a young girl such as ye were to hear. They gave ye wrong ideas. The world's not the sort of place ye can always order to yer will. Nothing but grief can come of thinking that. Who do ye believe ye is to have everything yer own way all the time?'

Elinor kept silent, but in her mind she damned him: 'Stupid, blind old fart!'

'Look at me and yer mother,' Jago went on. 'Do *we* have things our own way all the time? Not on yer life! I make sacrifices every day, girl. In the shop, here at home. Everywhere. If ye only knew how much . . .'

'I hear ye has something to tell me,' Elinor interrupted. 'Something *special*.'

Jago leaned forward in his chair, stabbed a finger at her, opened his mouth. But he obviously thought better of what he was about to say for he sat back, sighed again, ran a hand over his balding head. 'There's somebody I want ye to meet,' he said finally.

Elinor blinked.

'He's waiting in the other room.'

Before she could think of anything to say, Jago had got up and left the room. She glanced at her mother, but Genna was busily looking out of the window and would not meet her gaze. Elinor swallowed nervously. It was the middle of the morning. Jago ought by rights to be in his workshop. Who could it possibly be they wanted her to meet? And why?

He came back with a man in tow.

He looked about Jago's own age, this one, but where Jago was all hard sinew and bone this man was soft and pudgy. He had thinning grey hair in a long plait, a round florid face, and wrinkly bags under his eyes. They were dark, shifting eyes, and they reminded Elinor uncomfortably of the eyes of a rat. In fact, there really was something rat-like about the man in general, Elinor thought – an over-fed, over-pleased rat.

'This is my daughter, Elly,' Jago said by way of introduction.

The man bowed to her. It seemed a ridiculous gesture to Elinor. His belly stuck out like a melon over his expensive silk trousers, and despite the elegance of his clothing – his shirt, too, was silk, and he wore a finely dyed linen jacket – he had no more grace in his movements than a turtle.

'You did not exaggerate, friend Jago,' the man said. 'She is indeed a young beauty.'

To Elinor's surprise, the man's voice was rich and pleasant to hear.

'This is Master Hadelbert of Swallowvale,' Jago said.

'Good day to you, young lady,' Hadelbert said. He strode up to Elinor, lifted her left hand, and pressed it gently to his lips.

She snatched it away.

'Mind yer manners, girl,' Jago snapped.

Hadelbert shrugged. 'She is only young, Jago. And she has spirit. I like that in a woman. Particularly a young and beautiful woman.'

There was silence in the room for a long moment.

Elinor blinked uncertainly. Who was this Hadelbert? He had the appearance of a well-to-do merchant. She looked at her step-father. He swallowed and glanced away.

The silence held for long moments further.

Elinor felt her belly begin to cramp up. What was going on here?'

Jago coughed, ran a hand over his balding head. 'Might as well . . . get right to the . . . um, heart of the matter,' he said. He turned to Elinor and smiled. But it was the false smile of a conspirator. 'Master Hadelbert here has . . . um, he has asked me for . . . for yer hand in honourable marriage.'

'Wh-what?' Elinor stammered.

'I have told him we would be delighted to plight yer troth to him, and so unite our two families in . . .'

'*What*?' Elinor all but shrieked. She scrambled up, sending her chair rattling to the floor behind her.

Genna sprang up and took her by the arm, leading her off to the far corner of the room. 'Elly . . . Elly girl!' she whispered fiercely. 'Now ye *listen* to me!'

'I will *not*!' Elinor hissed back. 'How can ye expect me to . . . to . . . He'll have me like a fat old sow, producing babies till I drop. I've better things in store for me than *that*.'

'And what's wrong with having babies?'

Elinor scowled. 'There's more to life than babies, Mother!'

'Oh, aye? Such as what, then? What great plans has ye worked out for yerself, girl? What great skills, what special gifts, has ye that mark this greater destiny ye boasts of for yerself?'

Elinor hesitated. 'I . . . I . . .'

Genna nodded. 'Aye. I reckoned as much.'

'I'll find whatever it is, Genna. I *will*! I'll not end up like ye, scrimping and struggling just to make it to the end of each day. Crawling to the likes of Jago for sustenance. I swear it! I'll make something better of myself.'

Genna sighed. 'This marriage *is* making something better for ye.' She reached out and laid a hand on her daughter's arm, softly. 'It's time to put aside girlish fantasies and romance, girl. Ye've got to grow up and take up a proper woman's role. With a household of yer own to manage. That's far more than *I* had at yer age. It's an honour, what Master Hadelbert is offering ye. He's one of Long Harbour's importantest merchants. Owns six trading ships no less. Six! And with a match such as this, ye'll benefit the entire family. With ye as his bride, Master Hadelbert's says he's more than willing to give yer father all his ship-fitting business. Does ye understand what that means, girl? Jago will be set for the rest of his days. We *all* will be.'

Elinor pushed Genna away. 'How *could* ye?' she demanded shrilly, of her mother, of Jago, of them all.

'Elly!' Jago barked.

'My name is *Elinor*!'

Jago came up out of his chair, face white with anger, and pushed her into the corner of the room, grabbing her by the arms. 'Now you listen to me, girl!' he hissed. 'Ye lives here in *my* house. *I* provided for ye all these years, and ye not even my own flesh and blood. Ye will do as I say. Is that clear?' He shook

19

his head. 'Don't act *stupid*! This is a golden opportunity for ye. For us all!'

'I won't . . .' Elinor started.

'Ye *will*!' Jago glared at her. 'Who does ye think ye is? Ye has no understanding of the world yet. Ignorant child. Ye hasn't even reached yer eighteenth summer! Ye'll thank me for this, years from now, I tell ye that.'

Elinor shook her head, tried to pull away from him.

'Ye will do as I command, girl.'

'*Command*?'

'Aye, *command*.'

Elinor wrenched herself furiously out of his grasp, ducked beneath his clutching hands, and stormed out of the room.

'Come back!' Jago commanded. 'Ye come *back* here, girl, or I'll . . .'

But Elinor was out of the door already and away down the lane outside.

Genna ran to the door. 'Elly!' she called. 'Elinor!'

Elinor just kept on, ignoring her, fists clenched, legs scissoring furiously till she had turned the corner and left them all behind.

She had her Annocky. She could make a *far* better future for herself than ever Genna or stupid Jago could conceive of. She would go to her Annocky. Together, she and he would make that better future. Never again would she set foot in Jago's house. *Never*!

Elinor hurried on down the maze of familiar back alleyways she had known and used since she was a child, down towards the harbour, to The Anchor, to Annocky, to the future she dreamed of.

IV

'I tell ye, he ain't here, girl,' Mytch One-eye said. 'He *ain't* here!'

'But he's *got* to be here!'Elinor insisted.

Mytch shook his head. 'He's off on a job for Shilligen.'

'But he would've told me!'

'Left last night, girl. Whether he told ye or not.'

Elinor hugged herself. She looked about bleakly. The Anchor was quiet this time of day, dim and cool and empty save for a scraggle of men hunched disconsolately over half-drained beer flagons. Somebody let loose a bark of sudden laughter, and it seemed a strange sound. Elinor had never been here except at night, when everything was in full swing. It felt a lonely place now.

'Annocky'll be back soon enough,' Mytch said. 'No more than three or four days at the most.'

'Three or four *days*?' she cried in dismay.

Mytch nodded. 'I know that seems like a long time to young love, but the days'll fly by right enough and he'll be back to ye before ye knows it.'

'Ye doesn't understand. I've got to see him before then!'

Mytch patted her, as one might pat an agitated dog. 'Now don't take on so, girl. He'll be back soon enough.'

Elinor yanked herself away from him. She wanted to slap him, hard. But there was no point. She whirled and stalked out, stumbling into the grey daylight outside, blinking back tears.

It was drizzling, a cold, persistent rain off the sea. The day was grey and chill. A fitting match to her mood, she decided, gazing up at the clouds. She shivered, wrapped her rain-shawl tighter about her, hugged herself for warmth.

What was she to do now? She would *not* go crawling back to

Genna and Jago, tail between her legs like some whipped puppy. But how was she to get through three or four *days*?

Was it all for *this* that she had won her Annocky? So that he could go flitting off to unknown parts without so much as a fare-thee-well – and in the very time of her need?

She wished there were some Power she might evoke in her aid. Folk did such. There were shrines to the Powers – those great live forces that moved the world, animating all – and folk brought offerings.

Why, just along down by the quays there was a shrine to Sweet-water Kaila. Perhaps she might . . .

But Elinor shook her head. Such places were for the ignorant and the simple. The Powers were greater, or lesser, than human images of them. The Powers were . . . themselves. Like strong currents under smooth water, save that the water was the world entire. There was nothing in them for her to appeal to. They were simply . . . beyond her need. The easy appeals of simple folk over their little images – 'Revenge me, O great Kaila' – were not for her.

Which left her . . . what?

Elinor took a sharp breath. There was always Dame Sostris.

The front of Dame Sostris's house was a cascade of colours, vivid crimsons and greens and glowing yellows, glistening wetly in the persistent drizzle. It stood out from the block of dingy buildings into which it was spliced like a great bright flower thrusting itself out of a manure pile – a shock and a joy to the eye.

The front door, amongst all that colour, was a startling coal black. Lettered above it in large, careful script was: *DAME SOSTRIS: WISE WOMAN*. Underneath that, and somewhat smaller, was: *Farseer & Prognosticator Extraordinary*. And under that, in smaller lettering still: *with a wicked pack of cards*.

Elinor stood before the door with her hands on her thighs, gasping, for she had run most of the way, skidding on the wet pavement once, tearing her trouser leg and skinning her knee. She could not help but smile, seeing the familiar words before her. It took her time to work out writing, but, unlike some, she could read well enough if she had to – thanks to Corki, who had done more than just tell her stories.

Looking at the sign, Elinor laughed softly. A wicked pack of cards indeed . . . She pushed the door open and walked in.

The door gave on to a little entrance hallway which, in turn, led to a small waiting room, dim and cool, with cushions to sit on. 'Dame Sostris?' Elinor called anxiously, doffing her rain-shawl. 'Is ye at home?' The Dame kept no schedule, and clients came as they could, for there was no telling when or if she might be seen.

'Dame Sostris?' Elinor called again, her hopes beginning to fade.

But then a voice called hoarsely from another room, 'Go away, girl.'

Elinor ignored the order and rushed through the little red door at the end of the waiting room. 'Dame Sostris, ye've *got* to help me!' she cried. 'I've . . .'

The Dame lay prostrate on a low couch. 'I said go *away*, girl. I've one of my headaches.' The room was cool and dim. A curtain was pulled across the lone window, riffling gently at the touch of the rain-soaked air outside. Elinor could hear the water going *slip slip slip* outside, down the stone of the wall and into the gutter. Draped across the arm of the couch and leaning languidly against the Dame's shoulder was a slender black cat which looked up, staring unblinkingly at Elinor with golden, strange, un-catlike eyes.

'Dame Sostris, ye *must* help me,' Elinor said, but softly now. 'Please! Oh, *please* . . .'

The Dame sighed. 'Always it's *please please please* with ye, girl, desperate and demanding, hands wringing, eyes bright with tears. And here ye is, back again, dripping water and tracking yer muddy footprints all over my rug. What is it *now*? Did the love-charm I devised for ye not work?'

'Aye,' Elinor said, shifting her feet self-consciously. 'It worked. But now . . .'

Dame Sostris held up her hand. 'A moment, girl.' She levered the slim black cat off, saying, 'Away with ye, Maulkin.' Then she sat up shakily, ran a hand over her forehead, winced. Getting to her feet, she went to a pitcher of water on a nearby stand, lifted a small towel from a rack, dipped it in the cool water.

Elinor had always thought that the Dame resembled a tall, plump duck. The woman moved with a duck's waddling gait, and her hands, where they stuck out from the woollen shawl she had wrapped about her, were pudgy and smooth and white. Even her face seemed ducklike, with smooth white skin, quick dark eyes, and a sort of beaky, soft chin.

But a very clever duck, for all that . . .

Dame Sostris returned to her couch and dabbed delicately at her eyes and temples with the wet towel.

Maulkin the cat settled herself on the couch's arm, staring steadily at Elinor. She shivered. Maulkin had always given her the wemblies. There was something about the animal, about those strange golden eyes, that was unnervingly knowing.

Dame Sostris sighed. 'So now tell me, girl. What is it? Ye isn't with child, is ye?'

Elinor blushed. 'No. Not that.'

'Then what?'

'It's . . . I . . .' Elinor slumped down on a nearby stool and sniffed back the tears that suddenly threatened to overwhelm her. She felt foolish, and shook herself angrily. 'It's Jago, my step-father. He and my mother want to . . .' She told of their plan to marry her off to fat old Hadelbert, the words fairly tumbling out of her.

'Well, well . . .' Dame Sostris said, when it had been told. 'But the charm worked for ye, did it?'

Elinor nodded. 'Oh, aye. Annocky's mine. But he's gone away. And I don't know where to find him, or get a message to him. And he won't be back for *days*! That's why ye *must* help me now. I can't marry that . . . that wrinkled old whale! Not now that I've found my Annocky! It's my *own* future I want to have, Dame Sostris. Not being locked up with the likes of stupid old Hadelbert!'

'This Annocky's gone away, ye says?'

Elinor nodded. 'On a ship. Something for Shilligen.'

Dame Sostris nodded musingly. 'On a ship. For Shilligen. I see . . .' She leaned forward, putting the towel aside momentarily. 'Ye're certain sure that this Annocky's the man for ye, then? Ye wouldn't . . .'

'I *wouldn't*!' Elinor said sharply.

24

For long moments Dame Sostris was silent, the towel still draped over her forehead. Then she sighed again and lifted the towel away. 'Ye always has been a strong-willed little thing. Come, then.' She got up slowly and wrapped her shawl more tightly about her. Then, beckoning Elinor to follow, she waddled through into a tiny back room where a single table stood, straight-backed wooden chairs on either side of it. 'We will read the cards first. That before anything.'

Elinor slid into position on one of the chairs. She leaned her elbows on the table expectantly.

Dame Sostris took her place on the table's other side, though far more slowly. She closed her eyes and sat there for long moments, simply breathing.

Elinor began to fidget.

'Patience, girl,' the Dame said, not opening her eyes. 'One does not plunge into things where the cards are concerned. Ye knows that well enough by now, surely.' She put two fingers gently to her temple. 'And remember my poor head . . .'

The Dame sat, silent.

The cat leaped noiselessly up on to the table and sat, licking delicately at one paw, regarding Elinor with her strange, golden non-cat eyes.

Elinor shivered. She had sat here before, and it was always an unnerving experience. Her future, her fate, all her possibilities, as if she were seated in the middle of a long web stretching away before her . . . and, through her cards, Dame Sostris could reveal some of the strands of that web, show where they led, or might lead, or might not.

What would the Dame and her cards reveal this day?

Elinor waited, trying not to move, tense as a wound spring, feeling her heart thumping, until, at last, Dame Sostris opened her eyes, sighed, gave Maulkin an absent-minded stroke behind the ears, and took out the cards.

They were large, colourful things, the backs elaborately decorated with bright abstract designs. Dame Sostris shuffled them, her pudgy hands moving with surprising grace in a mesmeric, rainbow riffling that went on and on.

Elinor felt the little hairs on the back of her neck rise up, her belly tight with anticipation. The Dame knew the cards like none other. Sitting in this very chair, Elinor had first seen the card named The Lover come up – the dark man's profile standing for a man-to-be in her life. And The Strand – changing tides, the cusp between one aspect and another, sea and land – which had guided her to the quays, to The Anchor, to Annocky and the promise of a new life.

And now . . .

Dame Sostris set the shuffled pack on the table. 'Cut,' she said.

Elinor reached a trembling hand forward and cut the deck.

The Dame began carefully to lay out cards in a half-circle. Elinor leaned forward so as to see better. Maulkin, too, her black, whiskered cat's muzzle following the movement of each card as it was placed on the table.

First came a card with a man's face pictured on it, a staring, wide-eyed face, the hair tangled with seaweed. 'The Drowned Sailor,' Dame Sostris said in a soft, strained voice.

She turned over the next card, which held the image of a circle, intricately laced with abstract designs. 'The Wheel,' she said. 'There will be change in yer life, girl.'

The next one depicted a man in a huge brimmed hat, with one eye. 'The Merchant. Luck, both good and bad.'

The next card depicted two identical women, wide-eyed, with long hair flowing about them like so much dark water. One of the identical faces was smiling, the other frowning. 'The Twins,' Dame Sostris said. 'Uncertainty. Ambivalence. Being of two minds.'

The next card Elinor recognized with a little bleak shiver. The Hanged Man. Dame Sostris said nothing, merely looked up at her soberly.

The last card, placed beneath the crescent of the first five, completed a half-wheel layout on the table. It was entirely blank. Dame Sostris frowned. 'That which I am unbidden to see.' She sat back in her chair and stared silently at the six cards.

'What?' Elinor demanded. 'Tell me!'

The Dame shrugged uncomfortably. 'This is like nothing I have ever read.' She gestured at the cards. 'The Hanged Man, the Drowned Sailor. Death and death. Yet also the Wheel, meaning Change . . . And not the change of death – the Wheel never stands for that. And the Merchant with the

Twins . . . luck, good and bad, being of two minds . . . a strange pairing.' She shook her head, staring at the cards.

Reaching down, she plucked up the blank card. 'The Unknown. I've never drawn the Unknown as the axle card.' The Dame shivered. 'Most, most strange . . .'

'But ye *can* help me, can't ye?' Elinor implored. 'There must be *something* ye can do to help me!'

Dame Sostris shook her head sadly. 'I'm afraid there's nothing I can do, girl. The cards are too obscure for me to see into properly. How can I possibly help ye if I cannot read the cards?'

'Throw them again, then! Get a clearer reading.'

Dame Sostris shook her head. 'That is not the way the cards work, girl. Ye knows that.'

'But ye've *got* to help me!' Elinor wailed.

Dame Sostris winced, put a hand to her temple. 'There isn't any way I *can* help ye, girl. Anything I tried or advised might just as well prove disastrous as not.'

'Ye can't just . . . *abandon* me!' Elinor said accusingly.

'I'm not doing any such thing!' the Dame snapped. 'But I have my limitations, girl.'

'There must be *something* ye can tell me!'

Dame Sostris sighed, ran a hand gingerly over her forehead, peered at the layout of the cards. 'There's the scent of death to this reading. But not true death.'

'Whose death?' Elinor demanded, her heart thumping anxiously. 'And what does ye mean . . . not *true* death?'

'I don't *know*, girl. That's exactly the problem.'

Elinor slumped in her chair. She stared at the cards. 'Stupid things,' she murmured.

'No,' Dame Sostris said. 'They are what they are. And that is never stupid.'

Elinor looked at the Dame imploringly. 'What do I do *now*?'

Dame Sostris shrugged her bony shoulders uncomfortably.

'I can't just go home,' Elinor moaned. 'I *won't*!'

There was a strained silence between them for long moments. The cat was still seated on the table, and Dame Sostris reached out a hand to her, stroked her under the chin. Maulkin purred.

Elinor felt like slapping the pair of them, so unconcerned and selfishly content they seemed.

Neowww . . . Maulkin said. *Nowww . . . nowww.*

Dame Sostris sighed. She pulled away from the cat, murmuring, 'Oh, very well.'

Elinor blinked, uncertain.

'There is, perhaps, one thing that might be done,' Dame Sostris said to her.

'What?' Elinor demanded quickly. '*What*?'

'There is a . . . a woman of my acquaintance. She . . . how shall I put it? She swims in deeper waters than I. Perhaps it is time I sent ye to her. Perhaps she can make sense of what I cannot.'

'Who is she?' Elinor was out of her chair. 'Where do I find her. Quick! Tell me.'

'I'm not sure ye wants to have anything to do with this woman, girl. She's not . . . easy to deal with.'

'Where do I *find* her?'

Dame Sostris sighed. 'Her name is Kieran. Folk call her Mamma Kieran. She lives out on the Ferth's north shore. Outside Long Harbour. Ye'll have to take the ferry across the Ferth and then walk along the north shore strand some, westwards, till ye comes to a long, sloping hill with a rock shaped like a bird atop it. Mamma Kieran's home is on that slope's other side.'

Elinor shivered. She had never been out of Long Harbour in her life.

'Perhaps it's a bad idea, girl. Perhaps ye should . . .'

'I'll go,' Elinor said.

Dame Sostris shook her head. 'Don't be so hasty. She's from foreign parts, is Mamma Kieran, and not like any woman ye've ever met.' The Dame put a hand gently on her cat's sleek black head. 'It was through her that I got Maulkin here. Maulkin's . . . *special*.'

Maulkin made a small, throaty sound.

Elinor felt a little shiver go through her.

'Mamma Kieran is no easy woman to deal with, girl. I'm a little blessed with the Sight, is all. But she . . . Well, perhaps ye needs to have a think about . . .'

'I'm *going*!' Elinor said quickly.

Dame Sostris sighed. 'Aye, I reckoned ye would.' She leaned across the table. 'But have a care, girl. Dealing with Mamma Kieran may bring ye more than ye wishes.'

Maulkin said, *Nowww*!

Dame Sostris sighed again. 'It seems the time is right. Now indeed.'

Elinor stared uncertainly at the cat for a moment, then shook her head and reached into an inside pocket and brought out a handful of battered copper coins – all the little bit of wealth she had in the world. 'How much do I owe ye?'

Dame Sostris shook her head. 'Keep it, girl. I was of precious little use after all. Ye'll need it for the ferry crossing. And ye might need it for Mamma Kieran.'

'How much does she charge?' Elinor asked uneasily, regarding the paltry little pile of coins in her hand.

The Dame shrugged. 'That isn't always easy to say. Mamma Kieran is not . . . She does not always charge what one expects.'

'Meaning what, exactly?'

Again, the Dame shrugged. 'Ye will see for yerself, girl.'

There was a long moment of silence between them.

The Dame beckoned Elinor closer, reached a hand across the table, and sketched a quick little sign of benediction over her brow. 'May good fortune smile upon ye,' she said softly. Then she put a hand to her head and winced. 'Now be off with ye. I need to lie back down. My poor head . . . Be off with ye, I say!'

Elinor turned and left, knowing the way out.

Behind her, she heard Dame Sostris saying, 'Luck, girl. Luck.'

Then she was back out in the rain, running.

V

Elinor wove her way through the littered streets quick as could be, running when she could, splashing through puddles, skidding on wet cobblestones, barging impatiently through the more congested parts of the route. Down along by the quays she went, then, taking the long, crowded slope of Topgallant Parade, eventually crested Rory's Hill and saw the Ferry Station beyond.

There was a crowd there, animated and noisy in the chill drizzle, waiting impatiently while, over on the far bank of the river, the slow ferryboat unloaded its cargo of people and animals before it could return once again. Across the water, Elinor could just glimpse that farther shore, dark and unknown.

She stopped, heart thumping. She had a sudden feeling, as if . . . as if she were on the top of some slippery slope, beginning a long slide down, down, with no way to halt.

Waiting along with the rest for the ferry to return, Elinor paced back and forth anxiously through the crowd, her rainshawl wrapped about her against the rain, breathless and out of sorts, back and forth, back and forth . . . until a fat, middle-aged woman nearby tapped her on the shoulder and said, 'Slow *down*, ducks. It's sure he'll be there still when ye arrives.'

Elinor only glared.

'Young love,' the woman said to a companion. 'In'it won'erful, now?'

Finally, the ferry made its slow way back to the Long Harbour shore, disgorged its load of passengers, and Elinor was able to board along with the waiting rest. She paid the ferryman from her small stock of coins and stood at the railing, feeling her heart thump.

The ferryboat jounced gradually across the water away from

the city. Behind, the buildings and serried roofs of Long Harbour crowded the Ferth's south bank, stretching away westward along the shore as far as Elinor could see before the coastline turned and cut the rest of the city off from view. A grey haze hung in the drizzly air above the rooftops, and winding coils of wet smoke rose everywhere. It was all the home she had ever known, this jumbled city, and seeing it now, like this, from a distance, left her with a strange sense of loss.

On the north bank, a new throng had begun to gather already, impatiently waiting. Elinor leaped from the boat and cut her way through it, passing quickly beyond. She paused then and cast about, trying to get her bearings. This northern shore of the Ferth was as unlike the southern as could be. Here, aside from a few buildings huddled about the Ferry Station itself, there was nothing but open country and a long, vacant, intimidating stretch of rocky strand.

Elinor set off determinedly, stumbling along the stony shore.

As she walked, to her pleased surprise, the drizzle began to abate and the clouds opened up. Shafts of sunshine cascaded down, making the Ferth water appear like so much liquid gold. She took it as a good sign.

But it was no easy journey. The stones hurt her feet through the thin soles of her shoes. Her pulse was thumping with exertion and anxiety. She felt altogether out of her element here, what with the empty strand, the huge sky with its shredded clouds overhead, the wind making odd sounds in the dripping undergrowth above the shoreline.

And where was the long, sloping hill Dame Sostris had claimed Elinor would find if she walked this way?

But then, rounding an elongated bend in the stony strand, she saw it: a sloping rise of ground ahead inland, with a jumble of rock on top that resembled a gull with one wing outstretched. She greeted it with a sigh of relief. Beyond, according to Dame Sostris's directions, lay Mamma Kieran's dwelling place.

It proved a wearisome clamber, but eventually she topped the rise, leaving the Ferth behind her. Standing next to the stone gull – which looked nothing like a gull this close up – Elinor gazed downhill. It was broken country, this, a jumble of rolling hills rising north and east, covered with high grass and scattered trees. In the far distance, blue mountains hovered.

At first, search though she might, Elinor could make out no sign of anything resembling a house nearby. But then she saw it, not so very far off downhill, partly screened by a little clump of gnarled trees: a large, rounded hut, the eaves hung all about with oddments that clashed and clattered and chimed in the breeze.

Elinor skidded down to it. 'Hallo!' she cried as she drew close, hailing through her cupped hands. And again, 'Hallo!'

There was no response. The hut looked empty. No movement, not a sound.

'Hallo!' she called a third time. 'Mamma Kieran, is ye there?'

Still there came no response. The place seemed quite deserted. There was not so much as a wisp of smoke from the crooked little chimney that stuck out from the hut's conical roof.

Elinor stumbled to a halt. She felt her heart falter. It seemed too cruel. First Annocky gone, then Dame Sostris helpless. And now *this*. It was as if the very Powers themselves were conspiring against her to rob her of her future.

Daylight was dimming now. True night lay still a farish ways off, but shadows were beginning to gather. The trees here seemed to crowd around the hut, hanging over her with a patient, malicious intent, their dripping leaves whispering secret things in the breeze. She felt a cold shiver prickle across her scalp and whirled abruptly, thinking she had caught stealthy movement out of the corner of her eye. But there was nothing.

Something shrieked suddenly, making her heart lurch. She stood ready to flee, limbs shaky with fright. But again it was nothing, only the cry of some beast or bird.

Elinor shook herself. She was acting like a stupid, frightened child. She would *not* give in. Not to her step-father or her mother, not to bad fortune, not to silly fright, not to anything.

She straightened herself and marched straight ahead towards the hut. It had mud and wattle walls, uneven and pocked with odd-shaped windows. The conical roof was wood-shingled, glistening green with wet moss. From the eaves, all sorts of queer things dangled, dripping.

She saw the small skull of some animal, yellow with age, swinging in the breeze, dead teeth chattering, as if it were a live thing shaking with cold. She felt a chill shiver go down her spine and moved quickly away from it.

There was a wind chime made of little bronze bells in the shape of wailing faces, *ching chingging* softly. Next to this hung a long spidery length of greenish knotted stuff in which some small, invisible thing seemed to wriggle desperately. A rattling tail of little bones dangled further along, like human knuckle bones but shining crimson and cobalt and ochre. An ugly, demon-faced thing with long tusks, old and cracked, like a combination face-mask and war helm, twirled slowly on a tether, huge yellow eyes seeming to stare at her angrily as it revolved . . .

Elinor slipped gingerly past these queer danglers, avoiding the water that dripped from them, and squinted through a little eye-level window. But she could make out nothing inside, only darkness. She turned quickly back and began to make her way around the cabin.

There was a door on the far side, an oval of age-dark wood which hung part-way open.

She pushed inside.

It took long moments for her eyes to accustom themselves to the darkness of the interior. There was one big room with an alcove off to the right. The mouth of a fireplace loomed at the back of the room, showing a dim red glow of old coals. A wedge of brighter light lanced in from behind Elinor, through the still part-opened door, casting her shadow across the floor.

She took a step further in, her soaked shoes squelching softly. Some small thing scuttled through the light, too quick and too little for her to make it out properly. Her heart missed a beat. She shuffled back, hesitated. She seriously doubted that Mamma Kieran would take kindly to intruders. But having come this far . . . Elinor took a hesitant step further in, her heart beating hard.

A sudden rustling brought her up short. Squinting into the room's darkness, she made out two shining eyes staring at her. Only the eyes could she see, unblinking, bright like cat's eyes, but on a level with her own. Elinor shivered. Mamma Kieran would have left a guardian, surely, in her absence. Elinor damned her own foolishness in brazening her way thus thoughtlessly in here. Slowly, trying to reach the door without turning her back on those eyes, she moved one foot back, feeling her way, moved the other . . . .

Something suddenly cried out in the darkness, *kra-ee ka kawww*, a soft rasping cry.

Elinor froze.

Again it came: *kraw-ee ka kree kaw*.

She heard a long, breathy sigh. Something popped, like knuckles being cracked: *kluple klup klup*. With a little *whooosh* the fire suddenly flared up, spilling crimson light into the hut's interior. Elinor turned to flee, but her feet somehow got tangled up with each other and she tumbled heavily to the floor. She twisted round, got one knee under her, her heart kicking in her breast.

By the fire's sudden light, she saw a sort of platform-cum-chair contraption up against the far wall – an intricately intertwined back rising very nearly a man's full height, a long bench-like platform strewn with tattered cushions and folds of woollen cloth. Upon this a figure that had to be Mamma Kieran sat hunched, legs folded under her, head tipped forward, as if gazing intently through the platform and floor, far down into the very substance of the earth itself – but with eyes tight shut.

As Elinor stared, the woman sighed again, a long rattling breath. She lifted her shoulders and arms a little, her joints popping with a soft *kluple klup*. Slowly, she raised her head. Elinor heard the bones of her neck crackle like kindling. Mamma Kieran's eyes opened, big and dark, shining in the fire's dancing light like twin, glimmering, dark stones. 'So . . .' she breathed, gazing at Elinor.

Elinor stayed frozen as she was, on one knee, heart thumping. Mamma Kieran was *old*. Her hair looked gossamer thin and dirty white like old snow. Her face was deeply wrinkled, long creases running down her cheeks, folded crescents of skin under her big dark eyes.

A long shudder seemed to go through the old woman, and she drew up a kind of wrap from the platform upon which she sat and folded it about herself, an intricately patterned thing, a tangled tapestry of shapes and figures.

A sudden skitter of movement drew Elinor's eyes to the top of the intricately fashioned chair behind Mamma Kieran's head. A sleek black raven shuffled along the topmost railing, as it might shuffle along a branch. It bent forward, regarded Elinor alertly with one shining eye on a level with her own, then with the other, then both at once, staring at her down its grey-black beak. *Kraw-eek ka kreek, kraw-eek ka kraww,* it said. There was something odd about its eyes . . .

Elinor rose gingerly to her feet and tried to back away, but Mamma Kieran beckoned her closer with a bony hand. Elinor did not wish to, but, somehow, she could not refuse that beckoning and came to stand before the old woman.

If Dame Sostris resembled a duck, then Mamma Kieran was a chicken. She was skinny as any plucked hen, her beckoning hand like a very hen's claw, all skin and sinew and knobbly bone, and the skin of her arms and face was pocked with a myriad tiny scars as if she had once indeed been covered in downy feathers which had been stripped away. Most of her teeth were gone, her cheeks caved in, her face wrinkled and cracked.

But Mamma Kieran's eyes . . . her eyes were big and dark and alert as those of the raven perched above her. She cocked her head to one side, regarding Elinor, and smiled a gap-toothed smile. It was not a comfortable smile to look upon. 'So . . . a girlie comes to me, does she? Welcome to me liddle 'ome, then, girlie.'

Elinor shuddered. Her bones seemed somehow to have gone all to jelly.

'You needs me, does you then, girlie?'

Elinor blinked. The old woman's voice was breathy, her words oddly accented. And it was an odd word, that *you* – in place of the familiar 'ye' that she was accustomed to. What queer, distant land must this woman be from, then, to speak so strangely?

'Well, girlie?' Mamma Kieran said.

'My name's Elinor,' she replied.

The old woman laughed softly, a sound like a rusty gate hinge squeaking. The raven squawked along with her, as if sharing in her mirth. 'My, but we *is* a twitchy liddle thing, isn' we now?'

Elinor was stung. 'I came to ye for *help*,' she snapped. 'Not ridicule. I can get *ridicule* at home!'

'Ah . . .' Mamma Kieran breathed. She leaned forward, tilting her head and regarding Elinor with one eye just as the raven did. 'An' jus' what sort of *'elp* is you lookin' to find from *me*, liddle girlie?'

Elinor swallowed. She felt suddenly that it had been an altogether bad idea to come here. 'I . . . I don't . . .' she stammered.

Mamma Kieran laughed again. 'Speak up. Speak *up*, then, girlie. Or you gets nothin'.' The old woman leaned forward, regarding Elinor more closely. 'You 'ave the feel o' the Dame about you.'

Elinor stared. 'It was . . . Dame Sostris who sent me to see ye.'

'Oh, aye?' Mamma Kieran responded, one wispy grey eyebrow going up. 'An' 'ow fares the Dame, then?'

'Well enough,' Elinor replied. 'Though she had one of her headaches.'

Mamma Kieran nodded, then lapsed into silence, her head hanging loosely.

Elinor waited. The whole of the world seemed to hush, till the soft snappling of the fire and the rushing of the blood-pulse in her own ears felt very loud.

The raven moved not at all; save for the glitter of its strange eyes, it might have been a statue. As might Mamma Kieran. Elinor could not even hear them breathing. The pair of them might as well be dead, for all she could tell.

Elinor sighed softly. Was this everything, then? Was this all there was to the great, ever-so-wise Mamma Kieran? A silent, creepy old woman with a creepy bird with weird eyes in a creepy little hut in the middle of nowhere? She took a careful step backwards, another. What was the point in staying further?

'Your problem'd be . . . what, then, girlie?' Mamma Kieran said suddenly.

Elinor hesitated, uncertain.

'I may be old, girlie. But I ain' gone stupid. Not yet. Tell me your troubles. Or go 'ome.' The old woman shrugged. 'Your choice.'

'They want to marry me off!' Elinor blurted, the words out almost before she knew she had spoken them. She put her hand to her mouth.

'They?' Mamma Kieran asked. 'An' who might *they* be, then?'

'My mother and Jago. They . . .'

'Want you to marry?'

Elinor nodded.

'Then what'd be your trouble, girlie? Marry your liddle man and be 'appy.'

'No. Ye doesn't understand! Ye must help me.'

The old woman sighed. For a long few moments she stared at Elinor. Finally, she nodded. 'Tell me, then.'

Elinor told her, about the winning of Annocky, about her step-father and mother's dire plans to marry her off, about Annocky's absence, Dame Sostris's unaccountable inability with the cards . . .

'An' jus' what,' Mamma Kieran said, once Elinor had finished, 'does you 'spect me to do for you?'

Elinor wrung her hands together. 'I don't know. But Dame Sostris said ye . . . ye swims in deeper waters than she. Those were her words.'

Mamma Kieran nodded. 'That's one manner o' puttin' it.'

'Maybe ye can see into what she couldn't? Maybe ye can see to help me in some way she couldn't? There must be *something* ye can do!'

Mamma Kieran shook her head. 'The world *is* as the world *is*, liddle girlie. There's times you mus' just accept things. There's nothin' I can do for you.'

'No!' Elinor cried. 'Ye cannot fail me, Mamma Kieran. Ye *mustn't*!'

'*Musn't?*' the old woman snapped. The raven perched behind her on the chair raised itself suddenly and squawked, lifting its black wings. 'And jus' who is *you*, then, to be tellin' the likes o' me what I *mus'* and *mustn't* be doin'?' She pointed at the still part-way open door with a long, bony finger. 'Get you gone, girlie.'

Elinor surged forward in dismay. 'Oh, Mamma Kieran . . . *please*! Ye're my only hope! Ask anything of me. *Anything*!'

Mamma Kieran laughed. 'You has nothin' I 'specially want, liddle girlie.'

37

'Out of . . . pity, then. Help me! I've my whole life ahead of me. And it looks to be spoiled before it's properly even begun. My *whole* life will be ruined!'

Mamma Kieran laughed again.

Elinor glared at her, outraged. 'How can ye . . .'

'Come 'ere, child.'

Elinor bridled at being called 'child', but the old woman's face was suddenly implacable as a hawk's.

'Closer,' Mamma Kieran ordered. She reached out bony fingers and took Elinor's wrist in a tight hold, pulling her to her knees. 'Closer still, child.' Mamma Kieran ran her free hand over Elinor's skull, not quite touching it. Elinor felt a kind of prickly charge shiver through her, and her hair crackled. She tried to jerk back but there was surprising strength in the old woman's grip.

'Easy,' Mamma Kieran whispered. 'Easy now . . .'

Elinor felt a surge of sudden dizziness. The room seemed to tip. Her head felt abruptly heavy as rock. Dark treacle seemed to fill the air. The breath came in and out of her lungs – slow, slow. She tried to move but could not. Her body seemed far off, a lumpen thing. A long, long distance off, she vaguely felt her heart beating like a frantic drum.

In her mind, she seemed to see a pair of eyes, a bronze face . . . a snarling dragon's head with glinting ruby eyes. The fanged mouth opened and crimson blood poured forth in a bubbling torrent.

Elinor shuddered, tried to cringe away. But the terrible image persisted. The bronze dragon had a long tail now, but not like any natural beast's tail. It was long and straight like a rod, but flat, shining like a mirror . . .

An uncomfortable, persistent buzzing filled her ears. Through it, she heard the flapping of raven's wings, like a bed sheet snapping in the wind. A croaking voice spoke: 'Aks-sel. She iss the aks-sel . . .'

'I sees it,' Mamma Kieran whispered.

Elinor felt herself held, felt her faraway heart beating, felt herself trembling helplessly. Something like spidery fingers seemed to be going through her insides, sweeping through her, searching through her.

In quick succession, a stutter of images filled her mind's eye:

a great, dark, shadowy figure, like a man-giant; a queer-looking female face, part human, part animal; a horde of strange, furred creatures; a crowd of struggling, fighting folk – all whirling about her, as if composing a spinning wheel and she the hub . . .

Then she felt herself collapse. The floor hit her face with a painful *thwump*. She levered herself to one elbow and shook her head, trying to shake off the queer, sick-making dizziness that still gripped her. She was wet and shivery with sweat. She sat up too quickly and her belly surged uncomfortably. She swallowed hard, refusing to be sick.

'What did ye . . .' she started, but her voice died. Mamma Kieran and her raven were staring at her.

'What?' she demanded. '*What?*'

'Aks-sel!' the raven said, or seemed to say.

Elinor shivered. She stared at the raven, shook her head, blinked, swung her gaze back to Mamma Kieran. 'What did ye *do* to me? Why are ye staring at me so?'

Mamma Kieran's wrinkled face was tight with some emotion Elinor could not read.

'Answer me!' Elinor cried.

The old Wise Woman let out a long, sighing breath. 'You's got the stink o' the destined 'bout you, girlie mine.'

'No!' Elinor cried. 'There *must* be some way out!' She raised both hands to Mamma Kieran in supplication, still on her knees. 'Ye's got to help me! My life's *ruined* if ye doesn't help me!'

Mamma Kieran laughed. 'Your life! You knows nothin' 'bout your life, liddle girlie.'

Elinor glared at the old woman in outrage. 'What . . .'

Mamma Kieran beckoned her to silence with one bony hand. 'You wouldn' understand, child. You isn' able for it. We scried you, me an' mine. We *saw*. You is more'n I first took you for, girlie.'

'Meaning *what*?'

Mamma Kieran shrugged. 'If I tried to explain it to you, it'd only make you a discomfort in your belly.'

'Why not let *me* be the judge of that?' Elinor demanded irately.

Mamma Kieran shook her head.

'But . . .'

'Enough questions!' the old woman snapped. 'You wearies me. Does you wish me to 'elp, or no?'

'With . . . Annocky?'

Mamma Kieran nodded.

'Aye,' Elinor said quickly. 'But why does ye . . .'

'I said, *enough*!' Mamma Kieran leaned forward, her face stern. 'You 'as not yet asked me price, liddle girlie. You knows, doesn't you, that I *always* charge a price for me 'elp.'

Elinor nodded and reached into her pocket for the coins she had.

The old woman only laughed. 'Oh, not like *that*, girlie. For you, I needs a *special* price.'

Elinor shivered. Dame Sostris, she remembered, had warned her about Mamma Kieran's 'prices'. What could the old woman demand? Services? Blood? Living flesh?

'I want,' Mamma Kieran said, 'your left 'and – '

'No!' Elinor all but shrieked, jamming both her hands deep into her armpits.

Mamma Kieran shook her head. 'Let me finish, child. Give me your left 'and. I'll do nothin' cripplin' to you. Does you wish me to 'elp you or no?'

Elinor shuddered, hesitated, held out her left hand gingerly.

The raven squawked and launched itself into the air with a sudden snapping of its black wings. It landed with a clatter on a shelf on the far side of the room, then returned with something in its beak which it held out to Mamma Kieran.

The old woman took the thing from the bird's grip. It was a golden signet, like a large coin, three finger breadths in diameter. Mamma Kieran held it in the palm of her wrinkled hand for Elinor to see. A face was inscribed on it, part human and part animal, long and slender of chin, with pointy ears and overlarge eyes. A female face, despite all the strangeness.

Elinor started. In the queer visionary fit that Mamma Kieran had somehow brought about in her, she had seen that same strange female face. 'But how . . .'

'Shush!' Mamma Kieran commanded. The golden signet winked and dazzled in the firelight. As Elinor watched, it began to glow in the old woman's grasp: gold-red, red, white.

Mamma Kieran smiled her gap-toothed smile. 'Here,' she said, offering the glowing signet to Elinor. 'Take it.'

Elinor only looked. The air about the signet rippled with heat.

'Take it,' Mamma Kieran repeated.

Elinor reached out her left hand, jerked it back. The thing was *hot*. How could the old woman hold it like that?

'Take it!' Mamma Kieran hissed. 'If you wants me to 'elp you, girlie, you mus' take it into your 'and.'

'But how can I . . .'

'No questions. Jus' *take it*!'

Elinor swallowed. She reached out determinedly.

'Palm out,' Mamma Kieran ordered. She tipped her own hand, dropping the signet into Elinor's grasp.

Elinor moaned. It *burned*.

'Keep it tight,' Mamma Kieran ordered. 'Close your 'and on it and 'old it tight!'

Elinor did, groaning, feeling the thing burn itself terribly, inexorably, into her poor flesh; feeling, at the same time, the image of that human-animal face burning into her mind. She swayed, on the brink of swooning.

'Stay with it,' Mamma Kieran said. 'Stay!'

Elinor shuddered, feeling sick. Her hand throbbed with agony. But she hung on grimly, refusing to falter, willing to brave any forfeit this queer old woman might exact, anything at all, if it meant she might gain her Annocky and the life she dreamed of.

'All right, then,' Mamma Kieran said softly. 'You can give it me back now.'

Elinor did, almost fainting with the pain of opening her hand. Mamma Kieran took the signet easily. Its burning heat seemed to cause her no distress at all. Elinor was afraid to look down at her hand. It was more than she had been prepared for, that agony. And now she would be a cripple for life, despite the old woman's promise to the contrary. Nobody could suffer a burn like she had and still have the full use of her hand afterwards. She shuddered sickly.

'Well done, girl,' Mamma Kieran said. '*Well* done.'

Elinor could feel the imprint where the signet had burned itself into her palm. She flexed her hand a little, experimentally,

41

and felt a flare of agony. She shuddered, took a breath, looked down at her burnt hand, gasped.

There was nothing: no burn, no scar, no sign at all.

'I don't . . . understand,' she breathed, staring at her palm. She could feel her hand throb, a circle of agony where the white-hot signet had branded her, lancing pain through her hand and up her arm. But her palm looked perfectly all right.

'Hold still,' Mamma Kieran ordered, bringing the signet closer once more. 'An' look!'

Elinor looked. As the signet drew close to her hand, the pain throbbed with new intensity. But now, faintly, she could make out the brand it had left. It was as if the signet cast a kind of invisible radiance, and only under that radiance was the scar it had left visible.

A face looked up at her from her left palm, the same human-animal, pointy-eared, female face that was imprinted upon the signet itself.

'She is known as the Lady,' Mamma Kieran said, drawing back the signet and gesturing to the image of the face on it.

To Elinor's confusion, Mamma Kieran's naming of it seemed to make the image more . . . alive somehow. It was not that the graven eyes actually moved, or that the face changed in any way. But there was . . . something. A subtle shimmer of difference. The face seemed to gaze back at her, somehow, when she looked at it.

Elinor stared at the signet, then at her own hand. The image on her palm seemed momentarily to clear, like a reflection on still water. The pain was all but gone now.

'What has ye *done* to me?' she demanded. 'What is this . . . *Lady*? Some sort of . . . of spirit imprisoned in the signet?'

Mamma Kieran shook her head.

'What, then?'

'Somethin' . . . complicated. The face of need, of balance.'

'I . . . I don't *understand*!' Elinor complained.

'You doesn' need to.'

'But . . .' Elinor started.

''Tis my gift to you,' Mamma Kieran said.

Elinor blinked. 'But I thought ye said this was to be a price *I* paid to *ye*?'

The old woman nodded. 'Aye. My price is that you mus' let me gift you.'

'But . . .'

'There be times, me liddle girlie, when one does what one does . . . unknowin'. The great world is no simple place. I gifts you 'cause I feel the need to. 'Tis in me bones, in the very air we breathe, you an' me. 'Tis a question of the greater balances . . .'

Elinor stared.

Mamma Kieran leaned forward. 'But there's no cause for this to prey on your mind, girlie. No necessity at all . . .'

The old woman reached out, fanning her gnarled fingers, as if drawing something invisible from the air. 'Let it sink, liddle girlie. Let your mind open. Let it sink down . . .'

Elinor blinked, confused. Mamma Kieran's eyes were huge and bright and deep as pools, somehow.

'Let it sink deep,' she said, her voice a mere half-whisper. 'Sink below memory. No memory. Sunk down, down, down. A stone in deep, dark waters. Forget. *Forget* . . .'

Elinor shook herself. She had the strangest feeling . . . as if someone were tickling the inside of her head with a feather.

'Forget. *Forget* . . .'

'Forget what?' Elinor said. She stared at Mamma Kieran wonderingly. What was the old woman doing?

'I've changed me mind,' Mamma Kieran said then.

Elinor's heart jumped. 'Ye's not going to help me?'

'Oh, aye. I'll 'elp you all right. But I've taken sudden pity on you, girlie. I won't be demandin' any price from you after all.' The old woman leaned forward, her face intent. 'Would that be all right with you, now?'

Elinor shivered. She felt . . . She did not know quite how she felt. There was something . . . She felt as if something had happened, as if she were missing something, or . . .

She did not know what.

'No . . . no price for . . . for helping me?' she stammered.

Mamma Kieran nodded. 'If that suits you.'

'It . . . suits me. But I don't . . .'

'"The rivers sing their flowing song,"' Mamma Kieran said, '"towards the sea, where they belong."' The old woman's voice had taken on a chanting, melodic quality, and she pronounced the words perfectly, with none of her previous slurrings.

43

'"There's not a river flowing free but cries its yearning for the sea."'

Elinor did not know what to think.

'From a book,' Mamma Kieran explained. 'A very ol' book.' As if that explained everything.

Elinor shook her head. 'What does that have to do with *anything*?'

Mamma Kieran smiled her gap-toothed smile. 'Never you mind, girlie. Never you mind. You's a river, liddle girlie, lookin' for your sea is all.'

'Meaning what, exactly?' Elinor said.

'You'll know, one day. Per'aps.'

Elinor stared at her.

Mamma Kieran smiled more widely. 'I'm learnin' to *like* you, liddle girlie. You has a long path ahead of you, and no easy one.'

Elinor did not know what to say. She had a sudden pang of doubt.

'Will ye . . .' she began. 'Will ye help me gain my Annocky?'

The old woman nodded. 'Aye.'

'*Truly*?' Elinor could not quite bring herself to believe it. 'What will ye do, then? Tell me! *What*?'

Mamma Kieran shook her head and smiled her gap-toothed smile again. 'The red blood do run hot in you, girlie, don' it now?'

'What can ye *do*?' Elinor demanded. 'How can ye get me out of this mess I'm in?'

'I know things, girlie. A powerful lot about 'erbs, for instance.'

'How can herbs help me?'

'There's 'erbs, and there's 'erbs. Some gentle and kind as mother's milk. Others, now . . .'

'Aye?' Elinor prodded.

'There's an 'erb I know that's a poison – of sorts. Give it to somebody an' it . . . kills 'em. Or *seems* to.'

Elinor stared, not sure what to make of this.

'I'll give you a tincture o' this special 'erb to take away with you. When you wishes, swallow the tincture – all of it, mind – and you will . . . die.'

'But what good will *that* do?' Elinor demanded despairingly.

'All who see you will think you dead. An' if you's dead, you can't marry nobody, can you, now?'

Elinor nodded with sudden excitement, seeing where the old woman was leading her.

'Your folks'll mourn. Your husband-to-be will mourn along with all the rest.'

'And me?' Elinor said. 'What about *me*?'

'The effects of the 'erb wear off eventual. Takes some days, mind you. I'll keep my eye on things, from a distance of course. See that all goes as we wish. An' then, in the dark, I'll pry you out o' the ground and . . .'

'Out of the *ground*?'

Mamma Kieran nodded. 'They mus' bury you, child.'

'But . . .' Elinor shuddered, thinking of herself shut up under the earth, trapped, in darkness and cold, coming to consciousness scrabbling at the unyielding belly of her coffin – one of Jago's stout pine ones . . .

'"T'will be all right, child,' Mamma Kieran said reassuringly. 'We'll have you out before you comes back to yourself. You'll never even know you was buried. An' then we'll 'ave you reunited with this young man you's so hot for.' The old woman leaned forward. 'But this is no *light* solution, girlie. You *will* die in a manner of speakin'. For your family you will. You can never, *never* come back to them. Does you truly understand this?'

Elinor swallowed, nodded gravely.

Mamma Kieran reached to the raven which had stayed at her side all this time. 'I can send my companion 'ere with you when you leaves. He'll keep his eye on you. If anythin' untoward 'appens, he'll let me know of it.'

'But . . .' Elinor began, eyeing the raven uncertainly. 'It can't . . .'

The bird squawked, snapped its wings, looked at Elinor and winked. 'I ca-can,' it said softly in a raspy, cawing, but entirely understandable voice.

Elinor gasped. It was one thing to hear – to *think* she could hear – the bird's voice when she was all swoony and unsettled in her mind. But for the bird to address her like that, to look straight at her, with eyes that seemed . . .

They were utterly human and knowing, those eyes. How had she not noticed such a thing immediately?

'What manner of creature *is* it?' she asked of Mamma Kieran, utterly unsettled.

The old woman ignored the question. 'Has you the courage to do this thing, then? I warns you . . . choosin' this path may lead you places you don' 'spect. Does you still 'ave the will to do it, knowing that?'

Elinor hesitated, confused and unsettled by the utter strangeness of everything. But in her heart she knew there was only one answer she could give. 'I'll do it! Give me the tincture.'

VI

'Now listen to me, girl, *please*,' Elinor's mother said. 'A marriage like this . . . ye'll be the envy of the neighbourhood. Master Hadelbert is a *fine* catch. Why, he's . . .'

'He's an ugly, fat old man!' Elinor snapped.

'Mind yer tongue, girl!' Jago snapped crossly.

Elinor turned her back on the two of them and stalked across the floor to stand where the sloping ceiling came down to meet the wall. Her little attic room seemed crowded and stifling with both Genna and Jago here berating her.

'Turn around and look at us,' Jago ordered her. 'It's been more than a few years since I took ye over my knee and gave ye a good birching, but I could still do it!'

Elinor half-turned, glared at him in sullen resistance. 'Stupid, bullying old fart!' she said, but in the privacy of her own mind.

He took a menacing step towards her.

'Jago!' Genna said in exasperation. She ran her hands nervously through her grey-streaked hair, shook her head. 'Ye *isn't* helping.'

Jago scowled, fists clenched. 'The girl's being wilfully stupid, Genna. She always was too headstrong. I shouldn't have listened to ye when she was younger. "Be easy with her," ye was always telling me. "Better to be kind."'

Jago stabbed an accusing finger at his step-daughter. 'And now . . . *now* we have this! Instead of being useful, she spends her time mooning her life away. She runs off away from home, spending the night who knows where . . . And refuses to tell us *anything*! I won't *have* it, I tell ye!'

There was silence between them all for a long moment. From outside the window, the sound of a raven's *kaww kaw* could be heard.

'And where,' Jago asked infuriatedly, 'did that sodding *raven* come from? It's been sitting out there ever since Elly got back. In *my* day we didn't have ravens – dirty carrion birds they are – perched outside our windows like sparrows. There's something uncanny about it, I tell ye. What's the world coming to?'

Genna went over to her husband, took him by the elbow, and ushered him firmly out of Elinor's little attic room. 'Let me handle her,' she told him.

Jago acquiesced with ill grace, shaking his head, scowling. 'What's wrong with young folk these days? Where's their *respect*? In *my* day . . .'

Genna pushed him out the door and closed it firmly behind her. She looked at Elinor and sighed. 'He's a good man, yer father, but sometimes he does get on that high horse of his.'

'He's *not* my father,' Elinor snapped.

'Now don't start *that* again.'

'Well, he *isn't*!'

'Yer father's gone. And good riddance to him, I say!'

'He'll be back, one day. And then Jago'll be sorry.'

Genna went over to her daughter. 'Oh, Elly! Ye doesn't really . . . Ye haven't been harbouring *that* foolish hope all this time, has ye?'

Elinor bit her lip.

'He's *gone*, girl. Time ye accepted that and got on with yer life.'

'My life . . . which ye and Jago wish to ruin *entirely*!'

Genna sighed. 'Elly girl, there's some things we just have to accept. Ye're not yearning after that . . . what was his name? That head banger from Shilligen's mob, are ye? Is *that* yer problem?'

Elinor said nothing.

'Ye has to wake up to the realities of life, girl. That fella's nothing but trouble. Sure, he may be a looker, but he'll leave ye in the lurch just as Corki left me. Why . . . I bet ye he isn't even in town now. Out on some *job* or other somewheres. Amn't I right?'

Elinor kept silent.

'I *am* right, then.' Genna put a hand gently on her daughter's arm. 'Give him up, girl. There's a proper future waiting for ye with Master Hadelbert.'

Elinor looked away from her mother. Outside, the raven *kawwed* once more. She thought of Mamma Kieran and slipped her hand into the side pocket of her tunic. She could feel the little stone vial of tincture that Mamma Kieran had given her, hard and solid in her surreptitious hold. Elinor felt a shiver go through her. Such a little thing, a little darkness for a time, and then she would be free to start her new life with Annocky.

'Elly!' Genna said. 'Listen to me, girl.'

Elinor turned round. Her mother was looking old and tired. For a moment, Elinor's heart went out to her. There had been hard years, she knew, before Jago came round. Genna could hardly be blamed for taking what opportunity she could for some security and comfort.

But she would *not* make the same mistakes her mother had.

'Ye musn't do anything *stupid*, now,' Genna was saying. 'Please!' She put a hand gently on her daughter's arm. 'I know it may seem cold, this . . . arranging of things. But it's all for the best. Why, if I'd only had somebody to arrange things for me . . .'

'All right, Mother,' Elinor said tiredly. She disengaged her mother's hold.

'All right . . . what?' Genna asked, uncertain.

'Whatever ye says. The marriage is arranged. There's nothing else to be done. Is there?'

Genna looked at her uncertainly. 'Ye accepts it, then?'

Elinor shrugged. 'What choice do I have?'

Genna smiled. 'There's my good girl. There's my *sensible* girl. It's no easy world we live in, Elly. A woman has to look out for herself as best she can.' She clapped her hands. 'Oh . . . ye'll not regret this, I promise ye. Ye'll have a better life than I.'

Elinor walked over to her bed and sat on it. She shrugged once more. 'I'm tired, Mother. Can ye leave me be. Please?'

Genna nodded. She bent down and kissed Elinor lightly on the forehead. 'My *sensible* girl,' she repeated. Then, without a word further, she let herself out of the room, closing the door softly behind.

Elinor heard the sound of Jago's voice through the door – he must have been hanging about on the stairs all the while – saying, 'Well?' Genna's answer was too soft for Elinor to make out. She heard the sound of their voices, their footsteps on the stairs dwindling away, then nothing. In the silence that was left, she heard Mamma Kieran's raven call again.

She felt after the vial of tincture, thought of Annocky, of his long strong body, his careless laugh, the way he threw back his head sometimes so that his braid of red hair swung like a horse's tail. She thought of the little house they would live in, just the two of them, free and together and happy as larks . . .

Slowly, she drew the vial out of her pocket and looked at it. It was a smooth oblong of red-flecked green stone, about as long as one of her fingers and thrice as thick. A little cork stoppered the top. Pulling the cork, she lifted the vial to her nose and sniffed. It smelled bitter and sweet at once, the scent of roses and gall combined. She shuddered and re-stoppered the vial.

What if it went wrong and the old woman abandoned her? What if she came to her senses in stifling darkness and cold, and she all alone . . . utterly, terribly alone while the life drained slowly from her until, finally, she dropped into the long falling journey to the Shadowlands of the dead?

After all, Dame Sostris's cards had read death – the Drowned Sailor and Hanged Man. But it had been no *ordinary* death that the cards had shown . . . This make-believe death she and Mamma Kieran were practising must be what the cards talked of, surely.

But what if . . .

Elinor drew her mind back, silencing the doubts. This was her chosen path – unless she wished to make a life with fat old Master Hadelbert. Which she did not! Such doubting thoughts as she was having were only useless torments.

She held all the promise of her future in her own hands.

'You's got the stink o' the destined 'bout you,' Mamma Kieran had said.

Elinor kept remembering that phrase.

Lying in bed nights as a girl, she had yearned for the lives Corki told her of in his tales – brighter, better, bigger lives than the one she knew. Those story-lives had been far more vivid for her than her own, and she had made few girlhood friends, yearning too much for escape from the drab cage in which she felt prisoned.

She felt herself different from all around her, like a foundling hawk abandoned in some dowdy wood pigeon's nest. Her father had flown, and she would too.

She was destined, aye.

No repeat of her mother's drab, sad life for her. She would have something better by far. She and her Annocky. Together, they would do grand things. And Corki, if he returned, would smile and nod at her proudly, and say, 'That's my grand girl,' as he used to.

Oh, aye . . .

But, staring down at the stone vial in her grasp, she felt her belly twist. Could it really be so simple as all that? A little swallow – and all her dreams come true? Mamma Kieran had warned her that this act might lead down unexpected paths . . .

She got up from her bed and went to the window. It was evening, the sky purpling into night, the first stars glimmering faintly. Opening the casement, she leaned out into the cool air. The dark shape of the raven sat hunched on a shed roof nearby. It looked up at her, its uncannily human eyes glinting knowingly.

Elinor took a breath, held up the vial for the raven to see. 'I shall take it now,' she called to the bird softly. She felt foolish and terrified and exalted all at once. Her hand, holding the vial, shook in little uncontrollable spasms.

The raven nodded to her, solemn and silent.

She drew back inside, closed the window, went back to her bed.

'Annocky,' she said quietly, savouring the sound of his name on her tongue. Then she unstoppered the little vial, put it to her lips, and drained it in one sputtering gulp.

It was as if she had taken a draught of liquid ice. Her throat and belly went freezing cold in an instant. She felt a sick dizziness rush through her and toppled backwards on the bed. The room about her seemed to heave, to expand, to shrink. Her head throbbed painfully. Her heart raced like a mad thing, then slowed . . . *thump ka-thwump thump ka-thwump thump ka-thwump* . . . slow . . . slower . . . slowest . . .

The last thing she was aware of was the raven's far cry:

kree kaw kaw kree kaw ... In warning or benediction, she did not know.

Then there was only a pressing darkness.

Then nothing at all.

VII

Elinor awoke to darkness. She felt cold, her skin all goose pimples. She found herself panting: there did not seem to be enough air to breathe. Her back was stiff, and her legs. She tried to lift her arms, to stretch, but could not – her elbows smacked up painfully against cold wood on both sides . . .

No! she thought.

She lay still, refusing to believe. Mamma Kieran had *promised* that nothing would go wrong. It must be her imagination, some after-effect of the tincture the old woman had given her, some queer, vivid dream or other. Something . . .

She tried to take a long, calming breath, but it was too hard to get enough air. The sound of her own panting was loud in her ears. Her heart was hammering now as if she had just run a mad race up a steep hill.

It could not be . . .

It was utterly, utterly dark, and Elinor could see nothing – might as well have her eyes tight shut, or no eyes at all, for all the difference having them open made. Fearfully, she lifted her hands before her face, reached upwards . . . and discovered a cold, hard, flat wooden ceiling only a couple of hand spans above her nose. She felt about, fingers scrabbling in panicky rushes here and there, like spastic spiders. Ceiling, walls, floor. She felt it with her hands, lifted her legs and pressed her knees upwards against it, shifted her hips and felt the cold, unyielding wooden cradle all around.

In instinctual panic, she surged up and cracked her forehead painfully against the ceiling, fell back and hit the back of her head on the wooden surface under her.

'No . . .' she whispered, dizzy and faint with pain and lack of proper air and very horror. '*NO!*' She hammered desperately on the ceiling, shrieking, writhing, kicking with her feet, thumping her fists against the unyielding wood above till her knuckles dripped with blood.

All to no avail.

Exhausted, Elinor fell back. She began to weep, great racking sobs that went through her in painful spasms, until she found herself spluttering and gasping for air. She seemed to feel the weight of the earth above pressing down upon her wooden prison, pressing down upon her lungs, a great, dank, choking heaviness. Was this to be her end, then? Alone in the cold and dark, alone forever and ever, never to see the light of day once again, never to feel the wonderful warmth of sunlit morning air . . . nothing but this chill, stifling, lonely prison till she sank inexorably down into the sheer darkness of the Shadowlands, a tortured, stricken spirit . . .

It did not bear thinking on.

Elinor snuffled, swallowed, shook her head. She concentrated on her breathing, trying to shake the hysteria from herself. Her mouth felt dry as old leather. With nothing else to drink, she sucked at the blood oozing from her knuckles – and had to content herself with that. She shivered, both from the horror of her plight and the pervasive chill all about her. She tried to wrap herself up more tightly in the shroud in which they had buried her – a long, loose robe. But the cloth was as thin as thin, with no warmth in it at all.

How could such a terrible thing have happened? she asked herself miserably. Had Mamma Kieran been lying to her? Deceiving her? But that was too terrible a notion to accept.

'There's the scent of death to this reading,' Dame Sostris had told her. 'But not true death.' Elinor clung to that.

She took a long breath, shivering, trying to draw what goodness she could from the too-close air, sucked at her bruised and bleeding knuckles.

She shuddered, remembering stories of bodies that had been dug up from the grave, poor souls who had been buried accidentally before their time, hands gnawed to the bone from hunger . . .

Then, thinking of graveyard stories, she remembered something. Folk *did* get buried prematurely sometimes. And sometimes, in case of that possibility, the family would set up a brass bell at the gravesite, with a pull-wire sunk down through the earth and set inside the coffin.

Jago had always been a cautious, careful, fore-planning man . . .

Elinor began searching around her.

It took a long, anxious length of scrabbling about, but eventually, in the coffin's upper back corner behind her head, she felt a little brass pull-ring.

She was saved!

All she had to do was tug on the pull-ring, jangling the bell above, and somebody would hear and dig her out.

She reached back, determined to give the pull-ring a good yank. Not too hard, lest she snap the wire – awful thought. Just hard enough to start the bell tolling smartly.

But she stopped herself, for in her mind she saw how it would be: she would be saved, returned to the living world. And then . . . reunited with her family, with the prospect of marriage to Master tub-o-lard Hadelbert to be faced once more. And no way out this time.

She forced herself to relinquish the pull-ring. She would have to wait for Mamma Kieran to exhume her, wait and hope that the old woman would act in good faith, that the air would not fail her, that her nerve would not fail her . . .

Her back became a nagging agony she could not stretch properly to do anything about, and her legs almost as bad. Her belly began to cramp from hunger and her mouth felt blistered it was so dry. She found it harder and harder to swallow, for her throat seemed not only painfully dry but swollen also.

Half a hundred times she started, thinking she had heard the scratch or thunk or whisper of a spade wielded from above, digging her out. But each time it proved to be nothing more than her own wishful imagination.

Nobody came.

The air became progressively harder and harder to breathe. She knew there had to be air circulating into the coffin through the earth above, or she would not have survived this long – but it was hard not to imagine herself lying helpless while the last of the good air ran out and she died writhing and gasping like some poor stranded fish.

To keep her mind off such notions, she thought of Annocky, of his fine hands, the way he threw back his head sometimes, the good feel of him. And she thought of the life they would make together, home and love, aye. But more also . . . she knew not exactly what yet, but something special. She could feel it in her bones. Her life, her future would be *special*. She was destined. Mamma Kieran had sensed it clear.

You has a long path ahead of you, the old Wise Woman had said. *And no easy one*.

No easy one indeed, Elinor thought. But she thought, also, of her and Annocky together, the two of them older, mellowed by years, sitting on the veranda of their own house by the Ferth's shore, watching the sun set . . .

It *would* come to pass – she would see to that. Or die trying.

Elinor shook her head, trying not to think such thoughts . . .

Where *was* the old woman?

Her hand crept to the pull-ring. Surely if Mamma Kieran were coming at all she would have been here by now? Surely she had better start ringing the bell before it was too late.

But she held back, waiting, hoping, desperately determined.

It seemed like half her very life had been spent in the cold, dank, stifling darkness. Hunger and thirst were a torment beyond any she had imagined. Her cramped back flamed with agony that made her weep, until she could take no more . . .

And still she held on, waiting, no more than a tight little bundle of will and pain now, waiting in agony . . . waiting . . . grimly determined not to give in.

Waiting . . .

A scrabbling sound from above made her start and crack her head against unyielding wood.

She thought she had imagined it, like all the other times.

But it came again.

And again. The definite thunk of a spade.

It struck the top of the coffin just above her face with a *thwack* that resounded through her bones.

'I'm here!' she tried to call out. 'Here!' But her voice was no more than a faint croak, like a sick frog's. She tried to thump the wooden ceiling over her with a fist, and was frightened to realize how helpless she had become; she could barely raise her arm, so cramped and sore and shivery it was.

But the spade from above kept thunking away.

Elinor heard the sound of earth spattering, the blessed sound of voices – though too muffled for her to be able to make out words.

Then, to her utter relief, she felt the coffin sway up under her.

When they pried the lid off, finally, she thought she was going to faint, the rush of light and air was so powerful. Her eyes were blinded painfully and she turned away, mewing like a sick kitten.

'Poor liddle child,' she heard Mamma Kieran say. Then, 'Lift 'er out, the poor thing.'

Strong hands took Elinor by the knees and shoulders and she was lifted up like a sack of beets. She had not the strength to do anything but loll helplessly in the grip of whoever it was had her in their hold.

They set her down gently on the ground. She felt damp grass under her, wonderfully yielding after the coffin's hard wood. She stretched her legs, arched her back, felt her spine crackle softly, *kuckle kuk kuk*, and groaned. But if felt good for all that. Blinking, she lifted her head and looked about, trying to make sense of her surroundings. The terrible bright light that hurt her eyes was, she realized, no more than a simple candle-lantern. It was night, she saw; a clear night, with the stars sparkling painfully bright overhead and the air pure and cold as ice in her nostrils.

She lay back and wept with the very joy of it.

VIII

'No, child,' Mamma Kieran said. 'You's too weak to go.'

'I'm *going*,' Elinor insisted. She sipped at the cup of herb tea Mamma Kieran had made for her, holding it in two hands, both for safety and to savour its warmth. It was true; she did still feel trembly and weak, and Mamma Kieran claimed she was white as a sheet still, but Elinor could not wait any longer. By the window of the old Wise Woman's little hut she could see the day waning. A full day gone since they had dug her out of the ground, and three days 'dead' according to the old Wise Woman – two before they buried her, one in the grave. Elinor shivered and sipped at the warming tea.

'Annocky'll be returned by now,' she said. 'What with him being gone away, and everything happening so quick, and me with no way to contact him . . . He'll think I'm *dead*, Mamma Kieran! What else *can* he think? He must be half out of his mind with grief by now. I've *got* to go to him!'

Mamma Kieran shook her head. 'You needs a good night's sleep at least. An' some proper food in your belly.' From the far side of the room, the raven said, *kraw-eek ka kree kaw* and glared at Elinor disapprovingly.

'Your family took too long to bury you, girlie. Too much time wi' you laid out in the front room o' the 'ouse, wi' them moanin' and mournin' an' carryin' on. We should 'ave 'ad you out o' the ground long since. You needs rest and warmth and food, I tells you.'

Elinor shuddered, remembering the dark.

'Anyways, you's nothin' to wear save the shroud they buried you in,' Mamma Kieran added with finality. 'You'll catch your death in that thin thing on a chill night like this. Summer's a long ways off yet. The sea air'll eat right through you. An' what would your precious Annocky think, seein' you dressed for the grave so? Follow my advice, girlie. Let me fetch 'im 'ere.'

'I'm going,' Elinor repeated. 'I can wear the shroud. What does it matter? Annocky'll know it's me, no matter what I wear. And it's been warm enough all day, and looks to be a breezeless, warm night. Let me borrow an old cloak or something to wear over it. Ye can get me rowed across the Ferth down along to the quays. It'll be night by the time we get there, and I can sneak through to The Anchor unseen. I can do it! I can see Annocky tonight!' She stood up. 'And I *will* do it! With yer help or without it.'

'Aye,' Mamma Kieran said with a sigh. 'All right.'

Mamma Kieran arranged to get her rowed across the Ferth by the two men who had dug her out of the grave. Father and son, they seemed, fashioned from the exact same mould, the older one grey and bearded, the younger smooth-skinned and chestnut-haired. Farmers, by the look of their thick trousers and heavy boots. They had spoken not a word in Elinor's hearing, not to her, not to Mamma Kieran, not even between themselves, and silently did whatever the old Wise Woman bid them.

Once arrived at the quays, Elinor left her rowers waiting behind in the boat. She had promised solemnly to Mamma Kieran that she would return before daylight – but that was a promise she had little intention of keeping once she met Annocky. Why should she? She was free now to do as she wished. Her mother and Jago thought her dead. She *was* dead for all intents and purposes.

The future for which she had yearned would begin this very night. She could swan off with Annocky, wherever and whenever she wished, and none could gainsay her.

It was her every girlhood dream come true.

She slipped away from the quays through the dark back-ways, avoiding folk as much as possible. It did not take her any great time to reach The Anchor.

Once there, however, she found herself at an impasse. She could not very well just march in looking for Annocky. What would folk say if they saw her, in her burial shroud, come walking in like one returned from the dead?

So what was she to do?

She solved the problem by accosting a likely young lad, somebody completely unknown to her whom she chose at random as he walked by. Clutching Mamma Kieran's cloak tight about her, she drew the lad aside. 'I want ye to take a message to somebody for me,' she told him. 'He's in The Anchor yonder. Annocky's the name. Tell him to meet Elinor at the Night Garden.'

The lad looked at her quizzically. 'The Night Garden?'

'He'll know where that is,' Elinor assured him.

He hesitated. 'And what's in it for me if I deliver this little message of yers?'

'It's . . .' Elinor swallowed. 'It's a matter of life or death.'

'For true?'

'For true.'

He looked undecided for a moment longer, then smiled. 'Done,' he said. 'For a kiss.'

Elinor bridled. 'How dare ye . . .'

'D'ye want this message of yers delivered or no?'

'Aye,' Elinor said, sighing.

'Then pay up.'

She paid, and a wet, sloppy kiss it turned out to be, with the lad's hands roaming about her like twin puppies in search of the nipple.

'There now,' she said, when she was finally able to push him away. 'Take my message for me and be off with ye.'

He grinned at her. 'My pleasure,' he said and scampered through the doorway inside.

Elinor turned and slipped off, making her own quiet way towards the little trysting place where she and Annocky had first known the pleasures of each other: Annocky's Night Garden.

All was deserted when she arrived. There was no cheerful fire, and the place was dead silent. Elinor remembered how her heart had beat so that first night here. It was beating now, too. She tried to imagine what Annocky's face would be like when he received her message and realized she must be alive. Would there be tears in his eyes? She hoped so.

At first, she had thought she would fling herself bodily upon him the moment he arrived here. But now she thought better of it. She wanted to savour the moment, to look upon him from some hidden vantage, to see the expectant gleam in his eyes, to watch him search desperately here and there: excited, confused, afraid it all might be some terrible hoax.

And then . . . his arms about her, his long strong body pressed tight to hers, and all the years of their life together, long years stretching ahead, ripe with promise as a tree full of fruit.

Elinor sighed happily, crouched down behind a tangled arm of ivy, and settled herself to wait.

Time crawled by.

The night air was chill, as Mamma Kieran had warned, but Elinor still felt herself sweating. She was hot and clammy, tucked away in her little ivy-sheltered corner, her heart thumping eagerly, and she slipped the borrowed cloak off her shoulders. It was better with only the thinness of the pale shroud about her. She wanted the waiting over, wanted Annocky just to *be* here!

But she had learned the virtue of hard waiting, and this was far easier than the last vigil she had kept – there was starlight, gentle air, she could stretch her limbs if she needed.

And, eventually, she heard the sounds of somebody approaching.

Elinor shivered, thinking of how it would be . . . Annocky questing about anxiously, her savouring just those few, precious moments more of anticipation, then flinging herself into his eager arms.

She heard him draw near. In the starlit dark, she saw his hand lift the three-board door that kept this special Night Garden of his secret. He came through, tall and lean and handsome. The oval blue tattoos on his cheeks gleamed dark and exotic in the starlight. His eyes seemed bright as any cat's. He looked about, his braid of hair swinging like a horse's tail, took one step in, another . . .

Elinor leaned forward. She would let him come in altogether, she decided, let him feel a moment of despair, thinking the message a fake. Then she would leap upon him, laughing . . .

Ah, but he was a lovely man, she thought, watching the way he moved. *Her* lovely man . . .

He stepped further in, cast about him.

Elinor readied herself.

But Annocky turned then, reached back to somebody, and whispered, 'It's all right. Everything's quiet as can be.' He pulled somebody through after him.

It took Elinor a long few moments to see who it was he had with him. At first, she could not think why he would have brought *anybody*. Her message had been simple, but clear enough for all that.

But then she saw.

It was a woman he had in tow. Elinor heard her giggle softly.

A *woman*!

Elinor could not believe it. She felt as if somebody had just kicked her in the belly.

'Come in, my lovely,' Annocky said softly to the woman. 'I'll build us a fire. And by its bright dancing light we two shall know each other.'

Elinor felt a spasm go through her, clenching fists, jaw, belly. The very words . . . the very, exact *same* words he had used with her. The rotten, conniving, faithless scoundrel! She watched him reach towards the woman. Again came the soft giggle. 'Oh, . . . *Ann*ocky!' The two of them became one figure under the starlight as they embraced in a long, passionate kiss.

Elinor stared, her heart thumping, feeling dizzy and sick, as if the solid ground under her had suddenly been torn away and she were plummeting into dark, endless oblivion . . . For long, long moments she remained crouched rigidly down by the ivy, unable to move. Then a burst of fury set her abruptly free. 'Annocky!' she shrieked, surging up. '*Annocky*!'

The two before her split apart like a wooden statue riven suddenly by some invisible axe. The woman let out a terrified little squeal, her hands to her mouth. Annocky whirled, going six ways at once like a startled cat.

Elinor stalked towards them, her white shroud billowing about her palely. She raised an arm in bitter accusation. 'Ye . . . ye . . .'

The woman wailed, falling to her knees.

'No!' Annocky cried. '*No*!'

'A spirit,' the woman moaned. 'One of the unhappy dead!'

Annocky stared, his eyes wide and terrified. 'Ye's dead, Elly. *Dead*! Go back to the Shadowlands. Haunt me not. Leave me *be*!'

'Didn't ye get my *message*?' Elinor demanded furiously.

'Me . . . message?' Annocky said. 'I got no *message*. Ye's *dead*, Elly!'

'But I sent a lad to tell ye . . .'

Annocky made a warding sign with his fingers and spat between them at Elinor. 'A . . . a scathless journey in the darkness, friend,' he began to recite breathlessly, quoting the death litany at her. 'A scathless journey and a . . . a fruitful end. *Gone* from the world of living ken. *Gone* to the Shadowlands . . . to begin again!' He looked at her expectantly, as if waiting for her to disappear before his eyes.

Elinor stood frozen for a long moment, not knowing whether to laugh or cry or shriek. Then she pointed angrily at the still-kneeling woman at Annocky's side. 'So this . . .' she said, her voice hoarse with emotion '. . . *this* is all I mean to ye? Not four days dead and ye's already bedding a new woman?'

'Aieeee!' wailed the new woman, collapsing entirely to the ground.

'El . . . Elly . . .' stammered Annocky. He stared, shaking like a leaf. 'Now, Elly, how can ye . . . Ye's *dead*! I mean . . .'

'Aie-*eeeee*!' Elinor screeched. It was a sudden, wordless venting of all her anger and outrage and hurt, like the instinctual cry of some mortally wounded beast, or of some lost soul trapped between the land of the living and the dark Shadowlands of the dead.

The new woman turned and fled, scrambling frantically to her feet and out through the Night Garden's little three-board doorway as if her very life depended on it, mewling hysterically.

Annocky cast one last, terrified look over his shoulder back at Elinor where she stood in the starlight, white-faced, enveloped in her pale death shroud . . . then he too fled, leaping like a mortally frightened deer.

Elinor heard the crash and thump of the pair's retreat dwindling in the distance. She stood rooted where she was, unable to move for long moments.

Then she burst into a fit of hysterical laughter, falling to her knees, gasping with it . . .

After that, came the tears.

IX

The quays were all but deserted at this early hour. Dawn mist lay in wispy coils all about. Seaward, only the tips of the ships' masts showed clear, rising above the level of the mist like the crest of some odd, sparse forest.

Elinor moved along the quayside, shivering, for the air still held the night's chill. Her legs were shaky-weak, so that she tottered rather than walked.

She had not returned to Mamma Kieran. What was the use? Live the rest of her life on the Ferth's lonely north shore with the old woman and her raven? Hardly. Return to Long Harbour and seek refuge with Dame Sostris? Confess the truth of her survival to her mother and Jago? Not likely. Forgive Annocky and beg him to take her back? Out of the question! Seek a just revenge upon him? She was a little tempted by that one.

There was a certain satisfaction to the notion. She could cut her long dark hair, bleach it white-gold, say she was from the wilds of the Wold far inland. She could start a new life, work slowly towards the consummation of some terrible and fitting retribution . . . She felt a rush of fury, imagined herself cutting off Annocky's parts and leaving them dangling from some bush, saw his face white with shock, heard him pleading, pleading . . .

But it would never happen, she knew. Such thoughts were merely self-indulgent. The world did not move in simple and convenient ways, no matter how much she might wish otherwise. She was learning that.

She felt she had aged a decade overnight.

'I warns you . . .' Mamma Kieran had said. 'Choosin' this path may lead you places you don' 'spect.'

Unexpected places indeed! Her whole life had been taken from her, past and future both, and she left stranded high and dry like some wretched fish abandoned by a sudden tide. She thought of Dame Sostris's reading: the Drowned Sailor, meaning death; the Hanged Man, death again. She felt as if she had indeed died. There was only a cold lump where her living heart had been, and she felt numbed and sick.

But she would not go passively back. Not to humiliation and defeat and dependency. Not to a victim's life like her mother's. Never *that*!'

Which left her only the quays.

Corki had gone this way, never to return. She would too. And perhaps – who knew? – she might even meet him again one day, in some strange land. Her heart beat a little faster at the thought.

Elinor remembered vividly the fond love-light in his eyes when he had dandled her on his knee, remembered him taking her everywhere, The Anchor not least of all . . . She remembered his wide smile, his thin, calloused hands, the endless stories he told, the things he taught her: reading, writing, knot-tying, swimming. And she recalled his fond, exacting demands when he taught her to use the little knife. It had been a kind of conspiracy between the two of them, those games with the knife – and an occupation that drove Genna nearly berserk. Elinor smiled a little, remembering.

'She's a little *girl*, Corki,' Genna had all but screamed on one occasion. 'How *can* ye want to teach her something like the *knife*? The *knife*, for goodness' sake!'

It was as if it had happened only yesterday, Elinor could recall everything so vividly.

'The little knife's a thing everybody ought to know how to use,' her father had replied calmly.

'Hmph!' Genna had snorted. 'No daughter of *mine* is going to learn something like that. It's not . . . not *proper*. And she'll end up cut to ribbons in some stupid bloody street brawl or other.'

'Nonsense,' Corki replied. 'Ye never knows what life might bring ye, Genna. A little blade's just the thing to keep handy. Nobody can push ye around if ye has one.' He had smiled his wide smile then. 'Besides, this daughter of ours is a natural. Takes to it like a duck to water.'

'Well, she's no *duck*! I'll thank ye to . . .'

And so it had gone: Genna remonstrating, nagging, threatening; Elinor and Corki in smiling conspiracy all the while.

Until he had gone, forever.

'Oh, Corki,' Elinor breathed, gazing at the ships' masts gently bobbing above the mist. 'I *do* miss ye so.'

She no longer had the little, sharp-bladed bodkin he had given her. Absolutely nothing remained to her of her former life. The clothing she now wore – baggy coarse trousers, a homespun shirt, a peaked seaman's cap – she had stolen from some unsuspecting household's washing line. She even walked barefoot now, having found no shoes to steal. For the rest, she could let it all go. But she yearned for the little bodkin . . .

Everything gone.

For the first time in her young life, she was alone, with nobody at all to turn to.

She recollected once again the promise of the cards in Dame Sostris's reading: the Twins, the Merchant, the Wheel – uncertainty, shifting luck, and change. And the unknown of the blank card . . .

Elinor looked again at the ships. She could lie her way aboard, make up experience she had never had, get a berth as a deck hand. Lots of younger folk went off to sea.

It was the only action left her.

She would *not* stay on passively here in Long Harbour, a helpless victim of her own bad fortune. She had refused to give in to Jago and Genna, and she would not give in now. Far better to step purposefully into the unknown and the uncertainty the cards portrayed; to let the wind and the tide take her some new place; to let the Powers move her onwards, away forever from the un-life that awaited her here.

She coiled up her long dark hair and donned the purloined seaman's cap, big and floppy on her head. Then, with a deep breath, she strode determinedly towards the nearest ship.

'Of course we has a berth for ye,' said the Captain of the first vessel she approached, a whaler, fitted out to chase the small, white-bellied fin whales northwards.

Elinor smiled. This looked to be easier than she had imagined. The Captain seemed an ordinary, sensible enough man. Middle-aged, grizzle-whiskered, with sharp blue eyes set close together over a beaky nose.

'I've had more than a little experience aboard whaling ships,' she lied. 'I can do pretty much anything ye wishes.'

The Captain smiled. '*Anythin'*, ye says? That's good.'

They were standing at the foot of the gang plank, where Elinor had hailed him from ashore. The morning mist still curled about, briny-smelling, chilly and dank. And the quay stones were painfully cold under her bare feet. Elinor hugged herself for warmth.

The Captain gestured to the ship behind him. 'Why doesn't ye come aboard right now, then? I've a charcoal brazier goin' in the cabin. We can discuss yer wages.' He grinned at her. 'And I hankers after the first ride.'

Elinor shook her head, looked at him uncertainly. 'First . . . ride?'

'Now don't go playin' coy, girlie. Not now. Time for that game later, perhaps. We'll pay ye well enough. The men and I have discussed just this sort of venture. Ye's a comely enough little lass, sloppy dressed though ye is, and they'll like ye well enough, I'm certain sure. We'll all chip in to gets ye a new wardrobe.' He grinned some more and rubbed his hands together. 'A bit of the old in-out on a regular basis is just what we all needs on a longish cruise like this one's likely to be. But I wants the first ride, like I said.'

Elinor stared at him.

'Well, come *on*!'

She wanted to thump him, hard. Instead, she turned and marched furiously away.

'Hoi!' he called out. 'Where's ye goin'?'

Elinor ignored him.

'Little bitch!' he shouted. 'Little *teasin'* bitch!'

She just kept on, flushed and angry and mortified. Past two other moored ships she went, blindly, panting, fists clenched tight. Somebody whistled at her as she stormed past, a shrill *ta-weet ta-woo* of appreciation. She scowled at the man and he shook his head and laughed.

She wanted to smash something, or somebody. Instead, she

tried to let go of her anger – there was nothing left for her to do but try again.

Elinor approached the next ship warily. It was a freighter by appearance, a shoddy-looking short hauler, and not the sort that would have been her first choice. But perhaps she stood a better chance getting a berth on a vessel like this, which, surely, had to make do with whatever crew it could get. She knew from her father that the old timers chose long haulers for their berths: harder work but bigger profits.

The Captain turned out to be a small, barrel-chested man with elegant black moustaches. He gave a little mocking bow as she approached, not bothering to come down from his ship's rail to the gang plank to meet her. 'Already got one,' he called.

Elinor only stared.

'I *said*,' the Captain said, 'we've already *got* one.'

'Ye doesn't need any more deck hands?'

The Captain laughed, shook his head. 'Oh, aye. I could use a couple all right. But I'd not hire *ye* as one.'

Elinor bridled. 'And why not? I'm as good as . . .'

'Ye's a *looker*, girl. That's clear enough to see, even dressed like ye is. Only *one* thing I'd hire a *looker* for on *my* ship.' He twirled his black moustaches with the fingers of one hand. 'Shame, though. Looks like ye might be an improvement on our Suki. Younger and *firmer* at any rate . . .'

Elinor crimsoned. 'Why, ye . . .'

'Easy, girlie,' the Captain said. 'Take it as a compliment, can't ye?'

Elinor stalked off.

At the next ship she came to, a fat old man with white whiskers sat on a barrel beside the gang plank on the wharf, chewing on a piece of salted herring. He stank of the stuff.

'Is ye the . . . Captain?' Elinor asked uncertainly.

The man laughed and shook his head. 'Nay, lass, not me.'

'Can I talk with the Captain, then?' she asked.

'Aye.'

'Sometime this morning?' Elinor demanded icily when the man merely continued chewing on his smelly fish.

'Aye,' he replied equably.

Elinor stood tapping her bare foot on the cold cobblestones. 'Well?'

'Impatient lass, ain't ye?' the man said. He cocked his head and looked her up and down appreciatively.

'Don't start,' she snapped. 'Just don't *start*.'

He shrugged, chewing on his fish.

The morning was beginning to warm up a little now, the mist burning away. Two grey-winged seagulls sat on a mooring post nearby, eyeing the fat man's herring enviously. One of them squawked, reminding Elinor momentarily of Mamma Kieran's raven. She had a moment of panic. What if none of the ships would take her – except as a . . . a sea-going doxy? But she shook her head, refusing to give in to such thoughts. She would *not* go crawling back to her broken life in Long Harbour. Never!

'*Well?*' she said again to the fish-eating fat man. 'The Captain?'

The man sighed. 'Aye, all right.' He levered himself up off the barrel, belly foremost, pushing himself up with one hand on his lower back like a pregnant woman. 'A man can't even finish his own breakfast in peace,' he grumbled. 'Nice morning like this . . .'

Elinor shook her head, watching him waddle awkwardly up the gang plank and aboard the ship. But he gave her a little hope in a way; he was so ridiculous and . . . unpredatory.

And the ship . . . It was a two-master, not the trimmest she had ever seen, perhaps, but it had the look of solidity that was more important than a smart and orderly appearance. It was a ship that had been places, survived storms, seen far and strange ports.

She waited, trying not to get her hopes up.

When the Captain arrived, finally, Elinor was pleasantly surprised.

This Captain was a woman.

'I want a berth aboard yer ship as a deck hand,' Elinor said quickly.

The Captain was waspish and thin, with short-cropped silver hair. Her brows were dark, as were her eyes. She cupped her chin in one hand and surveyed Elinor.

70

'As a deck hand,' Elinor repeated.

'Aye,' the Captain replied. 'I heard ye well enough the first time.'

She regarded Elinor silently for long moments, then planted her elbows on the ship's rail, leaning down towards the quay and said, 'What else would I offer ye a berth as?'

Elinor opened her mouth, closed it.

'Is ye *interested* in working for me?' the Captain demanded.

'Aye,' Elinor said quickly.

'Then get yer gear and come aboard. We sail with the tide.'

'I have no gear,' Elinor confessed.

The Captain laughed. 'Running away then, are we?'

Elinor flushed.

'Well . . .' the Captain said. 'None of my business, what ye may or may not be running from. Since ye's got no gear, why not come aboard immediately?' She turned to the fat man. 'Show our new deck hand to her cabin, Smalt.'

He nodded.

'The aft cabin,' the Captain said. 'Ye knows the one I mean?'

The fat man smiled and nodded again.

'And throw that *fish* away, can't ye?' the Captain added.

The fat man frowned, shrugged, threw what remained of his herring overboard. The two seagulls raced in and began squabbling over it before it even had time to hit the water.

The Captain shook her head and laughed. 'Greedy things.'

Elinor came up the gang plank. A little thrill went through her as she felt the wooden deck under her feet – warm after the chilly stones of the quay, and swaying gently, like a live thing.

'My name's Anatasa,' the Captain said. 'But ye'll call me Captain. Clear?'

'Aye, Captain,' Elinor responded.

Captain Anatasa nodded. She held out her hand. 'Welcome aboard the *Kestrel*, deck hand.'

Elinor took the hand, formally sealing the bargain between them in the way such things were done quayside.

'Good,' said Captain Anatasa. 'Now follow fat Smalt here to yer cabin.'

'Aye, Captain.' Elinor turned and followed the fat man, her heart soaring. She had done it! Goodbye to Long Harbour. Hallo to a new life. Good, bad, or indifferent . . . it did not seem to matter to her at this moment. She had taken the first step along the only path open to her. She would make it through whatever might come next, of that she felt sure. She had a berth as a deck hand, with equal shares. She would survive. She would prosper . . .

'Down this way,' fat Smalt said. They had worked their way to the ship's stern by now, and he was gesturing her down a little set of steps. Elinor noticed a couple of the crew on the deck eyeing them quizzically. She was pleased to see at least one other woman amongst them. This was no all-male ship, then.

Smalt ushered her down the steps, then further aft along a companionway and through the interior of the ship till they stood before a stout little oaken door. 'In here,' he said. 'This is to be yer cabin.'

He lifted a locking bar from the little door and opened it. 'Ye first,' he said, ushering her through.

Elinor stepped down into a small, dark room, stooping to get through the little doorway. Inside, thick beams crossed the ceiling, and one wall bent sharply upwards and in, for the room was flush against the hull. But Elinor was rather pleasantly surprised for all that. The *Kestrel* was a stout enough ship, but certainly not overlarge. Remembering some of her father's old stories, she had expected quarters far more cramped than this. There was no gear, no sign of any other occupants. If she was to have the whole of this space to herself, it would be almost like living in her little attic room . . .

Behind her, the door slammed abruptly shut.

'Smalt?' Elinor said, puzzled. She reached for the door and tried to push it open.

It did not budge.

'Smalt?' she called, her heart beginning to thump in sudden anxiety. '*Smalt*?'

There was no reply.

Elinor smacked at the closed door with her fist, sending sparks of pain through the bruises she had there still from her time in the coffin. 'Let me out of here!'

Nothing.

She kicked at it, but the door budged not at all. 'Let me *out* of here!'

'Now calm down, dearie,' a voice called from the other side, a man's voice that Elinor did not recognize. 'Nobody's going to hurt ye.'

'Let me *out*!' she insisted.

'Not a chance of that, I'm afraid,' the voice responded. 'We're going to keep ye nice and safe and sound just where ye is.' There was a brief pause, then the voice said, 'My name's Pips. Captain Anatasa's First Mate, I am. She's given me ye as my responsibility for this voyage . . .'

There was a sudden commotion outside the door, a flurry of footsteps down stairs, voices raised.

'Who *is* she?' Elinor heard somebody ask.

'Some waif the Captain lured aboard,' came the reply from somebody else.

Elinor's belly clenched when she heard the word 'lured'. How could she have been so *stupid*?

'What's the Captain's plan, then?' she heard another voice say from outside the locked door.

'Captain knows folk in the far south who pay good money for girls like she.' It was the First Mate's voice. '*Good* money indeed, for one as young and firm as this one . . .'

Elinor sagged against the door. She could not believe what she was hearing. Captain Anatasa had lied to her, lied straight-faced to lure her aboard. To sell her off to . . .

'Now get going, the lot of ye,' she heard the First Mate's voice say. 'Ye've all got better things to do than to stand about here gawking at a locked door. We leave with the tide, remember. Get to it!'

There was a pause, some muttering, then the slow clatter of receding footsteps. Then silence.

Elinor slid down against the door and slumped on to the wooden floor, hardly believing, yet, that this was really happening.

Her first step into a new path . . .

She thought of Dame Sostris's cards, remembering how the Drowned Sailor had come up first of all.

That was her, she felt. The Drowned Sailor.

With no way back . . .

PART TWO

MINMI

X

'Let me out of here!' Elinor cried, thumping on the little door to her prison.

Silence. Nothing. Only the sway of the ship as it yawed over the deep-sea swells. The beams that braced the ceiling over her head creaked and cracked to the ship's motion; that was all the response she got.

Elinor kicked the door, and the wall, stamping on the floor in an excess of baulked anger. Two days now they had been at sea. She was starving hungry, thirsty as could be – she had found a little bottle of tepid water left in the room's corner, but it had been far from enough. What were they about, these stupid captors of hers? Were they going to leave her here to die of very neglect?

And there were moments when being trapped helplessly here in this dark, airless, heaving little room was altogether too reminiscent of her experience in the grave. She would feel herself panting, unable to get enough air . . .

She felt it coming upon her now. 'Let me *out*!' she cried, thumping the door some more.

This time, to her surprise, a man's voice replied from the other side: 'Step back from the doorway, girl. Stand over on the far side of the cabin, where I can see ye as I come in.'

Elinor stood where she was.

'Does ye hear me?' the voice demanded. 'I've food for ye. And drink. Be a good girl and I'll let ye have all ye wants. Be a bad girl . . . and I'll leave ye to starve. Clear?'

Elinor said nothing.

'Is ye listening, girl?'

She padded over to stand against the wall next to the doorway and placed herself in the blind spot that would be there behind the door when the man outside came in. She kept her silence, grimly determined. Let him get curious. Let him come in to see what she was about. She would jump him from behind the opened door, beat him into unconsciousness, take his weapons – surely he would have some sort of weapon upon him – and then she would make her way out of this stupid, dingy, uncomfortable prison.

'Very well, girl. Be it on yer own head, then.'

Elinor heard the sound of footsteps receding.

'No!' she cried. 'Wait!'

But he was already gone.

'Damn ye!' Elinor kicked the door angrily, hard as she could. It hurt her bare foot and she faltered back, hopping, holding the foot, cursing, blinking back tears of pain and outrage.

When he came the next time, it was a full day later.

'Step back from the door, girl,' he ordered her. 'Stand over on the far side of the room, where I can see ye as I come in.'

She did.

The door opened.

'My name's Pips,' the man said. '*Kestrel*'s First Mate.' He was a tall, gangling man in seaman's trousers. His eyes were sharp as a ferret's. 'The Captain's given me the charge of ye. Ye be a good girl, and I'll look after ye proper enough. But cause me grief . . . and I'll make ye rue it. Clear?'

Elinor nodded reluctantly.

The food he left made her near faint it was so good after her days of forced abstinence. And the water . . . cool and sweet and wonderful.

Once finished, she sighed, put down the empty dish. It felt so good to have food in her.

But . . .

But it was an empty feeling. She was still imprisoned, still helpless. Only not so hungry. And the same unpleasant fate still awaited her. There must be something she could *do* . . .

But there was nothing.

Search her mind however hard she might, she could come up with no way around the First Mate's careful feeding precautions. Each day he came to her, bringing food and water, eyeing her cautiously before entering.

Once, she tried disobeying his unvarying instructions. She neither ate nor drank that day.

And so the time dragged on . . .

She tried not to dwell on what might lie in store for her. There were days she cursed herself soundly for an utter fool. Even life with fat old Hadelbert was preferable to *this*. Why had she been so eager to fling her old life aside? If only she had taken more time, considered her options more carefully . . .

But this was the despair of the imprisoned eating at her. She realized that clearly enough in her better moments. She would have had to go creeping back like a whipped puppy with her tail between her legs if she had acted in any other way, back in Long Harbour.

Small comfort that seemed, though, as the days dragged past and she sat, alternately bored and despairing and furious in her dingy little prison.

Until the day of the storm.

XI

Thunder *karoomed* like a great, angry drum. The ship heaved sickeningly. Elinor swallowed, trying not to vomit. The beams overhead in her little cabin cracked and popped and *kreeked* so loudly with each roll and heave of the ship that she feared the vessel would split right apart and the sea swallow them all.

She staggered over to the door and hammered on it. 'Let me out!' she screamed. 'Let me *out*!' Her heart was pounding away in her breast like a mad thing. A dizzy blackness overtook her and she felt herself falling, tossed sideways by a sudden lurch of the ship so that she thumped painfully up against the wall, breathless and gasping.

The next thing she knew, somebody's hands were upon her, dragging her half to her feet. She blinked, shook herself, tried to make sense of what was happening. The door was open, banging back and forth in its frame with the heaving motion of the ship. Two men had her by the arms and ankles. She could see three more peering in through the doorway.

'Hurry!' one of these urged the two who held her. 'Quick about it or we're *all* lost!'

The two men hauled Elinor out of her prison, smacking her head against the door lintel in their haste. She struggled instinctively in their hold, her head ringing with pain, but they were too strong.

'Up the gangway!' somebody urged 'Quick . . . *Quick*!'

They emerged on deck, dragging Elinor behind – to be hit by what seemed a solid wall of screaming rain and seawater. She gasped, sputtering, unable for a moment to draw any breath at all.

She heard one of the men yelling something, cupping his hands and shouting himself hoarse, but the words were unintelligible. The deck pitched and bucked under her like some great animal gone berserk. Somebody cried out suddenly. Elinor looked backwards and saw a mammoth wave coming down upon them, a solid, careering wall of grey-green water high as the ship's masts.

She had one heart-stopping moment of clarity, as the wave seemed to hang over them unmoving for a long instant, poised to smash them to pieces. Then it was upon them, a great, furious, rushing torrent of icy water. She grabbed desperately at a stanchion, held on for her very life, felt the hands of the men who had dragged her up here slip away, felt the wave tearing at her, tearing at her . . . She found herself immersed completely in rushing, hurtling water, unable to see, to breathe . . .

And then it was gone, and she was left gasping and choking as the water streamed away. She felt chilled to the very bone, her ears ringing, her eyes stinging agonizingly with the salt water.

To her astonishment, the ship righted itself, wallowing and bucking sluggishly in the heaving sea as if exhausted but still afloat. Elinor gazed about her, stunned. She could not tell if it was morning or afternoon, day or night. The sky was a dark, restless moil of clouds, riven by painful bursts of lightning and booming thunder. The sea rose in great wave after wave, like a series of giant, moving hills, shifting sickeningly before her. The wind howled through the rigging, men screamed, the deck heaved . . .

It was a very nightmare.

'Grab her, lads!' somebody cried above the wind, and once again Elinor felt hands upon her.

'This way,' she heard one of the men clutching at her grunt.

Elinor kicked and struggled desperately, trying to wrench herself free.

Then a new voice called out, 'Stop!' loud and sudden and forceful enough to carry clear over the wind. 'And just *what* d'ye think ye're *doing*?' the voice demanded. 'Ye great *idiots*!'

Craning her head, Elinor made out the tall, gangling figure of the First Mate standing before her captors, barring their road.

'Out of the way, Pips!' one of the men shouted.

'Stop this!' he shouted back at them. 'Ye panicky *fools*!'

'It's her,' somebody said, yelling over the howl of the wind. '*She* brought this storm upon us!'

'Don't be *stupid*!' the Mate shouted back.

The ship bucked suddenly and all had to grab on to what they could to keep their feet.

'A woman's bad luck aboard a ship,' somebody cried.

'The Captain's a *woman*, ye thick-headed idiot!' the Mate returned. 'And ye serves under her willingly enough.'

'The Captain's different.'

'Oh, aye?' the Mate said scathingly. 'And what about Tiffy and Dorys? Are they different, too?'

The gathered men only muttered sullenly.

Again the ship bucked, slipping sideways under them. A sudden wash of knee-deep, icy water swept over the deck. Elinor felt the men gripping her stumble, right themselves. She tried to shake herself free, but they hung on too tight.

'A woman like this one's nothing but bad luck!' somebody cried.

As if in answer, a branch of blue lightning crackled suddenly through the storm-riven sky above them. Thunder *KAROOOMED*.

'See!' somebody shouted once they could hear again. '*Fatal* bad luck!'

The Mate shook his head and gestured at them angrily. 'Take her below again! She's valuable cargo.'

The men hesitated.

'*Now*!' he shouted. 'Take her below!'

One of the men gripping Elinor turned to obey, but the other refused. 'She'll be the death of us, lads!' he called to his companions. 'Over with her, I say!'

'Over with her!' shouted somebody else. Others took it up. 'Over with her. Over the side!'

'No!' the Mate shouted. 'Ye stupid pack of idiots. *No*!'

Elinor felt half a dozen pairs of hands upon her.

'Here comes the Captain,' she heard somebody say.

'Stop! *Stop*!' Captain Anatasa shouted. 'Don't ye *dare* move, any of ye!' She came rushing up along the heaving deck, one hand on the gunwale for balance, furious. 'Ye stupid, *stupid* louts! What d'ye think ye're *doing*? Might just as well toss all the rest of the cargo overboard while ye're at it and ruin this venture entirely!'

The men holding Elinor faltered. Several let go of her altogether.

'We've ridden out storms before,' the Captain went on. 'This one's no different from the others – just bluster and empty fury . . .'

Elinor looked about, panting for breath in the storm-driven wind. The sea roared. The deck bucked sickeningly under her. Giant waves heaved . . . But she *was* up on deck, free of her cursed prison . . .

She felt another pair of hands slip from her.

Anything was better than being re-imprisoned below, to await passively the fate Captain Anatasa intended for her . . .

Sudden lightning arced through the sky above. The great *KAROOOM* of the thunder rolled over them painfully, making the men cringe.

Elinor twisted sideways and kneed one of the men gripping her, tore herself out of the hold of the others, leaped for the gunwale.

'Quick, lads!' she heard First Mate Pips shout. 'Grab her. *Quick*!'

But they were too late. She felt one of them clutch at her ankle, kicked him hard in the face, vaulted desperately backwards and tumbled away from the ship, out and down, down . . .

Her fall seemed to take a ridiculously long time. She felt herself tumble slowly, seeing the ship above and behind her, the First Mate's face livid with outrage, the white, amazed faces of the men staring at her, the rigging flapping above their heads . . . then the great, heaving, grey-green expanse of the water, laced with yellow foam . . . then the ship's deck in her view again, further off now, the curve of the hull rearing above her, the men's faces becoming smaller, smaller . . .

Then the water came up and hit her, an impact at first like smacking into a solid wall. Then the wall seemed to dissolve and she was sucked down, down, into surging darkness and cold. Elinor struggled, kicking out, so tumbled and churned about that she did not even know which way might be up and which down, but refusing to let the sea have her so easily as this, swallowing her whole on the first gulp.

Somehow, she managed it, bursting through to air, her lungs burning, gasping and choking and retching sickly. But alive still.

She looked up and saw a mountain of water hanging over her. Her heart stopped. She did not think she would have the strength to struggle again out of the black depths. She was shuddering with cold, her muscles quivery-weak and unreliable.

The wave came down . . .

She choked on bitter seawater. But instead of being driven forever into the depths, she found herself bobbing along upon the surface, tossed about like the ship had been, or like a little cork, rather.

Another wave . . . more sea swallowed, more tossing . . .

She could do it, she began to realize. She could stay afloat, shivering and shocked though she might be.

Elinor looked about her as she was swept up on to the crest of a high-weaving wave. A lightning bolt illuminated the world, and she could see for an instant in every direction. There was no sign of the ship, no sign of anything save the violently churning sea and sky. Thunder KAROOOMED, making her head ring, and she was tumbled back down into a grey-green watery trough.

Elinor drew a shaky breath. Her shoulders ached, and her legs. Another wave was coming down upon her. She might be able to stay afloat like this for a time, aye. But for how long?

It was a simple thing that saved her.

Sliding blindly down a steeply curving, watery slope, she smacked unexpectedly against something hard, hitting it head first. The blow made her skull ring. She clutched desperately at the thing she had struck, her heart jolting in shock and fright.

It was a main-spar from some ship – whether from the *Kestrel* itself or some other vessel she was never to know. The spar was a longish length of wood, thick almost as her torso, rolling and bobbing and difficult to get hold of properly, but a sanctuary of sorts nonetheless.

She wrapped her arms about it and hung on. Her head throbbed agonizingly, as if some relentless demon were smashing at it with a hammer. The world phased in and out of darkness. Her thoughts grew scattered, like a flock of birds blown apart by some great burst of wind. The spar to which she clung heaved and rolled. Seawater choked her, blinded her eyes. Lightning slashed painfully across her vision. Thunder *KAROOOMED*, making her poor head echo to it painfully. Her thoughts seemed to spread and dwindle, like so many birds disappearing over a far horizon, leaving only the spar, and aching arms and legs, labouring lungs gasping for breath, her clutching the wet, twisting wood, refusing grimly, desperately, absolutely to let the angry sea swallow her.

XII

The strand was rocky and strewn with storm-wrack. Torn braids of red-green seaweed festooned the stones. Pewter clouds rolled overhead, lit by cold dawn-light. She lay as she was for long and long, shivering helplessly, merely breathing. It was all she felt capable of. Her head pulsed with blinding agony.

The sea still tugged at her, untiring, tenacious as some beast of prey, each new wave grasping at her with cold, frothy fingers, loosening the pebbly sand beneath her, trying to drag her back.

She struggled upwards. In the grey dawn-light, she could just make out the dark line of a little stone bluff walling the beach in on its landward side. She dragged herself along through the sand and the rocks towards it.

The breakers were behind her now, and she beyond their greedy reach. But the ground under her seemed to be heaving like the very sea itself. Her head felt as if some great giant were smashing at it with a hammer. She moaned, wrapped her arms about a shard of rough stone, tears flooding her eyes, willing the pain in her skull to go away, the earth to stand still.

Which, finally, gradually, the earth did, settling like sane ground ought to, a firm, solid base for her aching and exhausted body . . .

The next thing she knew, she was blinking sleep out of her eyes. The clouds were broken up overhead, and the morning sun visible. She felt its blessed warmth upon her. She put a hand tentatively to her throbbing head. There was an excruciatingly tender lump on her skull, and she winced when her fingers found it. The overall pain seemed to have lessened, though, settling into a bearable, aching throb, like a painful tooth. Shakily, she propped herself up on an elbow, looked around bleary-eyed.

She groaned. Every bone in her body felt bruised, from her toes to her ribs – flaring into sharp discomfort with every breath she took – to her throbbing skull. Each little movement, each twist or bend of sinew or muscle, caused her minor agonies. Her mouth felt dry as old wood. It hurt to swallow. And when she tried to lick her salt-encrusted lips, she found her tongue too dry to do it.

But she was *alive* . . .

Water. She needed to drink.

She tried to move, and found that her feet seemed to be stuck. Looking down, she saw her legs were all twisted up with a long braid of the red-green seaweed. She tried to kick free but it proved tenacious stuff, and it had somehow become twined about her lower legs, from knees to ankles. After a little, she gave up the struggle and rolled stiffly over on to her back as best she could, exhausted. Laying her sore head down on the sand, she gazed blankly up into the pulsing blue dome of the sky. The air was mild and soothing, the breeze a soft caress. Somewhere, gulls were crying, a mournful sound . . .

She had not the faintest idea of where she might be, and no clear recollection of how she had come to this deserted stretch of beach – spat out by the fury of the sea somehow. She remembered being flung about by great waves. She recalled small white faces staring down at her from above. She recalled . . .

It was as if a great blank wall had been erected in her mind. She could remember the tossing sea, see those white faces made small by distance and height. But nothing more.

She was . . .

She could not recollect who she was.

A long, cold shiver went through her. She might have sprung suddenly into existence here on this beach for all she could recollect of a past life. The sea, the little white faces, the stretch of beach upon which she was lying . . .

That was all.

She lay shivering, the blood-pulse thumping in her aching head, trying desperately to bring back something, anything, from her past. But it was fruitless.

Perhaps she *was* some newly created being.

A nameless being.

A gull came soaring into sight above her. It turned its head and eyed her, interested, as it passed. Carrion bird. She knew that about it. Gulls would eat any sort of refuse.

But how could she know what this flying creature was and what it did, and yet not know anything at all about herself? She felt herself shudder. It was too strange. To know, and yet not to know. Looking about, she recognized sky, rocks, clouds, gulls, beach, sea, horizon, gold-glowing sun . . . It was all perfectly familiar. She could recognize and name everything. Everything except for her own self.

She heard the sound of human voices.

It took her three attempts to get up on one elbow, and she still could not wrench her feet free of the seaweed tangled about them. Squinting down the beach, she made out three figures trailing along the shore, searching through the storm's jetsam. They had not seen her yet. She tried to call out, but her throat and mouth were too dry and swollen. She could not even grunt.

But the beachcombers spotted her soon enough, without her calling to them. They came running up, all eyes.

'What *is* it?' one of them called in a high-pitched, excited voice.

They were children, she saw, raggedly clothed, skinny, with hair like birds' nests.

'Is it a . . . a merperson?' she heard one ask, a boy, his eyes round with wonder.

'No, silly.' This from a little auburn-haired girl. 'It's a *person* person.' The girl pointed. 'He's dead, see? His eyes are open. Old Malby told me all about that. When a person dies, Malby says, the eyes stay open, 'cause the person's looking off into the Shadowlands and . . .'

The third child, another boy, shrieked suddenly: 'It *moved*!'

Lying supine and exhausted and tangled in the seaweed, she tried to make her parched mouth form proper words.

The children skittered hastily backwards.

'It's alive!' the girl whispered.

'Wa . . . Wa . . . ufpp . . .' she croaked.

'What's it saying?' one of the boys said.

'What're you saying?' the girl asked directly, creeping nearer.

'Wa . . . waa . . .' she struggled.

The girl tilted her head sideways, reached out a tentative hand. 'You're *cold*.'

'Wa . . . tur,' she managed finally.

The little girl's eyes widened with sudden understanding. 'There's a stream a ways along the . . .'

One of the boys grabbed at her arm. 'Penna!' he hissed. 'They're *coming*. I can see them over the bluff.'

The girl whirled and looked off in the direction the boy was pointing.

'Come *on*, Penna,' he urged.

The girl hesitated, then shook herself loose from the boy's hold and knelt down quickly.

Lying bound helplessly in the seaweed still, too exhausted for the moment even to be able to lift herself up to see who or what it was that might be coming upon her across the strand, she felt the girl tug sharply on her tangled hair, making the bruised lump on her skull thump agonizingly.

The girl did something, and a hank of hair came away.

'Come *on*, Penna!' the boy pleaded.

The girl stood up, stayed frozen for an instant, staring down wide-eyed, then scampered quickly off with the two boys, clutching the clump of stolen hair tight in one small hand.

She struggled up, managing, after two shaky attempts, to lift her head just enough to see what it was had sent the children scurrying away.

Several figures stood on top of the bluff that edged the sea strand, staring in her direction. One of them let out a whoop, and they came loping over.

These were not children, she saw as they came closer, but men, dour-faced as fishwives, armed and armoured. But the manner of their dress . . .

One of them carried a pike almost twice his own height, a long black pole of a handle topped with a glittering bronze halberd blade shaped like a crescent moon. He had on a huge leathern war helm, far too large for his head, and had to keep shoving the thing back in place.

Another carried three little swords in a row, slung from his belt like a fence. This one wore no helmet; instead, he had his hair twisted up into an elaborate double braid that had been thickly greased so that it stuck out on both sides of his head, flapping like little wings as he ran.

A third carried a huge hammer. The head was of black cast-iron, intricately worked with copper inlay, but the handle was a mere tree branch, crooked, with the bark still on it in some places.

Another, carrying a long iron-bladed sword thrust scab-bardless through his belt, wore a full-length scarlet cloak that dragged in the sand, the trailing hem soaked and tattered and stained.

The last was dressed all in black from head to foot. He had a black dagger in his belt and carried a long black spade in his hand.

The five of them came lolloping along the strand like a ragged pack of hounds.

She would gladly have hidden away from such a band if she could. But there was no chance. Her feet were still fast held by the seaweed, and she was too weak. So she could only lie there helpless on her side in the chill sand, watching, as the newcomers drew close.

The one with the black dagger and spade was first upon her 'It's a merperson,' she heard him say to the others as they drew up. 'See? There's its tail caught up in all that weed there.'

To her surprise he let out a great *whooop* of glee. 'Peer Lyle will deal with us well for this. The Lord Mattingly has been wanting a merperson for his own for a *long* time . . .'

'Are you certain sure, Pilchert, that it's a . . . an actual . . . an indeed and actual *mer*person, now?' This from the one with the sodden and dragging crimson cloak.

'Now let me tell you, you great potato you . . . I *know* a merperson when I see one. And I says . . .'

'Aieeek!' the one with the hammer suddenly spluttered. 'It *blinked*!'

'Pilchert, you's a fool,' the one with the long, bronze-headed pike said. He shook his head, which meant he had to reach quickly up to right the ridiculously overlarge helmet he wore. He pointed an accusing finger at the spade-man. 'I always told you you was. That's a *person* person, not a *mer*person.'

'And I suppose you even *know* about such things, you ignorant carrot!'

Lying helpless on the cold strand, she stared, not knowing quite what to make of all this. Almost, she laughed, for it seemed to her that there was something of the ridiculous about these men: their outlandish and ill-fitting fighting gear; their debate, so reminiscent of what the three children had said about her . . .

But there was nothing humorous about their dour, pinched faces.

'Lord Mattingly's not going to be especially interested in a *person* person, now is he?' one of them said.

'No . . .' came the response.

'What do we do *now*, then?'

The one with the black spade crept towards her. He poked her in the side with the sharp corner of his implement.

'Owahhh . . .' she moaned.

The spade-man leaped back. 'It's *alive*.'

'Wa . . .' she moaned, trying to say 'water' as she had with the children. But her poor parched mouth just would not work for her.

'It's speaking!'

'Not no language I ever heard. What does *whaww* mean, then?'

'It's saying hallo, of course, you stupid turnip,' the man with the spade said. He squatted down, though still some distance away from her, and carefully said, 'Whaww! Whaww!'

She tried to swallow, to make her mouth work, but the effort was beyond her. Her lips were too scabbed and salt-crusted, her throat and tongue too dry and swollen to be of use.

'It doesn't understand you, Pilchert,' one of the gathered men said.

'Leave it, that's what I say.' This from the man with the bronze-headed pike. 'Knock it on the head and leave it for the sea to take back. And then let's away from here.'

Pilchert, the one dressed all in black and carrying the black spade, shook his head. 'You lot leave if you like. Me, I'm staying.' Laying the spade down, he crept tentatively forward. He reached a hand to her, drew it back nervously, reached out again and pulled back some of the seaweed that still lay draped over her. He bent closer then, pushed aside the tangled, salt-thick hair from her face, wiped the sand from her cheeks. She shuddered under his intrusive touch but did not have the strength to make anything like resistance.

Pilchert let out a low whistle.

'What is it, Pilch?'

'It's . . .' He sat back on his heels and stared at her newly revealed face. 'It's . . .'

'It's what?'

'It's a *woman*.'

The men crowded about.

'What are we goin' to do with a woman, then?' the scarlet-cloaked one said querulously.

'Is you really that stupid, Dack?' the one with the hammer demanded.

'I know what *I'd* like to do with her,' said the man with the three little swords dangling at his belt. He tilted one of his swords up in a quick, obscene gesture, then collapsed into childish giggles, his elaborate, greased hairdo bobbing ridiculously.

'Shut up, the lot of you!' said Pilchert. 'We'll take her back with us.'

'But, Pilch!' whined the one named Dack. He wrapped his scarlet cloak closer about himself and frowned petulantly. 'What about all the valuable things you said we'd find here on the strand? What about all them things?'

'She's better than any of that,' Pilchert responded. 'Think, you great turnips, you! She's a woman. Thrown up here by Father Ocean. She's storm wrack. Nobody owns her. Nobody'll claim her. She's . . . *ours*!'

'Oooh . . .' said the pike-man and the one with the three little swords simultaneously.

They all looked at each other in sudden, excited conspiracy. 'Ours!' one of them murmured. 'Our very own woman. Our very *own* . . .'

*

They hauled her roughly across the strand. She tried to struggle, but she was too weak, her exhausted limbs too awkward and heavy.

At the little bluff that walled in the strand, they lifted her bodily, carrying her in a clumsy kind of cradle they made out of their linked arms. They almost lost her twice, once giving the back of her poor bruised skull a hard thump against a stone that left her breathless and blind with pain.

Once on top of the bluff, they set off at a quicker pace, holding her cradled between them still. She faltered into unconsciousness, fainting away despairingly into the dark . . .

Only to come out of it once again, feeling the jolt of their walking still in her sore bones and throbbing skull. She slipped back helplessly, came to once more, phasing in and out of awareness of her surroundings . . .

And then, as a sharper jolt shook her into fuller awareness, she opened her eyes and saw where it was they were bringing her.

The sound of the sea was still faintly in her ears, so they could not have come all that far from the coast, but she could see no sign of the ocean itself. Instead, everywhere she looked there were grassy hills, giving way towards the east to higher mountains in the far distance, their peaks thrust up into the bellies of dark clouds. For the sun was cloud-hidden now, she realized, the air chillier. She shivered, felt a spot of cold rain splash against her cheek.

Turning her sore head, blinking, trying to gather her shattered wits, she saw their destination ahead: a huge, sprawling stone structure, a single, enormous thing the size of a small city almost. The green humps of the hills rolled down towards it and stopped abruptly against the high stone walls. And behind those high walls, up and up, reared blocks and towers and roofs, all interconnected into a single, gigantic complex of stone.

As they drew closer, though, she began to see that the place was crumbling into ruin. The walls were shattered in places, tumbled down in rubble. The roofs beyond were ragged and hollow, with splintered holes and remnants flapping in the rising storm breeze.

Her captors were hurrying now, staggering a little, their breath coming in gasps. Thunder rumbled in the distance.

'Hurry!' one of them urged. 'You know how quick these cursed spring storms come on.'

Down a grassy slope they all skidded, past a great pile of shattered rock, like some giant's discarded toy of stone.

'Hurry, hurry . . .'

More thunder, the world gone dim and strange, the grass bluey-gold and moving like a live thing under the storm-wind, the stone of the strange, gigantic, crumbling structure glowing ochre and russet . . .

And then, suddenly, they were skidding through a low entrance way – little more than a tumble-down hole in the stone of the wall – and stumbling inside into dank, chill, echoing darkness.

XIII

As they dragged her along into the dark, she tried to struggle out of their hold, kicking and thrashing, but her strength was all gone, and the only thing she gained was a cuff on the side of her painful head that made the darkness come alive with sparks of light.

The men moved awkwardly, stumbling and cursing in the dark, but moving nonetheless as if they knew just where they were going. She could make out nothing at all. The utter, oppressive blackness made her heart fail, and she felt a rush of sudden, inexplicable terror. She struggled again, desperately, but too weakly now to merit even a cuff.

And then, in the distance, she spied a faint, sputtering light. A torch, it turned out to be: a smoky torch set into a rickety sconce. The hissing light danced off water runnelling down the stone wall.

On they went, back into more darkness, out into another stretch of torch-lit radiance, into the dark once more.

It was a huge place, this – endless leagues of dank stone corridors it seemed, lit by the sputtering, smoky torches set at irregular intervals. There seemed no design, no consistency. It stank of mould and stagnant water, of age and filth. And the air held a dank chill that went right to the bones.

And still onwards they went, up stairwells, along twisty-turny corridors, plunging through the pools of blackness between the hissing torches. There were old wooden beams in spots, shoring up the ceiling, rubble strewn across the floor from the mouldering walls. Her captors simply stepped over or around or through whatever might be in their path.

At one point they passed into an area where the wall itself had tumbled away all along one side of the corridor. The storm-wind wailed through the stonework. Rainwater and daylight splashed across the cold stone floor like liquid silver. Her captors blinked and stumbled. She had time for a single, cleansing breath of rain-rinsed air, and then they were back inside once again, immured in the dank, dark, noisome interior.

Onwards her captors dragged her, up a steep flight of broken stone steps, panting with the effort. There was a nervous speed in their movements now, and as they moved off along yet another dark corridor at the top of the steps, she heard them begin to mutter and whisper anxiously amongst themselves, too low at first for her to make out the words, then louder . . .

'We musn't . . .' one insisted in a harsh whisper. 'It's too dangerous coming this way.'

'Yes. *Yes*! We must. We *must*!' replied another. 'It's the only way through.'

'Remember what happened last time we came this way!'

'That was a mistake . . .'

'*Your* mistake.'

'No, it wasn't.'

'Oh, yes it was!'

'Now don't you go taking that tone with me, you great mushroom. I'll have you know . . .'

By now the discussion had become so heated that the men had stopped and were huddled in the dark spot between two torches, heads together, whispering fiercely.

'I don't want no repeat of last time. After they caught us, he nearly had our heads!'

'Peer Lyle was only toying with us, you silly apple.'

'Oh, yes? Easy for *you* to say! You weren't the one Lord Mattingly *pointed* at.'

They had dropped her by this point, leaving her against the cold stone wall. She tried to push herself up, get her feet under her, to run . . . But it was no use; her limbs were nothing but jelly.

Her captors' whispered squabble escalated to a fierce, hissing crescendo, then ended in quick silence as the sound of footsteps could suddenly be heard from the corridor ahead.

'Now you've done it!' one of them rasped. 'I *told* you we

96

shouldn't've brought her along this way. We're in for it now.'

The footsteps grew louder and more clear by the instant. A tall figure suddenly appeared bearing down upon them.

He was of a different cut from her captors, devoid entirely of their ridiculousness. He carried an ornate candle-lantern, and in its radiance his well-fitting clothing fairly shone with giltwork and precious stones. He wore thigh-high, dark leather boots that creaked softly with each stride he took. A fur-trimmed cape swung from his shoulders. He walked with a swagger, one hand held to the elaborate pommel of a needle-slim sword by his side, the other swinging the candle-lantern.

'And just *where* have you lot been?' he demanded, holding the lantern high and squinting at the little group before him. 'And what are you doing here?' He gestured at her where she hung in the grasp of two of her captors. 'And *what* is *that*?'

Pilchert, the black-dressed spade-wielder, stepped forward into the lantern light and made a clumsy, sweeping bow so low he almost toppled over. 'Pe . . . Peer Lyle . . .' he said.

'Peer Lyle,' all the rest murmured in uneasy unison.

'Well?' the man demanded. 'I *asked* you a question.'

'We . . . we found this . . . this person washed up on the strand. We were out looking for any jetsam we could . . .'

'In the interests of Lord Mattingly,' one of them put in quickly.

'And yours, too, of course,' added another. 'We weren't going to keep any of it for ourselves. Of course we weren't.'

'Of *course* not,' Peer Lyle agreed coldly. He lifted his hand from his sword's extravagant pommel, stroked at a little pointed black beard that grew from his chin, gripped the sword once more. 'I am *still* waiting for a proper answer.'

'We found this . . . person . . .'

'You already *said* that,' Peer Lyle interrupted.

'Yes . . . well. We . . . we . . .' Pilchert spluttered.

'Come *on*, you silly little man. Out with it!'

'We were taking her to . . .'

'*Her*?'

'Yes, Peer,' Pilchert said in a small voice.

'Taking this *her* . . . where?'

'To . . . why, ah, to . . . to Lord Mattingly, of course.'

'Of *course*,' said Peer Lyle thinly. 'And you simply . . . *forgot* to mention any of this to me?'

Silence.

Peer Lyle strode forward, lifted his lantern and peered at her, jerking her chin around so that her face was lit more clearly. 'Young,' he said after a little scrutiny of her. 'And perhaps not ugly under all that filth and salt and bruising.'

'Oh, no, Peer. Not ugly at all!'

'Why did you not wash her?'

'Wash her?'

'Yes. You have heard of washing, have you not, you ridiculous little men?'

Silence.

'If we are to take her before Lord Mattingly,' Peer Lyle said, 'we must have her washed.'

'*We*?' Pilchert said in a small voice.

Peer Lyle nodded, grinning through his pointed black beard. 'Young Mattingly might just like her.' He regarded the little group of men in silence until they began to fidget nervously. Then: 'Follow me,' he said. 'I will take you to the Chamber.' With that, he turned and began to stride off back the way he had just come.

She heard a combined murmur of relief and dismay from the little group huddled about her.

'Well, come *on*,' Peer Lyle called back at them over his shoulder impatiently.

They came, dragging her along.

It was more cold, smelly stone corridors, then. She slid away into unconsciousness, too weak and shaken to hold on to herself, and lost all track of events until she felt a sudden splash of frigid water inundate her. She fell back, spluttering and gasping. A rough hand wiped at her sore face with a wet cloth of some sort.

It was altogether an unpleasant experience, rough and fast and clumsy, leaving her bruised skull throbbing agonizingly. Then they were off once more. And the worst of it all was that they had given her nothing to drink. Her face was wet and cold, but her poor mouth and throat as dry as ever. She attempted to lick what moisture she could from her lips, but it was hopeless.

Onwards they dragged her, and she swooned away into a sort of twilight half-awareness . . .

And then, upon a sudden ringing *ker-laakk*, she realized that a set of huge, almost-intact, iron-bound doors was opening before her and she was being hauled across a somewhat cleaner floor into a large chamber.

There were patched and make-shift candelabras hung about, their myriad candles replacing the corridors' spitting torches. The ceiling, half hidden in shadow, was elaborately vaulted, but, like everything else in this mouldering ruin, beginning to crumble. One whole section was down in rubble against the far wall.

There were guards here, dressed in all manner of attire – long coats of dully glittering mail, short cuirasses, embroidered leathern surcoats, baggy crimson trousers, sleek dark leggings, helmets and little hats and elaborate hairdos and bald heads gleaming in the candlelight – but all armed alike: a short-bladed sword scabbarded at each belt; a long, intricately fashioned, bronze-headed pike in each hand. They formed a kind of human funnel channelling any who entered towards the chamber's back corner away from the rubble. There, up against the wall, was a dais of sorts.

A group of men and women stood congregated about that dais. They were dressed in the extravagant style of Peer Lyle, and with the same complete lack of consistency that marked the guards: jewel-studded sleeves long enough to drag on the floor, brilliant yellow tabards feathered like finch's breasts, glowing satin tunics trimmed with white and blue fur, waving headdresses of gold wire and crimson blooms . . . the whole clustered group of them a stunning, bizarre collection of silks and satins and shimmering feathers and jewels and flowers and intricacies of silver and gold, all surging and glittering in the dancing candlelight like a collection of exotic, bizarre, ambulatory flowers.

Upon the dais about which they clustered, nestled upon layers of softly glimmering, sumptuous, parti-coloured silken blankets, a man reclined.

'Peer Lyle,' a loud voice announced formally, and the vaulted chamber echoed it: *Lyle . . . yle . . . yle . . . yle . . .*

The man upon the dais winced at the noise.

99

Half a dozen of the pike-wielding guards detached themselves from the line and stood before them, barring their way. For long moments, nobody moved.

Then, from amongst the glittering congregation by the dais, a man emerged and walked softly over towards them. He was different from the rest; where they went in for extravagance and glitter, he dressed in sombre greys and black. A long iron sword hung from a scabbard at his hip – a sword meant for business rather than show. The man had long iron-grey hair caught back in a tight queue, and a close-trimmed beard of the same colour. He was lean as a greyhound, with sharp eyes the colour of a stormy sea.

He stood before them for a moment, then held out his hands in a silent gesture of command. Peer Lyle sighed and removed his slim, ornate blade, handing it over. The rest of the men followed suit, until all were entirely unarmed – even to Pilchert's spade. Then they were searched by the guards, initiated by a hand signal from the silent grey man. Only when the search was complete, and they found innocent of concealing anything, did the man motion for the little group to be ushered further into the room.

With their escort, they walked forward between the lines of guards – silent, stern-faced and unmoving as so many painted statues – and came eventually to stand before the dais. Her captors propped her up in front of them, facing the man reclining on the dais. She was too weak to stand altogether on her own, and they had to grip her from behind by the arms to keep her from falling.

The glittering people gathered about stared at her with cold curiosity.

'Lord Mattingly,' Peer Lyle began. 'I have brought . . .'

The man on the dais winced, waved him to silence with flip of the wrist.

In the wavering light, he had large, dark, liquid and oddly luminous eyes, this man. He seemed hardly to blink at all, but to stare constantly at his surroundings, his face set in an expression of habitual pain. He was frail-looking, all skin and sinew and knobbly bone, pallid as a mushroom, with thin, colourless lips and a beaky nose. His forehead was out of proportion to the rest of his face, broader and higher than it ought to be, giving him an oddly overbalanced look. He seemed young, but his hair was white, long and unconfined, like gossamer, and almost floated rather than fell about his face. He brushed it aside with a constant, habitual gesture of his thin hands.

His dress was at variance with the glittering throng about him, being simply a loose robe and baggy trousers. But those clothes had the same soft, luxurious satiny glimmer as the silken blankets upon which he reclined. He was stroking something on his lap.

At first, what with her own exhaustion, the piled silken wrappings about the man, and the chamber's uncertain lighting, she could not make out what it might be. Then she realized that he was stroking an animal of some sort.

It seemed about the size of a large cat . . .

She *did* have a memory of a cat, she realized with a sudden little flutter of excitement: a sleek black animal with strange eyes, its whiskered muzzle following the movement of cards as they were laid out upon a table . . .

But it was only a brief fragment, that memory, and the furred creature on the lap of the man before her did not truly resemble the animal she recalled. Its limbs were too long, its head too round, the ears too small and in the wrong place, and it had a too-long tail. And the eyes were huge and dark and strange, set above a little black-button nose in a round, honey-coloured face.

The creature slipped out of the man's lap and moved up to drape itself about his shoulders. It had hands, she saw, small and stubby like a baby's. It intertwined the little fingers of one of those hands familiarly through the man's white gossamer hair for balance, curled its tail sinuously about his throat – an action the man seemed to mind not at all – and leaned forward, its strange eyes fixed upon her.

She shivered. This little creature was not . . . *normal*. She did not know how she knew this, but, somehow, she did.

'And what,' the young man on the dais said, 'have you brought me, then, Lyle?' His voice was no more than a hoarse, breathy whisper.

'Lord . . .' Peer Lyle began.

'And not so loud, this time, Lyle. If you *please*.'

101

Peer Lyle was a different man entirely now, she saw. With her rough captors he had been arrogant, straight-spined, commanding. Now, he stood with head bowed, eyes downcast, and talked in a soft, placating voice.

'These men are bringing you a gift, Lord Mattingly. Something they found on the strand, spewed up by the sea. I sent them, Lord –' the men about her stiffened, but held their peace '– to search for you. To discover things for you. I think you will find what they have brought to be . . . ah . . . interesting.'

'Oh, really?' replied the young man on the dais. He reached up and stroked the creature still draped around his shoulder. He didn't seem to mind the weight of it there at all, or the furred tail that still lay curled about his throat like a slumbering snake. 'And just *why* would that be? This . . . *thing* you have brought me seems very sorry and bedraggled.' He waved a hand at the guards. 'Take it away.' He paused for a moment, then gestured at Peer Lyle and her captors. 'And take *them* away, too.'

'Lord Mattingly!' Peer Lyle cried quickly, taking an impulsive step towards the dais.

One of the guard escort stepped forward and smacked Peer Lyle across the forehead with his pike handle. Lyle tumbled to his knees, groaning, hands to his head. He looked up, blood trickling through his fingers. 'Lord Mattingly . . . *Please*! Listen to me. I have . . .'

The young lord brushed his floating white hair off his face with one thin hand, staring unblinkingly at Lyle with his queer, darkly luminous eyes.

Perhaps it was a trick of the uncertain lighting, but she suddenly realized that the creature on Lord Mattingly's shoulder seemed to have the exact same unblinking, dark-eyed stare as he. And it seemed to be following the conversation, its eyes going from one speaker to the next as if it understood every word.

'Oh, very well, then,' Lord Mattingly murmured in his hoarse whisper. 'I am bored today, Lyle. *Bored*! Stand up! Talk to me.'

The young lord turned his gaze to her then. 'Boredom is *so* irksome, don't you find?'

She did not know what to make of any of this. She tried with exhausted desperation to talk, to say something – anything – just to use her voice. But it was still no good. All she could do was croak.

'Is this a *frog* you've brought me, then, Lyle?' Lord Mattingly demanded. 'It croaks like a frog. It even looks a little like a frog. A sea-frog, perhaps. From the sea strand . . . I see a sea-frog on the sea strand, seeking such seaweed as seems sensible . . .'

There was an appreciative little titter from the glittering men and women clustered about the dais.

'Oh, *shut up*!' Lord Mattingly snapped at them.

They did.

She shivered. It seemed quite mad to her, all this: the dilapidated ruin, the false glitter of this queer, candle-lit court, this bizarre young man at the centre of it all, the strange creature draped upon his shoulder . . . She had a sudden notion that it was all nothing but a dream, a false nightmare conjured up in her own feverish mind, that she would awake any instant in some safe, sane place, remembering clearly who she was . . .

But no.

Peer Lyle had risen shakily to his feet by now. He brought out a kerchief from somewhere and began to wipe the blood from his face.

'You missed a bit,' Lord Mattingly said interestedly after a few moments. 'There, down your cheek.'

Peer Lyle swallowed, nodded. 'Tha-thank you, Lord.'

Lord Mattingly nodded back, brushed his floating white hair out of his eyes. 'Well?'

'These men have brought you a . . . woman, Lord Mattingly.' Peer Lyle waved at the men still propping her up, and they pushed her closer towards the dais to display her.

'A woman?' Lord Mattingly said. 'This doesn't look like any *woman*, Lyle. And she *smells*. Phawg! She hurts my nose. Take her away!'

The men holding her yanked her hastily back.

'She came out of the sea, Lord,' Peer Lyle said quickly. 'She needs to be more properly washed and cleansed. But I think, if you look closer, you'll see that she's not . . . ugly at all, Lord.'

Lord Mattingly leaned forward a little. 'And you brought her for me, you say?'

'Yes, Lord.'

At this point a man pushed his way suddenly from out of the glittering congregation about the dais. He was tall and thin and shrouded in an ankle-length, dark robe, his face hidden and shadowed by a large hood. He padded out to stand between her and Lord Mattingly.

Silence fell upon the room.

Slowly, the man raised his arms, the loose sleeves of his robe falling open to reveal bony, knobbly-elbowed arms. Branded on the inside of each of his forearms was an image of a tusked demon's head. The man tilted back his head and the hood of the robe fell away. His face was disconcertingly skull-like, entirely devoid of any hair, skin stretched tight over bone.

'Hiiii-eee . . . ah-ah-hah . . .' the robed man chanted. 'Hiiii-eee . . . ah-ah-*hah* . . .' He spun around, once, twice, thrice, whirling so fast his robe opened out into a spinning disc, revealing his skinny, blue-veined legs. Then he stopped, his dark robe settling back into place.

The glittering crowd of folk faltered back.

Slowly, the man came stalking over. He lifted thin, knuckly hands towards her, staring coldly, unblinking as a serpent, his eyes like glittering black marbles. 'She is . . .' he said, his voice high-pitched and nasal. 'She is . . . heavy. Too heavy. Danger in her.'

Nobody moved in the chamber.

The dark-robed man reached closer to her. She felt his fingers moving over her like so many dry, inquisitive worms. She shuddered, held fast, unable to pull away. He reached out and took her two hands in his, turning them palm up. He stared, blinked, squinted. His skull-like face wrinkled into a sudden frown and he dropped her hands. 'Who are you?' he demanded.

But there was nothing she could answer to that question.

The dark-robed man whirled about. 'Sink her back in the sea!' he said to Lord Mattingly. 'Bury her! Be gone with her. Be *done* with her. She is *dangerous*!'

She stared down at her palms, but could see nothing.

The dark-robed man strode to the dais. 'You must do away with her, Lord Mattingly! Chop her into small pieces to feed the carrion birds. Let the wolves gnaw on her bones. Have the eagles pluck out her eyes. Allow the . . .'

'Yes, yes, Skolt,' Lord Mattingly said, waving a hand to silence the man. 'I get the general idea.'

The young lord sat as he was, chin in his hand, staring at her with his strange, unblinking, dark eyes.

'Dangerous,' the dark-robed man repeated. 'Dangerous as a serpent, as a famished dog, as a . . .'

Lord Mattingly waved the man to silence with a sigh. 'Yes, Skolt, I *do* understand.'

At this point, the furred creature on Lord Mattingly's shoulder leaned its small face in close to his ear, as if whispering to him. He cocked his head towards it, and held out his hand for silence – though nobody in the room had uttered so much as a word since dark-robed Skolt had made his appearance.

The gathering waited.

She could hear little hissing sounds, as if the creature were indeed whispering . . .

Lord Mattingly looked up. 'Spandel wants to hear her talk.' He peered at the glittering, extravagant congregation. 'Ingland? Ingland, where *have* you got to?'

A fat old man with a long, dirty white beard splayed out across his big belly stepped from the cluster of glittering folk.

'Ingland,' Lord Mattingly commanded, 'give her a draught of something so she can talk. Wake her up properly. She looks half asleep! I don't *like* it when people are half asleep in my presence.'

'Lord,' the man named Ingland murmured. The closely gathered folk cleared a way for him, and he trotted back to the far wall and reached down to a low table. There was quite an amount of paraphernalia upon it, an array of multi-coloured flasks and jars, an intricate decanter of some sort, bottles and bags. The man brought out a green stone vial and poured a clear amber fluid from it into a little glass. Into this he mixed a pinch of yellow powder taken from a leather bag, a few drops of blue liquid from a bottle, another pinch of powder . . .

'Oh, do hurry *up*, Ingland,' Lord Mattingly said

exasperatedly. 'You always take so *long* to make these little concoctions of yours!'

'I'm hurrying as best I can, Lord,' the man replied.

'Well, *do* so, then,' Lord Mattingly said peevishly. 'And stop wasting time talking!'

'Yes, Lord . . .'

In a few moments, the fat, bearded man came forward with the little glass in his hand.

'Lord Mattingly,' dark-robed Skolt protested. 'You must not!'

The Lord Mattingly winced. 'Must not *what*, Skolt? And *must* you be so loud?'

Skolt bowed a quick apology. 'She must not be allowed to talk, Lord. Her tongue will weave plots. She will weave the *ruin* of you, Lord. The death of many precious things . . .'

'Really?' Lord Mattingly looked interested.

'Lord!' Skolt protested.

'Do it, Ingland,' Lord Mattingly ordered, gesturing the command as he spoke.

'Tip her head back,' Ingland instructed.

She tried to resist, having no idea what might be in the concoction the man had mixed for her, but she simply did not have the strength. A hand yanked at her tangled hair, sending a thrust of agony through her bruised skull, and she was forced to drink the stuff – a too-sweet, sticky liquid that made her gag.

'It should take effect very quickly, Lord,' Ingland said, stepping back with the now-emptied glass.

She felt a hot flush go through her, down her throat and into her gut, from her gut up again and into her throbbing skull, then out and through her limbs. It made her fingers tingle, her toes itch uncomfortably. She felt strength come back into her shivery limbs. She cleared her throat, coughed. 'Wa . . . wa-water . . .' she gasped.

'Ah . . .' Lord Mattingly murmured. 'She wants wa-water. Give her some wa-water, then, Ingland.'

The fat, bearded man brought a flask and an earthenware cup over from the table, filled the cup, offered it.

She drank gratefully, feeling the cool water soothe her delightfully. 'More . . .' she gasped, and was given a second cup.

'Enough,' Lord Mattingly said then, waving the man Ingland back. 'She can drink more later. Spandel wants to hear her talk.' He gestured. 'Talk.'

She cleared her throat, swallowed. 'I . . . I tha . . . thank ye for the water . . . Lord. Ye is . . .'

'*Ye?*' Lord Mattingly said. 'What is this *ye*?'

She blinked, confused.

Lord Mattingly turned to Peer Lyle. 'What does she mean, Lyle, with this *ye*? Can't she speak proper? Is she stupid or something?'

Peer Lyle opened his mouth, closed it, clearly at a loss.

'Are *you* stupid, then?' Lord Mattingly demanded of him.

'No, Lord,' Peer Lyle responded quickly. 'It's just . . . I don't . . .'

'It is a northern trick of speaking, Lord Mattingly.' It was the sombrely dressed swordsman who had overseen the taking away of weapons from her captors. He came now to stand next to her, regarding her with some interest, one hand on the hilt of the long iron sword at his waist, the other scratching musingly at his close-cropped, grey-beard.

'Ah . . .' said Lord Mattingly. 'You know such things, do you, Master Karasyn?'

'I have heard those from the north speak like this, Lord.' The man turned again to her. 'Are you from the north, then, girl?'

She blinked, trying to remember. 'I . . .' But there was only the great blank wall in her mind. 'I . . . may be.'

'No!' the dark-robed man cried. 'Do not let her speak!'

'Skolt, do you *mind*?' Lord Mattingly snapped.

'Long Harbour,' she said in sudden triumph, the name having come suddenly into her mind like a little fish swimming out of hidden depths.

'That is where you come from?' the grey-haired swordsman asked.

She tried to call up more. But it was no use. Just the name, devoid of anything else. 'I . . . I don't . . .' she started lamely.

'Have you heard of this Long Harbour place, Karasyn?' Lord Mattingly demanded.

'No, Lord.'

'Some desperate collection of dirty little hovels, no doubt,' the young lord said.

'It's a cleaner, better place than *this* dilapidated, filthy warren of yers, at any rate,' she snapped, bristling. It was out before she properly knew what she had said.

There was a collective gasp of astonishment.

The guards shifted closer, pikes coming up.

She swallowed, shivered. But there was something inside her that made her lift her head and stare at them all defiantly.

Suddenly, Lord Mattingly began to laugh. It was high-pitched, stuttering laughter, like the cry of some odd bird. He fell over sideways on to the piled silks on his dais, spilling the furred creature from his shoulder, like a man in a fit, body convulsed, hair falling in a wispy white cloud about his face.

Several of the gathered throng moved forward nervously. Fat, bearded Ingland came and knelt quickly next to the dais. 'Are you . . . all right, Lord?' Receiving no response save the high-pitched, spasmodic laughter, he reached out a hand in concern. 'Lord Mattingly?'

The young lord batted the hand away. He sat half up, still shaking with helpless laughter. 'You . . . you . . .' he stuttered, pointing at her.

She did not know what to make of it all. Apparently, neither did anybody else, for they all stood about, awkward, tense, staring.

The creature that had been upon Lord Mattingly's shoulder came over to the front edge of the dais and sat up there, flexible tail curled about its sleek flank, staring at her.

It was, she realized suddenly, quite a beautiful creature in its own way, slender and lithe-limbed and agile. Its short, soft, mahogany-and-honey-coloured fur shone in the chamber's dancing candlelight. Its little baby's hands were furred only on the back. The skin of the palm and the underside of the fingers was bare, a soft, gleaming black-brown. The fur on its long, sinuous tail was ringed with darker markings. And its honey-coloured, furred face was marked by dark circles ringing its eyes, as if it were wearing a mask. And those eyes . . .

They stared at her with all the knowing awareness of human eyes.

She shivered under that gaze.

There was silence in the room for long moments more, while Lord Mattingly's laughing fit slowly abated.

Finally, he looked at her and smiled, showing small, sharp, gleaming white teeth, like twin rows of carved pearls. '*Just* the creature I've been looking to find,' he said.

She did not know how to respond.

Peer Lyle, however, came forward a step. 'Then you're pleased with my gift, Lord?'

'*Your* gift, Lyle?'

'Of course, Lord Mattingly. As I have already mentioned, I sent those men out on a quest to find you the very best that could be . . .'

Lord Mattingly waved his hand. 'Wipe your chin, Lyle. There's blood on it. Can't you be a little cleaner? If there's one thing I cannot abide, it's men with dirty habits . . .'

'Yes . . . Lord,' Peer Lyle said, wiping his chin. He stood in stiff silence then, chewing at his lower lip.

'And don't look so glum, Lyle. I'll remember you for this gift. Don't worry. Can't you smile or something?' Lord Mattingly looked about him. 'What's wrong with you all? Have you forgotten how to smile? How to laugh? Laugh! Go on . . . laugh!'

Those clustered about the dais laughed obediently, awkward peals of forced mirth.

He stopped them with a gesture.

She stood, staring.

'You are staring,' Lord Mattingly said to her. 'It's not *polite* to stare.'

She shrugged self-consciously. 'I meant no . . . impoliteness. I've just never . . . never seen anybody like ye. Or –' she pointed at the animal still sitting on the dais's front edge '– like yer . . . pet there.'

'Pet?' Lord Mattingly reached over and stroked the mahogany-furred head. 'Spandel is no *pet*.' He put his chin close against the creature's shoulder, glanced at her sideways out of his strange, dark eyes. 'You must be a very stupid girl.'

She held her tongue, but only just. The potion she had been fed made her blood sing in her ears. She felt strong and confident, as if she had just awakened from a long, refreshing night's sleep. But she recognized the falseness of the feeling. Some part of her was too canny to let it get her into trouble here. And who knew how long the effects of the potion would last?

109

'Sensible girl,' the grey-haired man with the iron sword said quietly, moving closer to her.

She looked at him, uncertain.

'It's never a good idea to let Ingland's potions go to your head.' He stood regarding her curiously, arms folded across his lean chest. 'You look as if you've had a hard time of it, girl.'

She shrugged. He seemed the sanest one here, this man. But she wasn't about to trust him . . . or anyone, or anything, in this queer, nightmare place.

'Do you want her, Karasyn?' Lord Mattingly asked. 'She's yours.'

She stiffened.

'Lord!' Peer Lyle started, but Mattingly silenced him with a look.

'Most generous of you, Lord,' Karasyn replied. He took a few steps back from her, turned to face the young man on the dais. 'But I have no need of a woman.'

Lord Mattingly laughed his strange, high pitched, bird-like laugh. 'You mistake me, Karasyn.'

'Lord?'

'Train her.'

Grey-haired Karasyn blinked.

'You are my Weapons Master. Train her, I say.'

The creature at Lord Mattingly's side slid up his arm and perched on his shoulder once again. It bent its sleek furred head and whispered close into his ear – if that indeed was what it did.

She waited in silence with the rest, feeling her limbs still quivering with energy. Perhaps, if she were quick enough, she could make a break for it . . . dash out of this chamber, lose herself in the maze of ill-lit, dank corridors . . .

The creature suddenly leaped from Lord Mattingly's shoulder, its long tail twisting for balance as it flew through the air. There was a hasty, awkward scuttling as people cleared a way for it. It scampered nimbly up her thigh, its little hands clutching her still sea-damp, salt-crusted clothing, then up her side to perch on her shoulder as it had upon Mattingly's.

The men still holding on to her scuttled back and away in panicky haste. She flinched, tried awkwardly to brush the thing off, but it clung tight.

Then she heard a breathy little voice in her ear: 'He needs you, girl. Needs, needs, needs you!'

She felt her heart lurch.

'He needs, needs, *needs* you,' the little creature repeated.

'See?' Lord Mattingly said from the dais. 'Spandel approves of her.'

There was an uneasy murmuring from the gathered company.

'Train her, Karasyn.'

'But, Lord . . .' Karasyn said. 'She is a . . . *girl*!'

Mattingly nodded, smiling a thin smile. 'I *had* noticed that, Karasyn.'

'But no girl could ever . . .'

'Train her!' Lord Mattingly barked, and he was no longer smiling. 'Or do you wish to . . . disobey me?'

Karasyn shook his head. 'No, Lord. For your dead father's sake, I will obey any order you give me.'

'Good,' Mattingly said. 'Then *train* her.'

'Lord Mattingly!' It was dark-robed Skolt again. 'You must listen to me! Kill her. *Now*! Kill her fast. She is heavy with threat to us. She is *dangerous*. She . . .'

Lord Mattingly merely waved the man to silence.

She had been trying to follow the meaning of what had been passing, but with no success. 'Train me in what?' she demanded now. The creature still sat upon her shoulder. She tried to shrug it off again, to brush it away, but it stayed fast, its strong little hands firmly intertwined in her sea-matted hair.

Lord Mattingly leaned forward on his dais. 'Why . . . train you for the sword, of course. What else?'

'No!' dark-robed Skolt cried.

Lord Mattingly winced and glared at him.

She did not know what to say.

'No girl could ever . . .' Karasyn began again.

Mattingly's creature leaped unexpectedly from her shoulder, sending her reeling. It scampered across the floor and into the glittering congregation about the dais. There were squeals and little shrieks as it bounced about amongst them. Then it reappeared. In one of its small hands it clutched a dagger. Racing across the floor, it flipped the weapon at her, handle first.

She caught it. To her surprise, her hand seemed to know just how to hold the thing.

111

The gathered company stared at her.

Karasyn drew his iron sword, the weapon coming out of the scabbard in one fast, smooth motion, with a soft, unpleasant *whisss*. 'Put it *down*, girl,' he ordered, his voice hard. The sword came up menacingly. He had the look of a man who knew *exactly* what he was doing with a blade.

She went to put the dagger down, but Lord Mattingly interrupted.

'No, no, Weapons Master. Let her have it.' The young lord's face was glistening with sweat, as if he were flushed with a sudden fever. His strangely luminous dark eyes stared unblinkingly. He gestured to one of the men who had been holding her – the one with the ridiculous, flapping hairdo, who had had the three little swords in his belt, and who had three dangling, empty scabbards now. 'Give this man one of his blades back,' Lord Mattingly commanded.

The man so chosen blinked, brushed a drooping wing of greasy hair out of his face, glanced anxiously at his companions, at the room in general, at Karasyn.

Weapons Master Karasyn nodded slowly to one of the guards, keeping his own sword at the ready.

The guard went and fetched one of the short swords, returned, handed it over hilt first. The man held the weapon uneasily, his eyes shifting about.

'Take her,' Lord Mattingly said.

The man stood frozen.

'Take her!' Mattingly commanded.

The man came at her then, hair flopping, his short-bladed sword up.

She swallowed and hefted the dagger in her hand. It was a poorly balanced thing, with a dull, chipped iron blade . . .

The man lunged at her awkwardly, flat-footed as a goose.

She sidestepped easily enough, her limbs moving reliably thanks to the potion she had been given. She felt strong and confident. Falsely confident, perhaps . . . But, somehow, she *did* seem to know what she was doing. She had a sudden flash of memory – her with a little blade in hand, a man's wide smile . . . There and gone in an instant.

Lord Mattingly was applauding. 'Again. Do it again!'

The man came at her once more, lunging.

This time, she ducked in under his guard and snicked him with the dagger along his forearm, the movement coming naturally to her somehow.

The man howled and dropped his sword, clutching at his cut arm. It was over as quick as that. She stood back, dagger in hand, panting, her free hand to her bruised head, which throbbed painfully despite the strengthening potion.

The glittering congregation stared, mute.

Lord Mattingly, however, brought his pale, thin hands together in a loud clap. 'Well *done*!' He turned to Karasyn. 'See? Train her, Karasyn.'

'*Lord*!' dark-robed Skolt shouted in protest.

Lord Mattingly winced.

Grey-haired Karasyn still kept his sword at the ready. 'Drop the dagger, girl,' he said. 'Now.'

She looked at the long sword blade, at his hard grey eyes, and obeyed.

Skolt sidled up close to the dais. 'She is a *great* danger to you. I am your Seer, Lord, and you must listen to me. You must *not* do this thing! She is a danger. She is a . . .'

Lord Mattingly sighed. 'Leave me *be*, Skolt.'

He backed a few steps off, outraged. 'Do you deny my knowledge? Do you deny the long line of Seers from which I come? Your father listened to me. *Always*!'

Young Lord Mattingly sighed again. 'You weary me, Skolt.' He ran a hand over his pale face, brushing his wispy hair aside. 'And you *bore* me.'

Skolt backed away a few steps, his face white with outrage. 'I am a Seer. I will *not* be spoken to in this manner. Do you hear? Do you *hear* me?'

'Go away,' Lord Mattingly said.

Skolt only stared.

'Are you grown deaf, then?'

'No,' Skolt replied in a tight, angry voice.

Lord Mattingly gestured. 'Go. Leave my sight.'

Skolt hesitated for a long moment, looked around at the gathered throng but obviously saw no support there. Karasyn stared at him coldly, his sword still bared and ready. Skolt turned a black gaze upon her, scowling at her.

'Skolt!' Lord Mattingly snapped.

The Seer turned, bowed to the young lord, a shallow, brittle dip from the waist.

Mattingly gestured him away.

Without a word further, Skolt whirled on his heel and stalked furiously off out of the chamber.

Lord Mattingly laughed his odd, bird-like laugh. He turned and regarded her. 'My Spandel dreamed of you. Oh, yes . . . You are *just* the sort of creature I've been looking to find.' With that, he collapsed abruptly backwards on the dais, pale and panting and exhausted, as if a great, invisible fist had suddenly struck him down.

Fat, bearded Ingland rushed to the dais. 'Lord?' he said worriedly. He knelt and put a hand to Lord Mattingly's wrist, shook his head. 'Leave!' he said over his shoulder at the gathered crowd. 'Lord Mattingly needs rest. All this excitement has overtaxed him.'

Those gathered about hesitated. Some pushed closer to the dais.

'Leave!' the man repeated.

Lord Mattingly was collapsed on his back. Little webs of white spittle hung from his lips. His creature came scampering up and squatted next to him, stroking his over-broad forehead as a mother might stroke the fevered brow of a child.

'*Leave!*' Ingland all but screamed.

There was a general, confused shuffling about.

'Are you all deaf?' grey-bearded Karasyn demanded. 'Lord Mattingly needs rest.' He gestured a command at the two rows of guards, and they began herding the glittering congregation away from the dais. One man tried to resist. The guards beat him, a quick flurry of blows that left him groaning.

She stood as she was. Glittering folk spilled past her and out of the chamber's door. But she was too shaken and confused by the suddenness of everything to know how to move.

And the effects of the potion seemed to be wearing off. She felt her limbs becoming heavy. Her skull pulsed agonizingly. Her eyes stung. Without knowing quite how, she was on her knees. She saw grey-bearded Karasyn standing over her, long iron sword still in hand. His mouth moved, as if he were saying something, but she could not make out the words. He looked very far off somehow.

The room seemed to be tipping abruptly to one side. She saw the ceiling slide across her vision. Something hard and cold smacked against the side of her head, sending a wash of agony through her skull. She was on the stone floor . . . she saw a foot, another, before her eyes.

Then she saw nothing at all.

XIV

She rolled over, sighed, groaned. She ached still, everywhere. It seemed a duller sort of ache than it had been, though. Her head throbbed, but only distantly. She stretched, rubbed sleep-sticky eyes, blinked, shook herself.

She vaguely remembered a sea strand, the cold waves trying to drag her back into the depths after they had spewed her forth, and gulls spilling through the blue air above her, and . . . and rough men gripping her. Recollection filtered into her slowly. Dark stone corridors, a pale, skinny man with wispy white hair, a . . . a little creature whispering into her ear, the feel of a dagger in her hand . . .

'So . . .' a voice said. 'The mystery sleeper awakens finally.'

With a jerk, she snapped up to a sitting position. A lance of pain went through her bruised skull at the too-sudden movement, and she put a hand to the tender lump she remembered being there, finding it, to her surprise, considerably smaller than she had expected.

There were blankets about her. She lay on a pallet, she saw, in a chilly little room. A smoky fire sputtered in a small hearth. Somebody stood next to that hearth, looking at her. She clutched at the blankets protectively, suddenly self-conscious; some part of her did not at all like the fact that he – for the person was a he – had been staring at her while she slept, all unknowing.

He came forward a little and she got a better look at him, a slim young man, dressed in loose trousers and a long-sleeved tunic almost as sombre as that of the grey-bearded swordsman, Karasyn – she remembered the name – except for a blood-red sash about his waist. He had long dark hair pulled back in a tight queue, narrow moustaches, brown eyes set wide apart. A thin scar, like a carefully tattooed line, ran from his forehead down his left cheek.

116

She looked at him, looked around, swallowed. 'Whe . . . where am I?' she asked.

'In the Guardery,' the man replied.

Which enlightened her not at all. She blinked, trying to get the sleep from her eyes, from her mind. Her throat was dry and sore. She spotted an earthenware flagon on the floor next to her pallet.

'Water,' the man said, seeing her glance.

She reached for it, her stiff limbs complaining at every slight movement. She took a long drink, another. The water hit her belly like ballast. She splashed a little on her face, relishing the soothing coolth of it, closed her eyes, tried to piece together memory more clearly – greatly relieved she *had* memories. The big candle-lit chamber, the bizarre young Lord Mattingly on his silken dais, his even more bizarre little creature – *talking* creature – angry, dark-robed Skolt the Seer, the blade-fight they had forced upon her . . .

The room in which she lay was stone-walled, stone-floored. She recalled leagues of dank stone corridors. 'Where *am* I?' she repeated.

'In the Guardery,' he repeated back. 'In one of the sleeping cells.'

'But *where*?'

'In the *Guardery*!' the man said in exasperation. 'Are you stupid, then? Or just hard of hearing?' He shook his head. 'I've been stuck here for the better part of the morning, wasting my time when I could have been doing more worthwhile things . . . and you lie there repeating foolish questions.'

She felt like slapping the man. It was he who was the stupid one. 'This place. This . . . what would ye call it? This sprawling stone . . . place. What is it named?'

'Oh,' he said. Then he shrugged. 'This is Minmi City. One of the great Domains.'

'Domains?'

'Yes. The great southern Domains. Are you northerners all so ignorant, then?'

She bit her lip, took a sharp breath.

He stood over her, arms crossed, tapping his foot impatiently.

'How long has ye been looking at me?' she demanded,

feeling a stab of hot annoyance go through her. The man was irritating as a burr.

He shrugged. 'If I were you, I'd learn to speak properly.'

She bridled instinctively. 'And what does the likes of *ye* know about proper speech?'

'I know enough,' he replied, 'not to sound like a fool foreigner.'

She glared at him. 'Ye's the fool here!'

'You *do* have a temper, don't you?'

She shrugged sullenly.

'My name is Rannis. Third Rank . . .' He smiled. 'But not for long.'

'Third Rank, what?'

'Guard Rank, of course. What else?'

'Oh, of *course*,' she replied thinly. 'What *else*.'

'Up with you, now, girl,' he said, seemingly oblivious to her sarcasm.

His use of 'girl' rankled, somehow. 'My name,' she said, 'is . . .' But she could not recall her name.

It was like a great empty space inside her. *Everybody* had a name. She tried to think back, to draw up memory . . .

But it was no use. There was only the sea strand, her lying exhausted and tangled in a festoon of seaweed. It was as if she had truly been sprung into existence that very moment, with the gulls crying overhead . . .

Thinking of those gulls, she had a sudden, momentary image of a ship's rail, a fat man throwing a little fish into the water, gulls squabbling . . .

Kestrel.

The name came to her with abrupt unexpectedness. Was it *her* name? No . . . She did not think so. It was . . . She did not know what or whose it might be. But . . .

Kess.

She felt that might be a good name.

'I am called . . . Kess,' she told the man standing impatiently over her. The sound of the name felt strange on her lips.

'Well, up with you, Kess,' he said. 'Weapons Master Karasyn wishes to see you. You've slept long and long. Enough of girlish weakness.'

'I've slept because I *had* to, not out of weakness – girlish or

118

otherwise. And I'm nobody's *girl*!' She glared up at him from the pallet upon which she sat, still wrapped in the blankets. 'How . . . how long have I been sleeping here?'

'Three days.'

'No!'

Rannis nodded. 'Oh, yes. You were fevered for most of the first two. Ranting like a mad woman. I know. I was here for part of it.' He reached across suddenly and tore the blankets off her. 'But the fever's gone now, so *up* with you.'

The chill air of the room made Kess shiver. She hugged herself, feeling her salt-crusted clothing crumple stiffly. 'Ye's a buffoon!' she snapped at him.

'And *you* need to learn how to *talk* properly.'

She glared up at him, shivering.

'Not . . . how do you say it? Not . . . that barbarous northern *ye*. The word is *you*. Say it.'

Kess only glowered, confused, feeling her pulse thud painfully in the bones of her skull.

'Say it!' he insisted.

She kept silent.

Rannis shook his head. 'You'll never prosper here if you continue to act like some sullen . . . *girl*. You've got to learn to fit in. And you can start by dropping this ridiculous . . .'

'It isn't *ridiculous*. Where I come from, everybody . . .' But the words died on her tongue. She could not recall anything about where she came from.

'Well,' said Rannis, 'this isn't wherever you come from. And here, that *ye* of yours sounds purely ridiculous. Now say the proper word.' He glared at her, hands fisted on his hips. 'Say *you*.'

Kess set her hands on her own hips in mimicry of him and glared back. 'Make me.'

He sighed and shook his head. 'Don't be *stupid*.'

'Ye doesn't . . .' Kess began angrily, but then stopped herself. This young man was no enemy of hers. Brash and annoying he might be, but some part of her knew it was certainly not in her own best interest to antagonize him. She had come out of sleep stiff and sore and unbalanced. And there was something about him that seemed to bring out the worst in her, as if he reminded her unpleasantly of somebody . . .

She shook herself, took a long breath, trying to get her mind more clear.

'*You*,' she said finally. 'There. Is *you* happy now?'

Rannis shook his head. 'Not *is* you. It's *are* you.'

Kess scowled. He made her feel like a stupid child.

'Say it.'

'*Are* you,' she repeated sulkily. '*Are you* happy *now*?'

Rannis smiled. 'Oh, yes, happy indeed. Now come. Master Karasyn has been waiting for you far too long already. Up and out!' He reached down and hauled her off the bed and out through the door in one lithe, irrefutable motion.

Rannis dragged her through more of the dank corridors, walking too quickly for her stiff limbs, so that she stumbled with painful clumsiness behind him until light blinded her momentarily. She shook herself from Rannis's hold, blinked, tried to get her breath.

'Master Karasyn,' Rannis called softly.

Squinting into the brightness, she saw the Weapons Master, grey-bearded, lean as a hunting hound, sombre and solid as she remembered him; she felt a little surge of relief at the accuracy of that memory. He stood in a kind of open yard, she saw, two lines of grey-clad men behind him.

He gestured at Rannis and her to wait, then turned back to the lines of men who stood facing each other – with swords in hand, she realized. 'Thrust!' the Weapons Master called out. 'Parry! Riposte! One . . . two . . . three . . .'

The ranked men moved their swords against each other in unison, as if going through the steps of some odd, formal dance.

'Watch your footwork, Tasom,' Master Karasyn told one of the men. 'You're falling over your own feet!'

'Thrust . . . parry . . . riposte,' he repeated. 'Thrust . . . parry . . . riposte . . .'

The men were panting, and sweaty.

'Thrust . . . parry . . . riposte . . .'

'He's a demanding old bastard, is Weapons Master Karasyn,' Rannis said in Kess's ear. 'But he's the *best*. Last Master of the great Lightning Wheel blade school. You can think yourself lucky to be given the chance of studying under him.' He shook his head. 'Though I doubt it'll do you much good.'

Kess blinked. 'Studying?' The sunlight hurt her eyes still. She felt fuzzy-minded and not altogether certain of things. She recalled Lord Mattingly commanding the Weapons Master. 'Studying . . . what?'

'The blade, of course,' Rannis said. He took her by the shoulders and pointed her towards the twin ranks of men going through their ritualized dance. 'Watch.'

Kess shrugged his hands from her irritably and turned to look. The line of blades came up, out, *krangged* together, dropped, moved again, *krangged*, came down, then up to a guard position.

'Thrust . . . parry . . . riposte,' the Weapons Master continued. 'Thrust . . . parry . . . riposte . . .'

It went on till the men were gasping and exhausted, stumbling, their swords wavering weakly.

'Enough!' Master Karasyn called out finally. 'Break.'

The men collapsed, panting like hounds.

Only then did Master Karasyn turn and come striding over to where Kess and Rannis stood waiting. She opened her mouth, determined to demand answers from him, but he cut her off. 'You need to wash,' he said by way of greeting. 'You stink of the sea still. And your clothes look stiff as bark.' He turned to Rannis. 'See she's washed and issued with clean clothing. You should have done that first. Where's your brains, boy?'

Rannis bridled. 'I thought you'd want to see her right away, soon as she woke. I thought . . .'

'Just see she's washed. And fed, too. She looks hungry.'

'Yes, Master Karasyn.'

Karasyn turned from them and back to the lines of weary men. 'Right, you lot. Let's try it again.'

The men groaned.

'Thrust . . . parry . . . riposte . . . Thrust! Parry! Riposte!'

'Come on, then,' Rannis said to Kess, his voice tight. He grabbed her by the elbow and yanked her towards the doorway that led back into the dim stone interior.

It was breathlessly cold water she had to wash in, and none too much of it – a couple of buckets and a stone trough in a chilly room, with Rannis waiting impatiently outside. But it was clean, sweet water nevertheless, and it made her feel better. Discarding her old clothing in a stiff little jumble in the corner, she washed herself all over. She stood for a long moment, letting the water run off her, savouring the feeling of being clean again.

But the air was chill, and the wet stone floor freezing on her bare feet. She dressed quickly in the loose trousers, rough leather boots and long-sleeved tunic Rannis had collected for her.

'Kess?' he called from outside the room. 'What are you *doing* in there?'

She ignored him. She splashed the last of the water over her face, ran her fingers as best she could through her tangled hair – she was afraid she would have to cut it, so snarled and knotted was it – and tried to put it up, tucking and tying the long damp strands in upon themselves. A sudden flash of memory, or half-memory, rather, went through her: a little sharp bodkin. She had used it to pin up her hair. But where and when had she used such a thing? And what had happened to it?

She looked down at the sorry, crumpled mess of her old clothing and shivered. It felt like leaving a discarded skin behind – as some serpents did. Poor, sodden garments though they were, they were all that connected her with any past she might have had – if indeed she *had* any real past . . .

But she must! She knew things, understood things, was able to do things. What had happened to her to make her memoryless like this? It was as if somebody had amputated part of her mind . . .

'Kess!' Rannis called impatiently from the other side of the door. 'Come *on*!'

It was good to have a name.

'Kess, if you don't . . .'

As she emerged from the little room, he looked at her, started to say something, stopped short, mouth open, staring.

Some chord was touched in her, and she could not help but smile. 'Catching flies, are we, then?' she said.

Rannis closed his mouth, shook himself. 'Well, well . . .' he breathed. 'Who'd have thought it? You're a . . . a *girl.*'

'This comes as a surprise to ye?' Kess felt like laughing, and yet wanted to slap him at the same time.

Rannis shook his head. 'I . . .' He looked at her out of the corner of his eye, and she saw a new surmise in his glance now. She did not know if she liked what she was beginning to see there or not.

'Come along,' she urged. 'There was some talk of food, wasn't there?'

He nodded, blinked, shook himself. 'All right, then.'

It was to an eating hall he led her, through the usual meandering series of dim stone corridors – this Minmi was like a giant, jumbled, stone rabbit warren – and eventually into a large room with trestle tables lined with little benches. A dozen or so grey-clad men sat scattered about in small groups, already eating. They fell silent when Rannis and Kess entered.

There was rice and lentil soup, coarse bread, boiled turnips, dried herring, all served from a communal counter to which Rannis gestured her. She recognized the food and knew the good taste of it all. But despite her empty belly, she found herself too shaky to eat much. She had a little soup, soaking a slice of the bread in it.

She wanted to ask questions of Rannis, but the food kept her occupied. And the thick silence of the Hall subdued her, too, for none of those already here had said so much as a word since she and Rannis had entered.

She looked up at those silent others. None would meet her glance.

Then, abruptly, one of them pushed aside a half-empty bowl and stalked over. 'She's a *girl,*' he said.

'So what?' Rannis responded.

'So *what*? Have you *entirely* lost your wits, Rannis?'

The others in the room began to gather around.

'Only Mad Mattingly would have thought of something *this* stupid,' one of them said in disgust. 'A *girl* Guard, indeed. The only thing that keeps this sorry Domain going is the Guards. Without *us*, Mattingly and his mad like would have spun it all to ruin long ago. And *now* . . . now he . . .'

'And you, Rannis?' another said, interrupting. 'I suppose she's already given up her favours to you. That's why you're championing her then?'

Kess rose up, instinctively outraged.

Rannis pushed her back. 'Watch your mouth, Lotch,' he said. 'You know *nothing*!'

'I know enough to know a girl in the Guards is *trouble*!' the one named Lotch replied. He had a fringe of long dark hair about his ears and the back of his bald skull, tied in a loose plait intertwined with flashing silver beads. His face was flat, his cheek shadowed with stubble, his eyes dark and angry. 'Manny's right in what he says. We're the only thing holding this place together. The girl's nothing but trouble. Out of the way, Rannis. Let us deal with her now.'

The men began to sidle towards Kess like a pack of predatory wolves. Rannis stood up, blocking them.

Kess pushed herself up from the table, her sore limbs complaining, and tried to back away, her belly twisted up with anger and fright. Her head hurt with a sudden thrust of pain. 'I didn't ask to be taken into yer stupid Guard!' she snapped.

'Listen to her!' bald Lotch said. 'She can't even talk proper.'

'I told you to watch your mouth!' Rannis warned.

'Or what?' Lotch said, swaggering closer. He was shorter than Rannis, but more heavy-set, square-shouldered and thick-armed.

Rannis shoved him, a hard, sudden thrust of both hands, sending Lotch stumbling back until his legs caught on the edge of a bench and he spilled on to the floor.

He scrambled up, a knife in his hand now. 'Come on, shithead!' he hissed. 'Try that again . . .'

Kess stepped back, her heart thumping. She had seen no weapons in evidence before on any of these men.

But Rannis came forward. From somewhere he, too, produced a blade.

'Stop it!' Kess cried. 'This is all so *stupid*.'

'That's it,' Lotch taunted. 'Let a girl protect you.' He sneered. 'Coward!'

Rannis made towards him, blade at the ready.

But, '*Enough*!' a sudden, authoritative voice shouted.

Everybody turned. Weapons Master Karasyn stood in the

eating hall's entrance. 'Fools!' he spat. 'As if we haven't enough troubles already, without you lot squabbling senselessly amongst yourselves.'

'It's *her* fault,' Lotch said peevishly, gesturing with his blade in an accusing stab at Kess. 'You cannot let *her* become one of us!'

'*Cannot*?' the Weapons Master said. 'And just who are *you* to say what Karasyn can and cannot do?'

Bald Lotch went silent, lowering his gaze sullenly.

Karasyn glared. 'Put that blade away!' he snapped at Lotch. 'And as for the rest of you . . . Get out of here, the lot of you, and be *quick* about it!'

They went, but not without casting nasty looks backwards at Kess and Rannis.

'And you,' the Weapons Master said to Rannis with a sigh, 'put your blade away, too.' He gestured at Kess. 'Take her out of here and show her where she'll be sleeping. I've arranged things with old Haladin. See him about it. Do you think you can do that without causing further trouble? Or shall I get somebody else to do the task?'

Rannis flushed. 'I can do it, Master Karasyn.'

'Do so, then.' With that, the Weapons Master whirled and stalked out of the room.

Kess shivered. Her heart still thudded from the sudden threat of violence. She took a long breath, shook herself. 'Tha . . . thank you,' she said to Rannis. She had been utterly alone since coming to herself on the sea strand, trying to cope with her lack of memory, with all the things the world had thrust upon her. It seemed that now, unexpectedly, she had found an ally.

She felt a little warm shiver go through her. 'This is the first that anybody's . . .' she began.

'Oh, shut up!' Rannis snapped at her. 'You think I did this for *you*?' He shook his head disgustedly. 'Most of that lot's friends of mine. Or *were*, at any rate. Lotch is right. You're nothing but *trouble*, girl. It was just my bad fortune to be on duty when you awoke. Could have been Lotch himself just as easily. But it was *my* mischance to get stuck with the responsibility for you.'

Kess stared at him.

'Well, come on,' he ordered her brusquely. 'You heard what Master Karasyn said.' He turned then, and led the way out of the room without a backward glance.

XV

Kess sighed. She stood upon her hard little bed in her chilly little room and gazed out of the only window, a narrow rectangle too small to get her shoulders through. It was a jumble of crumbling stone walls and tattered rooftops she saw – except for a narrow slice of green hills and blue sky in the far distance, peeping from between an age-pocked tower and the grey slate roof gable of the Guards Eating Hall.

She had been to the Hall to eat her fill three times a day for three days now, traipsing the corridor between there and her little room. Thanks to the food and rest, she felt nearly recovered, far less sore and stiff. Her head was nearly without pain, the lump that had been so painfully tender almost gone entirely.

The only noticeable result left now of her being spewed out by the sea was that her hair had had to be cut off, for it was altogether too snarled to save. It had come as a shock to her, seeing how long and dark it was as it came tumbling down under the shears. It felt altogether strange to be short-cropped, like having a tight-fitting little cap rather than true hair, and a part of her mourned – though she was unsure why, exactly. But the hair would grow out again eventually . . .

Sighing, Kess turned from the window and sat down upon her bed. She ran a hand through her stubbly brush of hair. She felt stranded, caught between. Why had the sea spat her up on the strand here? Who *was* she?

She dreamed dreams at night. She would feel herself entrapped in suffocating darkness and awoke sweating and shivering, her heart hammering fit to burst. There was a place through which she would walk, a place of crowded buildings, like yet unlike Minmi. And a man, with tattooed cheeks and a long slim braid of red hair. Thinking of him made her belly contract in inexplicable anger. Like Rannis he was, a little. Yet unlike.

Once, she had dreamed of a black bird that came to her and said, 'Aks-sel, aks-sel,' then flew off to a conical hut. In another, she saw two middle-aged people, man and woman, looking down upon her, shaking their heads disapprovingly – though who these two might be and what, exactly, they disapproved of so strongly remained a mystery to her. Sometimes she would dream of cards, with faces and shapes of people upon them. And sometimes of a single female face, part human and part animal, long and slender of chin, with pointed ears and overlarge eyes. Like Lord Mattingly's little creature, perhaps. Yet not. Staring at her with those overlarge eyes, staring . . .

Flashes and fragments. Enough to confuse and upset her, nothing more. Sometimes, the palm of her left hand would itch and burn. Yet, examine it as she might, she could see no sign of any scar.

Three days alone . . . eating, sleeping, dreaming, trying fruitlessly to recollect herself. No one had spoken so much as a word to her, not in the Hall, not coming or going from her room. Rannis, when she passed him, had refused even to look her in the eye.

Kess sighed. There was so much she ached to know, not only about herself but also about this queer place in which she had been stranded. Who had built this great stone warren, and why? The days of its former glory were obviously long past. What sort of folk was it who lived here now, who held the likes of young Mattingly as their lord? Mad Mattingly, as the Guards called him, and his uncanny little talking creature . . .

They seemed mad enough themselves, most of the folk here – with the exception of Karasyn and his Guard. Perhaps.

Master Karasyn had ordered her to stay within the confines of her room and rest: a sensible enough order at the time, given her exhausted state, and accompanied by no apparent threat of any sort. But now . . .

She felt her strength return. She felt restless. And the day's-end meal was not for a long time yet, leaving her with nothing to do save sit upon her bed, or pace, or stare pointlessly out of the little window and roll the unanswered questions through her mind over and over and over again . . .

On sudden impulse, she whirled about, opened the door to her room, stuck out her head. The corridor beyond the door was empty and still. Always, so far, somebody had come to collect her silently for meals, and she had made her way dutifully along to the left, as she had been directed, down the corridor and thence eventually into the Eating Hall. Now, with no one about to witness it, she slipped out and turned right, padding off into unknown territory. It felt so good to stretch her stiff legs, to be moving . . .

Weapons Master Karasyn, she knew, would strongly disapprove of any such disobedient action on her part.

Let him.

Along the corridor she went, alert as an escaped prisoner. And that feeling began to give her ideas. Why not simply keep walking until she discovered a way out of this stone warren? She had been so weary over the past days, so totally immersed in eating and sleeping . . . But with no watch kept upon her door, who was to stop her from walking off through the corridors, out of Minmi entirely, and over to the far green hills and away to freedom? Some part of her had had more than enough of strange folk pushing her about, telling her what she must and must not do.

If she ever could find a way to those hills . . .

But the coridor along which she walked just seemed to go on and on, leading nowhere. It was empty and silent and dreary. This Guards' section was in better condition than the area through which she had first been brought – higher up, brighter, with occasional windows – but it was still the same apparently endless, chill, empty, stone-corridored maze.

This Minmi was a huge, confusing place. She had no notion of how many folk might inhabit it. Could she walk for leagues and never see a soul? Or would she turn the next corner and . . .

The corridor continued empty and silent as could be. But that silence began to take on a sudden menacing quality for her. Her own steps seemed to echo alarmingly loud. She stopped, listening, her heart beating fast.

Who knew what might be lying in wait for her around the next bend? Minmi was *strange*. She had learned that already. What if . . .

She shook her head, sending a little echo of pain shooting through her still-tender skull, took a breath, swallowed, pushed herself determinedly along. She was not about to go creeping back in defeat to her little stone cell just because the eeriness of this place gave her the tremblies.

Around the next corner she went, striding out purposefully, and came upon a row of three wooden doors set into the wall. She tried them, her pulse thumping. All but one proved solidly locked – or jammed shut. And the one openable door went nowhere, revealing only a small, deserted, rubble-filled room.

Disappointed, she continued onwards through the dim, musty silence until she came upon an empty window. Most of the windows she had passed held the remains of cloudy glass, set in octagonal leaded frames. This one, however, had nothing of the sort left in it. Propping her elbows on the cracked stone sill, she leaned out and took a long breath, filling her lungs with the sun-warmed air.

There was a pervasive, dank chill in this great, dim, stone edifice. Feeling the warmth of the sunlight on her face, she sighed with pleasure. It was a cloudless afternoon, the sun so bright she had to squint.

All her walking made no difference in terms of the view: it was still the same confusing jumble of mouldering old structures she saw stretched out before her – save that the far green hills were invisible now. In any direction she could see, there were only dilapidated buildings growing out of each other, like the accretions of some horde of gigantic, nest-building insects. It was a huge, sprawling place, this Minmi. Everywhere she looked, there was building after interconnected building after building, without lane or street that she could see. Brown stone, ochre stone, stone blackened with age . . .

Until she happened to glance directly below and spy a little patch of overgrown greenery. It stood out against the dull stone surrounding it like a shout in a silent room, and it was only because she had been intent on things distant that her eyes had taken so long to register it. From her vantage point directly above, she could make out a cluster of little trees surrounded by a garden wall, the choked remnants of what might once have been a pond. There was a gateway of sorts set in the wall on one side, the faint line of an old path leading from it.

She wanted to be amongst all that greenery suddenly. It pulled at her. She had had enough of dimness and dank air and chill stone. And – who knew? – perhaps, once outside, she might discover some way to those far hills.

But how to get down? The little garden was three or four times a tall man's height below her at least. She had seen no stairs anywhere. She stuck her head outside and looked down. The exterior wall was of large stone blocks set with mortar, old and crumbling, as was everything hereabouts. There just might be enough in the way of hand and footholds where the mortar had come away.

She went out feet first, impulsively, feeling her way gingerly for a first toe hold, easing further downwards, searching for finger holds between the big stone blocks. Bit by precarious bit, she edged downwards, her limbs trembling with strain.

By the time she reached the ground, her legs and arms both were quivering and numb, and her bruised skull throbbed painfully. She felt sick in her stomach and had to stand for long moments, hands braced on her thighs, panting, her vision hazed with red.

Finally, she straightened up, sucking on a split finger nail, and looked about. The stone wall hemming in this little place was higher than it had appeared from above, well over her head. It cast a long purple shadow. Thick trailers of creeping vine hung from it, splattered with small white flowers. She heard the busy *hrummm* of bees. A hedge of little trees bordered the wall along its sunlit side and halfway into the shadow, their branches intertwining with each other, forming a tapestry of shimmering leaf and limb.

Gazing at this, Kess saw sudden movement. A small body hopped along a limb, little wings fluttering. Blue and orange, it was, a handspan or so in height. It stared at her, its little bird's head cocked to one side curiously.

There was something odd about that little head . . .

She edged closer, trying to move slow and easy so as not to startle the little creature. It fluttered away, but not far. Clearly curious, it perched on a higher branch, staring down at her. It seemed a beautiful thing. Its blue wings shimmered like finest satin, while the breast and face were a pale, golden-orange. A striking contrast, the two colours made. A tuft of blue feathers capped the head, and the feathered face was dominated by wide dark eyes.

She gasped. It was entirely beakless, that face. The little creature had a mouth, with tiny, sharp white teeth. And the eyes . . . the eyes were like small human eyes, regarding her with the same knowing glance as Lord Mattingly's creature's . . .

With a little beating flurry of wings it was abruptly gone, out of the tree and over the wall, leaving Kess staring.

She shook her head, blinked. The garden was silent. She stood quiet for a long time, looking to see if the bird – if that was the right name for such an extraordinary creature – might return, or if another of its kind might be about. But there was nothing.

As the moments passed, she felt the sunlight seductively warm upon her after the pervasive stone-chill she had lived in for the past days. The green everywhere was soothing to her eyes.

Abandoning her fruitless vigil, she turned and swished through the tangled, knee-deep grass towards the remains of the pond she had made out from above, no more than a grass-choked, symmetrical depression now. She saw for the first time that there was a pair of stone benches on the far side, shadowed by the wall and half obscured by a sweep of the trailing vine. Somehow, they looked inviting.

She waded onwards through the grass towards them. A bee *thrummed* past her ear and she ducked out of its way. Lifting one hand, she pushed aside the fall of vine that obscured the farther bench, for that was the more intact of the two. She thought she would sit there for a while and . . .

'Took you long enough,' a voice said.

Kess froze.

Somebody chuckled. 'Don't look so shocked, now. I isn't going to harm you none.' More chuckling. 'Oh, no. Not me. I wouldn't. Not *me* . . .'

Kess stared about for a wild, confused instant, seeing nobody. Then she spied the owner of the voice: a figure seated on the ground, half hidden by a fall of vine-leaf and pale

132

flowers, swathed in a voluminous parti-coloured cloak, purple and black and orange. The figure's back was propped against the vines that trailed down the high stone wall. Bees buzzed about its hooded head, intent on their business with the flowers. The figure seemed to mind them not at all.

Kess stared.

The figure patted the ground in front of it. 'Come and sit with me, then, girl,' it said. Its voice was hoarse and breathy.

Kess backed away, uncertain. She had seen enough already in Minmi to make her wary.

'Now don't be getting all frighted about me.' The figure beckoned, patted the ground once more.

There seemed nothing actually threatening about it . . .

'Come *on* now,' the figure said. 'You've been making me wait long and long enough as it is. Don't play the skittery little birdie with me now.'

'You've been . . . *waiting* for me?'

'Indeed, yes. Waiting three days for you.'

'But how . . .'

'Old Seer Skolt thinks he and his are the only ones.' The figure made a dismissive gesture. 'Got his head up his arse, old Skolt does. 'Cause he likes the view from there.' The figure patted the ground again. 'Come. Sit.'

Kess padded gingerly over, not at all certain what it was she might be dealing with here.

'Nervous little creature, ain't you?' the figure said. 'Indeed yes.'

Kess peered at the figure's face. It was shadowed in the cloak's hood, and all she could make out was a pair of glimmering eyes. 'Who is ye?'

'Who *is* I? You do talk funny, girl.'

Kess scowled. She was getting tired of folk here ridiculing her speech. 'I didn't come here for ridicule,' she said. 'I can get *ridicule* at . . .' She stopped, mouth open. She had said the very same thing once to . . .

To who?

She could not remember.

The figure raised a hand placatingly. 'Sit. Sit. I won't do you the slightest little harm. I'm on *your* side, girl. Indeed yes.'

'My side? In what?' Kess said, settling herself down cross-legged on the grass.

'They're after you, girl. Oh, yes indeed.'

Kess stiffened. 'Who is after me? Why?'

'Arse-peering Skolt. That's who. Better look out, girl.'

'My name,' said Kess, 'is Kess. Not *girl*.'

'Right you are, girl. Kess it is, then. Indeed yes.'

Kess sighed. 'Who *is* ye?'

The figure reached up and slid back the cloak's hood, revaling a woman's face, round with fat, old and saggy and wrinkled as a dried plum, all but toothless, and smiling hugely. 'I was named Rotundalithaliths when I was born. But most folk find that altogether too much of a jaw-cracker. So they call me Malby. You could call me Brith, if you liked.'

Kess shook her head. 'I don't . . .'

'Or Kallie, if you like that one better. It's all the same to me.' The old woman scratched at her wobbly chin musingly. 'Always reckoned Tilda was a nice name. Or Tildie. That's it. Call me Tildie. Oh, yes indeed . . .'

Kess did not know what to say. It was another crazy person she was dealing with, apparently.

'I'd close my mouth if I were you, girl. What with all them bees about.'

Kess scowled. 'My *name* is . . .'

'My, but you're a prideful little creature, ain't you?'

Before Kess could respond, the old woman held up a hand, gesturing her to be quiet. 'No offence meant. Nothing wrong with being prideful. Oh, no. Pridefulness is good.'

Kess took a breath, shook herself. 'Ye said ye's been . . . *waiting* for me. How could ye . . .'

The old woman chuckled. She held out a pudgy hand, and Kess saw a little doll there. How it had suddenly appeared in the hand she could not tell. There was something about the little figure . . . She bent down, curious, wanting a closer look.

'No!' she gasped.

'Oh, indeed yes,' the woman responded, chuckling some more. 'Here. You can hold it if you wish.'

Kess took it gingerly. The little doll looked like . . . her. It was roughly made of twists of cloth and twigs and moss; yet, somehow, it looked *exactly* like her.

'Except,' said the old woman, 'you've cut your hair. That'd explain why you took so long to get here. Indeed yes . . .'

Kess fingered the little doll's dark tresses. There was something oddly familiar about them. With a shock, she realized what it was. 'This is my hair!'

'Of course.'

'But how did ye . . .'

'Little Penna got it for me.'

Kess only stared uncertainly.

'On the sea strand. Bright little whippet is my Penna.'

Kess recalled the little girl, the two boys with her, then the three of them racing off, a hank of her own dark hair clutched in the girl's hand. 'Who is ye?' she demanded again of the old woman.

'I told you that already,' the woman replied. 'You can call me Tildie.'

Kess shook her head. 'I say again, who *is* ye, Tildie, to be seated here claiming to wait for me? What does ye want of me?'

'Ah . . .' Tildie said. 'That's a *much* better question. What do I want of you?' She reached a hand up for the doll.

Kess passed it back to her, and the little thing promptly disappeared in a way she could not quite fathom.

'Well?' Kess prompted, for the old woman had gone silent.

'Seer Skolt hates you,' Tildie said then, leaning forward, her face abruptly serious. 'And that means I like you. That means I like you a *lot*. Indeed yes . . .'

Kess was not sure what to say.

'You made old Skolt look like a right rat's arse,' Tildie chuckled. 'And in front of Mad Mattingly and his court, too. Oh, it was a sight, girl. A sight!'

'My name is Kess.'

The old woman shrugged. 'Particular, ain't you?' She shrugged. 'As you wish, then. It's the least I can do if I'm going to be protecting you.'

'Protecting me? From . . . what?'

'Why, from Skolt, of course.' Tildie chuckled again. 'And his wicked minions.'

Kess was not altogether sure she ought to take this queer old woman seriously any more. Yet there was the little figurine. Had this Tildie actually used it to . . . 'call' her here? Had this whole excursion of hers somehow been of this old woman's causing?

'Skolt is a vindictive old scoundrel,' Tildie was saying. 'He'll do you a harm if he can, Kess. Indeed yes . . .'

'Can he . . .' Kess was not sure how to put it. 'Is he a . . . a sorcerer?'

Again, Tildie chuckled, her chins wobbling. 'Nothing terribly much to fear on that count. Oh, no. He and his kind strut about boasting of how they carry on the tradition of the great and ancient Seers, but they've lost most of it. Oh, yes. Ignorant blunderers they are for the most part. And full to bursting with their own importance.'

Tildie leaned forward conspiratorially. 'Once, there were terrible sorcerers in this land.' The old woman shivered. 'Real sorcerers. Men so powerful, they could shape-change the very world itself, create creatures in any form they wished. And they did so, too. But that was long and long ago. Four . . . five generations of folk, I reckon. Maybe more.'

She shuddered melodramatically. 'In their day, they held sway over this land, them and the Lords of the Domains. And each Lord possessed his own Seer. And they vied with each other, those Lords, for control. And the Seers gave them power, indeed yes. Such power. It is said that, with the Seers' help, the Lords were able to . . . replicate themselves. Imagine it! Two, five, seven exact same selves of the same man. Able to be in two, five, seven places at the same time. One man thinking as seven. Seven men thinking as one.'

Kess shivered at the notion, she who no longer felt she had even one intact self.

'They built Sofala and Hess and Minmi City, and all the rest of the southern Domains, those Lords. They carved out those great Domains with fire and sword, blood and pain and destruction. And behind it all were the Seers, like the hidden puppeteers at a puppet show.'

The old woman levered herself abruptly up from the ground. 'Come. Follow me a moment.'

She waddled like an old sow when she moved, did Tildie, and it took a time for her to barge a path through the grass to the little gateway that was set into the garden's wall. That gateway was without gate now. Trailers of thick vine lay draped across it, leaving only a narrow little tunnel through which to squeeze. Tildie pushed her way through the tangled green, brushing aside bees negligently, and disappeared.

Kess hesitated, then went after.

On the gateway's other side there was a stone patio, with the garden wall at their backs, thick with vines, and the remnants of an ornamental ironwork railing running round its other periphery. It was the stonework underfoot that first took Kess's attention: an elaborate, abstract whirl of dark and light coloured flagstones set in a series of interlocking patterns that made her still-tender head spin dizzily if she let her eyes follow the weaving design for more than a heartbeat or two. Hastily, she looked away from the flagstones, up past the sagging, ornamental railing . . . and gasped, seeing where she and the old woman were.

Kess had unthinkingly assumed the little walled garden to be at ground level. But she now saw that it was, in fact, on a rooftop. A chance placing of buildings gave her a view of Minmi unlike any she had had so far. Rank upon rank of buildings, going down to yet more buildings, like a series of huge, intricate stone steps leading nowhere and everywhere.

'This place was called Viewpoint, once,' Tildie said. 'Gatherings of the great were held here.' She gestured at the array of buildings before them. 'Imagine what Minmi must have been like in its day, girl. Folk bustling about, the buildings new and solid and shining. They used to paint them, back in those fargone days, reds and greens and oranges, bright as fresh fruit.' Tildie pointed away off to their left. 'Look. You can see the last bit of paint on that one over there.'

Kess looked and saw streaks of faded orange all across the side of one building. She would not have recognized it for paint if she had not been told. 'How did . . . how do folk get about?' she asked. 'There's no walkways, no streets.'

Tildie shrugged. 'Inside. Everything's inside. We learn the ways as little children. It was a fort, was Minmi, in the old, old days. Oh, indeed yes. Long and long ago. Then it grew, and each new generation added a bit here or there, building on to the last bit of work, until it grew to be as you see it. One of the wonders of the South.'

Kess gazed about her. There was a kind of wonder to it, in a dark sort of way.

'Nobody knows all of it now, not any more,' Tildie said.

'There's too few of us left, now. They ruined it.'

'Who?' Kess asked, after the old woman had gone silent for long moments.

'The likes of Skolt, of course! The old Seers. The old Lords. So intent on gaining power, on controlling each other, that they brought it all crashing down about them. Stupid creatures.'

Kess blinked, uncertain.

'The balances, girl! The Powers. The world's a great whirling dance, Power and Power balancing each other, fire and water, air and earth, movement and stillness, cold and heat, Shadowlands and living land, out and in, fall and fly, spirit and flesh, moving, changing, growing, but always, *always* balanced.'

Tildie shook her head, 'They wielded *power*, those old Seers. Terrible power. To this day, all the South is full of the signs of their plottings and manipulations. They tried to use this land to . . . to cultivate all manner of exotic creations. But they upset the balances, and their cultivations long ago ran to riot, and their great Domains tumbled down to ruin.

'They left us a terrible legacy, those old men – a world still out of kilter. In the arrogance of their power, the Seers tore loose the very moorings of the world. And now . . .' Tildie shrugged. 'Their secret knowledge is forgotten and faded. But Skolt and his like still root about, like pigs in a field, trying to revive that old learning . . .'

In the vines behind Tildie, Kess saw a sudden flurry of movement. Small blue wings flashed in the sunlight. 'Look!' she said, pointing.

Tildie turned. Seeing the little blue-winged creature, she smiled. 'Ahhh . . . We call them Carolells. Lovely small creatures, ain't they now? Indeed, yes.'

'What . . . are they?' Kess asked.

Instead of answering Kess's question, Tildie put her two index fingers to her lips and blew a complex little whistle. The Carolell cocked its head, its knowing eyes wide.

Again, Tildie whistled.

The Carolell leaped into the air, wings flashing sapphire in the sunlight. It arced across to Tildie, circled her three times, then landed daintily on the hand she held out for it, perching on her wrist.

'Hallo, my lovely,' Tildie cooed. 'Hallo, my lovely little

creature.' She stroked the small blue head with a finger, and the Carolell *chirrupped* with pleasure, rolling its knowing dark eyes.

'What *is* it?' Kess asked, staring. 'Its eyes . . .'

'Oh, yes,' Tildie said. 'His eyes. Indeed, yes.'

'I don't . . .' Kess began.

'He is of the Seers' doing, this handsome young lad,' Tildie said, still stroking the small blue head. 'Or, rather, his father's father's father's many times fathers were.'

'Of the Seers' . . . *doing*?'

Tildie nodded. 'Oh, indeed yes. I told you, girl. The Seers had knowledge and *power*. They could mould the very flesh of life to their whims. Terrible creatures, they made. And pretty . . . Like this one here.'

'Lord Mattingly's . . . creature, too?'

'His pretty Lamure, you mean?' Tildie nodded. 'She is of that sort, yes indeed. And there are other kinds, too. They are not uncommon here in the South.'

Kess stared at the blue-winged Carolell. 'His eyes seem . . .'

'Human?' Tildie finished.

Kess nodded.

'Some folk refer to creatures such as this and Mad Mattingly's ring-tailed Lamure as humanimals . . . As good a name as any, I suppose, for what they are become.'

'And that is?'

'Human spirit and animal flesh together.' Tildie lifted her hand towards Kess. 'Care to stroke his little head?'

Kess put a tentative finger out, felt the smoothness and warmth of the feathered head. The Carolell *chirrupped*. 'Is he . . .' Kess was not sure how to express it. 'Is he . . . mindful, then?'

Tildie shrugged. 'Do you mean, is he like a little man in spirit? Yes and no. Some humanimals are more . . . "human" than others. Some talk, some do not. Carolells, now . . . Nobody knows for certain. And the beautiful small creatures keep their own counsel on the matter.'

Pulling her hand away from Kess, Tildie flipped her pudgy wrist and sent the Carolell fluttering off into the air. 'Away with you, now,' she called after it. 'Begone to where it's more safe for you.'

'Safe?' Kess said.

'There are those who don't *like* creatures such as he. Abomination, some say, to so interweave human and animal. But nothing is ever altogether bad, and I think Carolells are *fine* small creatures.'

The old woman shook her head. 'We are a poor, sorry lot, we folk of Minmi. Half mad. Living a faded and fragile dream of former glories, the most of us, in borrowed robes too big for us. Filled with fire and florid convictions and destinies and designs. Oh, yes . . . A sorry lot indeed, sunk in the old, old dreams.'

'Why . . .' Kess began. 'Why are you telling me all this?'

'Why, to let you know what you'll be dealing with, girl.'

Kess frowned.

'Oops!' said Tildie with a chuckle, putting a plump hand to her mouth. 'I meant *Kess*, of course. Indeed, yes . . .' She gestured to the great pile of stone structures all about them. 'Minmi is like a hornet's nest. Full of intricacies and stings. You watch yourself, Kess girl. Old Skolt will be after you. Indeed, yes.

'You *watch* yourself. And I'll watch you, too.' She reached out and took Kess by the hand. 'I *like* you, girl. Remember that. Oh, yes indeed . . .'

The old woman stiffened suddenly. 'What's this?'

Kess tried to pull away, but Tildie would have none of that. She shifted her grip up to Kess's wrist, holding with surprising strength, and stared at Kess's left palm. 'And just where did you get *this*?' she demanded. Her pudgy face had gone strange and tense.

Kess peered down at her palm. It was the one that itched sometimes. But she could see no trace whatsoever of anything there. 'Can you . . . see anything?' she asked nervously.

Tildie looked at her, a long, hard searching look that made Kess's stomach quiver. Then she shrugged. 'You wouldn't understand it, girl. Waters too deep for the likes of you. But it changes things, does this . . .'

Kess shivered. 'Changes . . . *how*?'

'The balances, girl. It seems you are an axle.'

'An axle?' The word echoed in Kess's mind, but in a strange, croaky voice: 'Aks-sel, aks-sel . . .'

Tildie nodded soberly. 'The Powers work in subtle ways. Like water running downhill. If one channel gets blocked, the water will find another way.'

Kess only stared.

'You've no recollection, have you?'

'Of . . . what?' Kess said, her heart thumping suddenly.

'Of anything.'

Kess swallowed. 'How . . . how did ye *know*?'

Tildie shrugged. 'I have my ways.' She reached a hand to Kess's cheek. 'Poor little ducky . . .'

Kess pulled sharply back.

'I'm your *friend*, ducky. Remember that. Indeed yes . . .'

Kess stood, uncertain.

Tildie regarded her for long moments in silence, then abruptly gestured with one pudgy arm to the vine-hung wall behind them. 'There's a doorway set in the wall over there. It leads to a stairwell. Take it up three turns, then go left till you reach the fork. Take the right-hand branch. That'll get you back.'

Kess peered at where Tildie was pointing. It took her a few long moments to spot it, draped as it was in vines, but she finally saw the dark opening of the doorway. 'I see it,' she said. Then she turned back, and, to her profound confusion, realized she was all alone.

She whirled, stared this way and that, but there was no sign whatsoever of old, fat, slow-moving Tildie. Kess felt the little hairs along the nape of her neck prickle uncomfortably.

She took one last backward look at Minmi's jumbled architecture, shook her head in mute, uncertain wonderment, then turned and made her way through the vines and thence into the dark opening of the doorway Tildie had pointed out to her. She only hoped the old woman's directions were reliable.

There was a stairwell there right enough, stone steps going both down and up in a tight, curving spiral. Kess sighed in relief and went up the stairwell for three turns, as Tildie had instructed, feeling her way in the chill interior dimness, and found herself in one of the usual dank stone corridors.

She turned left, following the old woman's directions, and walked along till she came to the fork. Taking the right-hand branch, she kept on until, abruptly, the corridor came to an end. A closed wooden door barred her way.

After an anxious few moments, she found that all she need do was lift a crossbar to push the door open. She stepped into yet another dim corridor beyond . . . with a short row of doors set into its wall. Abruptly, she recognized her surroundings. She had come out through one of the same doors she had earlier tried unsuccessfully to open. Her room was not far away, then. Closing the door behind her, she padded off.

There was still nobody about, and she slipped into her room quickly, pulling the door to after her. With a long sigh, she went to stand by the narrow window, gazing out over the tops of the jumbled Minmi buildings at the hills beyond. They stood like far-off sentinels, tinted ochre and emerald by the lowering sun. She could make out a dark mass of storm clouds off north and eastwards on the horizon beyond them: rain this night, she reckoned.

Kess sighed and turned away from the window. She looked down and examined her left palm. There was absolutely nothing there as far as she could make out.

More unanswered questions to plague her, she thought disgustedly. She was grown very weary of unanswered questions.

She shook her head. She did not at all know what to think of this Tildie, or whether to believe what the old woman had said or not. Or how much to believe – for some of it had sounded quite incredible. Indeed yes . . .

She shook her head again, sighed, shivered. She was not sure if her talk with the old woman had helped to enlighten her or simply make her more confused.

It seemed typical of Minmi, that.

XVI

'So you've had some experience with the blade then, girl?'
Weapons Master Karasyn said.

Kess shrugged. 'Some.'

'Some?'

She shrugged again. She had no notion of what experience
she might or might not have had – but she was not about to let
on to this man any such thing. His very look was a challenge.
She felt the short hairs at the back of her neck rise like a dog's
hackles.

'Right,' said the Weapons Master. 'Let's see what you can do,
then, now that you've had your three-day rest.'

They were in the outdoor practice yard, in the early morning.
The air was chill and damp, the paving stones underfoot still
soaked and puddled from last night's rain. She was more alert
now than she had been on her first visit here, and knew more
of Minmi. All around, she saw the tumbled stone buildings.
This practice yard must be almost as high up as the little garden
in which she had met Tildie . . .

'Here,' the Weapons Master said. 'We'll work with the little
blade first.' He held out an iron-bladed dagger towards her. 'It's
only a practice blade.' He ran a thumb along the edge. 'Won't cut.'

She took it from him. It seemed awkward-feeling and
heavier than any blade she had ever held – what blades *had* she
held, then? she wondered.

'Now who,' the Weapons Master said, 'should we set you
against, I wonder?'

She stood in the centre of a rough circle of men, stiff and
self-conscious.

'I'll take her.' It was the balding man who had had the set-to
with Rannis back in the Eating Hall on the day of Kess's first
waking.

'Lotch,' the Weapons Master said.

The man came forward out of the anonymity of the group, his bald head gleaming in the early-morning sunlight, one of the iron practice daggers already in his grasp. He was grinning maliciously. 'Shouldn't take but a moment, lads,' he said to those behind him. 'I'll put her on her back, where she belongs.'

The gathered men guffawed.

Kess looked at Lotch, angry, uneasy. The man was husky, thick-shouldered, strong and heavy. She glanced at the Weapons Master.

'Do what you can, girl,' he said, and waved her to it. That was all.

Lotch leered at her. He flexed his broad shoulders. 'Come and get me, girlie.'

'Watch yourself, Lotch,' somebody called. 'I saw her in Lord Mattingly's chamber. You didn't.'

'Hah!' was all the response Lotch gave.

The gathered men backed away, making a rough circle within which Kess and Lotch faced off against each other.

'Come on, then, girlie,' he urged, gesturing her towards him. 'Tickle me with your little iron tickler.'

She wanted to slap him, arrogant brute that he was. But some part of her knew better than to let her temper get the best of her when blades were involved. She felt a vague recollection come into her, prompted somehow by the weapons, the shuffle of feet, the nervous quiver in her belly. It was the same almost-memory she had experienced when gripping the blade in Lord Mattingly's chamber, but clearer now . . . she and some man, circling each other, blades in hand. Yet the memory, such as it was, evoked no sense of animosity. What had they been about, this man and her, circling each other with blades in their hands and smiles on their faces?

'Keep your head,' she could almost hear the man say, in the faintest of memory-voices. 'Steady, steady . . . calm and steady.'

Lotch came at her suddenly in an unsubtle, overconfident, bear-like rush, clearly thinking simply to overwhelm her. Kess skipped back, her heart thumping, and ducked under the arc of his swinging blade as he went skidding past her on the slippery flagstones.

The gathered crowd hooted.

'Come on, Lotch,' somebody called. 'You can do better than *that*!'

Kess felt her pulse quicken. Her belly tightened. The weapon in her hand felt awkward as a stick. She hefted it, trying to get a feel for its balance. Her hand was slippery with sweat, which did not help anything.

Lotch came at her again, more carefully this time. She dodged away, waiting, trying to calm her heartbeat a little, trying to get the gauge of him if she could. 'They'll most always be bigger than ye,' she seemed to hear the faint memory-voice say in her head. 'But ye're light on yer feet and quick as any cat. If it's ever a serious scrap ye finds yerself in, stay back, keep yer eyes open. Watch him. Get the feel of him. Only a fool rushes in where blades are concerned . . .'

Lotch gestured at her with his blade, impatient. 'Come *on*, girlie.' He feinted, sidestepped, tried another rush.

Kess skipped away again. Her heel skidded on the damp stone underfoot, and she only just caught her balance, her heart thumping.

The crowd hooted at Lotch.

His face was flushed now as he tried to rush her yet another time. Kess faded away from him, leading him round the circle that had been cleared for them. She could see his temper unravelling with each further step she forced him to take. And he was beginning to signal, slight, betraying shifts of eye and hand and balance that he would never have made had he been in proper possession of himself.

It gave her a little confidence, and she fell back more slowly when he rushed her yet again, looking for an opening of her own. But he made a vicious, quick stab at her as he passed that very nearly took her in the side. She avoided it only by a hair's breadth, and wound up on her knees, panting, her heart kicking.

She scampered quickly back to her feet before Lotch could get the advantage – but only just. So much for being confident! He might not have been able to cut her with the edgeless blade, but he would have cracked a rib, at the very least, had he connected.

She circled, faded away, ducked and wove, feeling her legs

all atremble now with the strain of keeping her footing on the slippery flagstones. Her head was beginning to ache too.

The crowd hooted continuously now. Lotch was red-faced and sweating and furious. For all his charging about, he had yet to touch her.

But it could not go on. Kess was sweat-soaked, too, her breath coming in painful gasps, her skull throbbing with pain now. She had not the strength for anything such as this yet.

Lotch came at her again, but this time he stumbled, skidding awkwardly, and went down on one knee. She caught him a quick slash across his right shoulder – his knife arm – before he could get back up, then skipped aside.

'A hit!' somebody called. 'A palpable hit!'

Lotch lurched to his feet, livid. He fumbled his knife, had to scramble hastily for it, then stood panting, glaring at her, rubbing his shoulder where she had struck him. It was not much of a hit, but it must have left a bruise nonetheless. 'Little *bitch*,' he hissed.

Kess backed away from him. 'Come and get me, then,' she taunted. He was losing control, his temper beginning to blind him. 'A temper-blind man makes an easy target,' the faint memory-voice in her head said, or seemed to say. She grinned at Lotch, taunting him purposefully. 'Come *on* then, little man . . .'

But before he could rush her again, Weapons Master Karasyn intervened. 'Enough!' he ordered.

Ignoring Karasyn entirely, Lotch made to go for Kess yet again. The Weapons Master leaped in, spun him about by one shoulder, disarmed him, slapped him hard in the face, and spilled him on his arse, all in one quick motion.

Lotch looked up from where he had been dumped, stunned and furious.

'Not a word out of you!' Karasyn ordered. 'Go back to your place.'

After a moment's sullen hesitation, Lotch did so.

Karasyn turned on Kess, who braced herself. 'As for you,' he began. The crowd gathered closer.

Kess stood, the practice blade in hand, panting with exhaustion.

146

'You did . . .' the Weapons Master said '. . . quite well enough.'

From somewhere a hand came out and patted her on the shoulder. 'Good for you, then,' somebody murmured. Someone else handed her a kerchief so she could wipe the sweat from her face.

But most of the men still hung back, cold and aloof and sullen-eyed. Lotch stood surrounded by a little coterie of his cronies, scowling.

Kess saw Rannis standing with the rest, not close to Lotch, but no closer to her, either. She glared at him. He ignored her.

'What did you notice, then, about this little bout we were just witness to?' the Weapons Master was saying to the group in general.

For reply, there was only a shuffling about of feet in the mud. Someone coughed quietly. Then silence.

'Mutton heads,' Karasyn said disgustedly. 'The lot of you.'

There was a muttering amongst the gathered men, but nobody spoke up.

'Lotch here,' Karasyn began, gesturing to the man, 'let his temper get the better of him. Once again.' He turned and waved a finger at Lotch. 'I've warned you of it, man. Time and time again. That temper of yours will prove the undoing of you.'

'I'd have got her,' Lotch said sullenly. 'Given a few more moments, I would have *had* the bitch. She kept running away. She didn't fight fair. You all saw it! It was just a lucky hit she got on me when I slipped. I'd have had her in another moment, I tell you! Lucky thing for *her* you stopped things when you did.'

A chorus of muttered agreement followed this.

Karasyn shook his head. 'She used her brains, Lotch. I watched her lead you around like a bull on a string. We all did. She had you coming and going. And do you know why?'

Lotch shook his head, scowling still.

'She kept her temper. She thought about what she was doing.' Karasyn turned to Kess. 'I have to say, you're an intelligent fighter, girl.' He gestured to the gathered men with both hands. 'Something quite novel amongst this bunch. Most here use a blade like a hammer. You've had some sensible teaching, haven't you?'

There was a general murmur of disbelief. 'A girl given fighting lessons?' somebody said scathingly.

'Might as well give a frog dancing classes,' Lotch said in disgust.

Kess glared at them. Turning to the Weapons Master, she said, 'I had lessons from my . . . my . . . father.'

Kess put a startled hand to her mouth. She did not know why she had said such a thing. Could it be true? *Could* it be her father she almost-remembered? Did she *have* a father, then?

Karasyn was watching her. He scratched thoughtfully at his short-cropped beard, folded his arms, unfolded them. Then, as if having come to some decision, he nodded to himself.

The gathered men waited.

'When Lord Mattingly commanded that I teach you the blade,' Karasyn began, 'I thought it foolishness.'

'Too true!' someone piped up to general agreement.

'But . . .' the Weapons Master went on, silencing the gathering with a hard look '. . . I'm beginning to think that his command might not have been so . . . foolish after all.'

Lotch stepped forward from amongst his cronies, his face clouded still with sullen anger. 'Meaning what?'

'It's a skill that I teach, Lotch. A skill that comes hard to some, easier to others, that some master and some do not, despite training.' The Weapons Master shook his head. 'I have to show some of you lot the same movement half a hundred times before I can drum it into your thick heads.

'And then this girl comes along.'

'And?' Lotch prompted sullenly.

'And I see her – half your size, a mere colt of a girl – outclass you entirely, after all my months of training you.'

'She didn't fight *fair*, I tell you!' Lotch protested.

Karasyn shook his head. 'She fought *smart*, Lotch. She fought careful smart, *natural* smart.' He turned to Kess. 'You've had training, girl. But you have the gift, too.'

Kess blinked. 'Gift?'

The Weapons Master nodded. 'I can see it clear in you. I've been half a lifetime teaching these skills. I know the gift when I see it. I'll teach you . . .' He turned to the gathered men. 'I'll teach this girl . . .'

There was a general disapproving chorus of mutters and

148

complaints. Karasyn silenced them. 'I'll teach her out of respect for the gift in her. What matter if she's a girl or not? It's the *gift* that matters.'

Karasyn looked at Kess and shook his head. 'How Lord Mattingly saw it in you I'll never fathom, but he was right. I owe the lad an apology for that. I'll make you good, girl. Very good. If you let me.'

'I have a choice?' Kess demanded. She was not at all sure she liked the way things were tending here. The Weapons Master was looking at her with a kind of possessiveness – like a man with a new and highly prized hunting hound. She did not fancy being anybody's prized anything.

Karasyn stabbed his finger at her. 'It would be a crime to waste a gift such as yours, girl.'

Kess shrugged.

Karasyn shook his head, snorted in disgust. 'I teach these louts here day in and day out. They show some promise, some of them. But none yet like you. Like *you*, girl. And what do you do when I offer to bring out the gift in you? You *shrug*!'

The Weapons Master threw his hands up. 'What a waste! Might as well offer a frog dancing classes indeed.' He shook his head. 'Maybe Lotch here has the right of it after all.' He turned from Kess and addressed the gathered men. 'Right then, you lot. No point wasting further time. Let's get to the day's practice.'

Lotch made a rude sign at Kess with his fingers, smiling in malicious triumph.

'Wait!' Kess cried.

All eyes turned to her.

Kess swallowed. She was not about to let the likes of Lotch strut away like that, triumphant. 'I'll learn,' she said. 'If ye'll teach me, Master Karasyn.'

The Weapons Master smiled. 'Oh, I'll teach you all right, girl.'

Kess felt her stomach twist up. She had been out-manoeuvred here. She knew it. But what other options were there for her? It was not as if she had many roads open to her here in the stony maze of Minmi. And seeing the likes of Lotch and his cronies discomfited was worth it. Was it not?

Oh yes . . .

XVII

For a treble handful of days, Kess practised in the training yard
with the rest, going through the several series of movements
while Master Karasyn marked time: 'Thrust . . . parry . . .
riposte. Thrust . . . parry . . .'

Despite the Weapons Master's apparently high expectations,
she was noticeably clumsy at first, putting the wrong foot
forward sometimes, bringing the sword blade up when it ought
to go down, losing her balance too easily. None of what Master
Karasyn was teaching seemed to connect with the vague
memories that haunted her. She kept trying to put into effect
the notions she received from the nebulous memory-voice in
her head, but the Weapons Master only shouted at her when
she tried. It was disorienting and frustrating in the extreme.

And any slightest mistake on her part brought barks of cruel
laughter and scathing remarks about 'gifted' morons and
simpleton females.

'No, no, *no!*' Master Karasyn would shout at her, his face
close to hers. 'You're thinking too much. You're too intent. I'm
training your body, not your mind. Keep your mind *quiet*. Let
your hands learn on their own. Let your body learn.'

She tried, keeping her mouth shut, scarlet with anger and
shame and confusion most of the time, miserable and lonely
and ostracized. Mealtimes, she ate alone in the Eating Hall, for
the others ostentatiously ignored her. Whenever possible, she
took the food to her little room and ate there, gazing out of the
window past the crazed stone jumble of Minmi towards the far
distant hills. Her back ached, her arms, her thighs, her wrists –
and her mind ached with the host of still-unanswered
questions that plagued her.

But each morning, when she was in the yard with the rest,
sweating through Master Karasyn's regimen, she *tried*, giving it

all she had, going through the sparring exercises till her arms burned and her legs shivered weakly, thrusting and parrying with whatever man she faced as adversary till the *kringg* of the iron blades hitting each other formed a counterpoint to her dreams and her ears rang with it.

She was determined to face down the lot of them. It was all that seemed left to her, now.

Days blurred into days till she could no longer properly recollect how long she had been there.

Slowly, to her own and everybody else's surprise – except Weapons Master Karasyn's, perhaps – the instruction began to take.

They were training with the short sword, a longer, heavier blade than the one Kess had used in her bout with Lotch that first day in the yard, and far bigger than anything she could ever imagine herself having wielded before her arrival here. Huge and awkward though it had felt at first, like a great leaden stick in her hand, she had begun to feel the balance in it. Things were coming easier, somehow.

Kess started to realize that, as Master Karasyn had said, most of the men about her truly had no real aptitude for any of this. They were working on attack and defensive postures, patterns and series of movements, named and choreographed, like a dangerous dance – the Swift Current attack, the Windmill, the Double Tree defence, the Serpent's Tongue. Master Karasyn would have to demonstrate even the simplest of moves again and again, and even then, most would not get it. But she began slowly to see – or to feel, rather – the pattern behind the movements he was teaching them, and soon enough he need only show her a movement once, twice at most, and she got it.

One morning, the Weapons Master had gone along the line, showing each man in turn how a new defensive movement – the Falling Cat – was supposed to work, shifting an elbow here, a knee there, as was his wont, leaving those he had already shown to practise behind while he went on to the next and the next after. Coming back to inspect, he had looked at her critically. 'Do it again,' he said.

She did, lifting the blade in a quick defensive arc, her feet just so, balanced low and light – thinking she had somehow got it all wrong, readying herself for some caustic remark and for the grip of Master Karasyn's hands upon arm or shoulder, correcting her. Instead, he had merely nodded approvingly, murmured, 'Good,' and passed on.

And that was the moment she finally accepted that he had been right. She *did* have a gift for the blade. She watched others clumsily persist in wrong moves and postures, repeating the same awkward mistakes again and again despite all instruction, as if their limbs had wills of their own and were determined to resist any such training as Master Karasyn offered. But her own natural inclinations seemed to bring her always in the right direction, as if her hands had only been waiting for the hilt, as if her feet already knew the steps and only needed to be reminded.

How or why such a thing should be, Kess could not fathom. Perhaps what they did here touched some unknown, deep chord in her, connecting somehow with those half-glimpsed memories of the smiling man with the blade in his hands? She could not know. But she felt as if the emptiness left in her by her lack of any clear past was being filled up. With a blade in her hands, she was beginning to feel whole.

'Right, you lot,' the Weapons Master said one afternoon. 'Take a rest.'

The yard was treeless, shadeless. The sun felt hot as could be. They were all sweat-soaked and panting. Too tired to talk, they lay sprawled upon the hard flagstones, passing waterskins about.

As usual, Kess had sat down at the periphery of the group. A waterskin was passed to the man nearest her. She reached out a hand for it as her turn came round, but he ignored her completely and passed it on to the next man instead.

Kess felt a flush of anger. She was parched with thirst. She had put up with about all the petty snubbing and insults she was going to. Surging to her knees, she made to snatch the waterskin.

Somebody beat her to it.

Rannis.

The man holding it was in the midst of drinking, the waterskin held above his face, and he was squirted in the eyes. 'Kwa-uht!' he spluttered.

Rannis ignored him, passed the skin over to Kess, and sat down beside her.

Kess stared.

'Drink up,' he said.

She was still too surprised to do anything but stare. These were the first words Rannis had spoken to her since that day of her awakening in the Guardery. He had snubbed her completely since then.

'Well, drink,' he urged her.

Lifting the waterskin, she took a long, cooling swallow and handed it back to him. 'Thank you,' she said, remembering to use the southern 'you'. It had become almost second nature by now, and she seldom lapsed into the old 'ye' any more – save when she was upset and forgot herself.

Rannis nodded, took a drink himself, offered it to her a second time. 'More?'

Kess shook her head. 'Too much water sits badly in my belly on these hot days. I learned that the hard way when . . .'

She bit her lip. She had been determined not to speak with him, remembering all too clearly how he had treated her. But her tongue seemed to run off on its own, nearly. It had been so long since she had had someone to talk with.

'Hold out your hands,' he told her.

Kess kept her hands on her lap. It was too much like an order, the way he had said it, and she could feel her hackles rise. She felt prickly as a mother cat.

Rannis shrugged. 'Suit yourself, then. I was only going to pour some of the water into your hands so you could swill your face with it.' He made to get up and leave, taking the waterskin with him.

'No,' Kess said. 'Wait!'

He turned and looked down at her.

'I'm . . . I'm sorry,' she said. 'It's just that . . .'

Rannis nodded and sat down again. 'You've had no easy time of it, I know. And I'm to blame as much as the rest.' He reached over to her, put a hand on her arm briefly. 'Sorry.'

Kess blinked, shook her head. She did not know what to make of this sudden change of heart. 'Why?' she asked after a moment. 'Why come and talk with me now, all of a sudden?'

Rannis shrugged. 'It's about time *somebody* did. Master

Karasyn's right, girl. You do have a gift for the blade. And *that's* something worthy of respect.'

'Even if *I'm* not? Is that it?'

'No, no,' he said quickly. 'You're too prickly by far, girl.'

'Kess. My name is Kess.'

'Kess, then.' Rannis sighed. 'I'm trying to make peace, Kess.'

She shrugged. 'Make whatever ye wants.'

He glared at her. 'Now listen, you little . . .'

She held up her hands. 'Peace,' she said quickly, trying to smile. 'It's just . . . I don't know how I feel, Rannis. These past days . . .'

He nodded. 'Hard days.'

She nodded emphatic agreement.

'Well . . .' he began, but a sudden commotion silenced him.

Newcomers were spilling into the yard. Kess saw bright silks and feathers and jewels, heard the tinkle of bells and laughter. In the midst of this crowd, like a plain stone set in an ornate setting, came Lord Mattingly, carried on a sedan chair by four stout men.

The group of tired Guards leaped to their feet.

'Ranks!' Master Karasyn ordered, and they moved as quick as could be into formal ranks, four parallel rows, each Guard standing with feet apart and hands folded.

'Lord Mattingly,' the Weapons Master said, going forward in greeting. 'This *is* a surprise. I never expected to see you in my training yard. What brings you . . . outside? And here, of all places?'

Lord Mattingly was blinking like a bat in the sunlight. His gossamer white hair floated like thistledown in the outside air, and he kept pushing it away from his face. He gestured impatiently with one hand, and the porters set his sedan chair on the ground. A thin boy came trotting up with a parasol, a brilliant multi-coloured thing, which he opened up and held above Lord Mattingly to provide a pool of shade. Another started fanning the young lord with a large, hand-held silk and bone fan in the image of a gilded bird.

'Ahh . . .' Mattingly sighed. 'That's better.' Out in the open, Lord Mattingly looked pale as the underside of a fish.

'Lord?' Master Karasyn said enquiringly.

'Yes, Karasyn?' Mattingly responded in his soft, hoarse voice. He stretched, lifting his knees in the chair, blinked. 'What is it?'

The Weapons Master took a breath, let it out. 'I asked you why you had come to visit me here in my yard, Lord.'

'Ah, yes . . .' Lord Mattingly smiled. He put a pale hand to his mouth and coughed softly. 'It's been nearly a score of days now, they tell me, Karasyn. I am curious.'

'About . . . what, exactly, Lord?'

'Why, about the girl, of course.' Mattingly pointed at Kess. 'Come here, girl.'

After an instant's hesitation – Mattingly's unthinking arrogance set her teeth on edge – Kess came. His creature was crouched half-hidden amongst the silks draped over the chair, staring at her. Knowing now what manner of being it was, she could not help but speculate on just how much humanity there might be behind its extraordinarily human-seeming eyes.

'I see he's armed you,' Lord Mattingly said, pointing to the iron practice sword in its wooden sheath at Kess's belt. 'Has he been teaching you to use it?'

Kess nodded. 'Aye. He has.'

'He has . . . *Lord*,' Master Karasyn corrected.

Lord Mattingly waved a thin hand at the Weapons Master. 'She's a barbarian, Karasyn. From the north, you said. Remember? We can't expect *manners* from such as she, can we now?' He leaned forward in the chair. 'Show me.'

'Show you what . . . Lord?' Kess said, being careful with both her 'you' and Master Karasyn's 'Lord'.

'What?' Mattingly said. 'Show *what*? Do you think it's your private parts I wish to see? The blade, you stupid girl! Show me how you use the blade.'

Kess scowled.

The Weapons Master stepped up. 'Show Lord Mattingly what he requests, Kess.' He turned to Mattingly. 'Would you like to see a bout, Lord?'

Mattingly shrugged, nodded, sighed. He hunched further under the shadow of the parasol, blinking and squinting. 'But do it quick, Karasyn. I can't bear this sunlight. It burns my eyes like fire.'

'Yes, Lord,' the Weapons Master answered obediently. 'You there,' he called to one of the ranked men, gesturing him out.

Kess did not know the man's name – as she did not know the names of most of those here – but she knew him by sight well enough. He was not one of the best, but neither was he amongst the worst. As he came towards her, she could see his face stiffen with determination. He was intent on humiliating her in front of Lord Mattingly; it was clear from every line of his expression.

Let him try, she thought.

'Draw,' Master Karasyn ordered.

They drew their iron blades, the cold metal making a soft *shrish* coming out of the scabbards.

'Position,' Karasyn said.

They stood facing each other in the formal stance, blades up. A light touch, iron kissing iron with a little *chingg* . . . Then it began.

He went for her with a quick, hard lunge – using a gambit Master Karasyn called the Swift Current attack, trying to get in past her guard before she knew what he was about. But he was not near quick enough and she saw it coming. She skipped lightly aside, using the Crane Dance defence, feeling her feet, her arms, her whole body move quick and sure. As his forward momentum carried him just that slight bit off balance, she brought her own blade down in a quick sideways jab that caught him bruisingly on the elbow of his sword arm.

He grunted, stumbled, recovered, tried to go for her a second time. His face was clenched with anger now.

'Enough,' Lord Mattingly said. Given in Mattingly's soft, hoarse voice, it was far from a shout of command. But it somehow brought proceedings to an abrupt halt nonetheless.

'I've seen enough, Karasyn,' Lord Mattingly said. He looked at Kess and smiled.

It gave her the shudders, that smile, for it was not the ordinary sort of smile one person gives to another. There was no proper recognition of her as a person at all in his oddly luminous dark eyes. It made her feel like a *thing*.

Mattingly waved to his porters. 'Back,' he commanded, and they lifted the sedan chair obediently and started off the way they had come. Without a further word, he disappeared inside, his court followers trailing after like a swarm of colourful, noisy insects.

And then they were gone, leaving the yard in perplexed silence.

'Mad as a gadabout Mayfly,' somebody muttered.

'Without us Guards, Minmi would be nothing but stinking rubble by now.'

'Enough of that!' Master Karasyn snapped at them. But he was staring at the exit-way through which Lord Mattingly and his entourage had disappeared, brows wrinkled in thought, clearly as perplexed as the rest of them.

XVIII

The trouble started that evening, after the day's-end meal.

Kess came out of the Eating Hall with Rannis at her side. They had supped together, Rannis and she, and the Hall had been buzzing with it.

Bald Lotch was standing three steps beyond the door, propped against the wall, waiting. 'So mad Mattingly's doxy has finished her meal at last,' he said. 'And her puppy dog's tagging along behind her.'

Rannis started to push past Kess, but she held him back. 'Ignore him,' she said.

But Lotch shoved himself off the wall and stood barring their way. Behind him, suddenly, four or five others appeared.

'What is it ye wants?' Kess demanded.

'Listen to her, lads,' Lotch responded. 'Stupid girl still can't even talk proper.'

Kess bit her lip.

'You're not wanted here, girl,' Lotch said. 'Ever since *you* got here, everything's gone to pieces.'

'If that's so, it's because of *you lot*!' Rannis snapped.

'That's right,' one of the men behind Lotch piped up. 'You defend her, Rannis. Be her brave champion.'

'Piss off, Kurt!' Rannis said, stepping forward.

But Lotch intervened, raising his hands. 'I've a proposition for you, girl,' he said, ignoring Rannis entirely and looking at Kess.

'Such as?' she returned.

'A straight match. You and me. Short swords.'

'No!' Rannis said. 'You know Master Karasyn has expressly forbidden any such . . .'

'Stay out of this, Rannis,' Lotch warned. He regarded Kess closely. 'Unless, of course, you don't think you're able to look out for yourself – you with the great *gift*.'

Kess hesitated.

'Or is it all just trickery and flimflam, then?' Lotch taunted. 'Easy for you to pretend such a gift, sparring under Karasyn's watchful eye. But do you have what it takes to stand against a real man in a real fight?'

'Kess,' Rannis began, 'don't . . .'

'Or are you too frightened?' Lotch pressed. 'Is that it, then? Just a frightened little girl . . .'

Kess felt herself flush.

'Just you and me, girl. One against the other. Nobody else about. Nobody to help you when I put you down. And that's *exactly* what I'm going to do. Put you *down!*' Those gathered behind Lotch twittered appreciatively.

'Well, girl?' he pressed. 'What do you say?'

'Gulls have got her tongue, Lotch,' one of his cronies said.

'She's too frightened to face you,' another added with satisfaction.

'The great *gifted* Kess,' Lotch said with a sneer. 'Hah!'

Kess felt Rannis's hand on her arm, urging her away. She shrugged him off. 'All right,' she said to Lotch. 'I'll face ye.'

He nodded. 'Good.'

'Kess!' Rannis hissed. He tugged at her. 'Don't be stupid. They're just riling you. You're no match for Lotch. Not yet.'

She pushed him off angrily. She *was* a match for Lotch; she knew that in her bones. The man might outweigh her, but he was clumsy as a pregnant cow, relying on blind brute strength. She could take him, and any of his cronies, too. She was sure of it.

'Just you and me,' Lotch said. None else about.

'Done,' Kess replied.

Rannis grabbed her by the arm. 'Use your brains, Kess! It's a trick. Lotch'll never fight fair.'

She shrugged free. 'Let me *be!*'

'It's your anger making the decision here,' Rannis said. 'He's working you like a potter works clay. You're being stupid.'

'That's it, girl,' Lotch said sneeringly. 'Let him talk you out of it. That way you won't have to own up to your own hopeless, *girlish* cowardice.'

'Where?' Kess said. Rannis was right in what he said. Lotch was working her. In her heart of hearts she knew it well enough. But just looking at his stubbly, dark-eyed, sullen, triumphant face, was enough to make her want to spit. She had had enough of the man's constant, infuriating goading.

'There's a place I know,' Lotch was saying, 'where we can meet in private. It's just beyond Pontaree, on the high level.'

Kess shook her head, perplexed.

'Rannis here can tell you how to get there,' Lotch said. He turned to Rannis. 'Past Pontaree three-way, down the Scrimmish Long Hall and into the Skard. Then upwards along the Parapet till you come to the Scope. Third corridor on your right, then a hundred paces or so after that. It's a biggish hall, open to the outside all along the south side. So we'll have the light. Can you get her there?'

Rannis nodded.

'If you hurry,' Lotch said quickly, 'we can meet before sunfall.' He shrugged. '*If* you have the nerve, of course, girl.' He looked at her, a taunting smile on his stubbly face. 'Do you agree?'

'Done,' Kess said.

'I'll see you there, then,' Lotch said. 'Remember, just we two. Nobody else. Nobody to come to your rescue when I put you *down*.'

With that, Lotch and his cronies strutted off, laughing.

Kess burned. 'Stupid, arrogant, fart-faced idiot!' she muttered.

'You're the idiot,' Rannis said. 'Lotch won't fight fair in this. I know him. He'll . . .'

'Just lead me to this place, Rannis. All right? Just *do* it!'

Rannis shook his head, scowled, sighed. 'All right,' he said eventually.

'We'll have to sneak me a sword first,' Kess said. 'From the yard.'

Rannis nodded uncomfortably. 'Against Master Karasyn's most *specific* orders.'

Kess shrugged. 'Let's just *do* it, Rannis. *Now!*' The past days had created a reservoir of anger and frustration in her. She could feel it flooding through her now, as if some invisible membrane had broken, like liquid fire in her belly and limbs. Lotch would rue the day he faced her with this challenge. Oh, yes . . .

*

Kess walked the last hundred paces or so of the corridor leading to Lotch's hall. A purloined sword hung at her belt. Rannis had been left behind, with orders not to follow. She felt her pulse hammering. Her limbs seemed to quiver as she walked. Her palms were slippery with sweat and her breathing harsh. She felt frightened and angry, anxious and determined, nervous and exhilarated all at once. It was as if she had taken some drug; her whole self felt charged.

Ahead, the corridor led to a doorway. Through this, she came out into a large, empty hall. There was a forest of columns, like huge stone trees, leading up to the dim ceiling high above. Looking closer, Kess saw that, in fact, each column was carved in the image of a tree – chipped and cracked and split though they now were – the branches of each stone trunk intertwining with others above to form an intricate latticework that braced the ceiling.

All along Kess's right, the hall lay open to the outside air. The soft radiance of the waning day poured in, making everything a maze of light and dark. The stone of the columns glowed red-ochre in the light, shimmering against the dark violet of the shadows.

'Hallo!' Kess called, for the place seemed entirely deserted. 'Lotch? Is ye . . . Are you here?'

Silence, save for the ripple of an echo. Could the man have lost his nerve so easily, then?

'Lotch!'

'Here, girl,' he said softly, emerging from behind one of the stone tree trunks. 'Are you alone?'

Kess nodded. 'And you?'

'Oh, yes,' he replied. He held a sword two-handedly – not one of the dull-edged practice swords. Its ground and polished iron blade caught the light and glinted coldly.

Kess looked at the weapon and swallowed. 'That's no practice blade.'

Lotch grinned. 'So?'

Kess drew her own purloined sword. 'So all I have is one of the edgeless practice blades. See?'

Lotch grinned all the more. 'So you'll just have to be all the more careful, then, won't you, girl?'

'Now wait a moment . . .' Kess began. She remembered

Rannis's warning that Lotch would not fight fair. 'How can ye . . .'

'Ready yourself as best you can, girl,' he said, coming towards her. 'I've been waiting for this for a long while.' He stepped forward carefully, as if on eggshells, his sword up and *swishing* softly in the in-and-out crescent of the Petal – the first guard position.

Kess backed away. This was a new Lotch, cold, careful, dangerous. There was nothing at all hasty or bullish about him. She did not know how to react. She could do him no real harm with her dull practice blade. But the weapon he carried looked dangerously sharp. It was hardly going to be a fair contest . . .

'*Frightened*, girl?' he gloated. 'Feel your heart thumping, do you?'

Kess frowned, shook herself, took a fresh grip upon her blade's hilt.

He rushed her.

Kess parried. The swords *klangged*. He worked her back towards the row of tree-columns, his blade striking hers with bone-jarring force in a fast series of blows, the sharp edge of it biting against her own dull one.

But she began to check him, after a little, moving quick and sure in the patterns Master Karasyn had taught her – feeling that, indeed, she had been right: she could take this man. After the first flurry of hard blows, he was beginning to slow, his breath coming in gasps. He had over-extended himself, pressing her back so hard, so soon. So long as she did not falter, or miss her footing on some treacherous bit of the stone flooring, she could take him. She felt her heart leap. So long as he did not resort to some manner or other of foul play . . .

From behind, she heard the sound of soft footsteps. Rannis! she thought.

But it was not Rannis.

Glancing backwards, she saw a stranger appear from behind one of the columns, arm raised, hand holding a truncheon.

Then the back of her head exploded painfully and she fell abruptly away into dark nothingness.

XIX

Darkness, her head beating with pain . . .

She tried to move, but could not. Her limbs seemed paralyzed. A liquid surge of purest terror shot through her. *Paralyzed*. In the stifling darkness . . .

Like being in the grave again, all that weight of dark earth pressing down, her in her cramped, cold little coffin . . . Jago's solid workmánship, out of his carpentry shop. Jago and Genna . . .

Long Harbour . . . and Annocky and Dame Sostris and Mamma Kieran and her croaking black raven and . . .

It was the strangest feeling, being two persons at once . . .

Kess, I am Kess, a part of her insisted. *Pastless Kess. Kess of the blade*.

But *Elinor*, another part returned. *Elinor of Long Harbour*.

Like two strangers meeting for the first time. Yet not. Like sisters, perhaps. Twins parted by long years and finally reunited.

The Twins . . . Recollection of Dame Sostris's cards came back to her suddenly. The *Twins*! So this was what had been meant by that card, then . . .

She breathed a long sigh, letting the complexity of memory fill her, seeing and hearing and smelling, remembering, reliving. Like a long drink of water to a thirsty woman, it was.

Kess.

Elinor.

Whole again.

Two in one. One in two . . .

The pulse thumped in her skull, a rhythm of pain without let-up. She tried to put a hand to her head, but found she could not move.

Paralyzed.

What was *wrong* with her? Where was she? What had happened?

She tried to open her eyes.

No use.

She tried swallowing, moving her lips, her toes, her arms, her fingers.

No use.

She could breathe, think, fear. No more than that.

The sound of her breath was loud in her own ears. It came to her then that she could *hear*. At least that. She cast about with her ears, listening for something, anything that might give her a clue to where she was.

But there was nothing save the rhythmic sound of her own breathing. She held her breath, poised, all her self poured into her hearing.

Silence. Dark silence.

She began to panic, remembering all too clearly now what it was like to be buried like this. She recollected the fight with Lotch, the stranger's hand coming from behind her holding the truncheon. Lotch's doing, of course. Rannis had said the man would never fight fair.

And now?

Was this how he revenged himself upon her? Had he dug a hole in some out-of-the-way, lonely place and buried her, bound somehow into paralysis, to die a slow death, alone in the dark? Was he sitting above her on the new-shovelled earth at this very moment, gloating?

It did not bear thinking on.

She struggled desperately to move, her heart banging away under her ribs – she felt *that* at least. It could not be true. She could not be buried alive twice in one lifetime. Could *not*.

There was sound suddenly – a long, rusty *keer-eek* that made her heart kick with mingled terror and relief.

Then the dancing flicker of a torch. Her eyes stung like fire. They blinked and watered of their own accord, the tears spilling down her cheeks in little rivulets.

The torchlight came closer. She could hear the soft splutter of it, the tiny *hisss* as some burning part of it dribbled to the floor. A face stared down at hers. Looking at that face, she felt everything suddenly snap into perspective: she was lying on her back on a cold stone slab, a ceiling above her, walls all about. A room, then, not large. And the face?

Not Lotch's, she realized with surprise.

It was skull-like, entirely devoid of any hair, skin stretched tight over bone. Eyes like twin, glittering black marbles in the torchlight.

She knew that face.

'Ah . . . So you've come back to your senses, have you, girl? I can see the life-light back in your eyes.'

Familiar voice . . .

She tried to recall.

'I have you paralyzed, girl. No use struggling.' He laughed. 'As I'm sure you've already discovered.' He held the torch higher, casting more light upon his features. 'Recognize me?'

What she saw in the high-held torch's radiance was a tall man, shrouded in an ankle-length, dark robe. The loose sleeve of the robe fell open to reveal a pale, knobbly-elbowed arm holding up the torch. In the inside of that forearm, she could make out the branded image of a tusked demon's head.

It took her a long moment to recollect the name.

Skolt.

The Lord Mattingly's Seer.

Whom old Tildie had warned her against.

Elinor-Kess's heart lurched. So much for the old woman's promise to protect her!

The Seer stood back, regarding her. 'You are a puzzle, girl. And I do not like puzzles. You appear suddenly in young Mattingly's court, like a stone thrown into a quiet pond, disturbing everything. Your own Guard eagerly betray you to me . . .'

Bending forward, he stared into her frozen eyes. 'Who brought you here to trouble me and mine, eh? And why? You stink of some Power, girl.'

The Seer bent closer. 'There are many questions I wish you to answer for me. But I may need to . . . urge you a little.' He drew forth a needle-bladed dagger from out of his robe.

She could do nothing, not even blink.

'I shall enjoy that *urging* very much.' Skolt held the point of the dagger just over her left eye. 'I think I will begin by blinding you. Yes . . .' He held the torch closer. 'You may be paralyzed, girl, but you can still *feel*. Here . . . let me illustrate.'

He lifted the dagger away from her eyeball, took the torch and held it close to her left hand where it lay limply across her belly. With the dagger's point, he made a neat little incision across the back of her hand. It burned like fire, a sharp thrust of agony beyond all expectation from such a small laceration.

Skolt turned and gazed enquiringly into her eyes. He laughed softly then, and held up the dagger for her to see. 'I have taken the liberty of treating the blade. Every slight little cut will *burn*.'

He pricked her shoulder, her left breast, her thigh, in quick succession. Each burned agonizingly, as if he had embedded red hot wires into her flesh.

'Your eyes next, girl. Imagine it . . . the blade penetrating your eyeball, cleaving it like so much jelly. And *burning* . . . And all the while you can do nothing but feel the pain. *Feel* it, girl! Be *frightened*!' He bent closer, brought the dagger up towards her eyes.

She tried to turn away, to strike out, to move. But it was useless. She could not even blink voluntarily.

The dagger came closer, the slim iron blade glinting coldly in the torchlight . . .

Suddenly, the Seer drew back, laughing. 'Not so quick, I think. There is a rhythm and an art to such proceedings.' He slipped the knife back into his robe. 'By the time I allow your paralysis to wear off so that you can talk to me, you will beg me for release.'

Skolt laughed coldly. 'But after you tell me everything I wish to know, you will live a *long* time, and regret *most* bitterly what you did to me.' He bent so close to her face that she could smell his stale breath. 'I *owe* you, girl. Nobody makes a fool of me in public such as you did. You are *mine*, now. I will have my answers, and I will be *revenged*!'

She could do nothing, not even look away from the terrible, exultant triumph in the man's eyes.

After one last, gloating look, the Seer turned and stalked

abruptly off, taking the torch with him. 'Think on it, girl. Think on it and be *afraid*.'

Then he slammed the door behind him, leaving her alone and frozen, terrified and furious in the stifling dark.

XX

Strangely, it was the two-person split inside her that let her endure. It was like having a companion in the lonely dark, for she was somehow both one person and two simultaneously. She did not understand it. One moment she would be *I*, a whole person encompassing both Elinor and Kess. The next moment, she would be one or the other – Kess, amazed at some new revelation of the past; Elinor, hungry to know about Minmi, about how she managed to use one of the long iron blades so deftly.

Kess was the simpler soul, focused, proud of her new-found skills, astounded at Elinor's complexity of memory. Elinor's was the deeper experience.

She – they – lay in the dark and the two aspects of her – the two selves – gradually settled into each other, two in one, one in two, in a manner even she could not quite articulate properly to herself. The process frightened and exhilarated and engrossed her.

And kept her sane until Skolt returned.

It was the sudden *kranging* open of the door, the flickering blaze of torches, and rough hands upon her that brought Elinor back from deep inside herself. She was hauled up by three men, dangling like a carcass in their hands, and brought into another room. They dropped her upon a low stone platform, propping her half-upright, giving her bruised head a smack in the process that sent sparks scuttering across her vision.

When she could focus properly again, she tried to make sense of her surroundings.

She was in a windowless chamber, far less run-down than what else she had seen of Minmi, lit both by the usual sputtering torches and by several queerly glowing globes. On the wall facing her there hung a brilliantly coloured, woven tapestry. She took one glimpse of the images depicted, and it was enough – intricately stitched scenes, men with bladed weapons raised and . . . un-men, strange creatures part human and part animal. Impossibly scarlet blood, twisted, agonized faces . . .

In the wavering light, they seemed almost alive, and the utter bloody realism of it – the horror depicted so clearly on the faces, the queer, disjointed, butchered bodies of the un-men – made her feel sick. She desperately wanted to look away, but in her paralyzed state could not.

Skolt walked into her field of vision. He beckoned to the men who had carried her in. She had been so far unable to catch more than the merest glimpse of any of them out of the corner of her frozen eyes. Now she saw they were all dressed alike in imitation of Skolt: long, dark, cowled robes, their heads shaven, their faces thin and white, with coldly staring eyes like so many human serpents.

'My apprentices,' the Seer said, gesturing to the trio. He smiled a thin, cruel smile at her. 'They are eager to help me in my dealings with you – you who were sent to destroy me.'

He bent close to her, his stare fierce and unblinking. 'Oh, yes. I have divined your mission clear enough, girl. Why else would you appear out of nowhere in young Mattingly's court, pretending to have been thrown up by the sea? But I have been too clever for you – and for whoever intended using you as a tool to destroy me. All that remains is for me to discover who sent you, and to be revenged. I have enemies. Those who are jealous of my great learning, who would stop at nothing to destroy me . . .'

Elinor wanted to punch the man. His blind arrogance, his monumental self-centredness, made her sick.

Skolt straightened, stepped away from her, smiling. 'Your plot has failed, girl. Your own sort betrayed you to me. In fact, in the final analysis, you have done me a favour – despite your wicked intentions. Thanks to you, I now have a productive contact amongst Karasyn's Guards. And *that*, girl, makes the insulting things you did to me seem almost worthwhile.'

Elinor stared at him, helpless to do aught else. He must mean Lotch, of course. Somehow he had been in contact with Lotch, or Lotch with him, and the whole challenge Lotch had initiated had been nothing more than a ruse to deliver her into the Seer's hands.

Skolt was smiling still. 'Before we begin today's . . . entertainment, I will show you my hidden realm here. It is a privilege I grant only a select few . . .'

He gestured to one of the apprentices and she felt hands gripping her, turning her head.

'As you can see,' Skolt said, 'there is none of Minmi's usual decrepitude here. I have far too much pride in my calling.' He pointed to the tapestry. 'See? It is old . . . very old. But the dyes have faded not at all, and there is not a single loose stitch to be found anywhere in it.'

The Seer stood admiring the awful scenes depicted. In his hand, now, he held one of the odd, glowing globes. She could hear it hissing, ever so softly. It cast a steadier light than the torches, colder and less bright and smokeless. Skolt held the glow-globe up closer to the tapestry. 'A beautiful thing, is it not?' Moving closer still, he thrust a bony finger at one corner, where a demon-faced man in scale armour was depicted doing some foul thing with a blade to a creature that seemed half woman, half eagle. The creature's wings were smashed, a wreck of red blood and splintered white bone and trailing feathers. Its head was flung back, the eyes and mouth opened wide in agony. Blood spilled in a wet gush, glistening crimson under the light from Skolt's glowing globe.

'Something to think about, what the man is doing. Can you see it clearly from back there, girl? No? Perhaps we should bring you closer . . .'

The apprentices moved to shift Elinor.

'No.' Skolt waved them back. 'A little imagination is good. Let her wonder what, exactly, he is doing with that blade of his. I know well enough. Perhaps I shall do the same to you, girl, eventually.'

Elinor shuddered inwardly.

Turning from the tapestry, Skolt pointed to the chamber's far wall. The hands holding her head dutifully aimed her in that direction. There was a small, cloth-draped cage. Skolt reached over and lifted the cloth away. Inside the cage was . . .

The Kess aspect of her recognized it: one of the little blue-winged Carolells.

'Ugly, useless creature,' Skolt said. 'I trap as many as I can. They are, after all, part of my sphere of concern.'

Hanging the glow-globe on a wall hook, the Seer bent down, unlatched the door to the cage, and reached in. With a swift, deft movement, he caught up the little creature and plucked it from the cage. The poor thing shrieked and struggled. Taking the small head in one hand, the body in the other, Skolt twisted sharply.

Elinor heard the little *snappp* as the creature's neck broke.

The Seer merely smiled. 'Here,' he said, bringing the limp body over. 'Have a closer look.' He stretched out the slack wings. The little head lolled loosely.

Elinor felt sick.

'Ugly thing,' Skolt said. 'Nasty dispositioned. They should all be destroyed. Or kept as I keep them. For . . . experimental purposes. Look!'

He propped up the little head with his fingers. It was as the Kess aspect of her remembered, a beautiful thing. The tiny human eyes stared sightlessly. She remembered the *chirrupp* of pleasure the one in old Tildie's hand had made as she caressed it. Could this be that very same one? She could not tell.

Skolt flicked the head about. 'Looks almost human, does it not? But they have no minds. None of them do. Humanimals, the common folk call them. But they are mere . . . creations. A token of the power and the knowledge that once existed here in this land.'

He frowned, staring down at the broken creature in his hand. 'It is a sign of the sorry degeneration of things that such creatures roam freely.' He flung the dead Carolell aside, the pitiful little body arcing through the air and out of Elinor's field of vision. 'But all that will change once the world is returned to its proper order once more.'

Elinor felt her guts lurch at the man's casual cruelty.

Skolt turned and strode away. Hands lifted her up, hauled her after. Across the room they took her, then through a doorway and into another room entirely. This one was long and narrow and low-ceilinged. Down the middle of it ran a trestle table, upon which there was an array of strange objects.

She caught a glimpse of something squirming spastically in cloudy liquid in a large glass jar, white-blue sparks of energy spiking through the liquid like lightning . . .

And then they had hauled her past and through towards yet another room, so that, though the table was laden with queer things, she saw only that one big glass jar clearly; the rest was only a confused blur of strangeness.

Down a worn stone stairwell they dragged her. She could hear the sound of her heels knocking against the stone steps, feel each bruising *thwump*.

At the bottom, the Seer held up a softly hissing glow-globe. The walls here glistened with moisture, a greenish, glimmering sheen under the globe's cold radiance. At the room's far end . . .

A naked man lay upon the floor. Elinor took one look and was nearly sick. She could not turn her head away – the hands holding her kept her too well aimed – but she blurred her vision, trying to focus on the wall beyond the poor soul. Only one quick, clear glimpse did she receive, of seeping blood and wet flesh and a white, horror-filled, frozen face.

'He . . . insulted me,' the Seer said, gesturing at the man. 'Now, he regrets it. Isn't that right, Kabod?'

The man moved not at all. Only his eyes showed the utter horror and the agony he must be feeling.

'Ah . . .' Skolt breathed. 'Nothing to say, then?' He laughed. 'Five days, girl. That's how long Kabod here has been in this room. He is lasting rather well. Some, now . . . some expire in a very short time. And you? I wonder about you. I *do* hope you show some stamina.'

He gestured abruptly at the apprentices to turn Elinor's head. 'And here, now. Here is something I think you might find interesting.'

At the other end of the room there was a wooden table. Strapped upon that table lay . . .

She felt uncertain as to what, exactly, it was.

'Take her closer,' the Seer instructed.

The apprentices shuffled forward, propped her upright, directed her gaze.

A man, yet not a man. Green skin, huge, bulbous eyes, over-long legs, long webbed feet. Splayed out, strapped down. A horrible mixture of frog and man, it seemed. Its skin glistened slimily. It had a kind of snout rather than anything resembling a true human nose, with mere slits for nostrils. Little bubbles of wet phlegm ballooned out from those nostril slits with each breath, inflating, popping softly, inflating. She could hear the creature's soft, panting, gasping breath.

Her first reaction was disgust. This was a horrible travesty of humanity. Unnatural. Something that should never have existed, that had no right to exist . . .

But then she saw what had been done to the poor thing – the skin of its torso peeled back and pinned aside, naked white ribs glistening, wet red flesh, the pulse of organs underneath. And the eyes . . . The creature's eyes held the same look of frozen, agonized, altogether human horror that the tortured man's had.

Her heart went out to the poor, gruesome thing.

'Disgusting, isn't it?' said the Seer. 'A travesty. But not without its uses, it and its like.'

Skolt motioned to the apprentices, and Elinor found herself turned to look at him.

'Minmi was the greatest of the great southern Domains, once. And will be again, one day. I and mine work selflessly towards that goal.' Skolt's dark eyes had taken on a sudden, evangelical fire. 'It was my kind that made Minmi great. And it is my kind that will do so again. We *will* gain the respect we deserve! And the likes of this creature will serve us. It was my predecessors who created them. It and all the others of its sort are *my* inheritance.'

The Seer shook his head, scowling. 'The world has been overturned. Creatures such as this strut about as if they had every right and freedom. Creatures such as *you* insult me with impunity in front of the reigning Lord of Minmi. And that Lord *ignores* me! It is *insupportable*!'

Skolt was panting now, his face white. 'But we . . . *I* shall bring back again the greatness that once was. The world will be returned to its rightful order. No more of chaos and discomfiture. No more of confusion. No more of the rule of the worst and the least.'

He strode over to the poor cut-open frog-man upon the table and stood gazing down at it. 'And this creature shall serve me in my great destiny. From it I will learn . . .'

The Seer stopped abruptly, shaking his head. He turned back to Elinor. 'But you could not possibly understand what it is I am learning. Relearning, rather. Reconstructing the old knowledge. There will come a day, girl, when all of Minmi bows before me as the Great Seer. When all of the South will. The Great Seers held all the world in their hands, once. And so will it be again. It is my destiny. The great, secret order of Seers will be entirely resurrected, with me at its head!'

He leaned towards her. 'Why am I telling you all this? To give you some sense of the enormity of what you have done, and tried to do. It was not just *me* you insulted in front of Mattingly and his court, but everything which I represent . . . Look!'

Skolt held out his arms so that the loose sleeves of his robe fell away. On the inside of each bony white forearm, the image of the tusked demon's head showed, a blue-black scar of intricate detail. 'Look! See my mark. Only one man in each generation may be branded thus in Minmi. Only one man carries the wisdom and the knowledge, the dignity and the power. *I* am that man, descended from the long line of wise men who were once the real rulers in Minmi and all the great Domains. I, Skolt of Mamiatica, one-time apprentice to Tanass the Grim, *I* am the hope and the pride of that great lineage!'

The Seer flung his sleeves back, stalked over to Elinor, thrust his face close to hers. 'I am no *ordinary* man, girl. And I wish you to know *exactly* who and what it is that will be revenged upon you.'

Elinor felt sick, looking into his mad, triumphant face.

He laughed, then, reading how she felt in her eyes, perhaps. 'Put her over there,' he commanded the apprentices. 'Let us begin today's . . . entertainment.'

They dropped her on her back upon the cold stone floor, making her head ring with pain in the process.

'Today,' Skolt said, 'I think we shall begin with fire.' Bending down, he stroked a hand across her face. 'You have a comely enough face, girl. I think I shall change that.' Turning to one of his apprentices, he said, 'Collis, fetch the brazier.'

The apprentice nodded and scurried off.

'Or, perhaps,' Skolt went on, straightening up once more, 'I shall start on some of your more sensitive parts first. The hidden parts. Yes . . . With the hot iron from the brazier.' He smiled. 'It is always such a *satisfying* process.'

Elinor shuddered – at least she shuddered inside. She struggled furiously to move, her heart bursting, putting everything she had into the effort, straining till her vision went dark.

But it was no use whatsoever.

The Seer smiled maliciously down at her. 'Your *tender* parts, girl.'

Arms crossed in their sleeves, he stood awaiting the apprentice's return, staring at her. 'Who sent you, then? I look forward to hearing the answer. Was it Tinnikin? He has a devious enough mind to try such a thing. Or was it Ingland himself, perhaps? And what was it, exactly, that you were supposed to do?'

Skolt reached down, lifted Elinor's hands, peering closely, sniffing like a hound. 'You have the smell of some Power to you, girl. Somebody has been doing what he ought not.'

Dropping her hand, he straightened up. 'But there will be time enough for answers. First, the kiss of the hot iron . . .' He turned and called, 'Collis! Hurry up with that brazier. Do you think we have all day?' Then, when there was still no sign of a response: 'Where *has* the dolt got to?' He waved at one of the two remaining apprentices. 'Go and see what's keeping him. And hurry!'

The apprentice started off.

'Idiots!' the Seer grumbled. 'How am I expected to resurrect past greatness if I must deal with congenital idiots?'

Before the second apprentice could get through the doorway, however, the first returned. He carried a large, glowing iron brazier, holding it well away from his body by a set of wooden handles. He put it on the ground next to the Seer.

'The iron, you moron,' Skolt said irritably, gesturing at the brazier. 'Where is the iron? Go back and get it!'

The apprentice backed away, head averted. The cowl of his robe was up, hiding his face.

'What's *wrong* with you?' Skolt demanded.

The man stood at the very edge of Elinor's field of vision, but she, too, could see that there was something amiss. The apprentice's brown robe hung askew. And he seemed . . . hunched up in some manner.

'Answer me, fool!' Skolt snapped. 'What's the matter with you?'

In a startling burst of unexpected motion, the apprentice kicked over the brazier, tore the robe off himself, and flung it across the room. '*Now*!' he cried.

Red-hot coals scattered across the floor, and the Seer leaped back out of Elinor's view, spluttering curses.

Elinor could make out nothing further. From where she lay, all she could see was skittering shadows on the stone ceiling.

There was the sound of running feet, the thump of colliding bodies. She heard a scream. A man grunted with pain near her. One of the apprentices stumbled past, tripped over her frozen feet, and tumbled face first on to the stone floor, moaning.

The Seer cried out, furious, 'Get *out* of here, you rabble! You have no idea how . . .'

Skolt's voice died. Then, '*You*!' he cried.

The air in the chamber seemed somehow to crackle. Elinor felt a sudden sense of inexplicable vertigo. Her ears went *pop*. Her belly lurched. She seemed to hear a roaring . . .

'No!' Skolt shouted. 'You *cannot*!'

'Oh, yes I can,' a voice answered him. A woman's voice, hoarse and breathy. 'Oh, indeed yes.'

Elinor knew that voice.

She heard footsteps on the stone floor near her.

'It's all right, girl,' a voice said.

Rannis! He came into her vision, a fighting sword in one hand – no dull practice blade – with wet blood running from it. Putting the sword down, he lifted her to a sitting position. 'Are you all right, Kess? Can you talk?'

She felt her heart turn in her breast with very relief, but, try as she might, could not make any kind of response, still could not even so much as blink voluntarily.

Rannis stared at her, his face creased into a worried frown. Then he turned and looked outside her limited view. 'What have you *done* to her?'

She heard the Seer laugh. 'Too late, boy. You can never save her now, you and your crazed rabble. She's *mine*.'

Rannis turned Elinor then, and she could see the room. On the entrance steps stood old Tildie in her voluminous parti-coloured cloak. In her hand she held a little doll tightly, a miniature dark-cloaked, hooded figure. Her pudgy face was pale and tense, her eyes locked with the Seer's. Skolt glared back at her, a dark, furious, unblinking stare.

'Tricks!' the Seer fumed. 'Stupid, womanish *tricks*! I am stronger than you, old woman. You cannot hold me forever. And when your strength fails . . .'

Skolt was against the far wall, two Guardsmen about him, naked blades out and ready. Half a dozen other Guards, perhaps more, moved about, grim-faced, all with blades out. One of the apprentices lay unmoving on the floor, a pool of dark blood slowly forming about him. The one who had tripped over her nursed a bleeding arm. The third, clothed only in a little loincloth, stood shivering and white-faced, held fast by the threat of a blade against his belly. There was a soft *hissssing* as the spilled coals from the brazier drowned in the wet blood that pooled across the floor.

'You are making a serious mistake, boy,' the Seer said to Rannis, his gaze still locked unwillingly with Tildie's, face clenched into a mask of fury.

Rannis laughed a mirthless laugh. 'It's *you* who made the mistake, Seer. Did you really think that the Guard would stand idly by while you abducted one of its own?'

'*She*?' Skolt said incredulously. 'She's no part of your Guard, boy. She's a conniving bitch, a mere utensil, who's insulted you as much as me. By her very presence amongst you she drags your precious Guard into ridicule and disrepute. You should be *thankful* to me for taking her off your hands.'

Rannis said nothing.

'Admit it, boy,' the Seer went on. 'She's been nothing but trouble for you ever since she arrived. Isn't that so? What place can one such as *she* have in your Guard, then? You'd become a laughing stock, with her in your ranks. The ordinary folk would sneer. And then where would we all be, with the rabble laughing at you? How could you do your duty *then*? Leave her to me, boy, and I'll forgive you this intrusion.'

Rannis motioned back the two Guardsmen who held Skolt against the wall.

'That's better,' the Seer said. 'Now you're beginning to show some sense.'

Throughout his talk to Rannis, Skolt's gaze had been locked

with Tildie's. The sinews in his white neck stood out like cords with strain. He shivered and heaved, as if pulling at some invisible bond, and then jerked his head suddenly. Tildie's jerked in an involuntary echo of response. The old woman's face was damp with sweat and her breath was coming in panting gasps now.

The Seer laughed. 'While we're arranging matters, boy . . . this conniving old bitch here is . . .'

Rannis lifted his bloodied blade, and thrust the tip neatly into Skolt's right shoulder.

The Seer grunted in shock.

'Rannis!' Tildie called.

But Rannis ignored her. 'Tell me what you did to Kess,' he ordered the Seer. 'And tell me how to make it right.'

Skolt's hand flew to his wounded shoulder, blood welling up between his fingers. Elinor saw him struggle harder to pull away from the strange hold Tildie maintained over him, thrashing like a fish on a line. 'Release me, woman! Release me or I'll . . .'

Rannis's blade came up. This time, it took Skolt in the thigh, a quick, painful thrust.

Skolt staggered.

'Tell me what I ask, Seer. Or I swear I'll take you apart piece by bloody piece!'

'Don't be *ridiculous*, boy!' Skolt responded. 'You can't . . .'

Rannis's blade-tip took the Seer in the forearm, ripping through the sleeve of his robe and leaving a bloody incision. 'Don't call me *boy*!'

Skolt shuddered and grunted, slipped down the wall to his knees.

'Rannis,' Tildie panted. 'Don't! If you pushes him too far I cannot . . .'

But Rannis merely hefted his blade threateningly. 'Tell me what I need to know,' he ordered Skolt. 'Quick!'

The Seer faltered back against the wall, then staggered up. With a great, roaring, furious shout, he flung himself forward and tore free from Tildie's hold.

The room erupted into violent motion.

Skolt rushed for the doorway, his robe flapping. Rannis leaped after, to intercept him, as did the other Guards. The apprentices flung themselves against the Guards, trying to come to the aid of their master.

All Elinor could make out then was a chaos of moving bodies. The air seemed to shimmer. She heard shouts and screams, saw the glimmer of blades wet with blood. One of the Guards flew into the air, screaming. A cold blue light seemed to coalesce about the Seer. Tildie screeched and flung the little doll she held at him.

Then all went suddenly still.

The apprentices lay unmoving, limbs twisted in unnatural ways, limp as so many discarded rag dolls. Skolt was on his back on the stone floor, his hands to his guts. Blood welled up between his shaking fingers, forming in a wet, dark pool about him on the floor. He was white-faced and staring.

Rannis stood over him, grim, panting. 'Tell me what I need to know, Seer.' He brought his blade down so that the bloody tip centred on Skolt's sternum. 'Tell me how to free Kess!'

Skolt glared, his eyes like black stones in his white face. 'Stupid boy! You have no conception of what you . . .'

'Tell me!'

Skolt lifted a bloody hand, swiped Rannis's sword aside, and struggled awkwardly to his feet. Elinor saw his guts hanging out, like pink-grey sausage dangling from his torn robe. Looking down, the Seer saw the same thing. He let out a great, inarticulate scream of outrage and flung himself straight at Rannis.

Rannis's blade came up in instinctive defence, and Skolt skewered himself upon it. He clutched at Rannis, howling like some demented creature, the bloody blade sticking out of his back through his ribs.

Rannis thrust him away, wrenching his blade free.

Faltering back, the Seer stared about him. 'You can't do this!' he screamed. Blood poured from his ripped guts. He stood in a dark wet pool, flapping his hands about. 'My life can't end like *this*!'

Rannis and the rest only stared.

'Curse you!' the Seer cried. 'Curse you all for . . .' But his voice faltered. He collapsed, first to one knee, then to a slumped sitting position propped against a wall. 'I . . . I will *not* . . .' he rasped, his voice hardly audible.

The life-blood fairly poured from him now. He looked about, shook himself, gasped out something incomprehensible. Then, slowly, he went limp.

In the instant before his death, he cast one last, venomous glance at Elinor. She saw his eyes go from living, glistening dark marbles to dusty lumps as the soul went out of him.

Silence gripped the room for long moments.

Then, 'What do we do *now*?' one of the Guard said in a small voice.

Tildie lay in a swoon.

Rannis stared dazedly at the old woman where she lay supine on the floor, at the corpse of the Seer. He ran a hand over his face, shook himself. 'We . . . we get *out* of here. That first!' He walked unsteadily over to Elinor and bent over her. 'Kess,' he said worriedly. 'Kess!'

Try as she might, she could still say no word in reply, make no move in response.

Rannis wiped his bloodied blade and sheathed it, then bent and gathered her up, lifting her in his arms with a grunt of effort. 'Let's away from this place,' he said to those with him. '*Quick!*'

Two of them lifted up the wounded Guard – whom Elinor had seen fly through the air. Two others took Tildie. The rest began to surge towards the doorway.

'What about that poor soul over there?' someone asked, pointing at the mutilated man in the far corner.

'Bring him away with us,' Rannis said. He was by the doorway leading out of the room by now. 'But be quick!'

Two of the Guards went and lifted up the tortured man, gently carrying him between them.

'What about *that*?' somebody else said, gesturing to the cut-open frog-man strapped upon the table.

Elinor's head had lolled over, and she could only partially glimpse what was happening.

'Uugh!' she heard one of them grunt. 'Don't touch it. Ugly, unnatural brute . . .'

'No!' she tried to say, remembering the look of entirely human horror she had seen in the creature's eyes. But she could make no sound.

'Put it out of its misery,' Rannis ordered.

'Easy for you to say, Rannis, with your hands already full,' one of the Guard replied.

'Let's just *do* it,' another said, 'and get *out* of here. This place gives me the wemblies.' He lifted his blade and brought it down in a quick, merciful stroke.

Rannis turned then and stumbled out of the room, the rest following after.

Through corridors and echoing chambers, up flights of steps and across a windy, empty place they went, till Elinor scented the odour of growing things, the fresher breath of outside air.

Rannis let her down, then. She felt the soft touch of grass upon her back. Sunlight warmed her.

She was safe. Against all expectation . . .

But still she could not move.

The Guards clustered about her. 'What's *wrong* with her?' one of them asked.

'The other one's just the same,' another added.

'Some uncanny spell of the Seer's.'

'Can she hear us, do you think?'

'Kess?' Rannis said. 'Kess!'

The paralysis held unabated. She could make no response.

'Is her mind gone?'

Rannis shook her. '*Kess!*'

'It's no use,' somebody said.

She could only lie as Rannis had placed her, helpless and frozen, like so much dead meat.

'No!' Rannis said. 'There must be some way to . . .' A sudden commotion outside her view made him turn.

'It's the old woman,' somebody muttered. 'She's coming round.'

Old Tildie came stumbling into Elinor's field of view. She held her head in her hands, shook herself, sat down hard. She sighed. 'Impetuous boy,' she said to Rannis. 'You nearly ruined us all. Indeed yes. You nearly did. He's a tough old bird, is Skolt.'

'Was,' Rannis responded.

Tildie blinked. '*Was*, indeed.'

'What about Kess?' Rannis demanded. '*Look* at her!'

Tildie peered down at Elinor. She nodded. 'What about her, then?'

'But she's . . . she can't speak, doesn't move. She's completely *paralyzed*!'

'Oh, not to worry, boy. Indeed no. I knows how to remedy *that*.'

She knelt down next to Elinor, surprisingly limber for all her bulk. Her voluminous cloak fell about her in folds of purple and black and orange. From out of it somewhere she brought a little vial of cloudy blue glass. Unstoppering it, she held it under Elinor's nose. 'Here, girl,' she said softly. 'Breathe this.'

Elinor breathed. Still paralyzed as she was, she could not have resisted even if she had wished. The fumes from the little vial burned like ice. She felt a cold tide go through her, a rush of icy terror. Her heart raced, then slowed. Then there was warmth seeping through her.

'I told you I would protect you,' she heard Tildie say from far, far away. 'Indeed yes . . .'

Then there was nothing at all . . .

XXI

Elinor took a long, sighing breath, another, opened her eyes.

'How do you feel, Kess?'

It was Rannis, leaning over her in concern. 'Can you talk? Can you *move*?'

She shifted position, found she could, smiled weakly. 'My head aches.'

Rannis smiled back, his face flooded with relief. 'Hardly surprising. The bastard gave you a solid clout with that truncheon of his.'

She stretched her limbs, sat partially up, fingered the lump on the back of her skull. She felt creakingly stiff, and each separate muscle ached, as if she had been battered systematically with a stick. But even so, she luxuriated in the thrill of every simple motion. Looking about, she saw she lay on a pallet in the small, sunlit room. 'Where am I?' she asked.

'Out near the Brink,' Rannis replied. 'Not too far from the Guardery. It's a quiet, good place, this.'

'How . . . how long have I been here?'

'A day and a night.'

'No!'

Rannis grinned. 'Seems to me I recall us doing this sort of thing once already.' He lifted a wooden cup of water to her lips. 'Here, drink.'

She did. Then fell back.

'Kess?' he said worriedly. 'Are you all right?'

Elinor nodded wearily. 'I ache, is all.' But it was not just her limbs and bruised skull that ached. Her mind did, too. Kess. Elinor. How could she explain to Rannis? To anybody? Could she say: 'I am two people, the old and the new.' He would think her mad. She wondered herself if she was not a little mad . . .

'Do you feel you could walk a bit?' Rannis asked.

She hesitated a moment, then nodded.

'Sunlight and outdoor air will do you a power of good,' he said.

They did.

Standing on an old portico, leaning against a stone railing, she took long breaths. It was early morning, the sky clear, the air still cool and fresh. Below her lay a long slice of Minmi's tumbled stone confusion – a new and altogether bizarre sight to the Elinor part of her, but familiar enough to Kess. Raising her eyes, she saw, in the distance, the far-away green hills after which Kess had yearned in those first days in her lonely Guards room. They fairly shone in the new morning light.

It felt very, very good to be alive and free again. She lifted her hand, wriggled her fingers, just for the simple pleasure of the movement. Her horrifying encounter with the Seer seemed like a nightmare from which she had awakened. Each breath of fresh morning air filled her with new vitality.

'Lotch is still missing,' Rannis said quietly by her side. 'We'll find him, all right. But it'll take time.'

Elinor shrugged. At the moment, her mind was too filled with the simple thrill of being alive and whole once more, and with her own twin complexities, to be overmuch concerned with revenge. 'Rannis . . .' she began, then fell silent.

'Yes, Kess?' he prompted.

She wanted to explain to him about the two parts of her. But . . . But she did not know how. Simpler to let things lie. He knew her as Kess. Let it stay as that: Kess, skilled with the blade, member of the Minmi Guard. There were worse things to be known as. She would keep the rest to herself. For the time being, at least . . .

'Well, girl,' a voice said from behind.

'Tildie!' Elinor exclaimed, turning round. 'I . . .' She did not know what to say.

Tildie's pudgy face broke into a smile. 'Good to see you up and about, girl. Indeed yes.' She beckoned Elinor close and gathered her into her arms in a motherly hug.

'I followed after you, Kess,' Rannis explained. 'But too late. By the time I got to the place, there was no sign of Lotch, or you, or anything. We didn't know what to do. And then old Tildie here came to us . . .'

'You *know* Tildie?' Elinor said. Gently, she disengaged herself from the old woman's arms. 'But if you knew her, why . . .'

Rannis shook his head. 'I'd never seen her before in my life. Minmi's a *big* place, Kess. You're too new here to know. Mattingly's court is the centre of everything, of course, and anybody with any ambition at all is drawn to it. But there's all manner of other folk here, nobody knows how many, living in corners as best they can, tilling the old roof terraces some of them, coming and going . . .'

'There's many faces to Minmi,' Tildie agreed.

'But how did you *know*?' Elinor asked, turning back to her.

'I said I'd protect you, didn't I, now? Indeed yes. I have my ways of knowing what happens to them I befriend.'

'The way you held Seer Skolt like that,' Rannis said earnestly. 'Pinned him against the wall with your very glance . . . I've never seen anything like it. If you hadn't done that . . .'

Tildie smiled, shrugged.

Elinor took her hand. 'Thank you,' she said earnestly. 'I owe you my life. More than my life. If you hadn't been able to lift my paralysis . . .' She reached out to Rannis, too. 'Both of you. And all the others . . . It's a miracle you were able to find me and free me so quickly!'

Tildie regarded Elinor, shook her head, chuckled, tutted. 'No miracle. You're an axle, girl. Oh, indeed yes.'

'Axle?' Rannis echoed, puzzled.

But Elinor was remembering . . . Tildie had named Kess that before. And back in Long Harbour, she recollected old Mamma Kieran's raven croaking, 'Aks-sel, aks-sel.' A raven with knowing human eyes . . . She felt a cold shiver go up her spine. 'I have been called that before,' she said. 'And by . . .'

But Tildie was talking on. 'I knew you for an axle, girl. Indeed yes. But I had no idea . . . not the *faintest* idea of the strength and depth of you. Old Skolt and his nasty brood dead and gone, just like that. And we all standing here whole and sound, discussing it. Amazing!'

'I never meant him any harm,' Elinor protested. 'It was purest accident that stranded me here.'

'*Was* it, now?' Tildie said quietly.

'Yes!' Elinor insisted. 'The sea spat me up. Skolt was . . .
He saw plots against himself everywhere. He was going to . . .
to torture me to find out who had secretly sent me to destroy
him. He was mad!'

'He was right, though, wasn't he, now? You *did* destroy him.
Indeed yes. He saw the threat in you. He just didn't have the
wisdom to know it was his own fear and overweening self-
importance that brought the doom upon him. If he'd just let
you be . . . But then, Skolt was never very big on wisdom.'

Elinor opened her mouth, closed it.

'An . . . axle?' Rannis said again. 'Like in a wheel?'

Tildie nodded. 'One around whom the events of the world
turn.'

Elinor only stared.

'It *is* a little hard to grasp at first, I know. Indeed yes. There's
other words for it than "axle", if you likes. "Channel", for
instance, or "vessel". It's all to do with the greater Balances.
And the Powers.'

'The Powers?' Rannis said uncertainly. 'The Powers don't
intervene in human affairs. They're not . . . not of such a
nature. Everybody knows that!'

Tildie nodded. 'Indeed yes. The Powers is the Powers.'

'But then, how . . .' Rannis started.

'Listen,' Tildie said. 'And I'll try to explain. The Powers are
like strong currents under smooth water, save that the water is
the world entire. But they don't just move, they . . . intermove,
they balance each other: water and fire, air and earth, wet and
dry, dark and light, up and down, fall and fly. Indeed yes. And
so the world is balanced.'

'You're only telling us what we already know,' Rannis said.
'How can Kess . . .'

'Impatient boy! I'm *explaining*.' Tildie leaned her considerable bulk against the stone railing, settling herself with a sigh.
'The ancient Seers, Skolt's sort, they brought into the world a
kind of perversion. They controlled. They ruled. They had *great*
power. They forced and fought and fashioned and . . .'

'They brought greatness to Minmi!' Rannis interrupted.

Tildie shook her head and sighed. 'But at a *cost*, lad. Indeed
yes. The world is many, many things in an intricate, moving

186

series of balances. The old Seers would have made it only *one* thing. They would have controlled all things, fashioned all to their own will. In trying to do such, they upset the greater Balances.'

'But what does any of this . . . this ancient history have to do with Kess?' Rannis demanded.

'If you dam a stream,' Tildie asked him, 'what happens?'

'It . . . it forms a little lake,' Rannis replied. 'So what?'

'And how long does the lake last?'

'As long as the dam,' Rannis said impatiently. 'I don't . . .'

Tildie smiled. 'The water always finds a way, don't it? Indeed yes. Around or over or through. Dam a flow in one direction and it'll find a channel in another. Stop up that channel, and it'll find yet another. Endlessly. Always. Indeed yes. Water finds a way.'

'So?' said Rannis.

'So too with the Powers. They always find a way. Persistent as dammed water.'

'A way to what?'

'To balance, lad. Indeed yes! To the greater, moving *balance* of all things in the world.'

Rannis shook his head. 'But what does any of this have to do with Kess?'

'She is one of the ways. A channel. A vessel. An axle. Through her, and those like her, the Powers rebalance the world.'

Elinor shivered. She was not sure she liked any of this.

But Rannis shook his head and snorted. 'Kess? A horse upon which Powers ride? Hardly!'

Tildie merely smiled. 'You have a special destiny, girl,' she said.

Elinor felt the small hairs at the back of her neck prickle. She recalled Mamma Kieran saying the same: 'You's got the stink o' the destined 'bout you . . .' She looked at old Tildie, pudgy as a goose, swathed in her parti-coloured cloak. 'Do you know Mamma Kieran, then?' she asked. With memory intact, she could not help but wonder. There was something altogether uncanny about this.

But Tildie merely said, 'Mamma who?'

'Mamma Kieran,' Elinor repeated. 'An old Wise Woman, with a talking raven.'

Tildie shook her head. 'Never heard of her.'

Which left Elinor nonplussed. 'She . . . she said the same sort of thing to me that you have, she and her raven.'

'She saw the same thing in you that I have, then,' Tildie said. 'And channelled you here where you were needed.'

Elinor did not know what to say.

'I don't know about any of this . . . this *channelling* and such,' Rannis put in. 'But I do know I'm glad to have Kess here back whole and safe again.'

Elinor looked across at him and smiled, grateful for his uncomplicated support.

Then she turned back to Tildie. There were questions to which she wanted answers. Holding out her hands, palm up, she said, 'What did Skolt see? What do *you* see?'

Tildie shrugged.

'Answer me!'

'I cannot.'

'Will not, rather! You saw something there clear enough before.'

The old woman sighed. 'I don't *know*, girl. Truly I don't. There's a . . . a *feel* of some Power to you. As if your hands have touched it – your left hand, rather. But as for what it is, exactly . . .' She shrugged ruefully. 'I don't know. I nose my way through the world like a blind fish, girl. The Powers move me, as they move you. I . . . I too am a channel, though a minor one. How do you think I was drawn to find you? I know what it's like, girl. Indeed yes. A blind confusion . . .'

Elinor stared at the old woman.

'There are no answers, girl. Only the living through. Only the beating of your heart, the breath in your lungs, and the spirit in you being moved blindly, like a banner in the wind . . .'

Elinor shivered.

'It's hard,' Tildie said. 'Indeed yes. But it's . . . wonderful, too.'

Elinor swallowed, shook her head. She was not sure she liked any of this. It made her feel like . . . like a mere utensil. A sort of a *thing*, to be used and discarded.

If, in fact, any of it was really true . . .

She felt, suddenly, that it was all too much for her. As if she had opened a door on to an enormous and unexpected

188

landscape. She was still weak and woozy and achy. Her head hurt. She did not want to think further on such things . . .

Tildie put a hand on her shoulder, gently. 'Don't fret about it, girl.'

Elinor turned, opened her mouth, but did not know what to say.

They stood like that for long moments, looking at each other, silent, Tildie's hand still upon Elinor's shoulder.

Then the old woman said, 'Blessings,' softly, and turned and waddled away without a further word.

'But . . .' said Elinor. 'I don't . . . How can ye . . .'

But Tildie was already gone.

'Queer old duck,' Rannis said, shaking his head.

Elinor stared at where Tildie's portly form had disappeared round a ragged stone portico. She took a long breath, another, shook herself. 'I want to walk,' she said suddenly, impulsively.

Rannis looked at her. 'You sure?'

She nodded. 'Absolutely.'

He looked at her some more, uncertain, then shrugged. 'All right. If you really feel up to it. Where would you like to go?'

'I know *just* the place,' she said. 'Is it far to my room from here?'

'Not very.'

'Lead me there. I can do the rest.'

Back past her room, along the corridor and down the hidden stairs she took him, walking slowly, for she was still shaky on her feet.

'Where does this lead?' Rannis asked, peering about curiously as they descended the stairs.

'You'll see,' was all she said.

When they reached the bottom and had pushed a way out through the thickness of tangled vines and into the bee-loud sunlight, to stand in the middle of the swirl-patterned flagstone patio overlooking Minmi, she heard him gasp.

'I never knew *this* was here,' he said in amazement.

'I first met Tildie here. "Viewpoint", she said it was once called. And I first saw the little Carolell here. Or in there, actually.' Elinor turned and gestured to the overgrown entrance to the little walled garden.

'Carolell?' Rannis said.

Elinor blinked. 'Little blue-winged creatures. I thought you'd know. Skolt had one in a cage. He . . . he'd killed it.'

Rannis shrugged, shook his head. 'I never saw.'

'Let's go into the garden,' Elinor suggested. 'Perhaps we'll see one.'

They walked softly through into the walled garden. Morning sunlight cascaded over the wall in a golden wash. The bees hummed about the heavy, white vine-flowers. Leaves rustled gently.

'There!' Elinor whispered, pointing.

Perched high on a limb amongst the trees that bordered the wall was one of the little blue-winged creatures. It cocked its small head and stared at them. Then, softly, it began to sing. Not like any bird song either the Elinor or the Kess aspect of her could recall. A series of liquid notes that were hummed rather than piped, like a high-pitched human voice singing wordlessly. A chant, almost, strange and very beautiful.

For a few moments it sang, head thrown back, little orange throat swelling. Then it stopped abruptly. With a soft *snapp* it leaped into the air and was gone.

They stood unmoving, staring at where it had been.

'I've never seen *that* sort before,' Rannis said softly.

Elinor shivered. 'Let's sit,' she said.

'Feeling tired?' he asked quickly, putting a hand on her elbow.

She nodded. 'A little.' His continued solicitude touched her. 'There are benches over that way.'

Through the high grass they walked, till they came to the bench where she had first encountered Tildie. They sat there together for a few moments. But the old stone was chipped and chill and uncomfortable, and they slipped down to the grass and lay, side by side, protected by the wall and warm in the sun.

Elinor lay back, fingers interlaced carefully behind her bruised head, and gazed off into the cobalt sky. Her mind was swimming, with memory, with conjecture, with questions. 'Do you think . . .' she began. She swallowed, sighed, started again. 'What old Tildie said about me. What do you think?'

Rannis laughed. 'Tildie's odd as can be. Who knows? Maybe

she's right. Maybe she's as wrong as wrong. Me . . . I find it hard to imagine you as a horse for the Powers to ride.'

Elinor sighed. Powers and axles and currents and destinies . . . It all seemed overwhelming. She felt tired. She did not want to think of it any more. She closed her eyes, sighed. Her limbs ached. The sunlight felt wonderfully warm and soothing.

Rannis put a hand on her brow, ran his fingers soothingly over her skin. His touch was comforting, and she felt warmed by his continued concern.

She looked up at him through half-closed eyes. The long scar that went from his forehead down his left cheek – which had seemed so dramatic at first – was hardly noticeable to her now. She reached up and ran her index finger gently along it. 'How did you get it?' she asked impulsively.

He smiled ruefully. 'I was a fool kid.'

'And so?' she urged. 'What happened?'

He shrugged, looked away from her, looked back. 'I . . . my family was . . .' he sighed. 'We had nothing. Lived in a hole on Minmi's north side, near the Pit.'

'The Pit?' Elinor said.

'Doesn't matter.' Rannis shrugged again. 'You need to know Minmi to understand. I was hungry most of the days of my boyhood, not just for food. For *everything*.'

Rannis paused, swallowed, continued. 'You see, Minmi is . . . Minmi is two cities. Lord Mattingly and his court are the inheritors of all that is left of Minmi's one-time greatness. But where Mattingly's predecessors were absolute rulers of the whole of the city, and all the land for leagues about, Mattingly himself rules only a small part. Outside his boundaries, there is no order and no rule. It is the Guards who keep Mattingly's territory intact. Without us, the chaos that breeds in Minmi's dark corners would overwhelm the whole of the city. *We* keep the old order alive. *We* keep the rabble and the crazies off. *We* maintain order and justice and the necessary continuity of . . .'

Rannis paused, sighed. 'But you asked after my scar . . .'

Elinor nodded.

'I was . . .' He gazed blindly off into the air, reliving memory. 'I was a skinny boy full of desperate dreams. My sister was ill with lung fever – all skin and bones and fever-sweat and gasping breath, and coughing blood. I stood at the foot of her bed, I remember, and swore I wouldn't let her die . . .'

Rannis sighed. 'There's a remedy for lung fever, you see. But folk like us out by the Pit had no way to purchase it. So I made my great vow, and I set off to . . . to steal it.'

'And?' Elinor prompted.

'I made my way into the Lowe Lay Walk . . . the market district . . . and stole the remedy from a stall – as brazen and stupid as could be.'

'What happened?'

'I was caught. The merchant had a minder for his stall – somebody in the background to keep watch over things. Most merchants do, though I was too much the innocent to know about such things then. He was a nasty piece, that minder. Carried a little stiletto . . .'

'Is that how . . .'

Rannis nodded. 'Chased me through the market, me running like a very demon was after me . . . I almost made it, too, except that one of the other merchants tripped me. The minder, he thumped me a few times, then took out that stiletto of his and said, "I'm going to make an example out of you, boy. Thieving's too common round here these days." He grabbed me by the hair and slit me with his blade, hairline to jaw . . .'

Rannis shivered. 'He would have done more, too. But all the commotion – folk shouting, me screaming like a stuck pig – brought the Guard.'

'And?' Elinor said.

Rannis smiled. 'Three of them came striding up like they owned the world. Folk went quiet. "What's going on here?" one of them demanded.

'The minder held me up, bleeding like a fountain. "Caught this boy stealing," he said.

'"Stealing what?" the Guard asked.

'The minder held up the little bag of remedy I'd stolen. One of the Guards turned to me and said, "You know what you stole, boy?"

'I nodded. I thought I was finished. My sort didn't mess with the Guard. When we saw them coming, we ran. I expected them to spit me then and there with their pikes. But the same one asked, "Why'd you steal it?" instead.

'"My sister's ill with the lung fever," I told him. "She'll die without that remedy!"

'He looked at me and shook his head. "And your family have no way to purchase any. Right?"'

Rannis looked across at Elinor, looked away. 'I was mortified and furious that he had seen through me so easily, that I had been caught so easily. I tried to yank myself out of the minder's grip. He hit me. I squealed . . .

'"Let him go!" the Guard ordered.

'The minder refused. "The boy's a good-for-nothing thief!" he shouted.

'But the Guard insisted.' Rannis shrugged. 'You don't argue with the Guard in a situation like that. Even the slime-ball minder knew better than that. He let me go.

'Then one of the Guard said, "Give him the remedy." I couldn't believe my ears.' Rannis smiled. 'Neither could the minder. "Are you *mad*?" he said.

'The Guard insisted. "We'll pay for it," one of them said. There was nothing the minder could do then. He gave it to me. I remember standing there, the blood flooding half my face and chest, staring up at those three men in purest amazement. Then, "Run, lad," one of them said. "Get it home, quick!"

'I ran . . .'

Rannis lay back and stared up at the sky, silent for long moments.

'And your sister?' Elinor said after a little. 'She got better, then?'

He sighed, shook his head. 'I was too late.'

Elinor opened her mouth, closed it again.

'But I remembered those Guards,' Rannis went on. 'And I knew . . . I *knew* I was going to get myself out of the dismal life I had been born into. So when my mother died a couple of years later, I came here and hung about and begged and stole what living I could and pestered the Guard mercilessly till, one day, finally, I was accepted . . .'

Rannis sighed. 'I never found out who those three were. But I've never forgotten. Those men enforced justice, fairly and humanely as could be. In the olden days, there was order and rule in Minmi, in *all* of Minmi. Life made sense, then. None died needlessly. Folk prospered. Justice was the rule. Now . . .

now Minmi is all dark corners and chaos. And Mattingly . . . well, you've seen what Mattingly is like. It's we Guards . . . *we* hold Minmi together now. At our best, that's what we do. We make life better. We bring back a little bit of the order and sanity and greatness of the past. We make a difference. *I* make a difference. As a boy, I swore that I would make something better of myself, that I would escape from the Pit, that I would make the world a better . . .'

Rannis stopped abruptly, looked at her, looked away, ran a hand over his face self-consciously. He backed a little away from her, nearer the bench they had quitted. 'I didn't mean . . . I never intended to tell you all of that. It's just . . .'

'It's all right,' Elinor said. 'I know. I was just the same.' She thought of Rannis as a lad, yearning to escape the confines of his sorry life, and knew exactly how he must have felt. They were the same then, he and she – in this at any rate. She felt a sense of connection with him, like some invisible cord being woven between them.

'I struggled out of my own life,' she said. 'That's how I ended up on the sea strand.'

Rannis blinked. 'So we are the same, then, you and I.'

Elinor smiled, hearing her own thoughts echoed in his words. She reached across and ran her index finger gently along his scar. It made his face on that side a little stiff, his smile a little lopsided. The scar itself felt like a length of thin string that had been glued on to his skin. Running her finger along it was, somehow, a gesture of intimacy . . .

She looked at him as he half-lay beside her on the grass, his shoulders propped against a corner of the bench. Rannis had good shoulders, she thought, square and solid and muscular, yet not at all stocky or chunky. And a nice face: broad cheekbones, an elegant line to his nose, white teeth flashing brightly under his dark moustaches. His wide-set eyes were the rich colour of polished walnut.

He took her hand in his. His fingers were long and slim, like the rest of him. He looked at her, his brown eyes intent. 'Kess of the Guard . . . You are not like any woman I have ever known.'

'Is that good . . . or bad?' she returned. She felt her heart beating harder suddenly, felt a flush of warmth go through her. The look he was giving her made her shiver.

He did not answer her question. Instead, he grabbed her, pulling her close in a quick, hard kiss.

Elinor could hardly breathe, so flustered was she, and so tight did he hold her. His moustaches prickled uncomfortably. She levered herself back from him, panting a little.

'Don't push me away,' he said.

'I don't . . .' Elinor started to say, but then went quiet. She did not know how she felt. The Elinor part of her remembered all too well the heat that she was feeling inside herself now . . . remembered the joy and the agony it had brought her with faithless Annocky.

But Rannis was no such feckless wastrel, surely. The scar on his face was testimony to that. And they shared so much in common, he and she. And it had been *so* long since she had felt a shared bond of *any* sort with *anybody* . . .

'Kess . . . Kess! Come back to me.'

She blinked, shook herself.

'You were gone,' he said accusingly. 'Do I matter so little to you, then?'

'No,' she replied hurriedly. 'It's just . . . just that . . .' She shrugged. 'I don't know what to say, Rannis. I . . .'

He pulled her close to him once again. 'Then don't say anything. There's no need of words between us, my Kess.'

She felt his long strong arms about her, and he kissed her again, strong and passionate and forceful. It was like being kissed by a bull, all force and panting breath and insistent tongue.

Then he was pulling at her clothes.

'Wait . . .' she gasped, for she heard a seam give way somewhere under his brute tugging. 'Wait!' She tried to push him away, but he held on to her tightly.

'You know you want it, Kess,' he said, his voice husky. 'Don't pretend you don't!' He was yanking at her trousers now.

'I *do* want it,' she said, trying to fend him off. 'But let me go. *Let me go!*' She managed to wrench herself free, half laughing, half angered. 'Ye'll have my clothes in rags like this!'

She pushed herself away from him. 'Sit!' she ordered when he would have come after her. He half-started up to his feet, but she straight-armed him back again. 'Stay there!'

He squirmed, but stayed as he was.

195

Quick as could be, given her still-stiff limbs, she slipped out of her clothing and knelt back down next to him, blushing uncertainty. She was scarred and bruised and thin to the bone . . .

But he looked at her hungrily.

She both liked and disliked the way he stared. The hunger in his look made her shiver pleasantly, but it also made her feel rather like a side of meat . . .

'Now you,' she said quickly, bending close and reaching for his tunic.

He pushed her back. In one hasty motion, he swept the tunic over his head, yanked off his boots and trousers, and revealed himself to her, white and slim and hard and naked.

Ah, but he was a lovely man, Rannis was.

He clutched her to him, his mouth going to hers hungrily. The nice man-scent of him filled her nostrils. He lifted her off her feet, still kissing her forcefully the while, and hauled her over to the grass away from the benches. There, he dropped her on her back, bent down, put his strong hands on her knees, and pried open her legs.

Before she quite knew it, he was inside her. 'Rannis!' she gasped. It hurt. He was too quick.

But he was deaf to her, plunging and gasping like some wild creature, his face strangely blank, eyes turned inwards, plunging, rearing, plunging . . .

And then it was over.

He rolled from her, panting, lying on the grass by her side, his head across her breasts. 'Ah . . .' he breathed. And again, 'Ahhh . . .'

Elinor did not know what to say. She stroked his long dark hair, feeling the warmth of his breath against her skin. 'Rannis . . .' she began uncertainly. 'Rannis?'

But Rannis was asleep.

XXII

Weapons Master Karasyn came to her room that night.

'How are you feeling then, girl?' he enquired, standing in her doorway.

'A little stiff,' she replied. This was only the second time she had seen him since her rescue, and on the first they had scarce exchanged a dozen words. There was something about him now that made her uneasy. He stood rigidly, a little awkward-looking, not at all his usual self.

He nodded. 'A little stiffness is to be expected. Rannis conducted himself well to get you out as quickly as he did.'

The mention of Rannis made Elinor shiver a little.

Master Karasyn stood looking at her, his head cocked a bit to one side. His posture made her think of the little blue-winged Carolells somehow.

'I want to talk with you, girl,' he said after a moment. 'About something important.'

She nodded, gestured him further into her room.

'You have brains, girl,' he started. 'I've seen that. And you use them. And you *do* have the gift. Why, if you were only a man . . .'

'What difference would . . .' Elinor began sharply, but the Weapons Master cut her short.

'Listen to me, now, girl. You'll never have the strength, the length of bone, or the weight to make a great bladesman. Oh, you're good, true enough. Better than most. But it's not enough.'

Elinor shook her head. Karasyn had started so suddenly, without any sort of preamble. She felt a prickle of sharp resentment. Kess had just begun to feel a sense of comforting pride in this new-found skill of hers – a pride and a skill Karasyn himself had been responsible for instilling in her. And now the man had undercut everything. 'I don't . . .'

'I'm trying to warn you, girl. Don't get too full of yourself. This bunch you're training with are mere louts, the most of them. You've never even seen a real bladesman yet.'

'So?' Elinor said. She felt herself flushing with mixed anger and resentment.

'So, I've a proposition for you to consider.'

'A . . . proposition?' she repeated suspiciously, taking a step back from him.

Karasyn nodded. 'I've watched you. I respect your gift. But you'll never make a Guardsman.'

'I . . .' Elinor fell into confused silence. She did not know what to think.

'Long ago,' Master Karasyn said, 'there were three great weapons schools in Minmi, each teaching a different technique. Blood Star, Wind, and Lightning Wheel they were named. Young men vied with each other to join. And the three different schools vied with each other for supremacy. The Weapons Masters were great men in those days, respected by all, peers of both Lords and Seers.'

Karasyn sighed. 'But that was long and long ago. Both Blood Star and Wind are gone now, their teachings dying along with so much else over the years. Only the Lightning Wheel technique is still rememberd. And only through me. It is what I have been training you and all the rest in.'

Elinor regarded the Weapons Master uncertainly, not at all sure where he might be headed. 'Why are you telling me all this?' she asked.

'I reckon you could master the Lightning Wheel technique well enough. You have the gift for that.'

'But I thought ye just said I . . .'

'I am the last of the Lightning Wheel Masters, Kess. I have no sons. No apprentices. There's none amongst the Guard whom I'd consider to replace me. Rannis is one of the better ones, perhaps. But he relies too much on his own brute strength. As do they all. The *gift* is lacking amongst them, girl. I had begun to . . .'

Karasyn sighed. 'I had begun to think that the skills would die with me, as happened to Blood Star and Wind. There was nobody. Until *you* came along.'

Elinor did not know what to say.

Master Karasyn shook his head, shrugged. 'It is *most* irregular. My own Master would turn in his grave were he to know. But you, a girl, are the only person I can think of whose gift makes her worthy of the Lightning Wheel inheritance.'

Karasyn looked at her closely and his eyes almost shone now. 'There is *much* I could teach you, girl. Everything! You could learn it, I know you could! You might not have the brute strength to carry off a Guard's duties, but you could *teach* them the proper use of the blade. You could carry on the great tradition after I'm dead and gone. It need not die with me . . .'

'Would . . . would any of them be willing to learn from me?' Elinor said, more than a little bitterly. 'Me, a . . . a mere *girl*?'

Karasyn shrugged. 'I could make you good enough so that they would *have* to learn from you. And after I am gone . . . Who else *could* they learn from?'

Elinor closed her eyes, tried to imagine what it might be like. Master of the Lightning Wheel blade school . . . She thought of herself as she might become, older, stronger, respected by all. The Kess side of her was drawn to the notion. But the Elinor side . . . That part of her was less certain. Was this to be the fruition of all her Long Harbour yearnings, then? They had been entirely unfocused, those girlhood yearnings of hers – mostly daydreams and unrealistic fantasies, she now realized. But, even given that, a life spent here in crumbling, strange Minmi did not seem . . . enough, somehow. And Karasyn's dream seemed all nostalgia . . .

'Think about it, Kess,' the Weapons Master was saying. 'It would make a good life for you, a *good* life, worthy of respect.'

Elinor was not sure how to respond. She thought momentarily of old Tildie's insistence on her being an . . . axle. What if there was truth in what the old woman had said? How would that affect the outcome of anything? And what of Rannis and she? Where would *that* lead?

'Think on it, girl,' Karasyn said. 'No need to commit yourself on the spur of the moment. Just remember what I have said here this night. Remember what I have offered you.'

Elinor nodded. There was an intensity to the Weapons Master she did not really understand.

He stood staring at her.

It made her belly flutter, this silent, staring intensity of his. 'Is there . . . something you're not telling me?' she asked finally.

He shrugged, swallowed. 'Lord Mattingly has sent for you.'

She blinked. 'Now? It's the middle of the night.'

He nodded. 'He insists. The boy's stubborn as any mule when he sets himself to anything. Always has been. He wants to see you now.'

'But why . . .'

'Why did I make the little . . . speech to you that I did?' Karasyn shrugged again. 'I have no notion as to what Mattingly may want with you. But I *value* you, girl. I wanted you to know you have a future here with me and mine. In case . . .'

'In case of *what*?'

'In case Mattingly makes you some sort of . . . offer.'

'Such as?'

'I don't know. But he's taken an interest in you. It's unlike him, that. I don't know . . .' Karasyn shook his head. 'Come along now.'

'Now? This instant?'

Karasyn nodded. 'He's waiting.'

Elinor held back. 'I don't want . . .'

'There's no use refusing. Lord Mattingly gets what he wants. One way or another. I'd hate to have you brought before him bound and captive.'

Elinor stared at him. 'You would do that? After all you've just said?'

Karasyn nodded. 'Loyalties, girl. I have my responsibilities.' He looked at her a little anxiously. 'But such drastic methods will not be necessary, will they?'

She sighed. 'No. Of course not.'

He nodded relievedly. 'Come then. There is a man waiting outside. Lyle, his name is. You may remember him. One of the court flunkies. Odious little rats, he and his like. Climbing over each other's backs in a graceless scramble for position and influence.' Karasyn made a disgusted face. 'But we are stuck with them. Lyle maintains he has a special claim upon you, since you were his . . . gift to Lord Mattingly. So it is he who shall escort you. Are you ready?'

Elinor shrugged, nodded.

Out the door Karasyn ushered her, then down the hall a little ways to where Peer Lyle stood waiting.

'Ahh . . .' Lyle said, seeing them. He made an elaborate little bow. 'A pleasure to see you again, Kess.'

Elinor nodded. Lyle looked just as Kess remembered him, the fur-trimmed cape and fancy clothes set with giltwork and winking stones, the thigh-high leather boots, the elaborate-pommelled, needle-slim sword.

'Thank you, Weapons Master,' Lyle said formally. 'You may leave us now.'

Karasyn hesitated a moment, regarding Lyle coldly. 'Remember what I said, girl,' he said in a soft voice to Elinor. Then he turned and stalked off.

'This way,' Lyle said, picking up a candle-lantern at his feet. 'Follow me.'

Elinor did.

'When you talk with Lord Mattingly,' Lyle told her as they walked along, their footsteps echoing softly in the dark stone corridor, 'remember to show the proper respect. Always say, "my Lord". And, whatever you do, avoid using that barbarous "ye" you employed that first time. It sends him wild, that sort of thing.'

The corridor turned, and they took a flight of steps upwards. 'And don't forget that it was *I* who first brought you to him,' he added. 'You might mention that now and again.'

Elinor stayed silent, concentrating on keeping herself stable; her legs had a tendency to buckle unpredictably as she walked.

She felt off-balance. Too much was happening too quickly.

Horrifying capture and miraculous rescue. The return of her lost self. Tildie's revelations. Rannis – she had not had enough time yet even to begin to know how she felt about what had happened between them. Weapons Master Karasyn's offer. And now this sudden night-summons from mad Lord Mattingly.

She did not know where it all might be leading . . .

XXIII

Peer Lyle ushered Elinor past a contingent of Guards outside the big double doors, who removed Lyle's slim sword and searched them both thoroughly before allowing them into the dimly lit chamber where she had first seen Lord Mattingly. Two of the night-Guard came into the chamber with them as escort, flanking them on either side.

The first time she had been here, there had been lines of Guards, the glittering congregation of hangers-on. Now, except for the faint sputtering of the candelabras, the place was silent, vacant. Only Lord Mattingly himself reclined upon the softly glimmering, parti-coloured silken blankets of his dais, alone save for the creature that was his constant companion – a Lamure, Tildie had named it – sitting alert upon his lap.

Peer Lyle bowed deeply. 'As you requested, Lord. I have brought her.'

Lord Mattingly nodded. 'Good. Now leave.'

Peer Lyle blinked. 'But, Lord, I had hoped . . .'

'Take him away,' Lord Mattingly ordered the Guard. 'And shut the door behind you and stay out, the both of you.'

'Are you . . . certain you wish us to leave you alone with her, Lord?' one of the two Guards asked, an older man. Elinor recognized neither of them – she still knew only a limited number of the Guard, and those mostly the newer recruits.

'Go,' Lord Mattingly said, shooing them away impatiently. 'Go!'

They left, taking a downcast Peer Lyle with them.

'Sit,' Mattingly commanded her then, pointing to a little stool that stood waiting in front of the dais. The Lamure climbed lithely up upon his shoulder, curling its tail about his throat in the way that it did – an intimate, slightly sinister gesture. It stared at her with its small, uncannily human eyes.

Elinor sat looking back with new surmise, knowing much more now than she had her first time here. She tried not to fidget.

'I heard you have been causing . . . disturbances,' Lord Mattingly said. He looked paler than ever, if that were possible, his eyes like dark liquid pools in the flickering light of the candelabras.

Elinor did not know what to say in response.

'My Seer is . . . deceased, thanks to you,' he went on in his hoarse, soft voice. 'Or so they tell me.'

Elinor swallowed. Had Mattingly had her brought here to be punished? Was that the reason for this sudden summons?

He stared at her in silence for long, long moments. Then he shrugged. 'Old Skolt was always a pain. I'm glad enough to be rid of him.' He smiled, a quick flash of sharp white teeth. 'Are you recovered from your ordeal, then?'

Elinor blinked, nodded. 'I am . . . well enough, Lord,' she replied, remembering how she was supposed to address this man.

Lord Mattingly remained silent for long moments further, staring at her still.

Elinor coughed nervously. 'And . . . you?' she asked impulsively, to fill the uncomfortable silence. She shivered, not sure if she had blundered or not with such a personal enquiry.

Lord Mattingly sighed. 'I . . . suffer.'

Silence once more.

Elinor swallowed, uncertain how to continue.

'I suffer,' he repeated.

Surely Lord Mattingly had not summoned her here merely to complain about his ailing health? It seemed ridiculous. He must have all the eager physicians he could possibly need to attend him.

'I *suffer*,' he said a third time.

'I am sure you do, Lord,' she responded uncertainly. 'The cares of yer . . . your great office must lie heavily upon you.'

Lord Mattingly shook his head, his white silky hair floating in a pale aureole. 'You sound as if somebody has been coaching you.' He sighed. 'Nobody understands me.'

Elinor waited uncomfortably.

'Nobody *listens* to me,' he went on. His hoarse voice broke for an instant, and he stopped, swallowed, coughed softly. 'They're all so . . . so conniving . . .' He shuddered, fell silent, gazed off blindly into nothing.

For a moment, he seemed to Elinor like a lost little boy. His face was pale as new bone in the chamber's candlelight, the skin stretched like parchment. There were blue smudges of exhaustion under his eyes.

The creature seated with him reached one of its little hands over and stroked Mattingly's silky pale hair, as a mother might to soothe an ailing child. He pushed the animal's hand gently away and looked at Elinor from the corner of his eye. 'Do you not wonder what it is that ails me so?'

'Why . . . the cares of your great office, Lord,' she said, hoping to strike the right sort of placating tone with him that she had seen others use to soothe him.

'Oh, don't be so *stupid*!' he snapped with sudden viciousness, jerking upwards on the dais and spilling the Lamure from his knee.

Elinor faltered back, overturning the stool in her surprise and falling sideways to her knees awkwardly.

Mattingly laughed. 'See? That's what happens when you talk to me like all the rest.'

She lurched to her feet in embarrassment, not knowing what to say.

'Sit,' he commanded. He gathered his creature back to him, gesturing impatiently at the stool with the other hand.

After a moment's hesitation, Elinor righted the stool and resumed her place before him.

'Talk to me,' he said, 'as you would to any other person.'

'Lord?'

'*Talk* to me!'

'Aye, Lord,' she replied. 'But . . . what . . . what does ye wish me to . . .'

'Not that foreign gibberish! Hasn't Karasyn taught you to talk properly yet?'

Elinor bit her lip. 'Aye, Lord, he has.'

'Then *do* so!'

'Aye, Lord.'

'And stop "aye Lording" me. It grates on my nerves!'

'Aye . . .' She coughed, swallowed. 'Yes, Lord Mattingly.'

He stared at her demandingly with his big, dark, liquid eyes. 'Well?'

She coughed again. 'I . . . Lord, what is it you want of me? Why have you had me brought here?'

'Ah . . .' Mattingly breathed. 'Finally.' He brushed his spidery hair from his face. 'A good question, that.' He smiled a feral smile, showing his small sharp teeth. 'I *do* want something of you. A service.'

'Lord?' she said with unease. The Elinor part of her had too many bad memories to like the direction this conversation seemed to be taking suddenly.

'I suffer,' Lord Mattingly said, 'from a . . . a morbid *acuteness* of the senses.' He paused for a moment, reached one hand down and caressed the silken material of his robe. 'I can wear only the sheerest, softest clothing.' He stroked the mahogany fur of the creature on his lap. 'Only the finest of furs. The feel of coarse wool –' he shuddered '– makes me vomit. The odours of flowers oppress me.' He gestured to the large, dimly lit room in which they sat. 'Anything more than the softest of lights is a torture to my poor eyes. And only a few sounds do not fill me with horror.'

She did not know what to say.

Lord Mattingly shuddered. 'Presiding over the . . . the loud confusion of court here is *agony* for me.' He sighed a long sigh. 'Do you not pity me?'

She nodded in what she hoped would seem an understanding manner.

Lord Mattingly sighed again. 'The selfish, glittering, chattering rabble that crowd round me here are all shallow, posturing *ingrates*! Like that Lyle. He and his sort care nothing for my sufferings, nothing for the sacrifices I make every day to keep their precious court alive.'

'But surely,' she began, 'Master Karasyn . . .'

Mattingly laughed bitterly. 'He served my father well enough. But my father was a strong man – strong and dull and stolid like an old bull. All Karasyn cares for is his precious Guard and his old Lightning Wheel school. He cares *nothing* for me!'

'But that's not true!' she said impulsively. 'Why, I know that he . . .'

'*Don't* contradict me, girl!'

She lurched up off her stool. 'First ye tells me to talk to ye like . . . like I would any *normal* person, and now ye snaps at me for doing just that!' She stopped abruptly, panting, her heart racing. Mattingly was staring at her.

She felt a sudden chill go through her. Nobody, she was certain, talked to him that way.

'Well . . .' he murmured. Then again, 'Well, well . . .'

She did not know what to do, standing there awkwardly.

'Sit,' he said.

'And, '*Sit*!' when she hesitated

She sat.

His creature had come forward, its little hands gripping the front edge of the dais, staring at her. She tried to ignore it but as she had on her first visit here, she found herself struck by the uncanny similarity between the two sets of eyes regarding her – animal and human. She shivered under their dark, liquid, unblinking gazes.

'You *are* just the sort of creature I've been looking to find,' Mattingly murmured after a little.

Which enlightened her not at all.

'How is your training coming along, then?' he asked.

She blinked. 'I . . . Master Karasyn says I have a certain natural gift for such work.'

Mattingly nodded. 'So I understand. You handle a blade well enough, from what I saw.' He levered himself to the edge of the dais, swung his satin-slippered feet carefully to the floor, stood up.

It was the first time she had ever seen him on his feet. He was smaller than she had thought, hardly coming to her shoulder. Turning from her, he set off across to the back corner of the big chamber, the Lamure scampering along behind. He walked with a pronounced limp, dragging his left foot behind him. It was misshapen, she saw, club-shaped.

'Come,' he ordered, looking back over his shoulder and beckoning her.

She hesitated.

'Come *on*! And stop staring!'

She got quickly to her feet and followed after him, keeping her gaze carefully neutral.

He led her to the chamber's far back corner. There was a

small wooden door there, set into the stone wall. Mattingly lifted the latch, opened it, waved her in before him.

All was dark beyond. She hesitated, turned to him. 'What do you want with me, Lord?'

'A service,' he replied. 'As I told you.'

'What *manner* of service?'

Mattingly laughed softly. 'A service none other in all of Minmi can render me.' He gestured to the creature at his side. 'Spandel,' he said, and it skipped nimbly through into the darkness on the doorway's far side. Then he pointed at her. 'Now you, too.'

Elinor hesitated still. 'But, Lord Mattingly . . .'

He shoved her, a hard, unexpected thrust of both hands against the small of her back, sending her stumbling awkwardly through the doorway. Before she could gather her wits or limbs together, he had come through himself and shut the door behind.

There was a little *spluutt* of sound and Mattingly held up a candle-lantern. By its glow, she saw that they were in a small, windowless room. The walls were hung with tapestries, sub-dued designs that made no sense but, somehow, seemed to soothe the eyes. There was no sign of the door through which they had come – only the tapestries. In the back corner stood a little canopied bed.

'My own room,' Mattingly said. 'None but I has ever set foot in here.' He sighed. 'Until now.'

She stared at him. 'Why . . . *me*, Lord? I don't understand.'

'You will, soon enough,' he replied.

She backed away, staring about her.

At the bed's foot was a wooden chest. Across from that, a tall wooden cupboard stood against another wall, next to a fire in a little hearth fronted by an ornate iron gate – nothing more than a bed of barely glowing coals now. Mattingly went over to the cupboard, his satin-slippered feet making no sound on the rugs that lay scattered thickly across the stone floor. Holding up the lantern, he swung the cupboard door open – the hinges went *kreeek* softly – and drew out one-handedly a rod-like, arm's-length object wrapped in dark, soft felt.

'Here,' he said, turning and offering it to her.

She hesitated.

'Take it!' Mattingly snapped, thrusting the wrapped object at her.

She took it. Under the thick folds of cloth, it felt hard, solid, weighty.

'Unwrap it,' he ordered, stepping closer and holding up his lantern.

Slowly, uneasy under his intent and unblinking stare, she knelt and placed the thing upon the rugs, lifted back the folds of dark felt until it lay revealed.

It was a sword in an ornate scabbard.

'Take it up,' Mattingly commanded.

She shook her head, knowing that nobody was permitted to hold a weapon in Lord Mattingly's presence save the duty Guards in the court chamber.

'Take it up!' he insisted.

She looked at him. Under the lantern-light, his eyes were like black, burning coals in his bone-pale face. His creature had leaped upon his shoulder again and stared at her with the same uncanny fixedness of Mattingly's own gaze. She felt the hairs along her neck prickle uncomfortably. It was an utterly mad stare, that look of his, utterly fixed, utterly compelling.

'Take it up!' he repeated.

Slowly, she reached. The scabbard was lacquered leather, a deep alizarin crimson, bound round with an intricate braiding of glimmering bronze wire. The sword's hilt, too, was bronze, with a simple double tang. The pommel was cleverly fashioned into a snarling dragon's head with glinting ruby eyes. She seemed to feel a little tingling shock go through the bones of her fingers and hand as she took possession of the sword's hilt. The grip was strangely warm. She felt the weight of the thing in her hand. It was perhaps a touch longer than the iron swords she had been training with. But this one felt far lighter in her hold, more comfortably balanced – and this while still in its scabbard.

'Draw it,' Lord Mattingly said.

After a long moment's hesitation, she did.

She gasped. Holding this sword, the Kess aspect of her seemed to surge up, like a furled flower expanding. She felt a rush of energy thrill through her limbs. In the radiance of Mattingly's little lantern, the blade gleamed like a long, narrow length of silver mirror. It was a straight, double-edged blade, very like what she was now used to, but the gleaming length of it was perfect, without blemish of any sort. She felt along its shining edge and slit her thumb, it was so unexpectedly sharp. Holding the ornate scabbard in her left hand, she made a couple of experimental passes with the blade, all pure Kess now, all focused on the blade. It seemed to fit her grip perfectly, to balance perfectly. The blade shimmered like white fire as it arced through the air, like it was light itself.

'It's . . . *beautiful*,' she murmured.

'It is a named blade,' Lord Mattingly said. 'An old blade. Made in my grandfather's grandfather's time.' He smiled. 'See how it gleams and glitters? No common blade at all. My grandfather's grandfather witnessed a great bit of star matter come plunging earthwards, all fire and thunder. He retrieved the thing – a molten lump, like the severed head of some monstrous demon, flung from the heights with such force it had buried itself more than two men's height in the earth. From *that* he decreed that the blade be made. Stronger than iron, more flexible, sharp as any razor . . . There is no weapon like it.'

Mattingly held his lantern closer to the sword's perfect blade, making it gleam brightly. 'The smith who crafted this was uncommonly skilled. See how utterly perfect the blade is? It was his master-work. And afterwards . . . Afterwards, my grandfather's grandfather had him put to death.'

Mattingly shrugged, seeing her shocked look. 'It is a named blade, as I say. In those far-off days of my grandfather's grandfather, it was known as The White Tooth of the Great Shining Dragon.' He laughed softly. 'A long name, that. I have renamed it. Fang, I call it now. It is yours.'

'Wha-what?' she stammered.

'It is yours,' Lord Mattingly repeated.

She stared.

'Consider it payment for the service I will demand of you.'

She blinked, shook her head. She stared at the sword, shivering. Kess wanted the thing. The Elinor aspect of her was not so certain. She sheathed it in one quick movement and laid it down upon the felt wrappings. Her hand immediately itched for it. Kess ached for it.

Lord Mattingly frowned.

'Lord Mattingly,' she said as calmly as she could, regathering herself. 'Ye . . . you cannot give such a thing to the likes of me. It isn't . . . proper.'

'I can do anything I wish!' he snapped petulantly.

'But *think*! What would I do with such a fine thing? I am naught but one of the Guard. Do you think my companions would accept me with a treasure such as this dangling from my belt? Do you think Master Karasyn would accept it?'

'Karasyn has nothing to do with this!'

'But he *does*, Lord. I serve under him.'

Mattingly leaned closer to her. 'Take it up!' he commanded, pointing at the sword. There was a little gleaming ribbon of spittle dribbling from the corner of his mouth, she suddenly saw. His breath was harsh and rasping. The hand pointing to the sword shook as if he had an ague.

'What is it, Lord?' she asked uneasily. 'What's wrong?'

'Take up the sword!' he shouted.

'No. I cannot!'

Mattingly thrust his white, clenched face close against hers. 'You will . . .' he was panting like a hound '. . . do as I . . . *command*. Take . . . it . . . *up*!'

She backed away from him, looked desperately about, searching the hanging tapestries for some indication of where the hidden door might be. Suddenly, from the far side of the wall to her right, she heard voices. 'In here!' she called out impulsively.

'Shut up!' Mattingly hissed.

The voices grew louder, shouts of enquiry.

She shouted back, moved towards the wall.

Mattingly grabbed her by the shoulders and spun her back about, showing sudden, surprising strength. 'Shut *up*, you fool! You'll ruin *everything*!'

She tried to pull away from him, but he held fast. 'The service . . .' he panted, 'the *service* I require from you!'

The voices outside had grown louder, clearer. Somebody started thumping on the door with a sword's pommel or some such: *ta-wakk ta-wakk*.

'Go *away*!' Mattingly shouted at them. But it only served to make those outside – whoever they were – redouble their efforts against the door.

'Fools!' he panted. 'Fools, *fools*! I'm surrounded by stupid, insensate *FOOLS*!' He turned and glared at her. Picking up the sword, he started towards her. '*You* . . . you will do . . . as I *COMMAND*!'

She stumbled away from him.

'Here!' He held out the sword to her, hilt foremost. 'Take it, you silly, stupid little bitch. Take it!' He flung the thing at her. She had no choice but to catch it – that or get it full across her face.

The sounds from outside the room grew louder – more voices, more hammering.

'Draw it!' Mattingly cried, his voice a harsh croak.

She shied away from him, holding up the still-sheathed sword in self-defence.

Mattingly stood before her, having backed her into a corner. 'Draw the blade,' he ordered. 'Kill me.'

She only stared.

'Are you deaf? I said *kill* me. Now! Before it is too late.'

She could only stand, frozen, shocked.

'I cannot endure any more of it,' he went on. 'Do you think I haven't *tried*? I cannot *endure* another *moment*. Kill me and let me have done.' He ripped apart his silken robe, exposing his bony, white breast to her. 'Kill me and put an end to this torment I suffer. There's not a living soul else in Minmi I can ask this of. None of them would do it. Only *you*, the barbarian foreigner. Kill me! *Kill me*!'

The door hidden behind the hangings splintered suddenly, and Elinor saw half a dozen or so Guards come tumbling into the room, shoulder to shoulder, with more behind. They were strangers to her – all save one. With a shock, she recognized one for a companion of Lotch's.

'Mad *bitch*!' the man screamed. 'She's trying to assassinate Lord Mattingly!' He leaped at her, naked sword in hand

The Kess part of her instinctively drew the blade in her hands. Once again, she felt a little prickling thrill run through her at the touch of the sword's strangely warm hilt. Strength seemed to fill her, making her heart jump.

Three of them came at her together, Lotch's companion foremost. She parried his initial cut, her own blade a flashing arc of light, the two swords *kringging* harshly. With the scabbard in her other hand, she swiped at the eyes of the second man, driving him back. The third let her be for a moment, turning to herd Lord Mattingly safely to one side.

Lotch's companion cut at her again, a vicious low slash that would have taken her leg off if it had connected. Cornered as she was, she could only leap up. His blade rang against the stone wall behind her in a splash of sparks. In his fury, he overreached himself. She saw it plain. Before he could recover, she slashed at his arm, a blow intended only to stop him, a quick cut across the muscles of his forearm.

The razor-sharp white blade severed the arm entire.

For a long, stunned moment, nobody moved.

She stared, shaken as the rest. It was no feather-light weapon she wielded, for all that it seemed so in her hold.

Lotch's companion screamed, holding up the stump of his arm in horror, blood pumping from it in a wet, red fountain to soak the carpets underfoot.

Almost, she threw the blade from her in dread, the Elinor part of her appalled at what she – what the blade – had done.

But they came at her in a rush then, as many as could crowd forward in the little room.

The very press of them proved their own undoing, however, for they could not get proper elbow room and kept fouling each other's strokes. She parried and thrust, the shining sword light and perfect in her hands. She felt a kind of rush, part horror, part fear, part something else entirely – like nothing she had ever experienced. Her heart thumped. Her limbs shivered, quivered, thrilled with quickening energy. She leaped and whirled and dodged and struck in perfect, flashing balance. Holding the white blade, she was somehow stronger, quicker, surer than she ought to be.

Three men were down before her, groaning. She was not altogether sure how. Lotch's companion lay white as chalk, his limbs thrust out awkwardly. Her feet squished on the blood-wet carpet.

Those who could backed hastily away from her, pale-faced.

'Reinforcements!' somebody cried. 'We need more men here!'

'Stay clear of that sword!' another panted. 'It's . . . it's a spell-sword of some sort. We need pike-men . . . Look what it did to poor Barlinan!'

More men poured into the room, shouting. Seeing what had happened, the new arrivals were abruptly silent. Two slid nervously in and dragged away those whom she had wounded. For long moments after that nobody moved, nobody spoke.

She stood with her back to the wall, in the centre of a cleared, blood-soaked space. With a shock, she began to recognize some of the Guard who had just arrived. She had sparred with them. They were the closest thing to friends she had in Minmi. How could any of this be happening?

Abruptly, Lord Mattingly surged up from where he had been led for safety's sake. 'Back!' he shouted to the Guards.

They moved away, hesitant yet obedient still.

'Lord!' somebody called out. 'Do not . . .'

Mattingly flung himself at her.

The sword came up almost of its own accord. Mattingly thrust himself upon it, and the razor-edged, shining blade seemd to sink cleanly through his breast with almost no effort at all.

Mattingly laughed triumphantly. He pulled away, the sword jerking in her hands. She could not relinquish the thing somehow, but hung on so that it grated out of Mattingly's breast, running wetly with his life's blood.

She stared, horror-struck, as the young lord did a halting little turn then collapsed on his knees, hands to his breast. Blood bubbled through his fingers. His white face was aglow with mad triumph. 'Yes!' he cried. '*Yes!*'

The Guard stared, unbelieving.

Mattingly's little creature came skipping over to him. He embraced it with one blood-soaked hand, bent his head as if whispering some last words of farewell. He looked across at Elinor, his face creasing into a final, triumphant smile. Then he fell back weakly, blood gushing from his breast.

'Kill her!' one of the Guards cried out, and they launched themselves in a furious rush towards her.

XXIV

Mattingly's uncanny gift-sword arced through the air as they came at her, like white lightning in her hand. Kess was exalted, feeling the blood sing in her veins, the sword warm and sure in her hold and deadly quick as a striking serpent.

As before, she felt the terrible perfection of it: she took one man's sword hand off at the wrist, and laughed, doing it. She split another's face, sending him reeling back, shrieking, caught a third man in the belly and ripped him open like a wet sack.

It felt wonderful. It felt terrible. It felt . . .

She did not know what was happening to her. She danced through the steps and the motions of the fighting technique that Karasyn had taught her, quick and sure and untouchable. And though it struck her attackers with bruising, heavy force, the sword continued to feel light in her grasp – everything the clumsy iron blades she had been using were not – perfectly balanced, a shining extension of her own arm.

At moments, the blade seemed to have a mind of its own, almost, for she found herself guarding against the thrusts and slashes of those against her before she even knew properly where to turn. And nothing could stand against its gleaming razor edge. It bit into the iron blades pitted against her, sliced through flesh and bone as cleanly as any ordinary blade carving a garden melon.

The White Tooth of the Great Shining Dragon, Mattingly had named it. Fang. A wicked tooth indeed. She could almost feel the dragon strength flowing through her.

It was most terribly *strange*.

The Elinor part of her was appalled. The Kess part . . . not. Something there was in the blade that spoke directly to Kess, a hot, seductive, exciting calling.

*

The Guardsmen had rushed in, engaged her, fallen back, all in the space of twice a dozen heartbeats.

She stood with the white blade up in what Karasyn called the Double Tree, a two-handed defensive posture with feet braced, her back to the tapestried wall. Her breath came in painful, harsh gasps, and she was bloodied all across one side. But it was none of her blood. They had not managed so much as to scratch her.

'Rush her, you fools!' somebody cried. 'Cowards!'

A man came at her, his mouth contorted in a scream. She took him through the ribs, sidestepping his clumsy, hysterical rush and thrusting the white blade in and out before he truly knew what had happened. He spun about, eyes wide and shocked, then sank against the wall.

She resumed the Double Tree stance.

Silence, then, save for the sound of panting breaths and the soft, burbling moan of the man whose face she had slit open.

Lord Mattingly lay in his own blood on the rug-covered floor, sprawled on his back, staring with dead eyes at the ceiling. His face held the remnants of his final, triumphant smile, though frozen now into a kind of parody of itself.

Nobody moved for long, long moments. White-faced and stricken, the Guardsmen stared at her over the bodies of their dead and wounded.

Through the door to the room more Guards came pouring. Amongst them was Karasyn. The Weapons Master stared. 'No . . .' he breathed, his voice barely audible, even in the room's silence. '*No!*' He looked as if somebody had taken him through the belly with a lance. She could not meet his eyes.

Then Mattingly's creature came bounding forth suddenly out of nowhere. Before Elinor knew what was happening, it was perched on her shoulder, hissing in her ear: 'This way! This, this, this way!'

It yanked at her hair, turning her head. 'There's a hidden door. Here. Quick. Oh, quick, quick, *quick*!' One of its small hands reached out and gripped the edge of a tapestry, tugging.

She dived for it, shrugging aside the heavy length of fabric and finding a short, hidden passage-way beyond.

There was a howl of outraged fury from behind her.

A few paces ahead, she could see a small wooden door. She

grabbed at it, yanked it open, flung herself through, slammed it behind – all in one instant. There was a locking bar this side and she swung it in place just in time. The door buckled as something slammed into it from the other side. It shuddered and shook, but the bar held. She heard more howling from the far side.

'This way,' Mattingly's creature said, and she realized it was still clinging to her shoulder.

'Quick, quick, quick!' it urged.

She did not know what to make of such a creature, whether she could trust it or no. But there was scant time for dithering. The Guard meant to kill her, sure as sure. Following the creature was a chance of life, at any rate. She was not about to go Mattingly's route.

She went as it directed and hared off along one of the typical, torch-lit Minmi corridors, the sword out in one hand, the scabbard thrust crossways through her belt – though how she had managed to hang on to the scabbard and stick it there she had no idea.

'Quick! Oh, quick, *quick*!' the creature repeated in her ear, and she ran fast as her legs would go, skittering over the stone floor, bouncing clumsily off the wall when the corridor bent suddenly, running, running, till her lungs burned and her side cramped painfully – running till she could go no further and had to stagger to a halt, bent double, gasping, shoulder against the wall for support.

When she was able to breathe again, and think, she looked about. This corridor was no different from any of the rest: dim, dank, seemingly coming from nowhere, leading to nowhere. She could hear the sound of water dripping. Shouts echoed behind her, but distantly.

Mattingly's creature had slipped from her shoulder and was on the floor, looking at her. 'This way,' it said in its small voice. 'I will lead you out. To safety, safety, safety.'

'Safety?' she said. 'Where?'

'Outside. Beyond the walls.'

Elinor took a sharp breath. Could it be true? Could this strange being really lead her outside Minmi? She shivered, sweaty and chilled at the same time, sticky with men's blood, sick and exultant and confused and terrified, all at once.

She looked down at the sword. The blade glimmered whitely in the torchlight, webbed with drying blood. She shifted it in her grip, bringing the hilt up, and the little ruby eyes of the bronze dragon's head that formed the pommel seemed to stare at her challengingly.

She felt a sudden revulsion go through her. In her mind's eye, she saw the look of horror on the face of the poor man whose sword hand she had severed. Thinking of what she had done with this blade, and the terrible ease with which she had been able to do it, made her suddenly sick in the pit of her belly.

'Quick! Quick!' Mattingly's creature hissed at her. '*Quick!*'

Behind, she heard shouts and cries, drawing closer.

She could not quite believe any of this was happening. She had been on the cusp of a new life here, what with the promise of Rannis and Master Karasyn's offer and all. And now . . .

She recalled Mattingly's final, triumphant, mad smile. He had flung himself upon the blade with the desperation of a drowning man flinging himself upon a floating log. And the blade . . . the blade had seemed as eager as he.

Had Mattingly been planning it all since that first day he had seen her before him when she had been newly dragged off the strand? He and his creature . . .

'An axle,' old Tildie had said of her. 'One around whom the events of the world turn . . .'

She did not know what to think.

'Oh, hurry, hurry, *hurry*!' Mattingly's creature urged her. It leaped to her shoulder, grabbing at her hair, its limber tail curling about her neck for purchase – as she had seen it do with Mattingly.

She shuddered and wrenched the tail away, nearly threw the creature from her.

It looked at her, its eyes wide with shock.

'Not my throat!' she said. 'Keep your tail from my throat.'

It stared at her a moment longer, then nodded. 'We must go! Hurry, hurry, hurry!'

She started off again, moving at a staggering jog, too spent and shaken to run properly any more.

Behind, the sounds of pursuit were mounting.

The dim corridors seemed to go on forever.

'This way,' the creature directed. 'Along by here, here.' But each time they turned a corner, there was only more corridor, without end.

Elinor stopped, exhausted, shaking. Her arm ached. She still held the glimmering sword naked in her hand, up before her, ready, afraid to sheath it lest they came upon some of her pursuers unexpectedly.

'Run. Run!' the creature urged. 'Run!'

'I cannot,' she gasped. 'I have to rest . . .'

'No time to rest. Not now. Not yet!'

She heard echoing sounds from behind and staggered off, pushing against the wall to get started.

The corridor sloped downwards, took a sharp veer to the left. There was virtually no light down here, and she paused uncertainly.

But, 'This way. This way!' the creature directed, tugging at her to make her turn rightwards.

It must be able to see in the dark, she realized. She following its directing, stumbling along, her free hand out in case she walked unexpectedly into anything.

'Faster! Faster. Oh, faster!'

Along the corridor she went in a staggering run, round a corner, round another. The sounds of pursuit dwindled a little.

And then, suddenly, there was someone ahead.

The sword came up and she felt a sudden rush of strength. She charged the man, intent on spitting him and getting away before anybody else could come at her from behind.

'Kess!' he called.

She skidded to a halt. Against all expectation and probability, it was Rannis.

Rannis . . .

He stared at her, drawn sword in hand. 'What have you *done*, Kess?'

'I . . . I . . .' She did not know how to respond.

'They say you . . . you *murdered* Lord Mattingly. Is it true?'

She shook herself, lifted the shining blade for him to see. 'He . . . he flung himself upon the sword. I couldn't do anything to prevent it.'

Rannis stared at her, his face clenched with emotion. 'But

he's dead, Kess. *Dead*! And you held the blade that killed him! How could you *do* such a thing?'

'I tell you, it was all *his* doing. He said he wanted me to do him a service. He brought me into his private chamber. Gave me this blade.' She held the blood-laced white blade up again. 'He . . . he just *flung* himself on to it . . .'

'And the Guard, Kess? What of them? They say you've killed some of the Guard, too. Is it true?'

'They came at me, Rannis. They would have killed me! What was I to do?'

Rannis hesitated, shuffled his feet. He lifted the sword he held and pointed to the creature perched still on her shoulder. 'And what are you doing with *that*?'

She did not know how to answer. She did not know, herself, what the little creature was about. It had come to her on that first day, she remembered, as she stood before Lord Mattingly, whispering, 'He needs you, girl. Needs, needs, needs you,' in that odd, repetitive manner of speaking that it had. Had it known all along, then, about Mattingly's suicidal plans?

She shook her head, took a step forwards. 'Let me pass,' she implored.

'I can't, Kess.' Rannis brought his sword up to a guard position.

'I'm innocent! I didn't do anything. It was all a mistake. All mad Mattingly's doing. He *planned* it all, Rannis.'

Somebody shouted in the distance behind. They looked at each other. She moved closer to him. 'Let me pass. *Please*!'

She could see the tension in him. His hand, gripping his sword's hilt, quivered.

'We . . . we could have had so *much*, Kess,' he said, his voice hoarse. 'You and me. Why did you have to go and do this mad, terrible thing?'

'I *didn't* do it, I tell ye! Hasn't ye been listening? It was Mattingly's doing all along. Never mine!' She went closer to him, her own sword carefully down, point towards the floor. 'Let me pass.'

He shook his head. 'I . . . cannot.'

She looked at him. 'Rannis? *Please*!'

'Oh, *Kess*,' he said, moaning almost. His sword dropped slowly.

219

She stepped forward and reached her left hand to his. For a moment they just stood, looking into each other's eyes, neither knowing quite what would happen in the next instant.

And then there came a shout from behind. 'There she is!'

Followed by: 'Look! She has an accomplice. Get them!'

Men came tumbling along the corridor in a yelling, furious mass.

'No!' Rannis cried. 'Wait! You don't . . . I'm not –'

But his voice was drowned in the din.

Elinor dropped Rannis's hand, brought up her sword defensively. The blade flashed in the torchlight.

None of her attackers seemed eager to be the first to engage her. They bottle-necked in the narrow corridor, hampering each other, cursing. But then one man erupted from the mass and came at her. She took his first cut on her sword in a double-hand defence. It was a heavy overhand blow and his iron blade chittered along hers to *quangg* up against the hilt. She felt the force of the blow all the way up to her shoulder joints.

For an instant they were hilt to hilt, nose to nose, his face pressed against hers. She saw the hatred in him, like a fire that lit him from inside. He grunted, tried to bring his knee up against her, spat in her face, wrenched his blade away, raising his arm to strike another blow at her. But he was not quick enough. She dug the dragon's head hilt of her own weapon into his ribs, kicked him as he faltered, thrust her blade tip through his shoulder and danced away, all in no more than half a dozen heartbeats. The man howled, dropped his sword, fell back to his knees.

She glanced across at Rannis, who stood staring at her, his sword slack in his hand. Mattingly's creature had been spilled from her shoulder and danced about behind Rannis, shrieking, gesturing at her to run.

But she could not. She dared not turn her back and flee, no more than any cornered animal could, facing a pack of yelping hounds.

The man she had hurt was still on his knees. 'Get her,' he groaned, urging his companions on. '*Get her*!'

There was a cry from those pressing near, and the lot of them charged in a mass.

It was shouting and grunting and blades all a-whirl like a mad storm, then. Elinor hardly knew what she did, skipping here and there, dancing away from one thrust or under another, her limbs thrilling with strange energy once more, the white blade in her hand singing through the air.

At one moment, she found herself pressed shoulder to shoulder with Rannis, and realized in a rush that he was fighting for his life alongside her, branded by the mob as her guilty accomplice. She felt the warmth of his side against hers. She found herself grinning unaccountably at him, panting, the sweat dripping off her nose. For a timeless instant, they looked at each other and she felt . . . she was not sure what exactly it was. Her heart soared.

And then they were driven apart by the fighting and she plunged into the whirling chaos of it.

How long the conflict lasted, she could not tell. Not long. Long enough. She fell into a kind of trance, not knowing exactly what she did or how, and came out of it to see the Guardsmen were fleeing, clambering desperately over each other in their haste. She stood, gasping, the blood pounding in her temples, exhausted and exalted, drained and filled. The wounded and the dead lay round about. Her arms ached. The white blade was soaked with men's blood.

And she was still untouched.

At her side, Rannis staggered over to lean against the wall. He had a long, bleeding gash across his ribs, his tunic hanging open in a torn flap. She rushed over anxiously to examine the wound, and found, to her relief, that it was shallow and not life-threatening. He stared at her, pale and shaken, gestured to the dead that lay about her in astonishment. 'How . . . how did you . . .' He gasped, swallowed, tried again. 'What has *happened* to you, Kess?'

She shrugged self-consciously, not knowing what to say, hardly understanding it herself. She looked at the bloody sword and shuddered.

Mattingly's creature came bounding in, then. 'Quick, quick, quick!' it shrieked. 'Oh, *quick*! This way. Before they return. Come, come, come! *Run*!' It bounded a few steps along the corridor, stopped, looked back at them with its round dark eyes shining wetly in the flicker of the torchlight. 'Come, *come*!'

Rannis stared.

Elinor staggered after it. Passing Rannis, she put a hand on his shoulder. 'Come on,' she urged him.

Poor Rannis looked to be in shock. His face was white as white and he seemed able to do nothing but stare: at her, at the bloody, gleaming blade still in her hand, at the wet gore that soaked her, at Mattingly's bounding, impatient, frantic creature.

'Come *on*,' she said again, taking him by the elbow and tugging.

He shrugged away from her touch as if she were some demon.

'Quick, *quick*!' Mattingly's creature cried, waving its little human hands frantically. 'This way!'

Pulling Rannis along, Kess hurried after as best she could, moving by instinct rather than any conscious volition now. She was utterly exhausted, shaken beyond proper thought. The creature beckoned and she followed, one hand gripping the sword still, the other on Rannis. When he stumbled, she pulled him up and along, staggering onwards. The corridor turned and branched, then branched again, and they kept on, and on, downwards, water dripping everywhere now, their footsteps echoing, water splashing, the corridor growing darker and darker and wetter till they walked ankle deep in cold black water.

'Quick, quick, quick!' Mattingly's creature cried.

They had left the last of the torches behind – too late, she thought of lifting one from its sconce and bringing it along – and it was dark as could be. She had to feel her way along, trusting the little creature's ability to see in the blackness, the heel of her sword hand against the wet stone of the wall, the other hand still on Rannis – who had said not a word. The water was almost to the middle of her calves now, cold and slimy-feeling and stinking of mildew and dark decay. She gagged, breathing through her mouth, trying not to smell it.

Onwards still the creature led, and onwards. She followed it by ear now, the splashing sounds it made being her only guide. The close, underground dark of the corridor made her shudder, reminding her too easily of the grave. Her heart stuttered. What if the creature – which clearly knew its way about – was leading

222

them down here only to strand them in some dark and noisome tomb? What if . . .

She thrust such thoughts aside, concentrating instead on moving forward.

Under her searching hand, the corridor took an abrupt bend to the right. As they splashed around that bend, Elinor gasped. Ahead, distant but clear enough, the corridor was illuminated by a softly shining, pewter radiance. She hurried on as fast as she could, seeing Mattingly's creature bounding across the stinking water towards that distant light.

The ceiling angled down till she was forced to walk in an uncomfortable stoop, hauling Rannis along awkwardly behind her. The light here seemed blinding after the blackness.

The walls narrowed. The water gushed loudly, funnelled as it was. Behind her, Rannis skidded, dragging her with him, and the two of them smacked painfully against the wall, staggering in the current, ducking to avoid the low ceiling, until they burst abruptly into light and outside air.

Elinor stumbled forwards, almost knee-deep in the coursing water, and stared about. They were out of the corridor, out of Minmi itself. The water flowing from the corridor forming a dirty stream that wound a way down a long, deserted, grassy slope. Ahead, far off in the distance, she could make out the hills – the same she had stared at longingly from her little Guards-room window – dark grey-green in early dawn-light, silhouetted against the pearly shine of the sky. The chill morning air made her shiver, but it felt clean as clean after the foetid dankness of the interior.

She staggered to solid ground and stood gazing about. The sun was slowly edging up past the shoulder of one of those far hills, pouring colour into the world. The great bulk of Minmi reared up and up. Lit by the new sun, the complex, inter-locked stone structures glowed ochre and russet. But what she saw were the shadows, purple-black, intricate, hiding who-knew-what? She shuddered and turned her back upon it.

Rannis splashed out of the water a little ways down from her and collapsed on the grassy bank with a grunt. She saw that somehow, despite everything, he had hung on to his sword. She realized that she still gripped hers as well.

Elinor felt dirty, sticky, wet and uncomfortable, desperate to wash the gore properly off herself, to wash the blood taste from her mouth, the smell from her face and limbs. Thinking on the things she had done, she felt her belly twist up at the sheer bloody horror of it. She had killed . . . she did not know how many men she had killed. Or maimed for life. Looking at the sword, she shuddered. Almost, she flung the gleaming, blood-ied, terrible thing away. But she could not.

Despite all, it felt too good to hold. The Kess side of her had no intention of abandoning it.

Mattingly's creature sat across the stream and looked at her. Its round dark eyes, circled by the bands of dark-coloured fur, did not have enough whites to be truly human – they were more like animal eyes in that aspect, dark and glistening. Yet, somehow, they were nonetheless very human, *too* human. And too reminiscent of mad Lord Mattingly's dark, luminous stare.

Rannis got to his feet and stumbled over to her. He took a long, shuddering breath, bent over, slipped on the grass, sat down with a thump and a little groan. He stared about him, silent still. She knelt next to him. Hesitantly, he reached out to her and she leaned close, gripping his hand in hers, careful of the razor-edged blade she still held in her other hand.

'We're *out*,' she said to him. 'We're *free*!'

The very word made her shiver.

She had escaped the confusing, twisty, dangerous maze of Minmi after all. And Rannis, too. And now . . .

Mattingly's creature bounced to its feet and beckoned with one of its little child's hands. 'Come, come, come!' it said.

Elinor sighed. She let Rannis go, straightened her weary limbs, stood up with an effort. 'Come on,' she said to Rannis.

'Whe . . . where *it* bids us go?' he said hoarsely. His side was soaked with blood, his face pale and clenched.

She shrugged. 'It led us out. To freedom.'

Rannis regarded the little Lamure with distaste, looked about at the long, empty grass slope suspiciously.

From the depths of the stone structure behind them there came the sudden sound of a horn. *Kree-taah! Kree-taah!* A brassy, strident blare that made the small hairs on her neck shiver.

Kree-taah! Kree-taah!

'The Great Horn,' Rannis said. He stood up. 'Nobody's sounded that since long before old Lord Patheron, mad Mattingly's father, died. Why . . .'

'Oh, quick, quick, quick!' Mattingly's creature cried. 'They sound it for us, for *us*!'

'*Us*?' Rannis echoed.

The little furred head bobbed in a quick series of nods. 'Quick! They will chase after us. Chase, chase, chase!'

Rannis stared at the great, sprawling, tumble-down stone mass of Minmi. He ran a hand dazedly across his eyes. 'Outside?'

'Yes!' the creature replied. 'We must flee, *flee*!'

Elinor was already on the move across the stream, splashing through the knee-deep, murky water. She was more than willing to turn her back on Minmi and flee, whether the Guard mounted a hunting party against them or not. She had had a belly full of the place – queer, cruel, confusing, complicated beyond all easy understanding as it was. Bending down, she wiped sticky blood from the white blade with a double handful of grass, careful not to slice her fingers on the keen double-edge, which had not been dulled in the slightest. Once the blade was clean, she sheathed it and threaded the sheath properly through her belt.

She staggered, feeling suddenly emptied. The Kess aspect of her dwindled. She gasped, finding it hard to get enough air. 'Come on,' she urged Rannis weakly.

Rannis was shivering, staring about him as if he expected demons to leap up out of the grass. He stared blankly out at the open, broken countryside. 'Out *there*?'

'Yes. Come on,' she urged.

'Only the crazies go outside,' he said.

'You mean you've never been beyond Minmi's walls before?'

He shivered. 'Never.'

'But how can you . . .'

The brassy horn sounded again: *Kree-taah! Kree-taah!*

'Come *on*!' she cried.

Rannis came splashing awkwardly across the stream to where she stood waiting. She tried to tug him onwards, but he

225

shrugged her off, bent stiffly, and began cleaning his bloodied sword – refusing her help curtly when she offered it. Done, he sheathed the blade and stood up, wincing, holding his bleeding side. He still looked dazed and stood there shaking his head, as if he had water in his ears.

The horn sounded one more time: *Kree-taah!*

'Quick, quick, quick!' Mattingly's creature cried, scampering off through the grass. 'Follow me.'

They did, stumbling wearily along the uneven slope.

'It could be leading us anywhere,' Rannis complained.

Far ahead, the green hills beckoned. Elinor shrugged. 'Anywhere's better than Minmi.'

'For *you* maybe,' Rannis grunted, his hand to his ribs.

After that, they were silent, trudging along behind Mattingly's bounding creature, making the best speed they could, the grass whisking about their legs, while, slowly, Minmi began to dwindle behind them.

XXV

'The creature's *gone*, I tell you,' Rannis said in no uncertain terms. 'Abandoned us here in this forsaken bit of wilderness.'

Elinor said nothing. It was just before dawn, and cold, and the two of them lay huddled together against the chill, tucked up uncomfortably against the roots of a huge, gnarly old willow. They had walked till the light failed, yesterday, then taken refuge for the night in the willow copse, seeing it looming before them in the gathering dark as they stumbled exhaustedly along behind Mattingly's creature.

Rannis shivered, feverish from his wound. She felt him fretting and uncomfortable, and wrapped her arms a little tighter about him, careful not to hurt. 'What sort of being is this creature of Mattingly's?' she asked, to keep his mind away from the pain of his wound, of their cramped position, of her own discomfort, still dirty and unwashed and smelling as she was. It was too cold to sleep any more – they had managed no more than fitful snatches in any case, fireless and shivering.

'What manner of being is Mattingly's creature?' she repeated, trying to coax Rannis into an answer. 'What did Tildie call it? A Lamure?'

He grunted agreement, then said, 'Spandel.'

'What?'

'Its name is Spandel.'

She remembered Mattingly using the name, now that he said it. 'Well? What manner of creature *is* it, then?'

Rannis shifted in her hold, wincing, careful of his gashed ribs, turning to bring his face closer to hers in the dark. She could feel his breath warm on her cheek. 'Spandel is . . . There was once . . .' he stopped, sighed. 'It would take too long to explain it all to you, foreigner that you are.'

'Tildie explained it to me, a little. About the beings created

227

once by the old Seers. Humanimals, she said folk call them. Like Spandel and the . . . the poor frog-creature in Skolt's chamber, and the little blue Carolells. Are there . . . many types?'

Rannis nodded. 'Too many. I'd never even heard of those little Carolells of yours.'

'But what *are* they, Rannis? Are they . . . human? Or just clever animals? Or what?'

'Hardly human,' he replied quickly. 'Animals? Well, yes. But not in any simple sense. Mostly, folk just try to ignore them.'

'But why?'

'They're . . . unpredictable. Make no mistake, Kess. They might talk like human folk at times, but they're different from us. There's no telling what really goes on in those devious little minds of theirs. Those of them that *have* minds. Most of them are merely brutes with the trick of speech. Mimics and copyists without any true thought of their own. And no true human sensitivity at all. Don't be fooled by them. Not even those that look almost human – some of them do. Like that frog-man we put out of its misery in Seer Skolt's chamber. And don't trust them.'

'But Spandel led us to safety.'

'For her own purposes, no doubt. Or on a whim. Or because she wanted company. Or . . . who knows why?'

'Spandel is a she, then?'

'Oh, yes. The only woman in mad Mattingly's life. And look where she led him!'

'I don't understand. Do you mean *she* led him on to . . . to using me to kill himself?'

'They do that.'

'The . . . humanimals? They lead folk to *kill* themselves?'

'No, no. They kill themselves. Too fragile, most of them.'

'But then, wouldn't . . . How could Spandel lead Mattingly to . . .' She was finding all this most confusing.

'I told you it would take too long to explain,' he said.

Elinor sighed, lapsed into silence. She was stiff and aching and weary to the very marrow of her bones. It felt as if she had not had a moment's true rest since that day Jago and Genna had come to her with their disgusting arranged marriage. And that was . . . She had no idea how long ago that was. It felt like three lifetimes.

'It's dawning,' Rannis said at her side, pulling her out of her thoughts.

She noticed, then, that the sky was paling in the east. It was still too soon for any real warmth, though. She felt Rannis shivering beside her. 'Let's get up,' she suggested. 'It'll warm us if we move about a bit.'

Together, they struggled stiffly to their feet, using the big trunk of the willow for support. Rannis grunted, straightening himself. He put a hand to his ribs, where the sword-gash was.

'How is it?' she asked.

'Stiff. Sore. How do you *think* it is, girl, after spending the night knotted up and shivering here in this forsaken hole?'

She bit back a quick retort. He was, after all, in pain and a little fevered. She must make allowances.

He shrugged, looked at her. 'It *hurts*, Kess.'

'My name's Elinor,' she said, the words out before she intended them. She was not at all sure why she had said such a thing. It just seemed . . . Now that she was out of Minmi, she suddenly felt she wanted her own right name back again.

'Elinor?' he said.

'It's my name.'

'But what about . . . Kess, then?' He stared at her. 'You mean you lied to us – to me – and gave a false name?'

'I didn't lie to you. I . . .'

'What *else* did you lie about?'

'I *didn't* lie, I tell you!' She drew breath, swallowed, took refuge in his own phrase. 'It would take too long to tell right now . . .'

He grunted and turned away.

She felt a quick little pang of unease, seeing his hunched back, but kept her silence. He was too prickly this morning. Anything she said by way of explanation might set him more against her.

She sighed. The sun was high enough now just to be visible through the limbs of the willows. The dawn breeze riffled their leaves, creating a soft, rustling music. Overhead, the sky was turning from pewter to pale cobalt. The willow leaves hung in streaming sheaves about them. The old, thick trunks glowed ochre-green. Elinor breathed it all in, feeling the clean, cool air fill her lungs. Her spirits lifted. Whatever might lie in store for her, this was better than the dim, dank, twisty stone corridors of Minmi.

From the trees behind and above them, something called out.

They both spun about awkwardly, Rannis grunting at the discomfort of the sudden movement. Elinor reached for the blade that still hung at her belt.

A small body came down through the willows, springing from limb to limb with the agility of a squirrel.

Spandel.

'Up, up, up!' she cried.

Rannis glared. 'Where have you *been*?' he snapped.

Spandel looked at him with her dark eyes, looked away, moved her furred shoulders in an altogether human shrug. 'Looking. Looking for things.'

'What sort of . . . things?' he said.

She shrugged again. 'Things to tell us where, where, where to go.'

Elinor stared at the small, exotic creature. Spandel sat on her haunches on the grass, knees up near her shoulders, in a position that had nothing remotely human about it. She was fiddling with the end of her long, ringed tail. That little nervous gesture, somehow, *was* utterly human, and Elinor took a kind of reassurance from it.

'Come,' Spandel said. She skipped to her feet and stood, poised, her long, slim arms held out for balance. 'Come, come. Follow me.'

'Why should we?' Rannis demanded.'Don't trust it,' he said to Elinor.

But Elinor could not see anything especially threatening about Spandel. She was an altogether strange little creature, yes. But malevolent? Elinor felt not. 'Where do you want us to go?' she asked.

Spandel pointed. 'Away, away to the hills.'

It suited Elinor, that.

But Rannis shook his head. 'Go further into this . . . this empty, useless, dangerous wilderness? Not likely!'

'Well, we can't just stay *here*,' Elinor said.

Rannis only glared at her.

'Follow, follow me,' Spandel said.

'And just why ought we to follow *you*?' Rannis asked acidly.

'I feel the way. I dreamed, dreamed, dreamed it.'

'Wonderful!' he said, throwing up his hands. 'She *dreamed* it to be the way.'

'Dreams?' Elinor said curiously.

'I dream dreams,' Spandel answered. 'I dreamed you.'

Elinor leaned forward. 'Is that how . . .'

But Rannis cut her off. 'And so do I dream dreams,' he snapped at Spandel. 'And Kess here. And most everybody. But don't expect *me* to follow you around like some silly goat just because you say you had some dream or other.'

'Rannis,' Elinor said, looking at him uneasily. 'Why is ye so . . . against her? Why so angry?'

'You don't understand. No foreigner could. These . . . creatures are not to be trusted. You'll see. Following where this one leads us will only bring us to disaster. We ought to return to Minmi. Perhaps we can . . .'

'Spandel saved our lives.'

'For some dark purpose of her own, no doubt.'

'Oh, don't be such a . . . an *ingrate*,' Elinor snapped. 'You can do as you like, return to Minmi, whatever. *I'm* going ahead with Spandel. She's the best chance we have.'

'Best chance *you* have, perhaps.'

Elinor looked at him quizzically.

'What do *you* care?' he demanded. 'To you, Minmi's just a place you left behind. But it was all my *life*! And now . . .' He wiped a hand over his face. 'I had a life, a future, a place in the greater scheme of things. Gone, all gone!'

'You're alive, Rannis,' Elinor said softly. 'That's something.'

He laughed a bitter little laugh. 'Most of me died, back in Minmi. Thanks to this . . . creature.'

Elinor did not know what to say.

Spandel sidled up to her side. 'The man . . .' she looked at Rannis out of the corner of her eyes '. . . makes me tight in my belly.'

Rannis glared.

'We must go, go, go!' Spandel said.

'Why the rush?' Rannis demanded. 'Do we have an appointment to keep, then?'

Spandel turned away from him, looked at Elinor. She

hopped from foot to foot, clearly anxious to be moving.

Somehow, Elinor began to feel it too, a hovering sense of urgency. She did not understand why, or how, she should be feeling such a thing. But feel it she did. 'Please,' she implored Rannis. 'We have to go. You can't just *sit* here.'

'And why not?' he returned petulantly.

Elinor shook her head. 'There's no point in talking to you when you're like this.'

'Like what?'

Elinor snorted in exasperation. 'You suit yourself. *I'm* going with Spandel.' She turned to the little Lamure. 'Coming?'

Spandel grinned, a quick flash of small, startling white teeth in her dark furred face. She leaped away, and Elinor started off after.

Behind, she heard Rannis grumble and fume. But he came trudging along nonetheless.

Onwards they walked, up one long, grassy slope and down another. Behind, Minmi lay hidden now by the rolling countryside. Ahead, the far green hills stood waiting. Elinor glanced back from time to time, still anxious about the possibility of pursuit from out of Minmi. She saw Rannis do the same more than once. But there was nothing. All about, the land lay utterly empty, a grassy expanse unbroken except for, here and there, a copse of trees like the one in which they had sheltered the past night, or an occasional stony height of land.

Late in the afternoon, they began to draw close to the hills. Elinor could see the darker mass of what must be forest ahead. The land began to slope more sharply upwards. The walking grew harder. She felt it in her thighs, her heel tendons. Stony outcrops thrust out of the ground, odd, angular shapes rearing up through the grass like the mouldering remains of giant, dead creatures. It had been long since they had last passed water, and they were parched.

'Must be a stream somewhere,' Rannis said, his voice a thin croak. 'My tongue's dry as old boot leather.'

'There, there!' Spandel said, pointing. 'There!'

Ahead, they saw the sparkle of sunlight on a little waterfall, tumbling down the side of a rocky scarp. They made towards it.

Their route took them close to one of the upthrusts of stone

232

that littered the land hereabouts. Up till now, Elinor had assumed they were natural outcroppings. Passing close to this one, she stopped, staring. It was a stone portal, half buried by earth and grass, with intricate designs carved over it. She peered at those designs, but found them too weathered to make out. Stepping back, she realized that she was looking at the remains of a building of some sort.

It had been shattered, as if some giant had stomped on it with his boot-heel. More than that. There were places where the very stone itself seemed to have been . . . melted. She saw one section where it had flowed like molasses before hardening again, and shook her head in amazement.

'The ancients could do incredible things,' Rannis said quietly, coming to stand by her side.

'Terrible things!' Spandel piped up, staying some distance off from the shattered stone remains and peering at them suspiciously.

Rannis glared at her. 'What would the likes of *you* know about it? They were days of glory, those old days. The old ones had great knowledge and great power. Minmi was an important centre, a complex, beautiful place.' He stared at the ruin before them and shook his head. 'I would give anything to have been born back then instead of now. They *lived*, those men. Now . . . now we spend our days scraping and struggling uselessly to rebuild what once was. And things just grow worse and worse. The old ones were *great* men.'

'The old ones were *terrible* men!' Spandel said.

'You owe your very existence to them, you ungrateful creature! If they had never created your ancestors, where would *you* be?'

The Lamure turned her back on him.

'What . . . what *happened* here?' Elinor said to Rannis, gesturing at the ruin.

He shrugged. 'Who knows?'

'But . . .' she began.

'It was long and long ago, Kess. There were wars. Much was destroyed. There's no knowing what event took place here, or who was involved.' He sighed. 'We have lost so much.'

Elinor felt a shiver go through her. People had lived here in this stone structure once, gone through their daily chores, loved and hated and made their plans. And now they were forgotten, lost forever, and this utter, terrible destruction was all those human lives amounted to.

'Come *away*,' Spandel said. 'Away, away! It's a terrible place this. Terrible! Can't you smell the *badness* in it? We spend too much time here. Too, too much time!'

'What's the *rush*?' Rannis demanded irritably. 'You've been rushing us all day.' He looked about him suspiciously. 'Where are you leading us?'

'To the water,' Spandel said. 'The water.' She beckoned to them, anxious, standing up on her back legs. 'Clean, nice water.'

Elinor turned from the ruin and away. She felt again that odd sense of urgency nagging at her. It had risen and receded throughout the day, never quite leaving her. She did not understand.

Turning from the ruin, she felt a crawly shiver across her back. Perhaps it was only Spandel's obvious anxiety affecting her, or perhaps something more palpable, but it felt as if some hidden . . . *thing* were watching her. She could not help but wonder a little anxiously what uncanny beings might lurk in this forsaken land.

But whatever it might have been – if, indeed, it was anything at all other than her own imaginings – never materialized, and they walked unmolested to the little tumbling waterfall Spandel had pointed out.

The coolth of the falling water was completely wonderful, and they drank and splashed and luxuriated in it. For the first time since escaping Minmi, Elinor was able properly to wash the filth and gore and sweat off herself. She felt like a new person.

Spandel bounced away, calling for them to follow, as she had been doing all day. But Rannis shook his head and plonked himself on the grassy bank next to the stream and lay back, dripping, watching the little, churning, white-water whirlpool at the base of the falls.

Elinor felt the strange pull of urgency upon her, like an invisible hook set into her guts, tugging, tugging . . . but she joined Rannis, too weary for the moment to do aught else. She looked back across the land through which they had just walked, and shivered. It was such a wild, strange place. Who knew what creatures might inhabit it, or what dire events might have taken place out there. Or might yet take place.

She let herself down on the grass with a weary sigh. They seemed safe enough here, in this little grassy nook by the falls. Her very bones ached with weariness. She put her head down on the grass, felt drowsiness begin to steal upon her, like a bag of softest sand being poured over her. Her eyelids closed, she felt herself slipping away . . .

'No!'

Little hands gripped her, shaking her awake.

'Don't sleep,' Spandel said. 'No time to sleep. No time.'

'And why *not*?' Rannis demanded irritably from where he lay. 'There's no sign of pursuit. We're safe enough here. You've been rushing us pointlessly all day. Now we've water, soft grass to lie on, and there looks to be shelter over there by the rocks.' He looked over at Elinor. 'Why not spend the night here?'

'Oh, no. No!' Spandel said hurriedly. 'We must leave. Quick, quick, quick!'

'Why?' Rannis repeated suspiciously.

'Because . . .' Spandel answered. She hopped up and down agitatedly, looked at where the sun was in the sky. 'Quick. We must go up into the hills. Or we will be too, too late.'

'Too late for what?' Elinor said. But she felt the strange, urgent pulling.

'Don't trust it,' Rannis put in quickly. 'No knowing what might be in its devious little mind.'

'Please! Oh, please, please, please!' Spandel pleaded. 'Come quick!'

Elinor hesitated. 'What is it, Spandel?'

The small furred face wrinkled. 'I . . . They're going to . . . I . . . Oh, I *dreamed*! Oh, quick! Don't ask confusing questions. Just come. Quick! *Quick!*' She bounded off upslope, away from the waterfall, looked back. 'Please, please come.'

'Let her go,' Rannis said. 'Silly, wearisome creature. We have all we need right here.'

Looking up at Spandel, Elinor did not know what to think.

'Stay here, Kess,' Rannis said. 'Who knows what dangers this forsaken land might hold? Don't be *stupid*.'

He was right enough, Elinor supposed. But his calling her names put her hackles up. And she still felt the invisible, persistent tug upon her. She turned and left him.

'Come back!' he cried.

But Spandel bounded ahead and Elinor went after.

'What's wrong with you?' Rannis called, getting to his feet. 'Have you entirely lost your mind? Come back, the pair of you!'

But they did not.

Cursing to himself, he scrambled up after them.

The slope up which they moved became choked with brush – thick, shoulder-high stuff with tenacious limbs. It was the beginnings of the forest Elinor had seen. Spandel bounced through it easily enough, but the knuckly branches seemed to grab at Elinor and Rannis as they tried to force a way through, so that both of them, but especially Rannis, were soon panting and sweat-soaked.

'Slow down,' Elinor called out, for Spandel was beginning to lose them.

With obvious reluctance, the little Lamure stopped and turned, hanging above them from a twisty limb by a hand and her tail, staring back with her dark, ringed eyes. 'Hurry, hurry, hurry!' she urged as they drew close.

'Stupid creature!' Rannis gasped. He aimed a blow at her and she swung out of his way with a little shriek.

'Leave her be, Rannis,' Elinor snapped.

He glared at her.

She glared back.

And then, from the distance ahead, they heard a cry, like the wailing of a child in terror, or in pain.

'Oh, quick, quick, *quick!*' Spandel urged, and disappeared ahead.

Elinor and Rannis looked at each other.

'It's a trap of some sort,' Rannis said.

The cry came again, made thin by distance, but clear enough for all that, a despairing wail.

There was no faking a cry like that, Elinor reckoned. 'Come on,' she said, then turned and struggled off after Spandel as fast as she could.

XXVI

Elinor scrambled through the thick undergrowth, feeling the strange sense of urgency, strong enough now to make her heart thump. She was unsure which way Spandel had taken, and halted after a little to try and get her bearings. She had not heard the wailing cry again, but now, from ahead, she could just make out the sounds of . . . She stopped to listen, was not certain what it might be. There were voices. And she made out clattering and creaking and *chinking* noises, made faint by distance.

Rannis came puffing up beside her. Before he could say a word, she was off again.

As the sounds ahead grew more clear, she slowed, creeping along now. She could see nothing, yet, beyond the thick green tangle of the brush.

Then it came again: a long wail like a child in pain.

With a little shiver of leaves, Spandel returned. 'Hurry, hurry *hurry*!' she gasped, then turned and sprang off ahead, slipping through the tangle growth with ease.

Rannis came up, panting, and sat back on his haunches. 'Don't go,' he said. 'They've no real mind, these creatures. *Everybody* knows that. They just mimic human folk. Who knows what the little creature might be leading us into? It might be . . . trained to lead people to their deaths. As it did poor mad Mattingly.'

Elinor shook her head. 'You're not making any sense, Rannis! Why rescue us from Minmi and lead us all this way just to bring us to some trap?'

He merely grunted, shook his head.

'Come on,' Elinor said.

Rannis stayed as he was. 'What's the point?' The wailing sound came again. 'It's just trouble down there, of one sort or another. The last thing we need now is more *trouble*!'

'Spandel says . . .'

'Spandel *says* . . .' he mimicked.

Elinor turned her back on him and started off again.

The going became steeper. Chunks of stone thrust up amongst the tangled undergrowth, eventually forming a kind of rough bluff. She crawled up to the crest and peered down.

To her surprise, there was a rutted cart track below, dipping and curving through the rocky terrain between two hills, hemmed in on each side by ragged green walls of bush. Again, she heard the plaintive, wailing sound. The agony in it pulled at her. Peering carefully out from her hidden vantage point, she saw . . . Elinor blinked. It seemed to be a sort of small caravan approaching.

Several men on foot came first, armed men. Some carried long, wicked-looking, double-barbed fighting spears, one a crossbow, cocked and ready; all had blades of one sort or another hanging from their belts. Their weapons and accoutrements *chinked* metallically as they walked.

In the first instant of sighting them, Elinor pulled back, her heart thumping, certain they were pursuit from Minmi.

But no . . . The inhabitants of Minmi went in for eccentric gaudiness. Looking again, she saw that these men all wore identical, sombre, severely simple clothing. And they had durable, not at all gaudy-looking plate armour cuirasses about their torsos, and iron and leather fighting helms. On each helm there was a small crimson insignia. The distance was as yet too far for Elinor to make out the design. Behind this vanguard on foot, however, there came a cart with a little pennant waving and bouncing above it on a pole, and here again was the insignia. It took her a fair few moments of squinting at the fluttering pennant before she could make out the design of it: a stylized sun, with blood-red rays emerging to frame a pair of hands, gripped – whether in greeting or struggle, she could not tell.

She shook her head, not knowing what to think. Who *were* these men? And where was the wailing child?

The cart came jouncing along, the axle creaking and groaning in complaint. It was a boxy, small vehicle, drawn by a sway-backed, stocky little creature like an ox, which the single driver urged on with a flicking whip. A square wooden cage sat upon the cart behind the driver. Inside that cage . . .

A large brown bear sat, leaning forlornly against the bars. As Elinor watched, it lifted its head and made the long, wailing, child-like cry of grief and despair they had been hearing. The hairs along the back of her neck prickled at the sound of it.

'Save him,' Spandel said, appearing suddenly at Elinor's shoulder.

Elinor only stared. The bear was filthy and matted. What possible connection could there be between this poor creature and Spandel?

Again, the caged bear put back its head and wailed.

There were two guards behind the wagon, Elinor now saw. One of these came forward and rattled the cage's wooden bars with his spear. 'Shut up, *animal*!' he snarled. There was something in the man's tone of voice that somehow made the word 'animal' an insult.

The bear wailed again, and the guard thrust at it brutally through the bars with the butt of his spear.

'Save him!' Spandel repeated. 'It is the dream. You must save, save, save him.'

'Leave it be,' Rannis said, coming up. 'You don't want to get involved in this, Kess.'

She turned to him. 'And why not?'

He frowned. 'You . . . you don't understand what you're letting yourself in for, interfering here. Let's go away quietly. Those men down there are *trouble*.'

She looked at him.

'Only a *stupid* person interferes with the Brothers.'

Elinor bristled. 'And just who are these . . . *Brothers*, then?'

But before Rannis could answer, the situation below changed.

A large black crow came flapping up out of the undergrowth. It reminded her of Mama Kieran's raven – the same dark, flapping, feather-fingered shape. It slow-winged its way above the little caravan on the cart track, like any ordinary bird might, save that it was dead silent.

The men about the wagon craned their necks, watching. 'Shoot it, Cole,' one of them said to the crossbow-man.

And then, without warning, the crow folded its wings and dived at the guard who had been jabbing at the poor bear with his spear, its sharp grey-black beak going for the man's eyes. He screamed and dropped his spear, trying desperately to fend off the crow with both hands. The other guards came pelting to his rescue.

But then, out of the bush, a little horde came pouring.

Elinor did not know what to think. The caravan seemed under attack – but not by men. There was the crow, circling up now and away; two mangy-looking wolf-dogs; a long-legged stork; several hairless, pale-skinned beasts with long noses, unlike any animal Elinor had ever seen; a small, sharp-antlered deer-like creature; a big ferret-like beast; a yellow cat almost the size of the dogs.

The animals flung themselves against the dark-clothed guards. In an instant it was all surging, stumbling chaos, the men yelling and cursing, striking out desperately with sword or spear. The crossbow-man let loose a shaft with a *clakk*, and one of the dogs howled in agony.

And then, to Elinor's further amazement, she heard the crow call out, 'Bringg the bowman downnn!'

The remaining dog leaped at the crossbow-man's throat as he struggled to reload his weapon, dragging him down in a screaming, thrashing confusion of limbs.

Spandel vaulted into the air by Elinor's side, emitting a little high-pitched shriek.

'Quiet!' Rannis hissed at her.

Elinor's hand went instinctively to the hilt of the sword at her belt. She part-drew it, feeling the tingle of the blade's strange energy in her fingers.

But there was small chance of any of the combatants below paying attention to them.

She leaned out of the cover that concealed them. The men and animals whirled and struggled. Two of the guards were down now, she saw – the crossbow-man and the one whom the crow had first attacked. But though the sheer unexpectedness of their sudden ambush had seemed to give the animals the upper hand at first, they were losing it now. Elinor saw the cat end its life spitting and screaming, skewered on a spear. Two of the strange pale-skinned, hairless creatures were bleeding. The poor brave creatures did not stand a chance against such armed and armoured men.

With the sword still half drawn, it was impulse rather than conscious decision that sent her leaping down on to the cart track.

'Kess!' Rannis cried.

But she was loping along the track already, the white-shining blade unsheathed, her bones tingling with the thrill of it. Kess came surging up in her, purer, simpler than Elinor, feeling bone and muscle and tendon, blade and balance, movement and force all as one dancing pattern.

The first guard to spot her cried out, 'Help us! These cursed brutes . . .' But the man went silent, staring, obviously at a loss as to how to place her, a lone woman armed with a blade unlike any other.

She came at him, and he rushed her clumsily. Kess read his intent: as Lotch once had tried, he intended charging down on her like a mad bull, overwhelming her bodily, no doubt thinking her easy enough prey.

She sidestepped him and thrust into his side as he stumbled past, feeling the proper balance of the movement in her wrist and arm and thighs.

Whirling on one heel, she looked back to see the man down. And down he was, but the plate-armour cuirass he wore had turned her blade and he was unharmed. Another of them came at her now, this one with a spear. She skipped hastily back.

For a moment, the purity of her Kess self weakened. Elinor re-emerged, far from certain what to do with the blade in her hand. She glanced behind, hoping to see Rannis come running up to help. But there was only Spandel, shrieking and bouncing about hysterically. And no sign of Rannis at all.

The spearman lunged for her, and she skipped back again, her heart skittering. Her hand was slippery with sweat, and the sword felt uncertain in her hold. She stood shaken, uncertain.

One of the pale-skinned creatures attacked the spearman from behind, dragging him to his knees. She leaped in impulsively, then, trod the shaft of the spear to the ground with one foot, and took the spearman in the neck – where the scale-armour left him vulnerable – with a quick, deadly thrust. He fell face first on to the ground, desperately clutching at his torn and gushing throat.

She took a gasping breath. Over the spearman's writhing body, she looked at the creature that had attacked him. Its face was entirely hairless, broad, with a long, quivering snout, sensitive and mobile – not like any animal she had ever seen. It moved, more than anything else, like a dog, and was the size of a very large dog, but its four feet had a kind of thick thumb and four stubby fingers, or toes. It had small pointed ears and a cat's sharp teeth. But it was the eyes that held Kess; in that utterly strange, hairless, pale face, the eyes were as human as her own.

'Help us . . .' the creature panted in a queer, breathy, but completely understandable voice.

She stared.

And then something screamed and there came a rush of bodies and she found herself immersed in the midst of a shouting, cursing, squealing, roaring, howling fight.

A man hacked at her, an artless, brutal slash. She ducked, taking the force of the blow on her own blade, feeling the shock of it up through the bones in her arm. His iron blade skittered along hers. She shifted over, spilling him aside and away from her. Before she could fully recover her balance, another of the spearmen came charging at her. She threw herself desperately sideways to avoid his thrust, rolling to the ground on her shoulder and coming up on one knee.

The spearman whirled, bringing the spear back up quickly. But not quickly enough. She surged to her feet and lunged desperately at him, going for the vulnerable neck area once more. She saw the look of sudden horror on his face the instant before her blade tore into his throat. Then he was down, choking.

She turned, panting, her vision swimming. The sword's strength thrilled through her. She pivoted, regaining her balance, all Kess now, looking for the man who had hacked at her a moment before. But the remaining dog had him, going for his throat.

Another of the dark-clothed, armoured men came at her then from out of the swirling mêlée, a swordsman. This one, however, did not charge her blindly. He held his sword with the ease of long training, coming at her with a feint to draw her, then a vicious lunge that would have skewered her through the sternum if she had not been quick.

He was good, this one.

He came at her again, a combination: *stroke, stroke, lunge*, his heavy iron blade *kringging* off hers, a little shower of sparks dancing ... *stroke, stroke, lunge* ... and then a sudden and unexpected low slash she only barely managed to avoid by flinging herself backwards. It nearly landed her on her arse, and only by the slimmest of slim blade widths was she able to sidestep the follow-up lunge he made with his other hand – in which a wicked-looking dagger had suddenly appeared.

She skipped back, her heart hammering.

Out of nowhere, the black form of the crow came diving at the man's head. He batted at it with his dagger hand, driving the bird off before she could gain any advantage. He sneered then, gesturing dismissively at the crow, and called something to her, but in all the noise and confusion she could not make out the words. He dodged sideways, aimed a vicious kick at the dog who still worried at the downed swordsman who had attacked her, then leaped at her, blade up.

But she was getting the measure of this man by now; he liked the feint, the fake to one side to draw her out first. And so he tried: the kick at the dog, the leap, the blade high to draw her guard upwards, the low, slashing lunge to follow. But this was one too many times. She would not let herself be drawn.

When his slash came, she was poised and ready. As she had with the spearman, she saw the look of sudden shock on his face as he realized his mistake. She took him through the armpit of his sword arm, just under the edge of his plate-armour and up into his shoulder joint, a quick, perfect thrust and pull of her blade – the Serpent Strike, Master Karasyn called it – in and out almost before her adversary knew he had been hit. She felt her blade grate on bone.

Down on his knees the man went, sword and dagger spilling, his left hand clutching at his crippled shoulder, the blood runnelling through his fingers. The crow came at him again then, swooping down and fetching him a vicious swipe on the back of the skull which sent him sprawling on his face.

She whirled, looked about.

But there was only one guard left standing by now. And he, seeing how things were, turned on his heels and fled.

'Stopp himmm!' the crow called out from above.

But the man was gone already, throwing himself into the cover of the brush and disappearing.

She stood, her sword-arm throbbing, her pulse drumming painfully in her ears. About her, the animals hovered uncertainly.

Slowly, she wiped the blade clean and sheathed it. The Kess aspect of her subsided. Elinor re-emerged again. She felt herself to be two . . . two-in-one . . . one-in-two . . . Her heart felt as if it was going to spill up out of her throat, and the world tipped dizzily about her.

She put a hand to her face, took a long breath, looked about at the creatures surrounding her. They stared at her with uncanny eyes – for she saw that they all had the same human sort of eyes as the hairless creature. The same as Spandel. They were two-in-one, too, she thought suddenly. Animal and human . . .

The bear wailed again, softer now.

Spandel came, skipping over the sprawled, still form of one of the downed guards to reach up and grab Elinor by the hand. The little Lamure tugged at her, dancing awkwardly on her hind feet, pulling her towards the wagon.

The cage-lock was a simple contrivance, and Elinor had it undone in two breaths. The door creaked open, and she stepped back quickly. A full-grown bear was a formidable creature. This one, she reckoned, would easily be more than a man's height standing on its hind legs.

But the creature made no move to escape its erstwhile prison, merely stayed as it was, leaning forlornly against the cage's side.

Elinor bent forward. 'Come on,' she said, beckoning. Its brown furred face seemed unutterably sad to her somehow. The eyes were big and dark and, like all the rest of the creatures' here, uncannily human. 'You're free,' she said to it.

It took a snuffling breath, blinked. There were big tears in its eyes – or so it seemed. Could a bear cry human tears? Elinor reached in impulsively with her free hand and took a handful of thick fur, tugging at the creature. 'Come on,' she said reassuringly. 'You're free now. *Free.*'

It growled at her, a deep, menacing rumble of sound, more felt through the fingers that gripped it than properly heard with the ear. She jerked her hand away, skittered back.

She heard someone come up behind her and whirled, hand reaching for her sword hilt instinctively. But it was Rannis.

'Of all the mad, stupid, empty-headed things to do! What *did* you think you were playing at? You could have got yourself killed, you *stupid* girl.'

Elinor stared at him. She felt her belly clench. 'But I *didn't*, did I?'

'Only by the sheerest of luck. That last man was a *swordsman*, Kess. If the crow hadn't distracted him . . .'

'I took him because I knew what he would do!' she returned angrily. 'The man only knew one trick, and once I . . .'

'It was *luck*, I tell you! You were lucky to survive.'

'No thanks to ye!' she snapped back at him. 'A lot of help *ye* was. I looked for ye . . .'

His eyes slid away from hers, then back. He shook his head angrily. 'Look about you. Do you realize the *trouble* you've landed us in now!' Rannis bent to one of the dead guards, tugged off the man's leathern fighting helm. 'See *this*?' he demanded, pointing to the crimson sun-and-gripped-hands insignia. 'These are . . . *were* Brothers. You and these stupid, mad creatures have killed them!'

'So?' she snapped. 'They deserved it.'

Rannis laughed hollowly, throwing up his hands. 'Listen to you! Since when have you appointed yourself the world's conscience?' He pointed to the blade sheathed at her belt. 'That weapon has addled your mind, girl. What do you think you are? Some . . . some crusading paladin?'

She flushed.

But Rannis had gone suddenly very sober. 'You have no idea what you've done here.'

She shrugged sullenly.

'These were *Brothers*!'

'Ye already said that. So what?' She gestured at the fallen guards. 'And how does ye know they were all brothers? They don't look like kin to me.'

Rannis shook his head. 'No, you ignorant little whippet. Not kin brothers . . . *Brothers*! These men were all members of the Ancient Brotherhood of the Light.' Rannis lifted up the helm, showing her again the stylized blood-red sun, the gripped hands. 'This is their symbol. The Ancient Brotherhood of the Light. *Not* a group any sane person would want to antagonize. And you . . . *you* come along with that white-bladed sword of yours which makes you . . . every time you wield it you do insane things, girl! You come along here and *massacre* these men along with the help of this rag-tag rabble of beasts!'

The animals had been silent and still up to now, gazing uncertainly at her as she unlocked the cage, staring wide-eyed at the argument between her and Rannis. Now they came closer, forming a rough ring.

'Stay back!' Rannis ordered them, his sword out threateningly. Then, to her he said, 'Come on. Let's away from here. Nothing can undo the mess you've created, but at least let's not compound our folly by hanging about. There's no knowing if another squad of Brothers isn't nearby.'

But she stood her ground.

'What is ye talking about, Rannis? Who are these . . . *Brothers*?'

'Come *on*,' he said by way of reply. 'Let's away from here!'

Still she did not move.

'Kess!' Rannis snapped in exasperation. 'There's no time now. I'll explain it all later. Trust me.'

'Like I trusted ye to back me up during the fighting?'

'You don't know what you're saying. You don't know what you've got into here.'

'And ye will not tell me!'

'Kess . . . *Kess*!'

'My name is Elinor,' she said to him, out of patience with all his arguing and pushing. Ever since they had escaped from Minmi, he had been nagging at her, it seemed.

He stared at her, his face clenched.

The bear wailed again then, suddenly. But it was a different sound now. She turned from Rannis and saw Spandel in the cage, perched upon the bear's broad shoulder, whispering into its ear the way she had whispered into mad Lord Mattingly's

The bear lifted its head and cried out, but more softly.

Elinor did not know what to think. Neither, apparently, did the gathered animals. They clustered about the wagon anxiously. Then, before any of them could make a further move, the bear reared up, spilling Spandel off, and lumbered to the open cage door. In a clumsy rush, it launched itself out of the cart, landing with a grunt on the ground.

The animals rushed towards it in concern. 'I'm all right,' it growled at them.

The crow flapped over to land in front of it, waddled close. 'Stupiddd bearrrr!' it squawked.

The bear hung its head.

Elinor stared, not quite believing any of it. She felt Rannis tug at her elbow.

'Come *on*,' he urged in a fierce whisper. 'Now's our chance, Kess, while they're occupied with each other.'

But she shook him off. She took a few uncertain steps forward, addressed the animals clustered about the bear. 'Who . . . *are* you?'

'Who are *you*?' This came from one of the hairless, pale creatures. It stared at her out of the corner of its uncanny human eyes, licking at a long, nasty cut across its shoulder.

Rannis tugged at her again, and again she shrugged him off. 'I am named . . . Elinor,' she said to the hairless creature. She heard Rannis grunt behind her.

The crow waddled over towards her, wings out for balance. 'Why diddd youuu helppp usss?' it demanded.

'I . . .' She was not sure what to say. It had been an impulsive act. Perhaps even a stupid one, as Rannis insisted. The Kess aspect of her had just leaped in, sword in hand, all unthinking.

'Never mind the why of it.' This was the stork talking, a tall, gangling bird with large dark eyes. 'She aided us.' It blinked at her, staring. 'We owe you a debt of thanks, woman. You and your white-blade sword.'

Elinor shrugged self-consciously. She did not know what to say.

'The Bro . . . Brothers will ru . . . rue this da . . . day!' the ferret-like creature stammered.

But the dog laughed, a kind of hysterical bubbling bark of sound. 'They'll not be the only ones to rue *this* day . . .' It stood next to the other dog, the one the crossbow-man had got. The shot animal was sprawled out on the ground, panting faintly. It lifted its muzzle and whined. The crossbow bolt had taken it through the chest, and it lay in a puddle of dark blood. There was, Elinor reckoned, no chance of its surviving.

She went over to it, knelt down at its side. Gently as could be, she stroked its head with her left hand. The animal whined pitifully, its tail thumping in a weak rhythm.

'Kess!' Rannis snapped. 'Come away from there.'

She looked up at him, frowning.

'Come *away*,' he insisted. 'Or I'll leave without you. I'm warning you, Kess . . .'

'So go,' she said.

He stood there scowling at her like a petulant boy. He no longer seemed the same Rannis she had known in Minmi. And she felt . . . She was not sure what, exactly. That strange, urgent feeling that had animated her on their trek here was somehow a part of it. It felt as if she were sliding irrevocably down some slope, momentum building, headed in some direction or other that was beginning to feel . . . *right* somehow. And Rannis . . . Rannis merely stood there, nagging, cajoling, threatening, resisting . . . trying to prevent her, trying to have *his* way in everything.

Like Jago, her step-father.

Rannis was staring at her.

She did not know how to talk to him. 'Go,' she repeated. It seemed all there was left to say.

He shook himself, opened his mouth, closed it. 'Have it your own way, then,' he said finally. 'But don't say I didn't warn you.'

The dog growled at him, hackles up.

Rannis brought his sword round.

'Oh, go away, Rannis!' Elinor snapped at him. 'Before ye causes trouble here.'

'*Me*?' he said, eyes wide. '*Me* cause trouble? How can you have the . . . the effrontery to . . .'

'Just go!' she shouted at him.

Rannis glared at her, outraged. 'Fine! Just as you say. I'll leave. But you listen to me, my girl. You'll live to regret this. You don't know this land. You'll never make it without me. I could have . . .'

248

'Just shut up and *go*!'

He did, his face white with fury, backing away from the gathered animals, sword still in hand until he was far enough off to turn and crash into the bush.

And then he was gone.

Elinor blinked. It seemed to have happened so suddenly.

The wounded dog at her feet whimpered again. She looked down upon it in pity. The poor thing . . . Best to end its life now rather than let it suffer.

But Elinor brought herself up short. If it had been any simple dog, she would not have hesitated overlong to end its misery with a careful sword thrust. But this was no mere dumb brute, was it? What *were* these creatures, then? Rannis's contradictory explanations had left her with no real notion. She looked about. They were all staring at her. 'Who . . . are you?' she asked them again.

It was the stork that came forward. 'We are . . . who we are. And you?'

'You are not like any human woman we have ever seen,' one of the pale, hairless creatures added.

Elinor did not know what to say. 'Spandel?' she said uncertainly, turning to the little Lamure.

Spandel came skipping over from where she had been at the bear's side. 'Like the Hyphon says, this human woman is not like any you've ever, ever seen.'

'Who are *you*?' the stork asked. 'To bring us a saviour in our time of need?'

'I am a Dreamer,' Spandel said softly. 'And a Channel.'

'Ahhh . . .' the animals breathed together, apparently satisfied by such an answer.

Elinor stared at Spandel.

'Cannn wee trusttt herrr?' the crow squawked, gesturing with its beak towards Elinor.

'She came quick, quick, quick,' Spandel said, 'to fulfil the dream and save your friend the bear from the Brothers' terrible hold.'

'Perhapsss,' the crow admitted. It eyed Elinor sideways with one bright, black, human-looking eye. 'Perhapsss . . .'

The wounded dog whimpered again, lifting its head a little.

'Poor Nolly,' the other dog moaned. It bent forward and

licked its companion gently on the snout. Elinor saw very human tears in its eyes. 'Poor, poor Nolly . . .'

'We must *do* something for him,' said one of the pale, hairless creatures Spandel had named Hyphons.

'He's going to die,' the bear said. Its voice was deep and gruff, a half-growl. 'Poor Nolly's going to die . . . and it should have been *me*. Why did you interfere, you lot? Why didn't you just let things be?'

'But Scrunch,' the sharp-antlered little deer said. 'We could not just let you . . .'

'If you'd just let me be,' the bear replied, 'none of this would have happened. Poor Nolly here wouldn't lie dying.'

'He's not dying,' the unwounded dog insisted. 'Are you, Nolly? He's only hurt. Badly hurt. But he's not . . .'

'Don'ttt bee stupiddd,' the crow told the unwounded dog. 'Use yourrr eyesss.'

'He is right, Jubb,' the stork said sadly.

'I . . . I ammm . . . Oh, Jubb . . .' the wounded dog gasped. It lifted its head, looked up with its startlingly human eyes at its companion, tried to say more, but collapsed back again weakly.

The dog named Jubb howled. 'Nolly! *Nolly!*'

Nolly let out a long, exhausted, rattling breath, then was still as a stone.

'He's dead,' the bear growled. '*Dead*. It should have been me, I tell you! Oh, why didn't you all just leave me *be*?'

Elinor knelt down beside Nolly, pitiful in death, no different seeming from any other dog. Yet she had heard it speak, seen the hurting humanity in its eyes. Without thinking, she began to recite the death litany. It was something she would never have thought to say over any ordinary dog. But nothing was ordinary here. 'A scatheless journey in the darkness, friend,' she began. 'A scatheless journey and a fruitful end. Gone from the world of living ken. Into the Shadowlands . . . to begin again.'

There was a shocked silence about her.

For a long moment, Elinor thought she had done something awful. The animals stared at her.

Then the bear lumbered up to her, half-raised himself upon his haunches, and put a heavy paw upon her shoulder. His big, altogether human eyes stared into hers. 'Tha-thank you,' he said. His voice, his very body, shook with some powerful emotion, and his eyes filled with tears.

The remaining dog came and bowed at her feet. The pale, hairless animals knelt beside the dog, all staring at her with the same tear-filled eyes.

Elinor did not know what to think.

'Enoughhh!' the crow squawked. 'Misserable grovellersss, the lottt of youu!'

'Oh, shut up, Otys,' Jubb the dog said, and growled at the crow menacingly.

The bird leaped away into the air.

Elinor shivered. The animals' intent, emotion-filled stares made her uncomfortable. She looked away from them self-consciously, turning to gaze about her. For the first time, she counted properly the number of sombre-clothed guards. Seven lay sprawled upon the ground, seven dead men, some torn, lying in blood, one sprawled on his back, face upwards, mouth open as if in a silent scream.

She swallowed, hard, trying to keep her stomach down. Her sword-arm ached. In all the rush and confusion, she had not, until now, had a moment properly to notice such gruesome details.

Flies had begun to appear, buzzing busily about the sticky limbs of the dead. Elinor felt sick in the pit of her stomach. She shook her head, swallowed again, trying to keep her mind from dwelling on what she had helped to do here – what the Kess part of her had done, what the white blade had done. Perhaps, as she had insisted to Rannis, these men deserved to die. Perhaps not . . .

And what of Rannis?

Elinor shivered. What was she to do now? He was the only person she knew in all this land. What had she thrown away with that one, impulsive act of dismissing him?

The animals were still staring at her, she realized. All except the crow, who had gone over to worry at the dead. Horrified, she watched him peck at the eyes of one of the corpses.

Looking slyly over at her, something disgusting hanging from his beak, he winked in an altogether startlingly human fashion. Then he tossed the something into the air – a glistening little sac trailing wet strands of bloody tissue; the remains of a human eyeball, she realized – and caught it again nimbly in his beak. He swallowed, threw back his black head, and laughed, a squawking croak of a sound.

Elinor shuddered.

'Disgusting bird!' one of the pale, hairless Hyphons said.

The crow only laughed some more and bent in quest of another morsel.

Elinor turned away from the sight. But in almost any direction she could look there were dead men. A shadow flashing over the ground made her jerk. Overhead, she saw a pair of broad-winged buzzards circling.

She recalled what Rannis had said about the possibility of other squads of 'Brothers' – whoever they might be – being about. It was time to get away from this place. The buzzards were a sure indication of death, a clear sign for any who might be interested for leagues around.

But where was she to go? She looked at the animals. Could she go with them? But where? She knew nothing about them, strange creatures as they were. Despite all Rannis's warnings to the contrary, they seemed perfectly mindful. But were they trustworthy? Sane, even?

Whatever the outcome might be between her and these creatures, the practical side of her knew she ought to ransack the dead for anything that might be useful before quitting this place. A part of her shrank from the very idea, but she had only her sword, not even a sleeping blanket. It was the sensible thing to do.

She could not, however, force herself to start with any of the more bloody corpses, and looked about for one less distressing to begin on. The last swordsman she had killed – the one Rannis declared she had bested only by luck – caught her eye. The man lay on his face, a little puddle of blood under his shoulder, where she had stabbed him, and the back of his now-helmetless head matted with blood. But he seemed somehow less horrible to contemplate than the others.

She went over and bent down to look at him. His sword lay near his right hand, and she kicked it aside. He lay on his belly, dead as could be, it seemed, but, having learned respect for his deviousness, Elinor was determined to take no unnecessary chances. She retrieved one of the discarded fighting spears and, using it as a lever, pried the man over on to his back. Blood oozed from his wounded shoulder and he groaned softly.

Elinor jumped back.

But he seemed safely unconscious. She bent a little closer, looking for the dagger he had held.

He kicked out suddenly and tripped her. She hit the ground hard, gasping. The dagger had somehow appeared in his hand. He made to stab at her ribs, but she managed to catch his wrist. They struggled like that, on the ground, for a long, panting moment. One of the hairless creatures jumped him, grappling at him with its stubby hands, hauling him off.

Elinor lost her hold on his wrist as the man was yanked away. He screamed at her in baulked fury and aimed a last, desperate cut with the knife. It quite missed her belly, for which he had clearly been aiming, but somehow he managed, with the back-slash, to make a long, nasty tear down the outside of her right leg.

It was like a red-hot wire ripping open her flesh.

Elinor cried out.

She clutched desperately at her thigh. Crimson blood oozed up all along the length of the slash he had made, far more than she could hope to staunch with her hands. She felt a wave of sickness go through her. The world shivered out of focus. She rolled over on to her side and was painfully sick, feeling her life's blood emptying from her, her leg one long flare of agony.

The bear came in a lumbering rush and took the man in his jaws, shaking him by the back of the neck like a dog might shake a rat until he went utterly limp.

The animals clustered about her, then, calling, crying. But she could not seem to make out anything they said. The world seemed filled with a great, roaring *hrummm* that obscured all else. She vaguely saw the brown, furry face of the bear pressed close to hers, felt his warm breath upon her cheek. Her hands were soaked with shining dark blood. She felt sick again, and her belly heaved. A great frigid darkness closed about her, like it had when she had been plunged into the storm-furious sea. She felt cold, cold . . .

It was hard to draw breath. The darkness grew thicker, more encompassing.

The darkness grew to be all . . .

PART THREE

MARGIE FARM

XXVII

In the dark, there was sound . . .

Burrr burr-urr . . . Burr burr-urr.

Elinor felt the sound as a soft, pleasant vibration on her breast. *Burrr burr-urr . . . Burr burr-urr.*

Then a voice: 'Away with you! Away, I say . . .'

The sound stopped.

Elinor sighed. Her eyes felt sticky, the lids glued shut. It took a long few moments' hard effort to get them open.

A small, triangular face was pressed close to hers, golden and black and white furred, mottled in no particular pattern, one ear all black, the other white with a gold tip, white-chinned . . . Bright green, little human eyes stared into hers. '*Burrr burr-urr . . .*' the face said softly. 'Forrr surrre . . . be welcomme. Forrr surrre.'

Elinor blinked, confused.

'Away with you, Alix,' a voice said. 'Away!'

The face disappeared from Elinor's vision. A weight was suddenly gone from her breast. She sighed, relieved and yet disappointed at the same time, for it had been somehow a comforting little weight.

'Welcome back to the land of the living, girl,' somebody said.

Elinor tried to turn her head. The muscles were stiff and sore. Her very bones felt stiff and sore. She felt weak as weak could be. With an effort she focused on a person leaning over her.

A woman. Long hair the colour of ripe cherries, grey-streaked, hanging in two thick braids. Round-faced, big-bodied, solid. Eyes green as those in the little triangular face that had greeted her a moment before. 'Welcome back,' the woman repeated. 'Good morning to you.'

Elinor tried to say something, but her voice came out only as a little croak. Almost, she laughed. It was too reminiscent of the other time, on the beach at Minmi. Was she destined to be forever stranded in odd places, voiceless?

Where was *this* place? What did folk here want of her? She had had enough experience to make her suspicious.

Elinor looked about, saw she was in a smallish room, wood-walled, the ceiling raftered with rough-hewn logs. In one corner a fire danced in a stone hearth, filling the room with pleasant warmth. A half-curtained window let in subdued, early-morning light.

'Water?' the woman asked.

Elinor nodded creakily.

The woman reached down and helped her to sit – she had been lying on a low bed, wrapped snugly in a warm woollen blanket. The rough touch of the wool, and her own stiffness and confusion, made her recall her first awakening in the Guardery at Minmi, with Rannis standing over her, staring. An instant later, however, all such thoughts were torn away.

She bent her right leg to help shift herself, and a sudden, sharp thrust of purest agony made her cry out.

'Easy, girl,' the woman said, 'or you'll pull the stitches.'

Elinor gasped. The pain seemed to lance through her leg into her hip and thence straight up to the base of her skull, spiking into her mind, scattering her thoughts like a flock of dizzy pigeons . . .

'Easy now. Easy . . .' the woman soothed. There was something in that voice, somehow, that made Elinor settle, despite everything. She straightened her right leg – which she had cramped up instinctively – and lay back. The woman propped her on a nest of soft little pillows, then turned and brought out from somewhere a large jug and a small cup, both earthenware, glazed a stunning blue. She poured water from the jug and handed the little cup to Elinor. She stared at that cup. She had never seen anything quite so beautiful . . . The blue of it shimmered and winked, shifting hue subtly as she turned the lovely thing in her shaking hands.

'Drink,' the woman urged.

Elinor drank. Her hands quivered weakly, and she had to grip the little cup firmly in both of them to keep it from spilling out of her hold. 'Whe . . . where *am* I?' she gasped. It felt most strange to be asking that question yet again, of another stranger. 'What do you want with me? Who *are* you?'

The woman smiled. 'I am Gillien.'

She was no longer young, this Gillien, Elinor thought. Her eyes were cradled by wrinkles, and she was far from being slim. But there was a solidity of spirit about her that Elinor could almost feel like a palpable thing, like a kind of glow about her. She wore a long, robe-like dress, dyed a deep blue. Her grey-streaked, cherry coloured hair caught the firelight and fairly glowed – as did her brilliant green eyes.

'Welcome to my household, Elinor.'

'Ho-how do you know my name?'

'Those who brought you to me told me.'

'But who brought me here?'

'Why, the Free Folk, of course.'

Elinor shook her head, half-raised herself from the bed. 'I don't . . .' A stab of pain through her right leg made her moan and she fell back. The extent of her weakness unnerved her. There seemed to be no strength at all left in her limbs.

'Don't fret now,' Gillien said. 'You've had a hard time of it. That was a very nasty gash you received.' She reached forward again and took Elinor's face gently in her hands. 'And there is the other . . . ah, difficulty. Your spirit is troubled, girl. I can feel it plain.'

Elinor jerked her face away from the woman's hold. 'I don't know what you're talking about,' she said quickly.

Gillien stood back, shook her head gently. 'I think you do, girl. You have been somehow . . . torn inside, and the two halves have not set quite properly yet.'

Elinor stared. How could this woman know what had happened to her?

'I do not understand it, really,' Gillien was saying now. 'It is not like anything I have ever encountered before. But . . .' She held up her hands reassuringly. 'Don't fret yourself. I won't pry. I know enough to realize that whatever it is has happened to you, I cannot remedy it. If, indeed, it *is* something to be remedied. The human spirit is strange and mysterious. And with the likes of you, girl . . . Well, who am I to know what is affliction and what benediction?'

Elinor stared. 'The likes of me?'

Gillien nodded. 'Fulcrum that you are.'

'Fu-fulcrum?' Elinor repeated.

'Point of balance. Channel.'

'Axle?' Elinor said uncertainly.

Gillien nodded again. 'I've never heard it expressed like that, but . . . yes, "axle" is as good a way as any of putting it. Turning point for one of the great wheels . . .'

'But how . . .' Elinor began in confusion.

'Enough of that, now,' the woman said. 'We'll talk later of it, if the need arises. In the meantime, let's see how that leg of yours is doing this morning, shall we?' She bent and lifted off the blanket.

The movement, careful though the woman was, sent a shudder of pain through Elinor which emptied her of any interest in discussion.

The leg was wrapped cleanly in lengths of linen bandage which Gillien removed with delicate care. Elinor took only one glance, then looked quickly away. It was an ugly, puffy, swollen wound, discoloured red and yellow and blue, puckered up with a long row of neat black stitches. The blade that caught her had ripped her from mid-thigh to below the knee.

'A nasty cut,' Gillien said, 'but shallow for all that. You were very lucky, girl. None of the deep blood vessels were severed. You bled, but not enough to empty you of life. It was the infection afterwards that caused the trouble.'

Elinor lay back weakly, not looking anywhere near her leg.

After inspecting the wound, Gillien nodded to herself and gently laid her palms over the stitched seam, moving them along from top to bottom and then back again, not quite touching, repeating the motion time and again. Elinor felt a kind of soft warmth seeping into her, as if invisible, soothing liquid were being poured into her leg.

Gillien lifted her hands finally, rebandaged the leg, and replaced the bed-covers. 'It's doing well,' she told Elinor. 'As I said, the wound grew infected and you were badly fevered. I feared we might lose you at one point. But you're a strong girl.'

'How . . . how long have I been here?' Elinor asked.

'Four days.'

'No!'

Gillien nodded. 'You were lost in the fever. Raving on about playing cards and ravens, ships and bluebirds, white blades and coffins and corridors – none of it making any too much sense.'

Elinor felt a sudden stab of suspicion. 'Why are you doing all this?' she demanded. 'Why are you helping me? What do you want from me?'

Gillien blinked. 'Why . . . You were brought here hurt. What were we supposed to do, then?'

Elinor shook herself. 'I don't . . . Why should you . . .'

'You were *hurt*, girl, and helpless. Here at Margie Farm we help folk, when we can.'

'Just . . . just help them? Expecting nothing in return?'

Gillien's green eyes flashed for a moment. 'I don't know what manner of folk you've been used to, but here we do not turn our backs upon those in need. And we do *not* help folk merely in expectation of reward!'

Elinor looked away self-consciously. 'I . . . I didn't mean to offend. It's just that . . .'

'I know . . . I know,' Gillien replied softly. 'You've had a hard time of things. I understand. But here at Margie, things are different . . .'

Out of nowhere, a small cat leaped unexpectedly up on to Elinor's bed.

'Alix!' Gillien said. 'Be careful.'

The little cat trotted along the edge of the bed and came to sit neatly next to Elinor's shoulder on the nest of pillows. 'I amm alwayss carrreful,' she said.

Elinor stared. Another one . . .

'This is Alix,' Gillien said by way of introduction. 'She has declared herself to be your watch-cat.'

The cat had been fastidiously licking her paw. She looked up at Elinor and showed her sharp little teeth in what could only be a cat grin. 'Welcome, Elinorrr. Welcomme to Margie.'

Elinor blinked, recognizing the face she had seen upon first coming to. This cat was a beautiful little creature, slim and elegant as only cats can be – what some folk called a tortoise-shell, her fur a mottled mixture of black and gold and white. Elinor reached out a stiff hand and stroked her tentatively under her white chin. 'You're a beautiful creature, aren't you?' she said.

'Burrr burr-urr . . .' said Alix. 'Burr burr-urr.' Then she arched her back, stretched, yawned, struck a little pose. 'Do youu really think me *bee-yootifull*?'

Gillien snorted. 'She's the most conceited thing imaginable, is our Alix. The last thing she needs is flattery.'

'I am *nott* conceeted!' Alix said, wrinkling her nose in offence.

'But she *is* beautiful,' Elinor added.

'Sseee?' Alix said triumphantly. 'Not flattery. I *am* bee-yootifull. Elinorr says soo.' She sat up very straight, her head at an angle, little white chin in the air.

Gillien laughed. Elinor could not help but join in.

Alix glared at them, her green eyes flashing. Then she sprang down off the bed, turned her back, and stalked away to the far side of the room, tail up in the air, head high. Settling herself near the hearth, she sat down, curled her tail neatly about her slim haunches, and began to lick one front paw with delicate care, ignoring them completely.

'Do you feel strong enough for company?' Gillien asked Elinor then.

'Company?' Elinor repeated. 'But who could there be here wanting to see me? There's only one person in all this land I know, and he's . . .' She felt a small pang at the thought of Rannis – gone and parted from her now, and not likely to come back given the circumstances of his leaving. She was unsure how she felt about him. What had happened between them back in Minmi . . . It had not, somehow, borne the promise she had supposed it would.

'It's not a man with dark hair and a blade scar down one cheek, is it?' she asked uneasily.

Gillien shook her head. 'Nothing of the sort.' She regarded Elinor curiously for a moment. 'And just who might this man be, then?'

Elinor shrugged. 'Doesn't matter. Someone I . . . left behind.'

'A strange girl indeed, you are,' Gillien said. 'Brought in here like you were, by who you were, with that exotic blade strapped to you. They thought a lot of that blade. Where *did* you get it?'

Elinor's mind had been clear of any thought of Mattingly's

262

uncanny gift-blade up until Gillien's mention of it. Now, she had a sudden yearning for the thing. 'Where is it?' she asked anxiously.

'I have it stored away safe enough,' Gillien replied. 'We don't much like weapons here at Margie. It'll be there when you need it.'

'But . . .'

'What would you do with it now, in the state you're in?'

Elinor shrugged. Gillien was right enough. But her right hand itched to hold the thing. Kess quivered inside her at the thought of it.

'Shall I tell those waiting outside to come in, then?' Gillien asked.

'Who is it that wants me?' Elinor said.

'The Free Folk.'

Elinor blinked. 'But . . .'

'They've been waiting long days to see you. Let me bring them in to you now. Would that be all right?'

Elinor tried to answer, but for a long moment could not find her voice. She felt suddenly dizzy and sick and overwhelmed, her two selves still not wholly balanced. She felt weak and sweaty and feverish and shaken beyond any easy pulling together.

Gillien bent down and put a hand to Elinor's forehead, her touch warm and soothing. 'It's all right. I can send them away.'

'No,' Elinor said hoarsely. She wished to know who these Free Folk might be.

The first in was Spandel, bounding through the door and leaping excitedly on to Elinor's bed. 'Elinor! Elinor! Elinor!' she cried.

'Carefulll!' Alix hissed at her from the hearth. 'Youu'll *hurrt* her!'

Spandel did an abrupt, mid-air turnaround, stared at the cat. The fur all along her spine went up in a stiff ruff. 'Why don't you tend to your *own* business, stupid, stupid cat? Who made *you* her private watcher-over?'

'Ssspiteful creatuure,' Alix spat, arching her back.

'Enough, you two!' It was Gillien, shaking her head.

Following her, a large stork walked into the room, stepping and bending on long legs like a dancer. Behind the stork came a prick-eared dog, two hairless, odd-looking creatures, and a muttering crow.

Elinor stared.

'The Free Folk,' Gillien said by way of introduction. 'Some of them, at any rate.' She gestured to the stork. 'This is Pallas.' The dog next. 'Jubb.' Then the two hairless creatures. 'Patikin and Tuss.' Then the crow. 'Otys.'

Spandel had come padding along the edge of Elinor's bed to perch on the pillow near her head. She put one of her small hands on Elinor's brow soothingly. 'You'll be fine, now. Fine, fine, with Margie's Dame to tend you. You will. You'll see.'

'Margie's Dame?' Elinor said.

'Me,' answered Gillien. 'One of my names, that. It's what the Free Folk first knew me by, and it stuck.'

Elinor shook her head. 'I don't . . .'

The stork came stalking up to Elinor's bedside. His long, knobbly legs were a startling, vivid orange, his beak grey-red. His plumage was all white, broken only by blue, lacy feathers above his eyes, like absurdly long human eyebrows. The eyebrow feathers quivered as he regarded her. He made a kind of bow, bending over, head lowered, then raised himself slowly upright once more, very formal and graceful and serious. 'We thank you, Elinor Whiteblade, for all you have done. And will do.'

The rest gathered close. They all did the same as the stork, making the same sort of formal, respectful bow, each in a different way. 'We thank you, thank you, thank you,' they said together in a kind of chorus, some of their voices clear and easy to understand, others less so.

They stared at her then, silent, with searching eyes. All were still as so many carvings, except for the crow, which squawked and spluttered softly to himself, waddling back and forth, eyeing her with first one dark, humanish eye, then the other.

Elinor lay back, not knowing how to respond, looking uncertainly at them arrayed about her.

'Come,' Gillien said then. 'Elinor's still weak. You've seen her, and thanked her as you wished to. Give her peace for a little, now. Let her rest.'

Elinor's visitors bowed themselves out. All except Spandel who remained by her side on the pillows.

'Youu alssoo!' Alix the cat ordered from the hearth.

Spandel remained where she was. 'None of your business what I do. None, none at all, stupid cat.'

'Out. The both of you.' Gillien shooed Spandel off the bed, then turned to Alix. But the cat was already gliding out, tail haughtily in the air.

Bending down, Gillien placed a hand on Elinor's brow. '*Rest.*'

Elinor seemed to feel a quiet warmth coming from Gillien's touch, spreading through the bones of her face, down her spine, along through her weary limbs. She resisted it for a few moments, not trusting it, a little frightened.

But what was the use of such struggle? It was, she realized, mere reflex. There was nothing threatening here. The very air seemed to have a peaceful current to it.

'Rest. *Rest . . .*'

Elinor did.

XXVIII

Elinor awoke to see a shaft of golden sunlight filtering into her room through the window. Dust-motes swirled in it like flocks of minuscule birds. It splashed upon the floorboards in a glowing rectangle. The window was open and, from outside, she heard the sound of human voices.

Suddenly, she wanted to be out. Enough of being an invalid. It must be mid-morning or later of a new day from the feel of the sunlight pouring in. She felt stiff and sore, but stronger, and desperately in need of using her limbs. Enough of lying comatose.

Gingerly, she lifted the covers off and manoeuvred her leg away from the bed, using both hands to help support it. It hurt, but not unbearably so. Only once did she bend it too much, sending a lance of fire shooting up her thigh. She stood up haltingly, keeping her right foot off the ground. The blood rushed to her toes, making the whole leg throb painfully, and she felt sickly faint. Red splotches obscured her vision.

But it passed soon enough.

Somebody had dressed her in a long-tailed shirt of soft cloth, the tails coming down to her knees – so she was dressed enough and ready. Hand against the wall for support, she hopped a couple of steps towards the door. But each jarring hop sent a jolt of pain through the wound, and she had to stop, gasping.

Then, in the corner, she saw the crutches, nicely hand-carved things, slim yet sturdy-looking. She hobbled over and reached for them. The tops were well padded and fitted up against her armpits just right. It took a few awkward, experimental steps before she got the feel of them, but then it was far easier to get about.

Her heart beating fast with anticipation, she made her way out of the door.

'Let me help you,' Gillien said, looking up. She hurried over towards Elinor. 'Are you sure you're ready for this?'

Elinor found herself looking into a large, wood-panelled room. Sunlight poured in through diamond-paned windows in a brilliant cascade all along one wall. She blinked, feeling like a worm coming up out of the earth. 'I . . . I needed to get out,' she said. 'I heard voices through the window, saw the sunlight. I've had enough of lying in there.'

Gillien nodded, her thick, cherry-coloured braids swinging. She was wearing the same sort of long, loose dress Elinor had first seen her in, but this one was green instead of blue. It made her green eyes seem to shine. 'Would you like to sit in the sun out on the porch?' she asked.

'Oh, *yes*,' Elinor replied.

'This way, then,' the older woman said. 'Are you sure you don't want me to help you?'

'I've got to learn how myself,' Elinor replied.

Gillien led her across the room. It was a large, comfortable-looking chamber, with a big stone fireplace at one end. A high wooden cabinet took up almost one whole wall, and a trestle table lined with wooden benches and chairs took up much of the remaining floor space.

'Our eating room, this,' Gillien explained.

'How many people do you have here?' Elinor asked. It was a big table.

Gillien shrugged. 'It varies. A dozen or so, usually. Come outside now. The fresh air will do you good. You look pale.'

Elinor felt pale. And clammy with sweat. Her belly spasmed a little. It did that, getting used to food again. She followed Gillien slowly down a wood-panelled hallway, at the end of which was a stout double door, open now. Beyond, she saw green fields and blue sky.

It felt wonderful to sit on the porch in the sun's warmth, her leg stretched out carefully before her. There was a large tree on the near side of the house, its leafy branches fluttering in the little breeze. The green music soothed her.

'So!' somebody said suddenly. 'The wounded warrior is up and about again. Good!'

Elinor turned sideways and saw a big man come striding up. He was bald, with a great blond beard cascading down to the middle of his chest – like the sunshine coming in through the window of her room, Elinor thought. He had blue eyes set in a crinkly network of wrinkles, and shoulders broad as any oxen's. He smiled hugely at Elinor, showing large white teeth through his beard.

'This is Hann,' Gillien explained. 'My husband.'

'Pleased to see you up and about,' he said, putting a meaty hand on Elinor's shoulder. She shied away instinctively, expecting a hearty slap or something of the sort, but his touch was light and gentle.

'Haying in a few days,' he said to Gillien. 'All this sunshine so early in the season is working wonders. Can't remember a more perfect start to the summer.'

Gillien smiled, nodded.

'Just came to see about lunch,' Hann went on. 'The crew's getting a touch restless out there.'

'It's *you* that's getting hungry,' Gillien said, smiling still. 'I'll send Docky along with it soon enough. She's just packing it in the hampers now.'

'Good!' Hann went over and gave Gillien a huge hug. She was no small woman, Gillien, but he overtopped her by a full head and shoulders. He lifted her off her feet easily and spun her around, laughing. Then he put her down, turned, winked at Elinor, and jogged off.

Gillien laughed, too, looking after him, her green eyes shining. She shook her braids back in place, smoothed her ruffled dress. 'I've got to make sure that lot get their lunch,' she said to Elinor. 'Sit here and relax in the sun for a bit. I'll be back. And I'll bring you a little something too. Hungry?'

Elinor nodded.

'Good. See you in a short while.'

Sitting there, alone, Elinor gazed about. The house behind her was a large, two-storeyed structure built of logs. It had more windows than she would have expected, and the eaves were decorated with fanciful, brightly painted carvings – animals, plants, floral designs. From inside she could just hear

268

the clatter of pots and pans. It was a soothing sound. This whole place, in fact, had a soothing feel to it.

She wondered where her visitors of yesterday might be. There seemed nobody near about, human or not. At the very edge of her hearing, she could still make out the distant sound of voices. She looked off in the direction she thought the sound was coming from, but a dry stone wall impeded her vision. It was only about waist-high, but that was high enough, from her position, to hide the fields. The whole area round about was bounded by this rock wall, Elinor realized, a stone necklace encircling the house about twenty paces distant from where she sat. The only break she could make out was directly before her, where a curved lane led from the house down to a kind of entrance gate. Through that gate, she could make out a cart track meandering away into the distance.

Looking further off, she realized for the first time that the farm lay nestled in a valley, and that there were hills everywhere: green-sloped, rock-spined, rising in the east towards a chain of blue mountains. She had, indeed, made it to her green hills, then. It gave her a little thrill to realize it.

She sighed, sat back a little. From the tree by the house came a rustle. She glanced up at it, and froze. A pair of bright eyes was staring at her from one of the leafy limbs. Looking more closely, she could just make out a furred face, sharp little ears, a kind of mane, golden as the sunlight almost.

The face disappeared abruptly, and there was a soft, sudden little *wump* from the far end of the porch on which Elinor was sitting. She turned and saw Alix the tortoiseshell cat come padding elegantly over.

'Are youu welll?' Alix asked.

'Yes,' Elinor said.

Alix came and rubbed her head against Elinor's hip in a cat-caress. 'It iss *goood* to ssit in the ssun.'

Elinor nodded. It still felt most strange to her to be conversing casually thus with what appeared to be only an ordinary cat – save for the eyes, of course.

Alix curled up next to her on the warm wooden planks and closed her eyes, purring softly. Elinor rested a hand on her furry back, feeling the little wings of Alix's shoulder blades rise and fall under the fur with her breathing. Questions nagged at the back of Elinor's mind; there was still so much that confused her. But it was soothing just to sit for the moment in quiet companionship, eyes closed, letting questions and worries go, feeling the sun's warm caress . . .

It was Gillien's voice that roused her.

'Well, well . . .' the older woman said. 'So *this* is where you are, Alix.'

The little cat stretched, yawned.

'Here,' Gillien said, handing Elinor a tray upon which were a ceramic bowl of fragrant broth, a gracefully carved wooden spoon, a thick slice of brown bread, and a cup of steaming hot green tea. The broth bowl and the tea cup were both of the same stunning blue as the water-cup Elinor had seen the day before, elegant and lovely things, too fine, almost, to be used.

'Mee tooo,' said Alix, eyeing the contents of Elinor's tray hungrily.

'Oh, no,' Gillien answered. 'Sandy has been telling me there's a new family of mice in the pot shed. They messed up most of his new slip last night. He's been asking after you half the morning.'

Alix looked away and yawned.

'He told me he's heard from Lessie that old Stayne down at Sutton Farm has kittens. He said he's planning to get one. Since, he said, you're such a *lazy* thing.'

Alix snapped her head up. 'I amm *nott* lazy!'

Gillien shrugged. 'Better tell Sandy. He's the one who said it, not me.'

'Hmmmphh!' said Alix and stalked off.

Gillien grinned.

Elinor grinned back, but uncertainly. She watched Alix disappear round the corner of the house.

'You look . . . puzzled,' Gillien said.

Elinor shrugged. 'Where I come from, people are . . . well, people are people and animals are . . . animals.' But she thought, suddenly, of Mamma Kieran's raven. 'Except . . .'

Gillien sat next to her on the porch. 'We live amongst the shadows of the past here in the South in ways it must be difficult for you, a foreigner, to understand.'

Balancing the tray on her lap, Elinor dipped a hunk of the bread into her broth. It tasted nutty and rich, hot and delicious.

'Do you mean the . . . old Seers?' she asked, mouth still half full. 'And the things they once did.'

'You know of them, then?'

Elinor nodded. 'I have met one.'

'*Really*?' Gillien said, and shivered. 'I do not envy you. Those of today have lost most of the powers they once wielded, but still . . . They are not to be dismissed lightly.'

'As I discovered,' Elinor agreed. 'To my cost.'

'So . . .' Gillien said softly. '*That* is something I would like to hear about.' She gazed off at the green hills for a moment. 'The Seers and the old Lords once held great power here in the South. Yet it was never enough for them. They tore themselves, their Domains, their creations apart in their eternal struggling against each other for yet more and more power.' She shuddered. 'They tore the very balances apart. They were . . . insane.'

Elinor had finished the bread by now. She tipped back the bowl of broth and finished it, too. She sipped at the hot green tea. It was pleasantly astringent. 'And the . . . the humanimals were created by those ancient Seers?'

Gillien nodded. 'Their ancestors were. Long and long ago. And when everything came apart, they escaped their prisons.'

'Prisons?

'The Seers did nothing without reason, nothing without purpose. The humanimals were created to serve their ends, kept in pens, cages. The Seers considered them to be mere *things*, to be dealt with in whatever fashion was most convenient to their aims. There are . . . terrible stories from the old days.'

Gillien stood up. The sunlight made the twin braids of her grey-streaked, cherry-coloured hair shine like silver and copper. She gestured about her, to the house, the fields, the green hills all about. A lone bird sang out in the distance, a long, rising series of twittering notes, like a bright flute. Gillien sighed. 'It seems a peaceful land, doesn't it?'

Elinor nodded. She took another sip of the pleasant tea. 'More peaceful than any I have known recently.'

'It's deceptive.' Again, Gillien sighed. She came and sat beside Elinor once again. 'The old struggles are not finished yet. There are those still trying to revive the past . . .'

'I've met them,' Elinor said.

'I'm sure you have,' Gillien agreed soberly. 'Coming out of Minmi as you did. But the Minmi folk and their like, those that still inhabit the old Domains, are only one part of the whole here. The other part . . . Well, the other part would be happiest if the past could remain dead and buried.'

'And you?' Elinor said.

Gillien laughed uneasily. 'If you have to ask about me, I'm not so certain any more.'

'You have nothing to do with the old ways, then?' Elinor finished a last gulp of the tea and put the empty cup on the tray.

Gillien shrugged. 'It's not so simple as all that. The old ways permeate everything. Might as well try to breathe while having nothing to do with the air. But we do *not* wish to resurrect those old ways intact. It was a path to sickness and insanity that our ancestors walked. We have no wish to follow in their footsteps.'

'Who, exactly, is this "we"?'

Again, Gillien shrugged. 'No particular group, I suppose. We've no organization, no structure. Farmers, for the most part.'

'And the humanimals?' Elinor asked. 'How many *are* there?'

Gillien shrugged yet again. 'Nobody really knows, not even the Free Folk themselves – though it's not the sort of thing they'd tend to bother themselves about. My guess would be that there are fewer than most folk imagine. Humanimals breed true, you see.'

'Meaning . . .' Elinor said.

'If our Alix were to mate with an ordinary tom-cat, she'd produce entirely ordinary offspring. Only with a true humanimal sire would she have humanimal children.'

'But why should . . .'

Gillien shrugged. 'Nobody understands the why of such things. But it means that humanimals have never been very numerous. Especially given their gadabout natures. They're wanderers, you see. And restless, most of them. Never able to settle in any one place. The Free Folk range the wild hills, sometimes in small groups, sometimes alone, visiting Margie when the need strikes them.' Gillien sighed. 'I envy them their freedom at times, especially now with the summer upon us, and the longer evenings.'

272

'And what of the . . . human people hereabouts?' Elinor asked.

'The Free Folk avoid them whenever possible. People are unpredictable when it comes to humanimals. But the Folk know they're always welcome here at Margie. And a few of the other farms in the Valley, too. Though the Brothers like it not at all.'

'The Brothers . . .'

Gillien nodded. 'Those from whom you freed Scrunch.' She looked sober. 'The humanimals are a living, everyday reminder of the great power the ancient Lords and their Seers once held. And of all that was lost. They make many folk uncomfortable. There are those – like the Brothers – who think them a disgusting travesty of humanity, that they should not be allowed to run free and breed. They claim it to have been an abomination, the creation of such beings in the first place, and wish to wipe out the mistake once and for all.' Gillien shivered.

'Human is as human does, as the old saying goes. The Free Folk are human as any of us in their hearts. Save they are more delicate.'

'I'm not sure I understand,' Elinor said. 'Delicate?'

'Perhaps we human folk never can understand, not truly. But I have ministered to them over the years, and have seen their sufferings. They are dual-natured beings. Part human, oh, yes. But part not, also. They are . . . complex beings.'

Gillien looked over at Elinor, suddenly fierce. 'Make no mistake, despite what some would have you believe, the human part of them is like you and I, with all the same hopes and fears and desires and knowings – a dancing spark of complicated individual self-awareness. But there is the other side to them, also, the . . . animal side.'

Though she still did not as yet really understand it all, Elinor felt an instinctive sympathy for the humanimals' plight. She, too, knew what it was like to be a dual-natured being. 'Do you mean they are torn between the human in them and the beast?'

'Caught between human compassion and bestial aggression, do you mean? No.'

'What, then?'

273

'They are like fish out of water sometimes, poor souls.' Gillien shook her head. 'And sometimes it is too much for them. Too bright. Too hard. Too lonely. It was a terrible thing the old Seers did, hauling them out of their dark wombs and into the hard light of human awareness.'

Elinor shook her head. 'I don't understand, Gillien.'

'We are an old land, here in the south, with old wounds. Few things are simple.' Gillien regarded her, face gone dead serious now. 'And neither are you any simple being, Elinor of the shining blade. We have not yet talked about your past, girl, or about who and what you are.'

'*What* I am?'

Gillien nodded. 'You know what I mean.'

Axle, Elinor thought, remembering pudgy Tildie. *One around whom the events of the world turn.* She shivered. Looking at Gillien, she felt a sudden rush of uncertainty about this farmer-woman who seemed kindly enough, but in whom there were hidden depths.

'I mean no harm to you and yours,' Elinor said. 'Truly.'

'Perhaps,' Gillien agreed. Her face softened, and she let out a long breath. 'You are a little unnerving to have about, girl. Such . . . innocence and such depth. And, the times being what they are . . .'

'I don't—' Elinor started.

'Do you feel able to walk a little? There is somebody I wish you to meet,' Gillien said abruptly, rising up.

'Where?' Elinor asked.

'Not far.'

Elinor hesitated for a moment, then lifted herself carefully to her feet and fitted the crutches under her armpits.

Gillien led the way around the house, which was bigger than Elinor had supposed, waiting for her to catch up before they rounded the corner together.

Beyond the house's far side there was a rolling, gently sloping hill. On the near crest of this, set against the encircling stone wall, was a small log structure.

'It's not so far,' Gillien said. 'Can you make it?'

Elinor nodded, hobbling along.

The squat little log building had no door, just an

entrance-way leading to the dim interior. 'Scrunch,' Gillien called softly.

There was no answer from inside.

'We'll have to go in,' she said to Elinor after a few moments.

The entrance-way was low enough so that both women must crouch to go through. Gillien made it easily enough, moving with limber grace despite the fact that she was no thin woman. But it proved too hard on Elinor's leg, and she had to edge back out, sit herself on the ground, and drag herself in backwards, injured leg straight out.

Inside, the place was dim, and it was hard for her to make anything out. The air was close, and thick with a musky, strong odour that caught at the back of her nostrils. She heard something breathing, a snuffling, grunting sound, and craned her neck awkwardly, trying to catch a glimpse of what was in here.

There was a sudden, unexpected *spluuut*, making Elinor's heart skitter. With a little splash of sparks, Gillien had lit a lantern – just a hand-sized bowl with some oil and a wick floating in it.

By the bowl-lantern's flickering light, Elinor saw a pair of large, moist eyes looking up at her from near ground level, very human, set in a large, darkly furred face. She shivered a little, not knowing quite what to think.

Gillien raised the lantern and Elinor saw more properly who – or what – she was facing.

A large bear lay on his belly, back legs splayed out, his snout resting on his limp front paws. He snuffled and looked up at Elinor. 'You,' he grunted.

Elinor did not know what to say.

'Now, Scrunch,' Gillien said gently. She reached out a hand and fondled the bear's ears. He sighed a little, but otherwise ignored her.

'Come closer,' Gillien urged Elinor.

But Elinor only stared uncertainly. The bear was a big creature, its paws the size of her head, nearly. Gillien held the lantern out so that she could see more clearly. The bear looked sad and weary, and utterly forlorn. He blinked at her, snuffled softly, closed his eyes. 'You . . .' he said again.

Elinor was still seated, legs out the entrance-way, looking

over her shoulder awkwardly. She shifted position, bringing her legs part-way in and facing the prostrate bear more squarely.

'You saved me,' he grunted, still with his eyes tight shut. 'You and your shining blade.' He eyed Elinor steadily for a long moment. 'You should have left well enough alone. They all ought to have left well enough alone.' A large tear welled up in his eye and spilled over. 'Nolly would still be here if you'd all just left well enough alone . . . Poor Nolly!'

'Scrunch!' Gillien said sharply. 'Don't be such a fool.'

The bear looked at Gillien out of the corner of one sad brown eye. 'I *am* such a fool.'

'Nonsense,' she replied.

Elinor stared at the two of them.

'Tell her, Scrunch,' Gillien said then, motioning to Elinor. 'Tell her how it is.'

'What does she care?'

'She's a foreigner. She doesn't understand. I think she would care, if she knew.'

Scrunch sighed. 'I tried. I *tried*.'

'Tried . . . what?' Elinor said hesitantly. She felt uncomfortable and confused. Why had Gillien brought her here?

'I tried going away,' the bear said. 'Living with the pure ones. But it was no use.'

'The . . . pure ones?' Elinor said. She shifted position. Her leg hurt. 'What am I . . .' she began, addressing Gillien.

'Listen to him, girl,' Gillien said.

'I get *tired*,' the bear said. 'All that light, all that harsh, never-ending light. I want the dark. Peaceful dark . . .' He sighed, a long outpouring of breath that made his lips flutter. '*They* never get tired. *They* never hurt in their minds as if a fire was lit there, burning, burning, hurting . . .'

Elinor looked across at Gillien and shook her head. She was not understanding any of this.

'I tried to live in the blessed dark,' the bear went on. 'I *tried*. But the fire would not go out. The light never dimmed entirely. No matter how I yearned. And the pure folk, they knew, and never really accepted me. In their bones . . . in their hearts, they knew.'

Abruptly, the bear began to weep, giving long, gasping

sobs, the tears spilling from his sad brown eyes. 'It was too much! Too *much* . . .'

Gillien set down the bowl-lantern, put her arms about the bear's great, furred shoulders, and pressed her face to his. She looked like a little child against his large bulk, but she murmured to him reassuringly, too softly for Elinor to make out any words, perhaps not using words at all, just soft sounds of reassurance and comfort.

'Come,' she said to Elinor, after the bear had quieted. 'We should leave him now.'

Elinor pushed herself out of the dark little place, happy to get away and stretch in the open air again. She struggled gingerly to her feet, her leg throbbing, and stood waiting, staring uncertainly at the little log hut with its dark entrance-way.

Gillien came out a few moments later. 'He's getting better,' she said, nodding to herself in satisfaction. She straightened her green dress, dusted it off, set her braids back in place, smiled.

'*Better*?' Elinor said. Then: 'Gillien, I don't understand *any* of this. Why did you bring me here?'

'I wanted you to see him,' she responded. 'I wanted you to experience it first hand.'

'Experience *what*?' Elinor demanded in exasperation.

'Come,' Gillien said, beckoning. 'Let us return to the house. 'You'll be more comfortable sitting down, surely.'

Gillien led the way back to the porch. Only when they had sat down again, and Elinor had got her throbbing leg into the most comfortable position she could, did Gillien resume their conversation. 'We human folk take the fact of our own mindfulness lightly, but it is no light matter for Scrunch and his kind.'

'He kept saying he'd tried,' Elinor said. 'Tried *what*? And who were the . . . what did he call them? The pure ones. Who were they?'

'Scrunch tried to go back,' Gillien responded. 'He went off deep into the wilds, to try to forget his human mindfulness and live with his simpler cousins. The Pure Ones, the humanimals name them. The bears and crows and dogs and all else that walk or creep or fly and are simply, purely, themselves.'

Gillien looked at Elinor. 'What is the difference, do you reckon, between Scrunch and his wild cousins?'

'You mean . . . ordinary, natural wild bears?'

Gillien nodded.

'Well . . .' Elinor began. 'Wild bears don't talk, of course. And they don't . . . weep.'

'What else?'

'I . . . I'm not sure. I haven't really thought about such a thing before.'

'The wild ones are . . . how should I put it? The wild ones feel no sense of themselves outside their surroundings. They are untroubled by questions of their own being. This makes them more simple . . . What human person cannot out-think a wild creature if put to the test? But it also makes them something else. More . . . pure, as the humanimals say. More a part of the great patterns and Powers. Never lost. Never out of step. Never entirely alone. No . . . that's not how to put it. Never . . . never able to feel entirely alone, perhaps.'

'I still don't really understand,' Elinor said, shaking her head.

'Think of a carving, then. A face carved from a great tree. In the early stages, it is difficult to differentiate between the features of the face and the form of the tree itself. As the carving progresses, however, the face becomes clearer, though still part of the tree. Only at the final stage does the tree drop away and the face emerge alone.

'We are the complete face, we human folk. For better or worse, we are separate, mindful, apart. The humanimals are the half-completed carving, no longer entirely part of the tree but not yet entirely whole. The wild ones are the initial beginnings, still undifferentiated. Wild folk are altogether a part of the world in which they live, wholly and purely.

'We human folk are no longer part of the world in that pure fashion. The humanimals are caught between, uneasily, painfully, dragged out of their initial purity by the old Seers' dark arts, not fitting entirely comfortably in either, not knowing where they really belong.'

Elinor stared off at the far green hills for some moments, trying to take it all in. 'But Scrunch sounded . . . upset that he had been saved.'

'He had made the resolution,' Gillien said. 'It happens, sometimes. It gets too much for them, the burden of mindfulness. Scrunch had tried to become like his wild cousins and failed. So he had come back to make his goodbyes and to die, like others have done before him.'

'Do they often . . . kill themselves, then?' Elinor asked.

'Not often. But it happens. Scrunch had given himself up to the Brothers when you and your Spandel and the rest . . . liberated him. He had resigned himself to the end.' Gillien shrugged. 'But you spoiled all that.'

'*Spoiled?*'

'He's a confused soul now, is our Scrunch. But I think you saved him, girl. And saved the others, too, from the mad folly of their rescue attempt.' Gillien sighed then and shook her head. 'But I fear what else you may have started. The world feels . . . *charged*.'

Elinor did not know what to say.

'Do you understand better about them now?' Gillien asked. 'They are not simple beings, Scrunch and Alix and Spandel and their kind.'

Elinor nodded. She paused for a moment, still staring off at the hills. 'These . . . Brothers. Who . . . what are they?'

Gillien shivered. 'They inhabit old Sofala, one of the ancient Domains. They are . . . how should I put it to you? Like others, they feel themselves to be the inheritors of past glories. They believe men to be the chosen creatures, the only ones with true souls, and that the world is theirs by divine right. In Sofala, they have even gone so far as to set up an effigy they call Jara, a man-faced Power they claim as their divine guide.' Gillien shivered. 'The Ancient Brotherhood of the Light is their full name for themselves, but there's precious little light in any of their beliefs.

'They believe the past age of the Lords and Seers was a time of greatness, a "golden age" that is now lost. They believe that, in creating animals with human spirits, the men of the past transgressed Divine Law and that, as a result, they were punished and their Domains destroyed.'

Gillien shivered again. 'So they are convinced that the solution is to kill all humanimals, thus wiping out the original transgression and paving the way for the recovery of all that was lost.

'There is a kind of fatal seductiveness in such beliefs for some folk. The Brothers' numbers have been growing steadily over the years. They are rebuilding Sofala, extending into the land all about. We trade foodstuffs with them. But they are . . . ruthless men, fanatical in their actions. Scrunch gave himself up to one of their roving hunting parties, knowing he would be taken and put to death.'

Gillien turned. 'But *you* killed *them*. And in the cause of the Free Folk.' She stared at Elinor for a long moment. 'What you did will change the Balances, girl. Be assured of that. You're a fulcrum. The world turns on the actions of such as you.'

'I . . .' Elinor shook her head. 'How do you know I am this . . . fulcrum?'

'It is clear as clear, girl, to those who can see such things. You have the print of some Power upon you.'

Elinor shuddered. 'I don't *like* it.'

'The humanimals think you a divine creature sent to their aid.' Gillien's face had gone serious once more. 'As for me . . .'

'I'm no threat to you or yours, Gillien,' Elinor said quickly. 'You've been good to me. I would never bring harm to you.'

'The world is *charged*, girl. I can feel it. You will do what you have to do. You have the stink of the destined about you.'

Elinor jerked her hand away and froze. It was old Mamma Kieran's phrase, that. And Tildie's. She had a sudden dark suspicion of a great secret society of such women as these, in touch, somehow, over huge distances, all working together to manipulate her into . . .

'Do you know old Tildie?' she demanded.

'Tildie?' Gillien said. 'Never heard of her.'

'Or Mamma Kieran? Or Dame Sostris?'

'No, and no,' Gillien replied. 'What's this all about, then? Who are these women?'

Elinor was not sure what to say. 'They have . . . guided me, or pushed me, or . . . I don't know.'

Gillien nodded. 'They saw into your nature.'

'And you?'

'I have a little of the Sight. Enough to recognize you for no ordinary person.'

Elinor regarded her uneasily.

'I've upset you,' Gillien said. 'I'm sorry.' She shook her head.

'I have no business burdening you with all this so soon. But I wished you to *understand*. Being what you are, ignorance is dangerous.'

Elinor nodded. 'I'm sorry I . . .'

'Gillien!' a voice suddenly called out. '*Gillien*!'

A man came dashing up the lane leading to the house from the entrance gate.

'Collart,' Gillien said, surging to her feet. 'What *is* it? Is anyone hurt?'

The man she had named Collart shook his head. He was an older man, thin, grey-haired, stubble-cheeked, dressed in baggy trousers and shirt, splattered with earth. He stood panting, his chest heaving, trying to draw breath. 'Vis-visitors . . .' he managed to say.

'Who?' Gillien asked.

'Better come and see for yourself.' Collart bent forward, his hands on his knees, still panting. He shook his head. 'Don't expect you'll like it much.'

'Who *is* it?'

He shrugged uncomfortably, looked at her, looked away. 'I was up on Roary's Hill, with the sheep. Came fast as I could, soon as I seen these men in the distance. They looks like . . . like Brothers.'

'Brothers!' Gillien frowned. 'Go and fetch Hann and the rest. They're in the west field. Quick!'

Collart left at a gasping run.

'And you return to the house,' Gillien ordered Elinor.

'But perhaps I can . . .' Elinor began, her heart beating suddenly hard.

'Just get back *inside*!' With that, Gillien turned and strode determinedly off along the lane leading down to the entrance gate, her cherry-coloured braids swinging, dress swishing about her legs.

281

XXIX

Elinor reached for her crutches, started to go inside as Gillien had directed, then hesitated.

The big tree near the house caught her attention. If she stood behind it, she would be shielded from the view of anybody at the entrance gate – and who knew? Any search party might just march straight into the house and miss her. She did not think it would be good for Gillien and Hann and the rest if she were found sheltering inside their house.

She hobbled over, quick as she could, and concealed herself behind the tree's broad trunk. Peering cautiously round, she discovered she had a straight view down the lane to the gate.

A squad of sombre-clothed, armed men were marching up the cart track in the distance. The same sort of men she had already encountered. Elinor felt her heart clench up.

Gillien stood by the gate, straight-backed and seemingly unconcerned at the prospect of facing a dozen or so armed men alone.

'Ho, woman,' said the man in the lead as he came close.

Though she had to strain a bit to do it, Elinor could hear him clearly enough. He was a big, dour-faced man with thick black moustaches, dressed like all the rest in dark clothing and body cuirass. He wore a leathern fighting helm, as did they all, but the sun-ray-and-gripped-hands insignia which marked his was a shining brass plaque rather than red embroidery as the rest seemed to be. And where they carried both long blades and lances, he was armed only with a blade. In his hand, he carried a small, gilded staff.

Gillien closed the gate firmly in his face as he strode up, calm as could be.

He gestured at her with his little golden stick. 'I am Collis Tigh,

Squad Chief of the Imperial Armed Might of the Ancient Brotherhood of the Light. Where is your man?'

Gillien shook her head. 'You are not welcome here.'

The Squad Chief frowned. He stepped forward to wrench the gate open.

'Have a care, man,' Gillien said.

'Oh, yes?' he sneered. He put a hand to the sword at his belt. 'And just what will you *do*? Lash me senseless with your woman's tongue? Smother me with your dress?' The men behind him guffawed. 'Now open the gate in the name of Jara the Great and stand aside!'

Gillien did not move. Elinor could not see her face, but her back was still straight and she stood calmly, one hand set firmly on the gate. 'You have the manners of a stoat,' she said.

The Squad Leader's face coloured. 'Mind your tongue, bitch!' he snapped.

'And you mind yours,' a new voice put in. It was Hann, come from the fields, a hoe in his hand. Collart was with him, and a handful of others.

'And just who might *you* be?' the Squad Chief demanded.

'I am Hann.'

'Are you the Master of this farm, then, Hann?'

Hann shook his head.

'Well, fetch the Master!' the Squad Chief snapped. 'And be quick about it. I tire of wasting my time with stupid farm hands.' He gestured impatiently at Gillien. 'And get this woman away from me. She grates on my nerves. Who does she belong to? By the Ancients, isn't there anybody amongst you man enough to keep her in her place?'

Elinor saw Gillien's back stiffen.

But Hann only laughed.

'Are you *completely* addled in the head?' the Squad Chief demanded. 'Will you fetch the Master of this farm or not?'

'No need to fetch the *master*,' Hann said.

'And why *not*?'

'The *master's* already here.'

'I am losing patience, man,' the Squad Chief said. 'Make yourself plain or . . .'

'Or what?' Gillien asked coldly.

'I told you to be *quiet*, woman!'

Again, Hann laughed. 'You're not making a very good impression, man.'

The Squad Chief glared at him.

'Meet the *master*,' Hann said, waving at Gillien.

'Don't be ridiculous!' the Squad Chief snapped.

'Nothing ridiculous about it. This is her farm.'

'This is her *man's* farm!' the Squad Chief said.

Hann shook his head.

'This,' the Squad Chief said, 'is unbelievable!' He turned to the men at his back. 'Break the gate down. Search the house.'

But Gillien called out, '*Halt*!' and so forceful was her voice, her very presence, that the men hesitated. 'You *will not* pass here without my permission.'

The Squad Chief laughed. 'And just how are you planning to stop us?'

'Are you really as stupid as you seem?' she said. 'Or is it just an elaborate pretence?'

The Squad Leader took a menacing step forward. He aimed his little gilded staff at her as if it were a weapon. 'You need a good thrashing, woman.'

Hann came to stand beside his wife. 'And *you* need to learn some manners.' He gestured at the Brothers. 'We might have let you in, perhaps. If you had been civil. But now . . . We'd no more consider allowing you on to our farm than we would invite a pack of rats into the granary.'

'Right,' the Squad Chief said. He gestured to the armed men behind him. 'Take this man down.'

Old grey-haired Collart came to stand next to Hann defensively, gripping a rusty pitchfork he had got from somewhere.

The Squad Leader laughed. 'And the old man too, if he wishes to be so stupid.'

But again Gillien called out, '*Back away*!'

The Brothers hesitated.

'Do you wish a feud with every farmer in the district?' she demanded of the Squad Chief.

He paused, looking at her uncertainly.

'For that is just what you will get if you force your way on to this farm. And think how *that* would affect your precious Sofala. Force your way on to my farm and you will see no grain

284

this season, no mutton, no cheese. Every farm in the Valley will be closed to you.'

'Hah!' the Squad Chief sneered. 'That is a ridiculous bluff.'

'No bluff,' said one of those gathered behind Hann. He came up between Hann and Gillien, a thin young man, blond, with a wispy beard. 'I am Gault the younger, of Perry Farm. And I stand with Gillien and Hann.'

After Gault came a grey-haired, short woman in trousers and shirt. 'I am Lessie, of Sutton Farm,' she said. 'I too stand with Gillien and Hann.'

The Squad Chief was beginning to look uncertain.

'We farmers look out for each other,' Hann said.

'And we do *not* like your sort bullying our own,' blond Gault added.

For a long few moments there was silence.

Then, 'State your business, man,' Gillien said.

'And be civil,' Lessie added, 'if you expect us to listen.'

'You are,' the Squad Leader began, his words clipped and harsh, 'harbouring a woman here.'

Gillien merely looked at him.

'Don't bother to deny it. We know she is here.'

'So?' Gillien said.

'So we have come for her. She is *ours*!'

Hiding behind the big tree near the house, Elinor shivered. Faced with these armed men, what could Gillien and Hann and the rest do save hand her over? Words would not stop such men. Pitchforks, neither. She glanced about, looking desperately for a way to get away without being seen. But there was none. She could not move without revealing herself.

'In what way, exactly,' Hann was saying to the Squad Chief, 'is she *yours*?'

'She has committed wicked crimes against the Brotherhood. She is a dangerous criminal and must be punished!'

'What . . . *crimes*?' Gillien demanded.

'Don't play me for a fool, woman! You know very well what crimes. She has wantonly murdered members of the Brotherhood. None may commit such a foul deed without punishment.'

'And just how did she commit this . . . foul deed?' said Gillien.

'That is none of your business. She has killed, wantonly and without reason, and she must be *punished*!' He waved his gilded stick at them. 'I am Collis Tigh, Squad Chief. This is my Staff of Office. I come to you officially, in the name of Iryn Jagga and of the Great Jara himself. Now give this woman over to me for the punishment she so justly deserves.'

'Not likely,' Gillien said calmly.

The Squad Chief stared. 'What did you say?'

'Are you hard of hearing, then?'

'Don't *toy* with me, woman.'

'Oh, I'd never dream of such a thing, man.'

The Squad Chief stood there, face white with fury, one hand upon his sheathed sword's hilt now. 'Will you give me the woman?'

'No,' said Gillien.

'She is ours, this evil woman. We *will* have her, with your cooperation or not. It is up to you.'

'And you may eat or starve,' said Gillien. 'It is up to you. Set *one* foot upon my property, Collis Tigh, Squad Chief, and you and yours will find yourselves without food for the rest of the year. No farmer in the Valley will sell you *anything*.'

The Squad Chief shook his head. 'You are making a grave mistake, woman.'

'See that you do not make one, man,' Gillien responded. 'Now walk away.'

The Squad Chief scowled at her.

'You heard what I said. Walk *away*.'

He glared at the little gathering standing solidly against him. 'Nothing but trouble can come of this. You do not realize what you do.'

'Oh, we realize, all right,' said Hann. 'Now walk away.'

The Squad Chief hesitated a moment longer, then turned on his heel and waved his men back. 'You haven't heard the last of this,' he spat over his shoulder, white-faced and furious. 'I am Collis Tigh. Remember that name, for you will live to regret what you have done here this day.'

No one bothered to say anything in response.

The Brothers marched off, baulked and furious, down the cart track and into the distance.

'And good riddance to them,' grey-haired Lessie, of Sutton

Farm, said. 'Shit for brains, the lot of them.' She shook her head in disgust.

Gillien turned and strode back towards the house.

Elinor came out from behind her tree. 'Tha-thank you,' she said to Gillien. It seemed an altogether inadequate thing to say.

Gillien glared at her, green eyes flashing, hands on her ample hips. 'I thought I told you to get back inside. What if they'd seen you?'

'They didn't, though,' said Hann, coming up. 'The girl's got nerve, Gill, you must admit.'

Gillien nodded, shook her head, laughed a small, strained laugh. 'Indeed. She has that.'

'Thank you,' Elinor repeated. The whole group had come up to the tree by now. 'It's been long and long since anybody has . . . Oh, thank you. Thank you all.'

'The man's an inflated, overbearing fool,' Gillien said.

'I should leave,' Elinor said quickly. 'My staying here puts you in danger.'

'Nonsense,' Gillien said.

'But . . .'

'It isn't just you, Elinor,' Hann explained. 'The Brothers have been pushing at us for years now, trying to undermine our autonomy.'

'They'd like to devour us whole,' young Gault said. 'Like wolves with a pack of sheep.'

'Only we're not easy to devour,' Hann put in, grinning fiercely through his blond cascade of beard.

'But what if they come back?' Elinor said. 'If I were to stay here you'd be in real danger.'

'We're in real danger in any case,' Gillien said, and her face was deadly serious. 'Remember what I told you about the way things are here? The old conflicts are far from finished. Something like this was bound to happen, one day or another. It seems today is the day, and you are the fulcrum.'

Elinor shivered.

'Your leaving won't end things,' Hann was saying. 'The Brothers are only looking for an excuse. If not you, then something else.'

'But what if they . . .' Elinor swallowed. 'If they attack the farm?'

'They'd never do anything as drastic as *that*,' Hann assured her. 'It's not in their own best interest. That was no empty threat we made about cutting off their food supplies. They need our food, walled away up in mouldering old Sofala as they are. They need our good will. And they know it.'

'Much as it irks them,' Lonn added.

'Much as it does,' Hann agreed.

Everybody laughed, but it was strained laughter still.

'Come, then,' Hann said briskly. 'Back to work, you lot. We've still a fair bit to finish before sunfall.'

Off they all trooped, leaving Gillien and Elinor alone by the porch.

'I'm sorry,' Elinor said. 'If it weren't for me, you'd all be . . .' She sighed. 'I don't know what to say.'

Gillien shrugged, put a hand gently on Elinor's arm. 'Things are as they are, girl. And will be as they will.' She smiled, but it was a thin smile. 'You did not make us do what we did.'

She turned then and made a shooing motion towards the house. 'Now go and lie down and get some rest if you can. You need it.'

Elinor hesitated for a moment, then nodded. Hobbling along on her crutches, her throbbing leg held stiffly out before her, she made her way slowly back into the house.

XXX

The next day, Elinor went out on to the porch again, to soak up the sun's healing warmth – but she put herself at the end closest to the tree behind which she had hidden when the Brothers came, just in case the need arose again.

It was mid-morning now of another sunny day, the air warm and fresh. Her leg ached, but she felt good in herself somehow. The two sides of her self seemed to have settled, or gone dormant, or something. And she had, somehow, not even bothered to ask as to the whereabouts of the white blade that Gillien had stored away safely somewhere.

She felt whole – despite all frights and confusions and uncertainties. She felt at home, here. She felt like she belonged, somehow.

It was most strange.

Without warning, a small body came bouncing suddenly over the wall that circled the house. 'Elinor, Elinor, Elinor!'

Spandel.

The little Lamure came tripping along over the grass on her hind legs, long arms and ringed tail held out for balance, and leaped on to the porch at Elinor's side. 'You're well, well, well,' she said with satisfaction, then clambered lightly into Elinor's lap. Arms on Elinor's shoulders, she stretched upwards, craning her neck and sniffing and searching about. 'Where's the *cat*?'

Elinor smiled, stroked Spandel's furred head. 'I haven't seen her all day.' She lifted Spandel gently and set her on the porch. 'Where have you been?'

Spandel grinned, a flash of little white teeth. 'I've been running, running, running . . .' She did a little skipping dance on the boards.

This was a new Spandel. She looked sleeker, fuller. Her fur was glossy. Her small, dark, human-like eyes fairly shone.

'It's so very *big*, Elinor. Big, big, big! And so *interesting*.'

'What is?'

Spandel gestured about her. 'Why . . . *everything*. I never knew there was so much *world* outside Minmi.'

'Spandel,' Elinor said impulsively, 'did you know what Lord Mattingly was planning to do back in Minmi?' It was a question that had been lurking at the back of her mind all along. 'Spandel?' she urged.

Spandel fidgeted, shrugged, looked away.

'Tell me,' Elinor said, 'please. I need to know.'

Spandel hugged herself, tail and arms. 'It was a *bad* place, Minmi. Bad, bad, bad. Badder than I ever could know . . .'

'Did you know he wanted to kill himself?'

Spandel nodded.

'And that he would use me as his . . . instrument?'

Again, Spandel nodded.

Elinor took a sharp breath. 'How *could* you?'

'You don't *understand*!' Spandel said quickly. 'Mattingly was . . . like one of *us*. The light burned him. I . . . I felt for him. Understood his pain, his need. He wanted release.'

Elinor ran a hand over her eyes. Having listened to Gillien, and Scrunch the bear, she had some idea of what Spandel meant. But still . . . 'Just . . . to *use* me!' she said accusingly.

'It was part of the dream. You were. And you are . . . what you are.'

'What . . . dream?'

Spandel rubbed at her muzzle with one hand. 'I dream dreams, Elinor. I . . . *know* things. I dreamed you. I told Mattingly. We recognized you, he and I, the moment you appeared before us. You were his freedom.'

Elinor recoiled.

'Elinor, Elinor, Elinor!' Spandel pleaded. 'Don't be cross. Don't be! The world is a great dream. A wondrous, painful, mysterious dream, dreamed by the Great Lady. Dreamer and dreamed. And we are. Dreamers all.'

Elinor shook her head. 'I don't . . . The world is not a dream, Spandel.'

Spandel looked at her, saying nothing.

'Who is this . . . this great dreaming . . . lady, then?'

Silence.

'Spandel?'

More silence.

Elinor sighed. 'Did you . . . dream about the Brothers, too?' she asked, after a little. 'And poor sad Scrunch in his cage?'

'Oh, yes.'

'And you knew what would happen? To me?'

Spandel shook her head in vigorous denial. 'It isn't like that. Not at all at all. I dreamed pain and darkness and fear. I dreamed wetness and men screaming. I dreamed forest and rock. That was all.'

'Did you dream me in that dream?'

'Not with your poor leg hurt. Not *that*.'

Elinor looked at Spandel for a long moment, then leaned back, sighing. It was most strange and complicated, all of this. She did not know what to think. She stretched her aching leg, scratched tentatively at the long ridge of the stitch-puckered scar, which was beginning to itch a little – a good sign, Gillien had assured her.

Elinor closed her eyes and lifted her face to the sun, focusing on the bright pink on the inside of her eyelids. The sunshine was delightfully warm. She heard a bird singing somewhere in the distance, heard the comforting sounds of ordinary life coming from inside the house. It was such a good place, this farm of Gillien's. She wished with all her heart that things might be simple, that she might have come here under other circumstances.

But things were not simple.

She heard a sudden quiet chittering, opened her eyes and jerked backwards, sending a stab of pain up her leg.

Seated there before her on the grass was a humanimal she had never seen before. It was a pale, furry, four-legged creature, like a large rabbit with peculiarly tiny ears. The humanity of its eyes was unmistakable.

'Hallo,' Elinor said tentatively.

Rabbit-like, it hopped towards her. It had long whiskers which twitched nervously. Arriving at Elinor's feet, it reached out one human-thumbed, furred paw and touched her lightly on her hurt leg. It looked up into her eyes, its own shining with some deep emotion she could not begin to make out.

She stayed still as still.

Then, without a word, the creature whisked away and bounded off, disappearing behind the tree near the porch.

Elinor shook her head, staring after it.

'They . . . recognize you,' Spandel said then.

Elinor looked at her. '*Recognize* me?'

'As being . . . special. The wild ones. They come from far, far away to look at you. To touch you. They say you are the chosen of the Great Lady.'

'Who *is* this "Great Lady" you talk of, Spandel?'

But Spandel only looked away, silent.

Elinor shivered. She did not like this adulation. She did not like this being . . . special.

Almost, she laughed. This was one of life's great ironies. All her adolescent days she had felt herself to be *special*, had yearned to be. And now . . .

It gave her a pain in the belly merely to think of it. Everything seemed so complicated and mysterious. *Axle*, *Channel*. The world turning on her actions . . . She did not wish any such responsibility.

All she wanted now was to be left alone and in peace so that she might find what it was life had to offer her. All her Long Harbour dreams were gone. Not shattered, exactly. Evaporated like so much morning mist, more like. And now? She did not know.

'Look!' Spandel said suddenly, breaking into her thoughts.

Elinor saw a large white stork come slow-winging its way over the wall. It landed with a graceful-awkward hop and a skip on the grass before them, then strode over on its long legs. It bowed rather formally before her and said, 'Greetings to you, Elinor Whiteblade.'

'Ah . . . Greetings to . . . to you,' she replied, a little taken aback by the title he had given her.

'It is good to see you are recovering your strength.' The stork stepped closer, very dignified, lifting each leg with slow grace. He gazed at her down his long, red-grey beak. Feather eyebrows lifted over dark, steady, serious eyes. 'You feel well in yourself?'

Elinor nodded.

'That is good. You are in good hands. Margie's Dame has healed many a one here.' He looked down at Elinor's leg, nodding with sober satisfaction. Then he turned to Spandel. 'And you, Dreamer. You are faring well in your travels?'

'The world is large and wild and wonderful,' she said.

The stork clacked its beak disapprovingly. 'Large, at any rate. And wild, certainly. But dangerous, too. You are too new to the wide world yet to be safe. You must be more careful, little Dreamer.'

Spandel shrugged in an absolutely human gesture, and looked away.

'You were one of those who came to see me by my bedside, weren't you?' Elinor said, leaning forward. 'And you were in the . . . wild, too.'

The stork nodded. 'Pallas is my name. We came to thank you for what you did.'

'But it's I who must thank you,' she replied. 'It was you who brought me here to Margie, wasn't it?'

'It was Scrunch the bear who carried you,' Pallas said. 'And the rest, doing what they could when Scrunch grew too weary.'

'Thank you,' she repeated. 'I owe my life to you all.'

'It is we who owe ours to you,' Pallas replied, and bowed to her again in his formal way.

'Howw verry *sweeettt*,' a voice suddenly said from above them.

Elinor looked about sharply, and saw a large black crow perched on the lowest limb of the big tree near the porch.

'None of you heardd me cominggg,' the crow said. 'So caught uppp in flattering each otherrr, you werre.' He *kawwed* harshly, in a kind of laugh. 'How *sweeettt* you werre all beinggg. Sweeettt – and blinddd as blinddd to anythinggg beyonddd your own pleasantriesss!'

'Otys!' the stork snapped. 'Be polite.'

The crow *kawwed* its harsh laughter again. 'Be pol-ite. Be pol-ite . . .' it mocked derisively. It leaped off the branch into the air, squawking, 'Be pol-ite, be pol-ite . . .'

'Stupid bird!' Spandel hissed, glaring at it.

Kaww kaww kaww, it laughed, and flapped away.

Elinor was unsure what to think. 'He was with you all, wasn't he?' she asked.

'He was,' Pallas replied. 'And is. But he is . . .' The stork rustled his own wings, lifting them in a kind of dignified,

293

feathery shrug. 'He likes to pick at things, does Otys. Sometimes he cannot stop himself.'

'Stupid bird,' Spandel repeated.

'No,' Pallas said seriously. 'Never that. He . . .'

A sudden, fierce and unexpected *yeeowwwll* sent the stork vaulting up into the air with a very undignified squawk. Spandel shrieked and scrambled up the tree to safety amongst its branches.

Elinor whirled about, her heart thumping.

'Lunch,' said Alix, her cat-face split in a mischievous and entirely self-satisfied grin. She sat down and began to lick fastidiously at one white-tipped paw.

Inside, the big eating-room table was piled with food – fresh-baked bread, slabs of white cheese, frothy ewe's milk, lentil stew, salt cod from the coast, a brace of huge potato and onion pies hot from the ovens, a stack of tart, wrinkled apples. Every chair was taken, and folk were crowded about the table, a dozen or more, talking and reaching across each other and laughing.

There was a pause as Elinor entered, and they all glanced up. This was her first group lunch. So far, the farm folk had eaten their mid-day meal in the fields. Today, for whatever reason, they were all gathered here. She felt self-conscious, hobbling into the room.

Gillien ushered her along to the far end, where a thin, blue-eyed man with sandy-coloured hair and long moustaches was carting a chair in from an adjoining room.

'Thanks, Sandy,' Gillien said. Then, 'Elinor, this is Sandy, our resident potter.'

'Is it you, then,' Elinor said, gesturing to the elegant blue dish-ware laid out upon the table, 'who makes the blue bowls and such?'

Sandy nodded.

'They're *lovely*,' Elinor said.

He burst into a huge smile. 'Come sit with me,' he invited, gesturing her over with his chin.

Elinor glanced across at Gillien, who shooed her along.

Folk shifted aside willingly enough, and, after a bit of a shuffle with the crutches, Elinor found herself seated next to

Sandy at the table. The lentil stew sat in front of her in a large blue tureen. Somebody passed her a bowl and she began helping herself to the stew. Buttered bread appeared next to her, along with a cup of the ewe's milk and a steaming slab of the potato and onion pie. 'Enough, enough!' she spluttered. 'I'll never eat all that.'

Spandel appeared suddenly and hopped into her lap, reaching for a slice of bread. 'I'll help.' The little Lamure took a huge bite, chewed, swallowed, nodded her head vigorously. 'It's good, good, *good*!'

The table erupted into laughter.

'I should think so,' somebody said.

'Best bread in the Valley at this table,' somebody else added.

Elinor recognized the voice as Hann's. Looking round, she saw him seated at the foot of the table.

'Isn't that so, Gillien?' he went on, grinning at his wife.

Elinor turned to the table's head where Gillien sat, Alix perched beside her taking dainty bites out of a little slab of the cod in a bowl. 'And the hungriest eaters in the Valley, too, I should think,' Gillien replied to her husband, gesturing at the gathering.

'Here's to wholesome hunger,' said a grey-haired man whom Elinor recognized as Collart, the one who had first come to warn Gillien of the arrival of the Brothers. He lifted a cup of the milk. 'Hunger . . . and Margie Farm lunches.'

'Margie Farm lunches!' the gathering echoed.

Elinor found herself joining in. There was an easy companionship here that truly warmed her. On her left, Sandy smiled and nodded. On her right, a lanky man with a long nose winked at her and said, 'Eat up, girl. You need to build your strength.'

After that, they were pretty much silent, all their concentration on the serious business of eating.

XXXI

For a double handful of days, life went on quietly at Margie Farm. Elinor sat on the porch in the sun for much of each day, healing. The stitches were taken out of her leg. Gillien bathed the long, puckered scar regularly, running her healing hands over it as she had been doing since the first day of Elinor's arrival at Margie. Gradually, Elinor began to walk without the crutches, using a cane instead.

She spent time with Sandy in his pottery, watching him turn the beautiful blue pots he made. She would sit quietly sometimes with Spandel, the two of them mesmerized by his skill, the wheel creaking softly as it spun, the clay changing from a shapeless lump to a curving mushroom to a pot, as if growing by magic before their very eyes, coaxed into being by his hands. She envied the man, for he had found what he wanted in life. It was clear to see as he sat treading his wheel, his whole self intent, eyes shining, magicking another perfect pot out of a lump of blue river clay.

She tried it herself once, with Sandy treading the wheel for her, but only managed a lopsided blob.

'Looks a bit like something that came out of the hind end of a sheep,' was his laughing comment.

She laughed along with him – for it was true enough, and his good-humoured observation somehow anything but hurtful.

As well as watching Sandy, she talked with the various farm folk, growing to know them a little, hearing their stories of field and hill. There were several dozen farms in the Valley, she learned, all loosely affiliated, oft times helping each other with the farming work, sharing flocks and fields, inter-marrying, forming a tight-knit little community for all there was no central village.

As she had with Sandy, though, Elinor felt a pang of envy.

These folk *belonged* here, wedded to each other and to the land itself. She felt like an outsider, for all the kindness they continued to show her.

And she felt guilty.

There were stories. During one of the communal indoor lunches, old Collart had said, 'Hear tell from old Pattington that *they* have been combing the hilly borderlands.'

There was no need to name that *them* – none mentioned the Brothers by name unless they had to.

'He told me his eldest saw them,' Collart had gone on. 'Out with the sheep, he was. Saw them beating through the bush. More of them than he'd ever seen that far out, he claimed.'

'Did they give the lad any trouble?' somebody asked.

'Only the usual bullying. Took two of the sheep, though.'

'A right pain in the arse they've been lately.' This from an older woman named Lall, who was the head of a farm at the Valley's far end, and visiting for the day. 'What *do* they think they're about? I've half a mind to tell them to piss off and to sell my barley elsewhere.'

'Where?' somebody had piped up.

Lall nodded soberly. 'Aye. Where indeed? That's the rub.'

Elinor had kept silent. There had been no further sign of Brothers around Margie, and little talk of them, but she felt a guilty unease. Her very presence brought danger – no matter that Gillien dismissed the notion.

'I've told you, girl,' Gillien insisted one afternoon as they sat on the porch shelling new peas together, 'we've been trading with them for years and years. They've *never* been easy to deal with.'

Elinor had nodded, but there was something in the set of Gillien's face that had made her uncomfortable.

But the days went on peacefully enough. Elinor helped out with what farm chores she could, or lolled quietly in the warmth of the sun, with Spandel or Alix – the two had managed a kind of truce – or Gillien, or Hann, or one of the farm hands. Grey-bearded old Collart came by sometimes to visit with her, and to hear stories of the north. He had travelled as a young man, apparently, and had an abiding interest in far-off places.

Sometimes Jubb the dog came to visit, or one of the hairless, pale creatures called Hyphons. Of Scrunch the bear there was no sign. He had lumbered off into the hills.

As the days passed, Elinor felt her leg grow stronger and stronger. Margie Farm was a good place, and peaceful. Folk were accepting here, of her, of the humanimals, of each other. It was different from any place she had ever known. She felt herself to be in an island of healing *now*, separated both from the upsets of her past – Long Harbour and Minmi and all – and from any future uncertainties that awaited her. They were good days, quiet days. Healing days.

And then, in the chill, grey moment before dawn one morning, Spandel came to Elinor at her bedside, trembling, eyes huge and staring, and said, 'I dreamed. I dreamed, dreamed, dreamed!'

'Hurt and pain and help,' was all Spandel could say by way of explanation. 'Fur and blood and pain.'

'Who?' Elinor asked. 'Where? Is it one of the humanimals?'

'Oh, yes, yes,' Spandel said, nodding her head vigorously. And then, 'No, no, no.'

Which left Elinor entirely confused. 'Is it someone we know?'

'He hurts and is frightened.'

'He? Who *is* it?'

But Spandel only hopped about in agitation. 'We must go, go, go! We must find him.'

'Find *who*?' Elinor insisted. 'Where?' But it was no use. She could get nothing clearer out of Spandel. Only that they must go, quick, out across the fields towards the rising sun. Quick, quick.

Elinor was far from eager to go traipsing off through the dawn fields, and her previous experiences with the little Lamure's dream-led urgings had left her wary. But there was no denying Spandel in this mood, and no peace till she did as Spandel insisted.

Out behind the house there was a wooden stile over the waist-high rock wall – three steps up, one over, three down. Elinor ended up on the ground on the wall's far side, gasping, shoulder pressed against the rough stone of the wall for support. Her leg throbbed fierily.

'Oh, hurry, hurry, hurry,' Spandel urged.

'I'm *hurrying*,' Elinor snapped back.

But, 'Quick, quick,' was all Spandel said by way of reply, bounding ahead to lead the way.

Elinor followed as best she could on the uneven ground, leaning heavily on her walking cane, limping between rows of some leafy green plant she did not know. This was the first time she had been beyond the wall, and the fields lay stretched out all around her in a mottled green tapestry. Beyond, westwards, she saw rolling, open meadows, with another farm house in the distance, only a little dot far off on the sloping hillside. Eastwards, however, the Margie fields were bordered by a wood, stretching away towards the wild tumble of the green hills, beyond which, in turn, were the great, far-away blue peaks of the eastern mountains, the sun slowly rising in red splendour behind their ragged crowns.

It was towards the wood, with the rising sun behind it, that Spandel led her, scampering away through the field.

Elinor hesitated.

'Spandel!' she called – fruitlessly. She shook her head and limped onwards as quick as she could.

The ground sloped downwards, and Elinor had to be careful about her footing, lest she slip and tear something. Seeing her coming after, Spandel called, 'Hurry! Oh, quick, quick!' She had got well ahead by now, and was into the edge of the wood.

'Spandel!' Elinor called again, but too late, for Spandel had scrambled up into the branches of the nearest tree and disappeared amongst the greenery.

Elinor limped on, panting, her leg throbbing, till she reached the wood, a maze of rustling greenery out of which she could make nothing definite beyond tree and twirling leaf and limb. Beyond, she could just catch glimpses of the wood's dim, deeper interior, where the trees became bigger. It was like a moving, multi-layered wall at the field's edge, green, grey-green, brown-green . . .

She heard a rustling, whirled about, and saw Spandel springing out from the shadow under the trees at the edge of the field some distance away. The little Lamure came bounding out several paces into the field, then stopped and looked back as if waiting for something.

Elinor stayed as she was, her heart thumping, one hand gripping the handle of her cane.

Spandel went skipping back to the wood, disappeared into the shadows for a moment, then shot out once more. There was something back there in the green dimness. Elinor could make out a shadow-shape. Something large.

It came out slowly near the sunlit edge of the field, a half-guessed form amongst the leaves . . . suddenly transformed into what was clearly the figure of a man, staggering awkwardly away from the trees, Spandel circling anxiously about him.

A man, yes. But like no man Elinor had ever seen before. He was dark all over, as if covered by a tight-fitting, single garment.

He moved wearily, awkwardly, favouring his left leg. Elinor saw the wet, crimson glisten of blood along his thigh. He took three more steps, Spandel circling him still, softly chattering, then he stumbled to his knees with a little moan of pain.

'Spandel!' Elinor called. She saw the kneeling figure look up, startled – wide, glistening dark eyes in a dark face. He tried to get to his feet, but ended up falling face first on to the ground. Elinor rushed along the sloping field as fast as she could manage.

'Oh, quick!' Spandel urged her, jumping up and down. 'Quick, quick, *quick*!'

Elinor arrived, panting, little spasms of fiery pain shooting through her thigh. The figure before her rolled over on his side, looking up at her. Elinor stopped dead, staring.

He seemed altogether human in his body – and undeniably male, for he wore no clothing of any sort. But his slim limbs were sleek with fur. His whole body, in fact, was furred like an otter's: a short, thick, dark walnut brown, shading to cream on his belly and the insides of his arms and legs. Only the palms of his hands and his nose were bare, both showing black, gleaming skin.

His eyes were a glowing brown, big in his furred face, and utterly human in their expression.

Elinor shivered. She did not know what to do. He was not like any creature she had ever imagined. She did not know how she felt. He was too strange. Somehow, the humanimals were far easier to accept. They were non-human in shape, yet human in spirit. This . . . this was altogether different. He was no animal, clearly. And yet he was not a human man either.

'Help him!' Spandel cried, jumping up and down in agitation. 'He's hurt, hurt, hurt!'

Elinor reached a hand down tentatively. The fur-man flinched away, his eyes wide with fear. She could see his thin chest heaving. Her heart went out to him suddenly, seeing him frightened like that, knowing the pain he must be feeling, facing strangers. 'It's all right,' she said softly. 'I won't hurt you. Let me see . . .' She kneeled awkwardly by his side and leaned over to examine his hurt leg.

He had a shallow cut across his thigh, a gash somewhat like hers had been, but less severe. The dark fur was matted with blood, and the wound showed as a wet, red, gleaming ribbon of exposed flesh. She could hear him groaning softly. He rocked back and forth where he lay on his side, his hand gripping his thigh just above the cut.

From behind, she heard somebody call out suddenly. Turning, she saw two men trotting in their direction. 'Over here!' she cried to them as they came up over the crest of the slope above. 'Here!'

Seeing the men come running down the slope at him, the furred being pushed up from the ground, trying desperately to get to his feet. But it was no good. His leg buckled under him and he collapsed after only two steps, mewling like a hurt dog.

Elinor scrambled over, bent awkwardly down, and reached a hand to him reassuringly. He clutched at it, his fingers surprisingly powerful. 'It's all right,' she said. 'You're safe. Nobody's going to hurt you.'

She did not know if he understood or not. Perhaps he could not speak or understand words. Perhaps he was the other side of what the humanimals she had met so far were – and human in outward form only.

'Quick, quick, quick!' she heard Spandel saying.

The farm hands came skidding to a halt. Elinor expected them to stand staring, as she had, shocked by what they saw. But they did no such thing.

'Need to stop that bleeding,' one of them said – old Collart, Elinor realized.

'You go and get a couple more of the lads and bring a stretcher,' the other man said. Elinor saw it was Sandy, still with blue clay on his hands. 'I'll see if I can't stop the bleeding.'

'Right,' Collart replied and dashed off.

Sandy knelt next to the fur-man. 'It's all right,' he said. 'You're at Margie now. We'll see to you. You're all right now.'

The fur-man merely stared.

'You're at *Margie*,' Sandy repeated, as if he expected the very name itself to act as a kind of charm.

But it had no such effect. The fur-man flinched away, moaning, when Sandy reached to examine the wound.

'Now, now,' Sandy said, trying to be reassuring. 'I only want to . . .'

But the fur-man jerked back, scrabbling desperately to get to his feet and flee.

'No, no!' Spandel cried, leaping before him to bar his way.

He stumbled, got no more than three steps further, then fell heavily, face first. This time, he lay still.

'He's fainted, poor soul,' Sandy said. 'Probably best, all things considered. Didn't look life-threatening, that wound, but cursed painful nonetheless, and all that scrambling about only makes it bleed the more.' He shook his head. 'And he was terrified of us. A real wild one, this. Just look at him.' He shook his head. 'No telling what's happened . . .'

Sandy bent towards the limp furred body. 'Let's try to get him on his back and bind that wound up and stop the worst of the bleeding. That first . . . Then we can get him to the house once Collart and the rest come with a stretcher.'

Elinor nodded, intent on helping in any way she could.

302

XXXII

The fur-man lay on his back on the bed, unmoving, a blanket over him up to the chin. Gillien had given him a draught of something to make him sleep. Mid-afternoon now, and still he had not stirred.

Elinor stared at him. He was the most exotic being she had ever seen.

His face was entirely furred save for a small, black button of a nose, which glistened wetly, like a dog's. His eyes were closed now, and she saw that he had long eye lashes, but that his eyelids, somehow, were not quite shaped like a human person's – being less separate eyelids and more an extension of the furred skin about his eye sockets that merely folded shut when he closed his eyes. But his face was altogether human in basic design, though delicate-looking, narrow of forehead and jaw, and sharp-chinned. A little brush of stiffer, slightly darker, longer fur ran from the top of his forehead back, like human hair almost, to form a sort of mane. His ears were small and pointed, with tiny tufts of whitish fur sticking from the tops.

His black lips were parted slightly, and she could see his sharp, very white teeth. He snored softly, like a cat purring almost. She bent a little closer.

His eyes opened.

She backed self-consciously aside, a hasty shuffle that sent a quick stab of pain through her leg.

He stared at her, unmoving. He had big brown eyes, with hardly any whites showing at all. They glistened.

'I'm . . . I'm sorry,' she said. 'I didn't mean to . . .' She backed further away from him, flustered. 'They . . . they brought you here to my room, you see. Till you came out of your sleep. Your leg will be fine. Gillien put stitches in it. Like mine. She . . .'

Elinor stopped. She felt like a silly child, rattling on so. But he

303

just lay there, staring, stiff as a carving. Not a single word had he spoken to anyone yet, not even when he had come to, his eyes wide with terror, as Gillien was setting the stitches in his thigh . . . Elinor had no way of knowing if he understood her now or not.

He followed her with his eyes, staring completely unselfconsciously, as a child might, or a madman. Dark brown, his eyes were, almost the colour of his fur, gleaming and wide and unblinking.

There was something compelling about that stare of his. Their eyes locked, and for long moments they gazed into each other, intent . . . Until she could bear the strange, mute intensity of it no more.

He sat up in the bed then, craning his neck about. 'It iss very sstrange, thiss place,' he said, in a soft, sibilant, purring voice. 'I am . . . wherre?'

He *could* talk, then. Elinor went closer, relieved. 'My name is Elinor. You're at Margie Farm. Spandel brought you in. She dreamed you. I saw you . . .'

She paused self-consciously. He was staring at her still, his mouth a little open.

'You . . .' he said softly, 'An esspecially beautiful creaturre, you arre.' He smiled at her – at least she reckoned it to be a smile: a flash of sharp little white teeth against those black lips of his.

Elinor did not know what to say. She found herself blushing, and felt ridiculous.

He pushed himself up in the bed, wincing. The blanket fell away, revealing his thin arms and chest, and the long slim line of his legs. He was really quite a delicately boned creature, Elinor realized.

His hurt leg was bandaged from knee to crotch. He picked at the bandage with one hand, his face knitted in a frown of perplexity.

'Don't!' Elinor said. 'The bandage will keep it clean. And stop it from bleeding more.'

He looked at her uncertainly.

'I have one, see?' Impulsively, she lifted the frock she was wearing and bared her hurt leg for him to see. It was wrapped neatly in a layer of thin, translucent white cloth, more to help

304

keep it clean than anything else now. The line of the long scar down her leg showed plain enough underneath it. 'I was hurt like you. Gillien healed – is healing – me.'

He looked at her leg, up at her face, at her leg again. His own face took on an expression of sudden anxiety. He looked about – a series of quick, agitated motions of his sleek, furred head. 'You are a being of flessh, you? Or a being of sspirit?' He lifted up a hand towards her. 'Can I touch you, me?'

Elinor went closer to him, hesitant.

His touch was like a moth's wing against her forearm, warm and delicate. 'Flessh,' he said softly. 'Flessh being, you.' There was a soft, breathy, hissing undertone to his speech, sometimes more pronounced than at others. 'Me, I had thought you of the sspirit. All of you.'

He lay back with a snuffling sigh, letting her arm go. 'Sso . . . no place of dreamss, thiss. What kind, then, *iss* thiss place?'

'Margie Farm,' she replied.

He looked at her, his brows knitted together in an altogether human expression of confusion. 'Farm? What iss . . . *farm*?'

'It's a place where people . . . grow things.'

'What ssort of thingss?'

'Food. Vegetables. Livestock.'

He shook his head. 'A *very* sstrange place, your place, yess?'

Elinor shrugged, not entirely sure what to make of any of this. 'I'm a stranger here myself,' she ended up saying.

'A beautiful sstranger,' he replied. 'Like a ssmooth white bird, you are. Like a ssisster to the Moon.'

Again, Elinor felt herself blush. 'How did you come here?' she asked him quickly. 'How were you injured?'

His face took on a troubled look. He glanced down at his bandaged leg. 'It hurtss,' he said. Then: 'Men it wass, that did it. Dark men with ssharp bladess. Hunting me. Only jusst did I esscape from them. Dark men, all looking alike . . .'

Brothers, Elinor thought. Must be.

The fur-man went quiet for a long moment, shivering. His fur had been flattened out a little by the blanket and he scratched at himself nervously, smoothing it back in order. 'I ssaw thosse men come running . . . Me, I thought they wisshed to hurt me.'

'The farm hands, you mean?'

'Thosse who came after you, when the sspirit guide led me to you.'

'The what?'

'The sspirit guide. Little Dancer. Sshe came to me in the foresst, led me to ssafety . . .'

'Spandel, do you mean?'

He repeated the name. 'Sspandel . . .'

'But she's no spirit,' Elinor explained. 'She's flesh and bone, like you and me. She's –'

At that moment the door behind Elinor opened and Gillien came walking into the room. 'I *thought* I heard voices,' she said, smiling. Looking at the fur-man, she nodded approvingly. 'Welcome back to the land of the living.'

'The woman of ssmall ssharp thingss that prick,' he replied, and smiled shyly. 'I remember.'

Gillien laughed.

Spandel came in behind her then, dancing lightly on her hind feet as she did, arms and tail out for balance.

The fur-man looked to her, held out his hands in immediate, unselfconscious invitation. 'Little Dancer!'

Spandel skipped over to the cot and vaulted lightly on to it.

'Spandell!' Gillien said sharply. '*Careful*!'

But the fur-man seemed entirely comfortable with her there. He put out a hand and stroked her gently. She snuggled up to him as if they were old and dear companions. 'I thought you a sspirit creaturre, you,' he said. 'I thought ssurely I had dreamed you.'

'Oh, no, no,' Spandel replied happily. 'Not me.'

'My name is Gillien,' Gillien was saying. 'This is Elinor. And the small being in your arms is Spandel.'

The fur-man nodded. 'I know.' He rubbed at Spandel's ears gently, purring, 'Sspandel, Sspandel,' in his raspy, soft voice. 'Little Dreamer.' Then he looked up. 'I am called Gyver.'

'Well, Gyver,' Gillien said. 'Welcome to Margie Farm.'

Elinor saw no more of Gyver that day.

'Out,' Gillien ordered. 'I need to change that dressing and get some broth into him.'

And the next day the fur-man was fevered, and Gillien kept everyone away. 'Leave the poor soul be,' she said. 'What he needs now is absolute rest and quiet.'

So Elinor sat on the porch out in the sun as usual. But her thoughts were with the fur-man. She kept running their brief conversation through her mind, trying to understand what manner of creature he might be. He certainly seemed human enough, though his hissing speech was a little quaint at times. And some of the things he said seemed *most* strange . . .

'How's your latest getting along?' Hann asked Gillien the next afternoon, striding in from the fields to where she and Elinor were sitting together on the porch peeling small potatoes. 'Is he recovering well enough from that gash of his, then?'

'Healing fast,' Gillien replied. '*Very* fast.'

'It's because he has the best healer in the Valley looking after him,' Hann said, smiling.

But Gillien shook her head. 'No. He's resilient as a weed, that one. And wild. Never seen so much as a house before, far as I can reckon. He's come a *far* ways to get here. From somewhere up near the Blue Peaks, I think.'

'A far ways indeed,' Hann agreed. 'Did he say why?'

'Just came to . . . to see a new place, apparently. Just to look. That's my understanding of it anyway.'

Hann shrugged. 'Just to look . . . Well, I hope he doesn't live to regret visiting us.'

Gillien glanced at him sharply. 'Have you heard something?'

'Just rumours.'

'Tell me,' she said, setting aside the potatoes and rising.

The two of them walked away, then, heads together, leaving Elinor alone on the porch. She continued peeling potatoes mechanically, but could feel her heart thumping.

A sound off in the distance startled her – a deep rumbling, felt in the bones as much as heard with the ears. At first, she could not identify it. Then it sounded again, and she recognized what it was.

Distant thunder.

Elinor shook her head. The weather had been so perfect for so many days, she had almost forgotten such a thing as thunder existed. She looked about, but the sky ahead was still blue and clear. Setting the potatoes aside for the moment, she reached for her cane and walked around the house.

The thunder clouds were there all right, though way off on the north-western horizon, and no more than a dark, moiling smudge as of yet. Again, she heard – half-heard, rather – their distant rumble. The breeze was coming from the north, cooling now.

Storm to come, sure enough.

She went back to the potatoes, feeling her belly tighten.

'Just rumours,' Hann had said.

Elinor sighed. It was a good place, Margie Farm, peopled by decent, trustworthy folk – and the world held few enough of those, as well she knew.

Again, she heard the distant thunder – a little louder now, closer.

She *owed* Gillien and Hann and all the rest.

And there was only one way she could see to pay them back properly: she must leave before she brought the wrath of the Brothers down upon everybody here. She could very nearly walk again now.

She had been living in a kind of pleasant daze, it seemed, lounging here in the warm sun, day after day, unworried, untouched, content just to be here.

But it was time to move on.

The only question was – where?

XXXIII

The storm came through in the dark of the night, crashing like a great beast through the sky. Rain hammered upon the roof of the house. Thunder roared. Lightning arced through the night in jagged cascades of cold light.

Elinor lay in her room, dry and secure in her blankets. She shivered pleasantly. It was good to lie here, safe, only half awake really, like an animal tucked away snugly in its burrow . . .

It went on, the rolling of the thunder in the sky, the rhythmic, hammering roar of the rain on the roof, the sputtering bright radiance of the lightning flashing in through her window. Like a kind of huge music, it was, and Elinor drifted in and out of half-sleep, listening.

Gradually, it began to pass away, dwindling into the distance, leaving her behind. She lay dreaming, feeling the tug of the storm upon her like a hand, pulling her on towards the lightning again, tugging at her, yanking on her, pulling . . .

'Elinor, Elinor, Elinor!' somebody was crying.

She opened her eyes and sat up with a start. In the dark, she could only just make out what was tugging at her. Spandel.

'Quick, quick, quick!' she chattered. 'Oh, *quick*!'

'What *is* it?' Elinor asked.

'Oh, Gyver, Gyver . . .'

'What's happened, Spandel?'

'He's gone! Oh, quick, Elinor. We must go after him. I dreamed . . .' she paused, shivered. 'I dreamed great death.'

Elinor squinted in the dark, trying to see Spandel's face. Her little human eyes seemed to glow softly. 'Whose death, Spandel? How?'

'I don't know. I don't know, know, know!' She pulled

urgently at Elinor's hand. 'Only hurry now. Quick, quick! We must find him.'

Elinor sighed, rose from her bed, shivering, and dressed quickly in loose trousers and top – she had begun to wear trousers again, now that her leg was healing so well – and laced on her Minmi Guards' boots that Gillien had kept for her. This was the first time she had put them on since her arrival here, and it felt strange wearing them. She was not entirely sure why she did so now, and stood there, feeling uneasy in her belly. There was a kind of . . . stitch in her guts, pulling at her as surely as Spandel had. It was like before, when she and Spandel and Rannis had crossed the grassy country, an uncanny sense of urgency.

'Quick!' Spandel hissed.

Grabbing up her walking cane, Elinor headed out of her room, and crept through the sleeping house, Spandel skipping silently ahead of her.

Elinor stepped out on to storm-drenched grass. The air was chill and crisp and clean, with a blustery wind tugging at everything. Overhead, clouds whirled by, tearing and tattering as the storm died away. In the far sky behind them, a sickle moon glowed, appearing and disappearing as the clouds tumbled past. Washes of faint silver radiance poured across the land, replaced by darkness when the clouds obscured the moon.

Elinor felt her heart beat fast. It was a wild night. She could hear the distant trees singing in the wind, a rhythmic sea-sound that counterpointed the alternating pulses of shadow and silver moonlight.

'This way,' Spandel urged, and plunged ahead through the glistening wet grass.

Elinor followed as quickly as she could, using her cane, but the wet grass made for most uncertain footing, especially with the changing light, and she could not keep up. The pull was still upon her, though, and that familiar sense of momentum, as if she were sliding inevitably down some slope. It made her shiver.

Spandel flitted over the stile that surmounted the waist-high stone wall and disappeared. Elinor followed, leg beginning to burn now, then crossed the field. Overhead, the clouds slipped away from the moon for an instant, and, in the sudden wash of silver light, she saw Spandel way ahead, near the edge of the wood out of which Gyver had first appeared. 'Wait!' she called out softly, waving her cane.

But it was no use. Spandel had disappeared, swallowed by the wood's great dark mass. Cursing, Elinor hobbled on till she came, eventually, to the dark verge of the trees. There she stopped momentarily, uncertain. The forest was like a black wall. She shivered. She ought to have brought her blade, she realized suddenly. But, somehow, the thought had simply not occurred to her. She cursed herself for a thoughtless fool. Anything might lurk ahead.

But she could not stand here waiting interminably, and to return to the house to fetch the sword seemed altogether inadvisable – especially with that uncanny sense of urgency still drawing her on. So she took a deep breath and just pushed on ahead, fending off the grasping branches in the dark, feeling a way as best she could. The wet limbs showered cold water on her, and soon she was soaked to the skin and shivering. She felt foolish, stumbling blindly in the tree-tangled dark. And more than a little annoyed with Spandel, who had left her thus to struggle blindly along behind.

She kept on, though, and in a little while the grasping thickness of the undergrowth at the wood's edge gave way to more open ground further in, the trees bigger, the going somewhat easier. After a bit the ground began to slope, and the walking became all downhill. The *shroosh* of the wind calmed. The trees opened up, and through the black tapestry of their thick trunks, she caught the quicksilver glimmer of water in the moonlight in a little dell ahead.

Drawing closer, she spotted Gyver sitting at the water's edge on the far bank of a murmuring stream, Spandel at his side. There was an open space in the trees above them, and the two of them sat silent, unmoving, staring overhead at where the glimmering moon rode the sky.

'What are you *doing*?' Elinor demanded irritably. Her leg ached and she was panting and entirely out of sorts. All this desperate rush, all the uncanny urgency, the talk of death and dreaming . . . and the two of them were just sitting there calmly, moon-gazing.

She waited for a response, but they seemed oblivious of her. She waded across the stream, soaking her boots. 'I *said*, what are you doing?'

Gyver sat gazing fixedly up into the sky. 'Me, I came to ssay hallo to my grandmother the moon.'

'What?' Elinor said.

'I could not ssleep. The sstorm wass angry. The world here iss angry, yess? Me, I came to ssee my grandmother.' He lifted a furred hand to point at the sickle moon. 'Sshe is newly arissen. Alwayss, me, I ssay hallo to her when she rissess new in the ssky.'

Elinor did not know what to think.

Gyver looked at her and smiled, a flash of sharp, moon-lit teeth in his dark face. 'You and sshe are ssoul-ssissterss, I think, yess?'

Elinor snorted. But she felt her heart quicken. He seemed completely childish, at times, this Gyver. And yet . . .

'Alwayss changing, alwayss the ssame,' he said softly. 'Alwayss watching over uss, her.'

Spandel looked up at Elinor with moon-bright eyes. All her dream-spawned urgency seemed to have gone. She patted the grassy slope invitingly.

Elinor sighed and sat herself down. So much for dreams and death and destruction. She hugged herself, wet and shivering. It was all very well for her two companions, furred as they were, but, now that she was no longer moving, she was beginning to feel the wet cold down to her bones. 'Do you two intend just to sit here all night, then?' she demanded exasperatedly.

'You're cold, you,' Gyver said. He reached an arm gently about her, drawing her close.

He felt sinewy and bony, with not a shred of excess flesh under his fur. But he was warm for all that. She snuggled closer to him.

'The moon wass a woman, once,' Gyver said in his soft, hissing way. 'A very wise woman, long and long ago. With many children. But when her children were grown, and it came time for her to leave thiss world, sshe could not, would not do it. Sshe wisshed to remain and watch over them forever. Sso sshe wove a great magic, with the sstrength of her will. And when her time came, sshe did not die away. Insstead, her sspirit rosse up into the ssky where sshe could watch over all her children, and her children'ss children, and theirss, forever . . .'

He paused for a moment, looking at her. 'Me, I am one of her children'ss children'ss children, I think. I musst let her ssee me sso that sshe may know I am well, sso that she may be content, sso that no terrible thing will happen to the world.'

Elinor was not sure if he were being serious or merely joking with her. She looked up at the moon. It shone behind wisps of flying cloud. A faint moon-rainbow lit the clouds in their passing.

'Uss, we are the children of . . .' Gyver began, but stopped suddenly, his black dog's nose quivering.

'What?' Elinor asked uneasily.

'Ssmoke,' he said.

'So?' Elinor could smell nothing. 'That'll be chimney smoke from the farm. It's almost dawn. Somebody's up early, no doubt, and has started the kitchen fire.'

Gyver shook his head. 'Not chimney ssmoke, thiss.'

'What, then?'

Spandel was up on her feet now, peering back anxiously through the dark screen of the trees towards the house.

Gyver shivered, snorting softly as his nose tested the air.

'What *is* it?' Elinor demanded.

'Bad ssmoke.'

'Meaning what?' she said impatiently. 'Talk plain, can't you?'

The fur-man shrugged, a quick lifting of his thin, furred shoulders. 'Not hearth ssmoke. Sstinking ssmoke.' He gestured to her. 'We musst go to ssee, yess? They tell me ssomething bad iss happening, my boness . . .'

'Your bones?' Elinor said.

But Gyver had already slipped across the little stream with hardly a splash, despite the limp he still had from his hurt leg, and was beckoning her to follow. Spandel flitted away, taking the water in two light bounds and disappearing amongst the great dark trees. Elinor went across much more clumsily: her foot turned on a submerged and slippery rock, and she nearly measured her length in the water, cursing, her bad leg shooting fire.

'Sshussh!' Gyver hissed.

'I didn't do it on *purpose*!' she hissed back.

She began to follow him through the wood, stumbling in the darkness. Gyver moved with the elegance of a dancer, injured leg or not, slipping between the trunks of the trees in the dark with hardly a sound. She found herself envying this easy, animal grace of his.

Through the serried trunks ahead, she saw the sky beginning to lighten. 'Dawn,' Elinor murmured with relief. Now at least she could begin to make out what lay underfoot.

But Gyver stopped, crouched down against the bole of a tree and shook his head. 'Not dawn, thiss.'

'Of course it's . . .' Elinor began, then stopped short. The light ahead flared suddenly brighter, a flickering, uncertain radiance unlike any true dawn. And it was westwards she was looking. 'The farm!' she said, suddenly terrified. Without thinking, she leaped ahead, smashing through a little thicket that seemed suddenly to rear itself before her in the dark.

'No!' Gyver called out.

Elinor ignored him, her mind focused only ahead. The farm . . . It was firelight ahead, from a fire large enough to light up the horizon. She rushed on awkwardly, ignoring the slap of tree limbs, the pain in her leg, stumbling over the uneven ground. It was all upslope, heading back to the house, and far more difficult than coming down to the stream this way had been. She fell once, with bruising force, but struggled back to her feet and raced on, panting. The light grew brighter. She could hear voices now. Somebody screaming . . .

The screaming stopped dead.

Elinor threw herself onwards, panting, her heart hammering, wrestling through the thicker brush at the wood's verge, till she came out to the open air. The high hump of the field cut off any view of the house itself, but, looking up the long slope, she could see great petals of flame rising up. Smoke whirled in a plume, black and oily-looking against the scudding, moon-silvered clouds.

'No . . .' Elinor sobbed. She threw herself out of the trees, skidded on the wet ground, fell on one knee, struggled to her feet again. Something hit her in the small of her back from behind and she went down hard, face first into the dirt. She struck out blindly, sobbing.

'Quiet!' Gyver hissed. 'Sshussh!'

'Let me *up*!' Elinor wailed.

He clamped a hand over her mouth, silencing her. She tried to bite him, to twist out of his hold, but for all the slenderness of his limbs, he held on to her with a sinewy strength she could not overcome.

'Sshussh,' he hissed in her ear. 'Sshussh, or they will hear uss!' He pressed his face close to hers, his dark eyes shining like little lamps in the glow of the distant firelight. 'You musst be ssilent, yess?'

Elinor nodded, knowing it was the only way to get him to let up.

'It's *you* who doesn't understand,' she said then in a fierce whisper once he released her. 'That's the house burning. We've got to get there and help them put it out before . . .'

'Look!' Gyver said, pointing over her shoulder.

Elinor twisted round. There were figures to be seen now along the top of the field on the far side of the stone wall, silhouetted from the waist up against the leaping flames. She strained to recognize Hann, old Collart, Sandy the potter, perhaps.

'Who . . . is *that*?' she gasped. For the figures ahead were strangers. And there were too many of them, trotting about with far more discipline than would have been the case were it the farm folk trying to deal with this sudden catastrophe.

Then, abruptly, she knew . . .

Brothers!

'Come away,' Gyver urged, tugging at her.

'No!' she said. 'I've got to go up there.'

'It'ss too late!' he replied. 'Come *away*.'

Elinor shook herself free from his hold and began worming a way along the field on her belly towards the rock wall.

'Come back,' he hissed at her.

She ignored him and kept moving, fast as she dared, angling along the field to reach the stone wall a little way down from the house.

Nobody from above spotted her and she arrived finally, soaked and shivering and filthy with dirt, her clothes heavy with it, her mouth full of the taste of it. Carefully, she peered over the top of the wall.

The farm was in ruins. The house burned like a huge torch, flames spiralling and whirling upwards, crackling and snapping and roaring. As she watched, part of the roof fell in with a great *whoooosh* of flame and sparks whirling off into the darkness.

She saw figures silhouetted against the fire, moving about in an orderly way, hauling sacks and barrels away from the flames, heaping them together in a mounting pile. And then she saw one of them come up with something over his shoulder which she could not at first make out. It was no light weight, for the man staggered along and flung it to the ground with clear relief – on to a different heap from that of the ill-gotten loot, Elinor realized. Only as the man let the thing fall to the ground did she recognize it.

A human body.

It fell like a limp sack, arms floppy and boneless-seeming. No living person would fall like that, unconscious or no.

And there was a small heap of such bodies . . .

She heard Gyver come up beside her then, hissing to himself in distress. He put a furred arm around her, pulling her down and out of sight behind the protective cover of the wall.

Elinor wept, tears of rage and grief. 'Cursed, vicious, despicable *scum*!' she hissed under her breath. She half-stood, spat through her fingers over the wall in an old curse. 'An ill death upon ye all!'

Gyver pulled her back down.

'Oh, Gyver . . . Gyver, what can we *do*?' she whispered, feeling her eyes fill with tears. 'It's all *my* fault. They were after *me*!'

He tugged urgently at her, trying to pull her away. 'We musst go from thiss place,' he hissed. '*Fasst*! Before thesse terrible men ssee uss!'

Elinor shrugged him off. 'No! We must *do* something.'

'There iss nothing,' he said. 'What can we posssibly do, uss?'

'I don't know. There must be *something*!'

Gyver was shivering. She could feel it as he put his hand on her. 'Pleasse. We musst *go* from thiss terrible place. There iss death on the air. Me, I can ssmell it all too clear!'

'But what if there's some of the farm folk still left alive, Gyver? We can't just . . . *abandon* them!'

He shifted about uncomfortably. She heard his hissing breath. 'Me, I will go ssee,' he said. 'You sstay here.'

'No,' Elinor whispered.

'Yess,' he insisted. 'You are too noissy in the dark, you. They will hear you ssure.'

'But I can't . . .' she started. Then realized he was right. He had moved with uncanny ease through the dark woods, despite his hurt leg. Like Spandel, he must be able to see in the dark better than she. And her leg was painful now. 'All right,' she conceded. 'But be careful.' It sounded a lame thing to say. She reached one hand to his arm, gave him a little squeeze.

He gave her a quick flash of teeth in a nervous grin. 'Oh, *mosst* careful.' Then he was gone, slipping away from her along the safe side of the wall.

Elinor waited, fidgeting. She hugged herself, shivery and wet and sick in her belly. The moon sailed by overhead, divinely oblivious. Silver and shadow danced across the world. The moments passed, slowly. Gyver did not return. Elinor huddled in the wall's shadow, feeling utterly alone. Of Spandel there was no sign.

Finally she could not stop herself and peered over the wall to watch as the Brothers continued to garner their ill-gotten loot, building a teetering pile. Beyond, silhouetted against the still-leaping flames, the big tree near the house stood scorched but still standing. She thought of herself hiding behind it, mute witness to the Brothers' first confrontation with Gillien and Hann and the rest. She felt sick, remembering it. Why had she ever stayed on so long? It was as if she had been in a daze, unthinking. And now she had brought *this* upon them all.

A little rustling sound made her turn, her heart suddenly in her mouth. But it was Gyver returning. 'So?' she whispered.

He was carrying something in his arms, she saw. She bent closer, squinting in the uncertain light.

'*Hississi-oouowww*!'

It was Alix. Gyver lowered the cat gently to the ground. Her whole left side was burned raw, all the fur gone, and there was a long, wetly bleeding sword gash running from her ribs to her flank – deep enough that Elinor could see the white glisten of bone. Alix licked at the wound weakly, spitting and hissing to herself.

'Oh, Alix . . .' Elinor breathed. 'What *happened*?'

The cat looked up, her eyes narrowed with pain. Her breath came in short gasps. 'Sstinking *verrmin*!' she spat. 'They came ssneaking from the darrkness . . . All dead now. All *dead*.'

'Who's dead, Alix?'

'All.'

'Gillien?' Elinor pressed, feeling her belly rise up in her throat. 'Hann? Sandy? Collart?'

'All,' Alix repeated. She licked at her bleeding flank, hissed, lay back weakly.

Elinor slumped against the cold stone of the wall, stricken. '*All* . . .'

'Ssneaking verrmin!' Alix hissed. Raising her head, she tried to shift her position on the wet ground. A sudden gush of blood erupted from the deep gash along her side.

'Alix!' Elinor cried.

But Alix had gone limp.

Elinor stared at the poor blood-sodden little body.

'Let uss go,' Gyver said gently, putting a hand on Elinor's shoulder. 'There iss nothing here for uss.'

His hand was slicked with Alix's blood. Elinor shrugged away, shuddering. She felt such an anger in her it was like a solid thing in her guts, a molten lump of fury filling her. She found it hard to get breath.

She stared over the wall at the leaping flames, the dark figures bustling about. Men were bringing up armfuls of stuff for the growing pile of loot.

She felt sick, looking on, and gripped at the cold, wet stone of the wall so hard it hurt. Then she saw a man separate something from an armful he had just dropped. It was a long, slim object . . . her own sword!

The man drew it partly, so that the half-blade shone like a column of light in the flames. He resheathed it, said something she could not catch to a nearby companion, then placed it next to the growing pile and laughed.

'I will have to get my blade back,' Elinor heard herself say. Her voice was hoarse, and she found herself panting like a hound after a long race. It was the Kess part of her speaking, pure, intent. She turned and glared at Gyver. 'I'll not let scum like *them* have such a blade. And there *might* still be some of the farm folk alive.'

Gyver opened his mouth, closed it again. He looked her in the eyes, a long, searching stare, then nodded reluctantly. 'But we musst be fasst, yess? The ssun is almosst up.'

Elinor gestured over the wall to a shallow drainage ditch that ran near the house and out beyond, eventually to connect with the stream in the woods below she reckoned. 'We can use that to get near them.' The flames made for uncertain illumination at best, and if they kept to the ditch's deep shadow they stood a good chance of remaining unseen.

They made a careful way over the wall, well down beyond the house itself, and crawled from there with painful care, worming along on their bellies until they could slither down into the dark safety of the ditch. From there, they half-crawled towards the house. They could see nothing, but the snapping, hungry sound of the flames was clear, together with the voices of the Brothers, preoccupied with their looting.

Once near enough to the house, Elinor peeked cautiously up over the ditch's edge. She was at a loss, and wondering uneasily now if this little foray on which she had insisted was not entirely ill conceived. All well enough to say she would not leave her blade here for these bastards. But how *was* she to retrieve it? And if there were still farm folk left alive . . . how could she go about trying to find them?

Chance showed her the way.

'Hoi!' somebody called out nearby. Elinor peered over the ditch's edge again and saw three of the Brothers struggling along with a cask of the farm's home-brewed ale. 'Give us a hand, here!' one of them called out.

Several Brothers moved in from different directions. One came trotting along the side of the drainage ditch, no more than three or four paces from where Elinor and her companions crouched. In an instant, she knew what to do. 'Hoi!' she hissed up at the man.

He skittered to a halt and stared down at her suspiciously. Cloaked by the ditch's shadow as they were, Elinor knew it would be hard for him to make out exactly who it was had called to him.

'Help me,' she whispered, making her voice as harsh and low as she could. 'I slipped in the dark and sprained my cursed ankle.'

The man stood squinting down at her mistrustfully.

Elinor gestured to Gyver, putting her hands to her own throat then gesturing with her chin at the man above them, hoping he would understand. Gyver's eyes went very wide, but he nodded.

'Don't just stand there like an idiot,' Elinor called softly to the hovering Brother, trying to put all the masculine assurance and impatience she could into her voice. 'Help me up out of here!'

He came to her then, skidding down into the shadow-dark of the ditch. 'How did you . . .' he started.

Gyver gripped him by the throat.

The man fought frantically to break loose and cry out, but Elinor leaped upon him, digging her knee into his groin as hard as she could. Gyver held on desperately tight. Elinor scrabbled at the struggling man's belt, clumsy and awkward in the dark, until she felt a hilt in her hands. She drew the weapon quick – a long-bladed dagger – and plunged it into his chest, once, twice, three times in quick succession.

But he writhed and fought the harder, unhurt by her blows, undeterred. Cursing to herself, Elinor remembered the body armour the Brothers all wore. She smashed hastily at his face, then, a back-handed blow with the hilt of the dagger she had taken from him. She struck him again, and again, trying not to hit Gyver where he still clutched desperately at the man's throat, until, at a fourth blow, the man at last went limp. Elinor took the dagger, inserted the iron blade under the man's exposed chin above his plate-armour cuirass, and drove it up two-handedly, hot blood soaking her hands, till she felt the sharp tip grate against bone.

The man convulsed, thrashing about. She thought he would never go still.

But he did, eventually, leaving Gyver and her sprawled over him, gasping for breath.

Gyver was shaking helplessly. 'I don't *like* thiss!' he hissed.

Elinor could think of nothing to say. She wiped her bloody hands on the ground, peered up above the level of the ditch. The Brothers had managed to manhandle the big cask of home-brew into position against the pile of loot by now. As Elinor watched, they settled it into position and then walked off – presumably in search of more spoils. There was no indication any of them had noticed anything amiss.

She stripped the clothing off the dead man as quick as she could and put it on herself. She left the plate-armour cuirass on him, but took his belt and helm – it was the helm she put the most trust in to hide her identity. There was a sheathed sword on the belt as well as the dagger with which she had stabbed the man. Her hands shook as she hurriedly dressed herself.

'Stay here,' she whispered to Gyver, settling the sword belt and jamming the helm on her head.

Gyver nodded. He squatted down near the corpse, shivering. 'But hurry. The ssun will risse ssoon!'

Elinor scrabbled up out of the ditch. The leathern helm she wore felt too big, uncomfortable, clumsy. And it was clammy with the dead man's sweat. She tried her best not to limp – for she had had to leave her cane behind – gritting her teeth and attempting to put the sort of swagger into her step that the Brothers had.

The loot pile itself was a hodge-podge assortment of all manner of things, and she felt her stomach sink at the very sight of it. Where had the man she had spied upon placed her blade? The spot had seemed very clear and obvious from her vantage point by the wall. But now . . . The pile had grown, and there seemed no way she could find anything here in the uncertain firelight short of turning the whole thing upside down.

'You there!' a voice called to her suddenly.

Elinor's heart kicked in her breast.

'Don't just stand about like an idle fool,' the voice went on. 'Busy yourself!'

She turned and found herself facing a familiar figure – the big, dour-faced, moustached Squad Chief who had led the original party of Brothers to the farm to take her away. On his leather fighting helm, the brass sun-ray-and-gripped-hands insignia reflected the flickering light of the flames.

Elinor ducked her head, tugging the helm forward, trying to hide her woman's features. She had half-turned, about to walk briskly off, when another of the Brothers came up hurriedly.

'We discovered this near the house, sir,' he said. 'It was under the body of one of the farm hands. I thought you would want to see it personally.'

'Show me,' the Squad Chief said, holding out his hand.

The man handed him a long, slim object.

For a moment Elinor thought it was her own blade, and that she had somehow been mistaken the first time. But no. It was a blade, all right – a finely made thing with an ornate scabbard – but not hers.

'Well, well,' the Squad Chief said, examining the scabbard and finely cast, glinting hilt. 'Who would have thought a lout like farmer Hann might own such a fine weapon? It will make a nice addition to my collection . . .'

'Have you seen the other, sir?' the man who had produced the sword asked.

The Squad Chief shook his head. 'No. What other?'

'It's hereabouts somewhere. I saw Montag put it down . . .' The man cast about, kicking at things on the ground to shift them. 'Ah . . .' he said after a moment. 'Here it is.' Reaching down, he took up Elinor's blade and handed it to the Squad Chief, who let the first sword drop and took Elinor's in both his hands.

'It shines,' the Brother who had given it to him said.

'Shines?' the Squad Chief said.

'Yes, sir. Montag showed me. Try drawing it.'

The Squad Chief slipped it part-way free of its sheath – and gasped. The blade shone as always, catching the leaping radiance of the flames like a shard of bright mirror.

Elinor stepped forward quickly. The sight of the blade made her heart leap. There were still only the two of them before her. The rest of the Brothers were occupied elsewhere. 'Sir?' she said, trying to keep her voice as gruff as possible.

'What is it?' the Squad Chief demanded of her. He slammed the blade back into its sheath and clutched it possessively. 'Didn't I tell you already to get busy?' He peered at her with sudden suspicion. 'Who *are* you, lad? You aren't one of Chot Potelly's lot, are you?'

'There's a . . . a difficulty over by the far side of the . . . house, sir,' Elinor stammered hastily, making it up as she went, working her way closer to the Squad Chief with each word. 'One of the . . . the cows has gored somebody.'

322

'Have you been *drinking*?' he suddenly demanded. 'They haven't any cows here. You *know* I gave orders nobody was to touch any liquor. Come here!' He pointed to the ground before him. 'Let me smell your breath.'

Elinor came up.

'Closer,' he commanded.

She took one step, another, then launched herself at the man, taking him completely unawares. She kneed him in the groin and grabbed for the sword all in one quick, desperate motion. The two of them went down in a grunting, cursing confusion of limbs. With the surprise of it all, Elinor was able to yank her sword out of his grasp.

She gripped the familiar hilt in relief, and thrust herself away. Rolling to her knees – ignoring the pain in her bad leg – she flung off the awkward helm and drew the sword, keeping the scabbard in her left hand. The blade shone in the firelight like a bar of light, and the Squad Chief and the Brother next to him stared.

She felt a tingle go through her hand where she gripped the hilt, felt her limbs thrill with new strength.

'Stop him!' the Squad Chief ordered the man at his side. 'Take him *down*!'

The other man came at her, iron sword up.

The sword in her hand seemed to move almost of its own accord, and she with it. She was Kess, empty of anything save knowledge of the moving blade . . .

She took the man through the throat before he knew it had happened.

The Squad Chief stared. He yanked his sword hastily out of its sheath, but before he could make a move, Elinor was on him, thrusting at his throat.

He blocked her, a desperate parry that landed him on one knee. As she drew back for a second cut, he cried out loudly. She slashed at him. He was a strong man, and managed to half-parry. She felt her blade skitter off his sword and catch him across the side of his head. The razor edge cleaved the chin strap of his leather helm, the force of the deflected stroke taking off both his left ear and the helm itself.

He roared in shock and pain and leaped at her, coming up off his knees with surprising agility, so that it was all she could do to sidestep his blind, charging attack. She just managed to deal him a sharp, back-hand blow across the temple with her hilt. He stumbled to his knees again, fumbling his sword.

She drew back, ready to sink her blade into him, above or below the body armour, whichever should prove the easiest. But it was already too late. There were shouts and cries. She saw figures dashing towards her. Turning, she ran for it, pelting along, her bad leg a burning agony now, till she could dive into the protection of the ditch.

Gyver was ready for her. 'Quick!' she panted, leading the way back through the ditch in a desperate bent-over scramble. She heard the shouts behind but dared not stop to see what was happening, dared not even look up – for the footing was too treacherous in the dark and it needed all her concentration not to take a disastrous tumble.

With the very suddenness of it all, they somehow made the safe side of the wall before the Brothers had begun even to properly sort out what had occurred. Crouching there, panting, she peered back. The men below were gathered together in confusion around the two sprawled forms she had left behind her.

'It was one of Chot Potelly's lot that did it, I tell you,' she heard one of the gathered men say accusingly in the distance. 'I always knew they weren't to be trusted!'

'He wasn't one of *ours*,' another replied hotly.

'Then whose *was* he?'

'Borting's dead,' she heard one of them say then, crouching next to the man she had taken through the throat.

'*Dead*!' three of them cried simultaneously.

'It was that uncanny sword,' one said. 'Like very lightning in the hand. Squad Chief Tigh's lucky to be alive!'

'He *is* alive, then?'

'I'm alive all right,' the Squad Chief said, staggering to his feet. 'Find that man, curse you all!' He clutched at his head, where his ear had been. Dark blood glistened on his hands.

One of the men came up to him hesitantly, offered something. 'I found it in the grass, sir. It's your . . . your ear, sir. Part of it, anyway.'

The Squad Chief batted the thing away with a blood-soaked hand and gestured about furiously. 'Are you all blind and stupid? Which way did he go?'

324

'Along there,' said somebody.

'No! This way,' somebody else put in.

Gyver tugged urgently at Elinor's arm. 'We musst *go*, uss,' he hissed in her ear.

She resisted, dazed, the blade in her hand still dripping blood, her bad leg on fire, feeling herself still to be Kess, and yet not; feeling herself empty, and yet not. She shook herself. 'We cannot leave yet,' she whispered. 'What if there are still farm folk left alive back there?'

'There'ss nothing we can do *now*,' Gyver replied. 'Come. Fasst! Before they are upon uss . . .'

Elinor did not want to leave; it felt too much like desertion. But she knew Gyver had the right of it. Hanging about now would only get them taken, for the Brothers were as stirred up as a hive of angry wasps.

Hastily, she wiped the blade and sheathed it – its white glimmer would be like a beacon in the scudding moonlight. Then she turned and ran with Gyver as best she could, clutching the hilt for what strength it might provide her, placing her hope in speed rather than caution, making for the protecting dark of the wood in the distance.

And they made it, staggering into the wet embrace of the trees, gasping for breath. Elinor felt shaken, exhausted, belly-sick. She hung her head, gasping.

When she could, she lifted up and looked back, seeing the fire still leaping hungrily beyond the farm wall, hearing the angry shouting of the Brothers mingled with the crackling of the flames in the distance.

Such wanton, inhuman cruelty . . .

She felt a sudden rush of fury – so much so that she was doubled over for a moment, nauseous and shaken and breathless with the very force of it.

She ripped the dead Brother's clothing off and flung it into the darkness. The helm was already gone. She dropped the dead man's sword, but kept the belt, hanging her own scabbarded blade on it. The man's dagger, too, she kept. Then, blinking back tears, she turned with Gyver and staggered away deeper into the wood. The sky was beginning to lighten in the east now. A new day dawned. A new beginning . . .

For her, it was just more endings.

PART FOUR

THE WILD

XXXIV

Just after dawn it started to rain again, a steady, drenching, cold drizzle. Elinor staggered on, following Gyver. Of Spandel there was still no sign.

It was thick forest through which they moved now, dim under the covering branches of great, gnarled trees. There was little enough undergrowth but the footing was treacherous, what with muddy ground and puddles, rotting leaf drifts and twisty roots everywhere waiting to catch an unwary foot. And the terrain was a series of slopes, as if they walked upon the solidified surface of great ocean waves, one after the other, up, up, up, to the stone crest, then down, then up the next.

The trees wept, the sky wept, Elinor wept. It felt like the end of the world . . .

She still could not quite believe what had happened. This grey, wet, cold morning, she felt herself to be utterly cursed. It seemed that nothing had gone right in her life since her mother and Jago had come to her with their marriage ultimatum back in Long Harbour. Worse, it seemed that everything and everybody she touched was dragged down with her.

Like the poor, kind folk at Margie . . .

She felt angry, and outraged, but it was a cold, shivery, impotent sort of fury. She would dearly like to bring down some sort of just and terrible retribution upon those who had destroyed Margie Farm. But there was no way she could imagine doing such a thing. She wished she could roll back the past, change things. If she had only run off and left the farm. Or she might have given herself up when the Brothers first arrived. Or . . .

Not paying proper attention to her surroundings, Elinor tripped on a tangle of tree roots and fell, sprawling painfully into a cold puddle. She struggled to her knees, cursing, rubbing at a bruised elbow, soaked even more than she had been, spluttering, her bad leg agony. The belt she had acquired from the dead Brother had slipped part-way down her hips, the sheathed sword jammed awkwardly between her legs. She shook herself, trying to get things properly straightened out so she could stand.

Gyver looked back at her. His wet fur was sleeked to his body.

'What are you staring at?' she snapped, wiping wet leaf mould from her cheek.

He padded over to her and held out a hand.

She took the hand, letting him help her to her feet. His grip was strong and warm. For a moment she stood looking at him. He smiled a little shyly, a glimmer of white teeth in his dark face. For a moment, she felt . . . She did not know what she felt. He confused her, Gyver did, having no temper, it seemed, being able to keep going after everything, and to turn back and offer her a helping hand and a small smile – all the while limping still from his own bad leg, to which soggy remnants of bandage still clung.

But limping far less painfully than she. He seemed to be walking over the hummocky and treacherous forest floor with hardly any difficulty at all, compared to her own painful progress.

Elinor let go of his hand, rubbed at her aching thigh. In her tumble, she had somehow lost the stick she had been using as a walking cane – her old one having been left behind in the Margie ditch. She was cold and soaked and shaking so hard she could barely stand, with her leg throbbing miserably.

Gyver was staring at her.

'Don't just *stand* there!' she snapped accusingly. 'Help me find my stick.'

He pointed, and she saw that the stick had been under her foot all along, half buried in the soggy, leaf-strewn dirt of the forest floor. She grabbed it up, angry and aching and feeling the fool.

'We musst keep moving,' he said.

'Don't order me about,' she snapped back at him.

He only stared at her the more, eyes wide. He looked hurt, as if she had slapped him unnecessarily.

Which, in a sense, was exactly right.

330

Elinor sighed, shivering. 'I'm . . . sorry. It's just that I'm . . . I ache and I'm cold and I'm fed up to the back teeth with . . .'

Gyver suddenly whirled about, staring off into the tangled mass of the wet trees.

'What?' Elinor said, her heart thumping. There had been no sign of pursuit yet, and she had begun to let herself hope they had got clean away, sheltered by the forest as they were. 'What *is* it, Gyver?' she repeated, having received no response from him.

The fur-man gestured back at her for silence, intent on something.

She blinked away cold rain-water and stared at where he was looking. They were in a wet hollow, a longish slope leading off to one side. One of the great old trees had crashed to the ground, clearing an open space. Elinor stared, holding her breath, but could make out nothing beyond the dripping tangle of trunk and limb and leaf; hear nothing save the endless drumming patter of the rain itself.

'If there's something out there,' she whispered, 'let's get *away* from here. *Fast*!'

But it was already too late.

Two dark figures came leaping suddenly down the slope at them, vaulting the great fallen tree, blades out, yelling.

She drew her own blade, feeling the familiar, uncanny tingle go through her, feeling Kess surge up in her. Her heart was thumping, her belly knotted, but . . . but she also felt a sense of relief. Her Kess self was simple, pure. She could forget regrets, anguish. Nothing mattered save the moving blade, only the blade.

Hide!' she hissed at Gyver. Unarmed as he was, he would only prove easy meat.

He looked at the men leaping towards them, looked at Elinor. His eyes were wide with shock.

'Quick!' she said.

He turned away then, disappearing behind a brace of dripping trunks. Elinor stayed where she was, waiting.

Her attackers paused, drawing closer. She stood in the defence stance called Little Crab, feet lightly braced, breathing from her belly for calm, feeling her self pure and perfect and perfectly balanced, ready to move any way she might be required. The white blade shone in the rain.

Her attackers slowed as they drew near, until they stopped dead just beyond blade reach, uncertain. They had obviously expected her to run, or else attack recklessly in her turn, or something. Anything but just stand there facing them in silence, stock still, waiting.

The three of them stood face to face. She could hear the men's panting breaths, see the faint vapour clouds of their breath in the chill, rain-wet air. They were dressed in the usual sombre clothing the Brothers favoured, with plate-armour cuirasses and fighting helms. One had curling black moustaches. Each brandished a long iron sword at her.

'That's the blade, all right,' one said. He regarded Elinor, face creased in an uncertain frown. 'Who *are* you?'

'Give it up, boy,' the one with the moustaches ordered her. 'You'll never take the two of us. And there's more coming behind.'

'Give it *up*!' the other echoed, gesturing at her menacingly with his blade. 'Or we'll take you down where you stand, blade or no blade, whoever you may be.'

Kess laughed, a cold stutter of sound. 'Come and try.'

The one with the moustaches leaped at her without warning, sword out. She saw in an instant what he intended: catch her guard stroke with his blade, bull his way in, knock her to the ground with the force of his attack.

She had seen it before.

A quick crossways counter-stroke, the *klingg* of wet metal against metal, a sidestep, and she cut down at his neck two-handed as he stumbled past – the sword's perfect, shining razor edge did the rest.

The man's head shot from his shoulders, blood fountaining.

The remaining Brother stared aghast.

Elinor took him before he could recover, skewering him through the meaty portion of his thigh, tearing his sword out of his grip with a quick whirl and flip of her own blade, sending it tumbling tip over hilt to splash into a puddle.

The man stared at her, clutching his bleeding thigh and groaning. She stepped up to him, blade ready.

'No . . .' he said. 'No!' His eyes were white with fear and

shock. He lifted a shaking hand, palm out, helpless. 'Don't . . .'

But all she saw was the leaping flames in last night's dark and the limp tumble of the dead body as one of them had dumped it on to the pile . . . She grabbed him by the crest of his leathern helm, yanked back his head and decapitated him, all in one swift, ruthless stroke. The bright blade cut through him – flesh and cartilage and bone – like a knife through butter.

She let him go and jumped back, away from the blood. In the rain it diluted quickly, forming a spreading pool, pinkly crimson.

She stood panting and shivery, her leg throbbing. She looked round to where Gyver had gone. There was no sign of him, no trail she could see to follow. But he could not have got far. All she need do was head in the same general direction, surely.

But a sudden commotion upslope made her turn.

There were more of them. Half a dozen at least. And they had seen her and their dead comrades, for they let out a great collective howl of outrage and came hurtling down the slope at her.

She stood ready as she could be, feet braced, sword up now in what Master Karasyn had named the Double Tree, the same two-handed defensive posture she had taken in Lord Mattingly's room when the Guard had surrounded her there – the best she knew how to do, faced with an onslaught of many men. She took a long breath, another, centring herself.

Then they were upon her, and she was caught up in a whirling, shouting frenzy of blade and limb and grunting man-flesh. She took one of them through the sword arm, thrust another away, leaped high to avoid a blade, rolled to her knees and away, then up, blade out, to meet a man who had not expected it. She saw the shock of the blow mirrored in his eyes as the razor tip of her blade went in under the bottom edge of his cuirass, smelled his gasping breath, so close to her was he, then shoved herself away.

She stood, panting, her back to one of the trees. Two of her attackers were down. The one she had taken in the arm was cursing; the other lay sprawled and still. For a moment, nobody moved.

Then they were on her again, shouting and cursing, hacking and stabbing like madmen. She dodged and parried desperately, stumbled on her bad leg, nearly went down, only barely able to counter a vicious slash at her, and then another. Gasping, she struggled back to her feet. Only the tree at her back had saved her thus far. But it would not be enough. They would take her, this bunch, eventually. Even with the sword's uncanny aid, she did not have the strength left to resist them.

They knew it, too, and howled triumphantly, circling her position like a wolf pack, ready to bring her down. It was only a matter of time before she made some fatal mistake . . .

One of them almost took her in the side – a fast pattern of strokes: *kringg klangg kringg kringg*. The man laughed, seeing her falter, and stepped in to finish her.

But he came at her too fast and too clumsily, slipping on the wet ground, and she still had enough strength to deflect his blade and gore him in the groin – a clumsy, desperate blow, but successful enough nonetheless.

The man fell, screaming. His companions hesitated for an instant, then leaped at her with renewed fury. She took a hard blow on her blade that hurt her arm; barely managed to dodge another thrust. Her heart was hammering, and she was gasping, unable to get enough breath. She was on her knees now, struggling to get back up. One of them came at her, his face lit with hard triumph.

And then there was a sudden roar, and her attackers fell apart in disarray. Elinor saw a big furry body charging and whirling amongst them furiously, all claws and fangs and roaring rage. The men scattered, howling. Elinor took one as he stumbled past her. The rest went down beneath the terrible, bestial fury of this unexpected onslaught.

Elinor stood, gasping, her heart labouring. Her attackers lay scattered and still, torn and bloody. As she watched, a large bear shook the last, like a dog with a rat in its jaws. Then it turned, growling deep in its furry chest, jaws wet and red with blood, its eyes alive with fury. She drew herself up, the blade ready, though she did not fancy her chances against such a wild beast, infuriated as it was with the blood and violence.

But it did not charge her. Instead, it shook its head, snorting, and sat down abruptly on its haunches like a dog.

Elinor drew breath, staring at it uncertainly.

It was licking itself now, its great pink tongue glistening in the rain, cleaning the blood from its coat. It stopped momentarily, looked at her out of the corner of its eye. 'A "thank you" might be nice,' it growled.

Elinor stared. 'Scrunch!' she gasped. 'Where did *you* come from?'

From behind the bear, a little form suddenly came bounding through the rain, squealing: 'Elinor, Elinor, Elinor!'

'Spandel!' Elinor cried, as the little Lamure bounded into her arms.

'Me, me, me . . .' Spandel crowed. She pointed at Scrunch. 'I found him, Elinor. I found him, found him!'

Elinor laughed weakly. She put Spandel down for a moment, wiped her blade, sheathed it, took Spandel up again. She felt her Kess self dissolve away as she let go of the blade's hilt – not without a little pang of regret for that pure, simple focus. She did not understand what had happened – was happening – to her. No longer was she torn apart into two halves. It seemed only the blade, now, that called up the alter aspect of herself.

She looked about her, shocked at the pitiful human remains that lay soaking in the rain. She shuddered, not knowing quite how she felt – exhausted, exalted, joyous, shattered, confused. She looked down at little Spandel in her arms. 'How did you . . .'

'This,' growled Scrunch, 'is *not* a good place to sit and chat.'

Elinor looked at him quizzically. She had seen him previously only in a depressed and morose state. This sharpness in him was entirely new to her.

'We need to get *away* from here,' he said, rising. He froze, then, and for a long moment stood snuffling the rain-soaked air. Then, 'Come out!' he called suddenly.

Elinor whirled, spilling Spandel to the ground and reaching for her blade hilt, heart jumping.

But it was Gyver who appeared, staring wide-eyed at the bodies. He kicked at one with his foot and hissed. 'Nassty men!' he spat.

'Gyver, Gyver!' Spandel cried.

'Little Dancer,' he returned, smiling his sharp-toothed smile.

'Time to *go*,' Scrunch the bear said.

*

They pressed on without pause till mid-day, working a weary way through the trees. The cold rain did not let up. Elinor was soaked and miserable and sore. Her right arm ached from having wielded the sword. Her bad leg burned and throbbed. 'I have to rest,' she called to her companions, who seemed to be able to walk forever.

They paused under the half-shelter of a great oak near a swollen, frothy little stream. Hunkering down, they drank from the cold, rock-flavoured water. Afterwards Elinor half-fell back, groaning. She felt weak and sick. It was a blessed relief to be able to lie down.

Scrunch went over to the remains of a fallen tree, rotted and punky and green with moss, and began tearing at the rotted wood with his claws, ripping up great chunks.

He scooped out several fat white grubs from where he had torn the rotted wood open, licked them off his paw with his long pink tongue, smacking his lips appreciatively. Then, with delicate care, he lifted one up between a thick thumb and forefinger – his bear's paws were equipped with a long-clawed thumb, Elinor saw for the first time.

He held the white, squirming thing out for her. It was about as long as her finger but thicker. 'Yours,' he offered.

'No.' Elinor shook her head, nauseated at the very thought.

But Gyver stepped in past her to the ripped-open tree and lifted out a couple of the fat white grubs eagerly. 'Deliciouss!' he said dropping them into his mouth.

Elinor stared.

Spandel, too, was searching about now, picking out the ugly white things.

Elinor reached out gingerly for the one Scrunch still held out in offering. It felt a little squishy in her fingers, like something decayed. She watched it struggle and squirm blindly for a moment, then shut her eyes tight and popped it into her mouth quickly.

It burst when she bit into it, slimy and far from delicious. But she found she could keep it down. And her stomach was insisting on more. So, like the others, she got down on her knees and began pawing through the rotted wood.

Once the supply of grubs was exhausted, they all huddled together against the gnarly root-bed of the oak tree that stood on the stream's bank, where there was at least some partial shelter from the continuous rain. Elinor had started shivering uncontrollably, now that they were no longer moving, and Scrunch gestured her over to his flank, where she was able to curl into his warmth gratefully.

He grunted, settling her more comfortably, let out a long, sighing, snuffling breath. Elinor lay there, warming, wondering about him. He was not the same tormented soul she had first seen. 'Where have you been?' she asked him, feeling her shivers beginning to lessen.

'About,' he replied.

She could feel the rumble of his deep voice in his chest as she leaned against him.

'Nosing myself back into the world.' He patted her gently with his great paw. 'Thanks to you.'

Elinor did not know quite what to say to that.

'Thank you,' she thought to say after a long pause. 'For . . . for coming to save me as you did back there.'

'It was my turn,' was all he said by way of reply.

They sat in silence for a while, the four of them huddled close together companionably for warmth.

Scrunch began to snore softly.

Gyver stretched out, sighing. 'It hurtss, my leg,' he said softly, rubbing at his thigh.

'Mine too,' Elinor replied. They smiled at each other.

Spandel sat up suddenly. She scrambled atop Scrunch's back and stared off long-necked into the trees. The bear grunted and lifted his big head with a jerk.

'What is it?' Elinor whispered. She had come to respect her furred companions' keen senses. She herself could see nothing untoward, hear nothing save the rain and the burbling of the little stream at the feet of the oak under which they sheltered.

Scrunch stood up, raised his muzzle to snuffle the air enquiringly.

'Ssomebody there,' Gyver hissed.

They disengaged themselves quietly.

'Stay here,' Scrunch said. 'I'll go and see.' Then he lumbered off, moving silently through the trees despite his bulk.

337

Elinor put a hand to the hilt of her sheathed blade, waiting, heart thumping. She was not at all certain of her ability to face another such attack as the last. She was too sore and weary and stiff.

They waited, anxious. The rain drummed through the trees. Elinor began to shiver again. Chill rain water dribbled down her back. She wiped her face with her forearm.

There was no sign of Scrunch.

'Where *is* he?' she whispered.

And then, through the trees, she spotted him. Through a little thicket he barged, then half-turned and reached up a big thumbed paw to hold back the branches. Behind him, the figure of a man appeared. Elinor squinted, trying to make out what might be happening.

Just the one figure, it seemed, an older man, thin, grey-haired, stubble cheeked, dressed in baggy trousers and shirt, soaked and splattered with mud.

Elinor gasped. 'Collart!'

'Aye, me indeed,' he called. He ducked through the opening in the branches Scrunch held up for him and came limping over. He was a ragged, sorry-looking figure, his clothing torn and scorched, limping badly. The whole left side of his face was one purple bruise, his left eye swollen all but shut.

Elinor rushed to him and gave him a hug. He winced, but smiled all the same. 'Good to see you alive, girl. Thought I was the only one to make it away from Margie in one piece.'

'But what are you doing here?' she said. 'However did you *find* us?'

Collart shrugged wearily. 'I didn't. I've been wandering pointlessly about in these cursed, rain-soaked woods all day. Got myself lost, I'm afraid. Heard something ahead of me, came creeping along to see what it might be – might have been some of the Brothers, curse them! But it was Scrunch here, come to find *me*.

'What about you, girl? How is it *you're* here? And the rest?'

'I was out after Gyver,' Elinor explained. 'Spandel and I both were. We found him in the woods. He smelled the smoke. We went back to see . . .'

'Ah . . .' Collart said. He pointed at the sword that hung at

338

Elinor's waist. 'Was it *you*, then, that caused all that commotion last night?'

'You were *there*?' Elinor said. 'Why didn't you . . .'

Collart shook his head. 'I was off in the fields, crawling like a worm for the safety of the woods. Just heard it, is all. Something about one of their own attacking them?'

'I disguised myself as a Brother.'

'Did you manage to get any of them?' Collart asked, a sudden glint in his eye.

Elinor nodded. 'One.' Then she smiled. 'Took the ear off that Squad Chief, too.'

'No!' Collart slapped his thigh, then winced again. Elinor saw that his hand was burned badly all along the back.

'Come,' Gyver said. 'Let me ssee to your hurtss.'

Collart looked at him uncertainly.

'I have a little of the sskill,' Gyver said. He looked at Elinor. 'Help me to get him sseated by the water.'

The fur-man seemed to know what he was about. Elinor helped him get Collart comfortably seated against a moss-cushioned stone on the bank of the little stream. Gyver went off a little way, searching, then squatted by the water's edge and began to dig with his hands.

'What happened, Collart?' Elinor asked gently while they waited for Gyver's return. She did not know if the man was ready to talk about it yet.

He sighed a long, weary sigh and stared off into the empty air with his one unswollen eye.

'You don't have to . . .' she began.

He waved her to silence. 'It's all right. It'll do me good to get it out.' For a few more moments he continued staring, then turned to her. 'I'd had a dark dream. Couldn't sleep. Heard something, so I got up to have a look see.'

Elinor nodded him on encouragingly.

'I came out of the house and heard voices in the night. Couldn't make out words. A vandal, thinks I. I'll give him something to remember Margie Farm by, all right.' Collart shook his head sadly. 'But it was me who ended up on the receiving end. I thought there was only one of them. Took him by surprise by the scruff of his neck, all unprepared. Threw him against the wall good and proper. But a second one jumped me then.'

Collart sighed, felt gingerly at his bruised face, winced. 'I didn't do too well. Not as young as I once was. But I took him down eventually.'

Gyver was back by now, hands full of black, oozing mud. He took Collart's arm and began spreading the mud carefully over the other's burns.

'Feels good,' Collart murmured, sighing in relief.

'How did you get those burns?' Elinor asked.

Collart shook his head. 'I tried to get into the house after it was burning. Foolish notion.'

'Did you . . . Was there anybody . . .' Elinor did not know how to finish the question.

'Don't think anyone else survived,' he responded soberly. 'Cursed cruel bastards! How could they do such a thing? Have they gone *completely* mad?'

'It was my fault,' Elinor said in a small voice. 'They came for *me*. If I hadn't . . .'

Collart put his good hand on her arm and said, 'Don't torture yourself, girl. Who'd have guessed the Brothers would do such a mad, cruel thing?'

Scrunch nosed his way up to them. 'Can you walk, Collart?'

Collart nodded. 'Reckon I can, Scrunch. If I have to.'

'Then let us walk,' the bear urged. 'We are still too near human lands.'

Elinor groaned inwardly at the prospect of more trekking through the rain. But she knew Scrunch to be right. Their best hope of safety now lay in putting distance between them and any possible pursuit. As quickly as they could.

So they set off, straggling through the trees.

'Cursed rain,' Collart grumbled.

Elinor nodded, halting for a moment, leaning on her stick to ease her aching leg.

'It will cover our sspoor,' Gyver said. He was ahead of them, looking back. 'Water iss *good*!'

'To drink, maybe,' Collart said. 'But I ain't no fish!'

'Come on!' Spandel called to them. 'Walk, walk, walk!' She was perched now upon Scrunch's broad shoulder.

'Easy for *you* to say,' Collart answered accusingly.

Spandel bounced down and danced over to him. 'I will walk

with you, then.' She reached up and tugged at his trousers. 'Come, come, come!'

Collart smiled and started walking.

Elinor followed after, soaked and cold and weary. But, somehow, despite it all, she too smiled, watching little Spandel urge old Collart along. She had known far worse companions than this unlikely bunch. Far, far worse . . .

XXXV

They walked for two days, deeper and deeper into the woods, passing through patches of broken, more open country sometimes, and twice encountering cart tracks – slipping quickly across after making sure there was no sign of travellers.

They headed eastwards, into the high wild of the hills, and the ground sloped more and more upwards as they walked, making the going increasingly difficult. They sky was a great moil of black clouds still. It had kept raining, off and on, as they trudged along, as if some deep core of the world were disturbed.

Now they were working their way along the bank of a little gushing river – white water dancing over a scree of green rocks. The ground underfoot was treacherous, and they went slowly.

The bank along the far side began to rise, turning eventually into a bluff of red-ochre stone about the height of a tall man, with dripping green moss festooning it. As they rounded an elbow of the river, a little grotto appeared. The racing water sent up spumes of mist, half covering, half revealing it.

Scrunch stopped precipitously, visibly upset.

Elinor looked about, expecting trouble. But there was nothing to be seen. Just the river and the cliff and the grotto.

'What is it?' she asked.

Collart was staring about, too, and Gyver seemed as puzzled as she was.

'What *is* it?' Elinor repeated, turning to Scrunch.

The bear avoided her look. He glanced at Spandel, who fidgeted uneasily. Both cast sideways looks at the grotto.

Elinor squinted through the coiling river mist, but could make out nothing save moss-draped ochre stone and the darker shadow of the grotto itself. Water swirled in a little sheltered pool there. There was a bit of gravelly strand, and . . .

342

She blinked. Her left palm itched suddenly, and she scratched it, not thinking. Was that the outline of a face she could see in there?

She stepped tentatively forward to the river's edge and peered at the grotto. There *was* the image of a face there, inscribed into the red rock, crudely done, and yet somehow not crude at all. A female face, part human and part animal, long and slender of chin, pointy-eared, with overlarge eyes . . .

For a moment, it seemed she recognized that face, had seen it before.

But no. How could that be?

'What . . . what *is* it?' she asked, turning to the humanimals.

'Dreamer and dreamed,' Spandel said. 'Dreamers, dreamers, dreamers all.'

Elinor stared, completely perplexed.

'Come on,' Scrunch growled. 'Let's be away from here.'

'Wait,' Elinor said. 'I don't . . .'

'Come *away*!' Scrunch said. 'This is not for your eyes.'

But Gyver was in the river, thigh-deep already, staring at the face in the rock. 'She iss grandmother Moon. And . . . not.'

'Not,' Scrunch said gruffly.

Elinor walked into the water by Gyver's side. The fast current tugged at her, cold enough to make her bones ache. But she felt beckoned, somehow, and waded across to the little stone grotto.

Standing knee-deep in the frigid water, she reached out a hand wonderingly to the face on the rock before her. Her right hand, her sword hand . . . And snatched it back, knowing with a strange and sudden certainty that it was the wrong hand altogether. She put out her left instead, putting it palm flat against the cold, rough, mist-soaked surface of the stone.

She felt a tingling, a sense of something flowing through her, like water through a chute, filling her and yet not. The face seemed to encompass all her vision for a long moment. Overlarge eyes, pointed, animal ears, sharp chin. She could almost see the eyes shining with life, gazing at her, into her . . .

And then, somehow, she was back across the other side of the river and up on the bank – with no recollection at all of how she had got there. She blinked, shook herself, shivering, shaken.

Spandel was staring at her.

Gyver came up out of the river, his lower body streaming water. He shook himself like a dog. 'Sshe iss very beautiful, thiss sspirit Lady,' he said.

'Who *is* she?' Collart asked.

Scrunch looked at him. It was not an especially friendly look.

Elinor felt her heart jump. So far, Scrunch had been entirely friendly. But what could they do to protect themselves against such as he, should he suddenly turn on them?

'I have heard, friend bear,' Collart said softly, 'of a Lady . . .'

Scrunch sat down, dog fashion, and sighed a long, snuffling sigh. 'You have heard things, friend man, that you ought not.'

Collart shrugged. 'The Free Folk made themselves easy at Margie.'

'Too easy,' Scrunch growled.

Suddenly, Elinor recollected Spandel on the porch back at Margie, saying, 'Life is a dream dreamed by the Great Lady.'

'The Great Lady,' she said aloud, 'who dreams us all.'

Scrunch snuffled in surprise. 'And what do *you* know of her, newcomer as you are?'

Elinor shrugged self-consciously. Her left palm itched, and she scratched it. 'Dreamer and dreamed, are we, dreamers all . . .'

'Dreamer and dreamed, indeed,' Scrunch agreed. 'She walks our dreams, the Lady. Or we walk hers.' He looked at Elinor and Collart. 'We dream of her – or she of us – but never clear. Some of us fashion places such as this, with her likeness, trying to dream more true, to bring her more into the world. I did not know this place was here, or . . .' He shrugged. 'This is not a place for human folk to see.'

'But we have seen,' Collart said quietly.

Scrunch nodded. 'You have seen.' He regarded them uncomfortably, glanced across at Spandel.

'It is meant to be,' Spandel said. She pointed at Elinor. 'For her. She is *touched*.'

Elinor felt a long, cold shiver run up her spine.

'You are sure?' Scrunch said.

'Yes!' Spandel insisted. 'Oh, yes, yes! She is, is, *is*!'

'What are you talking about?' Elinor demanded. They were

344

looking at her as if she had suddenly turned to some other person entirely before their eyes.

'The Lady,' Scrunch said softly, 'has come into the world through us. As a part of the Balances.'

Elinor shivered. Old Tildie had used the same word back in Minmi. And Mamma Kieran in Long Harbour before that – Mamma Kieran with her talking, knowing raven.

'The . . . Balances of the Powers?' Collart said.

Scrunch nodded. 'You human folk do not experience the Powers as we do. It is our curse and blessing, both. The Powers move our purer cousins like wind moves a pennant. We feel the echo of that in our blood and bones and minds . . .

'The world has been . . . disturbed. The ancient Seers reached into the fabric of things and ruptured them. *We* are part of the great unbalance they provoked. But we are part of the Balance, also. As is the Lady.'

'And Elinor,' Spandel added.

They were still staring at her, Collart and Gyver too, now.

'Don't *do* that!' she snapped at them. 'Don't stare at me like that.'

Scrunch lifted his big furred shoulders in a shrug. 'If you are *touched* . . .'

'Well, I'm *not* touched,' Elinor insisted. 'By this . . . this dreaming Lady of yours or anything else. All right? I'm not anybody's axle. Nobody's channel. I'm not anything. Just Elinor, that's all. Nobody's . . . *tool*. I'm just an ordinary person struggling to find a life for herself. And I'll thank you all just to let me be!'

She turned from them and stalked a few paces off, her soaked boots squishing. It was too much. *Everybody* seemed to want her to be their own special saviour. *Everybody* had great plans for her life. Well, she was none of the things anybody saw her as. She was . . .

But for all the vehemence of her denial, she felt with sickening certainty that there *was* something here, some core of truth she felt in her guts – though she could not make proper sense of any of it.

She stared at the mist-hidden face on the rock across the water. A half-memory played at the edge of her mind. Something to do with Mamma Kieran . . . She felt the strange tingling in her left palm once more.

That half-animal, half-human, pointy-eared female face . . .
Her palm. The face golden and shining. A sudden pain. A
terrible burning . . .

Almost, she had it.

But it slipped from her.

She stared down at her left palm. There was nothing there,
no mark or sign of any burn.

Elinor shivered, frustrated and confused and uncertain.

Scrunch let out a long, breathy sigh. 'We shall see what we
shall see,' he said. 'You are what you are, Elinor. And neither
we nor you may change that. In the meanwhile . . .' He
regarded Collart and her soberly. 'The Lady is our secret. Very,
very few human folk have ever heard of her.'

Collart put his hand over his heart. 'None will hear of her
through me.'

Scrunch looked across at Elinor.

'Nor through me,' she said.

Gyver nodded his own solemn agreement.

'Good!' Scrunch growled. He looked at all of them, his big
head swinging from side to side. 'No more about such things,
then.' He glanced towards the image in the grotto and lowered
his head in a quick sort of bow. Spandel did the same. Then
Scrunch turned and said, 'Let's away from here.'

They went.

But Elinor could not help looking backwards through the
trees, trying to catch one last glimpse of that mysterious face.
The great dreaming Lady . . . She felt her heart beating fast. So
familiar, that face.

It was all *most* confusing.

They walked on and on, endlessly. The rain came and went,
shrooshing through the trees. Up hill and down they traipsed,
across cold little streams, over fallen logs mouldering under coats
of white mushrooms, through thickets, and out into open glades.

Day was beginning to wane.

'We must find a place to rest up,' Elinor said.

Collart nodded wearily. All the upslope walking was hard on
the legs, and she could see he was near the ragged edge of his
strength. Even Gyver was limping again now. Her own leg
throbbed at each step.

346

Through the trees ahead, there was a more open bit of country. A long, jagged cliff face of dark stone reared itself to their left. 'Over there,' she suggested, pointing. 'There might be caves.'

'I'll go,' said Scrunch. 'I know caves.' He peered through the trees, then waddled rapidly away.

'Might as well rest,' Elinor suggested.

Old Collart nodded relievedly and went to sit by the tangled roots of an old hill oak. But so weary was he that he nearly sprawled face first. Gyver helped Elinor to prop him comfortably against the tree bole. Collart was covered in sweat, and his forehead, when Elinor put her hand to it, was hot with fever. She knelt next to him, silent, knowing not what to say.

'Don't look so glum, girl,' he said to her.

Elinor shrugged.

'You've got the same hang-dog look I used to see on a constipated hound I once owned.'

Elinor blinked, took a sharp breath. She had been about to ask him about the image of the Lady they had seen back in the grotto, but his remark – so like one of her mother's – put her suddenly in mind of Long Harbour and Annocky, and of her mother and Jago and the twins – she had not spared them so much as a fleeting thought in all the days since her departure.

She was suddenly overwhelmed by a paralyzing sense of loss. It seemed everything had been taken from her, one thing after the next, with no let up, culminating in Margie: Gillien dead, and Hann, and Sandy, who would never again make those beautiful blue cups and dishes, and all the rest. She felt a stab of fury, and of anguish, remembering the greedy flames, the strutting, dark figures of the Brothers.

And now, nothing but the dead – the *innocent* dead – behind and the empty wilderness ahead . . .

Collart sighed. 'It's never easy – losing.'

'I've lost too much,' Elinor said, looking morosely down at the ground on which she still knelt. She picked up a little broken twig and snapped it into smaller pieces. Spandel tried to crawl companionably on to her lap, but Elinor pushed her away, too glum, too tired and wet and out of sorts. The little Lamure looked at her accusingly, then padded off to sit with

Gyver. Elinor felt a quick pang of guilt, but was too weary to try any remedy.

'We're still alive, still whole,' Collart said. 'And who knows what greater pattern all this might be a part of?'

'Ha!' Elinor spat morosely. 'Greater pattern of disaster.' She shivered, feeling the cold rain-water runnelling down her back under her soaked shirt. Her leg ached fiercely and she shifted position, trying to find a dry – or less wet – spot to sit on.

She glanced over at Gyver who sat against a nearby tree, legs out straight, Spandel curled against him. Water runnelled across his dark fur in little rivulets, and he began to lick himself like a cat, smoothing the grain of his fur, his pink tongue glistening. Elinor found herself envying him. He seemed unaffected by the disasters that had swept upon them all, moving through them as a fish might through storm-tossed waters.

'You learn,' Collart said softly. 'You learn to lose.'

Elinor frowned.

'It's what happens, girl. As you grow older, you learn. The Powers give and the Powers take away.'

'So I have to *like* it?' she demanded irritably. 'I have to surrender, while those great, uncaring, impersonal Powers thunder through my life and wreck it entirely? I've lost *everything* I ever had. I don't even know properly who I *am* any more! And I'm just supposed to . . . what? Get *used* to it?'

Collart smiled wearily. 'No. Not at all. Rail against it all you can. But don't *deny* it. Don't spend your life trying to prevent it. Learn to accept loss. It's the final virtue.'

Elinor shook her head. 'Don't you *care* about what happened back at Margie?'

'I care, all right, girl. I *grieve* for Margie, and for poor Gillien and Hann and the rest. But life goes on, whether we will it or no. And we who remain must . . . lose.'

'But . . . but . . .' Elinor spluttered, 'learning to . . . lose. That's not what life is about!'

'It's the final virtue,' Collart repeated. He smiled again at her, tiredly. 'I've lost many things in my life. But I'm still here, and still able to manage a smile.'

Elinor rounded on him, but before she could say anything further, he pointed to the sword at her belt. 'It hasn't all been loss, though. Has it?'

Mouth still open, she looked down at the sword. Her right hand went to the bronze dragon hilt, and she felt the strange tingle of it. Her heart beat in quick excitement for a moment and she felt Kess stir in her. Kess the pure. Kess the dangerous.

Elinor the confused . . .

She laughed, bitterly.

'What?' Collart asked.

Elinor shrugged. How could she talk of it?

'It is no ordinary blade,' Collart said softly.

'No,' Elinor agreed. She gazed at it. The alizarin crimson of the lacquered leather scabbard was soaked with rainwater and glimmered like wet blood. The scabbard's bronze wire braiding shone. The little ruby eyes of the snarling dragon's head seemed to stare at her challengingly. It was a beautiful thing. A terrible thing . . .

It was hers.

She felt that suddenly in her guts. The one certain thing in an otherwise changing and altogether confusing landscape. For better or worse, the blade, and all it brought, was *hers*.

'Elinor?' Collart said.

She blinked. 'I don't . . .'

At that moment, Scrunch came lumbering back with a splash and snapple of wet branches. 'Found one,' he announced with obvious satisfaction.

'How far?' Collart asked.

'Not far.' Scrunch turned and headed back the way he had come. 'This way.'

'Come on,' Collart said wearily, prying himself away from the support of the tree at his back. 'Last leg of the day.'

Elinor and Gyver helped him to his feet. They all straggled upwards, following the direction Scrunch had taken, till they saw the bear ahead, awaiting them on a bulge of crumbling stone. He gestured with one paw. Elinor looked up and saw, off in the distance, a little black opening in the cliff face. A cave indeed. But to get to it, they had to traverse yet another wooded hollow, working their way down this side and up the other before they would come at the cliff face proper. She groaned, thinking on it.

Scrunch beckoned them, and they clambered on.

It turned out to be relatively easy walking at first, but the bottom of the hollow was choked with brush and dead trees, and they had to fight a way through, gasping and struggling. The trees here were evergreen and tangled together in a great thicket.

As they paused to take a much-needed breather and survey the likeliest route ahead, Gyver came up to her. 'May I ssee your ssmaller blade?' he asked.

Elinor looked at him, uncertain. He had shown no interest in weapons up to this point. 'What do you need it for?'

He pointed to a downed evergreen nearby, lightning riven. 'It iss good wood, thiss tree. No longer green.'

'Good for *what*?' Elinor returned.

Gyver grinned at her, his sharp little white teeth flashing. 'You will ssee if you lend me the little blade, yess?'

Elinor shrugged and handed her dagger over, hilt first, too weary to try disputing with him. She watched him take the hilt in his hand awkwardly, as if it was the first time he had ever held such a thing. 'Be careful. It's sharp.'

'Here?' He ran his thumb down the edge, winced, quickly pulled it away, blood dripping.

'I *told* you,' Elinor said exasperatedly. She reached for the dagger. 'I think you'd better . . .'

'No!' He skipped back. 'I need thiss, me.'

Elinor sighed. 'Be *careful* with it, then.'

'I will. Promisse.' With that, he padded over to the downed evergreen. It was a large tree, split by the lightning bolt that had killed it, dead limbs spread out in twin, brown-needled fans. Gyver searched through those hanging limbs and began hacking away at one with the dagger, sending chips of wood flying, till he was able to snap it off. Then he stripped the little branches away so that he was left with a straight staff, a couple of finger widths in diameter, perhaps chest high.

He came back and handed the dagger over. '*Very* good, thiss,' he said, lifting the staff for Elinor to see.

'What do you want it for?' she asked. His leg seemed near healed, and he was walking well enough, so that he did not need a walking stick. And it looked too light for a club or striking weapon of any sort.

'You will ssee,' was all he said.

Spandel came bouncing downslope towards them. 'Scrunch says to come on, on, *on!*' she urged them.

It was upslope, punishing going until, at the last, the trees thinned out and they found themselves on the rocky scree at the cliff's base.

Elinor plonked herself down exhaustedly, along with the others, gasping. Collart was white-faced and shaking. She rubbed at her aching leg, shook herself, feeling weary beyond belief. But the cave was not far now. She could see it clearly up above. All they had to do was work a way up along the tumble of rocks.

A sudden noise nearby startled her, and she snapped about. But it was just Gyver rummaging about on his knees a little ways off amongst the rocky scree. He came up with a grin on his face, holding a rock shaped like a big stone egg.

'What do you want *that* for?' Elinor demanded. The fur-man seemed so childish at times. First the evergreen staff – which he had done nothing with, only trail it along behind him – and now this collecting of stones. Could he not see that there were more important things to do than play about, she thought with weary irritation. How did he have the energy to do it?

He came back, juggling the rock in his hold, the staff stuck under one arm awkwardly.

'Come *on*,' Scrunch growled and headed across the rocks towards the cave.

The cave turned out to be better shelter than Elinor had expected. It was located next to a stream that tumbled down the cliff face in a little white cascade, forming a pool amongst the rocky scree at the cliff's base before draining downwards into the forest. Inside, the cave was spacious enough to stand up in, though only just, and went back far enough to give them all plenty of room. It was damp and chilly, and smelled musty, but their body heat would soon warm it up. All in all, it looked to be the best shelter they could hope for.

Scrunch nosed about a bit, pronounced the place safe, then settled himself comfortably up against one wall, muzzle on his big paws, and closed his eyes sighing contentedly. Collart collapsed at his side, Spandel with him.

Elinor left them there and backed out into the wet evening light.

Standing outside the cave's mouth, she gazed into the distance. From this height, she could see folds of wooded hills, like some huge grey-green ocean frozen in the act of breaking against the flanks of the distant eastern mountains, the peaks of which were buried in the dark bellies of the clouds. Thick woods hid all trace of the route they had taken to get up here, and she could see no sign of any path they might use to get out.

No back-path. No path forward. Only the desolate wilderness which led everywhere and nowhere. To such had her life come.

It felt to her as if she had been driven remorselessly by events to this desolate, rain soaked bit of stony hillside. She had struggled onwards from one disaster to the next, like somebody thrust down a long slope, unable to stop, leaving a trail of destruction in her wake.

And through it all, like an undercurrent, was . . . She did not know quite how to think of it. Dame Sostris with her cards and her dark, strange-eyed cat. Mamma Kieran and her raven. Old Tildie in Minmi. Gillien. The humanimals with their mysterious dreaming Lady. All claiming to see some-thing *special* in her.

She felt her belly twist in sudden outrage. She would not be *driven*, not like some hapless sheep.

Elinor sighed. At least the sheep could see the shepherd, and the slope. She was passing through a landscape she could not discern, one of half-guessed Powers and channels and cryptic faces, and the shepherd, whatever it might be – if indeed there was anything shepherding her – was entirely invisible and mysterious and the way ahead entirely pathless.

'Learn how to lose when you must,' Collart had told her. 'It's the final virtue.'

Well, she was learning. But it was a *hard* learning. And one she resisted. Her bones ached. Her heart yearned for some-thing more than loss and confusion.

Her right hand slipped to the dragon hilt of the sword at her belt, welcoming the faint tingle it provoked in her bones. *Hers*. The solid heft of it was a comfort.

Elinor sighed, let the sword go, rubbed her eyes. She was *tired*. She could see no answers, standing here. She needed sleep.

She looked to the stream that cascaded down near the cave's mouth. They had seen precious little in the way of food, and there looked to be nothing to do about her empty stomach now. But she was thirsty, and dirty, and wanted at least a drink and a wash before sleep. She picked a way towards the rushing water.

Gyver was already there, seated on the ground with the egg-shaped rock in front of him. Slowly, he twirled the thing, examining it minutely – though for what, Elinor had no idea.

Finally satisfied, it seemed, with what his examination had revealed, the fur-man reached up a chunk of stone and struck the crown of the egg-shaped rock smartly with it. The top quarter fell away neatly at the blow, leaving a flat surface, darker in colour than the outside.

Gyver grinned and made a satisfied hissing noise. Then he turned the egg-rock a little, bent over, and struck at it again. This time, he angled the blow so that the force of it went from the centre of the egg-rock towards its outside edge. A long, slim flake fell away. Revolving the egg-rock, Gyver struck it again, and again with the same sort of angled blow, each producing another long, slim flake of stone.

Elinor watched, fascinated now. She had had no idea that such a thing was possible.

When Gyver was done, he had produced a dozen or so stone flakes, each almost as long as his slim hand and perhaps two fingers' breadth in width. Seeing her, he held one up for Elinor to examine. It was thin and brittle looking, slightly thicker on one side than the other.

'You musst be careful, you,' Gyver said. 'The edge, it is sharp.'

'You mean here?' Elinor replied. The flake had a long, wavery, almost serrated edge along its thinner side. She ran her thumb along it experimentally, winced, quickly pulled away, blood dripping.

'I *told* you to be careful, you,' Gyver said, grinning.

Elinor scowled for a moment, then could not help but grin back ruefully. She handed the stone flake to him.

353

He produced a piece of stick about the thickness of his finger and began to work at the flake's edges, pushing against them with the tip of the stick, breaking off little tiny chips of stone. When he was done, he had a blade of stone about the length of his index finger, with a sharp, serrated edge along one side, and a dulled, thicker edge on the other. He held it up for her to see, tucking it between his thumb and index finger, the dull edge against his hand. 'Ssee?' he said proudly. 'Thiss iss *my* blade.'

Then he turned to the evergreen staff and began to peel off long lengths of bark.

What are you doing to it?'

'You'll ssee, you,' was all he said, grinning.

Elinor watched him for a few moments longer, as he started whittling the staff, hissing softly to himself all the while. Then she turned and bent down to the water, too exhausted to be much curious any more. All she wanted now was a drink, a quick swill of cold water on her face, and sleep.

Long, deep, undisturbed sleep . . .

XXXVI

Sometime in the dark hours, Elinor came awake with a start. She lay where she was, snuggled up against Scrunch's warm flank, her heart jolting. Outside the cave, the rain had stopped, the world was silent. For long moments she could not decide what it was that had wakened her. From the regular sounds of their breathing, her companions all seemed to be slumbering peacefully enough. She scratched at the palm of her left hand, which itched.

A dream . . . Her heart was still thumping. An after-image hovered at the edge of her mind. A face . . . A woman's face.

She thought of old Mamma Kieran and her raven. But it was not that. Her mother, then? Genna come to haunt her dreams? No. Gillien? Tildie? No again. She struggled to recapture it. A familiar face . . .

And then it hit her: it was the face of the humanimals' Lady that she had seen scribed on the rocks.

But the dream had held more. Blood and pain and . . . another face, dark as deep night. And there had been fear . . . Her heart still pounded with it. Fear that had thrust her out of the dream and into wakefulness. Elinor shuddered, remembering the sense if not the form. Something terrible . . .

There would be no more sleep for her this night. Gently, she pulled away from Scrunch's side and crept out of the cave, stiff and awkward-limbed.

She stood outside, shivering, trying to soothe sore muscles, massaging her bad leg which throbbed fierily when she put too much weight on it. The rain had ceased. The eastward sky was just pearling into dawn. A chill wind cut into her.

She heard a little noise from behind. Turning, she saw Spandel.

'I dreamed, dreamed, dreamed,' she cried anxiously, scampering down from above the cave mouth.

Elinor felt her heart jump. 'Dreamed *what*?'

'Dreamed *her* and you, and . . .'

'And a dark face,' Elinor finished for her.

'Yes, yes, yes!' Spandel responded. 'How did you *know*?'

'I dreamed, too,' Elinor replied. She looked into Spandel's little human eyes and shivered.

Spandel hugged herself. 'Dark, *bad* face.'

'Whose?' Elinor asked. 'What face was it?'

Spandel shook her head in distress.

Elinor held out her arms and Spandel leaped into them. It felt better, somehow, to have the warm, furred little body curled up against her. 'What does it mean, Spandel?'

'A dark dream,' she said, 'and unclear, unclear.'

Elinor felt the little Lamure shudder, and a cold shiver passed down her own spine in response. She could recall no proper details from her dream, just a vague, dark, male face, huge and threatening and fearsome, and the remembrance of her own fright, and blood, and pain. 'The dark face?' Elinor pressed.

'The face of Jara,' the little Lamure whispered.

'Who?'

'Jara. He whom the Brothers follow.'

Elinor had heard the name before, she was sure of it. 'A man the Brothers follow?'

Spandel shook her head.

'What, then?'

'Like . . . like the Lady. And not.'

'Like the Lady?'

'Dreamer and dreamed,' Spandel answered. 'Dark dreams. Unbalanced dreams. Sofala dreaming.'

'Sofala?'

'Home of the Brothers.'

Elinor blinked, shook herself, trying to understand. Sudden memory came to her: she and Gillien on the porch at Margie, Gillien explaining, 'In Sofala, the Brothers have even set up an effigy they call Jara, a man-faced Power they claim as their divine guide.'

Elinor shivered. 'The brothers have this . . . this Jara, just as you have the Lady? Is that what you're saying, Spandel?'

'It's a matter of the Balances,' Spandel responded. 'Balance and balance and balance.'

Elinor shook her head. 'I don't understand! What *are* these . . . these mysterious faces? How can I be dreaming the same as you?' She felt frustration well up in her like a tide. There had been altogether too many unanswered questions in her life of late. 'What does it all *mean*, Spandel?'

'Dark and terrible things in the world,' Spandel said. 'Terrible, terrible things.'

Elinor looked at her, uncertain.

Spandel said, 'Wings.'

'What?'

The little Lamure pointed with one slim, furred hand up into the lightening sky. 'Wings.'

Elinor looked and saw a black bird-shape. It circled, the feathers on each outstretched wing's-end like delicate fingers.

She envied it such easy freedom, feeling her own stiff limbs. No days of weary struggling up soaked, tree-thick slopes for such a creature. Just the easy oaring of wings through the empty air.

It came closer, and she saw it was a crow.

With a sudden dip, it landed on the rocks before her where it waddled back and forth, turning its head and regarding her first out of one eye, then the other.

She stood looking at it, uncertain. Its beady black eyes seemed familiar.

'Youu,' it said. 'The meddlerrr.'

Elinor stared. Spandel gave a little squeak, leaped from her arms, and skipped away.

'Because of *youu*,' the crow said, darting its sharp beak at Elinor accusingly, 'the whole world'sss upsidde downnn.'

Elinor felt herself flush, took a step back.

There was a sudden scuffling from the cave mouth and Scrunch's voice said, 'Otys!'

The crow *kaw-kawwed* softly. 'Me indeeeddd. I see the meddlerrr hasn'ttt manageddd to killl youu yettt.'

Scrunch came lumbering over, Spandel bouncing at his side. He snorted. 'You're in the same mood I last saw you in.'

The crow *kawwed* and jump-flapped away into the air. 'Stupiddd bearrr! She'lll onlyyy gettt you killeddd. She'll onlyyy bring griefff. Like shee diddd forrr themmm attt Margieeee!'

357

'So *you* say,' Scrunch responded. 'You didn't see what happened yesterday back at . . .'

'I don'ttt *carrre* whattt happeneddd!' The crow flapped back to land at Scrunch's feet. 'You'rre such gulllible foolsss.'

'You're such a doubting fool,' Scrunch returned.

'The worlddd hasss come aparttt,' the crow said. It glared sideways at Elinor out of one beady eye. '*Her* faulttt.'

Scrunch shook his big head. 'Many faults.'

Elinor felt a wash of irritation and guilt. 'Speak plain, can't you?' she demanded, glaring at the crow. 'If you want to accuse me of something, then accuse me plain!'

The crow blinked, peered at her out of one eye, shuffled sideways. His beak opened and closed with a soft *clakk*. 'Youuu don'ttt knowww what'sss beennn happeninggg. Terrrible thingss . . .'

Elinor started. It was Spandel's words from their talk of the strange and frightening dream they had shared.

'Tell us,' Scrunch urged Otys.

The crow *kaw-kawwed* once again, shook himself, fluttered his black wings. He cocked his head, staring at Elinor out of one eye for long moments.

'Otys . . .' Scrunch began.

'I'll *showww* youuu!'

Scrunch growled, 'Otys!'

But the crow had already leaped into the air, calling, 'Followww meee!'

'Well?' Scrunch said, looking round.

Elinor was not sure what to say. Part of her longed to be away from all this, all the expectations and accusations, the confusions and demands.

But there was the dream – surely no ordinary dream. And she remembered gazing out at the pathless wild last evening. Looking up now, she saw Otys high in the air, circling, waiting. Here was a path, of sorts. She felt for the sword's dragon hilt. She was tired of running – she had never run from things back in Long Harbour – tired of asking questions to which she received no clear answers. Things were happening in the world. It was time she began to play her part in events. She felt it in her guts, like a hook.

'*Well*?' Scrunch repeated. His big brown eyes were clear and demanding.

'I'm with you,' Elinor said.

He looked at her for a long moment, then nodded. 'Good.'

'Where's Gyver?' Spandel asked suddenly.

Everyone turned. There was no sign of the fur-man.

'Still back in the cave?' Elinor suggested.

Spandel bounced over, disappeared into the darkness of the cave's mouth, bounced out again a few moments later. 'He's not there! Just Collart, still sleeping.'

Elinor felt her belly clench up with sudden dread, imagining any one of half a dozen things that could have happened to the fur-man – none good.

But Spandel gave a little bounce and a gleeful squeak and pointed. Elinor whirled and spotted the figure of Gyver coming clambering up from the woods across the rocky scree towards them.

He arrived with a big grin on his face.

'Where have you *been*?' Elinor demanded. 'Don't you know better than to go traipsing off like that?'

Gyver's grin lapsed, but not quite entirely. 'I've been working on *thiss*!' He held out something for her to see.

It was the wooden staff he had cut the day before. But it was different now, bent somehow, and there seemed to be other, thinner sticks tied to it, and leaves, and string, and . . .

It took her a long, confused moment to work out what it was he held out to her so proudly.

A bow and arrows.

The staff had been skilfully whittled and shaved and strung with some sort of braided twine to make the bow. The arrows – half a dozen or so of them – were long and slim and straight, tipped with little chips of sharp stone, fletched with green leaves.

He must have worked half the night to finish this, Elinor thought.

Gyver was grinning again now, his dark eyes sparkling. He hefted the bow in one hand, the arrows gripped in his other so that they made a kind of fan. 'Eassy to get food, now. Eassy to do many thingss. Me, I feel *much* better!'

Scrunch came lumbering up, sniffed at the bow in Gyver's hand. 'Good,' he grunted. 'Let's wake Collart and be away.'

*

So they walked again through the woods, along uneven, treacherous ground, following Otys the crow, who flitted in and out of sight above them beyond the dark latticework of the trees, periodically disappearing into the far distance and then returning. Though the rain had ended, the woods were still soaked, the early morning air chill and wet.

Across the jagged ridge of one hill range they struggled, and down the other side. They found a stream and drank and rested a little – Otys hovering impatiently – and then went on. The crow led them up the long slope of the next range, and then through a little pass. Finally, after a last, wearying clamber, they found him waiting for them near the crest, perched on a mossy bit of stone, preening his wing feathers.

Collart slumped against a tree, gasping.

Elinor glared at the crow. 'What do you . . .' she started.

'Quiettt!' Otys said. Then, 'Thisss wayy . . .' He hop-flapped off the rock and away upslope. 'Buttt *carefulll* . . .'

Elinor dropped to her hands and knees and crawled onwards, feeling the cold wetness of the ground soaking her trousers, her bad leg complaining. Collart followed her example, grunting, moving stiffly.

'You all right?' she asked him in a whisper. What with one thing and another, she had not been able to exchange so much as two words with him so far this day.

'Some breakfast would have been nice,' he panted.

Elinor nodded. Her own belly was painfully empty.

'*Quiettt!*' Otys hissed, glaring back at them.

Collart shrugged, began to work his way slowly upslope after the crow.

Elinor followed, having no notion at all as to what it was Otys might be leading them to, or why there was such a necessity for caution. He had refused to listen to any of the questions they had tried to put to him on this journey. She felt her pulse jumping nervously. The absolute craziness of what she was doing suddenly overwhelmed her: here in the middle of some forsaken wilderness amongst these bizarre creatures, crawling towards some unknown and terrible . . . something.

But she felt in her guts a strange certainty that there was no way back to anything for her. She could only go on.

She worked a silent way through the woods along with the

others, following Otys's lead, until they found themselves at the very edge of the trees, peering out carefully from between the serried trunks and down from the crest of a rocky bluff.

Elinor could see nothing special. A little open, sloping grassy hollow, more trees on the far side. There seemed to be a path of some sort, a cart track perhaps, winding across the hillside.

'Why did you bring us here?' she hissed at Otys.

'Quiettt!' he said. 'Watchh.'

A red squirrel with tufted ears flitted out to the end of a branch on the hollow's other side. Looking about quickly, it skittered down to the grassy ground, bushy tail twitching behind. It took a quick hop, another, and started to dig about, chattering softly to itself.

Then it froze suddenly, cocked its head, the tufted tips of its ears quivering, and stared off down the hollow.

With an agile bound, it was across the intervening ground and had disappeared back up the tree from which it had come.

Elinor tensed. It had heard something, or scented it. She turned a quick, questioning glance at Otys, but the bird, too, was staring off in the same direction as the squirrel had, his head craned forward around a tree limb.

They waited, tense.

The wood was silent save for the little whisperings of a breeze in the leaves, and the barely audible gurgling of a stream somewhere below. Elinor felt suddenly thirsty.

A bird cried somewhere: *Chitta chitta chit*! Then there was silence again.

Elinor swallowed, shifted herself a little to ease her leg, levered a bit of twig away from her hip where she lay. And then she heard a faint creaking, and a murmuring sound that could only be human voices in the distance.

She lay frozen, tense, and watched as human figures slowly came into view below. She saw darkly sombre clothing, the glint of iron, heard the complaining creak of cartwheels jouncing over rough ground.

Brothers!

It was, she began to realize, a little caravan very like the one that had taken Scrunch. Only this one had three . . . no, four small carts in all. She could make out furred forms in cages, something with wings, a flash of hairless skin that had to be a Hypon . . .

And then she blinked and gasped.

Behind the last cart came a straggling column of ordinary human people, men and women, chained together, neck and ankle, in a double file of misery. Perhaps two dozen of them all told, the iron chain binding them together clanking with each stumbling, group step.

Most of the prisoners went unshod, their feet and ankles streaked with blood, and they staggered and limped and moaned and struggled weakly to keep up with the pace the carts set. A Brother strode along beside them, a long leather-ribbon horse whip in hand. Any that faltered were lashed onwards with a quick, ruthless stroke of the whip.

'*Thattt*,' Otys squawked softly, 'isss what the worlddd hasss comme tooo!'

Collart swore softly.

Scrunch grunted, shook his big head, growled deep in his chest.

Elinor slithered backwards until she came to a little open space between the trees. She got to her knees, shaking, then levered herself to her feet, reaching instinctively for the sword at her belt. She remembered Margie Farm, the devouring flames, herself watching helplessly as one of the dark Brothers dumped a dead body on the pile, like a limp sack . . .

The blade shone when she drew it. Her hand and arm tingled with the strange feel of it. She felt dangerous Kess surge up, pure and hard and ruthlessly determined.

Collart came crawling back after her, Spandel and Gyver following behind. Otys flapped to a fallen tree and perched there, eyeing Elinor challengingly. 'Welll?' he demanded.

'I *won't* let them harm more innocent folk,' she said.

Scrunch came scrambling down the slope, growling deep in his chest.

Gyver suddenly threw up his head, nostrils quivering, staring off into the trees.

Something flashed past Elinor's ear with a nasty *kwissss* and thudded heavily into a tree. She flung herself sideways, stumbling to her knees. A crossbow bolt quivered in the tree's trunk. With a shout, dark figures came leaping out of the trees.

'Scouts from the caravan!' Collart gasped.

Two came leaping forward side by side, one armed with a long fighting lance, the other with a sword. Behind them was the crossbow-man, who flung his discharged weapon away, yanked out a sword, and charged Elinor.

She leaped to meet him. He was a huge man and wielded a great, double-handed sword with a broad iron blade. He used the weapon without any art, merely swinging it in wide, deadly arcs, the force of which could have felled a small tree.

But with the weight of the thing, he was slow.

Kess knew better than to face such an adversary head on. As he came at her swinging his blade, she rolled sideways and down – in a movement that Master Karasyn had called the Striking Snake – and caught him a quick, glancing slash on the shins. He howled and fumbled the sword. She had him then. First, a quick thrust through the arm to immobilize him, then another in his groin, under the plate armour, and a last cut across his throat, opening him up. He went down screaming, blood gushing.

Kess smiled, thinking of Margie and of the poor captives below.

All this had taken no more than a dozen heart beats. She whirled with the quick, elegant strength the sword lent her, looking to see other adversaries. But none was left standing. Scrunch stood over one, growling, his jaws wet and red. Collart knelt beside the third.

She looked about, worried one of their own might have been hurt. Spandel seemed fine. Otys *kawwed* from a branch. But there was no sign of Gyver. 'Gyver!' she said to Collart. 'Is he . . .'

'I am all right, me,' the fur-man said, creeping out from behind the cover of the trees a little distance away.

'Oh . . .' she said. She regarded him in silence for a long moment. He was an odd being, and she would never have expected him to be anything like heroic – he seemed far too mild. But just to have . . . run off like that, to have hidden behind the shelter of the trees to save his own skin and let his companions face the danger alone . . .

'You are ssafe and all right, too, you?' he said.

She turned her back upon him, painfully disappointed. She

had come rather to appreciate his strange, unassuming, quiet nature, she realized. He was unlike any man she had ever known. But now . . . Now it was as if she had suddenly opened a door into an unexpected room and seen something disgusting.

'Elinor?' he said, uncertain.

She ignored him, the bloodied sword *thrumming* softly in her hold, and went over to Collart. 'You hurt?' she asked.

He shook his head, panting.

'How did you take him?' She did not want to say it bluntly in so many words but it surprised her that old Collart had dealt with this man so quickly. It was the spearman he had downed.

Gyver came padding over. Kess gave him a look so cold he faltered back.

Collart, seeing this, said, 'It wasn't me, Elinor.' He rolled the Brother over and showed her where two leaf-fletched arrows protruded from the man's throat.

Collart embraced Gyver shakily. 'You . . . saved my life, Gyver. Thank you is . . . is too small a thing to say.'

The fur-man smiled shyly, muttered something none of them could make out. Then, gently pushing Collart away, he pulled his arrows out of the Brother's throat.

The man shuddered and moaned wetly. Kess lifted her blade and despatched him with a quick, surgical stab, feeling no compunction at all.

'Gyver ducked for the cover of the trees,' Collart explained. He stared at the dead Brother. 'And put two arrows in this man from there while I tried to keep the bastard from skewering me with this nasty pig-sticker of his.'

Elinor swallowed. She felt herself flush. 'Gyver,' she said, turning to the fur-man. 'I didn't . . .'

He shrugged his thin shoulders. His face was troubled. 'It iss not our way, my people, to run at each other like thiss in mad fury, sshouting and sscreaming and waving ssharp bladess.'

'It is not our way, normally, either,' Collart muttered.

Elinor reached out, putting her left hand gently on Gyver's furred arm. She still felt hot with shame. Gyver grinned shyly, a little flash of sharp white teeth in his darkly furred face. They looked at each other – they were nearly the same height,

364

he just a shade taller – and, for a heart beat or two, their eyes locked.

'You can trusst me,' he said softly.

It seemed altogether foolish, given her experience with men so far, to believe him. He was not even human, really. She had no notion of just how strange he might actually be. But there was no guile in his soft, direct brown eyes, his open gaze . . .

Scrunch suddenly reared up behind them, growling. 'More of them coming,' he grunted.

'Quick!' Collart urged.

They sought cover.

More Brothers come pouring through the trees, perhaps eight or ten, cursing when they saw their fallen comrades.

'Spread out!' the leader ordered. 'Whoever did this foul thing cannot be far away. I want his head on a stick, you hear me?'

They fanned out, splitting into little groups of three or four.

'Must be fully half the caravan guard out,' Collart whispered in Elinor's ear.

They had hared quietly off, and lay safely a fair distance away by now, crouched behind a large, fallen oak. Elinor had sheathed the blade and lay shivering and panting against Scrunch's solid flank, her bad leg on fire. She hugged herself, missing Kess's hard purity.

Collart ran a shaking hand over his grey stubble and shook his head.

'Not ssmart of them, to ssplit up like that,' Gyver said softly. 'They have no woodcraft, them.' He pointed. 'Look!'

Not fifty paces off, three Brothers were working their way rather clumsily through the trees.

Elinor felt her heart jump and snatched at the hilt of her sword. The familiar tingle went through her. 'We can take them piecemeal.'

Collart swallowed, and nodded. He had acquired one of the dead Brothers' swords, she noticed, and was hefting it experimentally. To her surprise, he seemed to know what to do with it.

'Worth the try, anyway,' he whispered, staring at the sombre figures of the moving Brothers. 'The bastards deserve to be taken down.'

Drawing her blade, Kess laughed softly, though her heart was thumping hard. 'All right. Let me catch their attention. Then you take them from behind. But *fast*! There's others of them nearabouts. Spandel, you keep sharp watch.'

'Yes, yes, yes!' Spandel responded.

'Right,' Kess said. Blade in hand, she slipped off through the trees, half limping to save her leg, quiet as could be until she was about twenty paces from where her companions lay hidden. By now, she was behind the little group of Brothers.

'Heya!' she called, but not too loud, waving the blade so that it caught the forest light like fire.

They whirled round in surprise.

'Come and get me, stupids!' she invited them.

They charged towards her like hounds after a hare, crashing through a patch of briar and skittering through the trees.

She turned and ran, leading them on, her heart thumping. She leaped a fallen log, stumbled, her bad leg buckling, struggled back to her feet.

They were almost upon her.

And then, abruptly, one of them went down, a leaf-fletched arrow through his thigh. He screamed, doubled over. Another arrow took him in the throat and he fell to his face, making little drowning sounds.

The remaining two skidded to a halt, looking about them wildly. Scrunch appeared suddenly from nowhere and crashed one of them to the ground, going for the man's face with his formidable jaws.

The remaining man turned to flee but Collart got him, slashing him across the back of the knees with his purloined sword, then hacking at the downed man's head and throat in a furious onslaught until there was only bloody pulp left.

Elinor stared. There had been nothing for her to do.

Gyver slipped out from between the trees and silently retrieved his arrows. The second broke as he pulled it free. The man he had shot thrashed, still not dead. Gyver produced one of his slim stone blades and slit the man's throat, then leaped back quickly.

'Next?' Collart said, looking across at Elinor. He was gasping and bent over, but hanging on to his bloodied iron sword and grinning wolfishly nevertheless.

Scrunch growled, peering into the trees, ready.

Elinor looked at Gyver.

He was blood-spattered, shivering, his face tight. He let out a long, gasping breath, swallowed, nodded agreement.

The white sword shone. 'Let's do it, then,' Kess said.

With the help of Spandel, who could move about unseen by the questing Brothers, they were able to take two more small groups, ambushing them amongst the trees with variations of the same successful tactics they had used the first time.

'Like hunting boar,' Collart said grimly, gazing down at the latest dead.

But Gyver shook his head and shuddered. 'Not like hunting at all, thiss!'

Collart shrugged. He was a grim-looking figure indeed, blood-splattered, with the gory iron blade in his hand. But under the grim covering, he looked weary.

'You all right?' Elinor asked him. Her own blade was sheathed, and she was feeling weary herself and sickened at the carnage they had created. Collart was, after all, no young man, and he did not have the uncanny resource she had in mad Lord Mattingly's gift-blade.

He looked at her and half-smiled. 'Haven't done anything like this in years.'

'You've done this *before*?' she said.

He nodded. 'When I was young.'

'But you never said . . .'

Collart shrugged. 'It was long ago. Not anything I'm especially proud of.'

Elinor put a hand on his arm. 'I'm glad you're here.'

'I'm not,' he replied, smiling thinly.

She nodded. 'Hard times indeed.'

'Hard times,' he agreed.

She looked down at the dead Brothers. 'This makes eleven.' The Elinor part of her was appalled. But Kess counted the dead with satisfaction, feeling the sheathed blade's hilt firm and sure in her hand, ready for whatever else might come.

'All gone out of the wood now,' Spandel informed them, coming slipping in. She spat at the dead, her hair standing on end. 'Gone, gone, gone. Returned to the carts. Frightened.'

*

They crept back to the rocky bluff from where they had first glimpsed the caravan. Below, the chained prisoners were spread out in a ragged line, sprawled upon the ground, some of them dead asleep – or truly dead perhaps, so brutal was the treatment they had received.

There were only six or seven Brothers in sight, milling about, quarrelling with each other, glancing into the trees with scared, angry eyes.

'I say we *wait*!' Elinor heard one of them say. 'Potch Kory and his lot's bound to come back any moment now.'

'They won't be coming back!' another responded.

A third gestured at the trees. 'There's something *in* there. They're dead, the lot of them. *Dead*!'

Kess smiled, a grim, satisfied little lifting of her lips.

Below, one of the Brothers said, 'Let's get *away* from this cursed place!'

For long moments, none of them said anything, just looked at each other.

Then, 'What about *them*?' one asked, pointing at the double row of sprawled, chained captives.

'Kill them and be done with it, I say.'

'Right!' agreed another. 'I'm for that.' He strode towards the captives, taking up a lance.

'And the cursed animals, too,' the first one said. 'Kill 'em all. Quick! And then let's be *away* from here fast as we can.'

Kess surged to her feet.

The Brother with the lance had already reached the first of the chained captives. He raised the weapon.

Before he could strike, the man sprawled on the ground at the end of the chained line kicked out, entangling the lance wielder's legs and bringing him down.

Kess leaped from cover, skidded precipitously down the steep slope, and raced for the caravan, naked blade up and shining. She heard Scrunch scrabbling down the slope alongside her.

He was quicker than she, for all his bulk, and first to throw himself against the Brothers.

It was a wild, terrible few moments, iron and blood and screams and grunting, blade on blade, contorted faces, the *tlanggg* of her sharp blade biting into their iron ones. The sword was like a bar of blazing light in her hand, deadly and quick and unstoppable. Her blood thrilled with the tingling strength it lent her, and she danced and leaped and cut, bringing down all who stood before her.

And then it was over.

She stood leaning on the sword, panting, gazing blankly about. Her heart beat hard, and she was soaked with sweat. The thrilling strength ebbed. The Brothers lay dead or had flown. She spotted the disappearing back of one as he scrambled madly up the slope to escape, saw branches shake where another fled. But, even with the sword's strength, she was too weary to give chase. They all were. Scrunch sat slumped and panting, his fur mottled with blood and gore. Collart leaned against a cart, gasping. There was a nasty cut over his left ear, blood running down to soak his shoulder.

'You all right?' Elinor asked him in concern.

He nodded, chest heaving. 'I'm too old for this.'

Gyver came padding out of the trees. 'Me, I sstopped one. The ssecond, he got away.' The fur-man held up his bow. 'No arrowss left.'

Elinor sighed, nodded, shrugged. She turned to look at the column of chained prisoners.

They stared back at her, eyes wide. There were men and women, young and old. Some were weeping, some blinking and rubbing their eyes as if they could not believe what they saw.

'Who . . . who *are* you?' one man asked, the one who had tripped up the Brother with the lance, Elinor realized. He was short and stocky, with long muscular arms. His hair and beard were black and tangled with muck. His clothing, such as was left, hung in tatters about him. He stared at Elinor open-mouthed, at her companions, at her shining, bloodied blade. It was towards Collart, however, that he had addressed his question.

'We are from . . . from Margie Farm,' Collart answered.

'*She* never came from Margie,' the man replied, pointing at Elinor. He turned to stare at Gyver. 'Nor *him* neither.'

Collart shrugged wearily. 'Have it as you will, man.'

Elinor wiped her blade self-consciously, sheathed it. 'My name is . . . Elinor,' she said. Without the sword, she felt shaken and queasy. The smell of blood was in the air. 'And I *am* from Margie. Though I was only a . . . a guest there.'

'Where are the keys, man?' Collart interrupted, rummaging about amongst the sprawled forms of the dead Brothers.

The stocky, black-haired man blinked, staring at Gyver. 'Keys?'

'Yes, *keys*!' Collart said. He wiped at the blood that was still leaking from the cut above his ear. 'Which one of these guards has the keys to your manacles?'

'Him,' said somebody else further down the line. 'Over here.'

Collart went over.

'In his belt pouch,' the manacled man directed.

Collart reached into the pouch and pulled out a ring of large iron keys. 'Separate keys?' he asked. 'Or one for all of you?'

Elinor stood shivering as the sweat dried on her. Her bad leg was an aching agony. Her vision pulsed. She staggered over to lean against one of the carts for support.

Inside the cage that rested on the cart there was a dog – or something nearly a dog – and a smaller creature like the short-eared rabbit she had glimpsed briefly at Margie Farm.

'Whiteblade!' she heard one of them say softly.

Reaching up a weary arm, she unlatched the cage and swung the door open. The imprisoned humanimals spilled out.

'Whiteblade . . . Whiteblade!' she heard them repeat. It was taken up from the other cages in the other carts.

It was what the stork, Pallas, had named her.

'Whiteblade . . . *Whiteblade*!'

Gyver was unlatching the other cages now, and the ground between the carts was filling with moving shapes which came to settle before her in a half-circle, staring.

'Whiteblade,' they murmured in unison, and bowed to her in a little ripple of concerted movement.

She flushed, did not know what to say or do.

For a long moment none of them moved.

Then there was a shout and the sudden clanking of chains. People began to stagger up and the group of humanimals shied away.

Gyver came up to Elinor. 'Come and ssit,' he urged.

She nodded thankfully, too weary and disconcerted and self-conscious to speak.

*

'What happened here?' Collart asked of the freed prisoners once they had a sort of order established. The group was gathered near one of the carts, the humanimals on the periphery. Elinor sat a little apart, for none seemed eager to settle themselves too close to her. She felt people staring at her. There had been food in the carts, and everyone was chewing on hard bread and cheese and wrinkled winter apples. Collart held a wad of bandage to his ear.

'How did you end up like *this*?' He gestured with his free hand to the bloody manacles left lying on the ground.

'Where have you lot been, then?' demanded the stocky, black-bearded man who had first talked with them. He waved a gnawed hunk of cheese about. 'If you're really from Margie Farm, you must . . .'

'Who're you?' Collart asked him.

'Smitt. My name's Smitt. And as for what happened . . . The Brothers, curse them, have come boiling out of Sofala like a plague of hornets. They fired Geldy a couple of days ago, and –'

'Geldy?' Elinor said. The bread and cheese was filling her like ballast. She could feel strength returning with every bite. It had been . . . she could not recall how long it had been since she had last eaten proper food.

'Geldy's a farm community some leagues away,' Collart explained. Then, to Smitt, he said, 'How bad?'

Smitt looked at Elinor suspiciously, then said, 'To the ground.'

Collart swallowed. 'Go on,' he urged soberly.

'Something's happened,' Smitt said. He took a quick bite of bread, one of cheese, chewed. 'Don't know what. The Brothers have . . . changed. They're out in force now, armed and . . .'

'Vicious as mad dogs,' put in a thin woman with short-cropped grey-blonde hair. 'They burned down my farm, destroyed *everything*. And for what? I've traded with them for a decade now. Never cheated them. Why should they suddenly do this? Why? *Why*?'

'Why, indeed,' said Smitt. He looked at Collart and Elinor and Gyver and the rest. 'And you? Are you really from Margie? Is the farm all right, then?'

Collart shook his head. 'Like the woman's. Three days back. Burned to the ground.'

'That was when it began,' somebody said. 'Three days back. Seems like a month . . .'

'You must be Collart, then,' said the thin, short-haired woman whose farm had been razed.

Collart nodded, a little surprised. 'Have we met?'

'No. But I've heard of you. Nobody else at Margie's grizzle-grey like you, far as I know. Good man with sheep, they say. And lambs.'

Collart shrugged. 'And you?'

'Getta's my name. I run Carringan. *Ran* . . . rather.'

'Name's familiar,' Collart said.

'You two can chatter all you like,' another of the ex-prisoners butted in, a stocky, bald man. 'But me, I'm getting myself away fom here fast as my poor feet will carry me. Who knows but that more of the bastards aren't on our tail?'

Collart nodded. 'Good advice, that.' He turned to Elinor. 'Let's be away from here.'

'Where?' somebody wailed softly. 'I've nowhere to go now! It's burned . . . all *burned* to *nothing*!'

There was a general chorus of the same.

'Don't leave us!' an older man begged. He rushed to Elinor, grabbed her wildly by the arm. 'You saved us, you and your gleaming blade. Take us with you!'

She shook loose from him, and he fell back whimpering.

'Take us away! Take us!' they cried, crowding close, the ones behind pushing those in the forefront at her. 'Save us!'

Elinor tried to calm them, but there were suddenly too many, pressing too close about her.

Scrunch lifted himself, growling. He reared up on his hind legs, standing taller than any man, yellow fangs bred in a menacing snarl.

The pushing, pleading people fell back, shrieking in sudden fright.

Black-beared Smitt had somehow got hold of one of the Brothers' lances. He lunged menacingly at Scrunch with it.

Some of the ex-captive humanimals gathered in Scrunch's defence.

'No!' Elinor cried. She drew the shining blade. 'Stop it. *Stop it*!'

Everyone froze, humanimals and human folk alike.

372

Elinor stood, the blade out, glowing like a bar of purest light.

'Enough of this! Hasn't there been enough violence already?'

There was a sullen grumbling from the human crowd. 'We'll starve here in the wild lands if you leave us behind!' somebody complained.

'Nobody will be left behind,' Elinor promised. 'We'll go together. All of us.'

'Where?'

She shrugged. 'Away from here, first. And fast as can be. After that . . .'

'There's more food in the back wagon,' somebody said then. 'We won't starve for the next few days.'

'Mutton from my farm!' said the thin, grey-blonde woman named Getta.

'And spring potatoes from mine!' a man added.

'Let's go and get it, then,' said Getta. She turned to Elinor. 'With your leave, I'll start getting these folk into some sort of order so we can get the food packed and ourselves *out* of here.'

Elinor blinked, stared at the woman for a moment. In all her life, nobody had ever asked permission from her for anything. She swallowed, nodded. 'You have my . . . leave by all means.'

Getta turned and trotted away. 'Right, you lot. Let's get things organized here!' She pointed at a pair of younger men. 'You two! You look like strapping lads. Why don't you go start unloading the back wagon while . . .'

Elinor looked about her, searching after their own little group. Spandel was with Scrunch, she saw. As she watched, Otys came spiralling down to join them. Collart was trying to help Getta get things organized. She spied Gyver a little way off, trying to mend an arrow. He looked up and waved at her. She waved back. All were safe, then.

Resheathing the white blade, she turned away and leaned back against the nearest cart, needing the support. Folk were staring at her.

'Is she . . . real?' she overheard somebody say.

'I touched her,' a man answered.

'It's magic,' added another, pointing at Elinor and the blade at her hip. 'Deep magic of the Powers.'

'She'll save us,' one of them said softly, fervently. 'We're saved now.'

Collart came over, shaking his head.

'What do they think, these folk?' Elinor said to him, running a hand tiredly over her face. 'That I'm some . . . some all-powerful paladin out of a child's wonder tale, who'll come striding miraculously in from nowhere waving my magic weapon and make everything all right again?'

Collart smiled a thin smile. 'Something like that.'

Elinor took a sharp breath, swallowed, slumped against the cart.

'Can you blame them?' he said.

Elinor shook her head, shrugged, sighed. She was not sure what to think.

'What are we going to do with this lot?' Collart went on. 'That's more to the point. There's twenty-seven of them. I counted. And maybe eight all told who can walk properly.'

'What else could I have done?' Elinor replied. 'I didn't *plan* to have it turn out like this.'

Collart nodded soberly, patted her arm. 'I'm not blaming you, girl.'

'Where should we keep the food?' a man said to Collart, coming up suddenly. He nodded to Elinor with a little bow, but said not a word to her.

Collart took the fellow by the elbow and steered him away.

Elinor gazed at the semi-organized, jostling mass of folk and sighed. People kept glancing towards her, as if to reassure themselves she was still there.

They looked to her for salvation.

She fingered the sword where it hung, sheathed, at her hip. The White Tooth of the Great Shining Dragon, mad Lord Mattingly had called it. Fang. Mirror bright and deadly. And hers.

And hers, too, were the consequences of wielding such a blade.

A cold shiver went down her spine. Looking back on the events of the past weeks, she seemed to see a pattern, step and step and step, all bringing her here, to this moment, leaning against the rough, weathered wood of a cart, surrounded by scatterlings and refugees who looked to her for their future.

They seemed to be the same decent farmer folk as those at Margie – who had died because of her. Elinor swallowed. She thought she knew what it was that had set the Brothers on this path of terrible violence and destruction.

'The worlddd hasss come aparttt,' Otys had said before he led them here. And, his beak pointing accusingly, '*Her* faulttt.'

Her, and what she had done with the white blade.

It did not bear dwelling upon.

Elinor shuddered. These folk did not know it, but they were looking for salvation from the very source of their misery. The irony of it was like a stone in her guts. She wanted no part of this, wanted no such blood-guilt on her conscience.

But it was already too late.

She gripped the sheathed sword's dragon hilt, feeling the strange soft *thrum* of it in her bones. She was already a part of things, as caught up in the current of events as surely as any leaf swirling along on the surface of a fast moving stream.

She looked at the milling, weary folk about her. 'I'm with you,' she said softly, a private vow, the same words she had said to Scrunch. 'I'm with you.'

XXXVII

By day's end, they had found a place to camp for the night, a little dell in a concealing fold of the hills where a clear brook splashed through an open, grassy clearing surrounded by thick willows. It seemed an ideal, secluded haven for the night.

After some discussion they chanced a fire. Some of the ex-prisoners were simply too weary and too battered and mis-treated to stand the ordeal of a cold night. They had food, and several were soon busy grilling spiced sausages and bread over the flames. The odour of the cooking was delicious.

Collart regarded the fire uneasily. 'Might as well light a beacon while we're at it.'

Elinor shrugged. 'We need the nourishment.' She pointed at the more feeble of those they had liberated from the Brothers' caravan. '*They* need it.'

'True enough,' he agreed. 'But the Brothers will not take lightly what we have done. They'll be after us soon as they can.'

'Not tonight,' Elinor replied. 'Not this soon. And we're hidden up here.'

'The Brothers . . .' Collart started.

Spandel came springing suddenly out of the evening twilight and climbed lithely up Elinor's side to perch on her shoulder. 'The Brothers will be sorry, sorry, sorry!'

'Simple for you to say, little one,' Collart responded. 'But the world is a harder place than you imagine.'

Spandel shook her little head. 'I *know* how hard, hard, hard the world can be.'

Collart looked at her for a long moment, then shrugged. 'Perhaps.'

At that moment, Gyver came padding along the stream's verge out of the twilight towards their camp, a string of fresh-caught trout dangling from his hand. 'Fisshess!' he said, grinning from ear to ear. 'Lotss of fisshess in thiss water!'

Elinor smiled at him, waving.

'Over here!' somebody called by the fire. 'Bring them here.'

Gyver veered over and handed the fish to one of the cooks. He kept back a couple for himself, though. 'Flamess ruin the tasste,' he said, and walked off a little way to the clearing's edge where he squatted down to eat by himself.

Elinor watched him bite the head neatly off each trout, then peel it open with his sharp teeth. Such an animalistic tearing of raw flesh ought, she thought, to appear gross. But somehow it did not at all. He was so neat and precise, so . . . mannerly – that was the only word she could think of to describe him. He ate with the manners of a courtier, for all that it was raw fish and fingers and bared teeth.

He looked across at her and grinned and held out part of one half-eaten fish. 'It iss good! You sshould try it, you, before it iss ruined by the flamess.'

After a moment's hesitation, she left Collart and went over.

'Here,' he said, offering up the trout to her.

It was all glistening skin and pink-white flesh, a little slimy in her hand and altogether unappetizing.

'Eat, eat,' he urged her. 'It'ss *good*. It will give you sstrength!'

She took a nibble; another. She had expected it to be strongly fishy-tasting and as slimy to chew as to hold. It was neither. The flavour was hardly delicious, but it was not so terribly bad, either. And the flesh had a certain chewy consistency. It went down with unexpected ease.

Gyver smiled at her. 'Well?'

'It's . . . good.' To her own surprise, Elinor realized that, if she had to, she could eat such raw fish and keep it down and enjoy it – well, almost enjoy it. It was like the wood-grubs.

'It'ss *deliciouss*!' Gyver responded, taking a neat bite of his own fish.

Elinor laughed. 'Maybe not that.' She handed back the trout. 'You have the rest. I'll stick to having it cooked.'

He looked hurt for a moment, then shrugged. 'Eat with me?'

'I should go back with Collart. We have to . . .'

Gyver nodded quickly. 'Go, go,' he said, shooing her off. He was smiling, but there was something brittle about it.

Elinor turned and walked towards Collart. After a few paces, she glanced back. Gyver was gazing at her, the fish held limp in his hand. His eyes glinted like a cat's in the gathering dusk, and it was impossible to tell quite what expression was on his face. He looked away quickly. Elinor felt her heart flutter just the tiniest bit.

He was such an odd being, was Gyver. Gentle and soft-spoken, never arguing, never forcing his opinions. She remembered him slitting the Brother's throat with quick dispatch, leaping back to avoid the blood, his face tight. He had fought with them – for all that he had no experience of such fighting as they had been forced into – when he could just as easily have slipped away through the woods and headed back home. Wherever home was for him . . .

'Trust me,' he had said to her. She remembered his open brown eyes, his dark-furred face, his shy smile, sharp little white teeth flashing through black lips.

He was like no man she had ever known.

She heard shouting, suddenly, coming from the cook fire, and hastened over.

Folk were gathered together in a body about the fire. Those on the edges parted for her, whispering and gesturing to the blade she wore. But the shouters remained oblivious.

'We've got to strike back at these bastards!' somebody cried. 'We can do it, I *know* we can!'

It was young, black-bearded Smitt, Elinor saw, the one who had kicked the legs out from under the Brother with the lance who had gone to butcher the chained prisoners. He was waving his arms about, eyes flashing angrily in the firelight above his beard. 'We can cripple them. All we need to do is strike hard enough!'

'Oh, you reckon so, do you?' said a stocky man with an altogether bald head. He sat next to the fire, nursing his wrists where the manacles had bitten into them. He was an older man, with a ragged grey beard and bushy dark eyebrows over pale eyes. 'And just what are you suggesting we do? Storm Sofala? Rout the bastards from their stronghold?'

'No. Of course not!' Smitt returned. 'But we can harry them, worry at them.'

'Lot of good *that* will do, boy. We'd be like rats worrying at a bear. There's too many of them for us. All we'd accomplish is our own deaths.'

378

'Well, at least it'd be *something*! What are *you* suggesting, then? That we sit around the fire and nurse our cuts and bruises? And then slink away like whipped dogs?'

'Better than charging off like fools and getting ourselves killed for nothing!'

Smitt marched around the fire and stood before the bald man, glaring. 'And just who are *you*, then, old man, who counsels cowardice?'

The man looked up at Smitt and shrugged. 'Name's Passaly. And I counsel against stupidity, is all.'

'You're just scared, is all,' Smitt returned. 'You're just a coward!'

The bald man merely sighed and shrugged. 'Have it as you like. I'm too old and too tired to rise to your baiting, boy.'

'Fine!' Smitt said. '*Fine*! You do as you like. You sit by the fire and be old and frightened and useless. As for *me* . . . *I'm* going to do something!'

Some of those gathered muttered agreement. Others shook their heads.

Smitt pointed at Elinor. 'What about *you*? With that shining, deadly blade of yours, surely you . . .'

Old Collart cut him off. 'You're missing the point, you lot,' he said, raising his hands for quiet. 'The question isn't whether we're going to attack the Brothers or not.'

'Oh, no?' Smitt said. 'What, then?'

'The question,' Collart replied, 'is . . . how are we going to eat?'

That brought silence.

Collart nodded. 'Thought so. All you young hotheads hadn't thought of *that*, had you now?' He gestured about at the gathered company. 'How many do you suppose we are, all together?'

There was a quick tally of heads. 'Thirty, counting all of us,' one of them said to Collart, 'and you lot as well.'

'No more than a dozen or so who are fit for much, though,' Smitt added.

'We're all fit to *eat*,' Collart said. 'How are we going to feed thirty odd mouths, then? And that count doesn't include the humanimals.'

'The humanimals can feed themselves,' somebody said quickly. 'That only leaves . . .'

'No!' Collart said, cutting the man off. 'Let's not start *that*.'

'Start what?' the man responded.

Collart waved to the gathering: men, women, the various humanimals. 'We do *not* start things here by making divisions, by saying this one here will be fed and that one will have to fend for himself.'

'And why not? If some of them *can* fend for themselves, why ought they not? We've enough to do just . . .'

'*We*?' Collart said, interrupting. 'And just who is this *we*?'

'Why . . .' the man looked about him. 'Why, we . . . human people. We need to . . .'

A silence had settled suddenly.

The man swallowed, looked about him uneasily. 'I just meant . . .'

'I *know* what you meant,' Collart said.

'You're just soft on them 'cause you're from Margie Farm,' somebody put in then. 'Everybody knows Margie was always a haven for them. Gillien and Hann saw to that.'

'And look where it got them!' a man shouted.

'Not giving a welcome to the Free Folk didn't get you anywhere much, either,' Collart snapped back.

There was silence for a long few moments.

A ring of humanimals clustered around the human folk seated at the fire. They had watched in silence throughout the arguing. Now, people began to glance uneasily at them over their shoulders.

'What are they *doing* there?' somebody whispered. 'They're so quiet.'

'Look at them,' Elinor said then, addressing the group about the fire for the first time. Collart seemed to know well enough what he was doing, and she had hung back so far, uneasy lest anything she said might tip things in the wrong direction – for Smitt had tempers stirred up so. But she felt no patience with those trying to exclude the humanimals.

All eyes turned to her. She put a hand reassuringly to the sword at her hip then let it go again, suddenly self-conscious. The bronze dragon hilt glowed a ruddy gold in the firelight. The little ruby dragon-eyes flashed. She gestured to where the humanimals were gathered a little way off. 'They're in exactly the same plight as we all are.'

It was true. They were a ragged, weary-looking lot, some sprawled out in exhausted sleep, others huddled together for comfort, some eating the food Collart had made sure they received, some too weary even to do that.

'The poor souls,' some woman said. 'Elinor's right.'

'Poor souls, all of us,' another added, and laughed a soft, humourless laugh.

'Exactly,' Elinor said. 'Poor souls, *all* of us.'

'Well, *I* say . . .' Smitt began.

He was silenced by a general, hooting chorus.

'I don't want to hear *no* more talk!' one woman said. 'I'm *tired*. I hurt. I just want to finish eating and then go to sleep. In peace and quiet.'

There was a general murmur of agreement.

'Let's do that,' Collart said. 'Food and sleep and a peaceful night.'

'What about pursuit?' somebody asked.

'We will keep watch,' a growling voice answered from the shadows beyond the fire.

It was Scrunch. 'If the Brothers come near,' he growled, 'we will alert you. Never fear.'

Folk looked at each other uncertainly.

'Right,' Collart said. 'Thank you, Scrunch.'

Collart's reply was made with such authority that folk somehow accepted it. They needed reassurance, Elinor realized. And the simple finality of Collart's 'thank you' – as if he knew *exactly* what he was doing – had managed to settle things.

'Sleep and food,' she said, putting herself solidly with Collart and silencing the last of the grumbling. 'Sleep and food is what we need now.'

'Not necessarily in that order,' somebody said, to general soft laughter.

'Ahhh . . .' someone else sighed. 'Feels *good* to be free of those sodding chains.'

'Good to be *alive* . . .'

Somewhere, somebody was weeping softly. 'Hush . . . hush now,' a woman's voice said. 'It's over. We're safe now . . .'

Elinor looked at Collart. The older man shook his head. 'Not over by a long shot,' he said softly. 'Not yet.'

Elinor nodded, knowing that for truth.

XXXVIII

Elinor sat alone, staring off through the trees across a grassy hollow to the crest of a wooded hillside beyond. A little cascade fell splashing through a series of stone steps down the hill slope. Beyond the hill crest, the green-grey carpet of the forest ran unbroken up the jumbled, serried slopes of the farther eastern hills – the selfsame hills she had spied in the distance from the little window in her Guards cell back in Minmi, a very long while ago, it seemed. In the distance, the far-away blue peaks of the mountains rose up like great stone fangs.

Elinor sighed. It had taken two weary, terrible days of struggling through the soaked woods to get up here to this wild refuge. A straggling, crippled, weakening group they had been, dragging along what supplies and weapons they had managed to take from the Brothers' caravan. It rained, off and on, all the way. And then they had endured three further days of pouring, cold rain up here in the hill-camp they had put together, anxiously awaiting signs of pursuit.

But there had been no sign of vengeful Brothers on their trail, and they seemed safe enough now, hidden up here in the wild.

Safe, perhaps . . . but their camp was a destitute one. Despair was in the very air. One breathed it in with the rain, and grief, and frustration and anger. Days of argument, there had been, of confusion, of short tempers, of constant jostling and rearranging and soothing, and endless, endless talk . . . 'We must,' and 'You ought,' and 'I won't . . .'

Elinor sighed. At least it was quiet up here, away from things. And the rain had stopped, finally. Late-morning sunlight poured through the last, tattered remnants of the rain clouds. She flexed her leg. Days of no real walking had done it good. There were numerous things she ought to feel thankful for. Being alive and in one piece not least of all.

She gazed off into the distance. The wide world seemed quiet and huge and serene this morning. It was soothing on her eyes and her mind. She should have left the camp behind and come up here before, away from the noise and bad temper. She sighed, wishing she had somebody to share the healing quiet with.

But Collart had his hands entirely full with the fractious camp, and she had seen no sign of Gyver, or of Scrunch or Spandel, in days. They had their own pursuits, she knew, their own humanimal concerns, but she missed them. It was as if all she and the humanimals had gone through together no longer meant anything now that they were in the wild. She could not help but feel hurt and a little angry at their seeming desertion.

And what if one of them had strayed too far and encountered a squad of armed and angry Brothers?

Elinor sighed. She was tired of worrying, tired of feeling alone.

Collart was too occupied, the humanimals had abandoned her . . . and, despite the crowding in camp, the human folk, too, left her to herself. They were uneasy with her, staring at her when they thought she was not looking. It was the blade. They treated her as if she . . .

Something was moving through the trees on the far hillside before her.

Instinctively, she reached for the dragon hilt of the sword at her belt and scrambled for cover. Could it be Brothers? Was the camp discovered after all? She peered through the tangled branches of a bush, her heart pumping.

Whoever it was came barging along quickly but quietly down through the woods on the far slope ahead of her. She saw a flash of something brown. A sapling quivered near the wet rocks of the little cascade that danced down the hill slope. She heard a soft *krack*. Something trotted out of the green cover of the trees . . .

A large brown bear.

Scrunch. Or so she hoped. At this distance she could not be sure.

She watched the bear lap up water from one of the cascade pools, sit, lick himself. If it was Scrunch, she wanted to talk with him. She got up, started walking downslope to cross the little hollow that separated her from the cascade.

384

She hoped it was indeed Scrunch down there. She had no faintest idea what to do with a wild bear.

As Elinor drew close, she saw the bear waddle over to a log near the lip of a little pool at the cascade's foot. He snuffled along it for a few moments, then began tearing at it in one spot with his long claws. There was a *skreek* of ripping wood, and a wriggling clump of fat white grubs was revealed. He began to lap them up with obvious relish.

Elinor sidled closer. The air was filled with the soft sounds of the cascade. 'Scrunch?' she said tentatively. It certainly looked like Scrunch.

The bear peered at her, grunted, held up a pawful of grubs invitingly.

Elinor shook her head 'No, thanks. Once was enough.'

The bear laughed and downed them. 'You human folk are so picky.' He licked his paw, belched softly, grunted.

'Where have you been?' Elinor demanded.

Scrunch shrugged. 'About.'

She could not suppress a little stirring of irritation. 'We could have used you here these past few days. *I* could have.'

Scrunch sat down, tucking up his haunches like a dog, and looked at her, head cocked to one side.

'You just went . . . wandering?' Elinor said after a few moments. 'Just . . . deserted us? What about the watch? I thought you were arranging for humanimal sentries to keep watch over the camp. Instead, you just go wandering *off*?'

The bear lifted his big shoulders in a shrug. 'I needed wild-time.'

'Scrunch . . .' Elinor began. But she did not know what to say. The camp had been relying on humanimal sentries to give them warning of any approaching danger, sentries who would be invisible in the woods to any intruder. Now . . . She had a sudden, sickening image of a camp defenceless and vulnerable, the sentries gone wandering off willy-nilly, human folk none the wiser. She stared at Scrunch uncertainly, remembering all too well the state he had been in when first she had encountered him. He had seemed so solid since. But now? How unstable was he? How unstable were the rest of them?'

'I will not fail you,' he said.

Elinor blinked. 'How did you . . .'

'You had that look. Like all human folk. You think I will fail you.'

'No,' she said quickly.

'Yes,' he responded. 'You remember me as I was, back at Margie.' He heaved himself up and came towards her. 'You do not understand.'

Elinor backed away.

Scrunch stopped, shook his head, grunted to himself. 'See? You think me a danger. You think me unstable. You think . . .'

Elinor hesitated, then went to him on impulse and put her hand on his broad, furry back. 'No,' she said. 'We've been through too much together.'

He turned his big head and looked at her, blinked, snuffled. 'I set up the watch before I left, turn and turn about. None has run off. All is taken care of.'

Elinor nodded, feeling a little flush of guilt at her own readiness to accuse him of failure.

'You are a whole being,' Scrunch said. 'Complete. Like a fish in the waters or a bird on the wind. How can you know?'

'Know what, Scrunch?' she replied softly.

'I . . . I and my kind are . . . We are constantly *between*. We have no clear place in the world.' He let out a great, snuffling sigh. 'We need the silence and the solace of wild-time, but we need, also, the self-will and awareness of mind-time. We *need* the light of mindfulness, but it burns us, and so we need the healing dark of the wild. And, sometimes . . . it just becomes too much, the light, the tension, the *betweenness*, everything.'

'I understand, a little.'

Scrunch regarded her. '*Do* you? They were . . . *made* creatures, our ancestors, with no natural place in the world. *Between*. We, their descendants, are born like any natural creature, but still we search to find some place for ourselves in this land. Generations it has been . . .'

He took a snuffling breath. 'That was why we valued Margie so. Human folk have not been . . . kind to us over the years. But at Margie, we were free to go and return, as we needed, free to find the balance. Gillien and Hann and Collart and the rest . . . they gave us a haven and we loved them for it.'

Elinor shivered. She had been so involved with her own guilt over Margie that she had never once thought what its destruction might mean for the humanimals.

'A place in the world,' Scrunch said. 'It is our great hope and our great terror. Gyver . . . the likes of Gyver give us hope. He is more comfortable in the world than we. Perhaps we, too, will find such a place of comfort one day, such a balance as he has found. But Gyver is different from us. More like your kind. Perhaps there *is* no place for such as we . . .'

Scrunch shook himself. 'But we do have hopes. The Lady of Dreams gives us hope.' He looked at Elinor out of the corner of his eye. '*You* give us hope. And we will not fail you. When you saw me first, I was . . . directionless. Now, I have direction. Now, we all do. It is enough to hold us.'

'Hold you?'

'In the world. In ourselves. In the bright light of mindfulness.'

Scrunch put a big paw on her shoulder, a solid, gentle weight. 'We will not fail you,' he repeated. Then he turned and lumbered suddenly off through the trees, leaving her alone.

Elinor stared at where Scrunch had disappeared into the leaf-green tangle.

She sighed, turned, shook herself, gazed up at the white tumble of the cascade. Her guts were knotted with unease. She was touched by Scrunch's avowal, but sorely disturbed as well.

For he, it was plain, believed in her.

There was something stirring amongst the humanimal folk. Despite the sojourning in the wild, there was always a group of them in the camp close by the human people – unusual for them – and when they looked at her, there was expectation in their eyes. She remembered how they had gathered about her, the day she and the rest had liberated the Brothers' brutal caravan train, murmuring, 'Whiteblade, Whiteblade . . .'

What did they want from her?

Deny it though she might want to, she knew that she knew.

She had caught the camp's human folk with the same sort of look in their eyes, staring at her sideways, heard them whispering about her, pointing to the sword when they thought she was not looking. And arguing about her, over who knew what notions or fears or crazy expectations?

They looked to her, human folk and humanimals alike. She was their hope.

The Brothers ravaged the countryside, and had men out hunting them no doubt. And, back in camp, folk squabbled and argued endlessly. It made her belly twist into a cold knot, just thinking on it, for she had no clue how to save them.

She felt suddenly small and very alone and hollow, standing by herself in the great emptiness of the wild, severed from her past, blind to her future.

The cascade danced before her, splashing white water, filling the air softly with its water-music. A little rainbow shone faintly about it. How many mountain rills and streams had joined to feed this tumbling cascade? How many rivers would it join, in turn, eventually to feed the sea? Joining and joining . . .

There's not a river flowing free but cries its yearning for the sea.

The words came to her abruptly, something Mamma Kieran had recited for her all that way back in Long Harbour – during a different life, it seemed. It was simple enough for the cascading water before her. All it had to do was fling itself onwards and fall splashing over the rocks, and it would be fulfilled. But life was not like that for her. She had a sudden, overwhelming conviction that she had botched things somehow, that she had let her life be taken from her. Or she had let it drop, all unknowing.

But, standing here alone in this strange southern land, she did not know what it was she had lost, or what she lacked.

Or what she should do next . . .

There was too much of mystery in this land, too many hidden undercurrents with origins going back years and years. Terrible things had happened once here. Terrible things were still happening. And she was caught up in the midst of it all, blindly, not knowing how to stop the destruction, leaving a trail of death and confusion behind her wherever she went, it seemed. She thought of the poor folk of Margie Farm and shuddered. Her fault. And the camp refugees, whose lives had been shattered. Her fault again. Or so it would seem. For if she had never taken up mad Lord Mattingly's fell gift-blade, never attacked that first caravan train of the Brothers, if she had never been wounded and never stayed at Margie, if she had never stirred the Brothers up so . . . would not life here in this land still be what it always had?

And now *she* was their hope for a future?

Elinor sighed. She shifted her belt around so that she could bring the sheathed sword more clearly into view. Hand on its hilt, half drawing the mirror-bright blade, she could feel the faint, strange tingling it always evoked in her – and feel Kess stirring. It was a welcome sensation, for her Kess self was far less upset by things than Elinor. Kess knew little of the world, and needed only the blade.

The little ruby eyes of the snarling dragon's head hilt seemed to wink knowingly at her, as if alive. It was no simple weapon, and none who wielded it did so unchanged. She shivered, knowing that now for absolute truth. It was an old thing. No knowing who might have wielded it before her, or what calamitous history there might be behind it.

Letting the sword go, Elinor shuddered. She had done such terrible, violent things with this shining blade.

And it was all she had for direction in her life now.

The naked irony of that was painful. The blade had plunged not only her but also the folk of this land into blood and disaster. The blade would bring her, and them, through.

But how?

Life had been so much simpler back in Long Harbour. She had known exactly what she wanted then, and what to do to gain it.

And look where it had got her . . .

A little snapping sound from behind made her start suddenly. She scrambled to her feet, half drawing the sword.

And spied Gyver, of all people, padding towards her through the trees.

She slipped the blade back. She felt a little pleased thrill at seeing him again, and relief, for he had obviously come to no harm. Yet she was also resentful.

'I met Sscrunch,' he said. 'Sscrunch, he ssaid I would find you here. I do not dissturb you, me?'

She shrugged, shook her head. He had gone swanning off into the woods, no doubt, like Scrunch, gone for days, as at home in these wild hills as any of the four-legged humanimal folk. He had a new supply of arrows, she saw, fletched with grey-barred feathers now, and a proper quiver to hold them.

Laying down his bow and slipping the quiver off, he sat next to her on the grass, patting the ground for her to join him. He had twined a string of little white flowers, like tiny stars, through the ruff of fur that went back from his forehead, she noticed. They stood out in sharp contrast with his dark fur. He smiled up at her, a quick, uncertain flash of his sharp little white teeth.

Elinor thought of what Scrunch had said: 'Gyver is more comfortable in the world than we. Perhaps we, too, will find such a place of comfort.' The fur-man looked sleek and well, and she found herself envying him. Unlike her, he had a life and a home to return to. She sat down beside him, settling the sword to her side, tucking her legs under her. They gazed at the white-dancing cascade together in silence.

'I suppose you'll be leaving us, heading back to your own lands?' Elinor said after a little.

He shrugged.

'You have a family, there?'

Gyver nodded. 'I have a little ssisster, me. And a mother. And two mother-ssisstersss, and the menfolk of our band.'

It was somehow strange for her to imagine him with a family, to imagine a whole band of such furred beings together. It was as if, unconsciously, she had always considered him one of a kind. 'So you will go back to them now, your family?' Elinor shook her head; she was beginning to talk like him.

Gyver shrugged again, silent.

He was such an exotic-looking creature, so altogether human, and yet so not.

Silence settled over them once again. Elinor felt Gyver lean a thin, furred shoulder against hers. She stiffened against it momentarily, then shifted her sword and was content to let him stay like that against her. After her recent bleak confusion of spirit, she relished the simple, quiet companionship of it.

The trees rustled and creaked about them gently. The cascade sang its falling-water song. A woodpecker *tok tok tokked* in the distance. The afternoon drowsed, peaceful and clear after all the rain.

'The leaping sspiritss of the treess . . .' Gyver said softly.

Elinor glanced at him. 'What?'

'Do you not feel it, you? The treess leap their livess sslowly about uss. Up . . . alwayss upwardss, greenly.'

Elinor nodded, though not really sure what he meant. Gyver's view of the world was *very* different from that of any man she had ever known. 'What is it like, the land from which you come?' she asked impulsively. With a start, she realized that this was the first time she had ever actually asked him anything about himself – such had been the nature of the days they had lived through.

He smiled his shy, flashing smile. 'It iss a land much like thiss. With sslopess and many treess and much water. Clean, beautiful water.'

'Why . . . why did you leave it?'

He shrugged his furred shoulders. 'I am the Gyver.'

Elinor waited for some sort of further explanation. When it did not come, she said, '*The* Gyver? What does that mean?'

'My people, we name oursselvess by who and what we are. The furred and feathered folk, they name you Whiteblade. I have heard. Because of that.' He pointed to the sword.

Elinor nodded uneasily.

'You do not like it, the name they have given you?' he asked.

Elinor shrugged.

'It iss a good name.'

'It's . . . It's just . . .' She sighed. 'It's the way they all look at me, Gyver. Human folk and humanimal alike. Like I'm some special answer. Like I'm some *utensil* they aren't quite sure how to make proper use of yet. Like I'm some special saviour or some such. But I haven't *got* any answers. And I don't . . .'

She stopped, embarrassed. 'Sorry,' she said quickly. 'I didn't mean to . . .'

Gyver looked at her, his brown eyes clear. 'You are Elinor Whiteblade. It iss a *true* name.'

'I am Elinor Confused,' she replied, and laughed a bitter little laugh. She hefted the sheathed sword. 'It is no simple weapon, this. You have no notion of what it means to carry it, to wield it.'

'I have sseen,' Gyver said. 'I know.'

Elinor looked at him uncertainly.

'It iss a fell thing, thiss blade. And a dangerouss. And more than mere dead iron, yess? But it iss your river, I think.'

'My what?'

'In my land,' Gyver said, 'there iss a type of ssmall fissh we call the Darter.' He held up his thumb and forefinger, spread apart. 'Little like thiss. They are blind creaturess, the Darterss, with only ssmall white sspotss where their eyess sshould be. They live in little lakess and pondss, them.'

'Gyver,' Elinor said, interrupting. 'I don't see . . .'

'All their livess,' Gyver went on, 'the Darterss, they sswim their little waterss, blind.'

'How?' Elinor asked. She could not help herself. 'If they're blind, how do they get about?'

Gyver lifted his furred shoulders in a shrug. 'It iss their own ssecret. But sswim they do, little fissh in little waterss. Unless they find their river . . .'

'Their . . . *river*?'

He nodded. 'If the little Darter findss a way out of ssmall waters, everything changess. They dissappear, ssome of them, and sswim away, far away. To the very ssea itself, it iss ssaid. And when they return, they are . . . changed.'

Gyver held up both his hands, spread them apart a fair distance. 'Bigger, and with eyess. And teeth.' He flashed his own in a sudden grin. 'Sso my people, we ssay, "Sshe hass found her river" when we ssee ssomeone who findss a way in life that will lead her onwardss.' He pointed at the sword. 'That iss your river, I think.'

Elinor stared down at the sword. 'My . . . river.'

'That which leadss you out of ssmall waterss. That which changess you.'

Elinor sighed. 'It has certainly done that.' She looked down at the dragon hilt. The little ruby eyes seemed to wink at her mockingly. 'I don't know *where* this blade could lead me, if I let it.'

'The little Darter, sshe knowss not where the river might lead her, if sshe letss it.'

Elinor sighed again. 'It's so easy to *say*, Gyver.'

The fur-man nodded solemn agreement. 'Life, my mother ssays, iss lived in the bone and the belly.'

Elinor looked at him.

392

'We are like the waterss, Elinor. We musst . . . flow. Whether we will or no.'

'Whether we will or no,' she echoed.

'Sso ssays my mother . . .'

Elinor laughed softly. 'Your mother!'

She saw on Gyver's furred face a look of . . . she was not certain. Hurt? Confusion? Something . . . She reached out a hand to him in reassurance. 'I'm not laughing at you. It's just . . . I didn't expect you to go quoting your *mother* at me.'

He looked at her, head to one side, puzzled. 'Why not? My mother iss a wisse ssoul.'

Elinor shrugged self-consciously. 'The men I'm used to don't go around quoting their mothers much.'

She did not know quite what to say after that. She felt the fur-man withdraw into himself. And she found, a little to her surprise, that she did not want him drawing away from her. He was a strange man, with a strange view of life. And yet . . . what he said *had* comforted her, a little.

She felt the solid weight of the sword on her lap. Her *river*, leading her out of small waters. Just the sense that there might be something ahead for her helped. A river had direction, led somewhere, fed into something . . .

She felt Gyver stir.

She did not want him to leave.

'And you,' she said abruptly. 'What about you? I may be Elinor Whiteblade. But you said you were called the Gyver. What does *that* mean?'

He blinked, smiled a small smile. 'I am named Gyver becausse . . . becausse I am alwayss gyving about.'

'Gyving?'

The fur-man nodded. 'You do not know thiss word? To gyve?'

Elinor shook her head. 'No. Is . . . gyve an ordinary word, then? I thought it was your name.'

'It iss. But it iss a word, alsso. The little ssquirrelss gyve about ssearching for nutss. The great white heronss gyve about for frogss. The yellow beess gyve for flowerss. Me, I gyve about for . . . everything!' He laughed. 'Sso I am the Gyver. I cannot help it.' He put a finger to his black dog's nose. 'I have a nosse that musst be pressed into everything.'

393

Elinor smiled. 'So you . . . gyved your way here, to this strange land?'

He nodded.

'And put your nose into places you shouldn't and got yourself hurt.'

Gyver shrugged, grinning. 'I have sseen new thingss. I will have wonderful sstoriess to tell my people.'

Elinor sighed. He had come to say goodbye, she thought. That was what had brought him here. 'So now that you've gyved your way about in this land, seen your new things, you'll be returning home, I suppose?' Once again, she felt the pang of envy. Home. It was a nice word.

Gyver shrugged. 'Perhapss. One day. Me, I thought to leave. I . . . tried. But I could not. There iss . . . that which keepss me.'

Elinor looked at him, puzzled. 'But what is there to keep you here now?'

He looked back at her, his dark eyes unblinking. 'There iss you.'

Elinor felt herself blush suddenly, felt her heart jump. '*Me*?'

He nodded. 'You are mosst beautiful. Beautiful as the moon'ss ssisster.' He reached out a hand and brushed his fingers against her cheek, light and gentle as the touch of a butterfly's wing. 'And insside . . . insside you are like a young mountain willow. You bend, you fold, but you do not break.'

'How do you know?' she said, a little challengingly.

'I know.'

Elinor felt a long shiver go through her. There was complete certainty in his voice. His brown eyes were steady, glistening, open. A little flush of heat went through her loins.

What with one thing and another, it had been a long while since she had last felt that particular kind of heat.

Elinor stared at him in surprise. The little white flowers twined in his ruff of fur glowed like pearls. It was an almost feminine touch, and yet not. She reached out and ran her fingers tentatively along his furred arm. His pelt was short and soft and fine as puppy fur. She pushed against the grain of the hair, revealing the dark skin underneath, feeling the muscle there. For all his slenderness, Gyver was very strong.

She glanced up and saw his eyes still on her, intent. There was no bravado about him, and none of the ordinary male franticness of desire she had grown to expect at moments like this. She recalled Rannis's scrabbling, pushing, demanding hands, and Annocky's. Gyver simply looked at her – an open look, an intent look, a somehow intimately revealing look. It made her heart quicken. He ran his fingers gently over her cheek again, down across the line of her jaw to her throat.

Elinor closed her eyes. Little shivers went through her.

Then, on sudden impulse, she bent close and kissed him. The fur on his face was like softest down against her skin. His lips tasted salty. He spluttered in surprise, pulling back, staring at her wide-eyed.

It took her an instant to realize what was wrong. 'It's called kissing,' she said.

'Kisssing?'

'You've never done it before, have you?'

He shook his head, dabbed at his lips delicately with a fingertip. The little white flowers shivered above his furred brow. 'We . . . tasste each other?'

Elinor smiled. 'Well, in a manner of speaking.'

He pulled her to him. 'I like to tasste you.'

'Owww . . .' she said, for in his innocent enthusiasm he had drawn a drop of blood on her lip with his sharp little teeth. 'Careful, Gyver.'

He drew back in a quick contraction of uncertainty, his face wrinkled with concern. 'Ssorry,' he murmured. 'It iss new to me, thiss . . .'

She kissed him again, slowly, gently, letting her tongue intertwine with his. The surface of Gyver's tongue was slightly rougher than a normal human tongue would be, and it was more muscular. She could feel its strength.

'Let me see it,' she said, pulling back from him. And then added, 'Your tongue,' when he looked at her in confusion.

He hesitated for a moment, then stuck it out for her. It was longer and more narrow than a human man's tongue – wet and pinkly glistening, mottled with purple along the sides. She remembered watching him lick his fur with it like a cat, grooming himself.

He took her hand in his and brought it to his mouth. Softly, he licked her palm, a long, wet, hot caress.

Elinor shivered.

She ran her fingers over his upper arm, across his chest where the colouring began to turn from walnut brown to cream, down his belly. She felt him quiver. His fur was warm and dry under her hand, and he smelled faintly of . . . cinnamon and musk, she decided.

He reached for her, encircling her with his sinewy arms, pressing the two of them together. She felt his ribs move with each breath, his warm breath on her cheek, the warmth of him against her, felt his heart beating fast against hers.

'Will you take thesse off?' he asked, moving back a little and plucking gently at her shirt and trousers. He looked at her out of the corner of his eyes, grinning. 'I would like to feel it, your bare sskin . . .'

She stood momentarily, undid her belt and dropped the sheathed blade to the ground – with, first, a pang of unease, and then quick relief. She slipped her shirt off over her head, stepped out of her trousers. The air against her naked skin made her shiver.

Gyver made a little sound like a cat purring, but deeper, and reached out one hand, wonderingly. 'Lovely bare sskin . . .' He pulled her next to him, ran his hand over her shoulder, down the curve of one of her breasts, across her ribs and over her belly. His nails – claws rather – glided gently along her skin leaving little trails of shivery fire.

'Ahhh . . .' she breathed, feeling herself fill with warmth for him.

Looking into his brown eyes – with the little white starflowers dangling above them – she saw such sudden tenderness there that it near took her breath away. It was the look a mother might give a loved child . . . yet not. A look of incredible softness, yet a hungry look for all that.

She saw his eyes fill with tears. 'You are sso . . .' He blinked them away for a moment. 'Like the ssilver fisshess. Quick and pure and lovely. Like the moon hersself, you. Lovely and naked and wonderful . . . sso wonderful to me.'

She pulled him close and kissed him again, hungrily, and ran her hands down his belly.

His man's organ, too, was not quite human. It was sheathed in a way a man's was not, and the head stood out purple and pink and glistening, like his tongue. It near made her dizzy to look at it, so strange and beautiful did it seem to her at that moment.

His tongue glided wetly over her shoulder and neck. Gently, he nibbled at her with his sharp teeth. She felt little tingling shivers go through her from toe to head. Downward his tongue went, a gentle, wet touch, across her belly, her flank, him twisting sinuously in her hold to bring his head down, the little star-flowers trailing, licking across her.

She pulled him upwards to her. 'I want you *inside* me.'

She had thought perhaps he would be wild and rough, like an animal in rut, bucking and heaving. But he was nothing at all like that. He was gentle as could be, moving over her and in her softly. He felt warm and furry, hard and hot, sinewy and soft. She ran her hands through the fur of his back, feeling his ribs, the little wings of his shoulder blades, the rounded muscle of his haunches.

He was slow and sinuous as water atop her, beneath her . . . And every time she looked into his eyes she saw the same incredible tenderness there, and the little tears. She had never imagined seeing a man cry such tears for her. It brought unexpected tears of tenderness to her own eyes, and she felt such an upwelling of emotion that she thought she would burst, or dissolve, or melt away entirely – sadness and love, joy and grief and passion, all intertwined in a wondrous, inexplicable, melting knot that made her gasp for breath while he moved inside her in a deep caress.

When it was over, she lay panting on the grass, her limbs interlaced with his, feeling his soft fur against her side. Her body hummed. She felt utterly emptied and utterly filled.

'You are not like *anybody* I've ever known,' she said to him.

He smiled his flashing, shy smile. 'Nor you.'

She put her hand to his face. The little white flowers were dangling, and she tucked them back into the ruff of dark hair that went back from his brow. She felt the soft fur there, the curve of bone along his cheek.

She could not quite believe that such a thing had happened between them. And she was not entirely sure how she might feel about it, later. But for now . . . now she felt content just to lie here, feeling him close beside her in the sun-warmed grass, listening to the gentle water-song of the cascade and the intimate sound of his soft breath.

It was like a long drink of water after a terrible drought.

XXXIX

'Don't be so *stupid*!'

'Oh, yes? And I suppose you're never wrong about any-thing? Why don't you just . . .'

Elinor sighed. The day only just started, and more arguments already. She strode past this one as quick as she could, found Collart at the camp's verge, his face puckered into a worried frown.

'They're hungry,' Collart said.

'There's food, still,' Elinor said.

'Not enough. And where is there more? These are farmer folk, Elinor. They think food. They think seasons and crops and fields and planting. And they're *hurting*.' He gestured at the camp, a haphazard collection of stone fire hearths and lean-tos and purloined canvas strung up in a clearing amongst the trees, with folk clustered here and there in ragged groups. Collart sighed. 'They've had too much time over the past days to think of all they've lost. To think of the cursed Brothers out there, making free with their lands. It eats at them like a chancre.'

'They haven't learned your "final virtue", then?'

Collart scratched at the grey stubble on his cheeks that was slowly turning into a beard. 'I see you remember that conversa-tion. No. They haven't learned. And see where it leads them?'

A sudden shouting match erupted a little ways off. She saw one man go for another, saw them thrash into one of the camp fires, kicking up a backlash of sparks and burning brands, sending people leaping aside frantically.

She and Collart rushed over, along with half the camp, and the two combatants were yanked apart.

'What's this all about?' Collart demanded.

They had agreed, he and she, that he would do the most of the talking in this camp. Folk seemed more comfortable with him than with her. And they respected him, both for the fact that he had been one of those to liberate them, and for his calm commonsense. He seemed to be known by many here, if not in person, at least by name. Everybody appeared to know of Margie Farm.

'He called my mother a whore!' one of the two men who had been fighting said, a thick-shouldered red-head. Wiping a bleeding lip, he glared at his erstwhile adversary.

Elinor did not know him, but she recognized the other one: young, black-haired, with a wispy black beard. It was Smitt of the flashing, angry eyes; Smitt the hot-head.

The human folk here had begun to settle out over the past few days. The majority sat huddled by the fires, hardly talking except to argue with each other. And then there were those few who worked to try to organize what comfort could be got in this wild hill-camp. And those who agitated for one pet scheme or another. And those who were the trouble makers.

Like young black-bearded Smitt.

Somehow, whenever something went wrong with folk here, he never seemed far off.

Collart sighed and shook his head and glared accusingly at the stocky red-head. 'So name-calling has become a fighting offence now? I never knew you had such a delicate sense of honour about your mother, Molt.'

The other man shrugged sullenly, looking away.

'He's full of shit!' Smitt spat. 'He tried to steal some food. I caught him at it!'

The red-head surged forward. 'That's a lie! It's *you* who's the food-thief!'

Those gathered about erupted into shouting, some backing red-haired Molt, others Smitt, still others shouting at the shouters.

'Enough!' Elinor cried. '*Enough*!'

Slowly, they went silent.

She glared at them, one hand on her sword hilt. 'You're acting like sullen children.'

'You've got to stop this,' Collart said.

The red-head turned to him, gesturing at Smitt. 'Well, tell him and his cronies to . . .'

'I said . . . *enough*,' Elinor rasped in exasperation.

Collart glared at the crowd. 'Who needs the threat of the Brothers around here? You lot are *quite* happy to tear yourselves apart all on your own.'

There were lowered heads, sullen, self-conscious mutterings.

But Smitt stepped forward. 'It's no wonder we're at each other like cats and dogs. Sitting here doing nothing for days! We need to be out and about accomplishing things. While we sit here, those bastards are taking over our lands.'

'*Taken* over,' somebody corrected.

'It's already done, boy!' This from a stocky, bald, bearded man. Passaly, his name was. Elinor remembered him from his confrontation with Smitt that first night around the camp fire.

'I'm nobody's *boy*,' Smitt snapped at him. 'And if they've taken our lands, then we just have to take them back again! I've been saying that all along.'

Bald Passaly laughed bitterly and shook his head. 'Don't be stupid, boy.'

The men who had initally been restraining Smitt had let him go some time since. Now, he easily evaded their hasty grabs at getting him back, and moved towards Passaly.

Smitt glared. A handful of the younger men formed up about him. With them at his back, he advanced closer, till he stood with his face in Passaly's. 'You counsel against our just revenge, old man, against getting our own back, against what *must* be done, against . . .'

'Smitt!' Elinor said. She strode up and stepped between him and Passaly, altogether out of patience. 'Back off and shut up,' she told him, straight-arming him away.

Smitt stumbled back, glaring at her. He hesitated, took a menacing step forward, faltered, his eyes going to the sword at her waist. Then he turned from both Elinor and Collart and addressed the gathering. 'We can't just huddle up here like frightened children. I say we take the fight back to those bastards. I say we search them out and kill as many as we can. They *deserve* it! I say . . .'

'Shut *up*!' Collart snapped exasperatedly.

Half a dozen others chorused their agreement and Smitt shut

his mouth, looking around with a sullen glare. His followers gathered tighter.

'Back away and calm down,' Elinor ordered him. She drew the sword a little, just enough to show a finger's width of shining blade. It made her uneasy, using the threat of the sword in a situation like this – would she, *could* she ever use it if they called her bluff? – but she could see no other way of stopping what was happening here. The way tempers were flaring, Smitt could very well start a full-scale brawl. 'And tell your cronies to back away with you,' she added.

He cast her a single, sullen, smouldering look, then jerked his chin at his following, and they all shuffled sullenly back.

'We've got to stop this bickering,' Collart began, addressing the gathering. 'We've got to . . .'

'What we've got to *do*,' somebody said, 'is find food.'

'That's right!' put in a thin woman with short-cropped blonde hair whom Elinor recognized as Getta – one of those who had worked indefatigably to try to organize things here in the camp right from the early days of their liberation. 'We've got to solve the food question first of all,' Getta said. 'After that . . .'

'And just how,' Smitt interrupted, sidling back, 'do you expect to do so? Magic up a load of mutton from thin air?'

'Of *course* not. Don't be stupid!'

Smitt glared. 'I'm growing *tired* of folk calling me that.'

'Then grow up and show some commonsense,' Getta snapped. Before he could say anything in response, she went on quickly, 'There's food to be had in the woods. The humanimals have been bringing it in for us. All we need do is learn to forage for it ourselves.'

'There's not enough to feed us all!' somebody said.

'Yes, there *is*,' Getta responded. 'Look!' She pointed suddenly to the camp's verge.

There was a little ring of silent, staring humanimals about the crowd – as was usual when the human folk quarrelled. The humanimals seemed mesmerized by displays of human temper. Beyond that ring of furred and feathered folk, Elinor saw Gyver come padding softly out of the green shadows of the trees, the carcass of a little deer across his shoulder, bow in his other hand. He stopped, waved, stared at the gathering uncertainly.

Elinor felt her heart leap. She still could not quite believe what had happened between them yesterday . . .

'Look!' Getta was saying. 'There *is* food enough in these wild hills. Game and forage.'

Gyver stood, obviously unsure as to what was happening. He came closer into camp, let the deer drop from his shoulder, looked to Elinor for an answer.

He had such an open gaze, did Gyver, so guileless. In some ways he seemed such an innocent. And so defenceless.

'All we need,' Getta was saying, 'is . . .'

'I knowww wherre youuu cannn finddd fooddd!' a squawking voice cut in.

Elinor looked round, startled, along with everyone else.

It was Otys, the crow. He hop-flapped along through the edge of the silent humanimals and leaped atop the carcass of Gyver's deer. 'I knowww wherre you cannn gettt fooddd!' he repeated.

'What do *you* know about food?' one man demanded of Otys.

'We're talking about *human* food!' another said.

Otys hop-flapped from the dead deer's haunch up to its head. With a little flip of his sharp beak, he nipped out one of the deer's blind-jelly eyes, flipped it into the air, caught it deftly, swallowed it.

Somebody gagged.

Otys stared unblinking at the assembled folk. 'So ammm I, talkinggg abouttt humannn fooddd.'

There were soft hoots of derision.

'What would the likes of *you* know about decent food?' Smitt demanded.

Otys lifted his black-feathered wings in a shrug. 'I knowww whatt I knowww. If youuu are too stupiddd to listennn . . .'

'Don't call me *stupid*!' Smitt snapped.

'Thennn don'ttt *acttt* stupiddd,' Otys returned.

'Otys,' Collart said, stepping up. 'What are you talking about? Have you really found a source of food for us?'

The crow nodded. 'Oh, yesss.'

People surged eagerly forward.

'What *sort* of food?'

'How far from here?'

Otys *kaw kawwed*, flapped his wings.

'Speak up, bird!' Smitt snapped.

'Mennn and cartsss,' Otys said then. 'Heavy cartsss. Farmmm cartsss. Lotsss of gooddd fooddd. A supplyyy trainnn too Sofalaaa.'

'And just where is this supply train, then?'

'Passinggg throughh the nexttt valleyyy,' Otys replied. 'One of theirrr cart tracksss. Nottt farrr . . . asss the crowww fliesss.'

'Very funny,' Collart said.

Bald Passaly stepped up. 'Wait a moment, now.' He looked at Otys. 'Men and carts, you say. *What* sort of men?'

Otys shrugged his bird-shrug. 'Brothersss.'

The crowd rumbled.

'We can *take* them!' Smitt cried excitedly.

'We can get ourselves *killed*!' Passaly returned. 'How do we even know this is a food caravan? We've only the bird's word for it, and what does *he* know about proper human food?' Passaly turned on Otys, who perched on the deer carcass with wings half-stretched, head cocked to one side. 'Did you actually see *food*, good human food in those wagons?'

Otys lifted his wings again in his bird-shrug, then furled them. 'Whattt else do youuu reckonnn they'dd bee stockinggg in thossee farmmm cartsss, mannn? Rocksss?'

Passaly was not amused. 'So you *didn't* see any food. And now young Smitt here wants us all to go charging off down there like lunatics and get ourselves spitted on the Brothers' iron.'

'Not like *lunatics*,' Smitt said. Then, 'Thickhead!' he muttered, looking around at his little band of followers, who nodded encouragingly. 'We'd be canny about it. Ambush them.' He pointed at Elinor. 'And with *her* and that shining blade of hers, and us stout lads . . . the cursed Brothers will never stand a chance!'

An excited gabble went up from Smitt's cronies.

People melted away from Elinor, and she stood, self-conscious and alone, in the middle of an empty space.

'Will you do it?' Smitt demanded of her.

She shrugged. 'It isn't . . .'

'Will you *do* it?' he insisted.

She had been going to say that it was no easy thing to attack a supply train. That it meant blood and pain, hurt and death. That folk here did not know what they were getting themselves into, for none of them wielded the sort of weapon she did.

'She's not going to!' Passaly said, before she could think of how properly to express any of this.

'She'll abandon us,' someone else added.

The group erupted into confusion, into shouting and fist-waving.

'Enough!' Collart shouted at them. 'Enough! *Enough*!'

They settled, slowly.

Smitt pointed an accusing finger at Passaly. 'If he'd just stop acting like a frightened . . .'

'I'm the voice of *reason*, you half-wit puppy!' Passaly snapped back angrily.

'*Enough*!' Collart cried again.

Elinor stepped forward and folk went silent. They stared at her, at her sword. She glanced at Collart, who shrugged worriedly. Too much momentum had been built up here, she realized. Smitt and his followers, and the rest here who half-believed him, would not be deflected easily from the course they were setting for themselves. She had that plunging feeling again, as if there was a slope suddenly opening up before her and the only way to go was down . . .

She took a breath, accepting it.

But she had to stop these people from flinging themselves willy nilly, unprepared and unorganized, against armed and armoured Brothers. It would be a blood bath.

'Listen to me,' she said. 'We need food. This caravan Otys has spotted might indeed contain food.'

'So we *take* the food!' Smitt called.

The crowd started to erupt once more.

'*Quiet*!' Elinor shouted. 'Rushing down there is *not* the way to go about this.'

Smitt and the rest hooted in outrage.

She hurried on. 'But it's in our best interests to at least have a look at that caravan. Just a *look* is all. There's no point in arguing with each other about what we ought or ought not to

405

do till we know for certain if there *is* food in those carts, and how well guarded they may be.'

There was silence for a moment.

'I'll go,' a growly voice said. It was Scrunch the bear, seated dog-like at the edge of the gathering amongst the humanimals.

Elinor had not realized he was there.

She felt a stab of uncertainty. Was he really the right one to do this? He looked at her, eyes steady. 'I will not fail you,' she remembered him saying.

'Otys and I will go,' he told the gathering.

Otys let out a spluttering *kaww*. 'Nottt *mee*! Too manyy mennn withh crossbowsss. I don'ttt fancyyy beinggg stuckk like a pigeonnn on a skewerrr.'

'You know where those carts are,' Scrunch said. 'You can lead me easily enough.'

Otys glared at the bear for a moment, lifted his wings, *kaw-kawwed* in his throat softly. Then he settled, poked under one wing with his beak sullenly, shrugged. 'Alll righttt.'

'What makes you think *you're* going to be the one to go?' Smitt demanded of Scrunch.

'And why shouldn't he be?' Elinor said, irritated by Smitt's unstinting abrasiveness. 'He's more woodswise than any human person.'

'Why *shouldn't* he be?' Smitt echoed her question. 'Why, he's . . . How can you . . . He's not . . .'

'He's not a human person, you mean,' Collart finished for him.

Smitt nodded. 'I have nothing against his kind, Collart,' he added quickly. 'Don't get me wrong. But . . . well, how's he going to know what to look for? How's he going to be able to tell what's in those wagons?'

Scrunch lumbered up through the gathered folk and came to sit facing Smitt. He put one huge, thick-thumbed paw against the side of his nose. 'If there's food in those wagons, I'll smell it. Could you?'

Smitt frowned, chewed at his lip a moment, started to reply.

Elinor cut him off. 'He can do it. I know he can. Scrunch will not fail us.'

'Well, *I* say . . .' Smitt started.

An older woman interrupted him. 'If Elinor here vouches for Scrunch, I say let the bear do it!'

'Elinor's a *foreigner*!' Smitt responded. 'What can she . . .'

'She knows these furred folk,' a short man replied. 'She's lived with them. It was she and they who rescued us, remember. I trust *her* judgement over *yours*.'

Smitt started to reply, but whatever he might have been about to say was buried in a general mutter of approval over Scrunch's being chosen.

'All right . . .' Smitt grumblingly acquiesced. 'But you're making a mistake, all of you. Mark my words! A *big* mistake.'

Scrunch looked at Smitt. 'Mind you stay here in the camp, man. I don't want you blundering about on our tail.'

'I don't *blunder*, bear,' Smitt retorted.

The bear only eyed him silently.

'We'll make sure he stays,' Collart said. 'Him and his cronies both.'

Scrunch nodded. 'Good.' Then he turned and lumbered off. At the edge of the camp, where the trees thickened, he paused. 'Be back soon,' he growled. Then he gestured to Otys, who hop-flapped after him, and was gone.

'I tell you,' Smitt began, 'you're making a mistake, sending the likes of *that* off to . . .'

'Oh, shut your face!' three or four people chorused together.

A little titter ran through the crowd at Smitt's discomfiture. He scowled and stalked off with his cronies about him.

Elinor sighed. 'He's just a troublemaker, that one. He'll bring us all to blood and grief. He's too in love with violence and his own petty triumphs.'

But Collart shook his head. 'He had a young wife, an infant, a little farm he was just beginning to work. And he was ambitious, by all accounts. He had big dreams. All burned and killed and destroyed now. Everything gone. And he's all alone, with nothing left but his anger.'

Elinor looked across at where Smitt and the rest had gone to sit down. She felt a momentary rush of sympathy for him. She knew all too well what it was like to lose everything in one's life. It was the same story for all the folk here. Their lives had been ripped apart without warning. Oh, yes, she knew that feeling.

And the losing was not over yet.

She felt her heart constrict. If those carts did contain food, they would have to try for it. And if not this supply train, then some other. For food and vengeance – which was also a kind of food for folk such as these. Blood and fighting and the grief of people bleeding their lives away. *That* was what she could see ahead. That, or dwindling away up here in the wilds, dropping of hunger and weakness and very despair.

No. The losing was far from over.

Turning, she saw Gyver squatting patiently by the carcass of his deer. He looked at her, a questioning glance.

Elinor felt her belly clench uneasily. She wanted to go to him, but somehow she could not.

'Elinor,' Gyver said, padding over to her. 'You are . . . all right, you?' He smiled, but the smile faltered.

She thought of Collart and his 'Losing is the final virtue.' Perhaps it was true. But it was too painful a virtue.

Gyver's brown eyes were wide and searching. He was so . . . open. She felt some part of herself begin to respond to the promise of it, like an unfurling of tight-closed petals.

But it was too much for her. She averted her face.

He put a hand softly on her shoulder. 'Elinor?'

'I'm too weary of losing.'

He stared at her, perplexed.

'Go back home,' she said abruptly, feeling something close up tight inside her. 'You'll end up with a blade through your guts if you stay here. And I'll have to watch.'

'No . . .'

'Yes,' she insisted, seeing it with vivid, brutal clarity in her mind's eye. She turned from him and started away.

'Elinor!' he called.

Her heart lurched but she walked on, one hand on the sword's hilt for support. It was better like this, abruptly like this, with no looking back. A little hurt now and it would be over. And then Gyver would live, thrive, return to his own people with wonderful stories.

It was the best she could give him, under the circumstances.

And she?

She would take the lesser loss over the greater, and go on. Perhaps she was learning after all.

XXXX

It was dawn the next day before Scrunch and Otys returned.

The camp was just straggling into wakefulness, with people hunched round camp fires, nursing them back to life.

'The bear's back!' somebody cried, and a general shout went round.

Elinor was up with the early risers, having had a bad night's sleep, and saw Smitt come running, his little band of followers trailing along behind.

'Well?' Smitt demanded of Scrunch. 'Took you long enough! The bird said only the next valley. You've been gone all yesterday and all night!'

Otys came flapping in through the trees and skidded to a landing beside them, making Smitt skip out of his way. 'Weee camme quickerrr thannn youuu coulddd have, mannn.'

Other folk came straggling up, amongst them Collart, rubbing the sleep from his eyes. 'Tell us what you discovered,' he said quickly, before Smitt could start anything.

'A big caravan,' Scrunch replied. 'Slow moving.'

'Did any of them see you?' This from Passaly, who had just come up.

'None saw us,' Scrunch assured him.

'And what was in the carts?' Passaly demanded.

'Food, all right,' Scrunch growled. 'Farm produce. Spring crop grain, smoked lamb, new potatoes, little turnips.'

'Oh, *yes*?' said Smitt acidly. 'And just how can you know all that, if you never got close enough to . . .'

Scrunch put a paw to his nose and snuffled.

'And you expect us to believe you just because . . .'

'*I* believe him,' Elinor said.

'And I,' added Collart.

Half a dozen others chorused agreement, too.

410

Smitt shook his head. 'Well, *I* think . . .'

'Oh, shut up, Smitt,' Collart said.

'Hmmmpff!' grunted Scrunch, eyeing Smitt. Then he turned to the rest. 'There is more to tell. It's not just a food caravan.'

'Oh? What, then?'

'Mennn,' Otys put in. 'Lotsss of mennn, withh weaponsss.'

'Looks to me,' Scrunch said, 'as if they *want* somebody to attack this caravan. The carts are so obviously farm carts. And it's moving slowly, very slowly. And most of the men guarding it are kept hidden.'

'So you're an expert on tactics now?' Smitt demanded.

'Oh, do shut *up*, Smitt,' the woman named Getta chided him. 'Just let Scrunch speak, will you?'

A general chorus of approval greeted this, and Smitt went quiet, chewing at his lip sullenly.

'You think this caravan is a . . . a sort of decoy, then?' somebody asked.

Scrunch nodded. 'Just that.'

'But a decoy containing real food?'

Scrunch nodded again.

'Well, *I* say we *take* it!' Smitt burst out. He glared at those about him defensively.

This time, nobody told him to shut up.

The gathered crowd was silent, pensive.

'This is crazy!' one man said after a long few moments. 'We can't just go down there and . . . and *kill* them and take their food!'

'It's *our* food!' a woman answered him. 'They took it from us!'

'But . . .' the first man responded. 'But we can't just . . . just *murder* them.'

'They started it!'

'They murdered my Stanny quick enough!'

'But we'd be just like them if we . . .'

'It's kill or be killed!' Smitt said. 'And *I*, for one, intend to stay alive. We have to take that caravan. Or we starve. Simple as that!'

The crowd murmured uneasily. Eyes turned towards Elinor.

411

She stood silent for long moments, feeling their communal gaze upon her. So it had come, she thought. The moment of no turning back. 'Smitt just might have the right of it,' she said softly. 'For once.'

There was silence for a long moment.

Then, 'You'll be with us on this?' somebody demanded of her.

She nodded. 'I'm with you.'

'But it's a *trap*,' Passaly said. 'Even the bear sees that. It's obvious what they're doing. They need the farm produce just as they always have, crowded into rotting old Sofala the way they are. So they'll load up the cart trains, send them along with an extra-heavy guard, but hidden. If the food gets through that way, well and good. And if *we* try to attack, then they get *us* as well. All the better for them!'

The crowd broke in at this, some in agreement, some in outraged denial.

'What makes you think . . .' Passaly shouted. 'What makes you *think* we can spring such a trap, walk into the very jaws of the Brothers themselves, armed and ready for us, and come away unscathed?'

'We need the food,' a hollow-faced older man said soberly.

To that, Passaly had no ready response.

'We go down there,' Smitt started eagerly, 'at the dead of night, take them while they're sleeping. Then, once we have the carts . . .'

'It'll not be so easy as all *that*,' somebody said. 'Passaly's got a point, at least partly. The cursed Brothers won't fall over for the mere wishing of it.'

'They'll *fall*, all right,' Smitt replied, 'If *I* have any say in the matter.'

'Elinor's white blade will cut them down like so much chaff!' somebody else cried gleefully.

The crowd roared.

'Wait, wait!' Elinor said, holding up her arms for quiet. 'Blood and pain and fighting, that's what it will be. No easy cutting of chaff! Are you ready for that?'

There was a rumbling chorus of assent. Then silence.

'The question seems to be settled, then,' Collart observed soberly.

'Right,' said Getta, pushing her way to the centre. 'So how many of us are going?' It was to Elinor she directed the question.

Elinor blinked. 'As many as want,' she said. 'As many as can. How else can we do it?'

'Well, *I'm* going!' Smitt proclaimed.

'And I,' said Getta.

'Oh, no!' Smitt responded. 'We can't have *women* on an expedition like this.'

'And why not?' another woman asked, a beefy, middle-aged farm-wife.

Bald Passaly shook his head. 'Smitt's right. Women aren't built for such things as fighting.'

'Oh, yes?' said the farm-wife. 'Smitt's *right* now, is he? Well, let me tell you, I'm strong as *any* man. Ingra, my name is, one-time tenant of Rathissy Farm. I can butcher a brace of full-grown rams in a morning. And I reckon I can butcher men, too, if I have to.'

'But it's not . . . right!' another man put in. 'Women ought not to . . .'

Somebody said, 'What about Elinor, then?'

'She's different,' Passaly responded. 'She wields that shining blade. And she's a foreigner. She's not like a normal woman. She's . . .'

Elinor could feel a hot wash of irritation rising in her, but she kept her mouth shut. Butting in now might tip things over the edge. Better to let them sort it out amongst themselves if they could.

'She's *what*?' Ingra demanded.

'She's . . .'

'A woman like all the rest of us.'

'But you can't just . . .'

'Oh, shut *up*!' Getta snapped. 'Don't be such a moron. The cursed Brothers didn't make any distinction between men and women. They bashed us on the heads and carted us *all* off. I can use a bow good as any man. And I *owe* those bastards. They killed my boy, Len.' She scowled fiercely. '"As many as want", Elinor said.' She looked across at Elinor. 'Right?'

Elinor nodded. 'Absolutely.'

'So I'm going,' Getta said.

413

'And me,' added the farm-wife.

The two women looked at each other and grinned.

'Right,' Collart said after a moment. 'Men and women both, we're agreed upon that.'

There was some muttering, but before it could break out into anything, a man asked, 'What about the humanimals, then?'

'Not *them*!' Smitt said quickly.

Bald Passaly was in agreement with him on this, too. 'They wouldn't know what to do. We'd have to have somebody to watch over them all the time, or . . .'

'You have no idea what you're talking about!' Elinor snapped. 'Either of you.' She felt she had had about enough of this endless wrangling. 'How do you think we managed to free you all from the Brothers in the first place? It wasn't just Collart and I. And where has all the fresh food been coming from for the past several days? The humanimal folk are *valuable* allies. Have you forgotten so easily how it is that we know about this supply caravan in the first place? Be thankful they're willing to stay with us.'

'But it's a well-known fact,' Passaly began, 'that they don't have the proper mindfulness to . . .'

'You sound just like one of those cursed Brothers, Passaly!' Collart said. 'That's *just* how they talk. What's the matter with you, man?'

Passaly hung his head sullenly.

'What makes any of you think the humanimals would *want* to be part of this venture?' an older man called suddenly from the periphery of the group.

Scrunch spoke up, then. 'If Elinor goes after this caravan, we go with her.'

'Who is *we*?' Smitt demanded.

Scrunch gestured with his big paw. There were fully a dozen and a half of the humanimal folk, sitting silent witness to the human arguments. Each of them nodded solemnly. 'We follow Elinor Whiteblade. We are agreed on this.'

'How touching,' Smitt sneered.

But there was something about the humanimals' seriousness that seemed catching. The crowd went silent.

Elinor felt a long shiver go down her spine. Everybody – human folk and humanimal – was looking to her. She felt overwhelmed with sudden misgivings. Blood and grief and disaster . . . that was what awaited them.

But it was hope she saw in their eyes.

'We must do this together,' she said. 'If we are to do it at all. Human folk and humanimal folk together. We have a single, common enemy. We need every possible resource. *All* of us.'

She stopped.

Gyver had stepped out from behind the crowd. She stared at him, feeling her heart thump. Why had he not gone back to his home land?

The fur-man raised his hand, a little shyly, for everybody's attention. He stood near Scrunch, waiting till there was silence. 'We have a ssaying, my people.' He paused, blinked, went on. 'The green tree, she wasstess not a ssingle leaf.'

'Oh, *most* profound, that,' Smitt commented.

'No matter how big or how ssmall the tree,' Gyver continued, ignoring Smitt, '*every* leaf is needed. Whether they understand it or not, the leavess. Whether they wissh it or not. Whether they ssee it or not.'

The crowd murmured.

'Gyver has the right of it,' Collart said. 'We're all needed here, every last one of us: human folk, Free Folk, all of us.'

Elinor looked at Gyver.

The fur-man looked back, eyes clear and steady. There was no sign of any anger in him for what she had done. 'Together, uss,' he said. 'All of uss.'

'Together,' Elinor echoed, feeling her heart in her throat, wishing fervently Gyver were far, far away, wishing he were closer than he was, angered at his obstinacy, touched by his presence.

'I'm with you,' Smitt said, to her surprise. 'Human folk, humanimal folk . . . so long as we take the chance to strike at those bastarding Brothers, I'm *with* you!'

'Me too,' Getta said. At her side, Ingra the farm-wife nodded vigorous agreement.

'And I!' said one of Smitt's cronies, followed by a chorus of 'Me too!' from the rest of that little group.

'With her and that *blade* on our side . . .' somebody said, gesturing at Elinor.

'We'll make those bastards rue the day they were born!'

415

another finished, and a general, grim mutter of satisfaction ran through the group.

'Get our food back!' somebody shouted.

'Get our *own* back!' put in somebody else. 'Pay those bastards back for what they've done!'

'Create a *future* for ourselves again.'

The crowd surged up in a body, then, with folk suddenly shouting and darting about and slapping each other on the back in an excess of feeling – with the humanimals included as well. Elinor saw somebody clap Scrunch on his broad furry shoulder, saw one of the humanimal dogs leaping about yipping in excitement. Otys flapped above them *kaw kawwing*.

Elinor stood in the midst of it all, her pulse beating rapidly, thrilled and uneasy and not at all as certain about any of it as she was trying to look.

They might indeed be creating a future for themselves. But they might merely be rushing headlong to their own bloody deaths.

She shivered, gripping the sword. The only way to find out was to plunge onwards and see.

XXXXI

It was the black second half of the night, with nothing save starshine to relieve the absolute dark. They stumbled along, making a clumsy way through the trees, cursing under their breaths.

Making too much noise altogether, Elinor thought uneasily.

Finally, they gathered in a huddled group next to a burbling stream, waiting for the stragglers to be shepherded in by Scrunch and the rest of the humanimals who acted as rearguard – far surer in the night-black woods than the human folk.

The stream water spilled over a rim of stone and formed a little, star-lit pool, seeming very bright in the moonless dark. Somebody went for a drink and slipped and fell in with a splash.

'Fool!' somebody else hissed. 'Do you want them to discover us!'

'They're not within a league of here!' another answered.

'You *hope*,' returned another.

'Shut up, the lot of you!' This from Collart. 'And get that man out of the water.'

The man was floundering helplessly about, making choking noises. The little pool must be deeper than it looked.

Elinor sighed. The very notion of things being more than they looked made her uneasy. What if they had miscalculated here? They only had the one chance. If things went wrong here, they went wrong for good . . .

'Now this is the way of it . . .' Collart was saying in a hoarse whisper.

They had thought it best, he and she, that he continue to do the most of the talking; folk still felt more comfortable around him than her.

'We'll wait here,' Collart said, 'and let the humanimals scout ahead. Then, when we know exactly what . . .'

'Why don't we send *men* along to see?' somebody demanded in the dark. 'Why send just *them*?'

Collart sighed.

'*Because*,' Elinor answered for him, 'they can get places we can't. They can move silent and unseen, in ways we can't. All of which you *well* know.'

'We already know where they are, the bastards,' a man put in.

Elinor did not recognize this one. There were still too many she did not know in this group.

'I want a crack at them *now*!' the man went on. 'What's the point of sitting here waiting when . . .'

'Shut up!' a voice hissed.

There was a little scuffle, a grunt.

A different voice said, 'Go on, Collart.'

Somebody laughed, softly.

Collart sighed, shook his head, a motion only just discernible in the uncertain starlight reflected from the wavering surface of the pool. 'We wait, as I said, for our scouts to return. We wait till we know *exactly* what we're going to be facing. Then we face it.'

There was a general murmur of agreement.

They waited.

It seemed a very, very long time.

Of Spandel, there was still no sign – as if the wild lands had swallowed her whole. But Gyver was amongst the night-scouts flitting about the Brothers' camp, Elinor knew.

In his own way, the fur-man was as woodswise and sure in the dark as any four-legged humanimal. But things could go wrong.

Elinor shivered, thinking of it. She wished Gyver far away from here, safe and distant in his own land. She had not relented, had tried again to persude him to go home. But it had been a hurried, fruitless argument that had set both their teeth on edge – and only managed to put an uncomfortable distance between them. He was as completely immovable, in his unassuming way, as a stone boulder.

418

So now she sat in the dark with all the rest, trying not to fidget, trying not to worry about all that might go wrong, wishing she had not made such a mess of things between herself and Gyver, feeling her guts twisted up tight and her mouth dry.

Until, eventually, with a little rustling of leaves, the scouts returned.

It was Scrunch who, after a quick conference, relayed the information. 'One camp by the carts. Set up next to the track by a stream in plain view. Second camp's hidden away in the trees. That's where the main force is. With pickets out on watch.'

'Did everyone get back all right?' Elinor asked.

'Everyone,' Scrunch reassured her.

She spotted Gyver at that moment. He padded by her, ran a hand in a quick, soft caress across her cheek.

She did not know how to respond, caught between relief and aggravation, and he was gone again before she could recover.

'Did the Brothers *see* anything?' somebody demanded. Cautious Passaly, by the sound of him.

There was a soft, growly laugh.

'They saw nothing, heard nothing, suspected nothing,' a new voice answered.

Elinor squinted through the dark. 'Jubb!' she whispered, recognizing the dog she had encountered back when she had impulsively attacked the Brothers' caravan that first time – the dog whose companion had died. 'I didn't know you were here.' She had not seen him since her early days at Margie. 'Where have you been'

He grinned at her nervously, tongue lolling. 'Around and about.'

'Right,' Collart was saying, cutting off any chance of further talk. 'We go with the original plan. Are they camped on both sides, or just one side of the caravan?'

'One side,' Scrunch answered.

'Makes it easier,' Collart said. 'Every little bit helps.'

'How many of them?' Elinor could just make out Getta, squatting by the starshine-pool, bow in hand.

'Hard to count,' Scrunch replied.

'Wonderful,' said a voice – Passaly again. 'Just what I like to hear, that.'

'Can't be more than about forty, at most,' someone said, and Elinor recognized the voice as belonging to Smitt, who had been uncommonly quiet on this venture so far. 'We've *been* through all that.'

'Let's go!' a woman's voice urged – Ingra, the farm-wife, Elinor thought. 'My cheeks are getting cold from sitting here so long.'

'Pull your scarf up round your ears then,' somebody suggested.

'Not those cheeks, fool!' Ingra replied.

There was a general, soft tittering.

Then, 'Let's *go*!' came again from somebody in the back.

'Right,' said Collart. 'But *carefully*,' he added. 'We'll split up into the three groups as planned, each with humanimal scouts to lead. And nobody . . . *nobody* get any foolish notions of rushing ahead, right? Slow and careful. Follow the humanimals' lead. You'll need them in the dark. They know what they're doing. Down there, slow and silent, into position, wait for the signal. All together. Right?'

'Right,' a chorus of voices agreed.

'Let's be off, then,' Collart said.

Down through the trees in a careful line they went, creeping along in the darkness.

The plan was simple enough: each of three groups would slip into position under cover of the night's dark; the humanimals would bring down the picket ring of night-guards the Brothers relied on to give them warning; they would all creep closer, and then, at the proper signal, all charge down, one of their groups hitting that part of the camp near the carts, the other two taking on the main body of the Brothers at their hidden site in the woods – with Elinor and her blade spearheading that attack.

All of which was supposed to be done with utter surprise on their side, despite the Brothers' readiness for just such a foray against them.

Sneaking along through the night, her companions no more than mere flitting shapes in the dark woods about her, not knowing how – or even if – events were proceeding, it all seemed a very uncertain process to Elinor.

Could they truly rely on the humanimals? Scrunch himself might not fail them, but what of the rest? 'We have direction,' he had told her. 'It is enough to hold us.' She hoped so. She truly hoped so.

And what of the human folk? Were they necessarily any more dependable? With the exception of old Collart, none that she knew had had any experience with this business of killing. To her own astonishment, she had come to realize that it was *she*, of all those here, who was most practised at that dreadful game.

How in the world had *that* happened? What a long, strange path she had come since Long Harbour . . .

There was a sudden rustling commotion ahead. Elinor froze. She heard a man grunt, heard the soft thrash of bodies, a choking sigh. No more than a dozen heartbeats it took, from start to finish.

'Come,' a humanimal voice hissed. 'The way is clear.'

They crept onwards. Elinor's path took her past the still form of the night-guard. In the half-dark, she could just recognize his sombre, Brothers' garb. The man lay twisted unnaturally, his fighting helm spilled a little way from his still body. She glanced at him quickly, not wanting to make out any more details other than that he was down, and went on.

'You must all wait here now,' another humanimal voice said from the dark a little while later.

It took Elinor a long moment to recognize that voice. 'Jubb?' she said softly.

'Me,' he replied.

In the darkness, unable to see clearly any of the rest of those with her, the journey here had been eerily like crawling along alone. It was reassuring to make out Jubb's familiar form. The dog drew level with her, and Elinor reached a hand out to him. He nuzzled her. She felt him shiver with nervous excitement.

'Only a little wait, now,' Jubb said breathlessly. 'It will be soon now.' Then he was off again.

'Be careful,' she whispered after him. 'Luck to you . . .' But he was already gone.

Elinor sighed, waiting.

The world lightened, slowly. She shifted position, rubbing

her bad leg – though it was very nearly better now. A man coughed nearby. Someone else shushed him.

She could see nothing ahead through the trees. No sign of a camp, no sign of men, no sign there was anything to break the empty stillness of the dawn wood.

She did not like this waiting one little bit . . .

She fervently hoped Gyver was all right – wherever he might be.

There was a sudden shrill whistling.

The signal!

They surged forward, jogging ahead through the trees in a ragged line.

There was still no sign of a camp.

Nothing . . .

And then it was there: smouldering camp fires, sombre-garbed men scrambling desperately to their feet, white-faced and stricken.

The other group was a little ahead of them, and Elinor saw the first shock as they plunged into the Brothers' camp. There were shouts and screams and curses.

Elinor drew her sword, her heart beating wildly, feeling Kess surge within her. Everything became suddenly simple. The blade shone like a rod of lightning in the diffused silver dawn-light. She held it aloft. Somebody ahead let out a wild, triumphant cry. Those behind her echoed it.

'Whiteblade! Whiteblade!'

Then she was in the camp, amidst a whirl of struggling bodies. She cut one man down before he even knew her to be close, dancing through the chaos of bodies, moving in the graceful, deadly patterns Weapons Master Karasyn had drilled her in, the blade shimmering in quick, deadly slashes. She felt the blood singing in her veins, the blade like very lightning in her hold.

She leaped, exultant, bones quivering in tune with the sword's uncanny energy. It had been long days since she had last wielded it, and she revelled in the feel of it again, laughing for the sheer thrill of it all, knowing herself faster, stronger, more deadly than any who could come against her, filled with pride at her fighting skill, knowing the body-thrill of the white blade as it flashed in quick, deadly arcs in her hand.

Everything would be fine this day. There was none who could stand against her. She had never fought better. Like a dancer, she pivoted to take a sword cut on her blade, kicked the man aside . . .

And tripped over a loop of half-buried tree root, sprawling heavily on her face.

For one shocked instant, she could not believe it, could not move. Then she thrust herself up desperately, twisted about on her knees.

Too late.

One of the Brothers was lunging for her belly with an iron-shod lance, his face lit with gloating triumph. She raised her blade instinctively, knowing it would be no use, cursing herself for getting so carried away, like a stupid fool . . .

A body flashed in front of her. The lance took it, the sharp iron blade plunging right through, emerging wetly. Something howled in agony.

Jubb.

She recognized his familiar dog-form, writhing the last of his life out on the cruel point of the lance.

The Brother tried frantically to shake his weapon free, but Jubb had somehow managed to get his jaws round the haft, and hung on grimly.

Elinor took the man in one furious lunge, coming to her feet in a rush, sinking her blade into his breast almost up to the hilt – for he wore no body armour, yanked out of his sleep as he had been.

She turned to Jubb, shaking, dropped to her knees by his side. But poor Jubb was broken and bleeding, dead as he lay, jaws still clamped to the haft of the lance.

She stared, helpless and stricken.

Somebody stumbled up beside her, yanked her up. It was Smitt, white-faced and shaking, bleeding from a long, shallow gash across his shoulder. He grabbed her by the arm. 'Come on,' he cried, his voice hoarse. 'Come *on*!'

She stared about her, the sword limp in her hold, too shaken for the instant to move. They were in a momentary eddy. All around there was furious struggle and fighting, screams and crying and the wet stink of blood. She saw one of their own go down, spitted by an iron blade.

'Come *on*!' Smitt urged her again. 'I saw what the dog did! We need you. He knew that. We *need* you, Elinor!'

He pulled at her and she stumbled forward, gasping, bringing up her blade.

The Brothers were trying to regroup themselves, she saw, forming up near one of the camp fires in a bristling circle. She charged them, bursting their formation apart, her blade flashing, taking two men before they even knew she was upon them. She pivoted, mindful now, refusing to let the blade lead her too far, ready to take the next man that came against her.

But Scrunch had appeared out of nowhere, pulling down the man she had looked to see, smothering him with his greater weight. The man screamed.

She whirled the other way, then, striking at another of the Brothers who came at her, taking him with a long, double-handed stroke that severed his sword arm entire at the elbow, leaving him on his knees, blood gushing, white-faced and shrieking and staring at where his forearm lay on the wet earth.

When she looked up she saw Scrunch shaking the Brother he had attacked. Behind him, she saw another one of them, charging at Scrunch, from behind, howling, sword out, iron blade blood-wet and glinting.

'Scrunch!' she cried.

Too late.

It was all too horribly similar. Scrunch would never have time enough to whirl to meet his attacker properly. And she was too far away to do anything at all . . .

But somebody else came leaping out suddenly, taking the lance-man in the side with a body tackle. The two tumbled and thrashed, so tangled that neither Scrunch nor Kess could do a thing but watch, helpless. She saw one of the struggling men – which, she could not tell – get a blade loose. She tried to draw closer.

There was a scream, a sudden wilder thrashing, then the two men went still.

Scrunch rushed in, batting the two forms apart with a paw. The dark-clothed Brother lay sprawled on his back quivering. The man who had brought him down him rose to his knees, gasping.

424

Smitt.

There was no time for words, no time for anything but a quick baring of Scrunch's great ivory fangs in a hard grin, a nod, a grunt . . . And then more Brothers came charging at them, and they had all they could manage just trying to stay alive.

Elinor engaged one of them in a fast, desperate flurry of blows. He was a swordsman, and a good one, but he was shaken and uncertain what he faced. And he kept staring at the gleaming blade in her hands.

It proved his undoing.

The next she took with a quick sidestep and back-hand slash Master Karasyn had named the Scythe.

The next hacked at her shining blade, one blind, desperate blow, then turned and fled.

She stood, staring.

What Brothers remained unscathed were fleeing for their lives.

It was over. The Brothers' camp was theirs.

Elinor stood panting and shaking. Her sword arm throbbed, her bad leg too. She had taken a shallow cut across her left forearm, she noticed – all unknowing. It smarted fiercely.

She looked at the sword. The blade shone mirror bright as always, blood-laced now. She shivered, remembering how she had laughed, dancing through bloody chaos, feeling herself invincible. Kess's fatal overconfidence. Very nearly . . .

Had it been the sword's doing? The seductive power of it leading her too far? Or her own? Both together? It did not matter. She shook her head, and vowed to herself – to her *selves*, both Kess and Elinor – to be more vigilant in future. No more would she let herself be led into such self-inflated, criminal foolishness.

'You all right?' It was Collart. He stood, white-faced, breathing in great panting gasps, leaning weakly on the sword he had been wielding.

She nodded. 'You?'

He nodded back.

'Gyver . . .' she said. 'Where's Gyver?'

'Haven't seen him,' Collart responded. He looked about. 'We were lucky. They never recovered from their first surprise.' He was staring at her. 'Or from you and your blade.'

425

A few paces off Smitt stood, gasping and staring too. And behind him, others. She looked about and saw that almost everyone was doing the same.

For long, long moments there was a sudden utter and surreal silence. Not a bird cried in the wood. The very dawn breeze itself seemed to have been stilled. The whole of the world seemed to hang, poised and silent.

Then somebody laughed – or half-laughed, rather, a soft, stuttering, heart-felt burst of exhaustion and relief.

Then, 'Whiteblade!' she heard a humanimal voice suddenly cry.

'Whiteblade . . .' It was taken up in a chorus. 'Whiteblade . . . Elinor Whiteblade!'

She stood frozen, mortally self-conscious, not knowing what to do.

And still the chant went up, 'Whiteblade! Whiteblade!' as folk began to gather about her.

Gyver . . . Where was Gyver?

Not in the thick of it, she told herself. That was not his way. He would have been on the fringes, chasing after those Brothers who had got away, perhaps. She stared about anxiously . . .

And spotted him coming towards her.

He hesitated, what with that which she had put between them and her standing isolated as she was, with the 'Whiteblade, Whiteblade!' chant still ringing out. But she thrust the blade into the ground, opened her arms to him, and he came.

And after him, others, in a rush, till they were all clustered together, hugging and back slapping and shaking each other, all tears and smiles, weeping and laughing, humanimals and human both.

Elinor felt her eyes fill with tears. That they had not perished here on this mad venture . . . that so many of them were still whole and alive . . . that they had *succeeded* . . .

But on the other side of their jubilation lay the dead – theirs as well as the Brothers'. And there were the wounded . . . blood and pain and more souls to be well-wished on their final journey to the Shadowlands. And fewer of them alive now than there had been before this venture.

She felt filled, suddenly, with horror at what they had done here.

And yet . . .

Yet she could not help but exalt along with the rest. For they had survived. They had succeeded. They had carved out the beginnings of a future for themselves.

They had *won*.

XXXXII

It was three days later that the first group of refugees came straggling in, a ragged dozen or so, farmers all, dragging what few possessions they had managed to save. Gyver – gyving about – had discovered them, lost and half-starved and desperate.

'We heard,' they said.

'You defeated the Brothers.'

And: 'The white blade . . .' one of them murmured. 'Is it true?'

After those first came others, a trickle, a steady, gradual flow. Word had somehow got out – however such news was carried – and folk managed to struggle their way into the wild where, one way or another, they gravitated to, stumbled across, or were led to the camp up in the hills.

'If these refugee folk can find us,' Smitt said, 'then so too can the Brothers.'

'We would know in good enough time to avoid them,' Scrunch returned. 'Or deal with them. We have scouts out.'

'Only we must stay ready,' Smitt said. 'No letting them take *us* by surprise.'

Scrunch nodded soberly.

'Agreed,' echoed Collart.

'But what do you plan to *do*?' This from a woman who had recently come in leading a weary gaggle of refugees, amongst them some of the first children to arrive here, skinny little waifs with eyes like saucers. Adella, the woman named herself, stout, of middle age, with auburn hair in two long braids – she reminded Elinor heartbreakingly of Margie's Gillien.

'We can't just sit up here in these forsaken hills,' Adella said. 'My farm's going to ruin down there!'

428

The Brothers had overrun the entire Valley, it seemed, destroying and killing in a mindless excess of brutality at the start. But by now they had consolidated an iron hold on the territory, and were beginning to re-establish what farms they could, putting their own folk in place as overseers and using forced labour to do the farm work.

'My farm's been raped!' was the way one man put it.

'We can't just hide away up here and give them the free run of the land!' Adella complained angrily, her braids swinging. 'They're completely mad. We've got to organize ourselves. We must *do* something.'

'We're not just ... *hiding*,' Smitt answered her. 'We *are* doing things. But we need to be careful – sensible about our approach ...'

Elinor could not help but smile a little. Smitt was no longer the hot-head he once had been; the fight for the food-caravan had grown him up, quenching the most of his fire. He sat with bald Passaly, now, who nodded in sober agreement.

'No use rushing about like headless chickens,' Passaly said.

'No use flocking mindlessly about like *hopeless* chickens,' Adella returned, and there was a disgruntled chorus of agreement from many of the newcomers.

It was a general gathering, this, with most of the camp in attendance – more than five dozen human folk now, not counting children, and perhaps a third as many humanimals.

'We *will* do something,' Collart reassured them all. 'But young Smitt here is right. We have to be careful.'

'And meanwhile, while you're up here being *careful*, my farm's taken from me and ruined by *them*!' a man spoke up bitterly.

'What do you expect us to do?' Smitt demanded. 'Rush down there in a body and kill them all, everywhere, at once? All few dozen of us?'

The man who had spoken rubbed at his face and glared sullenly. 'At least it'd be *something*.'

'There's not enough of us yet,' Passaly said.

'There'll never be enough of us,' somebody put in bitterly.

'Well, we can't just give over and die!' said another.

Collart held up his hand. 'There's no easy answer,' he said. 'Whatever we do, it will have to take time.'

*

Leaning lightly against Gyver's warm, furred shoulder, Elinor sat gazing down at the camp from a little moss-carpeted stone promontory. It was evening, with the sun set already, the light waning. This was the first chance they had had to be quietly together, she and he, since the fighting – he out most of the time on scouting and hunting forays, and she caught up in endless discussions and planning and greeting sessions, for all the new arrivals wanted to be shown the white blade, to see it with their own eyes.

Elinor sighed tiredly. She did not know what to do or say. She felt utterly comfortable here, with Gyver beside her. And utterly ill at ease.

Why was everything so complicated?

He turned and nibbled ever so softly on her ear. She felt his warm breath, and an answering flush of heat inside her. But she pushed him away, gently.

'I . . . can't, Gyver.'

He looked hurt. But unlike Rannis or Annocky, who would no doubt have pushed against her, demanded reasons, chided her, nagged . . . Gyver merely pulled back, accepting.

Which she appreciated and admired in him no end.

Which just made things all the more difficult.

How could she explain? 'It's . . . it's too much, Gyver. The world is too shattered. There's been too much of death and grief already. I've lost too much already.'

'Life,' he said, 'it iss losss. And gain. If you never losse, you never gain.'

Elinor shook her head. 'Words, Gyver. Easy to say. But there's a part of me that won't let go.'

Gyver's brown eyes were sad and liquid and wide. 'It'ss better to have loved and losst,' he said, 'than never to have losst at all.'

She smiled, a brief little smile. 'I can't . . . can't let go inside. It's too much.' She thought of him lying splayed out on the ground, carved open, his guts spilled out. Which *would* happen, she felt certain. Him and his little stone-tipped arrows. It was only a matter of time. She picked up a stick from the ground and snapped it in half, in quarters. Without looking at him, she said, 'Why won't you go home?'

She felt him shrug, for their shoulders were still touching, slightly. 'Thiss iss where I wissh to be, me.'

430

She turned on him, suddenly angry. Why was he being so pig-headed? Why could he not see the sense behind what she wanted? Was she going to have to drive him from her, like some overeager, over-affectionate puppy?

But he was no puppy. He looked at her with his steady brown eyes and she found nothing to say.

'I will sstay,' he said, 'till I feel to go.'

'And me?' she returned. 'I have no say in any of this?'

He shrugged.

She turned away to leave, but he put a hand quickly on her arm.

'Stay,' he said. 'Pleasse. Ssit with me a while. Jusst ssit.'

She settled against him, took a long breath, another. The early evening air was pleasantly cool. She felt Gyver's warmth through his fur. She could not open herself to him, no. But she could not close herself altogether to him, either.

'What are we going to do, Gyver?' she said suddenly, meaning about their two selves, about the camp below them, about the threat that lay in wait for all of them, about the ominous future. About *everything* . . .

Gyver let out a soft breath. 'There are timess when one musst . . . wait. Like a bird, yess?'

She looked at him quizzically.

'The bird, she musst wait on the wind, not knowing, never knowing which way the wind will blow her. But ready, alwayss ready to fly.'

'Well enough for the bird,' Elinor replied. 'But me . . .' She sighed, shook her head. 'I feel trapped and . . . and confused.'

He looked at her with his big, brown eyes. 'And sso musst the bird. Until the wind blowss.'

Elinor sighed again. 'There's not enough of us. Somebody said it yesterday in the council session. There'll *never* be enough folk up here to seriously threaten the Brothers. They're too strong, too many. They can't lose! It's like . . . like we're a pack of silly mice thinking how to threaten . . .' She shook her head, rubbed a hand over her face. 'I can't even think how to finish the thought. Oh . . . what are we going to *do*, Gyver? I want to help these people. I *owe* them.'

Gyver put a hand to her cheek, gently. 'Ssometimess there iss

431

nothing to do but wait, like the bird, till it comes, the wind, and takes you up.'

Elinor looked at him, shook her head, sighed. 'Is that what your mother says, then?'

He grinned and nodded. 'My mother the wisse ssoul.'

They sat together quietly for long moments.

Then, 'Look,' Gyver said, pointing.

New arrivals were coming into camp, several men, by the look of them. Elinor saw Collart and Smitt go forward to meet them. It was a familiar enough sight: the greetings, the mutual questions, the gradual settling in of the newcomers.

'They'll be needing me,' she sighed. It was the custom for her to help greet new arrivals. Folk wanted to see the rumoured white blade. She got up, knowing it had to be done. 'I feel like a freak,' she muttered, 'with strangers pawing at me like that.'

But something below was different, she realized suddenly.

She heard voices raised excitedly, saw one of the newcomers waving about a piece of yellow parchment. Folk came running, human and humanimal. She heard her own name being called.

'What could it be?' she said.

'Perhapss,' Gyver replied, 'the wind, sshe hass changed.'

'Here she comes!' somebody called, heralding Elinior's arrival.

She came hurrying up, Gyver at her side. 'What is it? What's happened?'

'Look!' Collart held aloft the parchment she had seen from the stone perch above.

'They've nailed them up everywhere,' one of the new arrivals was saying, a dark little man with a wild shock of hair.

'Listen to this!' Collart said excitedly. He held the parchment before him and read: '"To Elinor, surnamed Whiteblade – greetings from Iryn Jagga, divinely appointed leader of the Ancient Brotherhood of the Light, ruler absolute of Sofala and all lands adjacent to it, Commander in Chief of the Imperial Armed Might of the Ancient Brotherhood, inheritor of celestial wisdom, instructor of the people, right hand of Jara the Great . . ."' Collart paused, took a breath. 'There's more of the same.'

'Doesn't think much of himself, does he?' somebody said.

There was general laughter.

'Get to the offer,' the shock-haired newcomer urged.

Collart squinted at the parchment, ran a finger along the lines of writing till he found what he was searching for. '"It has come,"' he read, '"to our attention that you have wantonly attacked our innocent caravans, killed and savaged our good men, liberated animals destined to be ceremoniously cleansed –"'

'Ceremoniously *what*?' somebody murmured.

'"– and given refuge to criminals and assorted miscreants who manifestly deserve to be punished."'

There were hoots and jeers, and Collart had to hold up a hand for quiet. 'Listen!' he said, then continued reading: '"You have, in short, become a thorn in our side, you and those who follow you."'

'Good for you, Elinor!' a woman shouted.

'Good for *us*!' somebody else cried.

'Listen!' Collart said again, and read on: '"Every physician knows a thorn must be removed, lest it fester. You have demonstrated yourself to be resourceful. We respect that. You have demonstrated yourself to be dangerous in battle. We respect that, also. But armed conflict, as all sensible men know, is the last resort of the ignorant. Therefore, we make you an offer."'

Collart paused, looked up.

'Read *on*, man!' Passaly urged.

Collart did: '". . . we make you an offer. Come to us at the field on the bluff above the Rannin River on the fifth day after the new moon, and we will meet you there to discuss the manner in which we can be reconciled –"'

The gathering erupted into excited shouts.

'Quiet!' Collart cried. 'There's more.'

When he could be heard again, he went on: '". . . we can be reconciled – you and all who follow you, we and all we command. There is nothing to be gained by further violence between us. Come to us. Talk with us. Reconcile yourself with us. Make a lasting peace through us. Trust us."'

Collart stopped. 'That's it. That's the finish.'

There were long moments of silence.

Then, 'It's a trap,' Passaly said. '"Nothing to be gained by further violence . . ." *Trust* them indeed! Sooner trust a venomous serpent as it rears to strike than trust *them*.'

'Fifth day after the new moon . . . that's three days from now,' somebody said.

'Enough time to reach the River Rannin . . .'

'She can't go!' a woman said – Getta, with a bow in hand. 'She *mustn't* go. Passaly's right. It's a trap!'

'But, if it's not, it's the answer to everything. It's our chance to make peace, to get our farms back!'

'*If* it's not!'

Elinor stood, blinking. Gyver had been right. The wind had changed indeed. But which way was it now blowing? 'Collart?' she said.

Collart frowned. 'I don't know.'

'But it's obvious,' one of the newer arrivals said. 'The Brothers have realized that they can't run the farms without us. This is their way of making peace.'

'This is their way of drawing us into a fatal trap!'

'No! It is not!'

'Oh, yes it *is*!'

'There's no talking with the likes of the Brothers,' Passaly insisted. 'They're like mad dogs, the lot of them!'

'Enough! *Enough*!' Collart shouted. He stood with the parchment in his hand, frowning still. 'It might be truth,' he said after a little.

A disgruntled muttering greeted this.

'*Might* be,' he said. 'And if it is . . . if there's *any* chance at all that it is . . .'

Elinor nodded, feeling the same thing herself. She swallowed. 'If there's any chance at all,' she echoed Collart, 'then we cannot say "no". You all must see that. This is the answer to everything.'

'If it's not a trap!' somebody snapped.

'*If*,' she agreed. 'But how can we say "no" even with such an "if"?'

'That's just what they're counting on,' Getta said.

At Getta's side, Ingra the farm-wife raised her beefy arms. 'Elinor, you *cannot* do this!'

Elinor shrugged uneasily. 'How can I *not* do this?'

There was silence then.

'We have to be very, very careful,' Collart said. 'No reason you need go alone, Elinor. We can go together, ready for trouble, send scouts ahead. If there's any sign of betrayal . . .'

Elinor looked across at Gyver, feeling her belly tighten.

If, if, and if . . .

It was a very weak support on which to build the possibility of a future. But it was more of a possibility than they had had only a few short moments ago.

Peace. No more blood and grief.

They could go carefully. They could go slowly, suspiciously.

But they had to go.

XXXXIII

'They're there,' Scrunch said. 'Waiting.'

Elinor swallowed, nodded.

'How many?' asked Collart.

'No more than a dozen and a half.'

'Is that all?' This from young black-beard Smitt. 'We out-number them two to one, then, not counting the humanimals. *Good*!'

'Are you *sure* there aren't more of them?' bald Passaly asked.

Scrunch shook his head. 'No more. We would have seen.'

'Horsesss alonggg nearr the toppp of the blufff,' Otys the crow said.

'They would have ridden here from Sofala,' explained Ingra, the farm-wife. 'Probably on *my* horses, too, the thieving bastards. They always did like my horses!'

'It bodes well, all this,' Collart said. 'The Field is a good place for such a meeting as this, plenty of tree-cover nearabouts for us, but open so we can see them. You can't make it out from here, but there's a long, steep slope down to the river behind them. Nobody's going to be coming up *that* to surprise us. And there's not too many of them. Good . . .'

Elinor nodded. She glanced about, hoping against hope to see Spandel's little dancing form come springing out of nowhere suddenly crying, 'I dreamed! I dreamed, dreamed, dreamed!'

But there was nothing. Spandel was disappeared into the wild lands. She only hoped the little Lamure had not fallen into the Brothers' ungentle hands.

Elinor felt her heart thumping. There was no point in delay. 'Let's do it,' she said. She looked across at Gyver, smiled a thin smile. It had been agreed that the humanimals would stay out of sight – since their kind brought out the worst in the Brothers – and this restriction included Gyver.

He reached a hand to her. 'I sshall be watching from cover,' he said softly, lifting his bow.

She nodded, gripped his hand hard for a long moment, then let him go and headed down to the bluff along with those who were to accompany her.

They emerged slowly from out of the trees at the verge of the field and saw the contingent of Brothers awaiting them.

They stood looking across at each other in silence. The early-morning sunlight shafted down, lighting the middle of the open, grassy place, but the two groups themselves stood in dappled tree-shadow.

For long moments, nobody moved.

Then one of the Brothers stepped forward. 'Which of you is Elinor? The one surnamed Whiteblade.'

Elinor stepped out towards him.

The Brother stared at her coldly, at the blade hung from her belt. He was a big, dour-faced man with dark moustaches. He wore a leathern fighting helm with the sun-ray-and-gripped-hands insignia of the Brothers worked on it in brass. He had a blade at his belt. In his hand, he carried a small, gilded staff. 'I am Collis Tigh,' he said, 'Squad Chief of the Imperial Armed Might of the Ancient Brotherhood of the Light.'

It took Elinor a long moment before she recognized him: the Squad Chief who had led the destruction of Margie Farm, the one whose ear she had clipped – it did not show with the helm he wore. She felt her belly clench. That this man should stand before her so calmly after all he had brought about . . .

'There is someone here,' he was saying, 'with whom we wish you to speak.' With that, he turned his back on her abruptly and walked back to rejoin the group of silently waiting Brothers.

Somebody else stepped out of that group, then, and walked slowly towards Elinor, standing alone in front of her companions. The man coming towards her was dressed in the same sombre clothing as the rest, but there was something about him . . .

'Rannis!' Elinor cried in surprise. 'What in the world are *you* doing here?'

He shrugged, smiling uncomfortably. 'It *is* you, then,' he said. 'Kess. I wasn't completely sure. When they found out I might know you, they asked if I could come and help with the talks.'

'But, Rannis,' she said, going a few steps towards him. 'When did you . . . How . . . Are you all right?'

'I'm fine,' he said. And he did look well enough. He was dressed in the Brothers' sombre garb, but apart from that seemed his old self, fit and well-fed.

'But what happened to you?' she pressed.

He shrugged. 'What's past is past, Elinor. It's not important. What matters now is that we try to stop the bloodshed.'

She looked at him, uncertain. There had been bad feeling between them at parting. Yet Rannis seemed to have left all that behind.

'We've got to stop the bloodshed, Kess,' he repeated. Then, shaking his head, corrected himself, 'Elinor.'

'Truly?' she said. 'That's truly why you're here?'

He nodded. 'Truly. There has been too much of blood.'

'You're not . . .' She stepped a little closer to him, lowered her voice. 'You're not *with* them, then?'

He shook his head quickly. 'No. Of *course* not! What do you take me for?'

'But your garb . . .'

Again, he shrugged. 'I was in . . . sorry straits after you left me. The Brothers took me in and helped. Theirs is the clothing I wear, right enough. But they do not insist I accept their beliefs. They are far from being the mad fanatics folk have made them out to be, Elinor.'

There were mutterings from behind her at this, for Rannis's words were loud enough to be overheard. Passaly advanced a few steps. 'Don't listen to him, Elinor. Saying that sort of thing . . . Well, he's *got* to be one of theirs. They're mad dogs, the lot of them. No sane man would ever . . .'

Smitt came up beside Passaly. 'Who *is* this man?' he demanded of Elinor.

'A . . . someone I know from Minmi,' she answered.

'Come away, Elinor,' Passaly urged. 'Let's get as far as we can from these cursed madmen. Quick, before they . . .'

'Tell your follower here to keep his mouth shut if he can't talk more sense than that,' Rannis said. Stepping closer to Elinor, he hooked a thumb backwards at the silent group of Brothers. 'Do they look like madmen? I tell you, they are much maligned . . . Elinor.' He put his hand on her shoulder conspiratorially. 'But they are not saints, either. If this man of yours doesn't ease up, there's no telling . . .'

'Let her go,' Smitt snapped. He stepped up, grabbed Rannis's hand, and flung it off Elinor. His other hand was on the hilt of the blade that hung from his belt. 'Step *back* from her. And be quick about it.'

Rannis stood his ground, though he bore no weapon. The gathered Brothers shuffled forward a menacing step.

'Smitt!' Elinor hissed. 'Leave off.' She gestured towards Rannis. 'I know this man. He's from Minmi. He's not one of *them*. He's here to help us talk with them. Now just back off and let me . . .'

Collart came up now. 'Let her talk, man,' he cautioned Smitt. 'That's what we came here for, isn't it?'

Passaly spat. 'There is no talking with *them*! I've said that all along.'

'Not with *that* attitude, there isn't,' Rannis said. Then, 'Tell him to back away,' he urged Elinor. 'Tell them all, this whole raggle-taggle bunch of yours. They make the Brothers nervous. If we're going to have any chance of success here, that's the last thing we need.'

Elinor looked at Passaly and Smitt. 'Please,' she said. 'I appreciate what you're trying to do. But this is the best, the only, chance we have. If we can only start some sort of . . . of dialogue here . . .'

'You're making a mistake,' Passaly replied quickly. 'Look at them. Just *look* at them! Do they look like normal, sane men to you?'

So intense was Passaly's warning that Elinor found herself glancing back uncertainly at the shadowed band of Brothers. They stood like so many spectres, silent, unmoving. It was sinister, the way they stood like that. Their pale faces appeared expressionless, like masks almost. She felt a little shiver go down her spine. Perhaps Passaly had the right of it after all. It was not yet too late to back quietly away.

'Don't *do* this, Elinor,' Passaly was urging her. 'Come away. Let's leave here, *now*!'

Almost, she did. Almost . . . But no. She shook her head. 'I can't. Not without trying, at least.'

'Yes!' Rannis put in quickly. 'We have to try.' He stabbed a finger accusingly at Passaly. 'Are you so frightened, then, that you would mindlessly destroy what may be your last chance of making peace?'

Passaly only glared.

'Or is it,' Rannis went on, 'that you do not really *want* peace? What do you stand to gain, man, that you want so to sabotage our attempts here?'

'How *dare* you?' Smitt said, outraged. He took a step forward, belligerently.

Collart put out his hand. 'Enough!' he said softly. 'The two of you. How can Elinor deal with this with you two jabbering in her ear?' He turned to her. 'I can bring them back with the rest of us, give you a chance to talk alone with this one.' He gestured at Rannis, lowered his voice. 'Do you truly trust him?'

Elinor nodded. 'What can possibly go wrong? The field's open. You can see everything.'

Passaly shook his head unhappily. 'You're making a mistake, I tell you.'

'How?' Elinor replied. 'We're safe enough here. And Rannis is guarantee enough against treachery, aren't you, Rannis?'

'Absolutely,' Rannis responded. 'You have my word on it.'

'Ha!' said Smitt. 'And why should I take the word of a . . . a mere servant?'

'I am no servant,' Rannis said, bristling.

'You serve *them*,' Smitt returned, pointing at the Brothers.

'No, I do *not*.' Rannis looked at Elinor. 'Tell him. I was one of the Court Guard in Minmi. No mere servant of anybody. And a Guard's word is worth something. Is that not true, Elinor?'

She nodded slowly, looked towards Collart. 'Take them back. I *know* this man. I trust his word. What he says is true. He was one of the Minmi Guard.'

'There will be no treachery here, man,' Rannis reassured Collart. 'You have my most solemn word on that. The Brothers come here only to talk. They wish for peace as much as you. Too much blood has already been spilt, on their side as much as yours. They wish only to end this pointless fighting.'

Collart stared at Rannis for a long moment, then nodded. 'All right, you two,' he said to Passaly and Smitt. 'Let's leave them to talk.'

Smitt and Passaly allowed Collart to shepherd them back, casting unhappy glances behind, leaving Elinor standing alone with Rannis.

'Are they really acting in good faith?' she asked, looking towards the silent group of Brothers. 'Do they really offer peace and reconciliation here?'

He nodded. 'They're sensible men. Come and talk with them.'

Elinor nodded slowly. 'All right. Bring them over.'

Rannis shook his head. 'Better you should go to them.'

'Why?' she asked, uneasy.

'It's a matter of face, girl. They make the offer. You come to them. It's the way such things work. Do you wish to offend them? What sort of a beginning would that be? There's no danger in it.' He stepped closer to her. 'Trust me in this, Kess . . . Elinor. Your people will still be able to see all that transpires. You said so yourself. It's just a question of walking those few extra steps. As a gesture of good faith.'

Elinor shrugged, nodded. She glanced behind her, made a reassuring motion with her hands. 'I'm going forward a few steps,' she told them softly. 'With Rannis. Everything's all right.'

Collart nodded, sober, watchful, tense.

Rannis smiled reassuringly. 'This way,' he said, hand on her shoulder.

Elinor walked with him across the grassy field. The Brothers stood still, waiting. She could see no sign of anything wrong, no hands sliding to weapons. And Scrunch had assured her there were no more of them hidden in wait – and she took quiet comfort from the knowledge of her own hidden supporters, invisible amongst the trees, watching, Gyver amongst them, with his bow and his grey-fletched arrows.

The Squad Chief who had first talked to her came forward. He made a sharp little formal bow from the waist, waving his gilded staff.

She nodded at him, keeping her anger in check. There was too much at stake here for her to indulge a personal grudge.

'Welcome, Elinor Whiteblade,' he said formally. 'There is much we must talk about. The very fate of this land rests with what we do here this day . . .'

Without warning, somebody suddenly shoved her, hard, from behind.

She stumbled, going down on one knee. Something hit her in the back of the head, and she fell, the field and trees about her throbbing into momentary dimness.

There were bodies in frantic motion all about her, then. Somebody was shouting. Several pairs of hard hands gripped her and began to drag her away. She tried to kick out, to dig her feet into the grass, but something hit her in the head again. Her vision burst into a confusion of painful, whirling sparks. She tried to cry out, but there was too much screaming and shouting, and her voice was lost.

They dragged her quickly away. She could hear the panting breath of the men holding her as they ran. One of them stumbled and fell, gasping, a grey-fletched arrow through his throat. Then the trees engulfed them and they jerked her along in a frantic zigzag course, her feet thumping against roots.

She tried to struggle, but her head throbbed too much and her limbs would not obey her wishes. She gagged, feeling she was about to throw up.

Then they were out of the trees, and she heard horses neighing. With a suddenness that made her stomach heave, they slung her face down across a saddle. She felt quick hands binding her, hand and foot. Then somebody shouted 'Haaa!' and slapped the horse, and it took off with a jerk that threw her painfully against the bonds holding her in place.

Away the horse went, neighing frantically, surrounded by other horses now, with men shouting and whipping their mounts.

With a sickening plunge, they plummeted over the side of the bluff which abutted the field, down the slope of it in a mad, wild rush, rocks and tree litter tumbling along with them in a noisy avalanche. Something smacked her in the face, and she could not move her hands to protect herself. She clutched desperately with arms and thighs, head down, vision swimming red, pressing her face against the horse's flank for protection, her heart hammering.

There were cries of outraged fury from above, but the sounds were dwindling fast.

Through thick undergrowth the horses plunged, greenery slapping and catching at her, and then on again, through a whipping confusion of more vegetation, downwards and downwards, skittering and sliding, neighing in fear and exertion. One horse stumbled and went down, flinging its rider heels over head to land with a cry of pain.

'On, on!' Collis Tigh, the Squad Chief, called – she knew that voice.

Onwards they went in their wild plunge, till Elinor was certain they were suicidal madmen, the lot of them, and that their madness could only result in painful death for all – herself included.

But somehow the horses managed to keep their footing. The slope of the bluff lessened, and they came out through a screen of brush on to level, grassy ground near the river. Collis Tigh held up his arm, signalling a momentary halt. The horses stood blowing, their sides heaving, throwing their heads about, eyes wide and white-rimmed.

Elinor felt her stomach churn and vomited painfully, spraying the ground, the horse's legs, unable so much as to wipe her mouth. She gagged, shuddering.

Above, she heard frantic shouting. Twisting round as best she could, she looked behind her. The upper crest of the bluff down which they had careered had to be something like a hundred paces above them. She saw the little shapes of her band moving about, starting the descent. But it was too late. It had all happened too suddenly.

Collis Tigh laughed, seeing it as she had. 'Too late,' he said. 'Stupid animals. They'll never be able to keep us from reaching Sofala.' He looked across at Elinor and smiled. He held her sheathed blade in hand, though when or how he had got it from her she could not recollect. Her head was ringing nd she found it hard to breathe. Her mouth tasted foul.

'You're *ours* now, girl,' he said gloatingly. 'And there's not a thing any of your ragtag, stupid little following can do about it.'

He laughed one final time, reined his horse about, and raised his hand. 'Forward!' he called.

The horses trotted on, reluctantly, spurred by their riders. One of the Brothers took up the reins of Elinor's horse and started it off with a jerk that sent blinding stutters of pain through her skull.

The ground flickered by beneath her face, grass and rock and hoof-scuffed dirt. Her vision wavered uncertainly. Her belly heaved. Pain thrust through her head. Then there was only darkness . . .

Elinor felt somebody untying the lashings that held her in place.

They dragged her off and let her fall on the ground with a painful thump.

'Get her to her feet,' a voice ordered.

Hands yanked her up, shook her.

She gasped, trying to breathe, trying not to faint as all the blood seemed to rush out of her head. Her hands and feet throbbed painfully. Something hit her in the face, a stinging blow, another. She blinked, squinted the world into focus, saw the dour, moustached face of Collis Tigh, the Squad Chief, glaring at her.

'Wake up, girl. Come back to us!' He slapped her once more, hard enough to make her head ring.

She tried to pull away, but the men grasping her held firm.

'So . . .' Collis Tigh said. 'The renowned Elinor Whiteblade.' He laughed. 'Not so clever now, are you? Not so dangerous now that we've pulled your fangs. Or should I say fang?' He held her blade up. 'A lovely weapon, this. Misplaced in such foolish hands as yours.'

Elinor shook her head, tasted blood in her mouth from a split lip. She felt sick, and would have gladly vomited all over him, but her belly was quite empty now, and it was only the dry heaves that shook her.

When she could look up again, she saw Rannis dismount from one of the horses and come over.

'Rannis!' she cried, her voice a hoarse croak. 'You've got to stop this! Make them see reason. What about the peace? *Talk* to them!'

But, '*You*!' was what Rannis said, and his voice dripped with bitterness. 'You destroyed *everything*.'

She stared at him.

'I had a life in Minmi. A *good* life. I had a place, a future, a self. And *you* took all that from me!' He slapped her, harder than the Squad Chief had, making her head rock violently. Did it again.

'Enough,' Collis Tigh said. 'We do not want her damaged.'

'This will not damage her,' Rannis said, and slapped her again. 'I owe her this. And more!'

Elinor reeled. She could not believe this was happening. 'Rannis!' she cried. Her lips were split and bleeding where he had hit her, and it hurt to make the words. 'How could you . . .'

'Shut up!' he snarled. 'You, who just abandoned me. You, who I sacrificed everything for, who *ruined* my life. You, who . . .'

'Leave it be,' Collis Tigh ordered. He scowled at Rannis. 'Behave like a man. You delivered her to us. We will not forget. Let that be enough.'

Rannis glared back at him. 'I will behave in whatever manner I like. And neither you nor . . .'

The Squad Chief motioned to one of the men behind Rannis. The man hit him in the kidneys, hard, and Rannis collapsed to his knees, groaning, face contorted with pain and shocked surprise.

'Behave!' Collis Tigh snapped. 'There is more at stake here than your trivial personal grudge. Do you think you are the only one with a score to settle with this girl? Look!' He yanked off his leathern helm and turned his head, showing the red nub of where his ear had once been. 'She took my ear from me, the sneaking little bitch. Do you think I suffer *that* gladly? But she is not our meat any more.'

Rannis said nothing, kneeling as he was, still gasping.

The Squad Chief shook his head. Then, 'Seat her on the horse and bind her tight,' he commanded to the men still holding Elinor. 'We have a long ways to make if we hope to reach Sofala by sunfall.'

The men did as he ordered, none too gently, and the whole

445

cavalcade rode off, with Elinor swaying in the saddle, her bruised face throbbing, her mouth dry as a stone and still foul tasting. The horse jounced under her painfully. She licked at the blood on her lip for the wetness of it. She felt her heart sink, and blinked back sudden, despairing tears.

She would not give her captors the pleasure.

XXXXIV

The ride went on and on. It was like a nightmare, an endless procession of clawing branches and thorns and wavering grass, jumbled ground, the horse jouncing down hill, up hill, splashing through water, on and on and on . . .

Until Elinor looked up, bleary-eyed and aching and exhausted, and made out square towers ahead, set against the evening sky in the distance like great blunt teeth on the horizon.

'Sofala,' one of the Brothers said, standing up in his stirrups and gazing ahead eagerly.

Onwards they went, pushing the horses till the weary creatures were gasping and shaky-legged and clumsy. Elinor felt her own nearly miss its footing coming down a little slope. She felt sick with hurt and exhaustion. No one had so much as given her a sip of water all the long, jarring ride.

The Brothers pressed on, heedless of all save speed, until, in the twilight of evening, they finally drew near to the Sofala Gates.

The gateway was huge, with double wooden doors fully twice the height of a tall man, set in a great, thick stone wall which surrounded the city, ivy-covered and broken down in parts, but still in better repair than the stonework Elinor recalled from Minmi.

Another of the old Domains, she realized. Huge and ancient and crumbling . . .

The big brass-bound double doors before them were a dark blue, the surface scarred by a myriad spidery cracks and dark chips. They were shut tight. A score of sombre-clothed guards, armed with long lances, stood in a double rank before them.

The guards' leader stepped forward with stiff formality. Collis Tigh rode up and addressed him, holding out his little gilded staff. 'Squad Chief Collis Tigh, with escort and prisoner. Bound for Iryn Jagga himself.'

The guards' leader bowed. 'Pass, Squad Chief.'

The gates grated open slowly, moved by some hidden mechanism inside the walls that squealed rustily.

They filed through, two by two, and into Sofala.

Inside, it was nothing at all like Minmi. Here, there were road ways and buildings and open spaces like those Elinor had been used to in Long Harbour – a lifetime ago, it seemed.

They rode along a narrow, cobblestone street leading off from the gateway. Two-storey buildings lined both sides, but there was no sign of life anywhere. Aside from the clatter of the horses' hooves upon the cobblestones, there was utter silence about them. Elinor shifted in the saddle, trying to find a position that eased her hurts. She shivered. In the dying evening light, everything was dim. No night-torches had been lit anywhere yet, it seemed. She became aware of a sweet-sour, sickly scent in the air.

All along the street's left side, she saw, there were largish, pale globes hung from the eaves of the buildings. Night-lanterns, was her first thought. A lantern lighter would be along soon to set them aglow, or the inhabitants of the buildings would light them themselves.

But there did not seem to be any inhabitants. And the more she saw of them, the less they began to look like lanterns.

Their cavalcade, moving in single file, two by two, rounded a corner and headed off along another street. As they turned, Elinor got her first proper, close-up look at one of the hanging, pale globes.

No lantern.

It was a severed human head, dangling by a black cord from the building's eaves. The cord had been threaded through the eye sockets, in one and out the other, then knotted. The head twirled slowly, staring blindly upwards out of its mutilated eyes.

Elinor turned quickly away, sickened. How many had they passed? she wondered. Two dozen? Three? What manner of horrid place *was* this?

None of those riding with her seemed even to notice.

The street they were moving along gave on to another. Elinor saw more dangling heads. And then, passing close as her horse made the corner . . .

One of the dead heads twirled slowly. She made out long hair the deep colour of ripe cherries, grey-streaked, hanging in two thick, ragged braids.

Gillien.

And dangling beside, poor Hann, the trailing remains of his blond beard matted with a dark crust of old blood, the skin of his dead face crawling with maggots.

Elinor's belly heaved, and for a long moment she could not get any breath at all.

Then, with a sudden rush, the horses were out of the narrow street and clattering into an open square – a large, empty expanse of cobblestones. The buildings they had been passing between had hemmed in Elinor's vision. Now, she could make out the great city walls, studded with squat watch towers, looming up in the distance all around, like a cage. Everything was silent, still, deserted. The sharp sound of the horses' hooves echoed eerily. Elinor shuddered. Sofala seemed a city of the dead.

They rode across the square, passing a complicated stone structure the height of three tall men that took up the centre. In the dim light, the stone mass showed grey and colourless. As they drew nearer, she tried to make out what it might be. It seemed to be composed of a series of platforms.

As the horses rounded the structure's far side, Elinor started. For there stood the first living people she had seen in this place – a dozen, perhaps, pale-faced, dressed in dark, tattered clothing. One of them held a smouldering lantern. They stood silently, staring at the stone structure rising before them.

Elinor squinted in the lantern's uncertain radiance. There were . . . things hanging from parts of that structure. With a sick feeling, she recognized dead humanimals. Her heart in her mouth, she looked to see if poor missing Spandel might be there. She made out a Hyphon, a dog-like creature, a stork dangling upside down by its long legs . . .

Elinor swallowed. Spandel, at least, was not here. But the dangling body of the poor stork explained why she had seen no more of Pallas since that sunny afternoon back at Margie. She

449

felt a sharp little thrust of guilt. He it was, in his formal way, who had first surnamed her Whiteblade. With all that had happened to her, Elinor had hardly thought of him since that day, and now . . . now here he was, limp and pitiful and sad. She bit her lip in anger and grief.

A little mewling sound made her glance down at one of the stone platforms – where the attention of the gathered Sofala folk was directed, she realized. There was a large furred creature of some sort there. Chained to iron rings set in the stone platform. Alive . . .

As they rode past, the creature shifted position slightly, to stare at them, mewling softly. She heard the chains clink. A pair of dark, sad eyes stared at her, catching the lantern-light. She recognized those eyes as all too human.

The people standing about said not a word. They glanced furtively at Elinor, at her captors, shied away as the horses came up.

'*Animal*,' one of the riders said, and spat at the furred creature as he passed it.

It did not flinch, merely stared sadly, listlessly.

And then they were out of the square and clattering into yet another dim, building-lined street. There were no hanging heads here – for which Elinor was quietly grateful. But she could take no real comfort. There was a feel to this place that made her sick in her belly – beyond the sickness of exhaustion and pain.

Onwards they rode still, clattering through the deserted, dark streets until they came eventually to a huge stone building. Elinor caught one glimpse of pillars and carvings and intricate stone scrollwork, and then they were riding through a great, open portal and into the building itself.

Inside, the horses' hooves echoed thunderously off the walls and high ceiling. Bright, flickering torchlight made her squint. Strong hands cut her bonds and hauled her down from the horse. Somebody cinched a set of cold iron manacles on her wrists. Then she was hustled off, a man gripping each of her elbows as she stumbled weakly along. There was commotion all about her. She heard voices raised, orders being shouted.

Men scurried about, grooms and servants who knew what.

And then they had pulled her through an open doorway and all the commotion was behind. The door slammed shut. Silence descended.

A man stood waiting for them. He was made from the same mould as all the rest, with the same dark, sombre clothing, the same set face that so many of them seemed to have. He wore no helm, this one. His short hair was iron-grey, his eyebrows dark black. His eyes were hard as two stones. 'It worked, then?'

'It worked, Commander,' Collis Tigh said. 'Exactly as planned.'

The man he had addressed stared at Elinor. 'And this is her?'

'This is her.'

The Commander nodded. He continued staring, a long, cold, unblinking regard. Elinor shivered. It was like being examined by a serpent.

'Welcome to Sofala, girl,' he said finally. 'We have prepared a *special* welcome for you.'

Elinor said nothing. It was almost all she could do just to keep steady. Her legs quivered. Her lower back ached viciously, as did her thighs. A line of fire ran down her scarred leg. Her bruised face was swollen and stiff and throbbing. She was actually grateful for the steadying effect of the hands gripping her elbows still.

'Take her to the dungeon,' the Commander ordered.

XXXXV

Down a long flight of steps they dragged her, through darkness and chill, then through a heavy wooden door and into what must be the dungeon itself.

It was dank and cold, ill-lit by flickering torches. There was an open area by the entrance where a large, smoking brazier sat. And other implements Elinor tried not to look at. Three men stood waiting there already, sombre-clothed like all the Brothers, silent and staring. But these three wore painted wooden masks, leering, demon-faced visages, with long ivory fangs and golden inhuman eye sockets through which their eyes peered. Elinor shuddered, seeing them.

The air here was thick with the stink of excrement and fear and damp and mould and rancid smoke. The chamber echoed with the sounds of suffering – moans, coughs, cries. In a far back corner somewhere, somebody – or something – was wailing, a high, continuous shriek that had nothing human left in it.

Elinor shuddered.

They put her next to a wooden bench by one wall. 'Stand here,' Collis Tigh ordered. 'Be quiet. Don't move.' Then he turned and marched out, his men trailing along behind. The last one slammed the heavy wooden door behind him.

Elinor stared at the door. She felt unnerved by the Squad Chief's sudden departure, as if it were a desertion of a sort – foolish thought. She glanced nervously at the demon-masked trio out of the corner of her eye. They stood or sat, unmoving, like so many statues. They seemed inhuman, with those bestial demon-masks. The wailing went on, but more hoarsely now, and less loud, as if throat or mouth or lungs, or all three, were giving out.

Time passed. They waited.

Elinor's scarred leg burned, and her lower back and thighs were a shivering misery. Her wrists were painfully chafed by the iron manacles they had her in. She shifted a little, trying to ease the discomfort, and the chains rattled.

'Be still!' one of the demon-masked men snapped. He reached up a leathern-handled, flexible switch, strode over and struck Elinor with it, three hard, stinging blows across her shoulders, making her gasp.

'Be *still*,' he repeated, swishing the stick through the air under her nose.

She tried not to flinch, but could not help herself. Her shoulders, where he had hit her, stung like fire. She tried to straighten up, doing her best not to let him know how much it had hurt.

They kept her standing there.

Her shoulders burned; her aching lower back, her thighs, her scarred leg, became an agony. The bench near her looked *so* inviting. She felt a little surge of anger, then. It was petty, making her suffer like this, trying to wear her down . . . But they would not succeed. They would *not*. They must need her for something, she reassured herself. Otherwise she would not be still alive, still uncrippled, still in her right mind. They were just trying to frighten her.

The door to the chamber was flung open, finally, and a new group of men came in. At their fore strode one who stood out. Like all the Brothers Elinor had seen, this one was dressed in the usual sombre clothing – breeches and tunic. But he wore no armour, and had on a knee-length cloak that fell in dark folds from his shoulders. His dark tunic glittered with gold, and he wore a little gold circlet upon his head, like a slim, glinting headband.

He stood regarding her for long moments. With something of a shock, Elinor realized he was a startlingly handsome man, tall and robust and clean-limbed. He was dark-haired, pale-faced, with a high, broad forehead. His clean-shaven jaw was strong, his lips thin and shapely, his nose elegantly straight. His eyes seemed to glow palely in the torchlight.

'Well, well,' he said, his voice deep and smooth and re-sonant. 'So we meet at last.'

Elinor did not know what to say. Who was this man?

'Come, come,' he said. 'No need to be shy with me. We are going to be friends, Elinor, you and I. The very best of friends.' He came over to her and put his arm about her shoulders. She winced away, for his touch hurt where she had just been beaten.

'Why don't you sit down?' he said. 'You must be tired after standing so.' He gestured at the bench. 'Sit down. Do.'

Elinor looked at him. He was more than a full head and shoulders taller than she, and she had to look up to see into his eyes. This close to her, he smelled of . . . violets.

'Who . . . are you?' she asked hesitantly.

He smiled at her, the sort of smile an elder brother might give his tired little sister, and patted her shoulder softly. 'My name is Iryn Jagga. I am leader of the Ancient Brotherhood of the Light.'

The wailer had never stopped, hoarse and soft and constant. Now, suddenly, the sound rose in volume to a shriek. Iryn Jagga looked across at one of the demon-masked men. '*Must* we put up with that . . . noise?' he asked.

The demon-mask hurried off. In a moment there was a sudden sharp yelp, a moaning grunt, silence.

'Ah . . .' Iryn Jagga breathed. 'That's better.' He smiled at Elinor and pushed her lightly towards the bench. 'Now sit down, do.'

Elinor sat with relief, looking up at him in confusion.

'Would you like something to drink?' he asked. 'Some water. Fresh milk, perhaps?'

'Milk?'

He nodded. Without looking round, he snapped his fingers. One of those who had come in with him produced a little bucket of frothing milk and a carved wooden cup. The man dipped the cup into the white milk and handed it, dripping, to Elinor. She took it in her two manacled hands and drank, feeling the creamy stuff fill her dry mouth deliciously.

'Give her another,' Iryn Jagga said when she had finished. 'She needs it.'

The man took back the cup, refilled it, handed it to her again. Again, she drank deliciously.

'Why . . . why are you . . .' she started.

454

But Iryn Jagga put a finger to her milk-wet lips and shushed her. 'I will be the one doing the talking, Elinor. Just sit there and listen. Can you do that?'

She nodded. Nothing in this terrible place had given her any hope. Sofala was worse than Minmi – far worse. But this man seemed saner than any she had yet encountered. She did not want to, but she could not help but feel a little trust in him, a little confidence. He was so calm, so mannered, so unlike the rest of the men here.

He stood looking down at her, arms folded across his chest. The long cloak he wore made him seem somehow bigger, broader, more solid than any of the others in the room. After a moment, he shook his head sadly. 'You have caused me considerable trouble. Do you know that?'

Elinor did not know what to say. Such was the force of the man's personality that she felt a kind of reflexive guilt at his accusation.

He waved a hand at her. 'No need to apologize. Such things happen sometimes.' He sat down next to her on the bench, put his arm about her shoulders gently. 'The question is . . . how are we going to put things right once again?'

His face was so close to hers that she had to squint to focus on him. The violet scent he wore seemed overpowering. For an instant, she entertained a wild notion of taking him by the throat, wrapping her wrist chains about his windpipe and semi-throttling him, using him as a hostage to make her way out of this terrible place.

But it was a hopeless notion. He was too big and too strong. And he was armed; she felt a sword at his side under the cloak. She would stand not the slightest chance.

She sighed. 'Wha—' She had to swallow, start again. 'What is it you want from me?'

Iryn Jagga smiled, gave her a little squeeze. 'Now that's my good girl, my cooperative girl.' He stood up then and walked a couple of steps away from her. 'What do I want? Why . . . cooperation is all. You see . . .' He began pacing slowly, back and forth in front of where she sat, his long cloak swirling about his legs, hands out as he talked. 'We have a destiny, we of the Brotherhood. We carry the torch of greatness. All is foretold, and we are the chosen of Jara.'

'Jara?' said Elinor. She recalled the name. Something Gillien had said. 'Who . . .'

Iryn Jagga laughed softly. 'Such innocence! *Who* is Jara?' He turned to one of the men gathered about. 'Who is Jara? she asks. Tell her.'

The man so addressed stepped forward a pace. He wore the same sombre colours as the rest, but was dressed in a long robe rather than tunic and breeches. About his neck hung a large golden medallion. There was a face depicted upon it, male, human, commanding. 'Jara is the great force, the moving spirit of the world,' the man said. 'The rain is his seed which he pours down upon the earth, impregnating her, making her crop. The wind is his breath. The heavens his domain, the stars his jewels, the sun and moon balls with which he plays, the . . .'

'Yes, yes,' Iryn Jagga interrupted. 'I'm sure she gets the basic idea.' He looked at Elinor. 'This is Ang Shen, Master Priest. He tends to be a little . . . excessive at times, I'm afraid.'

Ang Shen bowed. 'Only because of my great devotion.'

'Of course, of course,' Iryn Jagga agreed. 'A very devoted man indeed.'

To Elinor, Iryn Jagga said, 'The ordinary folk worship Jara at shrines. He's depicted as a handsome, robust figure of a man . . .' He smiled more broadly. 'Not unlike myself.'

Elinor stared. She felt an uncomfortable shiver go through her. They were playing with her, these men. She felt sure of it. But to what end?

'Folk make small sacrifices to Jara,' Iryn Jagga was saying, 'in supplication for his good will, giving him goats, fowl, that sort of thing. In their innocence, they believe him to be a real, existing being, whom they can ask to intercede for them in their daily lives.' Iryn Jagga laughed softly. 'We of the Inner Sanctions, of course, know better. He is . . .'

Turning to Ang Shen, he said, 'How should I put it?'

'Mere . . . personification,' the Master Priest replied.

'Exactly. Very nicely put. Mere personification.' Iryn Jagga shrugged. 'But if a personification keeps them happy . . . Who are we to deny them?'

He stepped closer to Elinor and raised his finger at her. 'But a personification must be a personification of *something*, must it not?'

'I . . . I suppose so,' she responded, seeing that he expected some sort of answer from her.

'She supposes,' Iryn Jagga repeated, looking across at the priest again for a moment. 'Well, you suppose correctly, girl. There is a great force that moves the world, a great, virile, *masculine* force. It has no face, but it exists nonetheless. Without it, the basic fabric of the world would collapse entirely. We name it Jara. It might be named anything. But it *is*.'

Iryn Jagga's handsome face had taken on a kind of light. His eyes shone eerily. 'The Ancients knew of this force. They were able to harness it and do . . . incredible things. And so will we again, one day. We are the chosen, girl, those who will carry on the great tradition of the Ancients. Ours is the task of recreating the world so that the greatness of the past can come to be once again.'

He shook his head. 'But first, we must correct the mistakes of the past. Oh, yes. Great though they were, the Ancients committed mistakes. In their greatness, they went too far, transgressing against the very laws of the vital force they served and used.' He bent close to Elinor, his face in hers. 'You have seen the results of that ancient error, girl. Abomination! Obscenity! Unclean mixtures of man and beast. A fatal sullying of the vital force of Jara. No wonder the world is in the sorry, disreputable shape that it is.'

Standing back, Iryn Jagga gestured to himself, and to the others behind him. 'But we of the Ancient Brotherhood of the Light have the wisdom and the power to change all that. It is our destiny to cleanse the world of these abominations. And then . . . *then* a new era will dawn. The force of Jara will flow through the world once more, unsullied, as it once did. The greatness of the past will return. Our great destiny will be *fulfilled*!'

At the last words, his voice had risen to a near-shout. He stood, arms extended, head back, panting with the very intensity of his speech. He took a long breath, another. Then he looked at Elinor accusingly. 'And *you* have been hindering that great destiny of ours.'

Elinor shivered. He was mad, this man. Mad as old Seer Skolt had been back in Minmi. Were they all like this, then, the inhabitants of these mouldering old Domains? Unable to accept

457

the ending of what once had been, seeing themselves as the chosen ones, those who would bring back all the lost greatness of the past. There was something pitiful about it.

'Well?' Iryn Jagga demanded of her. 'What have you got to say for yourself, you wicked, unnatural girl?'

Elinor swallowed. 'I . . .' She did not know how to respond.

'Ah . . .' Iryn Jagga breathed. 'Contrition, is it, that stills your tongue? That is good. Very good. I'm sure you must see the error of your ways by now. And you a *girl*. The fabric of the world is indeed in most serious disarray when the likes of you take up arms.' He shook his head sorrowfully, like a disappointed father. 'Whatever were you thinking of to do such a thing? What sort of upbringing were you given, then, in whatever crude, barbarian place you come from? Your mother should have known better than to allow such wicked, foolish notions into your head.'

Elinor bit back a sharp reply. It would do her no good to antagonize this man.

Iryn Jagga stood regarding her silently. Then he reached to his left side under his cloak and produced a sword, drawing it from the sheath.

With a pang, Elinor recognized it as hers.

The white blade shone like a bar of pure light. 'A beautiful thing,' Iryn Jagga said. 'Holding it, I begin to understand how you were able to do some of the things you did.' He made a little mocking bow to her. 'I thank you for it. I will make it my personal blade, treasured above all others. Does it have a name?'

'No,' Elinor lied, determined to deny the man whatever she might, no matter how petty.

Iryn Jagga shrugged. 'I will name it . . . Jara's Needle.' He ran the tips of his fingers along the gleaming blade in a careful, light caress. 'It is a beautiful thing, is it not? Who made it? From where did you steal it?'

'I didn't *steal* it,' Elinor replied, stung. 'It was given to me as a gift.'

'Oh, yes? And by whom, then?'

Elinor shrugged, regretting having said anything.

'I said, who gave it to you, girl?' Iryn Jagga's voice had gone suddenly hard. He stepped closer to her, lifted the sword, and carved a little chunk of flesh off her left forearm just above the manacle – all in one quick motion.

Elinor gasped, seeing the blood well up.

'I asked you a question, girl!' Iryn Jagga said. 'Are you going to answer me, or do I have to . . . persuade you further?'

Her arm stung like fire.

He took a menacing step towards her.

'It was Lord Mattingly,' she said quickly, unnerved by the very suddenness of what he had done to her. 'In Minmi.'

'So . . .' Iryn Jagga said. 'Mattingly's death gift. I heard something of that, girl. Though I had no idea it was *you* who had murdered him.' He shook his head. 'But I ought to have guessed easily enough.' He shrugged. 'See? Even *I* can make mistakes, overlook the obvious. Let that be a lesson to you.'

He examined the sharp point of the bright blade, where a little spot of blood dimmed its brightness. He snapped his fingers and one of his followers produced a kerchief. With this, he carefully wiped and polished the point till it was shining clean again, then flung the bloodied kerchief away, sheathed the blade, and slipped the scabbard back under his cloak.

He stood staring at Elinor for long moments. 'What *is* the world coming to,' he said finally, 'when a comely young girl such as yourself ends up committing such desperate and evil acts?'

'I haven't . . .' Elinor began.

But he cut her off. 'Don't try to deny it. I *know* what you have done. You must atone for your despicable actions, girl. You *must* atone. And we will be the means by which you can do that.'

He came close to her, put a hand upon her shoulder. 'You have been a confused and wicked girl. But we can remedy that. They will say of you: "Nothing became her in this life so much as the leaving of it".'

Elinor stared.

'I am grateful to you, in a way. For it was your violent and wicked actions that precipitated events. Without you, we would never have been *pushed* so. Who knows? It might have been decades yet before we moved to make all this land ours again, as it once was. Jara works in mysterious ways. Who would have thought he would use *you*, a wicked, ignorant

459

foreign girl, as his instrument to bring us to our promised destiny? Perhaps I shall live now to see the greatness of the past reborn in my own lifetime – something I never looked to witness. These are great times in which we live. Exciting times. Do you not agree?'

Elinor swallowed. She felt sick and numb.

Iryn Jagga looked at her and shook his head sadly. 'But you will miss all that, girl. For now, for you, there remains only the one last deed.' He smiled. 'You must recant.'

'Wha-what?' Elinor said, her voice hoarse.

'Here in Sofala,' Iryn Jagga said, 'we have traditions, ancient and venerable. The poor, atrocious spawn of our forefathers' errors must be cleansed. Oh, yes. But not in any haphazard fashion. They suffer, those walking, flying, crawling abominations. They suffer from the very unnaturalness of their condition. And we offer them surcease from that suffering. They should never have come into being, you see. They are too unnatural, too . . . fragile.'

Iryn Jagga bent close to her once again, the violet scent he wore encompassing her. 'So we offer them the Ceremony of Cleansing, where they may relinquish their poor, crippled selves and find the oblivion for which they all secretly yearn.' He smiled thinly. 'Public ritual is important to a community's wellbeing, don't you agree? The Ceremony of Cleansing serves to knit people together here in Sofala, to reaffirm basic values.'

'What makes you so certain you know what humanimals *secretly* wish for?' Elinor said, stung by the man's monumental arrogance.

'You are in no position,' Iryn Jagga said, 'to ask impertinent questions.' He slapped her then, hard, with his open palm. Her head rocked, thumping against the cold stone wall behind her, making her bruised skull sing with pain.

'You will be at the next Ceremony of Cleansing, girl. For, you see, it is not only the brute abominations who need to be cleansed. Sometimes human folk fall into error, such error as requires strong remedy. And, sometimes, an example needs to be made. So, before all of Sofala, you will publicly recant the error of your ways, recounting your evil acts, your wicked passions, your twisted desires.'

460

Elinor stared at him, unbelieving. 'I will do no such thing!'

'And then,' Iryn Jagga continued, ignoring her interruption, 'we will absolve you and give you the release *you* secretly wish for, and send your soul away to Jara, who will judge you as you deserve. Public confession, absolution, release. What more could one ask?'

'I will do no such thing!' Elinor repeated.

Iryn Jagga smiled. 'Oh, but you *will*, girl.' He gestured to the chamber in which they were. 'Look about you. There are numerous methods of . . . persuasion here. Would you like to see an example?'

Elinor only stared.

Iryn Jagga motioned to one of the demon-masked men. 'Show her.'

The man padded off.

He returned in a short while dragging a young woman after him. She was hardly more than a girl, Elinor saw, naked, filthy, all skin and bones, eyes wide with terror.

'Ah . . .' Iryn Jagga breathed. 'Good choice.'

The demon-mask flung her upon a sort of low wooden table and he and one of the others began strapping her in, by wrists and ankles.

'No!' the girl wailed, thrashing about. '*No!*'

The third demon-mask had approached the glowing brazier by this time and had withdrawn a long, slender skewer. It had a wooden handle and a sharp point which glowed white-hot so that the air about it shimmered.

The helpless girl screamed.

Elinor looked away.

'None of that,' Iryn Jagga said, wagging his finger at her. 'Hold her head,' he ordered one of the men behind him.

The man held Elinor's head with his hands in a vice-like grip, aiming her vision at what was happening. It was all horribly familiar, horribly like the time in Skolt's chambers. But there, there had been Rannis and the rest of the Guard to come and save her. And now . . .

No such thing was likely to happen.

The demon-mask was approaching the girl with his glowing skewer. He set the white-hot metal against the skin of her inner thigh.

461

The girl screamed.

Elinor closed her eyes. She could hear the horrible *skriss* of the metal searing the poor girl's flesh.

'Watch!' Iryn Jagga's voice said, and something hit her bruisingly hard, in the ribs.

She opened her eyes, shuddering.

The demon-mask worked on the prostrate girl, inserting the skewer's white-hot tip in tender places, pressing its length against others, working quickly, with the skill of a perverted master craftsman until his poor shuddering victim went limp and quivering, slack-mouth and drooling and vacant-eyed.

Elinor felt sick.

'Remember this,' Iryn Jagga said to her then. 'You will do as I wish. *Exactly* as I wish. Or suffer the consequences.'

Elinor stared at him, so utterly shaken she could hardly breathe.

'Start her,' Iryn Jagga said then to the demon-masks.

They dragged her off the bench. Elinor tried to struggle, but they were three strong men and she could do nothing.

They did not strap her down, as she had feared. Instead, they flung her on to the floor in the middle of the chamber. As she watched, crouched there, the three of them armed themselves, each with a kind of flexible, cloth-wrapped club.

They began to beat her, hard blows across her back and sides.

'Not the face,' Iryn Jagga cautioned. 'We will need her face.'

The blows continued, on her shoulders, arms, elbows, knees, thighs. She tried to curl up into a protective ball, but no matter what position she attempted to take, they found some spot to hurt her.

It went on and on till she felt herself to be one huge, throbbing, agonizing bruise.

'Enough,' Iryn Jagga said.

Elinor lay prostrate, gasping. She held herself in, refusing to weep, refusing to cry out.

Iryn Jagga stepped over her, holding in his hand one of the clubs the demon-masks had been using. 'The beauty of these, you see,' he said with surreal casualness, 'is the padding. They won't break bones or skin. But they bruise. Oh, yes. And the bruises stiffen and get tender. *Very* tender.' He thwacked the club against her shoulder, softly.

462

She winced away.

'I will leave you now, girl.' He smiled. 'To let you stiffen. To let those poor bruises of yours get properly sensitive.' He prodded her on a tender spot with the end of the club, making her yelp involuntarily. 'And then we will commence again. And then employ hot iron, perhaps. Till you come to see reason. Till you come to see that the only thing left for you is to do *exactly* as I wish.'

He turned from her then, letting the club drop. 'Take her to one of the cells.' Then he strode out of the chamber, never looking back.

Two demon-masks dragged her past the brazier to where a long corridor led away from the torture chamber into dimness. The corridor was lined with small, individual cells on both sides – three-walled cubicles, open to the corridor, with prisoners manacled to the back wall. One of the two demon-masks held a sputtering torch aloft, and by its wavering light she caught a series of glimpses of the pitiful, sprawled occupants as she was dragged past, their white, haggard faces seeming to leap out at her in the torchlight, their hollow eyes glinting.

The demon-masks flung her into one such three-walled cell at the corridor's farthest end. She fell with a groan, each muscle, each joint alight with throbbing pain. One of them grabbed up a short length of chain and quickly threaded it through her wrist manacles, securing it to the back wall.

Then they went, taking the torch, leaving her alone in utter darkness.

It was like being in the grave again, alone in stifling dark. The cold stone of the floor made her very bones ache.

She wept, quivering with pain, the tears stinging her eyes. There was nothing else left for her to do.

XXXXVI

Somehow, despite everything, she must have slept, for she came to, groggy and hurting and stiff, to find blinding torchlight in her eyes and hard hands yanking her up.

Her bruised limbs were an agony, and she cried out.

'Gently, gently,' a voice said. 'Lift her easy.'

Elinor stood shivering. Torchlight danced. She squinted, trying to make sense of what was happening. Her little cell was filled with dark silhouettes. Her whole body was one long, stiff ache. It hurt even to breathe. Hands gripped her, at shoulder, arm, and hip, propping her up, keeping her immobile.

'Bring her along,' somebody said. 'But gently.'

The chain imprisoning her to the cell wall was unfastened and she was dragged away, none too roughly, and taken back down the cell-lined corridor to the big chamber at the far end. Her legs were too bruised and stiff to be of any real use – save to give her pain – and mostly those bringing her along dragged her, her feet trailing awkwardly.

In the big chamber Elinor made out a group of silent, sombre-clothed men gazing at her. At their fore, she recognized the cloaked form and handsome face of Iryn Jagga. Behind him, she saw . . .

Rannis!

He stared at her, his face shocked.

'Put her over there,' Iryn Jagga ordered those who had dragged her. They set her down on her feet against a wall, near the bench she had sat on earlier. She worked her way clumsily over to it, sat herself down, letting her legs stick out straight ahead of her. The scarred one burned as if acid had been poured all along it. She looked about, blinking, trying to find a way to breathe that did not hurt so much.

'Well . . .' said Iryn Jagga. 'Good morning, girl. I trust you slept well?'

Elinor said nothing.

'A little stiff this morning, are we?' he enquired with false solicitude, stepping closer to her.

Involuntarily, she flinched away.

Iryn Jagga shook his head sadly. 'Now, now. This is no way for you to behave. What do you think? That I will step up to you and start smacking you on your sore parts? Like this?' He stepped up to her and gave her a hard thwack in her bruised ribs with his fist.

She cried out. It felt like being hit by a hammer.

He did it again, hitting her bruised ribs another time, her arm when she tried to cover herself, kicking her in her thigh, thumping her back as she doubled over protectively. She fell off the bench, quivering, entirely undone for the moment by the agony his blows caused. Her mind was a blank, lit only by the white fire of the pain.

She must have fainted, for the next thing she knew, she was seated on the bench once more, her back against the cold stone wall, somebody's hand on her shoulder holding her still.

Iryn Jagga stood before her. 'Stand up, girl,' he ordered. 'Up!'

She tried, pushing off from the wall with her elbows. It took her three attempts. Her back muscles were agonizingly stiff. Every little lurch and shift sent stabs of pain through her spine and up into the back of her bruised skull. Finally, she was able to stand before him, gasping, swaying. She lifted her head, biting her lip at the pain it caused her to do so, and tried to look him in the eye.

He shook his head. 'Defiance still, is it?' He made a quick motion to somebody. 'Strip her.'

She was still dressed in tunic and trousers. They ripped these off her, leaving her naked and shivering. Iryn Jagga walked in a little circle around her, eyeing her. 'Hmm . . .' he said. 'This looks like an especially sore spot right here, I think.' He pinched her on her back, digging his nails in and twisting her flesh hard, right on one of the worst bruised spots.

Elinor cried out, tried to writhe away. But he hung on to the little fold of flesh he held between his fingers, and her pulling away merely made the pain all the worse. He twisted, pinched,

465

dug in with sharp nails, till he had manoeuvred her to her knees, weeping.

He let go, then. Walking around in front of her, he squatted down and lifted her chin in his hand. 'See what happens when you fight me? You only hurt yourself.' He shook his head. 'Elinor . . . Elinor! Why must you persist in being such a wicked girl?'

All she could do was look at him. Her back, where he had mauled her, was pulsing with fire. She could barely breathe.

He held out his thumb and index finger before her face. 'This was all I used, Elinor. Just this. And it *hurt*, did it not? The body is such a frail thing. We can see all your sore spots like this, Elinor. You can hide nothing from us. I might hit you here, for instance . . .' He jabbed his fingers stiffly against her left side just under the ribs. A lance of fiery pain shot through her chest. 'Or here.' He reached over and smacked the thigh of her bad leg, hard enough to make her head swim sickeningly.

Once more, he shook his head. 'And still you defy me. Well . . .' He made a little beckoning gesture with the fingers of one hand, and Elinor saw two of the demon-masked men come up, padded clubs in hand. 'Do her again,' Iryn Jagga ordered.

'No!' Elinor cried. '*No* . . .'

But the demon-masks began on her with the clubs, going for the sore spots, hitting her harder and harder, mercilessly, the clubs smacking into her bruised flesh like great hammers, hitting her, smashing her, an agony of battering blows, on and on . . . till she was wailing and screaming and weeping and helpless, crawling across the cold stone floor, all her determination, all her pride, all her will beaten out of her, crawling to beg Iryn Jagga to stop it.

'What?' he said, looking down at her, arms crossed over his chest. 'I can't hear you, girl. What did you say?' He waved the demon-masks away. 'Speak up, then.'

'Please . . .' she sobbed. '*Please* make them . . . make them *stop*.'

Iryn Jagga smiled. 'I think not. Not yet.'

'*Please*!' Elinor cried. 'Oh, *please*. I beg of you . . .'

'And if I do as you ask, girl? What then? Will you, in turn, do as *I* ask? Will you do *everything* I ask of you?'

Elinor hesitated. Now that they had stopped hitting her, and she could draw breath, some last vestige of her old self came back, her old will still not entirely broken. She glanced about, desperately, looking for something, anything that might help . . .

It was a mistake. She knew it, too late.

Iryn Jagga saw it in her, that flicker of resistance. 'More,' he said.

But to her surprise, and uncertain relief, he raised his hand to forestall the demon-masks. Turning, he beckoned somebody over.

Rannis, pale-faced and staring.

'You do it,' Iryn Jagga said to him. He motioned to one of the demon-masks, who held out a padded club.

Rannis shook his head, staring at Elinor where she lay sprawled and gasping on the cold stone floor.

'Do it!' Iryn Jagga snapped.

'No!' Rannis said, fending off the club that was being thrust at him. 'Not that.'

'Do it,' Iryn Jagga repeated, his voice cold as ice. 'Or *you* will be next.'

Rannis shook his head. 'No. you can't make me do this. This is . . . you *cannot* do this!'

Iryn Jagga smiled. 'A simple enough choice, boy. You or her. Which is it to be?'

Rannis stared about him, stricken.

'Decide,' Iryn Jagga said. 'Quickly!'

Rannis took the club in shaking hands.

'Do it!' Iryn Jagga snapped.

Rannis hit her, a soggy blow.

'Harder,' Iryn Jagga ordered. '*Much* harder. Or it will be you next, boy. Remember.'

Rannis hit her again, harder. 'Forgive me,' he gasped. 'I never . . . How could I . . .'

'*Harder*!' Iryn Jagga commanded.

Rannis went at it, then, in a ragged, gasping frenzy, urged on by Iryn Jagga's harsh commands, thumping her with the club, blow after blow, with him weeping, her weeping . . . till she wailed and screamed and begged Iryn Jagga to end it, giving up all pretence of resistance, begging shamelessly like a dog,

467

crawling under Rannis's blows, pleading and crying and blubbering.

Iryn Jagga waved Rannis to a stop then, smiling. 'I ask you again, girl. Will you do *everything* I require of you?'

Elinor did not hesitate this time. 'Oh, yes,' she said quickly. 'Anything. *Anything.* Only make it stop.'

'Very well,' he said.

Rannis staggered back against the wall, flinging the club away, and doubled over, head in his hands.

Iryn Jagga walked over to him. 'Good boy,' he said, patting Rannis on the head like a hound. 'Sensible boy.'

Rannis glared at him. 'How could you . . .'

'Shush,' Iryn Jagga said. 'Be still.'

Rannis stared at Elinor, his face crumpled with grief and guilt and confusion. 'Elinor . . .' he gasped. 'For . . .'

'I said, be *still*,' Iryn Jagga ordered. He slapped Rannis once, hard, on the face.

Elinor lay on the floor, gasping, moaning. Her body was all one terrible, blazing, throbbing, agonizing hurt. Her chest heaved from the sobbing, and her breath came in short, painful, blubbering gasps. Her mind teetered . . .

But they let her be for long moments, and, slowly, she recovered herself a little. She lay on her side, curled up foetally, her head buried in her sore arms.

'You are mine, girl,' Iryn Jagga said.

Elinor kept silent. She did not dare even lift her eyes.

'*Mine*,' Iryn Jagga repeated. 'To do with as I will.'

Elinor shuddered. His words rang in her mind. There was something oddly familiar about them . . .

It came to her in a sudden flash of recollection: Seer Skolt gloating over her, she paralyzed and helpless. 'You are *mine*, girl,' Skolt had said. 'To do with as I will.'

Elinor felt a little jolt of recognition go through her. Skolt had been just as arrogantly, absolutely certain of himself as this Iryn Jagga. Her situation then had seemed just as hopeless as now . . .

There was no reason, she cautioned herself, to think that anybody would come to her rescue here – least of all Rannis. But, somehow, the fact that Iryn Jagga had used the very same words as Skolt gave her a little burst of hope. It was utterly foolish, no doubt. But she could not help but feel that Iryn Jagga had somehow damned himself by using those selfsame words.

The notion was like a little glowing ember inside her, warming her. She knew better, though, than to let any slightest hint of such a thing show.

'Elinor,' Iryn Jagga was saying. 'Come here to me.'

She tried to rise to her feet.

'No,' he said. 'On your hands and knees. Crawl.'

Elinor almost hesitated then, but caught herself in time and did her best to make it seem like mere painful stiffness on her part. She crawled to him, slowly, stiffly, groaning and panting.

'Kiss my boots,' Iryn Jagga ordered.

She did, without hesitating.

What did it matter? She would grovel. She would crawl. She would agree to do whatever Iryn Jagga demanded. But inside herself, she would cherish that little, buried ember of hope, of secret resistance. And if the right moment ever did come . . .

'That's my good girl,' he said, patting her head as if she were an obedient hound. He took her face in his hands, then, and turned it up to his so that he was looking into her eyes.

She was afraid he might see the hidden spark in her. But no. He was too certain of himself, too sure of his own power. He looked now only to see beaten submission in her – and saw only that.

'I am nobody's girl,' she said to him in the safety of her own mind, looking him straight in the eyes. 'Least of all *yours*.' It was the old trick from Long Harbour that she had used so often with her mother and Jago – she had all but forgotten. Contrition, submission, being a good girl . . . all that for appearance's sake. But she could say what she liked, silently, in her own mind, and none be any the wiser.

'Stupid, shit-for-brains maniac!' she cursed Iryn Jagga silently, looking straight at him, keeping her face empty.

Letting her go, he straightened up.

For a moment, she thought he had seen into her. Her heart lurched.

But no . . . He was smiling down at her, all self-satisfaction.

It was a secret victory she had won, for all its pettiness, and it warmed her.

'Now, girl,' he was saying, 'I will tell you what you must say. It is all most simple, really. You must say you were led astray, and that you committed wicked acts, but that you now know better and repent.'

Elinor only looked at him.

'Here. These are the words you will use.' Iryn Jagga took out a roll of ochre parchment from inside his cloak somewhere, opened it out, began to read aloud. '"I have been most wicked. I have committed acts against the will of Jara, terrible acts, violent acts. I have killed and violated innocent men. I have tortured innocent men for the very pleasure of it . . ."'

Something in Elinor revolted at this. She could not help it.

Iryn Jagga glanced coldly at her, went on reading. '". . . tortured for the very pleasure of it. I have associated with unclean animals. I have had unlawful knowledge of unclean animals . . . I committed these terrible deeds in wilful ignorance. But now I see the error of my ways. Now I repent. Now I am most heartfelt sorry. Forgive me. Forgive me. I beg from you absolution . . . absolution and peace."'

Iryn Jagga looked at her over the parchment. 'You will commit this to memory. Exactly these words. Is that clear?'

Elinor nodded quickly, knowing the price of hesitation, keeping her face scrupulously free from anything but compliance.

'Good,' Iryn Jagga said. Then he turned to some of the men standing near. 'Take her to one of the guest rooms,' he ordered. 'Feed her, clothe her. Keep her there.'

The men reached down to her and lifted her up, not ungently.

'We will talk again, girl,' Iryn Jagga said. He handed the parchment to one of her guards. 'To make certain you know your lines for the Cleansing.' He took a step towards her, reached a hand out. 'In the meantime . . .' He struck her in the ribs, hard enough to take her breath away. 'I can bring you back down here at any time. And there is still the hot iron, remember.' With that, he turned his back on her and stalked away, his dark cloak swirling behind him.

His entourage followed after, as if sucked out of the chamber by his departure. She glimpsed Rannis amongst them, white-faced, staring back at her, looking as if he were going to be sick.

The sight of him filled her with anger and pity. He had taken one too many steps down a bad road. It was a road she determined never to go down herself, not to be turned so to betrayal of friends and allies, whatever the cost . . .

As the men hauled her up into daylight, their hard thumbs digging into her sore flesh, she vowed silently, fervently, to herself, with all the strength of will she had remaining, that, do as he might, she would never, ever allow Iryn Jagga to possess her wholly.

Never.

XXXXVII

It was days before she could move again, so stiff and agonizingly sore was she. And more days after that before her bruised limbs became anything like reliable in their movements. She suffered blinding headaches, could not keep any sort of food down. Even simple sleep was hard, for the pain nagged at her too unremittingly.

Iryn Jagga shook his head, visiting her, clucked his tongue like a doting father. 'Poor girl,' he said, patting her softly. 'Do you see now the results of error?'

He sat down next to her on the hard little bed that was all the furniture in this stone cell in which they kept her. Without further preamble, he took out the parchment. 'Now repeat after me: "I have been most wicked. I have committed acts against the will of Jara . . ."' He stopped, looked at her, jabbed her with a hard finger in her bruised ribs. 'Repeat it!'

'"I ha . . . hav . . ."' she coughed, swallowed, tried again. '"I have been most . . ."'

'Wicked,' he finished for her. 'Say it.'

'"I have been most . . . wicked."'

He nodded, smiled, his handsome face lighting up. 'Yes. Good.' He turned to the parchment again, began reading. '"I have been most wicked. I have committed acts against the will of Jara, terrible acts, violent acts."' Again he stopped, looking at her.

'"I . . . I have been most wicked,"' she said, and went on to repeat what he had read so far – though stumblingly. And added, silently, in her own mind: 'An ill death may you die, you arrogant arse-hole!'

'"I have killed and violated innocent men,"' he read on, oblivious. '"I have tortured innocent men for the very pleasure of it . . ."'

472

Over and over he made her repeat the parchment's contents, a dozen, twice a dozen times.

And then he walked out and left her for a day – or two, perhaps; she was none too certain about the passage of time.

He came back again, once, twice, more times than she could keep straight in her pain-fuddled mind, reading the words to her, demanding she recite, correcting, slapping, smiling, scowling, pacing back and forth . . .

He was utterly mad, she decided. *Utterly*.

Time passed. She ate when she could, slept when she could, a sleep troubled by nightmares of clubs and the laughing face of Iryn Jagga that would send her shooting into wakefulness, her heart pounding.

Mostly, she sat or lay on the hard little bed, unmoving, staring dazedly at the stone ceiling, grateful with all her heart to be here and not down in the dungeon . . .

There were times when she could not help but wonder anxiously what might be happening in the world, what Gyver and Collart and the rest were doing . . . hoping against hope that they had done nothing foolish and were still safe and whole and alive.

She lay, sometimes, and made wild, impossible plans for escape, aching to be free from this terrible place, imagining herself overpowering her guards, her friends magically appearing to spirit her away to safety.

And there were times she lay in despair, feeling herself irrevocably cut off from everything and everybody that mattered to her and cast adrift, feeling in her guts that she was doomed here, that all she would ever see again of the world would be this little stone cell – and whatever terrible ceremony or other it was for which mad Iryn Jagga was grooming her.

But, as much as she could, she lay on the hard little bed and tried to will herself simply to recover, grimly determined, putting all the will she had left into encouraging her beaten flesh to restore itself, rebuild itself.

And, slowly, she did recover, feeling the strength begin to come back to her limbs – blue and yellow and green with bruising though they still were. The headaches lessened, stopped. Her bruises diminished, her swollen lips began to feel normal again.

And then, one morning in the chill grey light of dawn, she came out of sleep to hear the sound of footsteps outside the locked door of her cell.

The door was flung open and Iryn Jagga himself stood there. 'The day is here, girl,' he announced, smiling hugely, as if it were the best of news he was bringing her. 'Up, you lazy bones. Up!'

Men came rushing in, hauled her from the bed. With rough speed, they stripped her of her own pitifully ragged clothing and dressed her in new garments, sombre as all the Brothers' clothing was, pushing her into long trousers, leather shoes and a long-sleeved tunic. Only her head and hands showed, and all her bruising was hidden.

They hustled her out of her cell. In the hallway outside, Iryn Jagga looked at her critically for a moment, then nodded. 'Remember your lines,' he said, prodding her once in the ribs, hard, with a stiff finger. Then, without a word further, he whirled and marched off.

The men holding her took her away in another direction entirely.

Through a long series of hallways and corridors they dragged her, till eventually they came to what seemed to be a small stable. There was the musty odour of straw, a series of little stalls, and a cart standing there in an open area. It was smallish, square, with big wheels. An ox-like creature stood hitched to it, chewing patiently on its cud.

The men hauling Elinor along lifted her bodily up into this cart and chained her in place, by waist and ankles, so that she stood in the middle with the sides of the cart hip-high about her.

A driver climbed on to a little perch in the cart's front and flicked a whip at the ox-beast. The cart started off with a jerk that made Elinor gasp, sore as she still was, and nearly toppled her. The chains held her roughly in place, but not enough to support her, and she had to grab at the cart's rough wooden sides with her hands to steady herself.

The stable doors opened, letting a flood of bright, early-morning sunlight stream in. The cart moved outside on to a lane, the iron-shod wheels making a great clatter on the cobblestones. The air was cool and fresh after all her days inside. Elinor took a long, revivifying breath, and another, throwing back her head and opening her lungs to it.

Down the lane the cart went, and thence out into a broad street. For an instant, Elinor could not make sense of what lay ahead. The street seemed to be lined on either side with queer, shuddering walls. A great *hruummm* filled the air. Then she realized it was people, hundreds of people, packed into a jostling, noisy mass on both sides of the street.

The crowd hooted and jeered and screamed at her as she was drawn past. Somebody flung a rotten fruit of some sort. It splattered against the cart's side near her, leaving a wet red strawberry mark – with too much of the look of fresh blood about it.

She tried to flinch away, but there was nowhere to go. More pieces of fruit followed the first, one smacking against her ear with enough force to make her reel. The crowd laughed.

The cart's wheels rattled and thumped on the cobblestones, and Elinor was pitched about. Rounding a corner, they hit an unexpected pothole and she was flung violently against the side. One of the crowd reached out and grabbed at her, trying to drag her down. A hate-filled face was thrust against hers, shouting something unintelligible. Only the iron grip of the chains kept her from being hauled away into the screaming, seething press of people.

Armed guards waded in, then, thumping at the people with long sticks they carried, and the cart went onwards.

Elinor did not understand any of this. The screaming. The hate. The very air seemed thick with it. She felt faint and sickly. What was *wrong* with these people?

There were more carts on the street now, she realized, ahead and behind hers, forming a kind of procession. She tried to ignore the screaming crowd as best she could, concentrating instead on the other vehicles, trying to see what passengers they might hold. She was frustrated by the curving street, the bumping and uncertain cart, the distraction of objects hurled at her. But she did catch one quick glimpse of what seemed to be a large bear a few carts ahead. She immediately thought of Scrunch, and her heart quailed. But it was impossible. Scrunch could not be here, no more than any of the others could. Surely they would not be so stupid as to walk right into the ruthless arms of the Brothers?

The carts clattered on through the lines of screaming people, following a road that curved into a long arc, eventually giving on to a large square, bright in the morning sunshine. Elinor gasped. The whole of the square was packed. There must be a thousand people. Only a narrow laneway lay open, roped off and cordoned by armed guards, leading to a sort of stage in the square's centre. Down this open lane the line of carts went, with people screaming on either side, hands reaching out threateningly. The very air quivered with the force of emotion that was let loose here. Elinor shuddered, cowering instinctively.

The cordoned laneway ended in a clear space before the stage – if that were the right word to describe such a structure. It was partly a wooden platform, constructed of raw new wood, shining in the morning sunlight. But it was also part stone. Huge blocks of old, red-grey, black-veined rock. With a start, Elinor recognized it as the same stone structure she had passed in the empty square, the evening she had first entered into Sofala, where she had seen the pitiful, dangling form of Pallas the stork. But now the stone structure was altered. Along with the wooden stage, a kind of huge platform had been added, forming a dais. And upon this dais . . . For the first time, Elinor saw a representation of what had to be Jara.

Iryn Jagga had been right, the statue did resemble him, tall and broad-shouldered, with regular, extraordinarily handsome features. It stood twice the height of a tall man, hewn from some kind of pure black stone, without blemish or flaw of any sort. Whoever had created it must have been more than a master craftsman for the dead stone appeared to hold life itself. Jara stood, legs wide apart, arms out as if in greeting, or threat, or dismissal – Elinor could not tell. The great black limbs seemed to quiver with hidden life and strength. The face seemed alive, the expression intent, the eyes to look out at those of everyone in the square with a cold, supreme intelligence.

Elinor shivered, staring up at that perfect, ebony face. She felt sick in her belly. Her head swam, her left palm flared up in a sudden torment of itching. She remembered, suddenly, the dream she had shared with Spandel, of the two faces, the Lady's and a great, dark, menacing male face, and of blood . . .

That great face was before her now, utterly implacable, the expression one of all-powerful control. She felt herself in the presence of something greater than herself; greater than anyone or anything here in the square.

As she stood, chained helplessly in the cart, staring wide-eyed and shaken, Iryn Jagga stepped out on to the wooden platform of the stage, handsome and imposing in his dark garb, the gold circlet glinting on his brow. Elinor's own sword hung at his belt, shining and looking like new. The crowd erupted into a frenzy of cheering and shouting and wailing. Iryn Jagga raised his arms, both hands high, then partially lowered them till he stood in exactly the same position as the great black statue of Jara. The pose was one of benediction. But also one of calling up, of beckoning.

Iryn Jagga played the crowd, opening his arms in a kind of encompassing gesture that made the jam-packed people shriek all the louder, then lowering them, hands out flat, palms down to soften the noise. Louder, softer, in, out, drawing them in, shrieking and shouting and wailing like the damned; letting them out, panting and pale-faced and almost silent.

In . . .

Out . . .

Elinor felt her heart surge involuntarily when the crowd leaped up at Iryn Jagga's bidding, her ears ringing with the shouts and cries, and she felt her muscles go lax and her lungs empty when he let them go.

In . . .

Out . . .

Elinor felt herself reelng dizzily. It was like a great breath that animated all here. In . . . Out . . . Binding them into some manner of uncanny union, all focused on Iryn Jagga and the great dark statue of Jara. She saw men and women in the crowd flinging themselves mindlessly into the air, their mouths open in wordless screams, faces white and ecstatic. The square was a sea of seething, surging, ebbing chaos.

And then Iryn Jagga raised his arms high above his head and held them there for long climactic moments before lowering them, slowly, till he had again resumed the exact same pose as the statue, his whole self as immobile.

The crowd settled, till all movement, all sound, had ceased, and the people stood about, eerily silent, eerily intent, staring expectantly at the stage.

For long, long moments, Iryn Jagga stayed entirely motionless. The utter stillness of the crowd held, while an invisible tension built, like a cord being wound round about and through all those gathered here, pulling tighter and tighter and tighter till it seemed human flesh and bone could bear no more and the crowd would break apart into wailing bits.

But Iryn Jagga moved, lifting his arms. The crowd let out a great, communal sigh.

'We are gathered here today,' he shouted, his strong voice carrying easily across the square, 'for a great *Cleansing*!'

The crowd roared.

Iryn Jagga held up his hands to quieten them, a little smile on his face. When they had stilled, he repeated, 'For a *Cleansing*, so that we may move ourselves further along towards the great *destiny* which awaits us!'

Again, the crowd went wild, shouting and screaming themselves hoarse.

When he could be heard once more, Iryn Jagga continued: 'Many years ago, our forefathers brought forth into this land a great promise . . . a *wonderful* promise. They ruled this land, as they were *meant* to, for they were the *chosen* ones. But what happened to them?'

The crowd murmured; it was like the sound of an uneasy sea.

Iryn Jagga raised his hands, palms down, quieting the mass of people once more. 'What happened to them, I say? They went too far. They created too much. They defied the very laws of Jara himself and brought into the world things that should never have been. And what happened to them then?' Iryn Jagga let his arms drop, hung his head momentarily. 'They were . . . *punished*. Their world was torn apart. And now *we*, their descendants, must build again. We must atone for their mistaken deeds. We must create a new order, a new world, a new destiny. For now it is *we* who are the destined, *we* who are the chosen, who will rule the world once more as we are destined to. But we will not make the same errors our great

478

forefathers made. For we may be weaker than them, but we are wiser. We will cleanse the world of their mistaken creations. We will make the world ready for the power of Jara to flow through it!'

Iryn Jagga paused, shook himself. 'And then . . . *then* we will take our rightful place amongst the great and fashion such a paradise as has never existed before in this world and will never exist again!'

The crowd roared out its approval in a great, ragged wash of sound.

'Bring on the first!' Iryn Jagga cried.

From one of the carts, a brace of guards dragged a furred creature. Initially, Elinor could not recognize what it was. Then she saw it was a sort of huge rabbit, with tiny ears – not unlike the one which had come to see her back at Margie. The poor creature was quivering and wailing pitifully.

'Bring it to the altar!' Iryn Jagga shouted.

The guards dragged it to a cupped platform set into the stone at the feet of the statue of Jara, flung the poor creature down and quickly chained it in place there. The crowd hooted and screamed and threw things. The furred creature cowered, whimpering.

'Here!' Iryn Jagga cried, pointing an accusing finger at the poor, shuddering humanimal. '*Here* is the living embodiment of our forefathers' errors. *Here* is the living embodiment of that which prevents us from achieving our great destiny. *Here* is that which must be destroyed to make the world a better place!'

At a sudden gesture from Iryn Jagga, a kind of curtain was flung aside and a group of men filed up on to the stage to stand behind him. To her surprise, Elinor spied Rannis amongst them, white-faced and staring.

From the ranks of these men, two came marching out on to the stage. One was the Master Priest Elinor had seen in the dungeon, dressed in the same dark robes he had been wearing then, with the same large golden medallion he had carried. He held it up now from a gold hanging chain, for the crowd to see, the image of Jara glinting in the fresh morning sunshine. The medallion itself seemed to shine like a little sun.

The crowd roared.

479

Next to the Master Priest stood the second man, dressed all in black: trousers, tunic, boots and gloves. He wore a painted wooden demon-mask, like the torturers in the dungeon had. In his hand he held a long, intricately bladed implement, a cross between a sword and a lance. It was polished iron, and glinted coldly in the light.

At his appearance, the crowd stilled, tense and expectant.

'The Liberator of soiled souls!' Iryn Jagga cried.

The masked man held aloft the intricate blade he carried, and the crowd cheered raggedly.

The Master Priest stalked over towards the furred creature on the stone altar at the feet of Jara. '*You*!' he shouted harshly, holding the gold medallion on high. 'Abomination in the sight of all true men. *Animal*!'

The furred creature looked up, eyes wide and white with terror.

'You, who burn with the light of human awareness, who burn with the bright light of human thought. Pitiful, unnatural creature that you are . . . You must be cleansed, so that the world may be cleansed!'

The demon-masked man, who had drawn close to the dais, lifted his blade, brought it forward in a swift, glinting thrust.

The furred creature shrieked, a high, terrified, shrill cry that was cut off in mid-note. The blade went in, the complex, intricate edges of it tearing flesh and rupturing bone. Blood flooded the altar. The poor furred body was lifted from the stone by the force of the blow, seeming to hover in the air for a long, terrible moment, shuddered, pouring blood. Elinor saw its eyes flash white, saw the final horror and agony clear in them.

The demon-masked man tore his blade out, leaving the body in a quivering heap on the stone for an instant. Then he brought the blade down edgeways in a sharp, hard stroke, and severed the head from the body entirely.

The Master Priest darted in and grabbed the head before it had a chance to topple off the altar. He stepped back, holding the dripping, grisly thing aloft triumphantly in one hand, the golden Jara-medallion swinging from its hanging chain in the other.

The crowd roared and stamped and shouted frenziedly.

Elinor thought she would be sick.

They brought on another trembling, helpless humanimal captive, and another after that, and yet another, murdering them all on the altar before the black statue, till a row of dripping, grisly trophies dangled from a rack to one side, and the stone cup of the altar ran red and wet with the poor souls' blood.

When it came to the turn of the bear Elinor had seen earlier, she expected a struggle – he was big enough and strong enough to cause trouble. But there was none. The bear shuffled up to the dais, pushed and hauled and prodded by armed men. He aimed a single, listless swat at one of them, that was all. He must be in the same despairing, self-destructive state she had seen Scrunch in, Elinor thought, come to the Brothers for release. Or perhaps it was the very power of the screaming crowd itself . . .

On the stone altar, the poor creature cowered, whimpering, and the blade took him as it had all the others.

Then the next was brought up to be butchered.

And the next.

The crowd became a wild, seething thing, like some single, great ferocious entity, surging forward and back at each fatal stroke of the demon-masked executioner's intricate and deadly blade. Elinor felt her hair standing on end, her belly tight as a clenched fist.

And then it was her turn.

The people packed into the square went silent as she was unchained from the cart and dragged up to the stage by four big men who held her tight.

'Remember your lines,' Iryn Jagga warned her in a coldly quiet voice, leaning close.

Elinor nodded quickly, compliantly. But she had no intention of reciting any part of the confession he had made her memorize. She had come to a bleak acceptance that there would be no miraculous, last moment escape for her from this. She would end her life here as the poor humanimals had, spitted and torn by the demon-masked executioner's weapon.

But if that were to be . . . then she was *not* going to cooperate with Iryn Jagga. She would not become another Rannis for him.

Iryn Jagga was addressing the crowd: 'We have here a woman . . . a woman who has led a bloody and misguided life, a woman who has done wicked, wicked deeds, a woman blind to the divine and inviolate dictates of great Jara.'

The crowd shouted, roared, shivered with riotous, righteous fury.

'But Jara works in mysterious ways. For he has used this woman as the instrument by which our great destiny is furthered. And, through her, we have received a *special* gift.' He unhooked Elinor's sword from his belt and held it aloft, still sheathed. 'Jara's Needle, it shall be named.' He drew it, then, waving it above his head, the perfect white blade shining bright and sharp.

The crowd roared madly.

'Not only . . .' Iryn Jagga went on, sheathing the blade and hooking it to his belt once more. 'Not only does Jara use her to deliver this gift, but he has also been the force through which she has seen the error of her ways! Such is always the way with those who oppose Jara. And so with she. She *has* seen her error and *does* repent.' He gestured to the men holding Elinor, and they thrust her forward on to the gory wet altar before the great statue of black Jara.

Elinor stumbled, going down on her knees, feeling the bloody, wet surface of the stone under her. She tried to get up, in a sudden desperate attempt to leap away – for with the chains off her there was nothing securing her to the altar. She could leap off, away through the crowd . . .

But her limbs would somehow not obey her. Try as she might, she could not lift herself from her hands and knees. A strange buzzing filled her ears, making the bones of her skull vibrate uncomfortably. She blinked, squinted, keeping her vision in focus only with difficulty. Staring up at the black stone face of Jara, she gasped. It seemed to move, the stone eyes to gaze down upon her with cold, pitiless awareness.

It had to be an illusion of some kind. Cold stone did not suddenly take on life!

But her skull resonated painfully, and she found it hard to get enough breath. The cold black stone eyes stared down at her, transfixing her, freezing her.

'Speak!' Iryn Jagga commanded her. 'Speak your

renunciation, wicked girl, before we grant you the final release you crave. Speak before great Jara and be cleansed. Speak! *Speak!*'

Elinor bit her lips. She would not. Not one word . . .

But her mouth opened, and the words came: '"I have been most . . . wicked. I have committed acts against . . ."' She tried to stop it, tried to close her mouth, to bite her own tongue. But to no avail. '". . . against the will of Jara. I have committed terrible acts, violent acts . . . I have killed and violated innocent men. I have tortured innocent men for the very pleasure of it . . ."'

It was a nightmare, she trapped and helpless, reciting everything Iryn Jagga had demanded of her, whether she willed it or no. A helpless ineffectual pawn.

A sudden fury filled her, then. It was insupportable, this. She would not . . . would *not* allow it to continue.

With every shred of will and strength and effort she had left in her, she flung herself flat against the bloody stone surface of the altar, smacking her face painfully against the stone, tasting blood: her own and the poor humanimals' who had died before her.

The words coming from her faltered.

'Speak!' Iryn Jagga shouted. '*Speak!*'

The Master Priest stood over her, the golden medallion swaying in his hand from the hanging chain. He held it aloft, the golden Jara-image swinging.

For long, frozen instants, the world seemed to stand still for Elinor. The swinging, golden medallion before her was suddenly . . . familiar. She had seen something just like it once. Before coming here to Sofala. Before Minmi. Before . . .

She remembered dim firelight, shimmering air, a golden visage . . .

And then buried memory awoke, like a current suddenly loosed inside her: Mamma Kieran's hut, the old Wise Woman holding a small golden signet before her, the air shimmering with heat, the female face on the signet glowing, a face part human and part animal, long and slender of chin, pointy eared, with overlarge eyes.

Elinor shuddered. The humanimals' dreaming Lady . . .

It all came back to her in a rush, and she remembered how, in

483

Mamma Kieran's hut, she had envisioned a snarling dragon's head with glinting ruby eyes, the fanged mouth open, blood pouring forth in a bubbling gush – a bronze dragon with a tail unlike any natural beast's tail, long and straight like a rod, but flat, shining like a mirror . . .

The blade, surely . . .

And she recalled how a succession of strange images had filled her mind: a great, dark, shadowy figure, like a man-giant; a not quite human female face; a horde of furred creatures; a crowd of struggling, fighting folk . . .

It had all come to pass.

She blinked, seeing the Master Priest swing the golden medallion above her. She remembered the searing pain that Mamma Kieran's signet had caused her, the imprint of the Lady's strange face branded agonizingly into her left palm. She felt the pain again now, suddenly, her hand throbbing with it, as if memory had brought it to life. Looking down, she saw the image of that face gazing up at her now from her palm, watered with the life blood of the poor sacrificed humanimals.

She recalled her dream of the two faces, and remembered standing in the deep woods grotto, knee deep in cold water, staring at that same female face scribed on the moss festooned, mist-soaked rock, feeling her hand tingle upon the rough stone, sensing only the faintest stirrings then of the memory that filled her now . . .

The face of need, Mamma Kieran had named that image.

She saw, or seemed to see, that face before her now, the eyes alive, the pointy ears quivering. A long shiver went through her. Every hair on her body prickled erect.

The face seemed to grow. The eyes held hers. They were dark and alive, those eyes, shining and clear. Looking into them, Elinor felt something sweep through her in a sudden dizzying rush. Memory, and the bloody altar, and the crowded square about her dimmed, and for a timeless instant she experienced a kind of vision, perceiving the world wholly in all its moving complexity. But it was not the familiar world of trees and rocks and sky and breath and body that she saw. Instead, it was flowing shapes, like complex forms of patterned liquid, the Powers as great glowing currents moving through all, inspiriting all. And the myriad beings – of flesh and almost-flesh, of wood and leaf and air; she perceived them all as glowing, flowing vessels – danced the most intricate of dances about each other, and all was moving, all constantly changing, all in shifting, mutual balance.

And then . . . not.

She watched as the great balances were disrupted, the great dance clogged, the underlying shape of the world warped. Somehow, she understood what she was witnessing: the acts of the ancient southern Seers.

She saw now how their actions had deformed the deep patterns of the world, how they had bent all their energies into certain aspects of existence, culturing those, force-feeding them with their powerful wills, controlling and ordering and, in their folly, believing they had the strength and the wisdom to rule and direct the very forces of life itself. Until they had gone so far down that road that the world teetered, unbalanced, and the Seers wrought utter ruin upon themselves and all with whom they had dealings, tearing each other and all else apart like a pack of dogs driven mad by their own deeds.

But the very unbalance they left after them brought about a counterforce. Blind, groping, unguided – but there. Not of the nature of black Jara or the humanimals' Lady. Not even the Powers themselves, perhaps. Something larger, or wider, some enormous, blind will to balance.

Like water running down a complex slope, the force of rebalance flowed inexorably onwards. Except that the slope was composed of the world itself, and of people's lives – of *her* life. And the water was composed of moving forces the like of which no ordinary mortal person might easily comprehend.

Mamma Kieran, Tildie, Gillien . . . herself, others. Each a channel through which something flowed . . . something blind as water, persistent as water, groping, dribbling, gushing, pushing through lives like a current, blindly, with unhuman patience, unhuman persistence, each small aspect worked into the pattern feeding the next, and the next, endlessly, with painful slowness, but happening, rebalancing . . .

With an abrupt, shuddering wrench, Elinor lost the vision and came to herself upon the bloody altar. She gasped, shivered, tried to adjust, for her eyes insisted on seeing the shapes of the world about her as flowing, glowing vessels, moving like pulsating bladders, like limber snakes of soft radiance, like . . .

Above her, she made out the looming figure of the Master Priest.

Memory and vision, all of it . . . all the matter of only a few heartbeats, then. The priest was shrieking, swinging his golden Jara-medallion at her like a weapon, his face white and contorted.

Her left hand came up, of its own accord it seemed, and she caught the medallion in mid-air. The priest dropped the hanging chain, clutched at the medallion, tried to wrench it from her grasp. The air about her shimmered. The medallion grew hot, hotter. It was like the first time with Mamma Kieran, her hand burning agonizingly. But she had come to know pain by now – Iryn Jagga had taught her well. She was no longer the innocent girl who had timidly crept into Mamma Kieran's hut.

She howled, for the pain, for her fury, for very defiance at everything about her, howled like a mad woman, gripping the medallion, while the stink of burned flesh filled her nostrils.

The priest faltered, staggering back and letting the medallion go. He stared down in horror at his charred and ruined hands, wailing.

Elinor heard a sudden commotion nearby, startled shouts and curses and scuffling. Glancing quickly round, she saw Rannis struggling with the men about him on the stage.

Iryn Jagga was screaming something she could not make out. He drew the white blade in a flash of brightness.

Above her, the black statue of Jara towered, the stone eyes seeming to glare at her in monstrous fury. She stared at the burning hot medallion in her hand. The face of Jara stared back at her. Then, somehow, the Lady's face was there instead, as it had been on Mamma Kieran's small golden signet. Elinor turned and hurled the medallion, hard as she could, straight into black Jara's glaring stone eyes.

What followed was like an explosion.

And not . . .

The very air itself seemed to split asunder. Strange voices howled. For an instant it seemed to Elinor that she knelt amongst a great ethereal throng of ghostly humanimals, all the

486

poor souls who had given up their life's blood on this pitiless stone dais before this pitiless, awful black stone image.

And then the statue came apart above her – a little crack, a split, a shudder, an explosive collapse, black stone chunks tumbling everywhere, as if a great storm were blowing it apart. She felt herself lifted, thrown, landed with a painful, jarring thump on the wooden platform of the stage.

She dragged herself to her elbows, gasping. Her left hand throbbed. She saw the image of the Lady fading. She stared, shocked. Her hands were unhurt, both left and right.

About her, men were struggling to their feet, staring about glassy-eyed, gaping and shaken.

She saw Rannis elbow his way up. He rushed over to her, took her by the elbow. 'You all right, girl?' he asked, his voice no more than a hoarse croak.

Elinor nodded numbly, too shaken for words.

The dais and the towering black statue lay in tumbled and smoking ruins. Iryn Jagga knelt, stunned, staring. The bright sword lay gleaming by his side on the wooden stage, where he must have let it drop in his shock.

Rannis dived for it.

Iryn Jagga saw him, and clutched hastily after the sword. The hilt was beyond his reach, and so he reached for the blade itself. His hand went out, fingers encircling the bright metal, and he tried to jerk it over so that he could reach the hilt properly.

Elinor would never have done such a thing, having learned the terrible razor-edge of that blade.

Iryn Jagga jerked his hand back, howling, leaving the better half of three fingers behind.

Rannis darted in and lifted the blade away, gripping the hilt safely. He stood then, glaring down at Iryn Jagga, who knelt, clutching his maimed and bleeding hand to his breast. They stayed like that, frozen, for a long moment. Rannis's jaw worked spasmodically. His face was white and stricken, and the hand holding the sword shook.

Then Iryn Jagga threw himself backwards, over the stage, tumbling to the ground beneath, leaving behind a little trail of blood and the abandoned sheath of the bright sword.

Rannis took two steps after him, hesitated, then grabbed up the sheath, whirled round, and came dashing over to

Elinor. He hooked the sheath to his belt, pulled her to her feet, panting.

They had the stage to themselves. The square was in an uproar, with people screaming and scattering panic-stricken in all directions.

'Let's get *out* of here!' Rannis shouted.

She stared at him.

'Come *on*, girl! Don't stand there like a silly goose and stare at me! Now's our chance. Run. *Run*!' He grabbed her with one hand, the shining blade still in his other, and dragged her after him, taking the steps down the platform three at a time, hauling her along, keeping his feet she knew not how, the two of them spilling on to the cobblestones of the square and staggering away.

The crowd was in utter turmoil. 'Come *on*!' Rannis shouted, still holding on to her, and burst into the seething chaos of bodies, hewing a path with the bright blade. People scattered away from him, screaming.

The two of them ran, slipping and sliding, Rannis hacking mercilessly at those too slow to get out of their path. Bodies littered the square everywhere – dead or comatose, there was no telling. They leaped over them, kicked them aside, running till Elinor thought her heart would burst out of her mouth, running till they had made it out of the square and into a side street down which they staggered, away from the screams and shouts and panicking surge of the crowd.

Rannis sagged against a brick wall, gasping. 'You all right?' he asked.

Elinor nodded, bent over, lungs heaving, too spent for words.

She could hardly believe what had happened. The strange vision she had experienced . . . was it truth? Had there indeed been a hidden undertow to her life, then? A subterranean current running beneath all her actions, culminating, somehow, in the act back there for which she had been a channel. As if she had been a conduit through which something larger than herself had moved.

The Lady? Something more?

She did not know how to know. She felt emptied and filled, exhausted and exhilarated, shaken and shaking and confused.

'Come on,' Rannis urged. 'We're still not out of this yet.' He looked about him, shook his head worriedly. 'I'm not sure where we are. There's a gate . . .' He turned, peered down the street. 'That way, I think.' He looked the other way, scowled, shook his head, turned back in the first direction. 'At least this way takes us away from the square.'

'Rannis . . .' Elinor gasped.

He turned to her.

She looked at him and did not know what to say, how to begin.

He smiled a weary smile. 'Later,' he said. 'If we're still alive.'

She nodded, put a hand quickly to his cheek.

They ran, then, skittish and anxious and desperate, Rannis with the bright sword still in hand.

The street was deserted. And the next they entered. Turning the next corner after that, they startled a little ragged group of men who stood and stared, and fled the instant Rannis brandished the white blade at them.

'We're going to make it, girl,' he panted, grinning. 'I know where we are now. The gate's along by here.' He held up the sword. 'With *this*, we're going to make it!'

He set the pace, sprinting down the street.

Elinor struggled after him as quick as she could, catching up with him at the far end as he crouched at a corner, peering round. She knelt next to him, peeping cautiously round the corner as he was.

There was a gate all right, smaller than the one by which she had entered Sofala, but there and open before them.

And guarded.

'There's too many of them,' she said. 'Must be nearly a dozen.'

'So?' Rannis said.

'You can't, Rannis. We'll never . . .'

He hefted the shining blade and grinned at her. 'With *this* I can. I've seen what it allowed you to do. I can *feel* the strength it gives me. With this blade in my hand, none can stand against me!'

Elinor reached for him. 'Be careful with it. It's not what you think. It can lead you too far if you aren't . . .'

But Rannis had already leaped away, calling, 'Follow me,' over his shoulder.

He hurtled into the gate guards, the blade a shining, deadly arc of white lightning. Three of them were down before they even knew he was amongst them. Two more he took, in quick succession, and then a third.

'Behind you!' Elinor shouted.

Rannis whirled and cut down the lancer who had been about to take him from behind.

The guards had managed to recover a little now. Those remaining grouped together before the gate, a hedge of blades against him. Rannis leaped at them, but they drove him back. Again he attacked, skewering one of them, the man going down screaming. But they managed to hold firm, shouting out loudly for help and reinforcements.

Elinor heard answering shouts in the distance behind her. She ran back to the corner. Peering round, she saw a throng of armed Brothers running along the street.

Rannis looked towards her.

'More coming,' she called.

He launched himself at the guards again in a wild fury, striking and dodging and slashing at them like a mad thing. One went down, then two.

Only three left now.

One of them threw down his sword and fled.

Rannis laughed, leaping for the remaining pair.

And then it was that the blade betrayed him.

He cut down one of the remaining guards with a wide, swirling slash, a virtuoso movement that caught the man totally off guard. Rannis carried the movement through like a dancer, whirling, perfectly balanced, the blade out, ready to take the next man unawares with a back-hand slash.

But the last guard was ready for him.

Rannis had been too sure, too flamboyant, too extravagant in his movements, feeling the tingling strength of the sword no doubt, as Elinor had, feeling himself faster, better, stronger than those he faced . . .

Round he came, the white blade up, face glowing with fierce confidence – and whirled straight into the guard's sword, the man's blade plunging into his abdomen up to the hilt.

490

Rannis stared, shocked.

The guard stared also, as if he, too, could not believe he had done such a thing.

Elinor rushed in, lifting up a dropped lance, bashed the staring guard over the head with it.

Rannis looked at her. 'Go!' he gasped. He held out the white blade to her. 'Here. Take the cursed thing. *Take it*!'

She took it from his trembling hand, feeling the tingle of it go right up her arm. Rannis unhooked the sheath and handed it over, gasping, the guard's blade still protruding from his belly. 'I . . . I never meant . . .' he began, then gagged, his face crumpling momentarily.

She held out a hand to him.

'Why did you *leave* me?' he demanded.

'Rannis,' she started, 'it was you who . . .' But she did not have the heart to try to correct him.

'We could have had a life together, you and I,' he went on. 'Even after Minmi. We could . . .' He gagged again. 'I . . .'

There were shouts from up the street, closer now.

Rannis reached down and fumbled for one of the guards' dropped swords. He shoved at her weakly. 'Go. Get away! I'll hold them.'

'Rannis . . .' she said.

'Go,' he gasped. 'Just *go*!' He shoved her towards the open gate. 'Or it's all for nothing.'

Reluctantly, she went.

'Don't . . . don't hate me, girl,' he called after her.

She turned, opened her mouth.

'*Go*!' he shouted at her.

Her eyes blind with tears, Elinor stumbled through the gate and out of Sofala.

Down a long grassy slope she fled, the sword's crimson sheath in one hand, the white blade itself in the other, feeling the strength it lent her, running fast as she possibly could, slipping and skidding on the grass, weeping still, hearing shouts and cries from behind, running till her lungs burned and her legs felt like sticks, running and running and running, gasping for breath, her vision full of crimson spirals and darkness, her mouth full of the iron taste of blood, running and running and running with desperate intensity till she found herself somehow in woods, splashing across a cold stream, struggling up a hillside, weaving between trees, gasping and heaving and struggling until, finally, she could do no more and tripped, sprawling on her face in the root-laced dirt.

The white blade fell from her grasp. It was all she could do just to lie there, her lungs heaving, the old bruises on her alive with pain, the world spinning sickeningly about her . . .

She heard somebody come up behind her, felt a hand pull on her shoulder.

She struggled despairingly, flailing out for the dropped blade, striking blindly with her fists . . .

'Elinor!' a voice said. 'Elinor!'

A familiar voice . . .

'It'ss me. It'ss *me*!'

She blinked, trying to focus, saw a furred face, bright eyes, a flash of white, sharp teeth . . .

'Gyver?' she gasped. '*Gyver*!'

He gathered her up in his arms in a tight, tight hold, his eyes full of tears. 'Oh, my Elinor, my Elinor!'

'But . . . but how?' she managed to say eventually, when he had let her go and she had enough breath to speak.

Gyver smiled and motioned behind him.

'I dreamed, dreamed, *dreamed*!' a familiar voice cried and Elinor saw Spandel come bouncing through the trees.

She hugged the little Lamure to her, then Gyver, laughing and weeping and dizzy with relief and unexpected joy.

'Where have you been all this time?' she demanded of Spandel.

The little Lamure shrugged her slim shoulders. 'The world is big, big. Bigger than ever, ever, ever I thought. I wandered far. I could not find the way back before . . .'

'You were *lost*?' Elinor said.

Spandel nodded, her masked, furry face wrinkling up.

Elinor threw back her head and laughed weakly. She thought of her vision, of great unseen forces moving lives. Spandel missing, her walking blindly into the trap that had brought her to Sofala and . . .

Spandel and Gyver were staring at her.

How could she even begin to explain any of it?

'Come,' Gyver urged. 'We musst away, quickly! It iss not ssafe here.'

Elinor nodded. She struggled to her feet, reached up the dropped blade and sheathed it hastily. For a second she stood staring at the fur-man, unable to believe it was really him, that she was really here, that *any* of it was real. She put a hand on his arm, felt the solid warmth of him.

Gyver smiled. 'Come,' he said, taking her hand and urging her along.

They went, the three of them together, moving as quickly as Elinor could manage, away into the safety of the woods where the Brothers could not reach.

XXXXVIII

They walked for three days.

Elinor and Gyver went hand in hand much of the time, for Elinor could deny him no longer. She had been hurt enough, and changed enough, to lose the arrogance – she could think of no better word – that had once made her believe she knew what was best for him, for them.

The vision she had experienced on black Jara's altar hung in her mind. The world was a great moving, balancing dance and nobody, finally, could stop that dance, or order it, or control it. All one could do was live it – in the bone and the belly, as Gyver's wise mother would say. If living it meant loss . . . then one lived loss. The great dance went on, within and without, and one went on with it.

So she and Gyver walked together hand in hand through the woods, looking into each other's eyes often, smiling, with Spandel bouncing along, happy for them. At night the three of them lay together, snuggled up like a litter of puppies, and Elinor could not remember ever having felt more at home.

And late in the afternoon of the third day, they walked back into the hill camp.

Folk came spilling out, wide-eyed and shouting, staring at Elinor as if she were a ghost.

Old Collart grabbed her, hugging her hard enough to make her half-healed bruises throb and her bones crack. 'You're *alive!*' He looked over at Gyver. 'I'd given *you* up for gone, too. And little Spandel . . .'

Gyver grinned. Spandel leaped and pranced.

Collart stared at Elinor and shook his head. 'We *tried*, Elinor,' he said. 'We tracked you to Sofala. We argued it out, skirmished, scouted the walls . . .' He sighed, ran a hand wearily through his grey beard – it was a full beard now. 'Sofala's a walled city. As impregnable now as it ever was in the olden times of the great Domains. We debated it, for days, thought up wild schemes to rescue you. But in the end . . .' Collart sighed again. 'In the end we were too few, too ill equipped. There was nothing we could do to save you. Nothing . . .'

He hugged her impulsively again, grinning hugely. 'And now you come walking in amongst us impossibly, still with that blade at your hip . . . How do you *do* things like this, girl?'

The whole of the camp was crowding about by now, all the faces familiar to Elinor – black-beard Smitt, bald Passaly, Getta with her bow, Ingra the beefy farm-wife, Adella with her swinging auburn braids – and others, familiar, not familiar, more than she remembered being here. And the humanimals, too. Scrunch the bear came barrelling through the press of people, nearly knocking her down with the enthusiasm of his welcome.

She laughed, wept, twirled about, surrounded by laughing, weeping, shouting folk.

'What *happened*?' they all demanded to know.

She told them the story, from the wild horseback ride, to the terrible days in the Sofala dungeon, to the outdoor ceremony in the packed and seething square. When it came to the uncanny destruction of the statue of black Jara, though, she faltered.

How to explain it to them?

When she had told Gyver and Spandel of the strange vision she had been given, they had nodded, accepting it with an ease that surprised her. 'The Deep Dream,' Spandel had said. And Gyver, 'The deep, deep currents.'

But what was she to say now? Elinor wondered uneasily. She was not sure she entirely understood herself what had occurred. And she did not anticipate from this motley, multi-minded group any such easy acceptance as Spandel and Gyver had given her.

But she had to say something . . .

So she told them of the Lady – leaving out her own vision – and of the burning medallion and the shattering of black Jara and the ensuing chaos that had allowed her to escape.

'The Lady!' humanimal voices whispered. 'The *Lady* . . .'

There was silence when she had done. People looked at each other, uncertain, staring.

'This . . . Lady,' Adella of the swinging braids said, 'who *is* she?'

The humanimals shuffled uneasily. They were scattered amongst the crowd, Elinor saw, with none of the original segregation of the two groups that there had once been. Human and humanimal in this camp had come to rely too much on each other for that.

'The Lady,' somebody repeated.

'The *Lady*,' humanimal voices whispered.

'She dreams us,' little Spandel said then. 'Or we dream her. She is . . .' Spandel seemed at a loss. 'She is the . . .'

'The face of your need,' Elinor finished for her, recalling Mamma Kieran's words. She felt the little hairs on her neck shiver erect. Mamma Kieran, she realized, had spoken like these folk in the South, Mamma Kieran with her talking raven.

'But is she . . . *real*, this Lady?' one of the men asked.

'What iss . . . real?' Gyver said. 'Sshe iss a sspirit persson. Sshe iss what sshe iss. Both real and . . . not.'

'Very enlightening, that!' black-bearded Smitt responded.

'Real or not,' Getta put in, 'she came to your aid, Elinor.'

'To *our* aid,' somebody else added.

'It's the end of the Brothers!' one of the men said, then.

'Oh, no it isn't,' another answered.

'Oh, yes it *is*!' replied the first. 'They'll never recover from a blow like this. We can have our farms back! Our lives back!'

A ragged cheer went up at this.

But Collart held up his hands, shaking his head. 'Don't underestimate them. This Iryn Jagga, their leader, is still alive by all accounts, and . . .'

'And in no especial good mood, either, I reckon,' put in bald Passaly.

The crowd tittered.

'Likely so,' Collart agreed. 'Alive and angry. And looking for vengeance.'

'But it'll take time for him to recover, surely,' a man said. 'For the Brothers in general to recover. Now's the time to strike at them! Hit them while they are weakest. Now's the time to . . .'

'To *what*?' Passaly said. 'To trot into Sofala and tear the place down stone by stone? All four or five dozen of us against . . . what? A thousand or more?'

'We've the Lady on our side!' somebody shouted.

'Don't be naive!' Collart snapped. 'Something happened in Sofala, something uncanny, something of the Powers. But it's not something the likes of us can easily comprehend. And certainly not something the likes of us can *command*!'

'She came to Elinor's aid!' a woman cried.

'And can you guarantee she will do so again?' Collart demanded. 'To our aid? On call when and as we need her help?'

There was an uncomfortable silence at this.

People turned to the humanimals. 'Will she help?' they demanded. 'Can you call her up?'

'Can *you* call her again?' a man demanded of Elinor.

She shrugged. 'I did not . . . call her at all. She . . . *something* moved through me, I think. Like . . .' She did not know how to explain it to them, they who had not experienced a vision of the world as a moving, patterned, balanced dance, like she had; who had not felt themselves moved by Powers beyond easy understanding.

Scrunch came forward. 'The Lady is not the sort that can be . . . commanded. She is . . .' He shrugged his large furry shoulders. 'We do not know what she may be. She is . . . *was* our secret companion, coming to us in our dreams. As Elinor said, the face of our need, perhaps. We do not think she is what you human folk call *real*. She is a force, maybe. Or some aspect of a force. Or, perhaps, she is some aspect of *us*. We do not know. How can we know?'

The human crowd murmured.

'We can defeat the Brothers without this mysterious and unknowable Lady!' a man said.

Half a dozen others cheered at this.

'Now is the time! Now is our chance!'

'With Elinor of the white blade!'

'Elinor! Elinor Whiteblade!' the shout went up.

'There's still too *few* of us!' Passaly said, shouting them down. 'Elinor and her blade or not. Are you all gone completely *crazy*?'

497

'Well, what do you expect us to do, then? Spend the rest of our lives skulking about up here in the hills?'

'Of course not!' Passaly replied.

'What, then?'

'I *owe* those bastards!' one man said.

'I, too!' another added.

'Then let's *take* them!' a third shouted. 'Now! While the time is ripe!'

'No, no, no, no!' Smitt yelled at them. 'We need to plan it. We need to be careful and clever and . . .'

'That's just the counsel of fear!' somebody accused him. 'We need to *strike* while we can!'

'There's not enough of us,' a woman put in. 'Passaly's right. There'll *never* be enough of us to defeat the Brothers!'

The man next to her glared. 'With an attitude like that, we certainly won't!'

Elinor stood a little apart, uneasy. It was the same old debate, this. Going in the same circular direction, round and round, and always back to violence and blood. She was bruised, and she ached, and she was weary of it all. She had seen far too much of blood, and did not relish seeing more.

Gyver stood forth then, holding up his arms for attention.

Folk quietened.

'I,' he said, 'know what there iss for you to do.'

'What, then?' half a dozen voices demanded simultaneously.

'Walk away,' he said.

Silence greeted this, for long moments. Then, 'Walk away? Walk *away*? What kind of counsel is *that*?'

'I *owe* those bastards!' a man repeated. 'I'm not going to just turn my back on them and run away like a whipped cur!'

'No, no!' Gyver said. 'Walk away. Not run away.'

'What's the difference?'

'Not running *from*. Walking *to*,' he said softly.

'To *what*?' the man who owed the Brothers demanded.

'The sserpent, it sshedss itss old sskin,' said Gyver. 'The birdss, they moult, letting their old featherss drop. The caterpillar, she becomess a butterfly.'

People were staring at the fur-man, uncertain.

Elinor stood next to him. What he said made sudden, vivid sense to her. She had gone through just such transformations,

498

had died and been reborn to a new and different life. But more than that.

Once, she had thought herself, resentfully, a mere tool, a utensil used by some Power. Now she no longer felt that way. She was, had been, a vessel, yes. She no longer doubted that something greater than herself had moved through her, shaping her life. But she was no mere passive vessel, doomed to blunder eternally on like some automaton. There *had* been choices for her to make. She had had to act, to do, to live her life herself. For though the Powers moved her, undeniably, she also moved the Powers. In the great complex dance that was the world, each being had a place. And, no matter how small the act, what each did . . . *mattered*.

For the pattern formed the dancers, but the dancers also formed the pattern.

The old Seers had disrupted the balance of that pattern. She, and others, had been part of something that took the pattern one little step towards a new equilibrium.

What they did or did not do here was a further part of that. Their actions *mattered*, not just to themselves but to the greater world as well.

Elinor looked at the folk before her, swallowed, took a breath. 'Margie Farm was a good place,' she began.

'Damn' right!' Collart agreed, along with a handful of others.

'It's in ruins, now!' Adella said.

Elinor nodded. 'It's in ruins, agreed.' She paused, trying to think how to say what she was feeling. She remembered her vision, the blind force in the world striving for balance. 'Margie was a good place, a *special* place. It was unlike any other place I have ever been.'

'So?' a man demanded impatiently. 'So you liked Margie. So did we all, those of us who knew it. It's gone now. Destroyed!'

Elinor swallowed. She was getting nowhere with this line of talk. She thought desperately for a moment, tried another approach. 'What is it, then, that we are fighting for?'

'Our farms!' several people shouted at once.

'Only that?' Elinor responded.

'Freedom,' came the answer.

'Freedom to do what?' she said.

There was a general muttering.

Elinor held up her hands. 'Let me try to answer my own question. You say you're fighting to get your farms back. But I say there is more to it than just that. I have seen Minmi and Sofala. I have seen what remains of the old Domains. Twisted people clinging desperately to illusions of their past, using brute force to try to bind the world to the old designs.

'But you folk, you're fighting for a future aren't you? Fighting to keep alive a way of life you've built for yourselves. A way of life that has balance and meaning. The way things were at Margie, and other farms. Where folk can live easy with each other, where nobody lords it over anybody else, where folk of all sorts can mix on equal terms.

'You're fighting to keep the Brothers from forcing you to fit into the mould of their mad fanaticism, their twisted attempt to revive the doings of the old Seers. You're fighting to preserve ordinary, decent folk who can look each other in the eye and ask after each other's welfare, and mean it.'

'That's it, right enough,' somebody said, to general agreement.

'To stop the Brothers from destroying everything that matters!' somebody else added.

'Do you wish to relive the past?' Elinor demanded of them. 'To live on cold dreams of what is no more, to lust after what no longer exists, to live only to recreate the world as it once was? Do you wish to live as the Brothers do?'

'Of course not,' came the reply.

'But the cursed Brothers have taken our future from us,' somebody complained.

'No, they have *not*!' Elinor said quickly. 'The Brothers have given us a future.'

The gathering stared at her.

Elinor licked her lips, trying to think how to express what she was feeling. 'Look about you,' she said finally. 'What do you see? Folk from different farms. Folk of different ages. Human folk and humanimal folk. Come together, all of us. And what is it that brings us thus all together and gives us common cause?'

'The sodding Brothers,' somebody answered.

Elinor smiled. 'The sodding Brothers indeed. It used to be that humanimal folk and human folk kept uneasily separate in this camp. It used to be that folk did nothing much but sit about in despair. It used to be that all we did was argue with each other.'

'We still do *that*!' somebody called, amidst general laughter.

'But we argue to a point, now,' Elinor said. 'Don't you *see*? Don't you understand? The world had been changed and we've been changed.'

'The world's changed for the *worse*,' a man grumbled.

'And us?' Elinor asked. 'Have we been changed for the worse, too?'

Nobody had a ready answer for that.

'It seems to me,' she went on, 'that there are two choices facing us now. We can fight.' She drew the white blade suddenly, feeling its tingling strength, feeling her Kess self surge into clarity. 'We can fight!' she repeated, brandishing the blade. 'I have fought. You have fought . . .'

The gathering gave out a rumbling cheer.

'But what are we fighting for? And how do we fight for it?' Elinor slipped the blade back into its sheath. 'The Brothers outnumber us . . .'

'The Brothers are cruel bastards and deserve to be killed!' a man shouted.

'But at what cost?' Elinor returned. 'Oh, we can kill them, some of them. But in the end what will be the result?'

'I don't care about the end. I *owe* those bastards for what they've done. That's what *I* care about.'

'And so you would give up the rest of your life for that?' Elinor said. 'And the lives of those here? To punish the Brothers for what they did in the past?'

The man started to reply, but she held up her hand. 'I said we have two choices. The first is to fight. The second . . . as Gyver says . . . is to walk away.'

There was a general uneasy grumbling.

'As Gyver says,' Elinor went on quickly, 'the serpent sheds its skin. The caterpillar becomes a butterfly. They become. They leave the old behind. They *change*.'

'But we can't just . . .' somebody started.

Elinor cut him off. 'I have changed. I have left the old behind and walked away into a new life. More than once. I had no choice. The world changes. We who live in the world change. It is all a great dance, complex and moving. Turn and turn, balance and change and balance. *That* is what destroyed the old Seers.'

'Balance?' somebody said, confused.

Elinor shook her head. 'No. Their very lack of balance. They tried to rule the world, to control it, to fashion it to their wills, to control all change. But all they did, in the end, was bring about their own destruction. And leave a legacy of disruption that we must all endure.'

She looked at them. 'What we do *matters* to the world. What we bring into the world *matters*!'

She paused, took a breath. She felt the familiar plunging feeling again, and her heart jumped. She had thought it finished, surely. But now . . . Could it be that what she had endured was not the end after all?

Everyone was looking at her, looking *to* her.

She swallowed. Whether she was channelled or not, she felt clearly what she must do here, for she truly did feel Gyver had the right of things . . .

'I'm with Gyver in this,' she said. 'We have everything . . . we *are* everything we need already. And we either spend the rest of our lives in hopeless bloodshed and hate – like the Brothers themselves – trying to punish others for what they have done to ruin our dream of the way things ought to be, trying to force the world to fit our notions of what it ought to be. Or . . . we walk away into a new life. We change. We find a new point of balance and bring something else entirely into the world.'

'Bu . . . but . . .' a man sputtered. 'Just . . . just to walk away . . . That would be . . . *defeat*!'

'No,' Elinor said. 'It would be victory.'

She took Gyver by the hand. 'Come,' she said, 'let us walk away.'

Gyver grinned. 'I am a sserpent, me. I sshed my sskin.' He did a little shimmying movement with his hips, as if divesting himself of a too-tight suit of clothes. 'I find new balance.'

Elinor and he walked a few steps away from the gathering, she stiff and limping a little still, the blade swinging at her belt. A little way off, they halted, hand in hand. Elinor looked back, questioningly.

The humanimals spilled slowly out of the human crowd.

'Where Elinor goes, we go,' Scrunch said. 'We have had a dream, always, we who are neither entirely one thing nor the other, we who are caught between . . . we have a dream of a place of belonging. It is not here, has never been here in this land we are coming to believe. Perhaps what we have dreamed will be where Elinor walks.'

'Perhaps it won't,' a man snapped from the crowd.

Scrunch shrugged his broad shoulders. 'Perhaps not. We shall see.'

There was silence, then.

Collart came walking out of the crowd. 'I shed my old skin,' he said, joining Elinor and Gyver and the humanimals. 'Long ago, I learned the virtue of letting go, of losing and loosing. I'm with you on this.'

They stood together, Elinor, Gyver, Collart, Scrunch, Spandel – with the rest of the humanimals grouped about them.

'Join us,' Elinor urged. 'Walk with us into something new, something changed, something . . . other. A new balance.'

Passaly was the first to come out of the group of human folk, followed by young Smitt.

'I shed my old skin,' Passaly said, echoing Collart.

'And I,' Smitt said.

The rest of the human folk stood for long moments, tense and staring, muttering uneasily amongst themselves. Then, slowly, haltingly, with many an uncertain step, they straggled across . . .

This book is for Jane O'Connor,
my sister and good friend